A REVOLUTIONARY BALLAD

Book two of

Memories from Oblivion

Atlas Hill

Rhapsody Books

This is a work of fiction. All the characters, organisations, and events portrayed in this novel are either products of the author's imagination or are used fictitiously.

First published by Rhapsody Books in 2018

Cover art by Zicuta
Map art by Shovel

ISBN 978-0-6482852-2-9

eBook ISBN 978-0-6482852-3-6

The Island of Skybed
Vinawell
Sequiposa
Astilow
Easterclem
Trubannis
Cetal
Pichreuse
Saffron
Whitesand
Farella
Noel
Cellarsy
Zenith
Strombolith
Kraga
Fernusin
Busparen
Seniblum
Aizary
1 Zorlia
2 Bastion City
3 Cetal City
4 Dcrellsdale
5 Frey
6 Dawnsdale
7 Poppaross
8 Aragon
9 Harper Springs
10 Millenzburg
11 Spheria
12 Illudia
Sill

To Felix.

Contents

PART III

ONE

A trek to remember

It had been more than a month since Alpheus left Zorlia. Although he knew the map of the land like the back of his hand, it was certainly an experience to trek across the plains, the hills, and the forests—or in his case, riding on a chestnut mare for most of the way. The journey itself had been smooth thus far along the main path of the network of trade routes collectively known as *Seeds Lane*, which had long been established to expedite trade among cities and towns in Western Trubannis, extending also to the country's foreign neighbour in the west.

Alpheus's destination was *Poppaross*, the capital of Vinawell. Once there, Alpheus would be competing for the chance to be wedded to the Princess of the West. But before he could even consider the challenge, Alpheus must first overcome his phobia for large bodies of water and hence the challenge of crossing the considerable stretch of water that separated Vinawell from Trubannis.

Alpheus had disguised as a travelling merchant selling herbal medicine. He had maintained a new hairstyle, letting his hair fall naturally in long tresses rather than tying it into a braided ponytail as he had before. He donned a long mantle of olive green knitted with a hood, carrying a stock of herbs on a simple straw knapsack. Basic healing was one of the many things he had learned as a scholar, but this would be the first time he had applied those skills in practice.

It had actually been thrilling picking plants along his way and providing immediate help to those with mild ailments. Not only was he making a difference, but he had avoided suspicion from Empire personnel at the various checkpoints. On the rare instances where he had been asked, he had assumed the name of *Albert Moon*.

And, in truth, Alpheus had hardly been himself. He had been watching the world flow before him without any spectacles. He had kept his only pair of glasses within the layers under his mantle—the pair that Agnes had given him as a parting gift.

Also beneath his mantle was his double crescent pendant which he had expected to pull out more often. But it was something else that he had found himself fish for—the unfinished thesis penned by Reeling. The paper was only about fifty pages long, but Alpheus had grown ever more fascinated by the ideas discussed within it, which contemplated a range of natural phenomena with particular attention paid to why and how to perceive those processes.

Reeling had authored the paper in such a way that employed witty references to explain convoluted philosophies. Alpheus had re-read parts of it almost every evening. Of particular interest to him was Reeling's emphasis on teleology, or the study of purpose in nature. In the paper, Reeling advocated for the seemingly simple idea that in order to fully understand something, one must undertake careful observation where the most critical part of the observation was an account of a thing's purpose. In parts of the dialogue, Reeling spoke of rain, snow, and hail, but not about how each phenomenon benefited or hindered human activity, instead considering the purpose of each phenomenon as part of the land and the cosmos on a much grander scale.

Everything had a purpose, from the welcoming cool breezes that swept away the gruelling heat of summer to the unnoticed droplets of rain that dabbed the tip of a flowering bud. But Reeling warned against the temptation to use man as the measure of these natural processes, and instead urged philosophers to consider, in the former scenario, why the wind blew at all and whether the wind as an entity itself was achieving its purpose, which had nothing to do with relieving anyone.

In an everchanging world, the role of wind was critical to erosion, Alpheus had noted, which in turn affected plants and animals as much as the landscape in which they inhabited. And while his faith had waned at least slightly since Reeling's death, Alpheus was still glad that the arguments presented in the paper did not contradict the central teachings of Ionianism and the doctrine that everything followed a predetermined cycle.

There *was* a difference, however, between the church and what Reeling implied in the paper. Adherents of the church generally accepted that natural phenomena and nature itself was a creation of the Immortal, and hence they considered it both meaningless and disrespectful to question what purpose any of it served. Reeling, in contrast, was clearly advocating an extensive inquiry into why nature flowed in the way it did, promising that truth resided in the physical world. As a result, Alpheus had begun to observe the weather carefully while searching for insights assured not only by Reeling, but most of the scholar community.

On some of the quieter nights, Alpheus had also recalled more than once his encounter with the angelic spectre that manifested out of the marble statue in the private basement of his home in Zorlia. He had admired the mysterious being then, and he still admired her now. And that was despite not knowing what she even was. She couldn't have been a sorcerer, not only because she had breathed out no grace, but also because she clearly didn't belong to the temporal world. In contemplating the encounter, Alpheus had also realised that he had never questioned the spectre's existence or its decency even though the teachings of the Immortal expressly classified all *other* spiritual beings or occurrences as the work of The Eternally Damned.

In any case, Alpheus considered it a blessing that he hadn't encountered any actual sorcerers since his departure. His own identity as a sorcerer remained an enigma and a major source of irony to him, especially when he considered that he couldn't access the potential powers sorcerers supposedly possessed, not when he had no one to guide him, anyway. His past research on the subject had been much more focused on the history rather than its application. And like anything else, one didn't simply become a powerful sorcerer. Practice was crucial to one's level of skill. Compared to Julian who had been in training since a child under the expert guidance of his father, Alpheus had yet to even fully accept the fact that he was a sorcerer.

Alpheus considered himself a traveller, merchant, herbalist, and philosopher in the past month—but not a sorcerer. He had managed to journey the span of the state of *Pichreuse* from east to west, finally slowing his step today, even selling away the horse that had made the journey with him, upon entering the important industrial port city of *Dorellsdale* on the west coast of Trubannis.

Dorellsdale was a major city of Western Trubannis, dwarfed only by Cetal City, with trade markets bustling in every corner. And despite the active exchange of goods, economic activity was largely self-regulated. Apparently, the Empire had decided years ago that the free market was the best system for the port.

Alpheus stepped into a local tavern now, trailing a figure whose style of dress and overall presentation was eerily similar to how he himself used to look. The young man had been his companion for the past week. His name was Joe Hendron, a hunter who had been raised in Vinawell but was of Truban heritage. The resemblance in Hendron's dress was no accident, of course. In order to divert unwanted attention in certain precarious situations, including a critical one that he anticipated would come soon, Alpheus needed someone to look like him—someone to be his scapegoat.

The hunter's relatively thin frame was only slightly wider than Alpheus's, and it allowed him to be tremendously nimble, which ultimately attributed to his success in his profession. He was now donning a cultured robe of grey whose cutting, length, and general flair were an imitation of Alpheus's usual preferred style. He was wearing glasses with thick circular frames and a pair of boots with enormously thick soles which boosted his height rather conspicuously. Indeed, the hunter's entire outfit had been Alpheus's doing. The mantle, the glasses, and the heightened boots had been presented as *gifts* which would add greatly to the hunting experience.

Alpheus had even managed to sway Hendron into tying his usual wavy hair into a braided ponytail in the same style as he himself had preferred. All that, and the hunter still only knew Alpheus as Albert Moon.

In addition to Hendron's outward appearance, Alpheus was betting on the hunter's curious background to divert attention. It was rare to see anyone call both Trubannis and Vinawell home. But Hendron could rightfully do so as he had been born and raised in the Vinan port city of *Aragon*, which was the first transit point into Vinawell.

Hendron hunted primarily in Western Trubannis, claiming that the beasts of Vinawell were too tame for his liking. His routine was three months of hunting followed by a month spent telling his stories in Aragon. He drew a wagon with a large cage sitting at the back that kept his prey alive, saving him the trouble to preserve its freshness were he to slaughter them. On his latest trip, Hendron had managed to capture an infant bear. He was ready to return to Aragon, and with Alpheus, they reached the city of Dorellsdale today—the final stop before crossing the sea to Vinawell.

As Hendron sauntered further into the tavern under that guise, Alpheus glanced about, noting that its patronage comprised of a fair share of foreigners from the west, mostly merchants whose Vinan heritage was apparent with their paler skin tone, soft amber hair, and blue eyes as opposed to the regular Truban's dark hair and brown eyes. There seemed to be little racial tension, though, if any. Even in here, the men continued doing business, making the most out of their trades. It was a wonderful sight for Alpheus to see people working in harmony, even if it was for monetary gain.

Alpheus settled on an empty stool, relieving himself of the knapsack that had been heavy on his shoulders and laying it under the stool. He then flapped his hood out to reveal his hair that now fell behind him past mid-spine. As he had expected, no one knew who he was in a place so far away from Zorlia. And as he peered about, he did not expect to see any familiar faces in return.

"Black beer," he said to the bartender, who winked at him in affirmation.

He downed a mouthful of the dark liquor, savouring the malty taste. He regarded the froth that still bubbled in his glass and began reminiscing his visits to Rogers.

Zorlia seemed ever so distant. Sometimes, it felt like it had all been a dream. Behind the contemplation of philosophy and natural phenomena among other experiences, however, vivid scenes of the tragedy that had driven him away continued to creep into his mind every once in a while, haunting him without mercy.

Alpheus blinked hard to shake of the forthcoming nightmare. He sighed and then turned to the other customers, gradually breathing easier as he watched the men mingling, sharing stories, and showing an apparent zest for life.

I had thought I could learn everything from books, he thought with a wry smile. *But no amount of books could explain or detail the experience of being there.*

Zorlia had been the centre of the world to him. He had believed there was no good reason to visit anywhere else, since all other places would prove inferior to what he had known. And while it was true that Dorellsdale or all other places he had passed lacked the imposing structures like Vondra Dawn or the Church of the St. Bernard Order, these places also saw far less grim, stress, and tension regularly witnessed in the capital. These people outside of the capital, at least upon appearance, were more content and more genuine. They were not envious of the sophistication Zorlians often presented themselves with.

The reverie ended when Hendron tapped him on the shoulder. "Hey," he said, gesturing toward the centre of the tavern. "You should listen. Sounds like they're talking about your profession."

Alpheus turned, noting that a group of nearly thirty merchants had gathered together, some of them throwing their hands in the air, fuming. "All of it!" one of the men cried. "Not just the money, even my pottery!"

"That damned Sail Band!" another man inserted. "They're destroying us."

"We have to make a stand!" a third voice cried.

"We want justice!" another hollered. And soon the tavern was filled with angry chants of *justice*—an inappropriate word to use in favour of merchants who were generally cunning, often cheating their customers in both quality and price. It was also ironic that the competition between merchants was often fierce—and yet, in times of crises, they were oddly united.

The Sail Band, Alpheus thought, having heard about the notorious crew of bandits who had been terrorising trade in Western Trubannis. Although some accounts described the crew as diplomatic and inherently good despite a few queer tendencies, merchants always spoke of them with scathing tones. Alpheus had learned that the thieving crew often targeted merchants, and that the nature of the trade made them easy targets—the fatigue from carrying stock and travelling alone.

The crew itself was apparently led by a former mercenary of war by the name of Sailanson. If the rumours could be trusted, the thieves were a dangerous lot that had achieved some remarkable feats in recent years, which included overthrowing a notorious ring of outlaws that operated in the eastern states of Noel, Zenith, and Cellarsy.

Their stories were told across the land, yet no one seemed to know exactly who they were or what they represented. A point that the story tellers agreed on, however, was that the thieving crew had never failed to get what they wanted.

"But what can we do?" asked one of the men, his question silencing the others. "The soldiers cannot help. They're probably more terrified than we are."

Another man grumbled, shaking his head. "Rumour has it that the thieves are mercenaries from the war—one of them a madman who slaughtered hundreds of his own comrades."

Alpheus remained silent but cringed on the idea, a lump forming in his throat.

"Don't know if it's true," that man continued. "But if they managed to break into the Monarchal Castle, who's to say just how dangerous they are?"

"This isn't getting anywhere," said the man who had started the discussion. "If anyone has any ideas, let's hear them!"

Other than a few hums, no one made a sound. Alpheus peered at the hopeless expressions the men wore. He didn't forget that he was only a merchant in disguise, but having acted as part of the community for the past month, he sympathised. These merchants might be ingenious when it came to thinking up new ways to sell their goods, but they were close to terrible in coming up with solutions for problems of a larger scale.

The silence was broken when a man scurried in from the entrance. "I have news!" he cried in a wheezing voice. "They left Dorellsdale! The Sail Band. They left! I saw them on the ship to Aragon!"

"What…?!" Hendron remarked quietly. "That's not good."

The merchants, meanwhile, erupted into mumbles. While it was good news for some, most were unsure how to react. Many merchants actually used the ferry on a regular basis, moving across the sea between Dorellsdale and Aragon, which was part of the Seeds Lane network.

Alpheus turned away, regarding the froth in his beer again. It might be inevitable that he would encounter the thieving crew sooner or later. But at least, at that time, he could be Alpheus Hindlow again instead of Albert Moon.

* * *

Together with Hendron, Alpheus rolled along the last of the Truban part of Seeds Lane. Just beyond the horizon of the setting sun was the sea that also served as a territorial border. The dully-shaded shipping yard was essentially a large, rigid garrison, the final checkpoint administered by the Empire before one departed the country.

The queue was long, even with four separate lines. And while this wasn't the only place that posted portraits of wanted criminals, they were certainly affixed in generous amounts here. Just like the ones Alpheus had seen in Dorellsdale and the other towns he had visited, his picture was here as well, sketched in charcoal. He was depicted with a braided ponytail, donning spectacles, and wearing a rather wicked grin that he didn't think he could actually manage.

The accompanying text beneath the portrait detailed his height, weight, and build, but mentioned nothing about what Alpheus had been accused of—not of the Lord Count's murder, and not of his escape from prison. It was likely that the Empire wanted the soldiers here to remain ignorant of the prison break fiasco, most likely to avoid embarrassment at a place so close to foreign territory. The only thing Alpheus could be sure of was that the soldiers had been pressured to seize anyone suspicious, apparently having recently made three or four times more than the usual number of arrests.

And yet, Alpheus was calm now under the disguise of Albert Moon, riding next to Hendron who invited all the attention. He glanced over to the hunter then who held onto the straps of the horse drawn wagon. This was where they would part ways. While Hendron had been a wonderful companion in the past week, bringing with him fascinating stories of his hunts, Alpheus had never considered not using him.

When they finally rolled along to where the inspecting soldiers were visible, with about twenty people still lining up ahead of them, Alpheus shot one last smile at Hendron who didn't notice it.

"I want to go on ahead if you don't mind," he whispered as he hopped off the vehicle. He pushed forward, gently brushing past a few travellers in the line, deftly sliding a silver coin to each, quieting them before they had even complained. He didn't look back at Hendron who must have been confounded by this action. The hunter didn't call out to him, however, not among a crowd of frustrated commuters who were already losing their patience.

"The sack," one of the soldiers demanded when Alpheus finally reached the front of the line. "And lose that hood."

Alpheus flapped open his hood and passed his simple bag over, noting that the soldier didn't focus only on him. As Alpheus had wanted, the soldier was keeping an eye on Hendron and his conspicuous wagon about four paces behind. And as Alpheus had assumed, they all knew the hunter. His drastic change of style—a combination of the spectacles, cultured robe, and ponytail—since his last transit through the garrison invited more attention than he otherwise would have received.

The soldier passed the knapsack back to Alpheus, exchanging a glance with the fellow soldier next to him and then eyeing Hendron together.

"May I…?" Alpheus said, taking a step forward.

The soldiers said nothing, reaching for their swords now, one of them brushing his other hand to gesture Alpheus to move away as they treaded slowly toward Hendron, who was still perched on the driver's seat of the wagon.

"Seize him!" the soldier cried.

Alpheus moved along without looking back, even as yelling resounded in the air behind him. He was sure he heard Hendron's voice somewhere in the receding cries of an argument or perhaps even a brawl. Still, Alpheus strode through safely. He had dreaded this day since departing Zorlia—not because of the soldiers who might recognise him, but because of having to board a ship and sail across the largest body of water he had ever crossed.

Alpheus held his breath now as he looked up at the two giant masts attached to even larger sails that fluttered in the wind. This could possibly be his greatest obstacle—to overcome the sea. He huffed out a sigh and then boarded the ship with careful steps.

TWO

A foreign land not so foreign

The voyage lasted for a day and a half, and the ship finally arrived in the port city of Aragon in the early hours of the second morning just before dawn. Alpheus acknowledged that the open sea was special, and that was in spite of a terrible ride where the vessel had rocked without end against roaring waves. Since almost drowning as a child, his fear of large bodies of water had never ceased. Logic had told him to stay at the rear of the vessel to minimise motion sickness, but his instincts then had him hiding deep inside the cabin, which resulted in a trip filled with constant vomiting.

Alpheus realised that the ship had been docked now, and as much as he wanted to step off the vessel, he simply had no energy with which to move. The crew on the ship were reluctant to nurse him and Alpheus was sure they were ready to dump him out. It wasn't until he offered them a silver coin that they then responded by giving him bread and fresh water.

Alpheus spent another hour in the cabin with his eyes closed. When the first glimmers of daylight poked in at him through the window facing the sea, he finally forced his eyes fully open. He rose to his feet, doing his best to steady his balance and shake off the wobbling sensation. He then thought for a brief moment before reaching his hands behind his neck, stroking his hair that he had let fall behind him in long tresses. He pulled his hair together and started weaving it into braids, tying the same ponytail he had been accustomed to for years—though his hair was a little longer now. He then reached into his knapsack for the spectacles from Agnes, fitting them on. He swung the knapsack on his back again and treaded out to the main deck.

And there it was, Vinawell—the country of the west.

A tremendous port docked vessels of vast proportions, and between them were a scatter of smaller boats sailing in and out. Beyond the pier was a host of men, women, and even children—all of them blending into a bustling fair of colourful clothing, tented stalls, and street entertainers ranging from magic performers to dancers and musicians. Behind the lively activity was the great protective wall, together with its gate, which was the entrance to the actual city.

The sun had only just risen, but Aragon was well awake on this clear morning. Across the bay, behind the great wall, was a cluster of warehouses facing the sea, and more ships of all shapes and sizes. Strips of triangular-shaped, colourful banners woven from tapestry ends hung from building to building, flapping like sea waves in the gentle breeze in a cloudless backdrop of blue sky adorned by gliding gulls.

Alpheus hopped off the vessel, pausing at the moist wooden pier to marvel at the port's spectacular presentation. His first interaction with a resident of this foreign country came immediately, in the form of a fortune teller, an old woman with a hunchback.

"Welcome, stranger," she said with a gruff voice. "Allow me to speak your destiny. I shall—"

"I'm sorry," Alpheus said, raising a dismissive hand. "I believe in making one's own fate."

He treaded past the fortune teller with a smile, verifying that he was finally liberated. There was no need to hide, physically or otherwise. He didn't have to be Albert Moon anymore. In Aragon, in Vinawell, he could start afresh as Alpheus Hindlow once more. Here in this country, Trubans were the minority. Trubans were the foreigners.

And as Alpheus strolled deeper in the fair, he noted how rare it was to spot his compatriots. While a Vinan generally had lighter hair and skin than a Truban, the two races weren't all that different in appearance. The blue eyes which occurred in approximately a third of their population, however, was a feature unique to them. Like Dorellsdale, there seemed to be little racial tension in Aragon.

Alpheus soon came across a perfume stall with a cluster of women, young and old, crowded about. He wasn't one to wear perfume, but despite the fresh air carried by the pleasant sea breeze, he was still feeling nauseous from the smell of the sea itself. Something to cover up that smell might not be a bad idea.

He waited patiently at the back until some of the people cleared away, opening a path for him to finally see the merchant who ran the stall—a woman. Female merchants were rare, and she looked no older than thirty years of age, at the same time diffusing an air of vibrancy common in younger women barely in their adulthood. It was unlikely that many younger women had her qualities, though—that of her capacity to run a stall in this lively fair all on her own.

"I see," the merchant said to Alpheus with a radiant smile, looking at the selection, and then picking out one with a blue tint.

She's charming, too, Alpheus thought, noting her soft amber hair and green eyes common to the people of Vinawell.

"This is an exotic fragrance—even in Vinawell," the merchant boasted, handing over the small glass bottle to Alpheus. "It's extracted from a flower native to certain woodlands. A flower called the bluebell."

Alpheus removed the cap, running the bottle just beneath his nose. Although he had never seen the bluebell flower, he thought the perfume accurately captured the hyacinth sweetness reminiscent of bell-shaped flowers. That sweetness was splendidly fused with an earthy and wet sense that represented the misty woodlands. It did its job in covering up the sea smell, and indeed did more to send him into a trance, to a faraway land covered with trees and shrubs.

Alpheus finally returned from the trance when he screwed the cap back on. He needed no further convincing in making his first purchase in this foreign land.

The next stall Alpheus stopped by was one that sold spectacles, its wide range simply piled on the floor atop a large drape. What had caught his eyes was the only monocle among the selection, which seemed to glint at him as it reminded him briefly of a certain, important person. But as Alpheus leaned down for the eyeglass, a figure flashed into the air behind him, leaping over him and then crashing down right in the middle of the stock.

The merchant gasped, and by the time he cried for help, the figure—a child no older than twelve—had snatched away half the selection and then fled away back into the sea of people.

"That scoundrel!" the merchant cursed, stomping a foot on the ground.

"Does this happen often?" Alpheus asked.

The merchant crouched down to clean up the mess. "Often? No. But lately, yes. It's always them."

"*Them*?" Alpheus asked. "You... know the thieves?"

"The child just now is a regular urchin," the merchant explained as he dusted a pair of spectacles. "The Sail Band is the one behind it all. They're exploiting the urchins to do their dirty work."

Alpheus cocked his head. "Are you sure it's them?"

"Well, of course," the merchant said. "The community's always updated. We usually prevent theft after only one attempt. But this Sail Band is something else—a nuisance we cannot rid ourselves off."

Alpheus climbed to his feet, his face splitting into a smile. "I'll see if I can recover your stock."

The merchant finally looked up then with furrowed brows. "And how will you do that?"

"With this," Alpheus said, holding out the fragrance he had bought earlier. He then swung open his knapsack, pulling out a piece of dried meat. "And this."

"Entice the thieves with food?" the merchant asked, scratching his chin.

"No, but I'll need a dog to help. I suppose there are some strays in town?"

"Well, yes, but—"

"I can handle it," Alpheus said, rather excited to finally meet the infamous Sail Band.

He then turned to leave, promising to return soon. Of course, the merchant had no way of knowing that Alpheus had left a mark on the thief just now. He had shot a bead of the bluebell perfume at the boy, rooting the essence into his neck with the technique passed down from none other than Jeffery Reeling. And while it was impossible for anyone to ordinarily follow the trace of only a single drop of fragrance, Alpheus was confident that any stray dog could help him on the trail. That was where the dried meat came in handy. Indeed, Alpheus treaded into one of the quieter spots in the fair, waving that piece of meat in the air. It was barely a minute later when a mongrel with patches of brown, white, and black trotted over to him.

"Good boy," Alpheus said, treating the dog to a bite and patting it on the head. "Now, if you help me, I'll give you the rest."

The dog squealed and Alpheus ran the perfume bottle across its nostrils. The dog then barked before turning, racing off with haste. Alpheus gave prompt chase, opting not to make a scene with the Glider Steps. After dashing through the enormous gate and into the city, Alpheus scrambled through tight alleys until the canine finally stopped between a set of houses that was four storeys high. No one was around.

Alpheus looked up. "Here?" he said quietly.

The dog barked, wagging its tail.

Alpheus stretched his arms out, touching both walls easily in the narrow lane. *All right*, he decided with a leap that shot him up to inches beneath the second-storey window, holding there against the opposite walls with all four limbs. He poked his head up a little, just enough for him to peek in.

The urchin. And he wasn't alone. With him were a middle-aged man slouched on a torn couch, smoking a cigar, and a younger man about the same age as Alpheus, standing. Next to the couch was a straw bag that Alpheus suspected held stolen goods.

Alpheus shook his head, turning his head back and looking down at the dog still waiting for the promised reward. He reached a hand into his knapsack, picking out the piece of dried meat, all the while, applying pressure on the other arm for balance. He dropped the meat, watching the dog snatch it away and then trot back off through the alleyways.

Thank you, Alpheus thought with a smile.

He then poked his head up again. Although he couldn't hear what the thieves were saying, it looked like the urchin was indeed being exploited. It all became evident when the young man struck the boy unconscious with a club. Alpheus shook his head and then climbed in, taking his time in doing so.

"Who in the hell are you?" the middle-aged man asked, spitting out the cigar and stepping to his feet, surprised but not startled by Alpheus's entrance.

"Glad you asked," Alpheus said, "for I haven't had the chance to introduce myself for a long time. My name is Alpheus Hindlow. And can I assume you are the Sail Band?"

The two men chuckled, the middle-aged man flicking out a knife from under his sleeves. "Yeah," the man said with a shrug. "We're them. But, you know, this is the first time we had prey come to us."

Alpheus eyed their weapons: a knife and a club. "Let's do this without anyone getting hurt," he said. "Return what you stole, and I'll let you go."

The two of them exchanged a look and then burst out in laughter.

"What's funny?" Alpheus asked, annoyed.

"You made my day," the man said, holding a hand over his stomach. "But the joke is over," he then said, swinging out his knife again. "Leave everything of value, and I'll *consider* letting you go."

Alpheus sighed. "That's just too bad, then."

He reached a hand beneath his mantle, fishing out small balls of clay the size of pebbles. He rolled one of those nearly spherical clay balls up to his thumb, with his index finger folded behind it. The thieves merely raised their brows in response, ignorant of what was coming.

It's been a while, Alpheus thought, swallowing and then stretching his arm out toward the two men and ready to flick out a bolt. *It won't kill them*, he assured himself.

And it didn't. No shining beam was fired out. Instead, the tiny clay ball lifted off into a slight arc before dropping to the ground with a click. All eyes, including Alpheus's own widened eyes, followed the clay ball as it rolled forward to make a brushing contact against the boots of its intended target.

The two men did nothing to hold in their laughter, cackling without restraint once again. "Funny man!" the middle-aged man commented, struggling to make out his words.

Alpheus groaned, swinging out his arm again, firing another couple of clay balls in quick succession. This time, two beams shot out, striking the thieves in the chests and choking them into a hiccup. They fell forward to their knees in pain, but even so, the middle-aged man glared up at Alpheus, already looking to slash at him with his knife.

Alpheus was prompt to respond, aiming for the thief's leg with another bolt that ended with the thief crashing to the ground at his feet. He crouched down with a frown and then snatched away the blade.

"You're not the Sail Band," he guessed, anger and disappointment in his words. "You don't have it in you to cause that kind of havoc."

The two thieves looked at each other, anxiety dawning on their faces.

"Will you talk?" Alpheus said, squinting at the younger man, who jumped in response while still holding onto his chest which must be throbbing. "Or will I have to force it out of you?"

"We're impostors!" the young man blurted before slowing down again. "We figured it was convenient since everyone's so afraid of them and all."

"What about the ones terrorising the merchants? From Western Trubannis to Aragon."

The thieves paused, still rather tight-lipped.

"Answer me!" Alpheus demanded, forcing a stronger tone—unnatural to him, but effective enough.

"It was us," the middle-aged man said. "I would believe the real Sail Band's rather selective in who they target. They wouldn't pick on just any merchant. As for why the journey from Trubannis to here? Well, it looked like they found out we were using their name. We figured to make our way here... but I think they might have chased."

Alpheus rose back to his feet, musing on the new information, in turn realising these men were only petty thieves. "Go," he said, turning away to face the window. "Leave the stolen goods and go."

"Wait, wait," the younger man said. "Are you serious?"

"Yes, before I change my mind."

The two of them, likely father and son, helped each other to their feet.

They didn't say another word as they limped away to the exit, the sound of their footsteps receding as they treaded down the stairs.

Alpheus looked to the urchin who still lay unconscious next to the torn couch. The child was far from innocent, but even so, Alpheus sympathised for the boy, who had various marks of neglected treatment across his small body—bruises and scars, old and new. The boy had likely been forced into a life of crime simply because there was no other way for him to survive. Alpheus reached under his sleeves for a bronze coin, which was enough money for the boy to live on for weeks.

"Live well," he whispered, clutching onto the straw sack of stolen goods.

Alpheus turned for the exit, but as he made his way to the door, a sudden, strange and overbearing aura swept at him from the stairs up.

A sorcerer?! he thought, but immediately realised that he sensed no grace.

As if by instinct, Alpheus turned for the window where he had originally entered from, leaping in that direction. But just when he was about to escape, something was hurled at him from behind—not hitting him, but it had him trembling as he looked down to make out a set of twin daggers rooted deeply just in front of his feet.

"Why the rush?" a voice cried from behind him.

Alpheus turned in sluggish jerks to come face to face with a man at the door whose grin spelled out a sense of having achieved what he had set out to achieve. The sinewy man was tall, but not wide. He donned a thick headband tied at an angle, flapping open a short shawl as the only piece of clothing covering his upper body, which showcased his supremely compacted muscles—particularly his abdominal brawn. A pair of olive green pants and an overlapping set of belts completed his outfit.

"Do you think to leave so easily after dragging my name through mud?" he said, slamming the door closed behind him.

THREE

Violanola Cottage

Alpheus was of two minds. For one, he was curious about the stranger and that ardent aura still brimming out of him. But at the same time, he was torn between an urge to clear a potential misunderstanding and his instincts that told him to run from the man who trampled in at over six feet of hot-blooded shapely brawn. At the end, he did neither. With his trembling legs weighing down on him, Alpheus found himself raising his hands as a barrier of sort.

"Are you...," Alpheus said, stuttering as the stranger treaded slowly toward him, "Could you... possibly be... the one they call Sailanson?"

More specifically, the question was whether this stranger standing before him was the madman who allegedly slaughtered hundreds of comrades as a mercenary during the war. The mere thought of the possibility manifested into fear in the form of a creeping chill that prickled up from Alpheus's spine to his neck. It finally occurred to him now that it was a bad idea to have voluntarily sought out the thieving crew.

"Not surprised you would recognise me," the man said with a smirk, confirming his identity before turning a glance at the unconscious urchin. "So it's true you use children."

It took a moment for Alpheus to realise the reason for Sailanson's aggressiveness, that the man saw him as his impostor "Wait!" he blurted. "No, this is a mistake."

"Damn right, it's a mistake!" Sailanson croaked, cracking his knuckles. "You had everyone thinking me a petty thief."

Alpheus turned for the window again. But before he could leap out, the man flashed over next to him, resting a sturdy hand on the window sill that he had wanted to step on. Stunned, Alpheus dashed away with an impressive leap, eyeing the door—in particular, the doorknob. But again, before he reached it, a dagger was hurled at him—not hitting him, but instead, gashing at the knob and splitting into two.

This is crazy! Alpheus thought, eyes snapped wide open. *I've got to—*

He turned back slightly, and the man was at it again, trampling directly toward him like a mad bull. Alpheus cringed, dashing to the left this time, making a sharp turn. He was conscious that there were more daggers hanging from Sailanson's set of overlapping belts.

If I could discombobulate him with my run, Alpheus thought, speeding up. *If I could only trip him up.* As he glanced back now in his haste, he saw a long trail of afterimages behind him with a sprinkle of glowing white dust.

It was as he remembered it should be. Except this time, there was more.

Immediately behind the fading afterimages was the raging man still giving unceasing chase. And along his way, Sailanson smashed every obstacle with his bare fists, tearing through walls, crushing down beams, and causing dust and debris to rain from the ceiling.

"Stop!" Alpheus cried, still running. "The whole place's going to collapse!"

Sailanson didn't stop at all, seemingly only interested in Alpheus's capture. All the while, parts of the wall near the door had started to shatter into a heap of rubble, brushing up thick sheets of dust.

No, Alpheus thought, eyeing the urchin who was about to be crushed by the rubble. *I can't reach him in time.* He dashed toward the boy with an outstretched arm, near certain that his effort was futile. But as the rest of the wall collapsed, the man who had caused the damage flashed across Alpheus, snatching the boy into his arms. Alpheus had no time to rejoice, however, because when he looked up, the wall was crumbling down upon him. He kicked back in desperation and managed to fall away just in time. He had just landed on his backside when all of it finally slammed down with a clap, sweeping up clouds of dust to smoke the chamber.

Alpheus coughed as he waved a hand to clear the smoke.

"You're good," Sailanson said, standing casually at an elevation on the rubble, slipping his twin daggers back into his utility belt. The urchin was lying on the torn couch once again, though the couch was now covered in layers of dust. "It's no wonder you were able to use my name for all this time."

"It wasn't me!" Alpheus cried, still perched on the floor. "I already told you—this is a misunderstanding. The ones who—"

Sailanson shook his head in pity. "It saddens me to see someone young and skilled resort to this."

Alpheus groaned, but when he slapped a hand on the floor in frustration, his urge to argue fell short as he noted the generous amount of rubble available to him which he could use as projectiles. He shut his hand into a loose fist, grasping onto some of the debris in the process. Sailanson raised a brow at him, and at that, Alpheus swung his arm out, shooting out a beam. To his delight, he fired with great power. And yet… this was the first time the technique itself failed.

Sailanson leaped into a reverse-flipping motion to evade the shot before *catching* the fired pebble between his fingers while upside-down airborne—all of this within the space of a fraction of a second. When he landed, he dropped the small piece of debris onto the rest of the rubble.

Alpheus gawked, collapsing to the floor in defeat. He was stunned enough that he was slow to realise that Sailanson had grown suddenly desperate and fearful about something, glancing left and right.

"We've got to get out of here!" the man said, darting toward the urchin.

Alpheus looked up to the ceiling where more dust was raining down. He then peered to the right end of the collapsed wall where the adjacent wall had started to tremble wildly.

You've got to be kidding me!

"Hey," the man said with a foot on the window sill and the boy on his back. "Can you walk?"

Alpheus looked down to his feet, which wouldn't respond. "I… I think—"

"Oh, never mind," the man said, looking out from the window.

For a moment there, Alpheus thought the man was going to leave him there to die. He changed his mind, though, when a figure flashed in from the outside, landing on the same window sill. The newcomer wore an eyepatch over his right eye, with dark wavy hair that fell just beneath the shoulders.

"Help him, Ro," the man said to the newcomer, gesturing to Alpheus, before leaping out with the urchin.

The newcomer groaned, but did as instructed, dashing at Alpheus and tossing him over his back. The next thing Alpheus realised was that he was plummeting down from the building. His natural reaction had him shriek. Only upon landing did he remember that it wasn't all that high. On top of that, the newcomer who had saved him seemed as good an acrobat as the man who had destroyed the building.

The two of them didn't stop there. Alpheus realised why when the entire second floor of the building tumbled down with a thundering clunk that reverberated in the air and perhaps resonated all across the city. All the while, a flustered cloud of dust and rubble rained down. As he was being carried away in haste, Alpheus gaped as he watched dust and smoke fill the sky.

Father of Heaven, please let no one be in there, Alpheus prayed with his eyes closed. When he finished the prayer, they arrived at the outside of what looked like a small house, which was one of the only single storey buildings around. The man with the eyepatch bumped Alpheus off from his back and then dragged him along by the collar into the house behind Sailanson. The urchin was nowhere to be seen any longer, and Alpheus could only wonder where and when Sailanson might have unloaded him during the hectic journey there. He tried to convince himself that Sailanson wouldn't have bothered to save the boy earlier had he wanted to hurt him.

Upon entering the building, however, Alpheus grew suspicious again. Every corner of the crude shelter was stacked with various goods—stolen goods, of course.

Another four people were already inside the house, sitting around a square table. It was apparent that they all belonged to the same crew. One of them was a young lady, petite, distinctly Truban, with wavy hair in a short bob. Only one of the other three men looked Truban—he also seemed to be the youngest of the men. A man with a rectangular face and downward slanting brows looked Vinan. And finally, perched at the back without expression was a giant of a man, tall but not wide, dark-skinned—possibly a man of Kragan descent.

"You got it all wrong, Marvin," the younger Truban man said with a wry smile.

Marvin? Alpheus thought with a wince, glancing over to Sailanson, the man who had demolished a building without breaking a sweat. *Marvin... Sailanson? He really is him... the infamous mercenary... a man loyal to the Lord Emperor.*

"The ones who assumed our name are over there," the young lady said, fiddling with the tip of a broken arrow. "And *this* is their hideout."

She pointed a thumb over to the far corner where a sturdy fishing net was wrapped around two unconscious men—the thieving duo Alpheus had spared earlier. Alpheus only realised now how naïve he had been to think that the spectacles was all they had stolen. But there was no point to be mad at those thieves now—not in the face of a much more frightening group of thieves.

"All right...," Sailanson said. "So can someone tell me what happened?"

"We found this place after you ran off on your own," the young lady said. "We've been waiting here for a while. In fact, the thieves only just came back."

Sailanson regarded Alpheus now with a sheepish frown. "I'm sorry," he said, scratching his goatee. "Are you... hurt? Oh, and by the way, the name's Marvin. The one who helped you just now is Rover."

The man in the eyepatch, or *Rover*, shot Alpheus a glance. He shook his head before retiring to a seat away from the others. Alpheus turned back to Sailanson, having trouble attributing to the man the name, *Marvin*, which was rather mundane for an alleged madman.

"I'm Tavie," the young lady offered with a wave.

"Ash," said the younger Truban man. "A geologist."

"Leo," said the Vinan man with a rectangular face. "Oh, and my friend here," he said, resting a hand on the broad shoulder of the giant. "He's Karl," he added with a wink, "and yes, he's Kragan."

"I see," Alpheus managed to utter, eyeing Karl who was certainly exotic in appearance. Other than his dark skin and tremendous height, the man had a long, blocky head, small eyes rectangular in shape, and protruding lips that were almost black in colour.

Alpheus jumped now as Marvin placed a hand on his shoulder. "Do I see that you're all right?" Marvin said.

"I...," Alpheus said with a slight frown. "I think I'm fine."

"Good to know," Marvin said with a sigh, stepping away to the shelves where all the stolen goods were stocked. "Didn't want to hurt you, Alpheus."

"Well, yes, but I...," Alpheus said, trailing off abruptly when he realised the thief had called him by name. *The criminal portraits*, he thought, the assumption springing to mind immediately. *He must have seen them.*

"Relax," Marvin said with a chuckle without looking back. "I don't work for the Empire."

"You... don't?" Alpheus said hesitantly as he watched the man inspect the stolen goods, certain that the man had at least once worked for the Lord Emperor.

Marvin had certainly proved reckless in barely an hour since they had met, but at the same time, the man seemed carefree. Perhaps he really had nothing to do with the emperor anymore. A more curious matter was the fact that Marvin looked to be only about thirty years of age. If the war had ended eight years ago, it meant he had barely been a man at the time when he had fought.

"Anyway," Ash said. "About you... Alpheus—if I can call you that. What's your crime?"

Alpheus trembled slightly, his eyes still on Marvin, who spared him no look in return. "Well...," Alpheus said, turning to Ash with a grimace and a disdainful tone to match. "Not theft. And no matter what crime I might have committed, it couldn't be worse than harming the innocent."

Ash raised a brow. "The innocent? What are you talking about? Are you still mad about... whatever Marvin did to you?"

Marvin perked up with a glance back at the conversation.

"I don't know," Alpheus said, shaking his head. "But if it were me, I wouldn't go on a whim and pulverise a building." He hissed, glaring at the ground. "The people there. They..."

Ash turned to Marvin, looking curious rather than questioning. "You destroyed the building?" he asked.

Marvin shrugged. "Figured I might as well. Have to give the mayor a lesson after what he did."

Alpheus squinted, his frown deepening as suspicion and confusion dawned his face.

"You got it all wrong, young lad" said Leo, the Vinan of the crew, as the other two shared a chuckle. "Other than chasing the impostors, we've been on the mayor's case—the mayor of the local municipality, that is. The man's covetous—as are many others in power. He's been embezzling from the civilians for years. That building is where he kept the things he robbed. But of course knowing Marvin," he said with a glance over at the crew leader, "those things aren't there anymore. As for the people, well—they're the first ones Marvin would have driven out."

Alpheus raised a suspicious brow. "Why should I believe you?"

"Don't," Tavie said, as if defending Leo. "You think we care what you think? You're the *only* criminal here."

"All right, now," Leo said, waving a hand. "Let's all be friendly."

"And you're *not* criminals...?" Alpheus challenged. "The infamous Sail Band? The last I heard, the Empire is on your case more so than mine. Don't try to make yourselves out as good and noble when you have the audacity to storm the Monarchal Castle without any respect for authority."

Rover, the man who had yet to say a word, shot a second glare at Alpheus now. "If you have so much respect for authority," he said with a gruff voice, "why don't you hand yourself in?"

Alpheus frowned again, but found that he had nothing to say. The others had turned silent too, and the collective mood suddenly grew dark.

"Anyway, Alpheus... *or* boy with many secrets," Ash said finally, breaking the tension. "We're doing what we think is right. We don't kill. We don't harm anyone aside from those who deserve it. And yes, we *take*, but we're selective in who we take from."

The explanation was more than Alpheus had expected, but he couldn't yet bring himself to believe any of it.

"You know, you can just go," Marvin said. "But leave that sack behind. It's not yours."

Alpheus looked down at the sack of spectacles. "What will you do with it?" he dared to ask.

"Not your concern," Marvin replied curtly.

Alpheus shook his head, realising that it was futile to even try recovering the goods from the thieves. "Very well, then," he said reluctantly, turning to the exit. "If you'll excuse me."

Alpheus fastened the strap to his knapsack, only to notice a sizeable tear on his right sleeve. He immediately turned his gaze toward Marvin, realising it was a result of his daggers from earlier. Indeed, Marvin grinned now, also noting the mark he had left. Alpheus gritted his teeth, raising an arm. And when he did so, a dark parchment fell to the ground from the sleeve, which was then promptly snatched up by Tavie.

No! Alpheus thought.

"What have we here?" she said, skimming the text. Seconds later, she waved it up into the air for the others to see. "It's from Poppaross," she said, sounding rather surprised herself, as she passed the parchment to Leo for examination. "Looks like *Alpheus* was hiding something more than his crimes. An invitation to... a Purification Ceremony. From *Lithia*."

As small in size as it was, the stamped, red-coloured heraldic crest on the top right corner of the parchment was too obvious to miss. These things were not easy to forge, and of course, it *was* the real thing, which depicted a mighty shield caressed by mythical beasts similar to lions on both sides.

"Definitely not a fake," Leo confirmed. "An invitation to the Purification Ceremony from the *Imperial Lithia Dominion*, the supreme authority of Vinawell."

"I didn't know the girl was coming of age already," Marvin said before squinting at Alpheus. "And of all people, they invited *you*? Who exactly *are* you?"

Alpheus swallowed, growing more and more anxious.

"The way you moved," Marvin said, treading toward Alpheus now. "And that beam you shot out. Just who are you? What did you do that had the Empire onto you?"

Alpheus could feel sweat building up all over his body beneath that thick mantle as he looked up at the imposing mercenary-turned-bandit tower over him. "I...," he said with a stutter. "I don't—"

"Don't tell me," Marvin then said, challenging him. "We can find out on our own soon enough. And if it turns out that you—"

"How do I know I can trust you?" Alpheus spat out on impulse.

"You'll know when you know," he said, finally backing away. "I won't ask you again. If you choose to tell me, then the decision will be of your own free will. You're headed to Poppaross, are you not? You'll have us in company."

What?! Alpheus thought. He thought he had said it out loud, but it was Tavie who uttered the word. The other crew members shared the sense of surprise.

"Relax," Marvin said to the others. "I was planning to go there, anyway."

"Why...?" asked Tavie, raising a brow.

"There's something I want from there. And Tav, I could use your help."

Tavie rolled her eyes. "Can you not call me that? Besides, do we really have to go? Castles are lame."

Leo began chortling, and soon both Marvin and Ash joined him. Affected by the contagious laughter, even the two seemingly emotionless men, Rover and Karl, began smiling.

Alpheus watched the crew mingle, exchanging jokes. It was a mystery how such a group had been put together, and how they managed to *stay* together. Every individual member seemed different enough that one would expect them to clash on nearly every decision.

And they do clash, Alpheus thought. *But it works for them. Somehow.*

* * *

The stigma that came with being a thief was inevitable, and no ornamental words could adorn the label. Alpheus had thought it laughable that the Sail Band self-proclaimed as treasure hunters. But as he watched the cargo ship sail off now, backdropped by a setting sun that caused the sky to bleed strokes of tangerine, he pondered about whether or not he had judged too soon. On his second day in this new country—and also the second day since he had met the thieving crew—Alpheus had seen a few things, and might have learned a thing or two as well.

Marvin and his crew were not passengers on that ship that was sailing away. The ones who had boarded the vessel were the two men who had committed multiple crimes in their name. And they had boarded neither as passengers, nor sailors. The Sail Band had arranged the *ride*—smuggling the two men onto the ship, netted together with a whole lot of fish.

And this had been their only act of mischief—even Alpheus had quietly agreed that it was funny and appropriate. Before this, under Marvin's direction, the crew had distributed the stash of stolen goods to people in the city—seemingly at random, Alpheus had initially thought. But in fact, the crew had been working at this since the morning in three groups, working from a list prepared by Leo and moving around the city passing out charity items to the less fortunate. The recipients were mostly made up of the elderly, the poor, the sick, or—more generally, those who had suffered some kind of tragedy. And the crew had managed to accomplish this without even showing themselves to the beneficiaries, leaving their gifts anonymously. While the goods being distributed had never belonged to them, it was more than commendable that anyone would go to the trouble. And they were efficient, too. It was clearly not their first time doing this.

Alpheus never found out what had happened to the urchin who had helped the two impersonators. But he could rest well knowing that the Sail Band had arranged something better for him than he himself could have.

Leo had a wagon ready the next morning. Their destination was forty miles west of Aragon, but unlike the convenient travel route from Zorlia to Dorellsdale, there was no paved path between Aragon and the Vinan capital. Soon after rolling out of the port city, they were welcomed by uneven hills and seemingly endless fields of lush green. This type of landscape was rare in Trubannis, but it was the kind of gentle and peaceful surrounding that Alpheus had always imagined was ideal for an artist.

Apparently, it was also Tavie's first visit to Vinawell. She had been poking her head out of the wagon in excitement as the gentle breeze slapped her face, reducing her to a squint.

It was a few hours later when the crew finally took a break. It was time for a meal, and—as nomads—they were used to *hunting* for food. Every one of them was a skilful hunter—everyone, that is, except Tavie. She complained that she didn't have a quality bow with her. And while it seemed a fair excuse at first, it was inadequate when no one else needed any equipment for something as *simple* as hunting. The others had picked up anything they could use to help as they utilised the environment in creative ways.

The same routine repeated itself for the next few days. And, during this time, Alpheus had begun to grow comfortable with a few of them. He was particularly fond of Ash, who was well-versed in geology. Unlike himself, who was familiar with the theoretical side of things, Ash was much more interested and skilled on its actual application. Behind his cheerful exterior was a grievous past. As a native of the southern state of Noel, Ash had experienced the horrors of war, as well as its aftermath. He had seen his family murdered before his very eyes, and his hometown turned into a bloodbath. He considered it to be a miracle that he had survived, and to respect the opportunity for a new life, he had vowed to treasure his existence. He had to live on, and live with passion, in order to honour those who had died. He also had to repay the one who had helped win him that new lease of life—and that man was none other than Marvin Sailanson. Their first encounter had been in the final year of the war. Marvin had managed not only to save Ash from near certain death, but the former mercenary had also lifted him from despair and guided him toward a meaningful life. Their second encounter had been years after the war, incidentally the time when Ash became the crew's first recruit.

Leo was another crew member that Alpheus had grown to appreciate. His full name was Leonardo Edward Bassing. He was indeed Vinan, from the central state of *Sequiposa*. He was genuinely friendly, having sought Alpheus out more than a few times in the last couple days to *remind* him of the etiquette expected around the crew, and in Vinawell in general. Leo claimed that he was no fighter, unlike the other crew members. He was reluctant to reveal too much about himself, though, often dismissing his life story as plain and stale, especially when compared to the others.

Everyone in the crew has a role to play, Leo had said to him. *Except me. I'm the only expendable member.*

Leo had described Marvin as much more than a leader. He didn't believe that he would ever meet anyone stronger and more courageous than Marvin. He had called Marvin one of the most selfless people he knew, one who genuinely cared for the state of the world.

Rover, too, was a good man—at least according to Leo. While the eyepatch and his general attitude of indifference might not give the best of impressions, Rover was inherently a good man. He was supposedly a prominent figure of the war, just like Marvin. Indeed, the two of them had supported one another since then. They had co-founded the thieving crew as a new chapter in their post-war lives.

Alpheus had yet to learn much about Tavie, or anything about Karl, the giant from Kraga. But on this third evening of travel, Alpheus decided to tell his story. As they all sat around a campfire under a clear night sky, Alpheus spoke for the first time at length about his circumstances, the murders, his criminal status, and why he was in Vinawell. Even as he was speaking, he thought for a moment the irony that he had somehow befriended a thieving crew.

His audience appreciated the honesty and the trust Alpheus had shown them. The surprise was that they seemed empathetic, rather than astonished, even when Alpheus spoke about sorcery and that he too was a sorcerer. The crew didn't seem wary of him even then, and Alpheus wasn't sure whether it was only because of his unintimidating build. But perhaps to the Sail Band who must have already heard many stories in their adventures, Alpheus's circumstances stood out less than they otherwise would.

* * *

On the fourth day of travel, Alpheus and the Sail Band reached the *Violanola Woodlands*. It was rumoured that an impressionist by the pseudonym *Cipher Nostalgia* lived out here. Alpheus recognised why an impressionist would choose this place, as he looked around him now at the variants of natural light that filtered through the canopies. It was midday, and despite plenty of sunshine, cool shades were cast off from the sparsely grown trees. Unlike the lush fields of the past few days, the woodland was home to only smaller animals such as those of the rodent order. Hunting was more difficult, because their targets were smaller—and also because that meant that they had to catch more.

"I'm feeling good today," Tavie said, stretching her arms and then pointing to the north. "I'll be over there. I'm not sharing my prey with anyone."

The others forced a smile in response. As it had been on the previous day, Alpheus elected to split off with Ash for today's hunting exercise. And it was the first time that he contributed to the cause. While Alpheus had never hunted before, he had a skill that might better any member of the thieving crew. It was his only means of offence, something that even Marvin had called remarkable. Alpheus loaded small stones at the tip of his thumb, and fired out beams with what looked like simple flicks of the index finger. The success rate was far from reliable, at times, missing his target by quite some distance. Even worse, he would sometimes only manage to propel those stones off tamely to draw nothing but thin air. But even so, Ash was duly impressed every time that it did work. The precision and accuracy of the technique was simply spectacular.

"Amazing," Ash said, gaping at another stone that Alpheus fired out like a small cannon. "Probably the closest thing to sorcery that isn't actually sorcery."

Alpheus sighed. "I've actually considered never lending to the ability again," he said. He breathed another sigh then, this one heavier than the previous as he dropped the rest of the stones to the ground. "I've killed people with it," he confessed.

Alpheus looked away to avoid eye contact with Ash, who said nothing. He sure that Ash would think less of him

"It's impressive all right," Ash finally said. "But it cannot kill, not with *your* power."

Alpheus looked up in surprise. "But, I—"

"Is this about how you were accused of downing some guards? Look, I cannot know how they died. But there's no way you could kill anyone with those stones."

"No, Ash, I—"

"Listen," Ash said, cutting in again. "If you grew stronger or if you managed to perfect the skill, then yes, perhaps you could kill. But now? No."

"You really think so?" Alpheus said, feeling his cheek muscles tense up to form a smile.

Ash beamed back in response. "You're still only a feeble scholar, Alpheus," he said, placing a hand on his shoulder. "It will take a lot more than that if you ever wanted to kill."

"You don't know how glad I am to hear that," Alpheus said, his eyes watering up in delight.

His joy took a brief hit, however, when a sudden scream reverberated across the heart of the woodlands, causing the leaves above them to rustle as a flock of startled birds fluttered over them. The two men turned toward where the scream had sounded from.

"Was that... Tavie?" Alpheus asked.

Ash frowned. "I wish it wasn't," he said, already stepping forward.

The perennials that had provided them with shade were now obstacles to avoid as they bolted through the woods. And after twisting through the mazy route in haste, they arrived in a relatively open patch void of trees. Instead, it was a domicile—a cottage one wouldn't expect to see there in that spot. The structure tinged in canary was ample in size with two storeys, encapsulated by an ornamental garden where luscious vines stemmed from the ground, caressing parts of the stone construction. Adjacent to the building was a fountain at the centre of a pond over which butterflies hovered. It was a combination of the serene sound of flowing water and the relaxing sight of gentle flapping of colourful wings that had both of them entranced for a moment. If there was anything that didn't belong, it was the opulent horse carriage and the couple of fine horses parked behind the fountain.

The wonder ceased, however, when Marvin arrived immediately to their right, chewing on a long blade of grass, and dragging behind him a sizeable sack of unfortunate prey.

Ash looked over to him. "Looks like she found herself in trouble again," he said.

Marvin spat out the blade of grass, shaking his head, looking annoyed rather than worried. Rover, Leo, and Karl arrived within the next minute. They each carried a sack of prey, though theirs weren't nearly as bulky as Marvin's.

Alpheus turned back to the cottage. This could be the home of the impressionist. He imagined the man—or woman—to be well-presented, polite, and, most important of all, a true genius of art. He looked toward the delicate wooden door and pictured that person stepping out from there. But his dreaminess was shattered when a dagger was hurled at the door, completely breaking off its handle.

"Come on!" Marvin said, already on his way.

"Wait," Alpheus urged, pulling him back by his shawl that fell from his broad shoulders. "No, we can't just—"

Alpheus paused when a squeak sounded. The door pushed out slowly with a gentle creaking noise. Stepping out to the porch were three women who shot curious glances out at the men. The women were vernal, perhaps not even twenty years of age, dressed simply but sensibly in dresses shaded in creamy yellow that fell to their feet. All three of them had that charm distinct to the women of Vinawell, that unassuming demeanour and general comfort in embracing their womanhood—similar to the merchant who sold the perfume back in Aragon.

Two of the three looked strikingly similar. Their round eyes were curbed in irises of transparent sky blue. Their soft amber hair was worn in the same layered fringes that brushed elegantly to the side, latched at the back with hair forks that pulled into half-ponytails. One of them, the apparent leader of the three women, also tied a ribbon-veil of light blue that fell delicately behind her. They were the closest thing to identical for two people who didn't seem like twins.

Their companion on the right meanwhile was slightly taller with hair of a darker shade and eyes of olive green. She also looked a tad more mature than the other two, who seemed barely in their womanhood. They were each fairly attractive in their own right, however, especially as the filtered rays of sunlight shone down on them.

"What is this commotion?" asked the young lady with the ribbon-veil, in a grumbling tone that didn't match her elegant appearance. "Who intrudes upon our peace?"

"I apologise if we caused you any inconvenience," Ash said. "But we believe you have our friend."

"I do have an ill-mannered lass stumble here not long ago," she said, studying her nails now. "She trampled on my garden bed, and is now repenting for it. She will stay here with me to learn some manners."

"I am sorry about your... garden bed, but we have a schedule to follow. I think it's best that you return her now."

The young lady looked up as her lips curled up into a grin. "No," she enunciated.

"Do you know who we are?" Marvin asked with a chortle, tensing up.

"I *don't* know who you are," she said with a shrug this time, "nor do I care."

Alpheus pursed his lips as he glanced back and forth at Marvin and the young lady, enjoying the exchange more than he should. The vigorous, sassy young lady was probably the worst kind of enemy for Marvin.

But young one, Alpheus thought as Marvin started. *You better run.*

The young lady remained ever so calm and arrogant. She lifted her thumb and index finger, bringing them to her mouth, blowing a gentle whistle, which was a strange thing to do given the situation. But, seconds later, leaves from above rustled as if by a brewing storm. And, soon, an enormous flurry of birds flocked in from behind the cottage—all of them swooping down at Marvin.

Marvin dived to the ground, lying flat on the grass to dodge the fierce sweep. After blowing past him, the birds glided in an upward arc before turning back to prepare for a second round of their aerial rave.

"Look out!" Ash cried.

"What is this...?" Leo uttered in shock as they all looked up to the *myriad* of birds—hundreds of them, all fluttering up in the sky. Each individual bird was small in size, but the sheer number that made up the swarm was frightening.

Alpheus swung his attention back to the cottage door, and specifically to the young lady with the ribbon-veil. *She's controlling those birds?!* he thought.

How?

Sorcery?

“I see that you are agile,” the young lady said, eyeing Marvin with a smug grin. “But how many times can you evade me?”

FOUR

The figurative salmon

The woman lifted her hand once more, looking to signal a second flurry. No one moved—no one dared to, not before learning what they were dealing with. But Alpheus, donning an olive-green mantle—someone who looked rather fragile compared to the others—flitted forward, brushing up a breeze that swept the fallen leaves into a spectacular swirl.

The young lady widened her eyes to Alpheus's sudden approach, to what would have been a blur to everyone including her. He rounded next to her, holding her hostage by the neck and causing her to let out a low moan. Her companions gasped, hands over their mouths.

"Azure!" one of them cried.

Alpheus ignored them, looking askance at the one he held, sensing not a hint of grace in her. "Send those birds away," he said instead, somewhat disappointed as he pressed gently onto her neck with his fingers.

She nodded, bringing a hand to her mouth again. She whistled and the birds took off, vanishing altogether in the same way as they had come. Marvin jumped back to his feet as Ash and the others rushed over to him.

"Thank you," Alpheus said and then withdrew his grip. "I apologise for being so rude," he continued, taking a step back from the slightly raised porch. "Can I assume your name is Azure?" he asked, looking into her gleaming eyes of sky blue.

"That is... indeed my name," Azure said, looking wary. "You are not of here. What do you want?"

"I thought we made ourselves quite clear," Alpheus said. "You have our friend, and we want her back."

"And why did you come here in the first place?" she asked, glancing out at Marvin and the rest of the crew. "And with such an odd bunch, at that."

"Enough of the pleasantries, Alpheus!" Marvin cried from afar, trotting in now. "We don't have the time."

"Alpheus...?" one of Azure's companions uttered musingly. "Would you share your full name?"

The curiosity stumped Marvin's advance. Alpheus, meanwhile, responded with a nod.

"Hindlow," he said. "Alpheus Hindlow of Zorlia."

The ladies exchanged surprised looks. They had apparently heard the name before. Alpheus was hopeful, however, that it had nothing to do with the crimes he had been accused of. In fact, he was wishful in thinking that Azure might well be Cipher Nostalgia, and that the woman had heard about him as an artist. Suddenly, he didn't mind whether or not she was a sorcerer anymore. If she were, she'd be the supposedly rare, dormant kind just like him.

Alpheus only realised he was staring when he finally noted that Azure was glancing elsewhere rather awkwardly. He blinked then as he turned his attention to her companions instead. It really was extraordinary that one of them looked so much like her.

"I feel discourteous to not have asked yet," he said then. "But may I know your names in return?"

"You can call me Carmen," answered the slightly taller woman with dark hair.

"I am Claire," said the other lady, who looked just like Azure.

Names that start with C, Alpheus thought, shooting his gaze back to Azure. *Cipher Nostalgia, though, is of course but a pseudonym.*

"And are you really who you say you are?" Azure asked with suspicion.

Alpheus simpered. "I don't believe anyone would want to assume my name."

"Why are you in Vinawell?"

Alpheus glanced over to Marvin, who simply shrugged. "I'm heading to Poppaross to be the Prince Consort," he said, regarding Azure again. "Well, to compete for it, anyway."

Azure exchanged another look with her companions. "This may be unprecedented, but I have a proposal," she said. "We want a favour. If you manage to help, we'll not only release your friend, but we will also support you in your bid to become the Prince Consort."

"And how do we know you can help?" Marvin cut in.

"You don't," Azure said. "You just have to take my word for it."

The implication that they had no choice—that they had Tavie as hostage—was obvious. And Azure seemed to trust that she could keep Marvin in check with that alone.

"What do you want us to do?" Alpheus asked.

"Not all of you," Azure said, her eyes on Alpheus. "Only you. We need a scholar. We've been scuffling with a nobleman whose name is Copper. He's also a scholar. I figured we can get you to talk to him."

"About what?"

"Lord Copper seeks to claim ownership of the cottage. He is adamant to have us moved."

"But in exchange," Claire added with haste. "He's offering a lavish dwelling in Poppaross. He's a good man."

"In any case," Azure said, taking over again. "Lord Copper's challenging us to the right of ownership. We think it fair that he has proposed a battle of wits rather than of strength."

"Well, *you* have a sharp tongue," Ash inserted from behind. "I think you'd do well yourself."

The crew shared a chuckle, and even Azure's companions giggled. Alpheus smiled, holding in a chortle of his own. *Agreed*, he thought, with his gaze on Azure, whose face was flushed. *Not many people are as witty*.

"And besides," Ash said, "if you wanted to rid this man off, your birds could do the trick."

"No," Claire said with a sorry expression. "As I have said, Lord Copper is a good man. We want him to understand."

It didn't make sense. But Alpheus couldn't bring himself to question Claire whose natural sensibility demanded deference. Despite sharing a strikingly similar physical appearance with Azure, she shared little of the apparent leader's vocal tendencies.

"Can I assume that this *battle of wits* has already started?" Alpheus asked with a glance over at the horse carriage on their right.

"Indeed," Azure said.

Alpheus smiled. "Looks like you owe us a *thank you* then. If it wasn't for us, you wouldn't have been able to excuse yourself."

Azure narrowed her eyes, in a way, to confirm that it was true. "I'm still waiting for your reply."

"You would need to tell me more," Alpheus said.

"Deductive reasoning," Carmen said, her dark hair and olive-green eyes a stark contrast to those of the other two. "Lord Copper is a top scholar of the *Academy of Astilow*. He is presenting to us certain propositions, and from that, we are to determine certain facts. In other words, it is a test of our ability to judge."

It still didn't make sense to Alpheus who mused over it as he continued to stare into the woman's olive-green eyes. It seemed less and less likely that these women were sorcerers, not even the dormant kind. After all, sorcerers were extremely rare. There was every possibility, however, that one of them might well be the famous impressionist who Alpheus would love to meet.

"Very well," Alpheus said finally. "I'll meet this Lord Copper. But I have a few conditions of my own."

"What are these conditions?" Azure asked with a slight roll of the eyes.

"I am with them," Alpheus said, nodding at Marvin, Ash, and the others. "They will be my side. As will Tavie, our ally who has fallen into your hands for damaging your garden bed."

"We can accommodate that. Except… we don't have the lass. Lord Copper does."

Some of the crew winced. "Perhaps we should be negotiating with this Lord Copper and not with you," Alpheus said, speaking for the others as well.

"Think that way if it helps your conscience," Azure said with a shrug. "But be warned: we are the only ones who can ensure the girl's safety."

They finally stepped through the front door now, into a corridor floored and walled with premium redwood timber. They saw no plants or flowers, and yet the scent of freshly picked flowers still filled every corner of the interior. A set of stairs was installed on the right side, while a couple of doors were visible on the left. The group proceeded to the second door, with Carmen leading the way.

A total of six men were perched inside. A well-groomed nobleman sat at the end of a long dining table, while the other five men—four of whom were soldiers—stood behind him. The fifth man was dressed oddly, donning a long dark robe complete with a hood that shrouded his eyes, revealing only the long, puffed goatee that fell from his chin. The man also held onto a wooden staff which could either be a mace or a walking stick. Curiously, there seemed to be an eerie energy around him.

"You kept us waiting," the nobleman said.

"We apologise," Azure said as she and her companions curtsied together.

The ladies found seats at the opposite end of the long table, looking a lot less comfortable than earlier.

"I see you brought some helpers," the nobleman said, eyeing Marvin, Rover, and Karl—all of whom would certainly appear formidable. "I welcome challengers and I have said that if you're able to find help, then by all means you are free to take it. I have my reservations, however, that such a group can—"

"Can what?" Marvin grumbled.

The man in the robe lifted his eyes. "It's him..."

The nobleman glanced over to his vassal, who looked weary with dark circles under his eyes. The nobleman then studied Marvin for a moment. He seemed to have recognised Marvin then, gawking openly at him before catching himself. The nobleman then stood from his chair and leaned forward in delight.

"You're *him*?" he said. "You're that man with the power of a hundred? And the rest of you... you are the group that make up the Sail Band? It is a pleasure to meet you all. Oh, and would you excuse my manners. I am Peter Ormond Copper."

Marvin eyed the nobleman carefully. "Ah, so *you're* Copper. Do I suppose you're a member of the Dominion court?"

"Proudly," Copper answered with a nod. He then turned back to the ladies. "To think that you managed to summon the Sail Band to your aid. But while that is certainly impressive, I'm interested to know how they could help... on a battleground of reasoning."

"They're here to spectate," Azure said before gesturing over to Alpheus. "Our representative is Alpheus Hindlow. From the renowned Villa of Zorlia, headed by Grandmaster Isaiah Felipe—*the man who knows all*."

Alpheus stepped forward. It was awkward even for him to be introduced that way. And now it became apparent to him that Azure didn't know about his alleged crimes. The nobleman who fell back into his chair at the far end, however, seemed to have heard, hinting it with a sudden, narrow squint.

"I'm not sure this is quite the person you can depend on," Copper said. "It is but a rumour, but Alpheus Hindlow has been pronounced a criminal in Trubannis—allegedly murdering four men, including Jeffery Reeling, the great Lord Count."

Alpheus winced at the mention of Reeling, glaring at the man who dared to say his name. Azure and her companions, meanwhile, eyed him with a sudden wariness.

"My criminal status in Trubannis stands," Alpheus said, eyes still on Copper. "But I do not admit to any of the crimes listed next to my name. In any case, it does not hinder my task of defeating you as a representative of The Villa. That is, unless you are afraid to compete."

"Me? Afraid of you?" Copper said, bemused. "You jest."

"Then let's get on with it."

Copper glanced over at Marvin and then back at Alpheus. "Very well, then," he said. "This isn't about you or me, anyway. I have only the Dominion's best interests at heart."

Alpheus turned to Azure. "Do you trust me?" he asked.

Azure exchanged a look with her companions. She then regarded Alpheus with her eyes opened wide.

"I... suppose," she finally said.

* * *

The collective intelligence of the three ladies had thus far solved three problems. A fourth problem was to be presented now, and perhaps a fifth and final problem if they managed to get that far. Azure had said that every subsequent problem had proved more difficult than the previous, and that was why they needed help. Perhaps to them, Alpheus wasn't the best person to rely on any longer. But Alpheus couldn't worry about that in the face of what could be a fierce intellectual battle.

"Shall we begin?" Copper asked.

"Please first allow me to explain the idea," Claire inserted, turning to Alpheus. "Syllogism is a logical argument made up of three parts. It calls for deductive reasoning in order to arrive at a conclusion based on two or more propositions. For instance, if I told you that all men are children of the Immortal, and then Mister Sailanson here is a man, then one could conclude that Lord Sailanson is a child of the Immortal."

Alpheus nodded at that while Ash and Leo looked like they might have understood without actually nodding. Marvin himself winked at Claire.

"The question that Lord Copper is about to present will follow the same three-part premise," Claire said. "But it is sure to be much more complex than the example I have just given."

Claire then eyed her companions, both of them nodding at her in agreement.

The nobleman cleared his throat. "Let us begin," he said, standing from his seat and then strolling to the right. "Consider George, a fisherman who lives in the country. He fishes every morning by the lake, early in the morning at precisely the same time. He has done this for ten years. It has become a habit of his to catch only two fish—one to feed the family, and one to sell at the market. That is all he needs, and he manages it every time, in a clear lake brimming with life. He fears that if he were to catch more, one day, the lake might run out of fish. He understands that custom is the great guide of life."

Copper paused there, looking out at Marvin, Ash, and the others in the crew who seemed to have no idea what he was getting at. The big Kragan at the back, in particular, seemed indifferent to the whole proceeding.

"Now, George lives a life of leisure," the nobleman continued, now strolling the other way. "He has a good family—three children. He enjoys a level of freedom that not everyone can afford."

He paused again, this time peering over to the women. "And yet...," he said, "George *considers* leaving—to turn his back on everything he has. Why he would do so is beyond me. He has followed custom for all his life, using his tremendous skill—but also his only skill he could live off, which is to fish. He has been given the freedom to do this, to trade, to do anything to his liking... within reasonable boundaries, of course. His family adores him, but they are also heavily dependent on him. Without his support, his presence, the family is not only incomplete, but is also at risk of breaking apart financially and emotionally."

Copper paused for the final time, now turning to Alpheus. "Tell me now, scholar of Zorlia, what can we expect if George actually leaves? What of the family and what of George?"

The answer seemed obvious but Alpheus said nothing just yet, wearing a slight frown on his face. No one said anything. Could there be a trick somewhere? Did it lie in the intricacies of the syllogistic combination, or in the definition of the given propositions? Indeed, the propositions themselves might be the problem. But which ones *were* the prepositions?

"I think...," Alpheus finally said, "if George were to leave, his family would fall apart, while George himself would also struggle to survive while living a life where he no longer fishes." He paused. "This is the answer you want. But, Lord Copper, your story is flawed... in more than one way."

The nobleman squinted. "Enlighten me, then."

"Ah, where to start?" Alpheus said. "First of all, you mentioned that custom is the great guide of life. I agree that that is true... in most cases. For George, it is logical that he *should* keep fishing, and that is regardless of the fact that he is supporting his family. And then you also mentioned that George enjoys freedom, that there is generally no external restriction on what he does."

"That *is* precisely what I said," Copper acknowledged. "Where is the contradiction?"

"There is none," Alpheus said, shaking his head. "The issue lies elsewhere—your standard about what you call freedom. It is oversimplified. Freedom—or liberty—is not restricted to external coercion. It is sometimes about *internal* interference. George might not be coerced by anyone to go fishing or to provide for the family. He is at liberty to do as he pleases. But it is his conscience that urges him to repeat what he has done for a long time. He knows he has a responsibility, and he cannot dream of ever escaping this destiny if he is to be a good man. In this way, he is *not* free.

"And now, while this *lack* of freedom is certainly for a good cause, there is an inconsistency when coupled with the argument that custom is the great guiding force of his life. Allow me to first say that custom is *not* a truth of logic. Sure, if George continues to fish at the same lake, we can assume that he will continue to be awarded the two fish every day. But this belief is simply the result of our conditioning, which teaches us that every day will be the same. It is not a truth, for there are *many* possible ways in which the lake could run out of fish."

Alpheus paused again as he shot a squint at the nobleman. "Lord Copper, you said that it is beyond you why George considers leaving," he continued. "From the picture you have painted, I am inclined to believe that George is a good man. I cannot imagine he would consider anything other than following the norm, had he suspected that his departure would be detrimental to his family. It sounds to me that George considers leaving because he *must* leave, and it is for the best possible outcome to most people involved."

It was a long response, and perhaps a little forced. The nobleman's frown, however, showed that he accepted at least parts of the answer. Azure and her companions eyed both Alpheus and Copper in turn, likely wondering if the answer was sufficient.

"Well answered," Copper finally said, forcing a smirk while maintaining an intent gaze on Alpheus, which rendered a moment of dead silence.

"You scholars sure are dull," Ash said, breaking the tension. He shared a chuckle with Marvin and Leo, who both agreed.

Alpheus simply shrugged, but Copper didn't take their frivolity well. He snorted in their direction, but then moved quickly to the next and final question.

"Let us end this lingering once and for all," Copper said. "I'll be presenting another syllogistic problem—and this time, it will be straightforward. Even so, I will only accept answers from Mister Hindlow."

Alpheus nodded in acknowledgement.

"The Meridian River is inhabited by a variety of fish, all of them exclusively freshwater species except for those of the salmon family. Salmons—all of which are strong and determined—spend their lives swimming *against* the stream in their attempt to break out from the crowd. But despite their liveliness, strength, determination, and grit in their effort to be different, it is only at the point when they manage to break the tide and make their way to the ocean that they realise the reality—that is, the arduousness of surviving in the real world.

"Even the salmon, when confronted with the unfamiliar, merciless, and hazardous tides of the ocean, are rational enough to return to their comfort zone—the Meridian River. By the time of their return, however, they are depleted of all energy, and there is no longer a purpose to their lives. After the routine spawning, they flow back into and *along* the stream, until they eventually die.

"*All* salmon species of the Meridian River suffer the same difficult fate of *regress* due to their *foolish* and *forceful* escape from what is their natural habitat—a place they should appreciate. In the end, what appeared to be courage is only an illusion, for if such behaviour should be classified as anything, it is obstinacy."

Unlike in his previous presentation, Copper was passionate and animated this time, the veins on his forehead almost having popped out, as if he were arguing for an important cause. He glanced over at the ladies, who looked away to avoid direct eye contact.

"The simple conclusion I ask for," Copper then said, "is the expected fate of a *king salmon* of the Meridian River."

It did seem like a simple syllogistic premise to Alpheus. The first proposition was clearly that *salmon species of the Meridian River swim against the stream*. And the second proposition was that *all of these salmon species suffer the same fate for their obstinacy*. The logical conclusion, therefore, must be that king salmons *also* swam against the stream and suffered a fate of *regress*. Despite it being a seemingly simple conclusion to derive at, no one said a word. Amid the silence, Copper stared intensely not at Alpheus but at the women, who all squinted away in different directions in response.

The question was genuinely uncomplicated. But Alpheus was reluctant to agree with the conclusion that everyone else could easily come up with—not only because it was too simple, but also because he didn't want to concur with the extreme collectivism the question alluded to.

Fables and legends often glorified individualism, usually telling fantastic tales of special individuals defying all odds along their way toward some great triumph. But in reality, almost every voice of authority, namely all the kings across the land and even the religious order of Ionianism, preached collectivism. Alpheus agreed that grouping everyone together and then embedding in their minds the vision that the group as a whole should strive to achieve was indeed the most effective way to control people. The most effective way, however, wasn't necessarily the most ethical way. Either way, the idea of the balance between individualism and collectivism was never a simple question of black and white.

But if Alpheus had to choose, he would easily lean toward the quality of being individual. The preference to be an artist, to create his own ideologies rather than be a *number* at either The Villa or the Truban Empire, was clear. It was also clear that he had been accused of being selfish more than a few times due to this behaviour.

Copper's *king salmon* was of course only an analogy for the idea that people should know their place, be satisfied with their circumstances, and refrain from diverging from them—to be content like the other freshwater fish. If Alpheus had believed in that ideology, all of the unfortunate experiences that had befallen him in the recent past might not ever have happened. Alpheus might have become a celebrated scholar rather than an infamous escaped prisoner accused of heinous crimes. He might have then joined the Truban Empire in an effort to become an important lord. But Alpheus didn't regret his decisions—at least not in terms of having to *settle* with his circumstances.

"I cannot derive a logical conclusion," Alpheus said, shaking his head. "But only because there is no true conclusion. You have made another mistake—in fact, two mistakes—one of which is an *enthymeme*. Your arguments result in only a suppressed conclusion."

Copper snorted, bemused. "The propositions were crystal clear and the king salmon most certainly *is* a type of salmon species found in the Meridian River."

"I am sure they exist," Alpheus said with a nod. "It is your reference to king salmons that is flawed. Your presupposition lies beneath the traditional syllogistic fallacies. You have failed to consider, firstly the existence of the *select* individuals within the class of fish. And, secondly, you have prematurely and without merit assumed the salmon's behaviour to be foolish and obstinate."

Copper laughed this time. "How so?" he said. "Fish is fish! And they're of the same species."

"No...," Alpheus said, his eyes sparkling. "You rely too much on theory and logic. The ocean west of Vinawell, with its strong currents, is certainly a most hazardous place even to people, and hence it was foolish—in theory—for salmons to search for a new lease of life there. Even so, empirical work would prove quite the opposite."

"Empirical work?" the robed man questioned, speaking for only the second time. "Lord Copper is a scholar of the highest esteem. If such empirical work existed, it certainly wouldn't slip by him."

Alpheus looked up. "Empirical work needs not be done only by scholars. Fishermen can be just as effective."

"Amuse me," Copper said, still wearing that smug grin. "Elaborate."

"Very well, then," Alpheus said. "Allow me to present my arguments on evolution. You wouldn't disagree that people of the past didn't have the luxuries of the modern day—simple things like paper for writing and oil lamps as a source of light. If everyone were content to conform to the masses, such inventions would never have been possible, because these milestones are the direct result of individuals in pursuit of making a difference.

"If everyone were content with carving marks with stones on rocks, there would never have been paper. Similarly, if everyone had been content to work exclusively during the day, then we'd have no oil lamps. Paper and oil lamps, invented by two separate individuals, became widespread and commonplace because people, as rational beings, believed that it was for the best that they exist.

"With these, among many other inventions and discoveries, we evolved as a race. Similarly, it was that *first salmon* that changed the history of the species. Fish cannot reason, but they are intelligent enough to be *conditioned*. They'd choose the best path when presented with alternatives. And it was that first salmon and its triumphant voyage to the ocean that changed the history of the species. Presented with an alternative, others of the same species followed suit—and, most importantly, this was achieved through the use of their rationality. Why is it, then, would you think their behaviour foolish?"

Copper frowned, growing impatient. "You still haven't explained how that *particular* salmon is better off."

Alpheus opened his mouth to continue his argument of which there was still plenty to say, but Azure had already spoken before him.

"It's true that there is no way to know if they are better off until much later," she said. "Even so, we can only try and hope for the best. Life is short. We cannot afford to ponder every step of the path. If we were to remain idle, we would lose even that slightest possibility of a better future."

FIVE

Daytime moonlight

Copper narrowed his eyes, but said nothing. His men, including the robed man with dark circles under his eyes, were all silent. Even Marvin and the rest of his crew, who had said very little, appeared as the short speech had resonated with them. Perhaps all of them had a past that they were either not proud of or hoped never to bring up again. But perhaps the past was also worthwhile in steering them toward who they were today.

Alpheus regarded Azure, noting with surprise that she had somewhat concluded the argument on his behalf.

"Lord Copper," Claire said, turning to the man. "We'll be fine on our own. Maybe one day, we'll be that first salmon."

The nobleman shot a disappointed gaze at her. He then stood from his seat. "Lord Hindlow," he said, peering to Alpheus again. "I concede my defeat. Let us meet again. At that time, let us be on the same side."

Alpheus smiled. "The next time is not far away," he said.

Copper simply nodded but didn't seem to think much about the implication as he instead proceeded to the exit. His retinue promptly trailed after him as he looked to leave in haste. He reached for the door knob, but before he got to it, Marvin stepped out to block his path.

"Not so fast," Marvin said.

Copper looked up to meet the eyes of the taller man. "What is it now?"

"I believe you have someone you need to hand over to us."

He pondered the claim, glancing over to his men who seemingly shared his ignorance.

"Don't play with us," Marvin warned, resting a stern hand on the nobleman's shoulder. "You'll live to regret it."

The noblemen squinted in response to the physical contact, reaching back for his sword and drawing it with spectacular speed. While it was possible that his only intention was to defend himself, it didn't matter to Marvin, who had the sword knocked off before Copper even realised it. The weapon, a sabre, was tapped up into the air, now spinning clockwise. All eyes followed its spin cycle, as if time had slowed down interminably. As soon as the sabre started to fall, Marvin snatched it from the air, pointing it at its startled owner.

The strange man in the robe thrashed out an arm in immediate response, thrusting a palm onto his liege's back, drawing a whiff that flapped off his hood to reveal his bald head. The focus, though, was neither on his lack of hair nor his long goatee that puffed back, but the luminous energy of green he seemed to have surged into the nobleman.

"Sorcery!" Alpheus cried softly.

But no one seemed to have heard him, distracted as they were by the fact that the nobleman had begun to emit a glowing aura of emerald green. Copper grinned behind that energy, slapping his hands together onto the sharp end of the sabre that Marvin was still holding. Copper pulled, seizing the weapon, which shot away from Marvin's grip and ended up in the robed man's hands. Marvin raised a brow, noting that the nobleman hadn't been cut in the process—that the green energy seemed to have actually created some kind of padding between his hands and the sword.

But while this was an initial advantage over the great Marvin Sailanson that anyone should have enjoyed, Copper and his entourage looked wary that they might have provoked the man and his formidable crew. Indeed, Ash and Leo jumped forward now.

"Stop!" Claire snapped, leaping in between everyone. "Lord Copper has held no one. He knows nothing about it." She then shot a glare at Azure. "Tell them!" she demanded.

Azure bit her lips as she cocked her head in shame, suddenly looking more like a servant rather than the leader of the women. "Lord Copper doesn't have her," she confessed. "I said what I said so that you would help us."

"Child's play," the robed man grumbled, withdrawing his arms with a heated swing and throwing his hood back on.

Copper shot a similarly irate gaze over at Azure. "One of these days, there is bound to be a mishap," he said before turning back to Marvin with a faint smile. "It would be a proud story to tell that I faced off against you, Marvin Sailanson. As for today, please pardon my leave."

Marvin nodded back in courtesy and he bid Copper goodbye, watching him and his men disappear behind the door.

The crew leader then turned back to Azure with a scowl. "This is the last time I'll ask."

Azure rolled her eyes as she walked away. "Come," she said, leading them back out to the corridor and then to a door opposite them under the stairs. She reached a hand to the back of her hair, pulling out a hair fork which turned out to be a key. She slipped the key into the keyhole, unlocking it with a click. Finally, she pushed the door open to reveal an expansive room with walls covered with impressionist paintings.

Alpheus marvelled at the sight, near certain that one of the ladies must be the famous Cipher Nostalgia. The intense colours of the art jumped out at him, and the dramatic effects of the light entranced him into a brief illusion in which he was back in the woodlands as depicted in one of the paintings.

"What is this?" Marvin asked, clearly uninterested in the artwork. "Where's Tavie?"

Azure rolled her eyes once more. "She's through there," she said, gesturing to another door halfway in the room.

They paced over to the door and stepped into a much smaller room, empty of paintings, furniture, and people. The glass window onto the outside was broken. Marvin jerked forward, as did Leo, as they skimmed the vandalism complete, with a note *carved* onto the wall.

I did a little more gardening, it read.

Azure leaped forward toward the broken window, peering outside. "That brat!" she cursed before storming outside through the front entrance.

Claire and Carmen trailed her promptly, sharing her concern from the expressions of their faces. Alpheus and the Sail Band followed, arriving at the outside of the room where a small garden bed sat—*destroyed*—with the women kneeled down now in despair next to it. The actual garden bed was undamaged, but the vines of a strange flower species climbing around the stone exterior had been trampled on and shredded into irrecoverable pieces.

No one from the Sail Band said a word, obviously suspecting that Tavie was the culprit. None of them seemed proud that their fellow crew member had managed to escape, however. Although no one had explicitly aired any grievances about Tavie, they had always referred to her in a tenor that she was spoiled and insensitive. Alpheus could only assume that Tavie had deserved being taken hostage.

He shook his head as he watched the three women collect the dead strips one by one. Barely a moment later, he tucked up his sleeves and trotted over to help.

Marvin took a hesitant step forward. "Here's a gold coin," he said, picking it out from under his blazer. "Get someone to replant them... or something."

Azure shot him a furious glare, her eyes in tears. "*Replant* them?" she asked. "Is that what it means to you? Can I slash away your limbs and replace you with someone else?"

Marvin cringed slightly.

"Sorry, Lord Sailanson," Claire said, visibly dismayed, and yet managed a much calmer tone. "Please forgive Azure. We have nurtured her—the flower—for a long time. And it is upsetting to see it come to this."

Azure huffed out a puff of air and then carried on with picking up the strips.

"Well...," Marvin said, scratching his stubbled chin. "If you don't want the gold, then we're off. Come on, Alpheus, let's go."

"You go on ahead," Alpheus said, looking up briefly as he continued collecting the dead strips. "I'll catch up."

Marvin nodded, and, with Ash, Leo, and the others, he soon disappeared into the woods.

It was another ten minutes before they restored the garden into a slightly more presentable display. The vines were obviously not going to twine out overnight, however, and it was perhaps that thought that had Azure grumble now at Alpheus.

"Don't expect any gratitude from us," she said.

"Azure," Carmen said, almost as if scolding her. "Lord Hindlow only wants to help."

"And he's helped us a great deal today," Claire added.

Alpheus flushed a pale pink. "If you really think that way," he said hesitantly, "would you offer your real names?"

The women shot him strange looks. "What do you mean our *real* names?" Azure then asked with a raised brow.

"Well, your name couldn't be just Azure, right?" Alpheus said.

Azure said nothing, retaining only her suspicious frown.

"Why don't we talk this over a cup of tea?" Claire then suggested.

* * *

Behind the main structure was a pergola upon which beautiful vines were trained. Under the roof was a delicate round table of painted metal, with a pair of quality crafted chairs to match. Alpheus was perched on the plush cushion latched onto his chair while he waited for the ladies. This really was a peaceful place, he realised, a secluded cottage hidden deep in the heart of the woods, illuminated by charming variations of natural lighting. The collective aroma of the various flowers cultivated there was tremendously satisfying, all of them resting in landscaped hand-sized blocks of neat moss elevated to waist height. It wasn't a particularly large display, but each of the dozen species there—all rather exotic—was a sight to behold.

I never knew Cipher Nostalgia as a botanist, Alpheus thought, realising then that flower arrangement was certainly an art.

The sound of footsteps caused Alpheus to look up, and he watched his hosts as they paced toward him with small steps hidden under the flaring hems of their dresses. While Claire and Carmen donned the same tent dress as before, Azure had changed into a dress threaded in a lustrous fabric of light blue, with a matching pair of loose hanging sleeves that covered the arm from the elbow to the wrist. She also had crowned herself with a tiara with a gem sparkling in the same colour as her dress. The rays of sunlight shimmering through the canopies sprinkled light upon her as if she were an angel. Other than the allurement, her new presentation also re-established her role as the apparent leader of the women.

Azure smiled as she sat down across from him. She then gestured Carmen over, who carried a tray with her and laid down a porcelain tea set, cups with matching saucers, and a teapot, wisps of smoke whiffing out. She poured two cups and then retired to the far edge of the pergola to join Claire who looked as if she was on watch.

"Please, Lord Hindlow," Azure said, gesturing at the tea as she, too, sipped gracefully on hers. Alpheus abided, and he found the tea sweet tasting with a strong aroma of flowers. He liked it, but didn't comment on it before placing the cup back on its saucer. Azure squinted at him with a grin, and he looked away.

"Allow me to extend my gratitude for the favour you have done," she said. "You have presented yourself eloquently before Lord Copper. And you have allowed more than a few of us to appreciate what it means to struggle for what we believe in."

Alpheus cocked his head slightly, not sure when or how she had seemed to change her attitude and etiquette. "Your praise is too much," he finally responded in humility. "I simply presented my belief… that social conservatism, while needed to maintain balance to the world, is also a major constraint to any advancement. Art, in particular, can never prosper if we live as restricted conformists."

Azure simply smiled before taking another sip of her tea.

Alpheus glanced out to the canopies and the light filtering through like waves. "So...," he said, "is Azure your only name?"

Azure looked up behind the porcelain, saying nothing until she laid the cup down again. "A strange question," she said. "Are you mistaking me for someone else?"

Alpheus looked away again. "Well, I—"

He trailed off when Azure rolled up the loose hanging sleeve on her left arm to reveal a brilliant pearl bracelet on her wrist. Alpheus met her eyes, confused about whether he was supposed to marvel at its craftsmanship. She then gently raised her arm higher until the filtered light dabbed onto the bracelet, at which time, it glistened a dazzling glow of bluish-white.

"Do you know what this is?" she asked, noting that Alpheus had widened his eyes.

Alpheus suspected he knew, but he said no word just yet. Azure then stood up from her chair and paced along the floral display, stopping when she reached a set of leafy vines climbing up a wooden net latched next to the stone wall of the cottage. The twining plant shied behind the other flowers on display as rather ordinary, with flowers that were closed. And it had seemed that the pergola provided the ideal environment for flowers to bloom.

"Please, Lord Hindlow," Azure said, gesturing Alpheus to join her in admiring the closed flowers. "Ladies," she then said to her companions. "We need some shade."

Claire and Carmen each collected a giant clover the size of a child from behind the beams erected next to them. They strolled toward Azure and Alpheus, holding up the clovers to shade them and the vines away from even the tiniest dabs of sunlight.

What now? Alpheus thought, intimidated by the sudden intimacy of sharing the darkness with three young women.

Azure removed her bracelet then, hovering it next to the shaded flowers. The bracelet pulsed, and its glow began to fade gradually, but rather than fading away, the illumination flowed over to the twining plant. The petals were suddenly sparked with life, opening up as a round flower emitting a magnificent white glow behind the shadow cast by the giant clovers.

"This is the *ipomoea alba*," Azure said in a whisper behind Alpheus. "Or the moonflower—an evening blooming flower."

Alpheus trembled slightly as he leaned in closer to the flowers. While the flower was spectacular, his mind was elsewhere. He was sure he knew what had happened, though he was reluctant to confirm it. There could only be two ways for the evening flower to bloom in the day. Sorcery was the first possibility, but Alpheus was convinced it wasn't that, having detected no grace breathing out of any of the women.

That left only the second possibility, which was even more frightening.

"This is the Child of the Moon," Azure said, whispering into his ear and confirming his daring guess. "It absorbs moonlight as its own source of energy, much like the process of photosynthesis. The energy collected can be transferred to other sources—for example, the moonflower."

Alpheus swallowed as a drop of sweat slid down from his forehead, unable to find the courage to turn back just yet. This was completely unexpected. How was he going to address the owner of the bracelet, who was none other than the princess of the Imperial Lithia Dominion?

"You're shaking," Azure said, maintaining her soft voice next to his ear. "You wanted to know who I am, did you not?"

She ran a hand gently down his ear, her fingers sliding into his cheeks until Alpheus jumped and stumbled backwards toward the table, stopping only when he bumped into it.

He then bowed down rather rigidly, but all he heard were giggles. When the tittering trailed off, he saw in his slanted position the flaring hem of the light blue dress approaching. He tingled, then, when the tip of a finger tapped his chin, lifting his head up gently until he was face to face with Azure, or the princess—their noses almost touching. Her warmth flooded over him. He stared into the swirling ocean blue of her eyes, seeing no end to the intricate whirlpool that felt as if it had pulled him in.

"Are you afraid of me?" Azure asked. "I promised to support you to be Prince Consort. I thought now was a good time to prove that I could."

"My apologies, Princess Steele," Alpheus said, backing away a few steps. "I was—"

"Who's Princess Steele?" she said with a slight frown, rising back to an upright position. "Ladies here are addressed by their middle names. It's Princess Flora."

"Right," Alpheus said with another bow.

"As for the name *Azure*," she said. "It's merely an assumed name I use when I am out and about. Now, Lord Hindlow, wasn't it a pleasant revelation to know who I really am… and who you are going to compete for once you reach the capital?"

Alpheus gawked at her for a moment. "Aye," he said, shaking off the confusion. "Yes, it was… wonderful."

"But, Lord Hindlow, I'm afraid we must part ways momentarily. I see that we're both headed for Poppaross, but it would be indiscreet for me to journey with a man."

"I understand," Alpheus said. "How about I stall behind while you... Your Highness and your attendants go on ahead?"

"No, Lord Hindlow," the princess said. "I need *you* to go on ahead. I still have a few errands to run before I return to the capital."

"Right," Alpheus said. "In that case, if you would excuse me."

The princess smiled at him, and her attendants did the same, with added curtsies. Alpheus bowed once more, and then turned to leave. He hadn't forgotten why he was in Vinawell. But only now did he realise he hadn't put much thought to the princess herself, who he had actually come for.

* * *

Tavie was about an hour late, but she had managed to return unscathed to where the crew agreed to meet. She was quietly proud to have gotten the better of the foreign women who didn't know their places, but she knew better not to let Marvin, Ash, and the others know about it. She could already anticipate how that conversation would end given that the insensitive thieves had always enjoyed painting her as a mischievous child.

Leo was the only one who might listen. But she couldn't remember a time when Marvin and Ash didn't mock her for almost everything she did.

In any case, she had to explain why she was late and also why she had failed once again to find any success in the original hunting exercise. Perhaps this time if she painted a picture with herself as the victim, Marvin would be easier on her.

"There were a horde of them," she was saying, thinking it was a drag. "Bandits, that is. They were barbaric... and *primitive*. They wore animal skin and consumed their prey raw. They outnumbered me and brought me to this... secret den. But I managed to fork out an escape path entirely by myself."

She grew confused as she spoke, though, as she realised her audience was losing interest. Marvin shook his head and was the first one to turn away. The others followed suit, leaving Tavie with no one to amuse.

"Hey!" she cried, leaping in behind them with a scowl and snatching Marvin by the wrist. "I didn't expect much from you lot. But a little solicitude would be good. I escaped by myself. Isn't that something?"

Marvin turned back with a forced grin. "Well then, how are you—our *princess*—doing? Did the primitive men keep you warm when they had you?"

She gasped. And though the former princess of Cetal was quick to realise it was metaphorical, she trembled at Marvin's inimical gaze. Her face turned blank and the others of the crew paused. It was rare to see Marvin like that. It was frightening, though not enough for Tavie to apologise.

"I'm still without a bow!" she complained instead. "I admit I'm not the best at hunting, but no one's helped. What do you expect?"

Marvin snorted and then took off again. Tavie grunted and thought to chase, only to be held back by Ash. Everyone else including Leo headed to the wagon, which was parked just behind the cluster of trees before them.

"What now?!" Tavie said impatiently. "Marvin can't always—"

"We were at the cottage just now," Ash said, silencing her immediately. "We can tell the story better than you could tell it yourself. Marvin couldn't care less for your hunting skills, but your reckless abandon has brought dishonour to the crew that he so proudly leads."

Tavie looked away with a sullen face. "But they really *did* tie me up," she said quietly in protest. "They had these birds—a lot of them."

"And *why* did they tie you up?" Ash asked. "Did you perhaps destroy something dear to them?"

Tavie looked down now, staring at the blades of grass. "It was an accident," she said. "I was chasing a squirrel. I lost my balance, and I reached my hand out for anything I could hold. There was no malicious intent."

Ash sighed. "One of these days, you need to think about what we represent," he said. "And think about whether or not you are a part of it."

Tavie said nothing. Those were the most solemn words she had heard from any member of the crew, and it hurt. It hurt that such earnest words were spoken in reproach of her.

How dare they...? was her first thought. *If we were in Cetal, I'd have you all kneel before me.*

But..., she thought in hesitation. Not even once had she considered a return to Cetal City. She missed nothing from her life as a child of royalty, except her mother, who had passed away. She suspected that her father, Pierre Morlan, didn't care to even search for her.

As the crew stopped by a lake to rest, Tavie reminisced what she had been through with them. It had been nearly half a year, and her experiences during this time were her only experiences of the real world. She could still remember in vivid detail that on only her second day, Marvin had clasped onto her delicate ponytails and mercilessly slashed them off with his dagger. She remembered the shock she had felt, for her hair had been one of the few things she wasn't only proud of, but also what she had spent most of her time on.

But now, as Tavie looked down at her own reflection in the clear water of the lake, she realised that her simple, short hair was indeed charming. Her outfit was a modest short sleeve top, woven from percale fabric and sturdy leather and matched with a light-weighted skirt and tall, durable boots. It wasn't the extravagant quality she had been accustomed to, but she had come to embrace the outfit and its practicality. She had come a long way. And although it was difficult to admit, she had grown attached to the crew, especially to Marvin, Ash, and Leo. Even Rover and Karl had their moments of charm, and were often gentle and forgiving to her.

She looked up, peering out to the men as they scattered about the grassy bank, a feeling of warmth spreading inside her.

* * *

It was nightfall when the Sail Band reached Poppaross. Despite Marvin's extensive travels, he had never visited the capital of Vinawell until now.

The city gate was a grand structure with elevated watch towers on either side high enough to survey great distances. Admission into the city itself was rather lax, though, with only several imperial guards on duty, watching the people pass in and out rather than inspecting them individually.

The general attitude of the city seemed to be of sensibility and reservation, which was a remarkable contrast to the exuberance of Aragon. The common streets were constructed with stone, while the buildings were erected side by side along a seemingly endless, winding strip.

According to Karl, these streets linked together to a larger spiralling stone path that circled up to the castle. The magnificent pearl white castle itself was erected on higher elevation, allowing it to be easily viewable from the city gate. It stood out, also, because it was cradled by mountains in the same way as a theatre stage was cradled by its auditorium.

Before Karl could elaborate, a raucous group of nearly a dozen men came stomping through the city gate on mean-looking stallions of a black shade that didn't look native to either Vinawell or Trubannis.

At the centre of the group was a young man who stood out in bright red who whipped forward a scimitar, pointing it in the air—almost as if leading an army to seize the city. He wore a tall helm with curved horns, the metal covering every part of his head except his eyes and mouth. The man had the dark skin of the Kragan people, and he wore a dashing grin behind the glitters of jewellery that adorned almost every part of him. Beneath his lustrous red coat was a skin-tight top and bottom that highlighted his slim figure.

Together with his cosmetic make-up and long hair, which fell out from his helm in a ponytail, one could almost mistake him for a woman.

The men behind him, draped in multiple dark cloths, blew into curving horns, wheezing out an unpleasant and arrhythmic, sharp pitch. The people near them cringed at the sound and the aggressive entrance, some of them trotting away while a mother covered her child's ears. At the same time, though, more people flocked to the gate, if only to see what the ruckus was about.

"You must be Lord Aryliel Trajetzky," one of the imperial soldiers said with a bow, halting the Kragan men. "The Dominion has anticipated your arrival. It is our honour that you have come for the Purification Ceremony. We shall do our best to ensure that you feel at home."

The young man nodded at him with a grin, his dark shade of skin now even more conspicuous next to the imperial soldier of fair skin. "Oh, I'll feel at home," he said pompously—his voice sharp and rather high for a man. "After all, your princess will soon be *my* princess."

He raised his scimitar to the sky again, and following that, his men blew their horns with even more enthusiasm. The people around them cringed again. Even the imperial soldiers, now four of them, winced slightly.

"Interesting invitee," Leo commented, glancing up at Karl, who didn't care enough to respond.

"He's here for the Purification Ceremony," Marvin said, changing the topic before any comparisons could be made between Karl and Trajetzky. "That means Alpheus will be going up against him."

"Lord Trajetzky," the imperial soldier said now, looking up at the man who did not dismount. "With all due respect, I ask you to tone it down a little."

Trajetzky looked down at him with a frown, his eyes glaring out from behind the intimidating helm. He snapped his sword back into its sheath at his waist and then raised a hand again to signal his men to stop.

"I apologise," he said, finally dismounting now with an agile hop. "I apologise that you have no appreciation for fine tunes."

The soldiers cocked their heads slightly, but then learned exactly what Trajetzky meant when he slammed the soldier who had been speaking at the chest with the pommel of his sword, sending him scraping across the stone ground.

The other three soldiers were prompt in attending to their comrade, but they could only watch as he coughed up blood. The aggressor's men, meanwhile, picked up where they had left off, blowing into the horns again, perhaps as applause for their liege. The people who had gathered around gasped, holding hands over mouths, careful not to criticise—even if accidentally.

"I apologise again," Trajetzky said, sparing his victim not even a glance. "I apologise for your fragility."

Trajetzky was vain and brash, not unlike the young Kragans Marvin had met in the past. With barely a swing of his sheathed sword and a few spiteful words, the young man had managed to humiliate the soldiers on their own turf. It was interesting to see what else the Imperial Lithia Dominion would do in response. Were any of their strongest knights in the vicinity?

Marvin perked up slightly when he noted a person approaching Trajetzky from behind and then dared to place a hand on the Kragan's shoulder.

"Show some respect for the host," the man said, a young noble draped in a mantle of a cloudy grey.

Trajetzky spun nervously, swiping out an arm to brush off the contact. "Take your dirty hands off of me!" he cried, almost hysterically. He hopped several steps away, pulling out a delicate handkerchief of silk beneath his coat, and began rubbing his shoulder obsessively, as if the nobleman had left a hand-mark there.

"You must be Lord Christopher Hartland," one of the soldiers said to the newcomer with a smile and a bow.

"Indeed, I am," Hartland responded with a bow of his own, as two men—his vassals perhaps—trotted next to him. "It is my pleasure to step foot in the capital."

Marvin glanced down at the longsword at Hartland's belt and noted the embossed Fenrir on the scabbard, which indicated his alignment with the Truban Empire.

Trajetzky had slipped his handkerchief away, and seemed to have also recognised Hartland's alignment. "A member of the Truban Empire?" Trajetzky said with a hiss.

"I am," Hartland said, wearing a proud grin.

"And you think to displease me with that backing?"

Hartland squinted. "I am only here for the Purification Ceremony."

The Kragan snorted. "How many people did they invite, and—"

"There are thirty participants in all."

"I wasn't actually asking...!" Trajetzky cut in. He narrowed his eyes and then reached beneath his coat again. "What I'm saying is: they only need one participant and that is *me*!"

At that, he whipped out an arm, sprinkling a fine powder at Hartland, who leaped back on instinct. After missing its target, the powder rained down to the stone ground, immediately incinerating the surface where it had made contact before evaporating into a heated odourless green smoke.

More gasps emitted from the crowd as glances shot over to the soldiers who simply gaped. While Marvin guessed that the destructive powder was but a mild variant of what he had seen in the war, it was clearly excessive and uncalled for. Trajetzky was only young, but his actions called to mind the viciousness of some of the vile men Marvin had once known. Warriors of the southern land were always keen to exhibit their power at their disposal at every chance.

And now, the young Kragan had managed to provoke Hartland, who groaned, drawing his longsword and slashing out in furious retaliation.

Trajetzky grinned, shooting out his own sword, defending that first strike comfortably before slicing out on offence a series of wavy but vicious swings. The men accompanying Trajetzky, all of them well-built, chanted their liege's name as the young Kragan quickly found his rhythm, easily dictating the pace of the battle.

It was clear that Hartland was no match for Trajetzky.

"Ro," Marvin whispered softly. "Can you…?"

Rover sighed. He then strode forward, stepping toward the fierce battle while slipping out his short sword which had been latched onto his right thigh. As he got within several steps away, Trajetzky groaned suddenly, shoving Hartland aside before slashing a cross at Rover, aiming at where he would have thought was Rover's blind spot, as he must have deduced from the eye patch.

"No…!" Hartland cried as he fell back.

But Hartland's worry was foolish, as Rover easily blocked off Trajetzky in a blinding clang of metal that stunned the crowd. Trajetzky stumbled back, falling into his men, who held him up to avoid what would have been total humiliation. Even as he stood, Trajetzky's sword-wielding arm was jolting, twitching visibly, as he wheezed out in fury, regarding his new challenger with a vicious glare.

"Trajetzky, was it?" Marvin said, finally stepping out next to Rover together along with the rest of the crew. "Now's not the time to show off your abilities. Leave it for the real thing."

Trajetzky peered across to regard Ash, Leo, Karl, and Tavie, too. "You people were invited...?!"

"No," Marvin said with a chortle. "But we'll be spectating. I hope you can make it worthwhile for us. Until then, I ask of you to quit blowing those horns. It's not pleasant."

Trajetzky nodded and then reluctantly called for his men to retreat, all of them riding off down along the stone path, and *not* blowing onto their horns. Behind the gradually dispersing crowd, Marvin regarded Hartland briefly, who was also walking away with his men. Somehow, the young nobleman appeared to be as frightened of him as he had been of Trajetzky. Had he perhaps heard something about him from the war veterans—Marvin's old comrades—still working for the Empire?

* * *

The traffic at the city gate was far worse than Alpheus had expected. Apparently, the soldiers were restoring order to an earlier incident which involved some ill-mannered foreigners barging their way through. With still a sea of bodies hoping to enter the capital in front of him, Alpheus worried about whether his own entry would cause yet more chaos. While he had no doubt been invited as a guest to the Purification Ceremony, the soldiers standing at the city gate would surely have been briefed about his alleged murders in Zorlia.

When he finally reached the actual gate, Alpheus presented his invitation parchment, which immediately prompted the guard to jerk forward slightly.

"Hold on, please," the guard said, turning anxiously to one of his fellow soldiers.

And *holding on* was exactly what Alpheus had to do for a while longer, forced to watch a handful of soldiers in a seemingly deep discussion about whether to allow him entry or not while other travellers behind him grumbled about why he was holding everyone up.

Alpheus managed a slight smile when the initial guard finally trotted back toward him with his invitation. "Lord Hindlow," he addressed him, handing back to him the parchment. "We apologise deeply about the wait. Please enter. And, also please report to the castle within the next few days."

Alpheus nodded in courtesy, knowing for certain that the guards would pass the message of his arrival to the castle, which would allow those with more authority to decide if he was still qualified to participate in the Purification Ceremony. No matter, Alpheus was prepared to convince anyone who might deny his right of participation. After all, he had reason on his side and perhaps even the actual princess, too, who could advocate for him.

Alpheus soon regrouped with the Sail Band after asking around for a group of *strange* people. It was late in the evening, now, and the crew had settled in at a local inn, one of the cheaper ones around. A few days ago, Alpheus would have suspected this to be some kind of act. But now, he realised that Marvin and the crew were often short on gold, and that they actually paid for goods and services, rather than compel others to provide them for free.

Alpheus found himself sharing a room with Marvin and Ash. Neither of them asked any questions about what had happened at the cottage after they had left. But Alpheus shared the story anyway, letting them in on the surprising information that Azure was actually the princess, the girl who was coming of age—that the Purification Ceremony was for her.

"I *thought* something was up with them," Marvin said, scratching his goatee. "Just couldn't put my finger on it."

"Really?" Ash said, eyeing him with a raised brow. "You didn't say a word about it back there."

Marvin shrugged with a chortle. "Well, I don't share *all* my thoughts." He shook his head, his expression turning more solemn. "Anyway, Alpheus," he said. "We ran into some competition of yours at the city gate. A man by the name of Trajetzky and another called… I forget."

"Hartland," Ash inserted, causing Alpheus to perk up. "Christopher Hartland, it was."

"Chris?" Alpheus said softly.

"Do you… know him?" Marvin asked.

Alpheus nodded. Other than the surprise that Hartland had been invited, Alpheus simply hadn't expected to see any kind of old acquaintance in Poppaross.

SIX

Cross-cultural candidates

Alpheus yanked himself up, his heart thumping and sweat building from the crown of his head as a wave of heat surged within his body. He shook his head and then held it, disoriented. His slumber had been a violent episode once again. He glanced over to the window where glimmers of daylight shone through the thin gap between the two sides of the thick curtain that wasn't completely closed off.

It was only early morning. No one else was around. He sighed and then fell softly back into the bed, eyes narrowed at the straw ceiling as his heart rate gradually steadied.

He didn't want to fall back into the dream, the same one he had dreamed recurringly since departing Zorlia. While he wanted to ensure that he didn't forget about Reeling no matter how far he trekked away, the man's death image which appeared in his dreams often and without warning was intense. The image was always followed by a sequence where Alpheus found himself consumed by the lust for power, fuelled by a voice that urged him on, asserting that strength was everything.

Alpheus could never quite remember the dream in detail, however, only that his own character was unrecognisable to himself. It was all rather disquieting, but he had refrained from analysing why he might be having such dreams in the first place. According to spiritualists, there were apparently deep meanings to be found in dreams, especially strange dreams that affected one's wellbeing. But Alpheus had never considered enquiring into the dubious field of spiritualism, which was neither guided by reasoning nor by the faith. He realised that he might soon have no choice but to be at least more accepting of the concept. After all, it was also true that neither reasoning nor the faith could explain the many otherwise inexplicable occurrences of the recent past.

He reached under his robe then, searching near his chest, and then pulled out the invitation parchment that had led him here to Poppaross.

Alpheus had studied it over and over in the last month—or rather, he had mulled over the implications of where his life was leading him while staring blankly at the sheepskin, which was no more than a simple note with his name, a date, and a brief message of invitation. The waxed heraldic crest was a phoenix that was more amicable than the fearsome Fenrir of the Truban Empire.

Alpheus blinked at the name of the princess then as an image of Azure sprung up to mind. His mental image of the vivacious princess was still attached to the name Azure whose real name was Clarissa Flora Steele. In any case, he realised that there was an opportunity before him, the possibility to carry on the phoenix crest and truly find a new lease of life as an esteemed figure.

And the only incentive to reach for the opportunity—the reward—was the potential to rise to a position of power, which would prove essential if he wanted to honour Reeling and find the man's murderer.

The beginning of the quest was today, the first day of April. All invitees to the Purification Ceremony were expected to confirm their participation at the castle. The actual ceremony itself and the subsequent events that would help the Dominion crown a Prince Consort were to begin seven days later.

Alpheus hadn't paid much heed to what the Sail Band had been doing these last few days, noting only that the crew hadn't returned to the inn since the prior evening. Marvin had promised to accompany him to the castle. And while Alpheus had playfully accused the crew leader to have simply invited himself, he actually wanted the company. He had often enjoyed solitude in the past, but ever since Reeling's death, his alone time was usually marred with the heart-wrenching memories he couldn't escape from, not even in a foreign country where it was supposed to be easier to forget about the tragic.

He freshened up now and changed into a mantle of ivory white. It was his preferred colour, and one that was popular in the Vinan capital. He fitted on his spectacles and tied his hair into a braided ponytail, flicking it behind his shoulders.

There was a knock on the door then. Alpheus looked up as the door was pushed open from the outside. Marvin stepped in with his usual grin, but almost everything else about the man was unrecognisable. He donned the same mantle as Alpheus—indeed, he did one better by sporting a matching beret—and that was despite wearing his slanted headband beneath it. The flaps that draped off of him did well to hide his imposing physique.

It was actually humorous, and Alpheus almost laughed. That was when

Ash trotted in, sporting the same look.

"Oh, Father of Heaven...," Alpheus uttered softly, his cheeks tensing up. Immediately behind Ash was Tavie, Leo, Karl, and finally, Rover—all of them dressed as scholars.

The mantles actually fitted Ash and Leo quite well. Rover, though, didn't blend in in the same way with his eyepatch and grave expression—Karl, too, with his giant frame. Tavie cross-dressed as a male, with her hair wrapped up under the beret. She applied no cosmetics but her feminine features, including her long eyelashes and luscious lips, were still evident when one looked carefully enough. In any case, the crew no longer looked like the mighty Sail Band that struck fear in their foes at the mere mention of their name.

"So, what do you think?" Ash asked.

Alpheus hesitated, trying hard not to laugh. "Well, I—"

"We're attending as your apprentices," Tavie cut in. "But don't think you have any actual authority over us."

Alpheus smiled at her. "I never dreamed of it. And... I do. I appreciate it. Very much."

Tavie returned the smile. "Well then, what are we waiting for? Let's go!"

Karl led the way. As an expert in cartographer who apparently drew maps in his mind, he led the crew through the narrow streets for what he claimed to be the most direct route to the castle. It had been said that the big Kragan had developed an ability to map out anything due to his extensive travels across the land. Alpheus wasn't convinced that that was all there was to it, however. And on the one occasion when he had asked Ash about it, he was told that no one really knew except for Karl himself.

They soon arrived at the foot of the castle hill. And as they looked up, they saw that it was a majestic structure of pearl white perched in front of the imposing mountains that cradled it. Its elevated location provided an ideal vantage point to watch for any potential enemies, and the mountains caressing it on all sides but one ensured that if anyone were to attack, they had no choice but to attack head on. The name of the castle was *Radiance's Nest*, a reference to the phoenix crest that represented the Dominion. With perhaps ten steeples, a few of which that shot up to heights levelled with the mountains that backdropped it, the castle wasn't as intimidating as Vondra Dawn. But *The Nest*, as the civilians called it, had a regal quality to it that was fitting for the home of a great king. The donjon, in particular, was a magnificent tower.

Alpheus proceeded toward the opened portcullis, which was connected to a wide-arcing bulwark, alongside his entourage who had now been disguised as scholars. The guards there—four of them—raised a brow upon their approach. As for their appearance, despite the crew's efforts, Karl and Rover attracted suspicion even behind the supposed outward semblance. Alpheus flapped out the invitation parchment and presented it to one of the guards. The creases weren't pretty, but the guard noted that it was genuine, glancing up at Alpheus now with a suspicious eye.

"Welcome, Lord Hindlow," said the guard, his words winning the immediate attention of the other guards. "Excuse my candour, but we did not expect you, especially as you are rather late."

Alpheus bowed his head slightly. "I *do* apologise," he said. "But if I am not wrong, it is still only morning now. What time did the Dominion expect its guests to arrive?"

"Precisely an hour earlier," the guard responded, sounding as if everyone should have known. "As it stands, Lord Hindlow, you are the last one here. I'm not sure if we can...," He hesitated, peering behind Alpheus to the Sail Band, who were now dressed in the disguise of scholars. "And who are they, if I may ask?"

"My apprentices," Alpheus said. "Is there a problem?"

The guard looked over to his comrades, all of them sharing that half-frown. "Well, we—" He paused, looking down the slanted ridge where a man on a horse galloped in. The man donned a mantle of maroon complete with a cape that flapped behind him. As he got closer with the horse kicking up dust, Alpheus recognised the bald head and the long, puffed goatee that belonged to the man who had been with Copper back at the cottage. Alpheus also noted the dark circles under the man's already wrinkled eyes which made him look rather ashen.

The grim man seemed to have recognised Alpheus in turn, as he now pulled on the reins to slow his horse. "So you have come," he said, glaring down from his mount, eyeing Alpheus and Marvin.

The guards bowed down to him. "Lord Ebenezer," they addressed.

"What is the holdup?" he asked them.

"Well..., we," the initial guard uttered in hesitation. "They have come rather late. And because Lord Hindlow is... well, we're not sure whether to—"

"The Dominion invited him," the man said with a frown. "There's nothing uncertain about it. Allow them to proceed."

"Aye, My Lord," the guard said, stepping aside and gesturing Alpheus to enter.

Alpheus smiled at the grim man. "Well, thank you," he said. "Lord..., uh—"

"Ebenezer," the man confirmed, stroking his goatee.

Marvin gazed at the man, musing upon something.

"Wait! Wait!" a voice cried out from behind.

On the same ridge, the only path to the castle, was a pair of foreigners trotting up. They had darker skin tones, similar to the Kragans, but their round eyes and protruding lips hinted that they were not people of the south. Their style of dress was exotic, with long robes of rich violet that hung loose, and separate shawls covering the head as well as the shoulders. They were short, too, and youthful in appearance, perhaps not fully grown yet. One of them was a man, and the other a woman—or perhaps they were boy and girl.

Marvin perked up, regarding the foreigners. "It's his son," he said with a beam.

"The resemblance is uncanny," Rover added with a rare smile.

"Whose son?" Ash asked.

The young man wheezed as he stepped to the portcullis. "We're finally here again," he said in a strange accent, resting an arm on his companion who hadn't broken a sweat.

"You're back again?" said the guard with a raised brow.

The young man held out a hand, still trying to catch his breath. "I was unable to find the invitation in the inn, but believe me. I am Tumaini Azan. I have come for Princess Flora's Purification Ceremony."

"As I have explained before, we cannot allow you entry without the invitation," the guard insisted.

"No, you must allow me inside," Tumaini pleaded with a wry face. "I am really who I say I am! I'm sure one of the envoys can verify my identity!"

The guards looked to Ebenezer again, who squinted at the foreigners.

"He is who he claims to be," Marvin said. "Please do him a favour."

Ebenezer considered it for a moment and then nodded at the guards who promptly opened the gate on his command. "Let us meet later in the day," he said to Marvin before pulling his reins and galloping his way into the castle.

"I owe you my gratitude," Tumaini said, stepping up to Marvin, who completely dwarfed him, his round eyes glistening in joy.

Marvin waved a dismissive hand. "Say, how's your father doing?"

"My Lord Father?" Tumaini said, cocking his head. "He is well—he *was* well when we departed. Oh, and she is my able maid, Layla."

His companion, or his maid as he claimed, looked to be barely an adult. She was slightly shorter even than the already diminutive Tumaini. And as she bowed down to Marvin now, she looked almost like a child. She wore her hair in a ponytail, with her entire fringe swept to the left. But despite her inviting round eyes and unintimidating petite figure, she emanated the aura of an assassin that was so unlike her liege, whose presence carried not a hint of malice.

"May I ask," Alpheus said, "how old are you two?"

"We're both sixteen, born just a month apart," Tumaini said.

Marvin nodded, his eyes wandering off to the sky as if counting something. "It's been that long?" he said finally.

"All right, little boy," Tavie cut in, rolling her eyes. "Are you going in?"

"Certainly," the young man responded. "May we accompany you?"

Soon after they stepped through the gate, a couple of servants rushed over. They were young women who curtsied to them. "This way, please, Lord Hindlow and Lord Azan," one of them said. "Allow us to be your guides."

"Many thanks," Alpheus said with a blush, the soft amber hair of the servants reminding him of the princess.

"Thank you," Tumaini said with a bow.

The servants curtsied again. "At noon, everyone shall gather at the central atrium. The Lord King will address you directly. Until then, allow us to take you on a brief tour of the castle, and also to show you to your rooms."

The group followed the servants east, circling along the bulwark. It was evident that the castle was well-manned, with plenty of soldiers on patrol. The courtyard was floored with what seemed like premium limestone and of a light tinge that beautifully reflected the natural daylight. It was pristine all around, with the pearl white hue reflecting back up. Tumaini, who strode ahead in glee with his maid, didn't hide his excitement about his surroundings.

"Say, Marvin," Ash whispered, as a few others including Alpheus listened in. "Who's the boy?"

"Didn't he say it himself?" Marvin said with a shrug.

"From his name and appearance, I'd think he's from the land of the deserts—from Seniblum. But I still don't know who he is."

"The boy's a prince," Marvin said. "His father is Adio Azan, the King of Seniblum."

Ash jumped, as did Alpheus, Leo, and Tavie, who were all listening in.

"I doubt he's the only child, though," Marvin said, "which means he's one of at least several princes."

The servants brought them to a wide hallway, floored with glinting marble and round beams that lifted up a high ceiling. "This is where you will stay," one of them said, gesturing to the right where there were more than ten doors. They offered Alpheus and Tumaini keys, but urged them to come back later as they were pressed on time to complete the tour. The servants then led them to the armoury, the chapel, and the stables. It was noon by the time they finished the tour which had apparently been conducted in haste.

The servants had grown more and more anxious about the time. They led the way now toward the central atrium where a crowd would have gathered. And while they strode with a sense of urgency, they seemed to be doing their best to hide their unease. Alpheus said nothing to add to their stress, doing the only thing he could for them, which was to trail closely behind them. He shot a glance over at the Sail Band walking alongside him, wondering for a moment if they had other ideas. Were they touring the castle, or were they probing it? Alpheus shook his head and tried to banish those thoughts. He looked up to one of the towers, noting how much of a privilege it was to tour a castle in a foreign land, wishing that one day he could be given the same opportunity in other countries.

So she grew up here, he also thought.

The servants stopped, bringing the group to a sudden halt. Alpheus peered about, as did everyone else. They were in a hallway that they hadn't visited earlier. The marble flooring was the same as the hallway into the guest rooms they had been assigned. But rather than an addition of ten rooms here, there was a solitary double door on their right. It was closed and latched with a sizeable padlock.

"Lord Hindlow and Lord Azan," one of the servants said, looking rather uncomfortable. "This antechamber is prohibited, and we wouldn't have come here if we weren't pressed for time."

"Is this where the king spends his time?" Ash said. "Are we skipping the party and meeting him now?"

"Certainly not," the servant said with a slight frown. "We are to pass through quietly. And if you could, My Lords, would you refrain from mentioning this to anyone?"

Alpheus looked over to Tumaini, who agreed promptly. Alpheus then nodded as well. The servants led them through the hallway, and then, after three or four more turns and another set of stairs, they finally arrived at the central atrium—a large open space watched over by the massive donjon on its northern wall.

Quite impressive, Alpheus thought, peering out at the crowd of over a hundred men. While Alpheus wasn't fond of crowds, the diverse range of cultures and nationalities blended together into the same space was a wonderful sight. Residents of the country still outnumbered the foreigners, though not by too wide of a margin. Alpheus glanced out, recognising more than several people of Truban heritage, though he knew none of them. He noted some men who hailed from Kraga as evident from their dark complexion, and also more than a few with the pale skin and bluish-grey hair of Aizary. Most of the men were youthful—as they should be, considering that they were here to compete to become the Prince Consort. They stood out from their companions of either advisors or vassals by donning garbs that were striking in either colour, style, or a combination of both.

"The King isn't here yet," the servant said, breathing a soft sigh. "We'll leave you be."

Alpheus smiled at the servants, who then turned away. "Marvin," he said, still looking out to the crowd. "Can you give me some time on my own?"

But when Alpheus turned, he realised that the crew had already trotted away, most of them in different directions. Tumaini had paced off with his maid as well. It was a good opportunity for everyone to get acquainted with a few strangers.

His inclinations brought him over to a man of pale skin and spruce-blue hair attended to by a small retinue—a group from the island country. Alpheus met the man's violet eyes as he reached a hand out to greet him. "Alpheus Hindlow, of Zorlia," he offered, wary that others might know of the false accusations of murder listed next to his name.

The man took his hand and reciprocated the greeting, seemingly ignorant of Alpheus's alleged crimes. "Walter Epari, of the Valhalla Kingdom." The man then raised a brow. "Lord Hindlow, can I assume that you are related to Charlotte Hindlow?"

Alpheus nodded. "She is my sister."

The Aizar man grinned. "A pleasure!" he remarked. "Your sister is but the most celebrated person in all of the Far East... well, after our King, that is. Our people adore her from the bottom of our hearts."

It wasn't the first time that Alpheus had heard praise for his sister, but Epari's visible admiration still seemed excessive. Alpheus did his best to feign pride in response for the woman who had not been there when he had most needed her—when Reeling most needed her.

"Is that so?" Alpheus said. "Can I suppose that the Academy of Illudia owes its success to my sister as well?"

Epari cocked his head, noting the negative undertone in the question. "I trust that you can see that I'm no scholar," he said, maintaining an amicable pitch. "So I'm afraid I have no answer for that."

"I suppose you wouldn't know Kathryn Trulips, then," Alpheus said, disappointment in his voice.

"The younger of the Trulips sisters," the Aizar man noted. "Well, I *do* know about her, and her visit to Zorlia. She's representing our country, after all, as only a handful of diplomats we send out."

"She has a sister?" Alpheus asked in surprise, interested only in the first piece of information. "And what's she like?" he added with growing curiosity.

"I don't know either of them personally," Epari confessed. "But from what I hear, it is harsh to compare the two—harsh on the younger sister. Fiona Trulips has been a household name in Illudia for close to a decade, both as an A-Class scholar and in her role as Baron in the Valhalla Kingdom. The young sister's achievements pale in comparison. Frankly, I wouldn't even know her name if she hadn't been elected as a diplomat."

Alpheus found no words to respond with, his jaws dropped open at the assertion. It was unthinkable that the brilliant Kathryn Trulips could be outshined, and least of all by a peer—her very own sister. Her circumstances were perhaps more similar to his own than he had thought.

"How much older is Fiona Trulips?" Alpheus said, assuming that a considerable age difference had given the elder sister a substantial advantage.

"Not more than an hour, I presume," Epari said with a chuckle. "They're twins!"

More surprise, leaving Alpheus speechless once again. He had been told long ago that the scholars in Aizary were brilliant, and that they had become more celebrated than the scholars in both Trubannis and Vinawell. Even so, he was astonished that Kathryn Trulips might only be considered mediocre in the scholar ranks there.

As he pondered the idea, Epari looked up at something behind Alpheus. "Is he with you?" he said, prompting Alpheus to turn.

Christopher Hartland.

Was this a day to revisit his scholarly roots? Alpheus had known that his old rival was in Poppaross and had also been invited to the Purification Ceremony. But as always, Alpheus had neglected to prepare for the potential encounter with the man. He simply wasn't ready now. And as it looked,

Hartland shared his disbelief of the encounter, the man's face blank and his jaws clattering but unable to spit out a word.

After a long blink and a shake of his head, Hartland's widened eyes transformed suddenly into an annoyed glare. It was then when Alpheus noted that his old rival was accompanied by a pair of attendants—soldiers—standing on either side of him.

Hartland waved his arms forward, gesturing for his attendants to seize Alpheus, who was too late in realising that the men were lunging at him. Bystanders in the vicinity gasped and scattered about.

"What are you doing?!" Alpheus cried, appalled by the audacity.

"Don't make this difficult," Hartland said before a brief glance about, in which he would have noted the glares from the other guests as well as the waves of people gathering around. "I am simply doing what the Empire asked of me," he insisted. "Cooperate with me and I promise—"

"What do we have here?" a voice said, resounding from the crowd that had flocked over.

Hartland turned to the voice with a frown, seemingly recognising the stranger who had spoken, a young man with a dark complexion and dark hair. Among the lighter skinned crowd, the man stood out as a guest from Kraga. He sauntered closer in with his slim frame, wearing a smirk, and dragging his long coat of red behind him.

"Come, everyone," the young Kragan said. "Come watch these cowardly, hypocritical Trubans duel it out."

"Trajetzky, this has nothing to do with you!" Hartland muttered under his breath.

More and more people flocked over now, many of them with the supposition that it was Trajetzky instigating whatever conflict was taking place. The focus soon shifted away from the Kragan to Alpheus and Hartland, though, as the potential story of two Truban candidates clashing against one another was too inviting. The incessant mumbling coupled with the unfounded accusations directed at the two Truban scholars had Trajetzky look rather pleased with himself.

Hartland hissed in response but refused to allow Alpheus loose.

"Are you at least going to defend your country?" Alpheus challenged him.

"Shut up!" Hartland yelled.

Trajetzky strolled closer yet, stepping in between them, his bold approach finally prompting Hartland's men to release Alpheus and instead prepare to defend their liege and perhaps themselves. "Do continue the squabble," Trajetzky said, flapping a hand in pleasure. "Entertain us."

Hartland grunted. "Would you *please* just let us be?" he asked again, as his attendants reached for their swords with visible fear blanching their expressions.

Alpheus winced, noting now that Hartland was trembling as the young Kragan leaned into him.

"We still have a score to settle," Trajetzky whispered in a sinister undertone. "You were saved last time. But don't expect those same saviours to come again. They're not—"

"What's going on here?" asked a cheerful voice from among the crowd.

Trajetzky jumped and then Alpheus looked up to confirm that the voice belonged to Marvin who paced in alongside Rover, Tumaini, and his maid.

"You again?!" the young Kragan asked, perhaps also thinking it strange that Marvin and Rover donned mantles. "So you really *did* come to spectate."

"We wanted to see you," Marvin said with a chortle.

Trajetzky shared a laugh before turning another smirk at Hartland. "Saved again," he whispered.

Hartland scowled as the boastful Kragan stepped aside. "Now, Alpheus," Hartland said quietly, trying his best to avoid any confrontation with Marvin and the crew, clearly not realising that Alpheus had befriended the Sail Band. "Come with me. The Empire summons you."

Marvin stepped forward now with a sigh. "You should probably leave him."

Hartland turned back slightly. But while he was cautious not to provoke Marvin, his attendants were less wise, daring to draw their swords now, whiffing out a breeze that startled more than a few men who had been watching the drama unfold.

Marvin rolled his eyes, reluctant to act. He opened his mouth now, with the intention to settle the matter with words. But he had no time to utter a word before a figure swept above him, somersaulting into the scuffle in spectacular fashion—confiscating the pair of unsheathed swords, spinning the blades the other way, and then snapping them back into their respective scabbards tied at the waists of their wielders—all in one fluid motion. Finally, with a gentle push at their chests, the two men stumbled back toward Hartland.

The crowd fell silent as they marvelled at the newcomer armoured in a stately knight's armour of mahogany red complete with a dark cape draped down from the shoulders, dark tresses of wavy hair falling over it.

A woman. A female knight.

She stood tall, dwarfing some of the men—a youthful woman whose athletic figure and confident beauty exuded womanhood in a rare majestic manner. She spun toward Marvin now, her blue eyes revealing her Vinan heritage.

"The king's arrival is imminent," she said, her voice crisp and overbearing. "Unwarranted force will be distasteful to His Lordship."

The men responded with subtle nods, most of them likely wondering who she was. Meanwhile, she maintained an intent gaze on Marvin, prompting him to grin back.

"I'll make sure nothing distasteful will ensue," Marvin said, narrowing his eyes slightly.

The female knight turned now, flapping out her cape and striding away as all eyes followed her. When she disappeared from view, Alpheus saw Hartland also trotting away with his vassals.

* * *

It was barely minutes after the commotion when everyone at the atrium was asked to be silent, for *His Lordship* had finally arrived.

Heads turned toward the base of the great donjon which cast a giant shadow onto the atrium. Noblemen and other lords strode out, half of them continuing to their left and half of them to the right. Copper and Ebenezer were both part of this group. Next came the knights, including the female knight from earlier. And then, finally, the king stepped out, his regal cloak and crown confirming his rulership. He was the only leader of any country who had preserved his position throughout the war and into the present. The man stepped up onto an elevated platform at the centre that had been arranged ahead of time.

At fifty-seven years of age, the king—his name being Francis George Steele—was the oldest monarch in the land. He appeared rather thin, perhaps fragile even, with barely enough flesh to cover cheek bones that protruded out from underneath his perpetually squinting eyes. His long steps, though, showed that he still had the bounce to attend every gathering expected of him.

Older yet than the king was the man who ascended to the platform after him as the only one with the privilege to share the same elevation—the Chief General of the Dominion, whose strands of grey hair and a rugged walking stick gave him away as the eldest but also the most experienced member of the Dominion. The man's name was Bradley Redford Gaston. He had the second most powerful voice in the court, and had been instrumental in the country's involvement in—and eventual withdrawal—from the war.

The king peered out to his guests now with an affable grin, contrasting with the solemn expressions his men wore. "It is my honour," he began, with a commanding voice, "and the Dominion's honour, to host you at Radiance's Nest. We are humble to have you come for my dear child's Purification Ceremony. She is unprepared to meet you today, though I am certain she anticipates this as much as I do. I trust that the details of your stay have been arranged, and that you will make the best use of your time in the next seven days prior to the scheduled date of the ceremony. For one, I encourage you to acquaint yourself with the members of the Dominion court."

The man paused there, glancing over to Gaston. "Please, Lord Gaston."

"Certainly, My Lord," the old man replied with a bow, and then went on to introduce the court members, about twenty of them, all of whom lined up on either side of him.

The first person appraised was the female knight, whose name was Morgan Palmyra Zabai. Despite her gender and relatively young age, she was named as *Dominus* with the authority to lead every army under the Lithia name. Gaston described her as the strongest of all knights within the Dominion and supposed that she might even be the strongest warrior in the land. A portion of guests raised their brows on the supposition. It was evident that most of the foreign guests knew the name but had never thought to associate it with a woman. But if her expressive vanity was anything to show for, then it seemed that Zabai herself also believed that she was indeed the strongest.

Copper was the fourth in the entourage to be appraised. Gaston named him as a steward who oversaw the day to day operations of the castle and the lands of the Poppaross area. He was responsible for harmonising relations between civilians on a macro scale.

The final member of the court to earn an introduction was Ebenezer. Gaston called him the *Great Mage* of Vinawell, a man who devoted his time and efforts on the abstractions of energy flow. Alpheus raised a brow when Gaston rather impishly hinted that the mage was on the hunt for sorcerers, a remark received by the crowd as humorous. And finally, Ebenezer was described to have only recently reprised his role in the Dominion after a nine-year absence.

The king soon retired from the atrium, leaving his men behind to acquaint with the guests. Gaston remained, too, perhaps to watch over the men on behalf of his liege. The guests weren't shy, flocking over to some of the court members who they believed they could win over, in one way or another. Lady Zabai, the only female member of the court, found herself somewhat isolated, and the thick air of intimidation that seemed to effuse out of her was to blame. It could also be that the guests who had come for the Purification Ceremony wished to avoid giving off the idea that they were interested in any other woman.

Alpheus spared the female knight no thought, pacing instead toward the only nobleman he knew. "Lord Copper," he greeted. "We meet again."

"Lord Hindlow," Copper responded with a half-smile, cocking his head. "I… really didn't expect you to be here."

Alpheus raised a brow. "Why…? You knew I was invited."

Copper frowned, his brow furrowing. "I don't understand. Or… do you *not* know—"

"I know," Alpheus cut in with a whisper. "She's the princess."

"She told you? And she still asked you to come?"

Alpheus shrugged, leaning away again. "Am I missing something?"

"Maybe *I* am." Copper shook his head. "I still owe you my gratitude for your part in bringing our great mage back."

Alpheus blinked, and then frowned slightly. "Now you've lost me."

"Lord Ebenezer," Copper said. "It was after what you said that he decided to return—your story about the king salmon."

"Right," Alpheus said, still confused. "So… where did he go during that nine-year absence? He became a vassal of yours?"

"No, no," Copper replied with a chortle. "I wouldn't dream of it. It was by chance that Lord Ebenezer was with me that day. And it was by god's grace that allowed you to tell us that story."

"I really don't understand. But just now, Lord Gaston was saying that your great mage is on the hunt for sorcerers. What's that about?"

"I could answer you myself," said a deep voice.

Alpheus turned to see Ebenezer's approach, pacing toward him with a wooden staff for support. The man's baldness reminded Alpheus of Victor Breunor.

"What do you want to know?" Ebenezer asked, stroking his long goatee.

"May we listen in?" Marvin said from behind Alpheus, trotting in with Ash.

Ebenezer nodded at them with a grin. He then turned his attention back to Alpheus.

"I sense some hostility," he said, narrowing his eyes. "If this is about what Lord Gaston said, then please know that it was merely a figure of speech. What I am pursuing isn't a hunt of sorcerers, but rather a study of them."

Alpheus met his eyes now with a stern expression on his face. "In that case, can I assume you know a thing or two about sorcery?"

Ebenezer smiled, stroking his puffed goatee once more. "Perhaps more than a few."

"Educate me, then?"

"First of all, there is a common misunderstanding about what magic represents, or even what it is. Magic and sorcery are interchangeable terms. The phenomenon is driven by an energy called grace. And grace is but a name incorrectly attributed only to sorcerers—for grace is energy given to us by the Immortal. Everyone shares this energy. A sorcerer is different, however, in that he is simply given a larger share."

Alpheus hissed, surprising himself as he heard the sound. The mage wasn't offended, though, and that had Alpheus begin to ponder. If what Ebenezer said were true, the argument that Reeling's murderer was a sorcerer no longer held true. He looked up at Ebenezer again, who had maintained his gaze on him.

"I have heard about what happened in Zorlia," Ebenezer then said, as if he knew what Alpheus was wondering. "It seems the court assumed the culprit a sorcerer due to what they have judged as death by unnatural circumstances—an astonishing accumulation of energy. But the evidence, as they have labelled it, is inconclusive. Any amount of energy can theoretically be collected through the correct channelling."

Alpheus winced but the others said nothing, waiting for the mage to elaborate.

"If it is examples of the phenomena you want to hear about," Ebenezer continued, raising an arm, "then allow me to mention the *Legendary Royal Bandit* who roamed the lands during the warring years. The man was no sorcerer, and yet he conjured unbelievable amounts of energy into his fists." Ebenezer paused there, glancing over to Marvin, who was glaring back at him. "And may I remind you, that was in the pre-Awakening times."

"The man was called a legend for a reason," Ash said, cutting in. "He might have been just that, a legend—a myth."

The mage said nothing this time, simply maintaining his modest grin. Alpheus exchanged glances with Ash, Marvin, and then Copper as silence filled the air around them.

"Lord Ebenezer," Marvin finally said. "Would you help Alpheus clear his name? I'm sure your reputation could help."

"I appreciate the candour," the mage answered. "But it is not possible for me to take the long journey to Zorlia." He paused there, musing. "Unless Alpheus Hindlow became our Prince Consort. In that case, it would be the duty of every member of the Dominion to clear his name."

SEVEN

To oppress or to defend

Alpheus followed Marvin out to a balcony hanging off one of the smaller towers. The sun had only just risen and the glimmers of orange stroking through the mountains, glinting now onto the pearl white of the castle, was nothing short of splendid.

Marvin's expression, however, did not reflect the beautiful view. The thief leader regarded him now with a narrowed, unforgiving set of eyes, similar to the time when they had first met. Perhaps he wasn't a morning person?

Alpheus was about to begin his first lesson in the combat arts, Marvin being his instructor, of course. The porch was large enough for the purpose, even if the fine view was distracting.

"Sorry to have bothered you," said Alpheus, stretching his arms forward. "It's time that I learned how to at least defend myself properly. I've been contained so many times in the past, and—"

Marvin lunged forward suddenly, grabbing onto Alpheus's arm and pulling him forward so that he stumbled to the ground.

Alpheus groaned, pushing himself back up angrily. "What was that for?!" he questioned, throwing an arm out in protest. And sure enough, that arm was clutched onto again and pulled forward before he realised he was thrown rolling across the floor.

As he picked himself up this time, Alpheus widened his eyes as he glanced down from his shoulder to the wide tear on his sleeves, and then at his throbbing hand which he had thrown out on instinct to break his fall.

"You don't choose what you learn," Marvin said, stepping toward him. "The first thing you need is the skill of survival. Stand up."

Alpheus rose immediately as demanded. If anything, the former mercenary surely seemed intent to help him grow tougher. After all, it was what he had asked for—to be trained in the combat arts, and to be strong enough to hold his own against the likes of Hartland's attendants. Given his circumstances and the probable trajectory he hoped to follow—which promised many more challenges—Alpheus had little choice but to finally learn what he had always deemed as unnecessary violence.

He snapped his feet together then, standing firm like a military man in training. As if to test whether he had indeed stood firm, Marvin started swatting him with his sheathed dagger, belting him at the legs and hips.

"Posture! Posture!" he cried.

That lasted for a good minute and had Alpheus roughed up early. He would probably have bruises all over him soon enough, but he couldn't worry about that yet—not while Marvin kept up his grimace.

"Throw me a punch," Marvin then instructed, snapping his dagger back under his mantle. "As hard as you can."

Alpheus pursed his lips and gave it his all. Still, Marvin parried the attack, brushing his arm away and then sweeping out his own fist, only tapping onto Alpheus's nose after his skilful retraction.

Alpheus widened his eyes, regarding the fist which had come as a blur. Marvin then finally withdrew his hand altogether.

"Can you tell me what just happened?" Marvin asked.

"My punch was too slow?"

"Are you asking me, or are you telling me?"

"My punch was too slow!"

"Speed wasn't the only problem," the thief leader said. "The main reason I was able to regain advantage after your initial offence is my ability to block and evade. It will take more than ten years to train you to a level where you can predict how others might attack. Instead, we can build on your instincts to dodge without having to think."

"Is that... even possible?" Alpheus asked, raising a brow.

Marvin tapped him on the backbone. "We can only try," he said, hitting him harder in the same spot a second time. "Shimmy. Use your hips. *Only* your hips. Forward, backward, left, and right."

It was awkward, vulgar even. But Alpheus did as he was told, albeit with a wry face. The exercise was meant to elasticise the part of the body that was most important in carrying out delicate movements. The logic made sense: while Alpheus could breeze away with the Glider Steps, he had no answer against close range attacks. Working on sly motions within the same vicinity would help to improve his instincts in order to evade precipitous strikes in close and cluttered combat.

It was more than an hour later when Alpheus was finally instructed to move onto the next exercise, which was to dance. "For your footwork," Marvin simply said. "It's called the *Zip Waltz*, a dance that focuses on hops, originality, improvisation, and elegance."

Alpheus nodded and complied, but wasn't convinced that the exercise would help. As soon as he began, however, he found that it was a rather gratifying experience, especially the improvisation part of it. The elegance and softness of the style matched the refined flavour of the island country of Aizary, which Marvin then mentioned was where the dance originated. With his favour for the Far East, Alpheus grew more motivated kicking out his feet as he hopped about.

* * *

Alpheus followed the same routine for the next two days, working on shimmies and waltzes. He started early in the morning and worked until the early hours of the evening. The view from the east-facing porch was wonderful, with mountains creeping up into the sky a defined ridge crawling up on the left, and the city on the right that sat as a base to the castle. The porch itself wasn't meant exclusively for his use, but it was isolated enough so that no strangers had yet intruded upon him. And it was made the more convenient in that it was only a short walk from the guest rooms.

Night had come again, and Marvin had left for a meal, leaving Alpheus with some rare alone time in which he continued to train. Alpheus wanted his steps to be perfect. On the back of his mind, he realised that his competition was using this time to acquaint with members of the Dominion court, and in turn, he noted that he was not. In fact, he still wasn't convinced that the training now would help much—not for the Purification Ceremony, at least, and maybe not even for the longer term. And yet, his legs continued to carry him in the waltz. He came to an abrupt halt when he spun around to see one of his many competitors—the pale-skinned Walter Epari—watching him from the arch that led into the corridor.

Alpheus met the Aizar man's eyes, panting, expecting mockery. Epari, though, shot him a smile.

"Where's your dance partner, Lord Hindlow?" he asked with no hint of sarcasm and a wink of his violet eyes. "If that's the Aizar Waltz, it's wrong."

"It's not the Aizar Waltz," Alpheus said, noting that the man had come alone, "but a derivative."

The man scratched behind his ears. "I am befuddled. Why are you here doing the waltz when you should be out there making friends?"

"Because this is more worthwhile," Alpheus said, unconvinced by his own words as he heard them.

"Would you care to enlighten me about why?" Epari asked.

Alpheus hesitated and struggled to conjure up any structured response.

The Aizar man then cleared his throat to break the silence. "Have you updated yourself about the talk in town?" he asked. "Can I assume that you don't know much about Aryliel Trajetzky? That he has made a name for himself in the past week as a ruffian but also a skilled combatant—and hence one of the frontrunners of the competition? And can I also assume that you don't know that the name of Alpheus Hindlow also has people thinking? Not only is your name now associated with a contemptible murder, but there are also rumours swirling about that speaks of your sorcery persona. Do you not have a few things you want to clear up?"

"I don't know what to say," Alpheus confessed, surprised by the candid mention of sorcery.

"Excuse my prying, Lord Hindlow," Epari said, now pacing forward with a hand to his chin. "I am just concerned for you, concerned that you are falling behind the competition. I am an admirer of your sister, and I have no wish other than to see you give your best effort."

Alpheus managed a slight grin. "I appreciate it. And I think—" But he trailed off as Marvin stepped into his field of vision, behind the Aizar man, stopping just under the arch. Marvin said nothing, but he wore a grimace that had Epari wince.

"Your attendant seems to be a strong man," the Aizar man said with a smirk.

"He certainly is," he said with a nod, thinking Epari's judgement correct but premature as he had not even seen the brawn beneath the mantle.

Epari then shrugged, turning for the exit. "I've said what I had to say. The rest is up to you."

Marvin shot the Aizar nobleman a cold stare as he passed him by. And when Epari paced away from view, Marvin looked out to the porch again to see that Alpheus had returned to training, hopping about as if there had been no intermission.

Does he think I said something? Alpheus wondered, trying not to look in Marvin's direction. *Hold on, what's he slipping out from his sleeves?* There was a glare to it, reflecting the moonlight. Metal, perhaps. He couldn't be sure until he spun once more at which time the thing was hurling at him. Alpheus widened his eyes as he prodded his head to the left, making out a... *butter knife?* as the metal seared pass him. Whatever it was, it continued off the balcony and into the darkness of the evening, off toward the mountains.

Alpheus swung himself back to Marvin, glaring at him in protest.

"Calm down," Marvin said with a wave of his hand. "Take a minute and think about what just happened."

Alpheus frowned, cocking his head.

"Did you think you managed the evasion because of luck?"

Alpheus looked down to his feet, which he had planted firmly to the ground after almost stumbling over just now. He had nodded his head away, but it had been his hips that saved him.

"The word is elasticity," Marvin said, finally showing a smile for the first time since their training had started. "Planning the evasion wouldn't have worked, but leaving it to instinct did. Do you remember our first meeting?"

Alpheus perked up with a slight grin. "I do. You pulverised a building, reducing the entire thing to rubble and dust. That memory will forever haunt me."

Marvin chuckled at the dry wit. "Yes, but more specifically, do you remember how I greeted you?"

Alpheus trembled as he recalled how the twin daggers had zipped at him.

"I wasn't aiming *at* you that time," Marvin said. "My intention then was only to announce my arrival. But this time, I *was* aiming at you… albeit with a dull knife. And this… is the result of your training."

"Then…," Alpheus uttered with both surprise and joy. "Are you saying my training is complete?"

"The first part is."

Alpheus's expression dulled. "How many parts *are* there?"

"Too many," he responded as if it were the standard answer. "But before we continue, I want to warn you about Ebenezer."

"What about him?"

"I couldn't remember who he was when we saw him at the cottage," Marvin said, his smile fading from his expression. "But I do remember a few things after meeting him again here inside the castle. As a supposed expert of energy flow, Ebenezer was famous for working with Dominion soldiers during the war. He conditioned them to specific sleep and exercise patterns, which allegedly allowed the soldiers to fight with far more efficiency. As for what's to be wary of? His ethics. The hearsay describes him as someone who treats people as… *subjects*—all of them a part of his *experiments*. I don't know what it is, but I can see that he's interested in you—most probably because you're a sorcerer."

"I have my own reservations about him," Alpheus said with a wince of his own. "I don't know what it is either, but I don't trust that man."

"Anyway," Marvin said with a sudden change in tone, "let's get to the next part of the training. Ro will be your instructor."

"Hold on," Alpheus said. "Rover? But I don't want—"

It was too late. The man with the eye-patch, always solemn and aloof, arrived to join them at the porch. It was still strange to see him donning a mantle, the neat style of dress unable to tone down his thick brows and high cheekbones that had always added a certain level of intimidation to his presence.

"I'll leave you be," Marvin said, already on his way.

"Wait! I thought we were about to finish up for the day!"

Marvin shrugged as he stepped toward the arch. "Ro's in charge now. If you can get past him, you can do whatever you want. The exit to the balcony is right here."

Alpheus hissed quietly. "You *do* realise I can glide past the both of you."

"Try it," Rover dared, crossing his arms as Marvin simply chortled.

Alpheus eyed the arch, his pathway to freedom—at least for the rest of this evening, and he hopped up, kicking a puff out from his boots. At the blink of an eye, he had rushed up to Rover, drawing a blast of air behind him. Building on the momentum, he caught greater speed yet, bolting to Marvin now. But before he could reach the arch, a gale from behind him swept him back into a ferocious rotating column of air that sent him whirling in the air before crashing down at Rover's feet. The man had held out a fist with his outstretched right arm which had brought out the seething twister. It was the closest thing to sorcery that clearly wasn't sorcery.

Alpheus looked up, stunned. "Did you... brew a storm with your bare hands?"

Marvin laughed, but managed to repress himself when Rover shot him a glare. The thief leader then turned away with a shake of his head and disappeared from view.

"I'm no sorcerer," Rover said as if he knew Alpheus wanted the confirmation. "I simply blasted onto the air trailing you. My task is to help you learn who you are facing."

Alpheus sighed and then pushed himself up. That was the most words he had ever heard out of the glum warrior.

"I have been tasked to help you build a solid offence," Rover continued, speaking more words yet. "The best way to achieve that is to fight and fight until one could fight no more. In other words, you and I will spar. Land one blow on me, and your training is complete."

"Well, that sounds easy enough," Alpheus said, unable to bite back the sarcasm.

As it turned out, it was indeed impossible on this first day. The benefit of having Rover as his sparring partner was obvious. The man was a former mercenary who rivalled Marvin in both skill and experience. And despite being a man of few words, Rover had much to say now with his immediate critique, which came out as rather blunt. Between his constant grouches and curses, however, lied rare instances of instruction that spoke about efficiency and endurance in combat. The man was reluctant to state anything expressly, but as he continued to hound, Alpheus noted his advice about finding one's balance between speed and power, attack and defence. The endurance part of it needed no further explanation, verbal or otherwise. Given that Rover was an instructor harsher even than Marvin, the activity would inevitably have Alpheus toughen up.

The guidance was undeniably valuable. Although Alpheus was constantly at the receiving end of crushing blows that sent him flying in every direction, he managed to convince himself, after some time, that the former mercenary was taking it easy on him. As the sparring went on, he also recognised that without the shimmies and hops that he had already learned, the session would have been far more challenging.

His training went on well past midnight. And when Rover finally called it a day, Alpheus was left exhausted with throbbing bruises all over. But as he fell to the ground in a sprawl, gasping for breath, he managed a smile as he noted how far he had come in only a few days. If he had managed to survive a sparring session with Rover—albeit with the man taking it easy on him—he assumed that he could perhaps hold his own, now, against even trained warriors.

A hand reached down to him then, a broad hand that had endured a thousand battles. Alpheus reached up, taking the hand which was indeed firm and strong.

"Thank you... Ro," Alpheus said, addressing the man with the shortened alternative which had seemed to be reserved only for Marvin's use. "I'm glad I have you on my side," he added.

Rover regarded Alpheus for a moment without a twitch. He then swung him to his feet.

"Marv is the only one you need to thank," he said.

* * *

Alpheus opted to fall right into bed rather than spending more time awake to draw a bath. Rover—who hadn't broken a sweat—had no need. In any case, sleep eluded Alpheus for the most part that night. His entire body was sore, and the collective snoring of the thieves with whom he shared the room seemed louder than ever. But what kept him from falling asleep most was a troubled mind overflowing with images of the barrage of attacks headed his way.

The fatigue was unbearable, and Alpheus found himself almost wide awake because of it. He didn't bother with checking the time, but he was sure that it was just a few short hours until his next rugged training session with Rover. If he were to last an entire day, he would need rest. He rolled about in frustration and then finally sat up, meeting Rover's gaze, who was lying on a bed across him, the man's lone eye glistening in the moonlight that shimmered in.

"Sorry I woke you," Alpheus whispered, pointing to the door. "I'll be at the balcony."

Rover closed his eyes and snoozed away. Alpheus threw on his mantle that had become ragged from training, tiptoeing his way out of the room. He looked to the left of the corridor, but then headed down the right, barely feeling his legs as he swayed about.

Without much thought to it, he followed the path he remembered from his first day at the castle. He found himself in an area that the servants had warned them all not to return to: the prohibited antechamber.

Why am I here? Alpheus thought with a yawn, his vision growing hazy as he made out the double door on the right. *Wasn't there a padlock on it?* he wondered. He shook his head and forced his eyes wide, staring into the oil lamp installed above the double door.

Alpheus jumped then when he heard a sound from behind him. Footsteps and muttering. *Guards?* Alpheus didn't know why, but he hopped forward, thinking that he had to hide. He pushed against the unlocked door, then slipped inside before shutting it behind him.

He had entered another hallway, and this one had no end for as far as he could see in the dim lighting. Alpheus prowled forward, still not sure why he had to. His eyelids grew heavier and his legs moved now as if independent from his head.

Sleep. I need to sleep.

He was almost snoozing as he wandered deeper inside. The light dream that came to him began with the eyepatch he had seen too much of already that day. He then finally collapsed against a wall and dozed off.

*   *   *

When Alpheus woke up, he didn't know how long he had been asleep. The closest torch attached on the wall was a distant away. He couldn't work out which way he had come in. He slapped himself in the face, and the gentle sting urged him to tread forward, possibly further away from the exit. He finally allowed himself a smile when a glimmer of daylight shone at the far end. He paced in that direction, pushing open the double door, but only to arrive at a small open courtyard he had never seen before.

A simple birch tree stood at the centre, surrounded by walls that shot up to heights that hid the courtyard from even the tallest towers of the castle. Beneath the solitary tree was a well, and next to the well were creeping vines that seemed to purposely conceal a set of stairs. A glance at those stairs had Alpheus shivering suddenly, as it reminded him of his time in prison. Even amid bright daylight, the stairs took in little natural light, partly because of the incredibly high walls. Curiosity won over, as it usually did for Alpheus, and he soon found himself descending the stairs lighted with candles mounted on both sides of the stairway. Every step of the way came, Alpheus found himself having to answer to his conscience.

Just what am I doing here, intruding this place?

After twenty or so steps, he came to a fork. He chose the right.

And I'm still going. What are you doing, Alpheus?

Somehow, it felt as if his legs were carrying him forward—independently from his head—deeper down the set of stairs. And after another minute, he saw the end of the stairway where ample light shone out.

He stepped inside to lustrous wonderment. It was an enclosed space, dome-shaped, with every part of the wall and ceiling covered in painted art—a contiguous painting of the natural outside world. The detail of the skyline—including the blue sky, the clouds, hills, trees, and even birds—was exquisite. At the centre of the ceiling was the sun, and just below it dangled a beautiful lantern emulating natural light. It was a piece of art that Alpheus wished he could paint. But after his brief, initial appreciation of it, a chill ran down his spine.

Why here? he thought. *And for whom?*

He desperately brushed his shoulders to dislodge the invisible creepers that had crawled into his imagination. He turned to see that there was nothing on him. As if to test him, a child's cough then reverberated inside the dome. It was the sound of a girl, and he had no way of knowing if it was in his imagination. He headed for the stairs with escape on his mind. But when he turned, he learned that he wasn't alone.

Two people stood at the stairway, stepping in. They were startled to see him, and Alpheus, in turn, tumbled over in brief terror. Looking back up at them at that height, he saw two people, one a lady and the other a child—or a doll.

No, she's a lady, too, Alpheus realised. The taller was dressed as any other servant of the castle, and the doll-like lady was small, looked like and dressed like a doll. Her big round eyes, puffy cheeks, delicate small lips, and fair amber hair was a perfect match for the neat ruff around her neck and the light purple coloured dress. Despite the supposed charm of her doll-like appearance, she effused an air of eeriness. She looked as if she had no soul, lacking both facial and physical expression.

"Forgive me for intruding," Alpheus said, trying his best to breathe normally. "I got lost, that's all."

The doll-like lady stared blankly past him and didn't say a word, as if she couldn't see him at all. Her maid didn't utter a word, either, but she studied Alpheus with suspicion. Perhaps she was evaluating whether or not he was a threat.

"I'm going to leave now, if that's all right," Alpheus said.

But still no word of response came. The continued silence prompted Alpheus to blurt out more irrelevant information.

"You know, actually, I know the princess—well, I mean..."

The maid's eyes widened suddenly. Yet still, no word.

"I don't mean today—I mean... I never meant to intrude. The Purification Ceremony—I'm here for that."

The maid seemed to calm down there. "Ah," she finally uttered, "so it is Princess Flora you seek."

Relief now. They *were* people after all. Not spirits, or whatever other supernatural beings he had imagined in his mind. Alpheus scratched his head in embarrassment and afforded a forced grin.

"This must not look good for my country," he said with a simper.

At those words, the doll-like lady grew suddenly interested. Her eyes turned sharp and focused.

"And what country is it that you represent?" she asked in a sweet, high-pitched voice.

As the word "Trubannis" came out of Alpheus's mouth, her innocent small lips curled up into a big, wicked smirk. At the same time, a sudden burst of grace-like energy effusing into the air had Alpheus' heart racing again. He immediately sought to escape, but it was impossible as the stairway was blocked and the strangers inching closer and closer to him.

"You want to leave now, do you?" the doll-like lady said. "You may, but you would have to leave *your head* behind."

The maid had pulled out a weapon from behind her back—a sickle. Stunned by the unprovoked aggression, Alpheus fidgeted his back up against the wall. A bead of cold sweat trickled down the side of his face as he realised that there was nowhere to run. Was this a dream? A nightmare? How could it not be? Was there a connection between this deviant room and Radiance's Nest? No. But here he was. The nightmare was more real than anything.

"Alpheus Hindlow!" a voice then resounded.

A dream, Alpheus thought, breaking a smile. But he didn't wake up. The strangers before him were still there.

"Alpheus Hindlow, are you there?" the same voice resounded again.

Alpheus looked up, thinking the voice familiar. "I'm here!" he cried at the top of his voice, which came out as almost a squeal.

Trampling footsteps started to sound, growing louder by the second. His saviour was approaching. The doll-like lady hissed and then reverted to her blank look. Her maid, meanwhile, slipped away the weapon. The newcomer—his saviour—turned out to be Ebenezer, a man Alpheus wasn't entirely fond of, except he was still grateful to see a familiar face. After rushing in, the mage shot a brief glance at Alpheus before bowing down to the doll-like lady.

"Apologies for the intrusion," he said without addressing her directly.

"This is unacceptable," the maid grumbled on behalf of her liege. "How did this person weave his way through?"

Her reproach was daring, yet the mage kept his head inclined to accept the blame. The doll-like lady, meanwhile, retired to the corner and stared at the painted sun.

"Take him away," the maid demanded, this time in a softer voice.

Ebenezer nodded and grabbed Alpheus by the arm. "Please excuse me."

Without another look at them, the mage led Alpheus out of the deviance and back into the quiet courtyard. The natural blue sky was a hundred times more pleasant than the disturbing artificial one he had just experienced. Ebenezer dragged him on into the same hallway he had come from, the two of them trotting away with a sense of urgency.

"Consider yourself fortunate that I came in time," Ebenezer mumbled.

"In time for what?" Alpheus asked in return, more annoyed than he thought he should be. He was most curious about the grace-like energy he thought he had sensed, but refrained from asking.

"And who *were* those people?" he added instead. "What was that room?"

"Couldn't have consciously found his way there," the mage mumbled to himself, ignoring the questions altogether. "He was drawn there. Has it come to this already…?"

"*Drawn* there?" Alpheus asked with growing suspicion, which seemed to finally bring the mage back to his senses, the old man blinking a couple of times. "What are you saying? I was drawn there? By *what*?"

"It's better not to know," Ebenezer then said with a frown. "More importantly, do *not* go there again."

"Oh, believe me—I won't. In fact, I'd have to rethink whether I want to be the Prince Consort after that."

"Think all you want. It doesn't concern me, but I repeat: do not go there again. I cannot promise that I can save you a second time."

His grave tone and the fact that he had bowed down to the doll-like lady would leave anyone suspicious. But Alpheus curbed his curiosity for now. He was in no mood to learn more—only wishing to forget it had ever happened at all.

Alpheus managed to ease up finally when they reached the familiar pearl colour of the main corridors and the magnificent pillars. He watched as Ebenezer slammed the double door shut, snapping a padlock onto it. Alpheus regarded it, praying that it would never open again.

EIGHT

The meaning of beauty

It was still morning. A sizeable clock attached to one of the pillars displayed the time as half past eleven. Alpheus hoped to avoid trouble. He didn't spare a glance at anyone he passed by, and he soon returned to the twin guest rooms assigned to him. Rover wasn't there anymore, though. The rest of the crew were also nowhere to be seen. Alpheus then paced away, with the balcony in mind, only to stop when a moan resonated from one of the other guest rooms, a few rooms across from his. The door wasn't closed all the way, the gap wide enough for a child to slip through.

Alpheus shook his head, unsure whether or not his mind was playing tricks on him. But as he blinked hard and then forced his eyes wide open again, another moan sounded from the same guest room.

Alpheus snuck up to the door and peeked inside through the small gap. He first caught a glimpse of a kneeling castle servant, a young man barely in his adulthood, seemingly pleading for forgiveness. He then glanced across the servant to see Aryliel Trajetzky and his men seated at a rectangular table. The Kragans were squawking about their meals, apparently not having been given the food they had requested.

It looked to Alpheus that the Kragans were tyrannising the poor servant. But Alpheus knew better than acting on impulse and being a foolish hero. He was ready to reluctantly turn away when he noted a knight sauntering in from the other end of the corridor. The knight carried a wide frame, donning full-plated armour, complete with a sword at his waist. Alpheus beamed, waving at him and mouthing his words of help rather than uttering them aloud.

The knight strolled over, looking both mean and reluctant, perhaps having recognised Alpheus as the alleged murderer from Trubannis—either that, or because he had been waved over as if he were a servant. When the knight crouched down to peek inside the room, however, he frowned instantly.

"Just sharing a conversation," he muttered softly with a shrug. "Nothing worth noting."

"What...?!" Alpheus said with his angriest whisper.

"I'll be on my way," the knight then said, maintaining a soft pitch as he rose to his feet.

And there he was, jogging away from where he had come. The knight had shamelessly turned a blind eye to Trajetzky's antics, probably out of fear. Alpheus shook his head as he watched him recede, but then he jumped at the sudden sound of shattered porcelain.

"Saiga," Trajetzky said, his discarded dish on the ground. "I wanted saiga. You had two days, and yet you still bring me this same trash."

The servant trembled. "Apologies, My Lord," he said, stammering as he spoke. "But we don't stock that meat. The saiga antelope is native to Kraga. We have instead prepared the closest alternative, an antelope we have here in—"

The servant trailed off when Trajetzky waved a hand to signal one of his men to grasp the poor servant by the head. A tap on the table then signalled the man to crash the servant to the ground against the shattered porcelain—head first. The resulting splatter of blood soaked the floor and even Trajetzky cringed at the sight of it.

Alpheus clenched his fists but resisted the temptation to jump in. His anger grew, however, when it became evident that this was all just amusement for the Kragans, who laughed at the expense of their victim's misery. They gradually grew silent when the servant coughed up a dribble of blood which dropped lightly at Trajetzky's boots, at which time, the mad Kragan sneered before leaping to his feet and dealing the servant a kick that sent him smashing into the far wall.

"No!" Alpheus cried, his loud utterance finally revealing his presence. He crashed in through the door, and on impulse, he drew a marble from beneath his sleeves and fired at a metal cup of milk which then exploded on the Kragans who all jumped to their feet at once, wincing at the splatter coursing through the air.

Alpheus leaped toward the moaning, young servant whose bloodied face had yet to render him unconscious. But if it were an indication of where it pained him most severely, the servant was in fact holding onto his injured shoulder, which had suffered the thumping blow from Trajetzky's heavy boot.

Alpheus turned his eyes to the assailants now, his brows knitted. "Servants are people, too," he said, his voice almost a growl.

Amid the anger, however, Alpheus quietly acknowledged his luck that the splattered milk missed Trajetzky altogether. The strange man even afforded a chuckle at his men, all of them bulked with much more brawn than him. But Alpheus did fear that he might have already said too much, and that he might soon be subject to the same fate suffered by the servant.

Trajetzky clicked his fingers then, a gesture to which Alpheus didn't know how to respond. And from the reaction of Trajetzky's men, they were also confused, until one of them signalled for the others—a total of three—to have Alpheus surrounded.

"What are you idiots doing?!" Trajetzky said, shaking his head with a scowl. "Get back over here!"

They complied immediately. "Lord Trajetzky," one of them said in a soft whisper. "The thieves aren't here."

Not offering even a glance at his vassal, Trajetzky had locked his eyes on Alpheus. He widened his eyes to study him, with a growing smile.

"I never knew a Truban can look like this," he said, stepping forward with a look of... *adoration?*

Alpheus grew awkward, shivering at the young Kragan's glowing eyes. "I apologise for the milk," Alpheus said. "I just wanted to— "

"Forget that. I'm more interested in who you are, rather than what you do."

"Interested... in me...?"

"All things beautiful attract me and are attracted to me. Your level skin, glistening eyes, perfect slim figure, and innocent charm make you a rare item of beauty. And to think I missed this the other day. Was it because of that pedant of the Truban Empire? In any case, be honoured, child. I shall make an exception to you, a man not of Kragan blood, to be my servant."

Alpheus gawked at Trajetzky, unsure whether he should be offended or pleased. Adding to the irony were the dropped jaws from his men, which showed that they deemed serving Trajetzky to be a privilege.

"When my business is done here, you will follow me back to Millenzburg. As my pet, you and I will form a winsome duo." He paused for a second, narrowing his eyes with a smirk. "Of course, you would have to pass the test first."

Trajetzky grabbed an empty plate on the dining table and launched it at Alpheus without warning, but Alpheus managed to maintain his calm and composure to perform an impressive evasion—the plate ended up shattered against the far wall. A simple bending of the hips, a slight nod of the head, and a hop away had saved him. It was Marvin's direct teachings on display, and an action that had Trajetzky beam at him now. But the mad Kragan didn't stop there, reaching now for his scimitar hanging beside the bed and, without unsheathing it, beginning to prod at Alpheus with supreme speed.

The barbaric chants of Trajetzky's men heaped more pressure on Alpheus and seemed to spur Trajetzky on as well. But at the same time, Alpheus realised that his elastic hip movements and his skill in the Zip Waltz were helping him respond almost routinely to the barrage. And soon he found plenty of encouragement that he was evading every single deft strike. This wasn't so different from sparring with Rover except now there seemed to be a real possibility of landing a counterattack. Indeed, Alpheus searched hard for an opening to strike back. It came when his opponent briefly lost his footing in a failed attempt to sweep him to the ground, to which Alpheus retaliated with a thrust of his own, aiming a jab at the Kragan's chest. Trajetzky managed to recover, though, narrowly brushing Alpheus away with a swipe of his hand before turning suddenly vicious.

Trajetzky slashed out his blade, slicing it with added power and speed. Even with elasticised hips and the craftiness of the Zip Waltz, Alpheus struggled to keep up. The young Kragan's lightning-quick tempo simply overwhelmed Alpheus who then soon fell in defeat with his neck at the mercy of the opponent's blade.

"Will you murder me at this castle?" Alpheus challenged with an upward glare.

The Kragan laughed in his usual boastful manner before withdrawing his weapon. "Had I wanted that, you'd be a dead man. But why would I destroy someone who I wish to join me? I told you that this is a test. In this world, beauty alone is not enough if he withers away for his frailty. Be glad that I consider you worthy."

With or without further elaboration, the idea was ridiculous. And Alpheus would have rejected the offer already if he knew how to do so without offending the man.

"I'm flattered," Alpheus said, almost cringing at the sound of his own words.

Trajetzky nodded with a proud grin. "I have no desire for romantic love," he said. "The notion is a silly one. Beauty is what I seek, and also and what I create. My role in this ugly world is an important one—it is to embellish it. I live to be surrounded by beautiful things and people. Make no mistake—women are beautiful creatures. I have heard the princess here is an item of exceptional beauty. But regardless of how charming women may be, the beauty is short-lived—it is inevitable that physical fragility and the susceptibility to age will always prevail. Real lasting beauty belongs to me... and perhaps only a handful of others... only to those of us with elegance on the outside and intelligence on the inside. And most critically, to those of us who are trained to endure."

He paused for a moment, shooting a gaze down at Alpheus, who simply swallowed. "Child, I can show you a higher level of beauty that is beyond the physical. It is called victory and conquest. Now, how does that sound?"

His grin split even wider then. But to his shock, Alpheus shook his head in denial.

"I won't be your servant," Alpheus dared to say, but with determination. "I actually thought your proposal warranted my consideration, but as you went on, it became clearer and clearer that your purposes are vastly different from my ideologies. Nevertheless, I appreciate the offer. And now I have every reason to fight to be Prince Consort, if only to ensure that you will not succeed."

That speech won Alpheus a fervent glare and then an audible slap across the face. Trajetzky was absolutely livid, and with a wave of the hand, his men pinned Alpheus against the wall, as the narcissistic Kragan himself irritably muttered words of threat.

"Submit now!" Trajetzky demanded, drawing his scimitar again and pointing it at Alpheus. "Or lose your fingers.... I'll slice them off one by one."

The man looked prepared to destroy anything he couldn't have, including Alpheus who had been naïve to bet on the madman's favour for him. With his arms clipped against the wall, Alpheus was helpless. And when he squirmed in futility, the men pressed harder, at which time, the double crescent pendant slipped out beneath his sleeve at his wrist. Eyeing the Ionian symbol, Alpheus prayed for power before squeezing his eyes shut. But the Kragan's blade edged closer to his throat and nothing of the supernatural cause rained down. He cursed in his head, cursing not at the Immortal, but at himself, who wished to be saved yet again. If it were a prayer, however, it was answered soon enough.

"What's going on here?" a voice said from the door, firm yet genial.

Alpheus turned to the direction of the voice, looking for the face he believed the voice belonged to. And indeed, it was Azure—*the princess*, together with her maids, Claire and Carmen. Her beauty shimmered across the room, the glistening blue of her eyes throwing giant waves crashing unto others. Trajetzky waved his men back, widening his eyes to appreciate the arrival of a lady of royal blood. The princess sported a dress similar to the one she had changed into that day at the cottage, but this one was tinged in a fabric of regal purple. She was without her tiara, wearing her hair braided in a long plait over her left shoulder. Her maids donned dresses of creamy beige, with less embroidery, but clearly a class above the regular servants. Claire, in particular, still shared a striking resemblance with her liege lady. Her round face and rounder eyes were nearly identical to Azure's.

And it was she, Claire, who paced forward now, peering across the room and meeting Trajetzky in the eyes. "Must I curb violence even in the castle?" she asked, her tone stronger than Alpheus had ever heard.

Trajetzky raised a brow, perhaps unsure which woman was the princess. "You must be mistaken, My Lady," he said, glancing at Carmen, and then at Azure. "I am wholly against violence."

Claire frowned slightly, peering down to the servant who had since fallen unconscious and whose face was soaked in blood.

"He slipped on his way out," Trajetzky said, maintaining a despicable smirk. "I was just about to take him to a physician when my friend.... *Alpheus*, came to visit."

Claire shot her glare back at their Kragan guest. "I do not wish for any early disqualifications."

"I am honoured for your concern, My Lady. And more honoured that you came to see me. Please be assured I will continue to persevere even when I become the Prince Consort."

"I look forward to it," Claire said. "As for now, we wish to take your friend... *Alpheus*, with us. We have a few things we would like to discuss with him."

Trajetzky scowled for a second, and then managed to smile once more. "Very well. Let us meet again in a few days' time. I shall convince you then that you belong with me."

* * *

Alpheus didn't mind walking the princess back to her chambers, not when she had asked for it. But he was embarrassed to have had to be rescued by her. He also noticed that the people they passed by were shooting them slight frowns. It wasn't good for the princess to stroll about alongside a foreigner, and it was worse that she was with a man—least of all, a foreign man who was an alleged murderer.

"These people will dramatize the story," Alpheus whispered behind the princess. "But rest assured, I'll submit a formal letter to the Dominion to explain this. I'll tell them it was my idea that—"

"You are a true gentleman," Claire praised, speaking for the princess again. "There is nothing to explain, however. There is no misconduct to be with a friend."

"A friend...," Alpheus uttered, still embarrassed about what had happened earlier.

Claire nodded and then eyed the princess. "I'm sure Princess Flora considers you her friend, too," she said with an innocent giggle so different from how she had spoken to Trajetzky. "Right, My Lady?"

The princess blushed a little. "Lord Hindlow's a friend," she said. "And so are you, Claire. And so is Carmen."

Claire giggled again, with her fellow maid joining her.

The princess sighed softly as she looked over her shoulder to Alpheus. "We came out today to see you," she confirmed. "After all, I promised that I would help you in your bid to become the Prince Consort. I was surprised, though, to see you in trouble. Perhaps if your friends had been in company, that wouldn't have been the case."

Alpheus sighed. "It's embarrassing," he said. "And I'm sorry that you happened by me at such a scene."

The princess and her maids paused for second, but asked no further questions. "Let us hold that thought for a moment," the princess said, as she nodded at the double door before them where a pair of guards stood on watch.

"My Lady," one of the guards greeted with a bow as they paced toward them. "May we dare advise you not to invite guests here? It would—"

"You may *not* dare," Claire said, cutting the guard short. "And be warned not to blabber, for I promise that your tongue would be sorry."

Alpheus tensed up, noting that the guards seemed as surprised by her tone as he did.

For a moment, Alpheus feared that it was the princess's private chambers that were behind the double door. He couldn't be sure when he found that they were now ascending a long flight of stairs.

"Can I ask you to continue your story?" the princess asked as they continued trotting up, all of them seemingly used to the journey.

Alpheus drew in a long breath. He briefly considered whether he wanted to say much more, but given that it was the princess who had saved him, he decided that he owed it to her. By the time he finished telling his story about how he wished to grow stronger physically, they had arrived at the top of at least hundreds of steps.

As it turned out, the end point of the journey was a private courtyard, private in that it was elevated above most of the high-rising towers of the castle. The patio was a replica of the pergola of the Violanola Cottage. From the vines that crept along the walls, to the closed moonflowers which were planted in bunches, it was all the same—albeit in a smaller space.

"You wanted to grow stronger," Carmen said as they all sat down. "But am I correct to assume that you have a distaste for combat?"

Alpheus turned blank for a second. "What makes you say that?"

The princess smiled. "Carmen can detect and dissect the smallest changes in facial expressions," she said. "She could read your thoughts from a slight turn of your eyelids."

Alpheus swallowed, suspicious whether or not that were true.

"But, Lord Hindlow," Claire said, weighing in. "If that is the case, I would think it's best that you discontinue from that path. Don't think of it as giving up. Think of it in the same line of philosophy that you used to convince us about how choices should be made. You showed that there are other paths than conforming to social standards."

Alpheus regarded Claire now, seeing more than a maid before him. *And are you of the assumption that I have conformed to learn combat arts?* He swallowed again. *That... may be true. It's the art of murder, something I have maintained I wouldn't commit.*

"Lord Hindlow," Claire said, bringing Alpheus back to reality. "There are good people who fight for good causes. But you don't belong in this category of people."

Alpheus frowned slightly this time. It was easy to say that he didn't *wish* to fight. But if he had learned anything in the recent past, it was that one's reality rarely coincided with what was ideal. He shook his head then, turning his focus on Claire, who seemed more and more like a noblewoman, and one with great wisdom.

"I am an artist," Alpheus said. "If I could pave a path of peace with my brush, I'd do it."

Claire smiled. "And like you, Lord Hindlow," she said, "I am also a scholar *and* an artist. We have done our research. We have learned about who you are, including your ability to wield magic. But, rest assured, we have nothing against sorcerers. If anything, we are intrigued by them."

"Is that so?" Alpheus managed to utter in response, unsure whether he should feel impinged upon or honoured by their interest. "Now, I have a question for you, then," he said with sudden force. "Where's Cipher Nostalgia? The impressionist. I need to know."

Claire twitched a brow at the mention of the name, as did Carmen and the princess. If the alias wasn't theirs, it would seem that they at least knew who the person was.

"He is... a friend," the princess said, almost as if answering for Claire.

"*He*? So... a man. I'd like to meet him."

Claire mused on that for a moment. "He would probably want to meet you, too," she said. "It is unfortunate, though, that we might not be able to arrange it."

Alpheus maintained his gaze on Claire, waiting for an explanation, until she turned away, clearly not interested to offer anything more.

NINE

Children of royal blood

Tavie had been dressed up as a man since her first day at Radiance's Nest. She had suspected that she would be bothered by it, but the only bother had been the fear that others would learn who she was. She had also suspected to grow bored of her travels with the Sail Band, and at times she hated that she was so attached to them. Every now and then, she would think about her royal heritage and the life she had left behind—essentially the right to live lavishly and be constantly pampered by pesky courtiers. Some of these were fond memories, she realised in spite of the outward hypocrisy involved, but not even once had she thought about turning back.

Sleep eluded her this evening. She wandered out into the hallways on her own, the passage dabbed by the red of Selene, its hue imbued now onto the mantle she donned. Her footsteps resounded gently in the near silence of the night. No one else was around. The beams that lifted the high ceiling almost seemed immense to her—just like the ones in the fort she had once lived in, *confined* within.

Tavie slowed her step as she looked up with a shudder. The tint of red fuzzing out on the glazed windows just under the high ceiling was something she had used to appreciate while praying for liberty. The stars and the moons had been her loyal companions, entities with which she would share her sorrows. It was almost laughable to her now that there had been no one she could confide in, and that she had had to alienate everyone around her by acting mentally ill. Her late mother was one of the few people she had been fond of, but she had detested even her at times. She had called the woman a craven, content with being just one of her father's many lovers. Tavie also dreaded the potentially large number of illegitimate siblings she might have as a result of her father's promiscuity. From the outside, it was a royal family, majestic and dignified. But on the inside, it was simply another dysfunctional family. Her recent experiences in the real world had confirmed that much.

Escape had been perhaps the best thing she could have dreamed of.

Indeed, she could hardly believe that it had been nearly half a year. She still remembered vividly what had happened on that eventful evening when the crew had stormed the Monarchal Castle. She credited the meeting to fate, and she quietly thanked the Immortal every evening before she went to sleep. The others knew nothing of this, however, instead often teasing her for clinging onto them.

After shaming the crew at the Violanola Cottage, she had made herself a promise to change. And while she had continued to disagree with the others over trivial differences, her renewed efforts to understand what the group represented had been genuine. She was keen to finally establish her own unique role within the crew—derogatory as it might seem, it was to be the woman who provided emotional comfort.

Tavie suspected that the others in the crew probably thought that her recent behaviour had been strange. She had been causing little mischief, and instead she had been clinging onto them tighter than ever. But this wasn't part of what she had planned. The reason for her behaviour had been in regard to one man, Christopher Hartland, who she knew had stalked her since the day that the crew had arrived in the capital.

She knew he was coming for her, and indeed, the man manifested behind a beam now, his head inclined.

"Lady Octavia," Hartland addressed her, speaking softly, perhaps to avoid attention.

Tavie swallowed, her pupils dilating under the shadows of the beams. Hearing that title which she had known for her entire life was more dreading than she had imagined. For at least a moment, it felt as if she was taken back to the fort that had imprisoned her.

"I apologise for approaching you like this, but the bandits are a dangerous group of people. It'd be foolish of me to confront them directly."

Tavie looked away as her discomfort grew.

"I believe you have already learned my name," Hartland continued. "I work primarily under the instructions of Lord Morlan—your father."

"I don't know what you're talking about," she finally said, clenching a fist into the thick mantle, knowing for certain that it was futile to deny who she was. Even the most inept of his father's vassals would have done his research before seeking her out and then showing himself.

"In case you didn't know yet, Cetal has since reverted to a Truban state under the authority of the Empire. As Lord Morlan's child, you will be granted with a noble title in Vondra Dawn. My task is to return you to Zorlia."

Tavie groaned quietly. "You speak of me as an item."

"Please come with me," he responded, either ignoring or simply ignorant of her displeasure. "We can leave here at once."

"*Leave*?" Tavie asked with a snort, meeting his eyes now. "Are you not here for the Purification Ceremony?"

"My priority is your safety. I cannot compromise that for anything."

"And by ensuring my safety, you mean from the Sail Band?"

"They are no ordinary bandits. In case you didn't already know, Marvin Sailanson was a mercenary and—"

"I know more than you think."

Hartland lifted his chin, his eyes glinting. "But you don't know everything," he said. "The man was once the Lord Emperor's most able soldier. He was a war hero. But he was also... a *monster* known as the *Judge*."

Tavie swallowed hard and pondered this claim, unable to associate that notorious cognomen to someone as carefree as Marvin.

Hartland grinned slightly as he realised he had her attention. "His stories are told everywhere. While I cannot adjudicate on his crimes, allow me to point out that a man doesn't earn the allegations to the massacres he is thought to be responsible for unless there is some truth to them. I trust that you have read upon the *Noel Gate Incident*, in which the man ripped apart more than two hundred men—all of whom were his comrades. I don't know why you're with them but be glad that I am here. Be glad that I will take you far away from their grip."

Hartland stepped forward, offering a hand. "Now, come with me."

"No!" Tavie cried, swiping his hand away. "Lies!" she said, shaking her head. "They're all lies!"

She regretted yelling the last words as her voice echoed through the corridor. So much for being discreet. But if it were any consolation, Hartland's frown and hectic scan of the surroundings showed that he was more afraid than her of being discovered. It was a moment later when Hartland must have confirmed that no one was around, for he soon turned his attention back on her.

Tavie was surprised to find herself all teared up, but she did her best not to shed even a drop. It was embarrassing to allow anyone to see her cry, least of all, one of her father's men who would surely report the incident. She bit into her lips to hold in the concoction of ambivalence that wrestled in her mind. A little part of her actually felt treasured that her father was trying to locate her. But the other part—a much stronger part—was struggling to hold in the anger she had for the man who she thought had no redeeming qualities as a husband or a father. She twitched then as she felt blood stream out from her lips from where she was biting.

The stream of emotions must have displayed on her face, for Hartland squinted in submission then as he turned away. "I'll give you some time," he said softly.

Tavie kept her head down as the sound of footsteps receded. When she heard no more sound, she looked up. Hartland was gone, but standing a distance before her was another man.

"Leo?" she said with a gasp. "How long…. have you been here?"

Leo wore a wry smile, pondering his answer before offering it. "Long enough to hear something that wasn't for my ears."

Tavie looked away. "Are you… going to say anything?"

"I don't know yet."

"Can you… not?"

Leo huffed in a long breath, followed by a sigh. "I can," he said. "It is your right not to speak of your past. The rest of us deserve this same right… given that you can still trust Marvin and the rest of us."

Tavie nodded, musing on the implications of that comment. She spoke no more, however, as she followed the man and his lanky figure back to the guest rooms. She trusted that Leo would help her keep her secret, and was surprisingly glad that someone now shared the secret. She did worry that he might start treating her differently, though. And if that were the case, this might be the beginning of the end of her time with the crew.

* * *

Alpheus looked at the young man sitting across from him, a diminutive figure whose bony arms and legs were made to seem that much more frail next to the sinewy frame of Marvin. The young man was Tumaini Azan, the Prince of Seniblum—one of the candidates who had been invited to compete for the honour of marrying Princess Flora.

In all fairness, Tumaini proved to be rather unique in positive ways, too. He was the only candidate of royal blood, hailing from the land of the deserts otherwise known as the *Kingdom of Sill*. He was well-mannered, gentle, and looked kind. But no matter how his honest qualities added up, it seemed that the Purification Ceremony—which claimed to have summoned only young men with special talents across the land—might have made a mistake in inviting Tumaini. It was no exaggeration to say that a relatively strong wind would sweep the young prince away. His claim of trekking the entire way there from Seniblum with only his maid was naturally met with raised brows. Stamina was an afterthought, as he looked too fragile to even have survived the journey.

As Alpheus regarded Tumaini, he thought about his own physical strength and his resolve to cease further training in the combat arts. He had already settled all potential differences with his instructors of three days, Marvin and Rover. After his meeting with the princess yesterday, he had hurried back to them with an earnest apology for not showing up for training. When he had told them he didn't want any further training, Marvin had only cared to ask if he was content with his current strength. Rover, meanwhile, really didn't seem to care at all.

Alpheus spoke openly about his confrontation with Trajetzky, explaining that he respected the Kragan's strength, and from the experience, he realised he could never reach that level. Marvin had responded by saying that a few days of training could never make up for years of hard work, and that in terms of hand to hand combat, Alpheus would never match Trajetzky—no matter how hard he tried.

While Alpheus certainly wasn't physically strong, he could rest well knowing that there was someone weaker than him in the competition—the Senil Prince. No one sharing the long table belittled the flimsy Senil, however, at least not outwardly. And it might have to do with Marvin, whose eyes had lit up since they had settled down at a larger courtyard close to the central atrium, with genuine interest and respect for Tumaini and his stories. Indeed, the young prince's actions were noble, but perhaps to his own detriment.

Everyone who had met Tumaini apparently thought him naïve. In the few days since he had arrived, he had sought out more than half the invitees—not to challenge, but to counsel. Some of those people had been initially wary of him, annoyed, especially when he seemed to know a lot about them, correctly quoting their desires and their circumstances in quite some detail. Upon sitting down with him, however, they had come to realise that he meant no harm. Tumaini didn't provoke. He was not a threat. He offered nothing materialistic, only words of wisdom, and he didn't force these upon anyone.

Tumaini was genuinely kind, and his efforts to find out more about everyone was only so that he could better understand each one of them and more efficiently sway them toward doing good. He spoke in accordance to the religious doctrines of his country, which promoted peace. And he was discreet to avoid the mention of his god as a measure against the risk of his words falling to deaf ears. At only sixteen years of age, it was rather remarkable of him.

All that, and he had made little effort to strengthen his bid to marry the princess. Perhaps he didn't care, because he was already a member of royalty in his country. What he might not yet understand, however, was that his title didn't command a whole lot of respect from the rest of the land. Seniblum's extensive desert landscape made them the least resourceful country and by far the least populated. And in a land where military power equated to dominance, Seniblum lacked even a proper army. In fact, the country was subject to grave insults during the war, likening their people and their land to tinsels and toil, and it was said that even the power-hungry Kragans saw no incentives to invading them.

The Senils had never sided with any country—not during the war, and not a hint after it. They were ever passionate in relaying messages of peace across the land, however, and for that, they had never attracted animosity from the previous Truban domain or their potent neighbours, Kraga, which was situated to their immediate west.

Tumaini's maid, Layla, sent out the same sort of reclusive ambience that indicated that she didn't crave the worldly gains that everyone else sought. They called themselves adventurers but their actions were more pilgrim-like, journeying into unknown lands and spreading good faith. Layla was an impressive fighter who wielded a pair of knives similar to Marvin, who preferred a set of daggers. And though her petite figure and delicate hands might fool some people, she was deceptively quick, earlier showcasing her cat-like movements when her arms had rippled out in a flash to catch a teacup from falling to the ground. It was difficult to judge just how strong she might be in real combat, but her quality of finesse was rare. Indeed, Alpheus thought that she would be an invaluable member of the Sail Band if Tumaini would spare her to Marvin.

It was out of the question, though. Tumaini and his maid were more than master and servant, and they had no intention to hide it. When Leo asked a question intended as a harmless joke, the young Prince openly admitted the relationship, as well as his plan to marry Layla in the future, in turn causing the maid to blush.

"But... you're here for the Purification Ceremony...," Ash said. "Wouldn't your father be vexing if he knew?"

The Senil Prince looked heavenward, nibbling on his bottom lip. "He was vexing, yes. And that's why we eloped. He doesn't know I'm here in

Vinawell. He'd be hopping mad if he knew I was here, but with no intention to compete."

The people turned silent, taken aback by both his truthfulness and his wilful ways. The awe ended with Marvin's chuckle.

"How dare he tell you what to do?" Marvin said with a pat on the prince's back. "How dare he, when he too had his own way of doing things?"

The young Prince blinked. "I wanted to ask last time. Are you personally acquainted to my Lord Father?"

"He's an old friend from before you were even born."

Marvin explained that his first meeting with Tumaini's father had been many years ago, a time before the war and even before the man was hailed as King of Seniblum. Describing Adio Azan as a wanderer who journeyed across the land, Marvin likened him to the young prince who was essentially doing the same thing many years later. In his travels, Adio Azan had helped and guided those in need, offering inspiration especially to the people terrorised by war. Alpheus saw that there weren't a whole lot of people Marvin was fond of, but Adio Azan was one of them—and that certainly meant something. But Marvin wouldn't go into detail about what the man had done for him, only claiming that he wouldn't be who he was today if not for that man.

As the conversation veered into details about Tumaini's journeys, Alpheus began to lose interest. His mind drifted back to the Purification Ceremony. It was in three days' time, and the event itself was scheduled to run for a day. He wondered what the other participants were doing to prepare, and he wondered if they were as anxious as he about what they would be tested on. According to Ash, almost all of the participants had attempted to bait clues out of court members, but only to see their efforts go to waste. Apparently, only a handful held the information, including Gaston, his advisers, and the monarch himself.

Earlier in the day, Ash had also advised that the news of his private meeting with the princess had spread about Radiance's Nest. Ash's investigations told him that more than a few people had earlier suspected Alpheus's seemingly carefree attitude to be a façade given his reputation as an alleged murderer and sorcerer. And now, they also thought him a hypocrite.

Alpheus didn't mind, though. Or at least he didn't let it bother him, for he had his own worries—not about his competition, but about the growing ambivalence within himself about what he wanted. He had realised his attraction for the princess, but he couldn't be sure whether that attraction had anything to do with her royal status. It was perhaps naïve, but having personally met the princess twice, it wasn't in his conscience to see the Purification Ceremony as a mere competition.

Alpheus hoped someone *good* would succeed. He didn't know if he belonged in the category of good, and his doubts on the whole idea of a marriage based on the obvious gains stemming from it had him in turmoil. He was no saint, and if there was a saint among the competition, he was prepared to help him succeed. But a saint? Did such beings actually exist? The only real thing he could do while remaining ambivalent was to prevent several other unworthy people from succeeding. Trajetzky was the first name on his mind. His old acquaintance and rival, Hartland, was another, albeit for his solemn personality rather than questionable morals. Next was the Aizar nobleman, Epari, who he had only grown wary of when Marvin labelled him as crafty and calculating. Those three were really the only men Alpheus had met out of almost thirty participants. And yet, he was ready to assume everyone else to be underserving.

TEN

A date with the princess

The word was that Princess Flora was an angel in disguise, a vernal lady of exceptional beauty. And while that was secondary to why most guests had journeyed to Poppaross, it was undoubtedly an incentive that had helped them make the decision to set out in the first place. To be chosen as the Prince Consort was a stupendous prize. But the majority of the invitees appreciated the potential of the grander prize which could be realised in the longer term.

Though young, the princess was in position to become the most powerful woman in the land within the next decade. With no male sibling to compete against, the princess was bound to inherit her father's reign and become the first queen regnant in recorded history. And the princess's transition into becoming the land's most powerful female leader was to begin from the day of her wedding.

Alpheus had struggled to think of it in that breadth, despite having initially shared that same ambition. He neither doubted the princess's ability to rule, nor her supposed destination to inherit the monarchy. He simply couldn't imagine the princess's petite figure perched on the throne, barking out orders to her vassals in her silvery voice. Alpheus suspected he was the only guest who had personally met the princess. And he appreciated that the time he had spent with her in relatively intimate settings was something that no other guest could dream of. His competition, however, seemed well aware of his meeting with the princess that had taken place in a private courtyard two days earlier. Indeed, Alpheus had attracted plenty of animosity from the other participants and court members alike.

And yet, he arrived now at the double door which led to the same private courtyard where he was ready to meet the princess for the third time, having received an invitation earlier that morning. And that was despite the fact that the Purification Ceremony was scheduled for the following day.

The men standing guard seemed to expect his visit, and they allowed him to pass through, albeit with a scowl. But Alpheus actually found the silver lining in the abuse—the people at the castle were loyal to the ones they served. He returned an innocent smile as he stepped through.

The long set of stairs was uneventful, especially as he journeyed alone. But the thought of the peaceful courtyard urged him on. When he finally arrived, Alpheus smiled as he noted the pergola was the same as it had been before, vines hanging from the top, creeping about so indifferently. Sitting at the table was a lady in a dress of purple, sniffing behind a semi-transparent veil that hung beneath her eyes, the veil draping down to almost her chest. Alpheus could barely confirm on first glance whether she was the princess or Claire. Their blue eyes were so similar, as was the way they wore their hair, with long, braided plaits cascading over their shoulders.

She looked up now, pale-faced, the blue of her eyes sparkling behind fresh tears. Her lashes were even more defined, now that her eyes were the focus.

"You're late," she said with a croaky voice, her tone confirming that she was the princess.

"I'm sorry," Alpheus said, wondering if the princess had been crying. "Are you all right? You look a little—"

"Ill? Yes, just a little."

"Then perhaps you should get some rest."

"I don't need rest," she said, rising to her feet. "But I do see the need to take a stroll away from here."

"Away from where?"

"The castle, of course. Now, will you accompany me to the city?"

Alpheus hesitated. "Actually, I'm not sure I should. If you want to go anywhere, you should probably go with Claire and Carmen. They—"

"They've abandoned me," the princess interrupted. "Claire and Carmen, that is. They're sick of all the talk of the ceremony, and now they're hiding from me." She now looked at Alpheus with a faint grin still discernible behind the thin veil. "That makes just the two of us."

Alpheus flushed, swallowing. A heat surged within him, forming drops of sweat that filled the scalp, almost stumbling as he stepped backwards.

The princess laughed in between another cough that briefly whiffed up her half-veil, revealing her colourless lips. "I'm only teasing you," she said. "But it's true that they have other errands today, so I'd really appreciate your company."

She didn't wait for Alpheus to agree, already entangling her arm onto his as she led the way back to the stairs, descending a few hundred steps and onto the double door, past the guards who gawked wordlessly at them. Although it was only a short trip from there to the front gate of the castle, it felt painfully long for Alpheus as he found himself at the receiving end of obnoxious looks from nearly every person that they passed by. It almost seemed as if the princess wanted the attention, though, as she kept up her extravagant coughs along the way.

Finally, upon reaching the front gate, the group of soldiers standing guard stepped in their path. "I apologise, Your Highness," one of the guards said. "We have been advised that no one, including Your Highness, is to be allowed to leave Radiance's Nest without His Majesty's word."

The princess scowled before coughing out another puff behind a loose fist and half-veil. She said nothing, but as her cough seemed to aggravate, she pulled out a rectangular token the size of her palm from her sleeves—and in the process, also revealed the famous pearl bracelet that resonated with the moons. The shimmering golden token, the Dominion's heraldic crest carved onto it, apparently equalled the king's own words. And upon its presentation, the guards were prompt in allowing passage.

Alpheus smiled wryly. "I'll ensure her safety," he said, his courtesy met with silence and untrusting glares. When Alpheus opened his mouth with the intention to strengthen his case, the princess clung onto his arm again and dragged him away and down the hill toward the city. Alpheus didn't bother looking back at the guards who were surely left frustrated and helpless.

* * *

The city was indeed more animated than Radiance's Nest—which despite its majestic qualities—demanded its occupants and visitors to adhere to strict social codes. The princess seemed to be itching to break free from those stern expectations today, now stretching her arms out wide into the air and taking in a deep breath amid the gentle breeze. Alpheus wasn't sure when, but the princess had stopped coughing altogether. Indeed, it seemed that ever since stepping out of the castle and into the city, her wan display had significantly subsided, and she had fully become the vibrant lady that Alpheus knew her to be.

It became clear now that she wasn't ill as she hopped about the stone path across stalls, sliding between civilians who didn't seem to know who she was.

But she really didn't seem happy, Alpheus thought, remembering the desolate expression on her face barely half an hour earlier. Perhaps she didn't want to get married. Or perhaps she didn't want her marriage to be dependent on what was essentially a competition between mostly ambitious men.

Alpheus watched her now as she poked her head into a confectionery shop just like an innocent child, among actual children. *Or perhaps that's who she is*, he thought with a smile. He sighed and moved closer behind her.

"Confectionery's *not* the best idea," he said, gesturing to their right, where a pair of soldiers stood watching them. "Not when you want others to think you're unwell."

The princess shrugged, returning her attention to the colourful selection of sweets on display. "Don't mind them," she said, looking over the children. "They won't stay for long. Why don't you pick some candy instead?"

"None for me, thank you."

"Oh, why not? I bet it's better than anything you can find in Zorlia."

"I wouldn't know," Alpheus said with a shrug. "I've never had candy before."

The princess laughed. "What kind of person hasn't had candy before?"

"The kind who knows that it's bad for you."

"You're such a good boy," she said, rolling her eyes. "It must have been easy to mother you."

Alpheus flushed with a slight frown. "What's that supposed to mean?"

"It means you are an obedient boy."

"No, my mother didn't...," Alpheus said, stammering. "It wasn't my mother. My sister raised me, and she was the one who..." He trailed off as he realised that it might be slightly embarrassing to speak about his relationship with his sister. But the princess was apparently already imagining him as a young boy being scolded by his sister, as could be seen from her deeper grin. Soon enough, she was laughing out loud with a hand over her stomach.

"I'm sorry," she said, trying to restrain herself.

Alpheus sighed again, hanging his head. The princess was a curious character. The more time he spent with her, the harder it was to imagine that she would one day be the monarch ruling over this country. But while her behaviour didn't reflect her royal line, she upheld the presentation of a cultured woman—albeit with a blend of vivacity and wit. Alpheus realised he was smiling simply from observing her as he tagged behind. But as he mused now, he was sorry that it was her last chance to be a child, to be carefree. Days later, she would have to marry a talented stranger and begin her transition toward ruling one of the greatest kingdoms in the land.

Their next stop was a florist. Attracting the princess to the stall were the many crafty flower arrangements on display under the colourful flaps of woven linen that created just the right amount of shade for the plants. In addition to some of the more popular varieties, like roses and orchids, were a collection of rare flower species, one of which was the moonflower. Although the nocturnal flower wasn't blooming at this hour, Alpheus was pleased to see the flower again. The princess, meanwhile, was talking to the florist-merchant, a kindly middle-aged woman, who seemed to enjoy her company.

Alpheus listened in on the conversation and noted that the princess's poignancy had all but withered. At least for a moment, anyway. When the florist-merchant turned to another customer, the princess's eyes grew suddenly hollow even in the face of the charming flowers.

Alpheus said nothing, only regarded her from the other end of the stall, wondering what had happened all of a sudden. Did the Purification Ceremony bother her so much? He paced over to her.

"Are you all right?" he asked.

The princess blinked away her daze. "Oh, I'm fine," she said, shaking her head. "It's just that I wanted to see it one last time."

"See what?"

But Alpheus didn't hear the answer, as a man crashed suddenly into the stall, shouting curses and sweeping his arms across the arrangements, destroying a heap in one go. The man, thin with bushy brows, kept at it like a maniac, screaming insults at the florist who was helpless to stop the rampage. It was far from Alpheus's forte, but he only knew to stop that man, grasping onto his wrist from behind.

"Stop at once!" he demanded. "Or else—"

The man met his eyes with a grunt. He then snatched an empty vase and swung it at Alpheus, aiming for his head. Alpheus widened his eyes, throwing up his other hand for cover, the impact shattering the crystal container into pieces and leaving his hand trickling with blood. The princess gasped, taking Alpheus's bloodied hand with no regard for the vivid red liquid now dribbling over her own hands. A pair of soldiers rushed over promptly, demanding an explanation from the man with the bushy brows.

"Hey, the hag's the one at fault," the man said, gesturing over to the florist-merchant. "If it wasn't for her and—"

"Excuse me?" the florist cut in with knitted eyebrows.

"Someone sent flowers to my woman from here," the man said, throwing an arm up in the air. "I've warned her that if we got even a stem more, I would—"

"That means nothing to me," the princess snapped, still holding onto Alpheus's hand. "I will not tolerate anyone to hurt my friends for any reason."

The man dared to snub her this time, eyeing her with a smirk. "And who do you suppose you are?" he said, clearly clueless. "You think yourself some sage because of a fancy dress?"

The princess scowled and the soldiers shivered. For a moment, Alpheus suspected that she was going to flaunt the golden token. Instead, she stripped away that half-veil and slipped a finger and thumb into her mouth to blow a gentle whistling tune, the same way she had done in the woodlands. The soldiers twitched as they recognised who she was. Alpheus looked up to the sky then, watching for the birds that he thought might soon flit their way here.

But that many birds in the city? Alpheus thought.

Nothing came after a second or two. But when the conceited man dared another smirk, an incessant fluttering of wings resonated in the air, followed by an infinite clicking that blended into a chorus of insect calls. A cluster of flying bugs buzzed in, zipping through the thick cloths of the stall shades, swooping toward the man with the bushy brows.

Cicadas, Alpheus recognised, noting the insects' prominent eyes and short antennae. Their concerted calls amplified tenfold now, and had the man scrambling and flapping his arms about wildly as he was chased away. In between his screams of distress, however, he managed to yell out a threat that this wasn't over.

Alpheus shared a brief laugh with the princess, despite his throbbing hand. The florist-merchant gawked—no doubt stupefied by the *magic* of the cicadas—as did everyone else in the vicinity, including the soldiers. The princess was intent to draw the attention away from her abilities as she now asked the florist for yarrow, a white, feathery flower, as she tore off a strip from her silk skirt. The pair of soldiers watched them for a moment longer, frowned and then paced away. And by the time they disappeared from view, Alpheus found that his hand had been neatly swathed up with what the princess claimed was herbal medicine that encouraged clotting while disinfecting the wound.

"The bleeding has stopped," the princess said, caressing his hand. "Is the bandage all right?"

"It's all right," he managed to utter, somewhat overwhelmed by the princess's kindness.

The princess flapped out a handkerchief now, wiping her face free of her ashen look, which was a result of some purposeful cosmetics. The glow in her skin returned, as did the colour in her lips. She then proceeded to the florist again, handing over some coins to her, presumably for the damage that would have otherwise been irrecoverable. The florist barely managed to mumble her words of gratitude, clearly still dumbfounded by the experience.

"Let's go," she then said to Alpheus, already on her way, heading along the stone path again.

Alpheus followed promptly, still unable to fully comprehend how he had managed to earn the princess's friendship. Despite her occasional mischief, the princess was a wonderful companion because her earnest tendencies always seemed to prevail. This city and its people seemed that much warmer with her by his side. Alpheus couldn't be sure whether or not he was fond of her for who she was, though. After all, the conflict of interest in winning the right to wed her was an incentive he couldn't simply ignore.

"Well, well," a voice said. "Look who it is."

Alpheus looked up to a pair of feet planted firmly on the ground. It took Alpheus a moment to place him, but the man who stood before him and the princess was someone he owed indeed—Joe Hendron, the hunter he had made his scapegoat back in Dorellsdale. The man was swaddled in bandages, in addition to the bruises on his face.

The princess eyed Alpheus. "A friend?"

Alpheus spared the princess no glance, instead he bowed slightly to Hendron. "I apologise, Joe," he said. "I didn't imagine they would treat you like this."

Joe shook his head with a scowl. "Then what *did* you imagine?"

"If it is compensation you want," Alpheus said in regret, "then I am sorry to say that I have no money. What I *can* do is get you a physician. Now, if you want to punch me instead, then be warned that I have a hard face that might hurt your knuckles, so—"

Alpheus stopped speaking abruptly now as Hendron raised an arm into the air. Alpheus shut his eyes tight, wincing—but not running from a smack he thought he deserved. But the hunter instead landed a palm on his shoulder.

"I'm not one to hold grudges," Hendron said.

Alpheus opened an eye, still cringing and growing more suspicious when the man turned to the princess, gesturing for her hand, which he kissed upon introducing himself. Alpheus recognised that it was next to impossible for Hendron to know she was the princess. The traditional way to greet someone was all well and good, but perhaps not when Alpheus had not yet had the privilege.

The princess offered her name as Azure once again and seemed intrigued about the history Alpheus shared with Hendron. Alpheus knew by now that the princess had a deep curiosity for learning about strange people and things. The hunter certainly qualified as a strange character, and he was also always prepared to boast about his experiences in taming beasts. It was too late for Alpheus to object when Hendron proposed to share his stories over a light meal.

The three of them settled at a teahouse called *Leaf*, an establishment with a refined presentation with dear prices to match. Hendron must have suspected from the princess's delicate dress that she had the gold to pay for any beverage they would want. As they sat down, the hunter began to explain his account of what happened back at the final checkpoint in Trubannis. That day, as he recalled, had been filled with chaos and confusion. Amid the accusations directed at him and the confiscation of his hunted assets, Hendron had also taken a beating from the soldiers who had demanded that he confess that he was Alpheus. Hendron had ended up confined in the basement of the garrison and questioned for days.

"It was then when he came," Hendron said. "A golden knight called Griflet. He cleared my name of all accusations."

"Griflet," Alpheus said, noting that the knight by the name was the Defender of Farella.

"He looked like a good person," Hendron said with a wry smile. "He asked if I knew where the real Alpheus Hindlow was hiding. I told him I knew no one by that name—only someone by the name of Albert Moon."

As that name rang in his head, Alpheus looked away in shame. He didn't understand why Hendron had covered for him. And while he was sorry for causing trouble for the hunter, Alpheus couldn't manage a word of gratitude.

"That was the name I used in disguise," Alpheus said, clearing the confusion for the princess.

"Now, don't get the wrong idea," Hendron said, maintaining his smile. "But between you and the Empire, I'd choose to side with you. I don't trust the authorities, and I don't believe you committed those crimes."

"But what makes you believe me?"

"Just a hunch," Hendron said. "It's what I have relied on all my life, including where I hunt and when I hunt."

"That's it?"

"Well, I also remember the time when we first met. I had sustained a few scratches, and it was you who patched me up. You also offered me the spectacles and boots."

Those were part of the act, Alpheus thought, glancing away again.

"I *was* mad at first," Hendron said. "But the spectacles and boots work like a charm. They revolutionise my profession. Even with the injuries, I managed to catch a fair share of beasts in the last two weeks. If not for anything else, I shall forgive you because of that."

Alpheus sighed again, the puff of breath carrying a weight of guilt. "I really am sorry," he said finally.

* * *

It was evening by the time they decided to depart the teahouse. Thinking that he owed the hunter an explanation, Alpheus had spoken about his objective which was to find a new lease of life away from Trubannis, but was careful not to include any information about the fact that he was in Poppaross to compete to become the Prince Consort or the revelation that the princess had been sitting there with them. It was all well when they stepped out of the establishment under an evening sky graced by the red hue of Selene, but their delight ended briefly when a group of men holding wooden clubs trampled down the street toward them.

For a moment, Alpheus thought they were soldiers. But on a more careful look, the men—five of them—though brawny, appeared more like butchers than trained warriors. The man at the centre was thin, unlike his companions. He wore a cone hat that dangled a shaded net over his face, like a beekeeper. He slowly lifted the net now, revealing a rash at his chin.

"As promised, I am back," the man said, before brushing aside the rest of the net to reveal more rashes across his face.

The princess was first to slip out a giggle, at which time Alpheus finally recognised the bushy brows in the otherwise plump face. He was the man chased away by the cicadas.

"You're going to be sorry," the man said with a growl as one of his allies slapped the club on his hand while another man cracked his knuckles.

Alpheus shook his head and stepped forward. "You just don't learn, do you?" he said.

The man grunted and then led a charge at Alpheus, who was ready this time. Alpheus waved away the princess and Hendron before he himself dashed forward, circling his foes with a mesmerising step shadowed by a glowing white dust that sprinkled behind him. He breezed by them, nullifying their formation and leaving them in a daze with fading afterimages that befuddled and confused them.

"Witchery!" one of them cried as a few bystanders gasped.

It wasn't witchery. It wasn't sorcery, either, but a motion skill that could be learned by anyone adept at recognising complex patterns. The crowd that was drawn in marvelled at the spectacle now, not wondering if it were sorcery, but simply in wonder of its elegance. They cheered with no suspicion as if it were a street show. As he glided here and there, Alpheus realised that he was moving with even more unpredictability than before—that after adding the Zip Waltz to his repertoire, he was as nimble as anyone. He timed his evasions with care now, embarrassing his foes, who crashed into one other.

The roaring applause was contagious, spurring even Hendron to join in the chorus. Alpheus was the star of the show, and yet he had eyes only on the princess, whose radiant laugh had him dashing about with even more gloss. Alpheus finally offered mercy when his foes held their spinning heads, at which time he glided toward the princess.

"Fly with me," he whispered, taking her hand.

Her face flushed pink as her lips opened gently and subtly.

"I'll take you on a moonlit stroll."

Alpheus held tighter to her hand, slipping his other arm behind her waist. Before she knew it, they had been propelled high up into the air, reaching the roofs with just a soft leap. The princess let out an initial gasp, but as they glided from building to building, she widened her eyes in awe at the new perspective and the wide-mouthed civilians who gawked at them from below. The crowd should have realised by now that this was not a mere street show. But Alpheus didn't mind what they thought when he had the princess in his arms.

The calm breeze that swept over the two of them almost blended into the gentle whiff of cool air they left behind. The red of Selene wasn't gleaming at its brightest tonight, but among the starry night and the abundance of lanterns on the streets below them, its tinge was enough to create a charming fusion of luminosity.

Alpheus turned to the princess now, watching her sparkling blue eyes, which more than replaced the heavenly hue of the absent blue moon. Her soft amber hair flickering and trailing behind her was a serene wave that seemed to have no end. Completing the enchanting allurement were her lips outlined and embellished by Selene's ruby luminance.

It was moments later when they settled on the roof of one of the taller buildings in the city. They lied down side by side on the partly slanted roof.

Reclined on the bevelled tiles, they looked up into the calmness of the night.

The dark of the clear sky was a never-ending canvas onto which the stars were brushed. From this angle, its far arching reach from horizon to horizon seemed infinitely wide. Those stars that were impossible to reach helped put things in perspective every once in a while, Alpheus realised. Reaching out for them perhaps wasn't as silly as logic might suggest, and the princess was now doing exactly that—extending an arm out. She clawed onto nothing but thin air, and also the chilly breeze at that elevation. A smile emerged, however, and an expression of contentment, fading away only as a cool breeze swept past her.

Alpheus was quick to remove his mantle, blanketing the princess, who smiled at him upon accepting it.

"Do you ever wonder what is out there?" she said softly, her eyes still heavenward.

Alpheus regarded a smaller cluster of stars. "Yes, many times. Scholars strive to explain everything. And as an artist, it fills me with wonder every time I imagine a world beyond ours."

"A world beyond ours. A world where there are no farewells." She sighed. "But even this world… I've always wanted to see it. I want to see it all. Will you accompany me?"

"Where exactly do you want to go?" Alpheus asked.

"Everywhere. But we could start with Zorlia. Will you take me there?"

Alpheus sat up on hearing the name of his hometown. He glanced back down at the princess who looked contented, still regarding the starry evening sky with her own glittering eyes. She clearly hadn't considered the implications of what seemed an innocent question that she had asked so casually. Or perhaps she was convinced that all of his problems related to Zorlia would be resolved in due time.

"If you want," Alpheus said, lying down again, looking heavenward once more, "I'll take you anywhere."

"Is that a promise?"

"Promise? But… it's not like you're any regular civilian who—"

"Promise me."

Alpheus sighed. "I promise," he said.

His eyelids soon grew heavy. He gave a final glance at his bandaged hand before his field of vision turned a murky grey. It had been an eventful day, the happiest he could remember since departing Zorlia. His ambivalence on how to approach the Purification Ceremony had since been replaced with a surge of motivation. He would give his all to be the Prince Consort—not just for the title, but for the princess. It wasn't going to be easy to triumph over the competition, but he slept on it next to the princess then, welcoming the challenge.

* * *

Alpheus woke to the rising sun of the next morning, the day of the Purification Ceremony. He rubbed his eyes with a quiet yawn, stretching his arms out under a clear sky tinged with the tangerines of dawn. He was still on that same roof, but the princess was nowhere to be seen. He remembered offering his mantle to her, but he was swaddled in it now.

Did she go back?

Alpheus rose to his feet, eyeing Radiance's Nest in the distance with a beam. The castle looked majestic from every angle. While he couldn't remember his dream from the night prior, he had grown confident with his chances of being eventually crowned as the Prince Consort. It wasn't about any advantage he might have, but about a strong belief that it was his destiny. It had all started when Reeling had first presented him with the opportunity, which had then carved out the path to Vinawell. Alpheus had since met Ebenezer, a court member who could clear his murder accusations. And finally, in meeting the mercurial princess, his zest for a meaningful life had somewhat been invigorated.

It was a little later in the morning when Alpheus headed back toward Radiance's Nest. But upon his return, he saw the castle clouded by a rare state of panic. As he stepped into the central atrium, he saw men running about with urgency, some of them stumbling as they seemed muddled about where they were even headed. The guests, meanwhile, glanced about at each other with frowns, sharing in the confusion.

"This is unbelievable," one of the guests complained.

Alpheus stepped up to the man who had spoken, a young nobleman of Vinan descent. "What is?" he asked. "What's going on?"

The young man eyed him with a dazed look. "The princess is missing," he said.

ELEVEN

The Purification Ceremony... called off

It was noon when every guest was herded into the central atrium. Almost everyone had already heard that the princess was missing, though no one could be sure whether it had all been staged, perhaps as a test on the contestants' ability to remain calm. After all, it was the scheduled day of the Purification Ceremony. The competition to wed the crown princess could well have already begun.

In any case, a host of court members were now at the base of the great donjon that towered over everyone present. More than a few of those Dominion representatives who had been present in this same venue a week ago were now absent, however. The noblemen and knights who *were* present shared troubled looks and quiet conversations amongst themselves. Alpheus raised a brow, peering about and noting Copper standing among a small group of noblemen. The man wore a dismal expression on his face. To his left was a group of servants setting up the elevated platform where the king had addressed his guests on their first day. Alpheus then peered back out toward the guests, prying through those faces for Marvin, Ash, and the rest of the crew. He saw none of them, instead noting Trajetzky and his smug grin, and then Hartland, who didn't seem to have noticed him yet.

Most of the crowd had turned silent as they watched the aged Chief General, Bradley Redford Gaston, ascend the elevated platform with the help of a rugged walking stick. The old man was wheezing when he reached the top, staring down at the crowd under the grey brows that hung over his narrowed eyes.

"Honoured guests," he began with a gruff voice that resounded out across the open space. "We have anticipated this day for years. It is unfortunate, however, that a detrimental turn of events has forced the Dominion to make a tough decision." He paused, peering out at the guests with a scowl. "The Purification Ceremony is cancelled," he announced, drawing gasps and gapes from the crowd.

Some of the people threw their arms in the air, crying scathing remarks after what sounded like a tasteless joke. Even the calmer guests frowned grimly.

"I ask you to accept our deepest apologies," Gaston said, maintaining a firm pitch and speaking over the commotion. "We are already exercising all our search efforts for the crown princess, but until we locate her, the appointment of a Prince Consort is to be postponed indefinitely. You are welcome to stay in Radiance's Nest, in which case we will endeavour to continue offering the hospitality befitting to the honoured guests that you are. But if you choose to leave, the Dominion will reimburse any travel costs. And, finally, please know that we respect your time and efforts in making the trip here. While I cannot promise anything, I anticipate the future day when everyone can be invited again."

The announcement ended there, as Gaston climbed down the platform before departing with an escort team. The guests—flustered as they were—soon dissipated, likely retiring back to their rooms.

Alpheus floundered through the sea of men, still searching for the Sail Band. He hadn't seen any of them since the morning prior. If anyone might know what was going on, it would be them.

"Lord Hindlow," a voice echoed behind him from the clusters of men still speaking to one another in hushed tones.

Alpheus turned to see a group of soldiers. He nodded in their direction, assuming that it was one of them who had spoken to him.

"Lord Gaston has requested you to the court," one of them said. "Please come with us."

* * *

The court of Radiance's Nest was smaller and less intimidating than the elevated court of Vondra Dawn. The creamy tinge of the beams and the walls didn't cry foul like they did in Zorlia. The heated debate that was going on, though, was as fierce as it could get. The king was perched upon his throne at the far end of the court. He didn't look at all like the kind man he had appeared to be a week ago. Standing to his right was Gaston, who had returned to the court after addressing the guests, and was now wearing a thwarted expression. Zabai, the imposing female knight, was also in attendance—as was Ebenezer, and a host of noblemen and other lords.

All the curses and blame thrown about now was probably not meant for foreigners. But it seemed that no one had the capacity to care. Alpheus wasn't sure how many men might have noticed that he had stepped in to join the crowd behind the rows and that was despite being escorted there by soldiers as well as being the only foreigner there among more than fifty or sixty men. He was quick to catch sight of Copper, however, who had also returned from the central atrium and was now standing only a short distance from the throne. The nobleman's dismal look from earlier had transformed into visible anxiety.

Most of the court turned silent when Gaston cast his arms in the air, his walking stick grasped tightly in one hand. "Let us summon the first informant," he said in a strong pitch, eyeing the colossal doors down the aisle opposite the throne.

Alpheus shivered, turning to the doors that slammed open forward. The informant was Carmen, who had a pair of soldiers hauling her forward by her arms. The maid was blanched—indeed, she was ghastly, with her head dropped forward and hair dangling over her face. It was evident that she had endured a recent beating that had resulted in her arms and legs hanging loose. She didn't utter a word, only whimpered helplessly as she was forced to her knees.

Alpheus dashed out toward the maid despite himself, his concern for her overshadowing the intimidation of the foreign crowd. "Just what is going on?" he snapped.

Although the question wasn't intended for anyone in particular, parts of the crowd began grumbling audibly about him. He ignored them and instead brushed Carmen's hair aside to reveal a bruise on her chin. He held his breath as he empathised with her pain, and then stroked away the rest of her hair to reveal yet more bruises. Carmen opened her eyes then, peering up at him with a surprised gasp.

"Why?" Alpheus asked, wheezing. "What happened?"

She offered no answer, instead shutting her eyes again and hanging her head.

"Alpheus Hindlow," Gaston said, his voice demanding. "Perhaps you could begin as our second informant."

Alpheus spun to face the king and his Chief General, among the host of other men scowling at him. It became obvious to him now that they had been well aware of his presence all along. He had been summoned to court, after all. For a moment, the memory of being accused of murder at Vondra Dawn came rushing back to him, surrounded by a host of faceless men, all of them gazing down on him with wicked grins spread across their cheeks.

Alpheus blinked away the memory and swallowed. *This isn't Vondra*

Dawn, he reminded himself with a heavy heart.

"This is all a big misunderstanding," Alpheus said, peering back at those who glared at him. "And it's all because no one ever cared to understand the princess."

The king narrowed his eyes. It was a frightening sight, but Alpheus dared to elaborate.

"If you did understand her," Alpheus continued, despite being spurned by parts of the crowd, "you would know why she's not here. You wouldn't need to worry that she's missing. She's carrying the weight of a country behind her back, but at the same time she's just like anyone else in that she wants a say in her own future. This Purification Ceremony essentially robs her of that right. I saw it in her eyes. She doesn't want to marry just anyone. She simply wants..."

Alpheus trailed off as remarks from the crowd grew more and more foul. Gaston, however, waved away these protests to allow him to continue. Once the court was silenced again, Alpheus abided but with a bead of cold sweat sliding down his forehead.

"I understand that I was summoned here because I was with the princess yesterday," Alpheus said, clearing his throat. "I understand the animosity I have attracted by meeting her, and I apologise if I have offended anyone. As to her being reported missing—well, that's news to me. But, frankly, she's much more clever than you all give her credit for. In this court alone, just now I have heard accusations of abduction, terrorism by religious sects, and even the possibility that she has been taken hostage by rival countries.

"She only departed early this morning. I thought she had returned to the castle, but while it clearly looks like she's not here, I'm convinced she's all right."

No one harassed him this time, but the knitted brows around the court remained ever so inimical. Gaston exchanged a brief look with the king. The old general then frowned at Alpheus.

"Where's Azure?" he asked.

"Azure?" Alpheus repeated with a confused squint. "No, I was with...," he said, trailing off as a terrible thought sparked in his head. Could it be that *Azure* wasn't actually the princess?

"You fooled a few soldiers when you left with her," Gaston said. "Can I then assume that your part in diverting attention means that you know a thing or two about where our crown princess has gone?"

Alpheus shook his head in disbelief. "No...," he uttered, holding his head now. "What's going on? Who was I with?"

Gaston raised a brow and thumped his walking stick into the ground. "Alpheus Hindlow," the man said, his voice growing gruffer. "We only have so much patience. If you are to continue acting ignorant, don't expect—"

"I don't know!" Alpheus cried, his own brows knitted together now. "You're telling me that Azure's not the princess? Who's the princess, then? Claire? Is she the princess? Where is she? Why is she not here? I have questions of my own to ask."

A brief silence followed. The court members seemed as surprised by his reaction as Alpheus was confused by their belief that he was hiding something.

"There is no Claire," Ebenezer finally said in his croaky voice. "There is no Claire," he repeated, speaking specifically to Alpheus. "If you are referring to the crown princess, her name is Clarissa Flora Steele."

Alpheus shivered as he gaped at the mage who had now turned to the king. *No*, he thought. *I don't believe it.*

"It appears that Alpheus Hindlow has mistaken Azure for the princess," Ebenezer said to the king, confirming Alpheus's fears. "I doubt he knows anything. He was used without realising it."

Used.

That word echoed inside his head. It ached. Had everything that had happened yesterday all been an act? Did it mean he had been played right into an emotional delusion ever since their first encounter in the woodlands?

Alpheus couldn't make sense of any of this yet, but the king was fuming. Gaston treaded down toward Carmen, shoving Alpheus aside.

"Explain yourself!" he demanded, lifting the maid's head with his walking stick. "Where is the princess? What mischief did Azure conjure up this time? Tell me."

Even as he was staring down at the marble floor, wide-eyed, Alpheus noted the implication in Gaston's questions. The old man suspected that Azure—apparently *not* the princess—was behind the actual princess's disappearance.

Carmen peered away from Gaston's glare. "I have nothing to explain," she said softly.

Gaston scowled and then swung the walking stick, striking her directly on the face. Silence filled the chamber again as the maid lay still on the floor, her hair sprawled around her on the ground.

"The mistake can still be corrected," Gaston said in seemingly the calmest tone he could manage. "Speak, lass!"

Carmen then sat up slowly, brushing her hair back to show a dribble of blood streaming out from her lips. She looked up at Gaston, her eyes even drearier than before.

"I owe the Dominion everything," she said, clenching a fist into her dress. "I understand what I've done, and I'm ready to return it all. Take my life, please. It is the only thing I can give."

"Fool!" said an overpowering voice from up ahead near the throne.

It was Zabai, and her expression was as frosty as anyone else's. "Do you think, even for a second, that there's any value in your life?" the female knight berated, now stomping her way down to them. "The reputation and, potentially, the wellbeing, of the entire Dominion and our country are at stake! The very idea of inviting people from across the land to the Purification Ceremony was to strengthen our stand toward foreign powers. But with it ending like this, our efforts have completely gone to waste. I wouldn't hesitate to stick a sword through your chest, or kill you again and again if it meant that we would be free from this conundrum. The only regret is that your life—or death—is of no meaning!"

Carmen wailed suddenly, her eyes flooded in tears. "I'm sorry," she muttered, almost unintelligibly, trying her best to hold in her emotions. "I'm so sorry! But... I couldn't—"

She abruptly trailed off when Zabai unsheathed a sabre, drawing a few gasps from the crowd who had been blinded by the lightning-quick draw. Carmen gasped, too, eyeing the blade that was inches away from her face.

"No!" Alpheus cried, knocking Carmen back to shield her.

His naïve heroics did little more than invite a vicious glare from Zabai, who didn't withdraw her sword after all. She did, however, glance over to the king, whose lips were pursed with rage.

"Know your place, Alpheus Hindlow," the king said in a grumble. "You are a guest, but I have my limits. Do not challenge my—"

The king stopped when Copper suddenly fell to his knees with a thud. "Your Majesty!" the nobleman cried with his head down. "Spare them, please! I am the one at fault. I am the one who allowed it to happen."

Attention immediately flitted to Copper. Even Alpheus was hopeful that the nobleman could explain more.

"What nonsense are you speaking?" Gaston asked.

Copper shook his head with a self-pitying frown. "There is no kidnapping," he said. "The crown princess... she... she voluntarily elected to elope with a man. And I was the one who paved the way for it to happen."

Men gasped at the claim. The mystery was finally unfolding, but it wasn't in a way anyone had imagined—least of all, Alpheus.

Elope. It was unthinkable to associate the word with the crown princess, whose popular image was of chastity and virtue. No one dared to comment, not even when Carmen shut her eyes tightly as confirmation of the truth of Copper's words.

The king held his head and said nothing, clearing struggling to come to terms with the idea. Only now did Zabai finally pull her sword back.

"I knew her intentions, and yet I did nothing," Copper said. "As for Azure, I don't know where she is. I suspect she had a hand in it. But, knowing her, I'm inclined to believe that the princess is safe and well."

"*Well...?!*" Gaston said, flabbergasted. "You're telling me she ran off with some scoundrel, and she's *well*?"

"I don't know how to explain this, Lord Gaston. But the princess—"

"Enough!" the king boomed, thumping a fist onto the armrest of the throne. "Lord Copper," he said, leaning forward. "Do you realise what you have done—what your connivance means to the country? The crown princess was destined to rule the country. And you allowed her to... *elope*?"

Copper hung his head. "I understand what I've done," he said. "And I accept the blame. But I think—"

The king swept an arm out, his signal for Gaston to whack Copper with his walking stick. Silence filled the air again until Copper lifted his head back up, showing a visible bruise on his cheek and blood on his mouth. The king grunted, perhaps upon the sight of the nobleman's face alone.

"Gaston, step aside," the king said. He then glanced to the soldier standing closest to him. "You," he said and then nodded in Copper's direction.

The soldier stepped forward toward the nobleman. He was young and had likely never been at the centre of such attention. He seemed reluctant, wincing slightly before swinging a gauntleted fist into Copper, who neither flinched nor uttered a sound. The soldier cringed as the blankness of the nobleman's eyes asked for more. He threw a second punch, and then a third, and a fourth.

"Harder!" the king demanded.

The soldier complied as more than several men shook their heads. It appeared that no one enjoyed watching this even though it also seemed that nearly everyone agreed that this was the least Copper deserved. Copper wasn't going to die from this kind of physical torment, but Alpheus feared that the king might actually have the nobleman pay with his life.

And then there was the thought of Azure again.

Her betrayal.

Her lies.

Alpheus clenched a fist and felt himself growing more and more agitated—for reasons different to most others in the court. As Copper finally spewed out a cry of pain, Alpheus dashed forward to swipe away the soldier hurting him.

"That's enough," he said, eyeing the king. A second later, several knights had lunged forward to Alpheus, pointing their swords at him.

"Lord Hindlow," the frail Copper uttered from behind, gasping for breath. "Please don't interfere."

Gaston gazed down at Alpheus. "We still consider you a guest," he said when he was sure Alpheus posed no threat. "But if you interfere one more time, you are leaving me with no choice but to have you imprisoned. And since you are unable to aid us in any way, I ask you to withdraw at once." He nodded at a few soldiers closest to him. "Escort him away."

Alpheus raised an arm in defence. "I will leave," he said, turning his glare back at the king. "But I will also search for your princess. In the meantime, I ask that Carmen and Lord Copper are held safely, at least until—"

"Who do you think you are, to negotiate with His Majesty?" Zabai inserted.

The king raised a hand to halt her, keeping his gaze on Alpheus. "Your help is unnecessary."

Alpheus shook his head. "I am not helping you, or anyone else, for that matter. I simply need to see for myself my place in this whole fiasco. Your soldiers can join the search, but I'll be the one to find her. I promise you that."

* * *

Tavie looked up at the giant portcullis of Radiance's Nest and the dulling tangerine sky behind it. Dusk was upon them. She was sitting under the shade of a tree watching a handful of men—most of them invitees of the Purification Ceremony—all of them seemingly ready to depart the castle, bidding farewell to one another now. Marvin was sharing a conversation with the Senil prince and his maid, both of them also ready to leave.

The first half of the day had been hectic. Together with the crew, she had learned even before the first glimmers of dawn that the crown princess of the country had gone missing. And since then, they had been probing the city for traces of the princess. Though they had yet to find any leads as to where Princess Flora might be, Marvin didn't seem bothered, at least not at this moment in which he was talking to Tumaini whose company he always enjoyed. Tavie peered back to the portcullis again as she contemplated the case of the missing princess which was certainly the most inimitable situation she had experienced even with the many unpredictable adventures with the Sail Band.

Tavie had never really cared for the reputation of the Kingdom of Cetal or her own honoured title as the Princess of Cetal. She did know enough, however, that it was always a tough ask for any major governing authority to maintain a reputable name, and it was inevitable that the land would soon learn about what had happened in the capital of Vinawell—at least superficially. Together with the crew, she had learned on the evening prior that the crown princess of the country had gone missing. And while her first suspicion had been that Princess Flora shared the same conundrum that she once had of wishing to escape from a predestined path in life, Ash and Leo's findings showed that that wasn't exactly the case. Princess Flora had apparently wanted more than a general escape from the Dominion. She had apparently run away with her beloved in an organised plan to seek true happiness. In simpler terms, she had eloped. And this narrative, even if it weren't true, would inevitably be a stigma that she would find difficult to shake off no matter how her life might pan out.

It was unlikely that any foreign invitees of the Purification Ceremony knew as much as Tavie now knew. While she realised that this wasn't about her, she emphasised deeply with the situation as she imagined the severe repercussions that would hurt the country as soon as word was spread about Princess Flora's alleged elopement. Even though the circumstances were similar to that of her own, Tavie was well aware that the magnitude of the current state of affairs in Poppaross was far greater than her own exploits. It was especially detrimental to Vinawell that this was the *crown princess* at the centre of attention—the woman who was to one day rule the country. Of course, irresponsible conjectures and the subsequent evolution of those stories might paint a more shameful picture than the truth. And then there were also those men—perhaps only a handful of them—who were prepared to defame the Dominion in any way they could, for reasons only they would know. For them, they couldn't have asked for a better ending than this.

Tavie looked down at her regular short sleeve top and light-weighted skirt and ran a hand gently down the percale fabric and sturdy leather. It was so much more natural to be fitted into this outfit again compared to the scholar guise she had had to wear in the past few days. She was a thief again—no, a treasure hunter.

"Are you going back to Sill?" Marvin was asking Tumaini.

"Not yet," Tumaini said, maintaining the smile he always wore. "We're not sure where we are to journey next. But Sill might be a few years away."

Marvin returned the smile and then pulled a dagger out from his belt. "Here," he said, offering the weapon to the maid. "Take this. The *S* on the handle might scare off some less friendly people you meet. Hopefully, you wouldn't have to use it."

Tavie watched Layla accept the dagger with wonder, remembering that Marvin had once lauded the maid as an incredibly gifted warrior.

"Take care," Marvin then said, turning back to Tumaini, who waved his arms out in circles as his way to bid farewell.

It was a tedious goodbye for Tavie, and despite her patience, she was left to rue the situation, as Hartland and his retinue now marched out from the portcullis. Tavie immediately rose from the shade of the tree and slipped back toward the rest of the crew, hiding behind Leo, who spared not even a glance at her. He had kept his promise so far and had maintained a rather carefree demeanour around her, even when he was alone with her. It seemed as though he had never learned about her secret.

"He's coming here," Leo whispered now, though.

Tavie poked her head out from behind Leo, and indeed, Hartland was headed their way. Marvin, who was watching the Senil prince hike away, didn't notice Hartland's approach until he was directly behind him.

"May I have a word?" Hartland asked.

Marvin glanced about. "With me?" he said.

Tavie shut her eyes tightly, slipping back behind Leo. *Please, no,* she prayed.

"Can you advise as to where I could find Alpheus?" Hartland asked. "I have given up on catching him. In seeking him—I only look to bring him a message from home."

"We don't know where he is," Marvin said with a shrug. "I suppose he's still in town, though. He can't have gone far."

Hartland narrowed his eyes. "Very well, then. I shall locate him on my own."

* * *

Alpheus had only just realised that evening had come when he could no longer see his shadow cast on the spiral stone path of the city. After departing the castle early in the day, he had wandered in the city rather aimlessly, still troubled by thoughts of Azure's betrayal. He looked up now when he noted a pair of boots standing in his path.

"Chris?" he said, uttering the words without a thought.

Hartland sighed. "Let's talk."

Alpheus gave him a quiet stare, nodding after a moment. They retired to a teahouse, but not the same one Alpheus knew. It had only been a day since.

"I'm going back to Zorlia," Hartland said. "Will you come with me?"

Alpheus met his eyes and then glanced elsewhere. "No. Not until I find her."

"The princess? It's not your job." He paused, waiting for Alpheus to respond. "Lord Morlan believes in your innocence," Hartland continued after another sigh. "Sir Tristan is doing what he can to help clear your name. And when I return to Zorlia, I will join him. But don't get the wrong idea. I'm doing it for the Lord Count."

Alpheus met Hartland's eyes again at the mention of Reeling's name. "Thank you," he managed to say.

Hartland shook his head. "I never imagined seeing you here... and with the Sail Band. None of that matters anymore, though. Alpheus, believe me when I say that I wish to see you again in Zorlia."

"I believe you," Alpheus said. "And I think part of the reason is so that I can see Agnes again."

Hartland squinted and then looked away for a moment with visible discomfort. Alpheus had always known that Hartland was attracted to Agnes.

"Her eyes," Alpheus said. "Is there a way to heal them?"

"There is," Hartland said, sounding hopeful. "At least, I believe there is. Part of why I'm here in Vinawell is to find the man known to some as the *Passionless Surgeon*. It is said that he is of Kragan blood, and that he was once a soldier, but for some reason, he defected to this country." Hartland sighed once again. "Unfortunately, that is all the information I have. My investigations have led me nowhere."

"The Passionless Surgeon...," Alpheus said, musing. "I'll help you to find him. That gives me another reason to stay."

Hartland gave a brief smile. "I wasn't going to tell you. But your sister is in Zorlia."

Alpheus raised a brow. "She *is*?"

"She was scheduled to arrive a week after my departure. I'd assume she's there for you, at least in part. With her defending your case, you're as good as declared innocent."

True, Alpheus thought. *But I still need to be there myself.*

"You've grown more stubborn," Hartland said. "Till this day, I still don't know how to look at you. Your luck, your encounters, and all the people you have around you... I don't know what to make of it."

"Neither do I," Alpheus said, sighing again.

Hartland rose to his feet, standing tall and proud. "Alpheus, we represent The Villa. Bring honour to our academy. Go out there and be what you can be."

Alpheus looked up. "Chris, you've changed."

"So have you."

Hartland bowed slightly as his farewell bid. He then turned to depart. Alpheus thought that his old acquaintance appeared contented, and the smile upon his departure didn't seem fake.

* * *

The civilians hadn't been told anything, and they were left to wonder just what exactly was going on, with the number of soldiers surveying the city growing tremendously in the past few days. The soldiers were far less forgiving than usual, trampling about the streets and searching private buildings with minimal notice, and yet giving no clue as to what they were searching for. But while the civilians were left frustrated and confused, the soldiers had it worst, interposed between curses from civilians and an enormous pressure from the court.

And worse yet, the Dominion had so far found little to no trace of the princess. Alpheus, too—who had promised to be the one to find her—hadn't been any more successful in his lone act. He had chased a few leads, but nothing of promise had resulted. He was aware that more than a few soldiers were on his tracks, perhaps only to ensure that he didn't get in their way. While he could easily outrun them with the Glider Steps, there was no reason to do so. After all, the soldiers were simply doing their job and Alpheus had nothing to hide. At least not until Ash suddenly appeared in front of him on the city's main road.

"Looks like our bookworm needs some guidance," Ash said, treading over to him with a grin.

For a moment, Alpheus hesitated, unsure that he wanted any help from the Sail Band when he had vowed to both the Dominion court as well as to himself that he would be the one locating the princess. But he soon threw away his pride and waited for the words he wanted to hear.

"We found her," Ash said in a whisper, almost mouthing the words, apparently also aware that there were soldiers around. "Not the princess, but her impersonator. Azure."

A surge of delight brimmed inside Alpheus as he swallowed the information, which confirmed to him that he had always been much more invested in locating Azure than the princess.

"Where?" Alpheus asked, maintaining a soft voice.

"East," Ash said. "The woodlands."

"The cottage?"

"Not that far. Somewhere in between. Let's get out of the city first. This way."

Ash glanced left and right at the few soldiers around and then dashed off into an alley. Alpheus tagged behind closely and decided that it was indeed time to lose the soldiers who were actually prompt in chasing. He gestured Ash to turn at the corner of the next building, and there, Alpheus grabbed Ash's wrist and dashed off behind cool whiffs of air. After another turn, they leaped up to the roofs.

As soon as they left the city, they jumped onto horses that Ash had prepared in advance, and then they began racing away. It was evening again when they finally arrived in a small town whose geographic northern location would form a wide triangle on the map with Poppaross and the Violanola Cottage. Only a few people were out at this hour, though most of the houses were lighted from the inside. They were humble dwellings, constructed with wood, and not of the premium grade common to the cottage. Leo waved them over from one of the dwellings.

"Go ahead," Ash said as he hopped off his mount. "I'll park the horses."

Alpheus nodded, climbing off his horse with Leo giving him a hand. Upon reaching the entrance, he eyed the simple door handle and took a deep breath. Alpheus pressed down and thrusted forward into a room lighted by a single oil lamp. The rest of the crew were inside, either sitting or standing around what looked like a dining table—all of them turning their eyes to Alpheus. And there at the far end of the table was Azure, whose gawk revealed her surprise in seeing him.

"You sure took your time," Marvin said, leaning back on his chair.

Alpheus shot him a brief glance. "Had to avoid the soldiers," he said, turning his gaze to Azure, who now looked away. It was probably to avoid attention, but she didn't look like a princess today. She wore no jewellery, and instead of the extravagant satin dresses Alpheus was used to seeing her wear, she sported a pair of puffy pants under a ragged over-blouse.

"Why is he here?" Azure asked Marvin, somehow annoyed.

"Thought you two should have a talk," Marvin said. "Come on, team," he then said to Rover, Tavie, and Karl. "Let's go for a walk."

Tavie rolled her eyes and Karl seemed reluctant. But in the end, everyone abided and left the house, closing the door behind them, leaving Alpheus alone with Azure.

Alpheus swallowed, having not moved an inch since stepping in, maintaining his gaze on Azure, who wouldn't meet his eyes. Not a word was exchanged for at least a minute under the flickering flame.

"Do you have anything to say to me?" Alpheus said softly, finally speaking to break the silence.

"What do you want me to say?" she said at the same volume.

Alpheus sighed. "I want to know who exactly you are," he said, his pitch growing suddenly aggressive.

"What are you so worked up for?" she asked, still looking away. "I'm sure you already have your answer."

"I want to hear it from you."

"All right," she said, finally turning to him. "My name is Azure, and I'm *not* the princess."

Alpheus jerked slightly. Words floated around inside of him, but nothing seemed right to say out loud.

"Are you disappointed?" Azure then said with a sarcastic smile. "I'm only a maid—a servant. It changes the way you see me, does it not?"

"There is a difference, I admit. But it is not your identity that bothers me—it is your lies."

Azure sneered this time. "I *do* apologise to have misled you. But correct me if I'm wrong as I cannot recall even once claiming to be the princess."

Alpheus cringed, realising that what she said was true. "No matter," he insisted. "You used me from the start. You purposely misled me to believe that you were the princess. And I was foolish enough to believe it. Lord Copper described you as an altruist. I cannot say that you are not... but only to the people you see as acquaintances. Clearly, I am not even that to you."

Azure shook her head. "If it is closure you want—then yes, it was all a set-up. A game."

Alpheus clenched a fist. He had expected this, but the pain of hearing it said aloud was greater than he had anticipated. He shut his eyes tightly, attempting to appease the pain. But that alone wasn't going to soothe his disappointment or anger, so he turned for the door, pulling it open and stepping outside without another glance at her.

* * *

If Alpheus had looked back, he would have seen Azure holding a loose fist over her mouth, holding in tears the best she could. *I'm sorry*, she thought, reminiscing back to that day. *But between you and the princess, I had no choice. And now... I have a job to finish.*

The door was pushed open from the outside then. Azure raised a hand to cover her teary eyes.

"Well, you did a good job of driving him off," said Marvin.

Azure frowned and looked away. "You're such a meddler."

"You know," Marvin said as he sat down at the opposite end of the table, "I can still catch him."

Azure sighed. "Let's just focus on our deal."

TWELVE

Compromised security

Alpheus glanced about the empty court. It was strange to see that no one was around, especially when his last visit had been a rowdy, almost chaotic affair. And where was Ebenezer? It was the mage who had arranged to meet him there at the court. Ebenezer was already an hour late and this made Alpheus suspect whether or not the mage had purposely wished for him to feel anxious about what he had teased—that he might be planning an expedition to Zorlia.

It had come as a surprise to Alpheus that Ebenezer sought him out, sending a messenger his way early that morning when he was just outside the capital. Despite his prejudice against Ebenezer, Alpheus was hopeful that the mage's knowledge of energy flow could help solve Reeling's murder case. The idea had taken his mind away from Azure's betrayal, if slightly.

His re-admission into Radiance's Nest earlier had attracted no suspicion from the guards on watch at the front gate. Apparently, Ebenezer had spoken to the guards earlier. The castle, though, was noticeably undermanned with most of its soldiers sent out to join the search for their crown princess. Even so, it was inexcusable that a foreigner had found his way into the court on his own.

Being the only one around, Alpheus's eyes had been naturally wandering toward the throne, the majestic centrepiece of not only the court, but the castle and indeed the country. From where he was standing, the throne was within reach. Its golden frame and upholstered dark velvet was a luxury exclusive to the monarch. The top rail, carved with a meticulous phoenix that shot up nearly ten feet high, completed the opulent chair in its show of regal splendour.

A guilty pleasure swept over Alpheus then as he eyed it from the bottom of the five-step dais that had seemed insurmountable the last time he was there. Without thinking about it, his legs brought him forward. And as he paced up, his legs weighed down on him. Each step was a momentous thud, almost as if ascending toward the highest peaks known to man. Alpheus finally hesitated, though, as he reached the top. He swallowed as he battled with the desire to fall into the chair, running his fingertips over the armrest of the cool precious gold. He closed his eyes then, imagining an unlikely scene in which hundreds—or perhaps thousands—of men were bowing down to him.

His eyes finally snapped open as he shook away that foolish image. *What are you doing?* he thought to himself as he paced back down in urgency.

It was another half hour later when Alpheus decided that he had waited long enough. He left the court and glanced down the hallway, which was again empty. *Lord Copper*, he thought with remorse. *Where are they keeping you? And... Carmen.* He sighed, realising the injustice in the fact that those two were confined while Azure was roaming free.

Alpheus looked up then at the sound of footsteps. A pair of soldiers a good distance away were coming his way, though they didn't seem to have spotted him yet. Alpheus slipped in through a door next to the court entrance, feeling suddenly guilty about the fact that he had fantasised about the throne earlier. The daylight filtering in through the tiny gap in the door he had left open was the only source of light in the compact chamber, which was likely used for general storage given the range of domestic tools filling the decks of tall cabinets.

Hiding was probably excessive when he hadn't done anything wrong, though the thought of having to explain why he was even there made him think twice. Alpheus carefully poked his head out now, noting that the soldiers were acting suspiciously, as if they were sniffing about for anyone who might have trailed them. The soldiers prowled closer now, perhaps heading to the court.

No, Alpheus realised a little too late. *They're coming here!* Within a moment, he pulled the door closed and slipped in between the tall cabinets, brooms and rakes leaning against him.

Alpheus held his breath and looked up. Beneath the high ceiling was a hand-sized opening that let in a glimmer of daylight, though barely enough for anyone to pick out the equipment stored there. Alpheus froze then as a tap sounded at the door, followed by a creaking noise accompanied by a growing amount of light streaming in from outside.

"This will do," one of the soldiers said softly, his words reverberating clearly inside the confined space.

"But are we really going to do this?" the other one said in the same soft volume, as they both snuck inside.

"It's not like we have a choice."

"Yes, but raiding the dungeon...? I don't know. What if we fail?"

"What are you so afraid of? Just do as we're told, and we'll be fine."

"That's what I've been telling myself, but it's hard."

Alpheus pressed his ear closer into the cabinet, but as he did, the entire thing started to shake. Alpheus futilely reached out his arm, only to watch the cabinet crash forward with a clap that slapped up a large cloud of dust.

The soldiers cried out when they looked up to what must have seemed to be a wraithlike figure beneath the faint rays of daylight. They managed to calm down, though, when Alpheus started to cough and sweep his arms out to clear the dust.

"Who are you?!" one of them demanded in a shaky pitch, clearly unable to recognise Alpheus in the darkness.

Alpheus was still coughing, but he soon realised why the soldiers hadn't run away. The fallen cabinet was blocking the door—the only exit.

"Identify yourself!" the other soldier said, drawing his sword with a clang.

Thinking on his feet, Alpheus heard himself cackling. "Why?" he said, assuming a taut voice. "I'm Alpheus Hindlow. A sorcerer. You have some nerve disturbing my slumber."

The soldiers had probably grown pale, if their gasps and shivering were anything to judge by. Their fear had been rationalised as they realised now who shared this temporary confined space with them—the alleged murderer of the Lord Count of the Truban Empire, a sorcerer believed to possess the ability to render their existence into nothing with the blink of an eye. While there was no way he could manage such a thing, Alpheus could tell that the darkness and confined space played into and even intensified the soldiers' fears.

"How can we... make it up to you?" one of them asked quietly.

It worked, Alpheus realised with a grin. "Now, tell me," he said with that same taut pitch, "what sinister scheme are you minions brewing? A raid of the dungeon?"

"Will you... promise not to harm us?" the other one asked carefully.

Alpheus swung an arm forward, the sleeves of his mantle drawing up a whiff of air that swept over the soldiers. "Speak now, or I shall do more than *harm* you."

"All right, all right! I'll talk."

"Then talk."

"We're just following instructions," the soldier began. "And besides, we're not doing anything malicious."

Alpheus snorted. "I'll be the judge of that."

"We're acting on the instruction of Sir Greene," the soldier said, speaking with reluctance. "He's a silver knight. And his plan for the raid is to ensure the security of our country."

"You're not making any sense," Alpheus said.

"The target is Lord Copper."

"You're planning to free him?"

The soldiers snickered. "Free him? He's defected to Aizary. We're going there to take his life."

What?! Alpheus thought, hiding his surprise. *Lord Copper... and Aizary?*

"Look," the same soldier said. "There's nothing more to it. We were only asked to warn them if the king returned. We don't know any more. Let us go, will you?"

"Who else is here?" Alpheus asked. "In the castle."

"No one, I think. No one with rank, anyway."

"What about Ebenezer?"

"Lord Ebenezer? Well, actually, he *was* here earlier. Sir Greene had him lured away. I think he was told that the king had called for him."

Alpheus puffed out a long breath. He then hopped forward and started pushing away the fallen cabinet, stopping after moving it only a few inches. He forced a grin, rising back to his feet.

"There," he said, pulling the door back until it hit the cabinet. It was enough of a gap for him to slip through. Alpheus turned back once more to the soldiers, whose frightened frowns were now visible under the ample daylight filtering in.

"Take me to the dungeon," Alpheus said.

"We cannot do that," the soldier said, growing anxious. "We're not going to mar Sir Greene's plans for anything. He's doing it for the country. He's a true hero."

"Your loyalty is admirable," Alpheus said. "But I *do* want to see if Lord Copper's really a deserter like you said. If he is, I might even lend Sir Greene a hand."

The pair exchanged a brief glance. "Here, take this," one of them said, offering a parchment from under his sleeves. "It's a map of the castle. I hope I'm right to trust you. Your voice just now... it was frightening. But it was only an act, right? You probably didn't realise when you stopped."

"You're a sharp one," Alpheus said with a smile as he accepted the folded sheep skin map. He flapped it out to confirm that it was truly what the soldier had claimed. "I appreciate this. Unfortunately, I cannot afford to have you blabber away to Sir Greene, so..."

"Hey, but we just—"

It was too late. Alpheus had darted behind them, swinging an elbow into one and a knee into the other, striking them on their necks to down them instantly. It was the same thing he had once seen Marvin do to easily knock someone unconscious. *But where he uses sheer force, I rely on my speed*, he noted, gazing at those soldiers now with guilt.

Alpheus dragged the soldiers away from the conspicuous place where they had fallen, shoving them clunkily into one of the cabinets. He flapped out the map again, which wasn't easy to understand with its confusing depiction of multiple floors and the fact that the number of floors varied across the castle. Alpheus was quick to note the dungeon, however, which was tucked away into the far corner of the castle where the structure was cradled by the surrounding mountains. The underground location of the dungeon likely required more than a key to get into. He flipped open his pocket watch now, noting that the small hand was pointed at five. Dusk was fast approaching. The soldiers had said that the raid was scheduled for midnight.

The armoury, Alpheus thought, closing his watch again with a click. *If this Sir Greene wanted Lord Copper's life, he would have to stock up.* He looked at the map again. *And it's not far from here.*

Indeed, it was a short walk, though he would never have thought to proceed through some of the stairs and passages that on first glance seemed to lead nowhere. Following the map, he found his way to the fourth and highest floor of one of the towers. Similar to the storage chamber, it was rather dark there with barely more than a few dabs of daylight sifting inside through the small windows. He had actually visited the armoury once during his castle tour on his first day there.

Alpheus looked ahead to an imposing double door, opened slightly on its right, sprinkling out a rusty orange luminescence out into the short hallway. Some indiscernible mumbling could also be heard trickling out. He squinted and then began to prowl ahead. As Alpheus got closer, he could discern a few different voices, and he suspected that there were at least half a dozen men inside.

Alpheus backed up against the door. *I suppose it's the same everywhere*, he thought with disappointment. *The lust for power means that there's always some scheme afoot.*

It sounded like the men inside were in the middle of a briefing. One of them was addressed as *Sir Dallon*, and that man's voice was somewhat familiar to Alpheus. Greene, meanwhile, was easy to identify, as he spoke with a commanding tone over the others.

"The guards can't stop us," said Greene. "But I don't want any unnecessary casualties. We have only one item on our agenda, and that is to efface the poison in the Dominion—to execute Copper. Now, what's the situation at the site?"

Alpheus allowed himself a peek inside. Among the group gathered at the rectangular table was a man in silver armour. *Greene*, Alpheus thought, trying to remember the faces he had seen from his first day in the castle. The silver knight was in his mid-thirties, bearded, with broad shoulders. Alpheus's attention then flitted to the man talking now—the man addressed as Dallon—who Alpheus now recognised was the same knight who had refused to stand up to Trajetzky, even when the Kragan was brutalising an innocent servant.

"We have secured the quarters," Dallon said. "I shall be there at the appointed time."

"We will see you there at precisely a quarter past eleven," Greene said with a grin. "Everyone, review your role one last time before we get going. Today will be the end for that traitor!"

Cries for justice filled the armoury and leaked out to Alpheus, who could only frown more deeply in response. He turned to leave now, and left through the same passageways down which he had come. Once he left the tower, he wandered off to the central atrium. Alpheus referred to the map again, noting that one of the towers closest to the dungeon was labelled as the servants' quarters. It was likely the *site* Greene had referred to.

But so what if I know? Alpheus thought as he paused under the great donjon. *It's not something I should meddle with. And besides, what could I do?* He sighed, wishing the Sail Band were here.

"What are you doing here?" a voice said then, which made Alpheus jump.

Treading in from the opposite side of the atrium between the grand columns was Zabai, the ever-majestic female knight in her armour of mahogany red. Accompanying her was a younger lady, also donning a knight's heavy armour, at least a few years her junior, and shorter. Like Zabai, there seemed to be an air of solemnity that swirled about this younger knight. She was far less imposing than Zabai, though, and even looked like she would actually entertain a conversation. After all, she was wearing a slight smile.

"Do you realise that I can imprison you for encroachment?" Zabai said, regarding Alpheus with a wary gaze as she approached.

"I didn't come here uninvited," Alpheus snapped. He then shook his head. "Anyway, that's not important! Tell me, Lady Zabai, did the king return with you?"

"And why do you think I should answer you?"

"I'm not asking for me! The dungeon is about to be raided. If you don't—"

But Zabai hardly lifted a brow. *Did she know about it already?* he wondered with sudden fear. For all Alpheus knew, Zabai could well be a partisan in Greene's scheme.

"What is this about?" her page asked, her tone firm, but not flat like Zabai's.

Alpheus hesitated for a second, but then went on to reveal what he knew, if only to do his part for Copper. He expected scepticism, because it was difficult to trust the word of a foreigner—an alleged murderer—especially against the honour of Dominion knights.

Zabai brooded over his statement for a moment and then suddenly grabbed for her sword. "Take it with you," Zabai said, handing it to Alpheus who thought for a moment that she was going to murder him. "I have no obligation to defend you."

Alpheus took the sabre from her, and when he looked up again, Zabai and her page were already on their way. "Wait!" he said. "Where are we going?"

"To the servants' quarters," her page answered with a quick glance back.

"*Now*?"

They responded not with words this time, but by moving further along with the clanging of their sabatons. Alpheus shook his head, but proceeded to tag closely behind.

"Are you in the belief that Lord Copper has defected?" he asked. "That he's a poison to the Dominion?"

Zabai didn't answer, instead just trotting on, her dark cape and even darker long hair waving from side to side behind her. But her page fell back slightly to match Alpheus's pace.

"The king is slated for a return later this evening," she began softly. "The search parties have had little luck so far. We don't want anything to add to the stress. As for Lady Zabai, she hasn't had a rest for days now. She's—"

"Robinette!" Zabai called back to her. "Enough talk."

Robinette hurried to Zabai, treading by her side. It was quite a long walk to the servants' quarters, which was made to feel especially long when no one was sharing a single word with each other while passing by barely any other souls in the castle. The sun was setting, and yet it was still too early when they arrived, with more than a few hours to spare until the scheduled raid. Alpheus doubted that even Dallon had arrived. He thought it commendable, though, that Radiance's Nest had its own tower in which to accommodate servants, unlike Vondra Dawn, where servants slept where they worked, and without beds.

Zabai led the way into the tower, trotting up a set of stairs. Like the rest of the castle, the quarters were empty of people. Perhaps even the servants had joined the search outside. Zabai stopped after reaching only the first floor, a large chamber cluttered up with narrow beds. She paced her way across the chamber and then finally sat down on one of the window-side beds, peering outside to the entrance of the dungeon which was clearly viewable from there. A group of guards stood vigil in front of the solitary building, and the scene reminded Alpheus of the prison he had escaped from. The small lantern that hung over the frame of the entrance was the brightest spot under a sky that was growing darker by the minute.

"We're just going to wait here?" Alpheus asked.

"Yes," Zabai simply said before hanging her head slightly, not in shame but seemingly in weariness. She then closed her eyes altogether, looking as though she was prepared to doze off.

Alpheus gawked in response and looked at Robinette for an explanation. She offered none, but instead peered out the window in alert, the gesture probably to relieve her liege from the vigil.

Alpheus perched on the thin frame of a bed a few across from where Zabai sat. The beds were all narrow, delicate, and much too close to the next bed. Despite that, it seemed that Zabai found the beds satisfactory, able to doze away even without lying down.

Alpheus flipped out his pocket watch, growing impatient. He looked up and met Robinette's eyes briefly, but the youthful attendant barely acknowledged him as she returned her attention outside. It was a while later when Robinette twitched, rising to her feet.

"He's here," she said.

Zabai snapped her eyes open, but didn't bother to rise from her seat, only peered over to the stairs. A moment later, light footsteps sounded from there.

It was indeed Dallon, the knight who was to secure the quarters. He was late in noting the company already there, and he was aghast as he recognised who was waiting for him.

"Lady Zabai...," Dallon uttered, barely managing to blurt out his words. He tensed up then and bowed. "A surprise to see you here," he said. "But an honour, as always."

"And why are *you* here?" Zabai asked, crossing her arms, still seated.

Dallon flushed, despite his brawny figure. "I was here to see someone, my second cousin. He's a cook. But... it looks like no one's here."

Zabai narrowed her eyes. "I hear that you are part of a dungeon raid. Will you enlighten me about that?"

Dallon paled immediately. "What?! No! Where did you hear that?"

"From me," Alpheus said. "You and Sir Greene."

Dallon snorted with a forced smile. "You must be kidding! And who are you again? An exile of Trubannis? I have no idea what this is about. But I'm completely dismayed that Sir Greene—a righteous knight—is being badmouthed."

Zabai stared into him for a moment, and then nodded. "Very well, then. Take your leave now. If memory serves, you are stationed at the front gate, not here in the quarters."

"I am grateful for your trust," Dallon said, bowing again. "But may I suggest that you stay away from certain people, especially those who have built a rather unsavoury reputation."

His hint was made the more obvious by his gaze upon Alpheus while speaking those words. Alpheus snorted quietly but then was shocked when Zabai actually allowed Dallon to leave. Her permissiveness was outrageous, and Alpheus scowled to show his displeasure as Dallon trotted away.

"Don't judge too early," Robinette said after Dallon had left, reaching into a small pouch hanging at her waist. "Watch," she said as she sprinkled a light-coloured powder onto the ground, which then revealed a set of shoeprints.

Alpheus leaned forward with a grin, impressed. There were many possible chemical reactions that would give that effect, but Alpheus couldn't see when either Zabai or her page had sprinkled that powder onto Dallon.

"Give it a minute," Zabai then said, betraying not even a hint of joy.

For that minute, Alpheus wavered on whether to apologise. In the end, he said nothing. And it was too late when Zabai rose to her feet. She stretched her arms out and shook off her fatigue, tossing her hair about in the process. Alpheus wondered if she was really so tired.

"Lead the way," Zabai said to her page.

Robinette nodded and began sprinkling down the powder to reveal Dallon's tracks. Once they stepped outside the tower, the spread between each shoeprint grew considerably larger. It was obvious that Dallon had begun running as soon as he had escaped their sight.

"Can you keep up?" Zabai asked Alpheus. "I cannot have you loitering on your own."

"I can keep up just fine," Alpheus said.

Zabai nodded to Robinette, and then off they went, dashing ahead along the trail. While Alpheus wanted to believe there was no intention to outrun him, a part of him suspected that Zabai wanted to do exactly that. In any case, it was easy to follow their pace with the Glider Steps. It seemed that they were only slightly faster than an average man. Alpheus noted that the cool vapour that was whiffing out behind him briefly won Zabai's attention as they were racing forward. He thought she would accelerate, then, but she maintained the same pace, trailing Robinette, who led the way without a huff.

Despite their speed, it took a while to arrive at the end of the trail, a sizeable rotunda near the front gate of the castle—a granary, a storehouse for threshed grain.

Zabai stepped ahead of Robinette now, who was wheezing quietly, while she herself didn't seem to have broken a sweat. Zabai swung the door open, taking charge, and the men inside gasped under the flicker of the oil lamp lighting the interior, gaping out at their intruders.

There were more than ten of them, one being Dallon, who was stunned and still panting from his own race away to reach the granary. The rest of the men shared his shock, most likely hadn't yet heard the end of Dallon's warning. They all sported simple black armour, looking more like bandits than knights and soldiers.

Zabai treaded deeper into the granary, and Alpheus followed with a hesitant step behind Robinette. Zabai stepped among the men before turning swiftly to face the leader of the pack, swinging her dark hair and cape with a swoosh.

"Explain yourself," she said with a glare at Greene, who had also changed into an armour of black.

Greene exchanged a brief look with Dallon. "I apologise," Greene then said, looking down. "I understand that this is against a knight's integrity, but Copper... he..."

"We're doing no wrong!" one of the soldiers snapped. "And we wouldn't have to do it this way if it weren't for you and all your hollow principles."

Zabai looked askance at that soldier, holding her position.

"What are you talking about...?" Greene uttered, fearing for the soldier.

"She's only a woman!" the soldier said. "It's humiliating that we are led by her. Women should know their place. They exist only to comfort us. They should be content to—"

Before he could finish that sentence, Greene sent him crashing into the bags of grain with a smash to the face. "Lady Zabai is our country's greatest warrior and asset. Without her guidance, people like you would never have been admitted into the Dominion."

Zabai didn't flinch, not even when Greene turned to her again. "I am deeply sorry for his insensitive words," Greene said. "The boy is new to the capital, hence his ignorance."

"And will one blow suffice?" Zabai said.

Greene trembled. "Then allow me to incapacitate his abhorrent tongue."

He hesitated for barely a moment before drawing his sword and slashing at the soldier whose terrified expression reflected the fact that he anticipated losing his tongue. Thankfully for the soldier, however, Robinette whipped out her own sabre to deflect away Greene's weapon, which was then hurled harmlessly into another bag of grain. Greene looked up in confusion, his hand shaking.

"There is no need for that," Zabai said. "And besides, his crime is far from the most serious among the group."

Greene held his head in shame, collapsing to his knees. "My men were working on my order. I will accept the consequences. But Lady Zabai, I ask of you to be vigilant. I do not hold the evidence of Copper's crimes, but I am certain that he has defected."

Zabai looked down at him with a squint. She then snatched the sabre off of her page, slashing it forward. A scream followed, but not that of Greene's.

Dallon screamed, growling as he raised his arms from which surged out dangerous amounts of blood. His hands had been unbound, severed from the wrists, and had landed now at his feet. Greene widened his eyes in shock and confusion, as did everyone else including Alpheus.

Dallon's eyes lit up in rage when he peered up at Zabai again. But before he could attempt anything foolish, Greene jumped on him, knocking him to the ground with a thud. Dallon squirmed about, but Greene just pressed down harder.

All eyes then turned to Zabai, whose sword was still extended. "Tell me," Zabai said, glaring down at Dallon, "what did Kraga give you?"

Dallon—flustered as he was—peered about in agony, perhaps searching for his hands which would never be a part of him again. Alpheus watched saliva gurgling out from his mouth, and realised that Dallon could no longer be a knight as he would never be able to wield a sword again. But the rest of the men there didn't seem to be sympathetic at all. They seemed more focused on Zabai's implication that Dallon had defected to Kraga. It became clear to Alpheus now that Zabai's words held much more weight than he had thought they would. And now, he also realised that he had inadvertently fallen into the middle of something he didn't want to be a part of.

No one said a word as the men exchanged looks, some of them regarding Dallon with squints and cringes as Dallon himself continued to wail in immense pain, thick layers of sweat coating his features.

"Will you confess?" Zabai asked.

"I don't know what you're talking about," Dallon finally said, still moaning in pain and fury.

"Denial won't save you," Zabai said, sliding her weapon from one side to the other.

She's not going to kill him here, is she? Alpheus wondered, sweat dampening his forehead.

Everyone paused then as the trumpeting of horns resonated from the outside, heralding the king's return to Radiance's Nest. Zabai frowned, handing the sabre back to Robinette who shared her worried look. Dallon, meanwhile, forced the beginning of a smirk despite his terrible pain, perhaps hopeful that the monarch might save him. It didn't last, however, as Robinette then knocked him unconscious.

"Sir Greene," Zabai said, already on her way out. "There's no way out of this. Bring your men with you, together with the traitor. We'll meet the king at the gate."

Greene obliged, hollering at his men to trail him, including the soldier who had dared to speak ill of Zabai. They trotted to the gate, where the monarch and his men strode in on sturdy mounts, some of them holding flags of the phoenix. Gaston and Ebenezer were part of the stately ensemble that numbered well over several dozen. Not a single knight was part of the group, and their looks of dejection foretold their failure in finding the crown princess.

Zabai dropped down on one bended knee with Robinette, Greene, and his men following promptly. Alpheus finally dropped when Robinette shot a frown at him indicating that he too must show his respect for the king, even as a foreigner.

THIRTEEN

Accident

While his earlier visit of the court during the day had been one of peace and even solitude, this second visit was an angry affair, similar to the very first time he had appeared there. Alpheus cringed now, thinking that he would never grow accustomed to the accusations thrown about in the world of politics. And he had almost forgotten why he had returned to Radiance's Nest until Ebenezer appeared. The mage had nodded at him, perhaps as an apology of sort, but had yet to speak a word amid the drama that was unfolding around them.

Zabai slid out her sword now, carving down from the collar of the unconscious Dallon. With the tip of her sabre, she tore open the drape and armour to reveal the burnt mark of a taurus on Dallon's back, a mythical creature resembling a bull with wings. One could imagine the pain, the intense heat, that one had to bear while being stamped on with that symbol. And yet it was the implication of what the symbol represented that had the onlookers aghast—the stamp of servitude used by the Kragans.

The mark was undisputable evidence that Dallon had defected from the Dominion, or at least had been threatened by the Kragans to do so. Either way, he couldn't be trusted anymore.

"Eyewitnesses have confirmed his meetings with Aryliel Trajetzky," Zabai said. "Unfortunately, Trajetzky has since departed the city and is beyond our reach."

The king shook his head in disbelief, groaning. "Ignoble," he uttered, regarding Greene. "To think you fell into the ploy and that you were about to kill Lord Copper. That you decided to disregard my word and the word of the court. You think yourself some saint, to be a superior judge than everyone here?"

"Your Majesty!" Greene cried, his head bowed. "Not once did I think that. But this mistake... I regret it so very much. I am deeply ashamed." He looked up then, wearing a frown of shame. "But this has nothing to do with my men. They were only acting on my instruction."

"Your Majesty," Zabai said, looking up to the king, the usual firmness in her pitch carrying a hint of indecision. "I ask you to pardon Sir Greene. He is a loyal knight who would defend the country with his life. If there must be someone to take responsibility, let it be me. After all, I am the Dominus, the regulator of the knights. This is a result of my negligence."

"Your Majesty!" Robinette cried, dropping to one knee. "If you must discipline Lady Zabai, then allow me to share the punishment."

"Robinette!" Zabai said under her breath. "What are you doing? Get up!"

"Your Majesty!" Greene said, also pleading. "I beg of you to pardon Lady Zabai. I am the only one at fault. I did my best to make sure Lady Zabai didn't know a thing about it. I can swear my life—"

"Enough!" the king said, slamming down a fist and then rising from the throne. "No one shall be pardoned. Sir Greene, I will have you demoted and banished from the capital. As for you, Lady Zabai," he said, turning to the female knight, "I will have your authority over our armies withdrawn."

More than several men perked up in shock. Zabai frowned slightly, but nodded to accept the decision.

"Your Majesty!" Greene cried. "Please! You cannot do that. Lady Zabai is the only one we can trust our armies to."

To Alpheus's surprise, more than a few noblemen joined in to defend Zabai with passion, bidding for the king to rescind the decision. Despite her cold front, Zabai was clearly widely supported and trusted among court members. Alpheus wondered if the knights would have protested even louder than the noblemen if they had returned from their search efforts. No matter, the king seemed unmoved.

"May I say a few words?" Alpheus said, stepping out to the aisle amid the attention, regarding the king who had barely noticed he was there until now. The ones who *had* noted his presence shook their heads in disapproval.

"I wouldn't dare lecture anyone here," Alpheus began. "Not when I made a promise here last time that I couldn't keep. I am not of this country, but I am fond of it—perhaps more so than my native Trubannis, where the court wants me dead. And for that, I do not wish to see the same disaccord I have seen in Vondra Dawn tainting the court here."

"Get to the point," Gaston said with a squint, the creases around his eyes pressed together.

Alpheus maintained his gaze on the king. "Can I assume that Your

Majesty is more worried for the country than for the crown princess?"

The king frowned, falling back into his throne, but otherwise appeared tolerant of what Alpheus was saying.

"You dread the thought that the princess may fall in the wrong hands," Alpheus continued. "Kraga have stamped your men with their symbol of servitude. If they happened to find the princess, one could only assume they'd do the same thing to her. And, of course, the Kragans aren't the only ones on your mind. You're wary of Trubannis, too, and Aizary, if they weren't so far away."

"You talk too much," Gaston berated, gesturing for soldiers to take Alpheus away.

The king held out a hand to halt them, studying Alpheus for a moment. "What might your suggestion be, then?" he finally said. "Excuse everyone who was involved?"

"No, not at all," Alpheus said. "I agree that there should be consequences. Without them, we would live in anarchy. And that is worse than any authority. But it is how we apply our laws that distinguishes a good realm from a bad one."

* * *

The king shot a surprising smile at Alpheus, which in turn seemed to brighten up all of the court.

Perhaps Lady Zabai will be excused after all, Robinette thought, peering over to Alpheus. *And we might have him to thank.* The sudden swing of the collective mood wasn't to last, however, when a panicked soldier lurched in from the back for an emergency report.

"Intruders! Intruders!" he cried, stumbling to his knees. "The dungeon," he said, pointing to the exit.

Attention flitted to Greene and his men, all of them still on their knees. "I don't know anything about this," Greene claimed, wearing a confused frown himself.

Gaston turned to the wheezing soldier. "Slow down," he said in an urgent tone that didn't match his words. "What intruders do you speak of?"

"I don't know who they are," the soldier said between breaths. "But no one could stop them. They downed all of the guards in a matter of seconds."

A host of glares darted to Greene again, who simply shook his head in disbelief, maintaining his innocence. The castle was thin on defence. The knights had not yet returned from their search for the crown princess. Greene, one of the only knights there, couldn't be trusted. The apparent defect of

Dallon to the Kragans further added to the uncertainty.

"Now's not the time for scruples," Zabai said before bowing to the king. "Your Majesty, allow me a chance for redemption."

"Very well," the king said. "Take the soldiers with you and remedy the disturbance. I shall trail you alongside the other lords."

Zabai bowed again and then turned, peering out to the soldiers there—barely ten of them—before beckoning them to follow her lead as she treaded out the court. If the intruders proved problematic, Robinette realised she was the only one to share the load. *But if it were the Guardians...* Robinette thought, paling at the possibility.

After pacing a short distance away from the court, Zabai turned to Robinette. "I'll have to go on ahead," she said. "You lead the soldiers."

"But—"

"Listen to me," Zabai said. "The king needs you. We don't know how many intruders we're dealing with. Now is the time to put your training to good use. You must use your judgement on when to fall back and when to rush ahead to lend me support. I'm relying on you, Quinn."

Robinette looked deeply into her liege's eyes, almost frozen over to hear herself being addressed as Quinn again. It was her middle name, reserved for only those intimate moments when she was allowed to be a just a woman and not a knight. Her parents had used to call her by that name, before they died in the war, anyway. Since then, she had trained to become a knight, and it had felt as though no one knew her *lady name* anymore. Zabai was the only one who knew everything about her. And Zabai was also the only one allowed to call her by that name.

Robinette frowned away her delicate emotions to see that Zabai had turned and was already dashing off ahead. She realised then that even Zabai feared the imminent confrontation with potentially frightening enemies. She pursed her lips, swinging back to the soldiers.

"Be vigilant," Robinette demanded as she led the way, moving at a conservative pace.

The soldiers—only nine of them now—followed her closely. The journey toward the dungeon was as uneventful as her prior visit only an hour ago had been. With not even a soul around, everything seemed strangely peaceful as she continued trotting forward, mindful not to outpace the king too much.

"Move!" Robinette cried, waving the soldiers on as she herself peered back again, waiting only moments before she caught a glimpse of the king and his retinue marching up from behind—quite swiftly, actually—but still not fast enough.

She was still a fair distance away from the dungeon where Zabai might already be in the midst of a rugged battle. Robinette had never doubted Zabai's ability to fend off foes, and she still didn't. But the ambivalence she saw in her liege just now was certainly a first. She hissed despite herself, rueing that the castle had never felt so large.

Robinette couldn't be sure how much time had passed, but now upon finally reaching the servants' quarters, she allowed herself a smile. At the same time, the tower almost seemed like a mountain of an obstacle on the other side which was the dungeon. She waved the soldiers closer to her now, still wary as she slowed her pace for the king.

"Listen to my command," Robinette said to the soldiers. "Lady Zabai may very well be fighting now. I trust that you all know how powerful she is. Make sure not to get in her way and—"

She trailed off there as the clanging of weapons sounded from the other side of the tower. "Dammit!" Robinette cursed. "Remember what I said," she maintained, reaching for her sword. "And prepare to fight!"

Robinette dashed off with the alerted soldiers tagging closely behind her. She led them to circle around the tower and further onto the lengthy wall that extended nearly to the edge of the castle.

Blast it! she thought, rueing that the wall was far too high to leap over. The wall was indeed the last barrier that a potential escapee of the dungeon was forced to confront. The irony was that no prisoner had ever reached that far, and instead, this same wall was stalling her advance in upholding the laws that governed the country.

They arrived eventually, and Robinette caught speed and darted ahead toward the entrance to the dungeon, leaving her allies to chase behind her. The evening sky was unkind to her, but the flicker ahead lighted her way. It was the only way. That flicker was, of course, the lantern hanging over the frame of the entrance to the dungeon.

Hold on, Lady Zabai, she thought with a hand on her sword. *I'm coming.*

As she had anticipated, Zabai was in the middle of a heated tussle against... *not one, and not two, but a total of five foes!* Robinette peered across the grounds where two prisoners lay unconscious among the defeated guards. *Lord Copper,* she recognised, *and... that maid.*

Robinette cried out and slashed her sabre toward one of the enemies, only for her weapon to be parried off by the end of a mere dagger. She noted that the man was draped in a dark mantle, sporting a white masquerade that covered his face from the nose up. She frowned, swinging out her sabre again, which the enemy evaded with an impressive leap backwards. He was powerful, and he was only one of *five*.

"Take the short one!" Zabai cried after fending off a couple of the men with a forceful thrust. "And the one closest to you!"

Robinette looked up, trusting that her liege was sending her to the weaker opponents. She lunged in at *the short one* who wielded a sabre similar to hers. As Zabai had gauged, this particular foe seemed too slow even to react. If it wasn't for another one of them lurching at Robinette from the side, five would have already turned to four.

But what is this...?! Robinette thought in awe as she looked up at the giant of a man who had jostled her away. She had barely given it much thought earlier, but now, as she perched at the man's feet, did she truly appreciate his colossal frame, which easily dwarfed even Zabai, who was known as a tall woman.

"Get up, Quinn!" Zabai urged, even as she sliced her sword against one of the stronger intruders. "Don't let his size scare you. He's no match—"

Zabai stopped mid-sentence as her enemy retaliated with a powerful thrust, pushing her into a stagger.

"Lady Zabai!" Robinette cried, leaping to her feet and sweeping her sabre out, only to be caught in a wrestling match against three enemies—including the giant.

"Let us!" a voice said then, resounding from the dark of the night.

Robinette turned to her right and saw that the soldiers had finally caught up. While the soldiers would prove no match for the stronger intruders, they could perhaps hold their own against *the short one*. That would at least make one less intruder to worry about.

* * *

Alpheus arrived at the same tower again, but this time alongside the king and his retinue. The journey here had been a hasty and hectic affair. But Alpheus thought that the king deserved plenty of credit for goading the large group of men as well as himself to keep within a safe distance to Robinette, who was supposed to protect all of them. Now that they had arrived, however, Gaston directed everyone straight into the servants' quarters for safety. Soon, they were all peering out from the same windows that had become familiar to Alpheus only hours earlier.

Alpheus recognised two figures donning the knight's armour currently in a heated tussle against a group who were clearly the intruders. The king and his men looked on anxiously, praying that their strongest warrior would come out on top. Alpheus, though, peered away briefly from the mighty battle, first to note a number of guards who lay scattered in the open—either unconscious or dead—and then two people donning the white prisoner's garb, hands in shackles, also lying on the ground.

"Lord Copper," Gaston said, the first to make the assumption.

Alpheus turned, narrowing his eyes, unable to confirm much more than the human shapes from the distance.

"That is the Valorous Viola Swordplay," Ebenezer said now behind Alpheus, referring to the supreme fencing style both Zabai and her young page were employing. "It is the most popular technique used by knights of the Imperial Lithia Dominion. But... it might not be enough against these foes."

Alpheus said nothing, still wondering what the intruders were trying to achieve. He held a fist, the sweat in his hands adding to an agony he couldn't understand. Was it the talk of Kraga that troubled him? Or was it his concern for Copper's wellbeing? Something seemed wrong, but he couldn't tell yet what it might be.

* * *

The scramble was growing fiercer by the second, but behind the masquerades and the shrouding mantles, all the intruders looked the same.

But that one, Robinette thought, glancing at the tall, lean intruder Zabai was fighting. *He's different. He moves with purpose, and he slides his dagger expertly. He's a step ahead of everyone else.*

Robinette had never seen Zabai fail to triumph against only one foe. With their numerical advantage now, Zabai was given that liberty, but her opponent had proved to be incredibly skilled. Armed with only a dagger, the man was forcing Zabai into a nimble clash of metals that sparked off a brilliant static.

But why? Robinette thought, as she turned back to the other four opponents with whom her soldiers were helping her fight. *These intruders... they almost seem reluctant.* She slashed her sabre out, catching a glimpse of the glimmer in one of her opponent's eyes. *Could it be they sought only to escape?* She shook her head, grinding her teeth. *No, this is not the time to be making guesses. Not when His Majesty is in the perimeter.*

Robinette whipped out the scabbard to her sabre then, using it to stave off the sword wielded by one of her opponents, the grating exchange of metal against metal clamouring out radially. She lifted the scabbard, laying it out almost horizontally with its tip at her chin. She spun the sabre up with her sword wielding arm, hovering the blunt edge across its sheath—assuming the stance of a fiddle player. No musical tune followed, but she slid out her sabre from there for a fierce slash that swept out a blast of air.

This was the Valorous Viola Swordplay of which she considered herself half an expert. Zabai was far more skilled than her, but even with her current skill level, she believed she would be a handful against some of the strongest warriors in the land.

She sliced away again, this time her sword was met by the gauntlet of the intruder who carried no weapon. The violent clash cracked into the armoured glove with a force that shook the entire ground at their feet. A jolt and a hint of hesitation indicated the intruder's awe, but he promptly found his feet again. Robinette believed that she was already waving the sabre and its sheath in tandem—and skilfully, too—using the latter mostly as a shield. But despite her best efforts and her continued aggressiveness, she realised that she wasn't about to down her opponent, who was immensely powerful despite still being obviously weaker than the man Zabai was fighting. The remaining three intruders had proved weaker than her—or so she thought—but their incredible tenacity made it extremely difficult if not impossible for her and her soldiers to gain any advantage.

Just who are these people?! she thought with a grunt, slashing away again.

The question of whether she could have done more became meaningless when she saw a few of her soldiers being downed now. The man who wielded no weapon knocked out four soldiers in quick succession, doing so seemingly as he desired. He was about to knock out the fifth now, when Robinette turned to him and sliced her sword out in rage. But her foe had anticipated this, dashing off with supreme agility. She chased, adamant to avenge those soldiers, but only to be caught in a futile racing match.

No! she realised suddenly. *He's luring me away.* Robinette forced her feet to a screeching stop and then peered back. The remaining soldiers were struggling mightily even as the giant man was trotting away from the brawl, carrying a prisoner over his shoulder.

Robinette cursed as she began dashing back. And, surely enough, the intruder she had chased just now returned the favour by dashing after her. Robinette hissed and then swung her sabre back in full force, hoping that the surprise would finally allow her to land the first and what might be a fatal blow on the foe. Instead, the intruder bolted to the side to evade a lethal hit, in the end sustaining a graze that drew a streak of red on the back of his forearm. The skill of the evasion was unbelievable, but the exchange bought her some precious time.

By the time she had raced back, however, the rest of her soldiers were defeated. The other three intruders were already trotting away now, hurrying for an escape, carrying a prisoner with them. Indeed, they were headed for their ally, who—after sustaining a graze on his forearm—was well enough to wave them over to him. Their goal was the opening at the end of that wall, the annoying detour for escape.

Zabai, meanwhile, was still caught in a hustle with the strongest of the intruders. She simply didn't have the liberty to do more.

Robinette didn't know when, but the lantern—which had been the only source of artificial light in the vicinity—had been snuffed out. All that anyone could rely on for vision now was the dull evening sky shrouded with dark clouds. Robinette snorted, turning her back against those who were fleeing.

"Lady Zabai," she uttered, sprinting toward her. *If we can down even one*, she thought.

As she was pacing there, a final surprise arose. A sixth intruder—donning the dark mantle and white masquerade—emerged from the dungeon entrance.

* * *

The king and the other lords widened their eyes, noting the petite figure of this latest member of the intruders. "Don't be fooled," Gaston said, reminding everyone that appearances were deceiving. The old man didn't seem to realise, however, that some of those lords were panicking because of something else—the fact that some of the other intruders seemed to be heading straight for them.

Alpheus paid no heed to their fears. His worry was elsewhere, on something he couldn't ascertain. This latest emerging intruder had shaken him, but he didn't know why. He squinted, supposing that it might be a *she*, a woman. With almost no light to see by, it was close to impossible to know for sure. But Alpheus thought he saw tresses of long hair that fell behind this newcomer, and that *she* was looking in the direction of the comrades who had fled. Alpheus squinted harder, and for a short moment, he thought he could see more clearly. Every stroke of motion out there seemed crisper, even if slightly. And from there, Alpheus made out a hand moving to the mouth, slipping into the delicate contours of what were definitely a lady's lips.

It's her, Alpheus thought with a flinch, his cheeks tensing up involuntarily. His gaze then darted away to Robinette, who rushed full steam ahead at the newcomer. She had thrust her sword forward, lunging ahead and looking for the kill. Alpheus gritted his teeth but managed not an utterance.

No, Alpheus thought, leaning forward. A clang of metals followed as a flying dagger deflected Robinette's searing sabre away. All eyes turned to the only other intruder there, who had surrendered his only weapon, having hurled it out with supreme precision and strength.

"Get out of there!" the intruder cried at his comrade, finally speaking now.

Zabai glanced back at Robinette and the newcomer. She hissed then with humiliation—probably on the thought that her opponent had the liberty to take his focus off of her. Their battle resumed immediately.

The newcomer did as told, fleeing now, but heading back for the dungeon rather than after the other intruders who had already fled. Robinette wouldn't allow it. She didn't need her sabre, instead dealing a deadly blow with her heavy gauntlets—striking the newcomer on the back of the shoulder and sending her crashing to the floor.

"Nooooo!!" Alpheus cried, his scream resonating in the air. He shoved a few men away and lunged out from the window, without consideration of the impact of the fall. He cringed as he rolled his ankle on an awkward landing, but he ignored the pain as he rushed forward. Robinette turned, perking up, only for Alpheus to dash right past her and ahead to her defeated foe.

Alpheus grabbed the injured intruder and held her in his arms. She was indeed a woman, a young lady, whimpering as the terrible scarlet of blood streamed out of her pale lips. He tore open the mantle at the shoulder where she had been struck, revealing a huge, throbbing, dark bruise covering the entire shoulder and parts of the dorsum. The wound looked lethal. Alpheus trembled as he grasped onto the masquerade. He lifted it to confirm what he had suspected.

Azure.

She coughed out a heap of blood, and her eyes were flooded in tears as she peered up to meet Alpheus's eyes. She gritted her teeth then and gathered all her strength to lift her hand to his face, running her slender fingers softly on his cheeks.

"Al-Alpheus...," she said faintly, managing a half-smile.

Alpheus stared back, his own eyes tearing up, too. "Why...?" he said. "*Why* is it you?"

Azure snapped her eyes wide open then as blood rushed up her thorax, which then resulted in a terrible expulsion from her mouth.

"No!" Alpheus cried, grasping tighter onto her as her eyelids flickered more and more slowly, until they finally closed altogether.

The skirmish had come to an end. The only intruder left had turned desolate, watching Alpheus and the dying girl. Zabai and Robinette remained vigilant, but now, as their foe removed his masquerade, their worry turned into ire. Alpheus didn't spare a glance back, knowing already that it was Marvin. The others who had managed to flee were Rover, Ash, Tavie, and Karl. Leo was probably just outside the castle, ready to expedite their escape.

Marvin frowned and said nothing. Zabai scowled in response, but finally slipped her weapon away as her page hurried over to her.

"Seize him!" the king demanded.

FOURTEEN

Sanction

Alpheus thought he had put it all behind him, but the memory rushed back now in vivid detail. That corridor. That storm. The torrential rain and the flashes of lighting that tore apart the evening sky. The roaring thunder that was deafening to his ears. All of that spurred his heart to thump harder. And finally, at the end of it all, was that streak of red that streamed out from the mouth framed by that neat moustache.

Jeffery..., Alpheus thought with a gasp, picturing the man's death image. He looked down now. It wasn't Reeling in his arms. But the feeling was the same. The burden of a dying person weighing down on his arms was more than he could bear. The bead of tears caught beneath her eyelashes added to the anguish.

"She's not dead yet," he uttered. "She's not."

Robinette, who had inflicted the damage, looked away with a squint. Zabai turned to her, shaking her head.

"It's not your fault," she said to her.

"But...," Robinette said with a wince, "I—" She struggled with the words, saying no more as Zabai gestured for her to fall on one knee. The king and his retinue had finally made the trip over to join them.

"Rise," the king said, still trotting in as he waved away the formalities. "Everyone trained in healing, please attend to Lady Zabai at once." He then peered over to Marvin. While the man was without a weapon, his storied *heroics* suggested to the king that he was a dangerous man regardless. The dismal look Marvin wore on his face, however, showed that he wasn't about to try anything violent.

The attention flitted back to Alpheus when he grabbed Azure's hand, pressing his palm against hers. "Don't die!" he demanded. "I won't allow it!" He inhaled a deep breath, pushing up the grace within him, amassing what he could in his hand. "I won't allow it," he repeated, forcing grace out from his palm, which then manifested into a light blue vapour dissolving into the atmosphere.

The men around them might have thought that he had gone insane, but even when Alpheus sensed that someone was approaching from behind, he couldn't bring himself to turn even slightly, not when he was still trying his best to save Azure.

It only works for inanimate objects, Reeling had said. And yet Alpheus knew no better than to keep trying, forcing his grace into her, wishing that it would save her.

"That won't do it," said a voice from behind.

Ebenezer.

The mage shook his head in disapproval, but then sat down behind Alpheus with his legs in a criss-cross. He whirled his arms in a semi-circle before thrusting his palms of luminous green onto Alpheus's back. The impact caused Alpheus to spew out blood, with an initial stinging pain that turned suddenly into an invigorating warmth that surged from his torso to his head. His grace immediately began to stream smoothly into Azure, her body glowing in that beautiful light blue.

A spectacular pulsing flow of colours surrounded them. Gasps from the spectators could be heard from every direction, but Alpheus didn't care, still concentrating as hard as he could in what looked more and more promising to him.

Azure finally opened her eyes then, still fragile and muddled. Alpheus beamed in response. He pushed out more grace, and even began to turn his head slightly to acknowledge Ebenezer's support, only for the man to dismiss him—howling at him to concentrate.

A revolving gust of wind surrounded them like a protection barrier, with luminous pulses of energy sprinkling around and about. Pulses of green mixed with sparkling pulses of light blue blended into a brilliant surge of energy flowing into Azure.

"Let go, now," Ebenezer said then, withdrawing.

Alpheus smiled, and then pulled back before laying Azure down gently. "Did we save her?" he asked, wheezing.

Ebenezer rose to his feet, breathing deeply. "For now," he then said.

"What do you mean?" Alpheus questioned, shooting himself up, only to collapse to the ground immediately due to exhaustion. He didn't know when, but as he studied his hands now with eyes that he could suddenly barely keep open, he noted that every part of his body had grown terribly numb.

"Why...?" he managed to say, before passing out completely.

* * *

The court bristled early the next morning. Copper had been released temporarily, shackles unbinded, and escorted there to share his word about all that had happened. Copper had been briefed on Dallon's murder plot, and he had been as shocked as anyone in learning that the man had defected to the Kragans. The culprit himself was there, unchained—but only because his hands had been ruthlessly severed. Adding to Dallon's mishap was a board collar around his neck and a strip of thick linen that tied his mouth shut.

The pitiable traitor was on his way out now, as Marvin and Alpheus stepped in. Dallon's judgement had likely been concluded, but Marvin had no interest in learning what had ensued or where Dallon was headed.

Marvin was the only representative of his crew, after the others had managed to flee the castle altogether. He was sure he could have managed to escape, too, but he had elected to stay, if not for Alpheus—who needed an ally in support of him—then for Azure, whose injury hadn't been part of his plans. Alpheus was pale now, having only just woken up from the drastic strain on his body of the evening prior. Alpheus had needed his help staggering his way here.

Alpheus wasn't the only one ragged by fatigue, though. The grim expressions that filled almost every face in the court showed that everyone had had it rough. The tireless search for the crown princess had already worn everyone thin, even before all the drama involving Dallon and then Marvin's own crew. The knights had returned earlier in the morning, all drained of energy, likely expecting to hear it from the king about their failure to find even a trace of where the crown princess had gone. The king said nothing to them, however, perhaps in part because of his own exhaustion. Other than an ailing cough that deterred him from speaking, his eyes drooped down almost to his nostrils. The other old man, Gaston, was speaking for the king, at the same time maintaining an inimical gaze on Marvin.

No one's glare was more hateful than Zabai's. The female warrior wore a hanging cast on her left arm, and was without her magnificent breastplate and the dark cape that was normally draped from her shoulders. The wheat-coloured, padded jacket she always donned underneath her plated armour sufficed, the gambeson illustrating a prominent chest which in turn reminded the people of her womanhood and that even she wasn't immune from injury. Zabai was most likely the kind of warrior who would hide all hints of weakness—especially from the knights who looked up to her. Her heavy wounds inflicted by none other than Marvin himself simply demanded the conspicuous bandages. Marvin's own chest and abdomen was patched up as well, nursing a few injuries of his own. Only then, Marvin noted a brief grin from Zabai's young page who stood next to her, likely smiling at the fact that even he hadn't come out of the hustle unscathed. Marvin glanced away from them now, agreeing that the ability to wound him *did* warrant some kind of proud smile.

Both Ebenezer and Azure were nowhere to be seen. But surely, someone in the court had information about what had happened to them. He realised that Azure was all that Alpheus cared about.

"Marvin Sailanson," Gaston said in a croaky tone, sounding as if he had lost his voice, yet still delivering his speech with nearly the same level of authority. "Would you care to begin with an explanation? We knew who you were from the start, since the day you entered the castle alongside Alpheus Hindlow. We elected to play the fool, only to extend to you the courtesy to be treated with equality rather than prejudice. Tell us, then, whether or not we have made a terrible decision."

Marvin regarded the old man for a moment. He then nodded, reaching down into one of the pouches hanging from his waist. He pulled out an item and then opened his hand to reveal a gleaming bracelet tied to a string which fell hanging from his fingers. It was the pearl band that belonged to the crown princess.

"Now, don't go making premature judgements," Marvin said. "I have nothing to do with the missing princess. But if you must know, *this* was our purpose. This bracelet. I made a deal with her—Azure. I'd do her a favour, in exchange for this."

Gaston frowned. "What favour?"

"She wanted to be a prisoner," Marvin said. "She wanted to change places with the one she called Carmen."

It sounded absurd even to himself as he heard it. But while the noblemen and the other members of the court exchanged wide-eyed looks, no one seemed particularly surprised. As some of them mumbled, Marvin noted that Alpheus said nothing. Marvin realised that if anyone was reluctant to accept that Azure should be credited for anything, it was Alpheus.

"She came to me," Marvin continued, eyeing Gaston and the king. "And, believe me, I was as shaken up as you lot when I found out the princess had gone missing. I wanted the bracelet. And that was when the bracelet found its way to me... delivered by Azure. I don't know why she had the bracelet or how she knew that I wanted it. In any case, she knew how to negotiate—telling us that we had to *earn* it. She had it cleverly hidden away somewhere, and would only tell us where to retrieve it once the favour was complete. As it turns out, the bracelet was *inside* the dungeon."

Gaston turned to Copper. "Is that your understanding?"

Copper nodded, still donning the simple garb of a prisoner. "It is true that Marvin Sailanson came down to the cells last night with Azure. I didn't know who they were initially, but when I realised it, I tried to stop them from doing anything reckless, but—" He trailed off, eyeing Marvin with unease. "But," he continued finally, "they knocked me out. I don't know what happened after that."

"After that," Marvin said, "Carmen was put to sleep, like you. As promised, Azure handed over the bracelet, and we were on our way. Well, except for Azure, who stayed in the cells as her friend's replacement. It was as it should have been." Marvin then shot a gaze at Zabai. "We did not expect to see you in ambush."

The female knight snorted. "And never did I imagine you to be part of a childish ploy."

"In any case," Marvin said with a shrug, "I can only assume the lass came up from the cells upon hearing the clanging of metals." He paused there for a moment with a sigh. "How is she? Will she... survive?"

More than a few people turned to the king with worried expressions, including Alpheus and Robinette, who were probably concerned for different reasons. "We don't know yet," the king said, finally speaking in a frail pitch. "The physicians are doing what they can. I trust that they are still hard at work now, not only to nurse Azure, but the lengthy list of wounded men who *you*, of all people, should know about."

Marvin met the king's eyes with a calm composure. The king was likely familiar with Marvin's stories—that he had been rumoured to be the greatest warrior in the land since the warring years. The Kragans had called Marvin a monster, one who terrorised armies on his own. The Dominion had, of course, never had to learn whether Marvin was really so fearful, having withdrawn from the war prior to his emergence as the Trubans' most feared soldier.

The king looked up now as the double door down the aisle opened from the outside. Ebenezer paced in with his wooden staff, alongside a small group of physicians.

"Your Majesty," the mage said in greeting as he fell down on one knee with his company. All of them looked fatigued.

"Skip the formalities," the king said, gesturing for them to rise. "Tell me, how are the wounded?"

Ebenezer rose to his feet with a tired smile. "I am glad to report that, of the thirty-two injured, there are no deaths." He paused then, stroking his goatee with a slight frown. "There is... an *impending* death, however. That... lass."

"No!" Alpheus said, swinging away from Marvin. "Why?" he questioned, grasping Ebenezer by his dark robe. "Our energy should have been more than enough!"

Ebenezer swung an arm to rid himself of Alpheus's grasp, tripping the scholar onto the floor. "I didn't give up any energy for the lass. I merely helped you direct your energy."

"What...?" Alpheus uttered.

"Her injury cannot be reversed by merely giving her grace. What will kill her isn't the right shoulder—it's the aftershock that has damaged and blocked the alveolar ducts. The respiratory system is compromised, and so too is the circulatory system. In other words, she cannot channel energy to where it is needed."

"Then I'll give her more grace—whatever it takes!"

Ebenezer shook his head. "Your grace would give the lass only a temporary boost. She cannot sustain the foreign energy. If you force it, the internal organs will deteriorate—the alveolar ducts would be blocked altogether. Her life may be prolonged by days, but she would end up dying a more gruesome death."

Alpheus held a tight fist, and a surprising number of people in the court shared desolate looks among themselves. And while Marvin felt he was at least partly responsible, and thus was feeling more complicated emotions about the news, the others in the court just seemed genuinely saddened for Azure. Even the king appeared troubled by the information.

"Enough of this," Gaston grumbled now, tapping his walking stick on the floor. "Lord Ebenezer, did Azure say anything about the crown princess?"

"I did as you asked, Lord Gaston," Ebenezer said with his head inclined. "The lass woke sporadically during her treatment until the morning. I interrogated her at every opportunity. In her weak, mumbled speech, she admitted to aiding in the princess's escape. But she claimed to know nothing on her whereabouts at this time."

"Lies!" Gaston said. "She knows something. Force it out of her. Beat her until she talks."

"She's dying already," Marvin said, shooting a glare at the old man. "Isn't that punishment enough?"

Gaston returned a smirk. "What would a brute know about what it means to run a country?"

Marvin narrowed his eyes. But as soon as he held a fist, every knight there drew their swords with a sharp jangle. More than a dozen swords were suddenly pointed his way. Surprisingly, Zabai was the only knight who wasn't part of the formation, but now meeting Marvin's eyes with that hostile gaze she had maintained since the beginning. Zabai turned away her gaze after a moment, meeting the knights with a subtle squint that made them pull back.

Marvin folded his arms then. "I agree that there is merit for Azure to be punished," he said, regarding the king again. "Regardless of any noble reasons, her involvement in sending the princess away cannot be excused. But what she has suffered now is already more than she deserves. As for where the princess is... well, I don't think she knows. Can we just let her live her final days without anyone throwing more guilt upon her?"

"You have some nerve," Gaston said, sneering. "To negotiate while carrying the burden of a crime yourself."

"Allow me to speak a few words," Copper said, raising a hand.

The king narrowed his eyes, but then nodded at Copper.

"I also wish to vouch for Azure," Copper said. "I have spent the last few days in contemplation. And while I can never accept that the princess has left us, I do not believe Azure is to blame. She was only helping a friend. She—"

"Then who *is* to blame?" Gaston interrupted with growing more and more impatient. "Is it *you*, Lord Copper?"

"Yes," Copper said regretfully. "I *am* at fault. I could have done more. But the one who ultimately forced the princess to depart is...," and he paused there for a moment, hesitating as he looked up at the king. "That person is you, Your Majesty... and all of those in your entourage."

"Absurdity!" Gaston cried, already gesturing for soldiers. "Silent that fool for me, and—"

"I am not done!" Copper retorted, his tone growing more aggressive. "I have given my life to serve Your Majesty and the Dominion, and I will honour that until the day I die. That, however, does not mean I agree with the Dominion's every decision and all its values. It is those values—those strict social codes—that drove the princess out."

Gaston was about to holler at him again, but the king raised a hand. "Go on, Lord Copper," the king said. "Elaborate."

Copper bowed in acknowledgement. "To explain why the princess chose to leave, allow me to begin with how she saw her life. It may surprise some of you that Princess Flora was a scholar, a member of the academy."

Marvin was surprised, and felt more so as he noted a few noblemen and some knights raising their brows at this new assertion.

"I do not expect many people to know this," Copper continued, peering about and meeting the eyes of his audience, "for she was never seen in the academy. She wasn't ranked alongside her peers, who barely realised that she was a peer. It bothered her, and she wanted to be involved. On a chance occasion, she made her own trip to a place all the other scholars had visited—the Violanola Woodlands. And that was where she met *him*.

"This man is a talented artist. Through his works, his charms, and his genuine care for *being*, he connected with Princess Flora almost instantly. I cannot disclose his name here, not before all the lords. If Your Majesty wishes to know," he said, turning to the king, "I shall tell you later in private."

The king shook his head. "So how is it that I drove the princess out? How is this man you speak of related?"

Copper sighed. "The man was not a nobleman, and that meant that he would never be admitted into Radiance's Nest to be recognised as the princess's partner. For the past year, the princess has hinted more than several times her wish to grant status to people from all walks of life, so long that they prove worthy. But her words were always dismissed before they were even given a chance to be up for discussion. The Purification Ceremony forced her into a dilemma she had wished to avoid—to contemplate escape. The truth is that I had hoped to convince her to stay. And I was confident I could do so... until..."

Copper trailed off, grimacing toward Alpheus. "Until *he* appeared," he said, causing Alpheus to raise a brow.

"The problem I presented that day," Copper continued, "and the way you negated it. It presented the princess with a viable alternative."

"I don't know what you're talking about," Alpheus said.

Copper huffed out a long breath. "Then allow me to remind you. I spoke about the king salmon and its undesirable fate of regress if it were to diverge from its comfort zone and swim against the stream. The story was based on *Going with the Flow*, an old fable that teaches people to be grateful of where and who they are, their place in society—and the virtue of cooperative effort. I added a twist to foretell the fate of *not* going with the flow." He paused there, turning back to the king. "The allusion was clear to the princess. I had hoped to stage the scenario for Alpheus Hindlow to convince the princess *not* to give up her royal identity.

"Except," Copper added, regarding Alpheus again, "he negated the theory and went on to assert that the pioneers of the world are those most willing to explore new possibilities, and that those who pave a path for themselves are the real champions of the land."

Those were not the specific words Alpheus had used, but the meaning behind it was the same. Marvin didn't know too much about it himself, but it appeared that Alpheus was finally starting to make sense of a few things now.

"But I am not here to indict Alpheus Hindlow," Copper said. "He did nothing wrong. His words inspired everyone there, including me. Though now, as I think back, I believe the princess's decision to leave was largely her own. As for Azure, she was simply doing what she could to help her liege. And as Marvin Sailanson said, I do not believe that Azure knows where the princess is. Ignorance, in this case, serves to protect both sides."

"A charming story, Lord Copper," Zabai said with a smirk. "But while you ratify the notions of forbidden love and noble friendship, you seem to have forgotten how the Dominion is affected. Need I remind you that this is high treason. You are a member of the court, Lord Copper. The crown princess's folly can be excused for her youth, but you and that foolish maid should know better than to connive—essentially telling her it was all right to leave her responsibilities behind. For that alone, both you and the lass are culpable of much more than you have thus far endured."

Copper frowned, unable to conjure any retort. He peered over to Gaston, who simply scoffed at him.

"The knights stand by Lady Zabai's word," one of the knights inserted with a gruff voice. "The least the lass deserves is execution. And you, Lord Copper, should also—"

"No!" a nobleman interjected, a middle-aged man with a dark beard. "Lord Copper did what he could. And Azure... she's already on her deathbed. She should be pardoned—if not for anything else, then at least for her health condition."

"What of the enormous risk her actions has placed our country's security at?" another knight remarked. "How is this even a discussion?"

The back and forth debate grew suddenly fierce. And as it went on, the king held his head in despair. What was going through his mind now was anyone's guess.

"Silence!" the king finally cried out, sweeping an arm out. He peered down at his men, then leaned forward as his eyes narrowed at Copper. "You have disappointed me, Lord Copper. I am not so foolish as to kill off someone who is as able and loyal as you. But from this day on, I never want to see you here at Radiance's Nest. Let your retribution be done away from Poppaross. Do you accept?"

Copper cleared his throat. "Yes," he said, nodding. He hesitated then. "And… dare I ask, what of Azure?"

The king fell quiet for a moment as he stroked his beard. "Azure shall be banished," he declared at a resounding volume. "For what she has done, Vinawell no longer considers her one of our own. She will be given a week to depart. That is more mercy than I should be giving. Once that time is past, it will be the task of every Dominion member to kill her if she is seen trotting within the domain. Am I understood?"

A few of the less forgiving people in attendance, including Gaston, Zabai, and Ebenezer, were the first to nod to the task. But even they must have been puzzled by the decision. A week to depart was meaningless when Azure would likely not even live for that long. Most of the other men, though, exchanged worried looks, several of them sharing mumbles of dissent.

"Am I understood?" the king asked again, in a roaring pitch this time.

The rest of the men bowed down then, despite their reluctance. Banishment was far from a merry result of a court meeting, and the demand for Azure to depart in such a short time was harsh. The death sentence was often seen as the worst punishment, but in Azure's current condition, it would have perhaps been more sympathetic. Ebenezer had promised that no one could save her, so dying in her homeland might have been a sad final wish.

The king dismissed the men there, asking only for Copper and Gaston to remain. As the rest of the men streamed out, Alpheus gestured at Marvin, who nodded in return. They eyed Ebenezer together. As they strode toward him, they noted Robinette also pacing toward the mage to ask the same question they wanted to ask. Ebenezer regarded them all with a squint. He then shook his head and sighed.

"Come with me," he said.

FIFTEEN

Driven by grace

Azure didn't have the capacity to worry about what had ensued in the court just yet. She was still unconscious, and dying. The physicians who had been treating her gave up on her as soon as the news of her banishment had reached their ears. Alpheus kneeled by her bedside now, holding her frosty hand. Marvin and Robinette watched from behind in lamentation.

Azure's face was pale. Her lips were colourless. Besides a faint heartbeat, she looked as good as dead.

Marvin had told Alpheus all he knew, or at least what he thought he knew. Marvin claimed that Azure had had it rough, that she had parted ways from the princess—her closest friend—forever. And that she had been trying to correct what she had done, in her own way. Alpheus realised as much—that Azure must be seen as kindly, at least in the eyes of many of those in Radiance's Nest. Not only had many lords pleaded for Azure's case in the court, but some of them had personally dropped by to see her.

It seemed implausible that a maid had somehow won over all those people, but Alpheus was too worn out to think. His mind was blank. In fact, he barely noticed how much time had passed until Marvin and Robinette retreated, and when he himself was overcome by fatigue.

Alpheus woke up again on the light sensation of something trickling over his ear—something cold and unforgiving. He snapped his eyes open and sat up to recognise it was Azure's fingers stroking his ear.

Azure had rolled her head to the right of the hard pillow and was now gazing out at him. She was finally awake. And in response, Alpheus forced the biggest grin he could manage.

"You're awake!" Alpheus said.

A long, weary blink was her only response. She then opened her mouth to speak, and Alpheus was quick to lean in, holding her hands. It seemed that her entire body was frozen stiff.

"How... how long do I have left?" Azure uttered.

"What do you mean?" Alpheus said, feigning confusion. "You have a lifetime!"

She closed her eyes and managed a half-smile. "Tell me the truth," she said, her voice almost a whisper. "I can handle it."

His eyes flooded. "No, really..., you'll be all right."

She blinked slowly again, barely managing to open up her eyes. "Don't expend any more energy on me."

He gaped at her, unsure what she meant.

Azure coughed hoarsely. "Don't underestimate me. I feel a vibrant energy flowing inside me—an energy flow I only knew about from publications... until now. This is grace... right? You're a magic user."

"I..."

"Thank you, Alpheus. But I can feel it rapidly draining away... it cannot last. One cannot rely on another to give them life."

More tears gushed out of Alpheus. Azure seemed to have somewhat made her peace with her own death, and now a stream of gurgling red blood surged from her mouth, driving her to cough and stain the bed sheets.

Alpheus hid his horror and panic the best he could. He wiped the blood around her mouth with some cloths that the physicians had left, all the while reassuring her that everything would be all right.

"I don't have much longer, Alpheus," the maid said. "I cannot worry about my life. But I value integrity. I want to know what the Dominion decided."

To save her from having to say more, Alpheus relayed to her the discussion at the court. He didn't lie about the outcome, her banishment, but he covered up other negatives with ornamental words.

"The king is wise... and generous," Azure said. "I really *don't* know. Carmen and I made sure we didn't know. Only that way could Princess Flora be free."

She coughed then, spewing out another few spatters of blood.

"I believe you," Alpheus said, wiping her clean of the scarlet red a second time. "But please, save your energy."

She held his hand this time. "No, I need to say this. About you..., I apologise. I *used* you. That's the truth. But it was only to aid in the princess's escape."

"It doesn't matter anymore," Alpheus said, shaking his head.

"I didn't want to involve you, but—"

She trailed off there, as her discomfort visibly worsened. She hollered in pain, her hands and feet tensing up as if the veins within them were going to burst. Alpheus held her down urgently, hoping to calm her and somehow alleviate her pain. But the contact, as careful as he was, only added to the aching. Azure jerked, kicking her feet up and clawing at what she could.

It was all chaos until Ebenezer treaded in. The mage rushed forward and pushed Alpheus aside, clasping the patient by the skull and then channelling his luminous green energy into her. Azure grew warmer immediately, and her pain soon subsided as she was put to sleep once more.

Alpheus glanced away from the bed to see Marvin and Copper standing at the door. It became clear to him then that it was Marvin who had sought Ebenezer, and only with Copper's persuasion had the mage agreed to come there. Alpheus smiled at them and expressed his gratitude.

"It's too early to rejoice," Ebenezer said. "I cannot perform miracles. As I have said, the damage is irreversible. She *will* die."

"Is there nothing we can do?" Copper asked.

Ebenezer shook his head. "Theoretically, a reconstruction of the damaged alveolar ducts is a solution," he said. "Unfortunately, such a surgical repair in this situation is impossible given that she would have to be cut open before one could navigate through to the specific organs that require reassembly."

Alpheus held his head in despair as his eyes wandered blankly.

"I do have a suggestion," Ebenezer said, stepping into Alpheus's blurred field of vision. "The maid is due for banishment. If we left her, she wouldn't last a couple days. But with your help, she could live for another month."

"A month?" Alpheus uttered.

"In this month, we will be on our way to Zorlia. The maid can live longer. And her banishment will be satisfied."

Alpheus looked up with a gape. *Zorlia*, the word ringing in his head, almost without meaning. Ebenezer frowned in response, perhaps reading Alpheus's indifference. The mage held a hand over his mouth, however, to avoid speaking too soon.

Amid the silence, Marvin chuckled once, which then transformed into full-throated laughter. It wasn't a time to be laughing, but his wide grin and glistening eyes showed that somehow, he had found a reason to.

"Alpheus, you take that lass!" he said in the most upbeat tone anyone had heard in a while. "But not to Zorlia. Head south—to the *Harper Ranges*, in Southern Vinawell. Find *that man*. He can save her."

Alpheus turned to him, feeling a sudden hint of hope. "*That* man?"

"The Passionless Surgeon. His name is synonymous with miracles in healing. There has even been talk of resurrection."

The name was familiar to Alpheus. Hartland had mentioned it once before departing the city. Legends described the man to be of Kragan ancestry, and despite the antipathy the Southerners attracted, this man was widely adored for his godly ability in healing. Rumours suggested that he had once represented the mighty Millenzburg Empire, the former ruling government of Kraga. But following the succession of the current government—led by Szaran Wandalvic—it was believed that he had left the country altogether. He was rarely documented in contemporary articles, and that meant his existence itself was a dubious matter.

"Why the Harper Rangers?" Alpheus asked.

"Don't know," Marvin said with a shrug, "but he was spotted there not too long ago."

Ebenezer smirked. "Over half a year ago."

"He's no adventurer," Marvin said, "so there's a good chance he's still there."

"And you are basing that on intuition, or just some wild assumption?" the mage remarked. "Even if he were there, did you consider the size of the mountain range? How would one navigate and pinpoint just where he might be?"

"The mountain range covers an enormous area," Alpheus acknowledged. "To locate a single man in that vicinity would be close to impossible, I know. But my knowledge of the area, even if from books, can help me. Working with the method of elimination, much of the range can be disregarded. I'll take Azure there and I'll find the physician."

Marvin nodded at Alpheus with a grin. Copper smiled as well. Ebenezer, though, was growing more and more frustrated with the discussion.

"What about Zorlia?" Ebenezer asked Alpheus. "What about your criminal status?"

Alpheus pondered for a moment, and then eyed Azure again. "I appreciate the offer, but I have to help her. And before you depart, Lord Ebenezer, I must know how to strengthen her vitality until I find the physician."

The mage's eyes flared. "You really mean to do this? For her? A maid?"

Alpheus nodded.

Ebenezer shook his head with a huff, but then went on to calm himself. "Perhaps you would change your mind if you knew the purpose behind my trip to the Truban capital," he said. He paused then and shot a glance at Copper and then at Marvin. "Very well, I guess it doesn't hurt if you all knew. The Dominion is sending me to probe into any hostile activity from the Truban Empire. We have learned about the rise of sorcerers in Zorlia, and the rift among the Truban court. We are wary of the Trubans. We want to trust them, but we do not."

"I don't trust them, either," Alpheus said.

Ebenezer sighed. "Yeremia Schim penned a letter requesting my services. We hardly expected it, but it's the perfect opportunity to see for myself just what is going on in Zorlia. The letter spoke about the sorcerers and the threat they pose. And the messenger who delivered the letter claimed that he had evaded the Truban emperor altogether."

"And what is it that you're getting at?" Alpheus asked, noting that Marvin raised a brow.

"As we see it, the Truban Empire is in the midst of a violent transformation. There shall be bloodshed, plenty of it. And, depending on what results, everyone else may be entangled in the mess. I don't want to see another war. That's why we are planning to—"

"Say no more," Alpheus interrupted. "I'm not the noblest of people, but I don't wait to see a war, either. I want to help. I really do, and I promise I will... as soon as this is done. Zorlia can wait."

"It can... *wait*?!" the mage bellowed, his eyes widening in disbelief. "The well-being of the world can *wait*?"

Alpheus furrowed his brow. "Please, show me how to prolong Azure's life. She'll have to live on my grace, right?"

The mage fell silent. It certainly didn't look like Ebenezer *needed* Alpheus's company, but for some reason, he had pushed for it time and again. Ebenezer looked over to Marvin, probably betting on the likelihood that the ex-mercenary would at least berate Alpheus, if not help with the convincing. But Marvin simply shrugged. And so, too, did Copper, who now nodded at him.

"Please help him," Copper said. "Teach him to channel his energy."

The mage glared at the nobleman and inhaled deeply, before finally breathing out a dejected sigh. "Very well," he said, turning to Alpheus again. "You will have two days, for I shall depart on schedule. And the maid shall be deported without delay."

* * *

Alpheus would be forever indebted to the training he received in the past two days, amassing even more knowledge than he actually needed, some of which he could follow-up on in the future. There was much to memorise and a heaping pressure to learn all he could in the limited time available. He routinely looked up to the heavens for inspiration, praying often to the double crescent at his wrist.

By the conclusion of the second day, Alpheus was done. He had even managed to earn some rare praise from his teacher. More importantly, however, he was confident that he could keep Azure alive for a month, and maybe more. He expressed his gratitude to Ebenezer, and he also whispered words of appreciation to his faith. His prayers were answered, he believed, attributing little of the credit to his own strong foundation in human anatomy.

Alpheus learned that powering lifeless objects was uncomplicated, because those objects didn't react. This was in contrast to living organisms which were sure to respond if suddenly surged with a foreign energy, whether the organism intended it or not. The biological processes of any being would make sure to trigger an answer, between accepting and rejecting a call. From a bee to the flower it pollinated, life was consistently active. People—as more complicated beings—were the most delicate of the chain, with a deluge of possible responses to the signal of another's energy.

According to Ebenezer, there were four categories of energy, each represented by the elements: earth, water, air, and fire. People possessed energy made up of all four, and the task needed for the efficient channelling of energy was to understand these proportions, as each reacted in its own way. As a start, each person could be classified under one of the four elements—this was the dominant or central energy which represented more than half of the person's chemical build. Earth was characterised by a rigid, glob-like flow. Water ran in smooth streams. Air whiffed about in puffs. And fire swelled with a forceful presence.

This series of elements matched the different groupings of sorcery that Alpheus had once learned from Kathryn Trulips. It was the same concept, but in disguise. The key difference was Ebenezer's emphasis on the claim that every living thing—and certainly not only sorcerers—possessed these powers.

While it seemed simple enough to match a flow to its element in terms of identifying one's dominant energy, the proportions of each was difficult to determine when all those conflicting flows of energy pulsed together.

In the case of giving energy, adjustments were made to suit the recipient based on the preceding analysis of the subject. The intricacy lied in regulating the correct strength and speed of the energy flow to match a given subject, and on the specific neurons that required attention. With thousands of unique neurons inside the body and multiples of that number of organs which could react in different ways, one had to be stringent—otherwise, the good intentions of trying to help could instead aggravate existing problems. The positive for Alpheus was that both he and Azure were *water dominant*, and that alone paved the way for a smoother process.

In the few times during these couple of days which Alpheus had allowed himself a breather, he had been approached by various people of the court. They had expressed their appreciation for his efforts to help Azure. According to some of them, Azure's stand on the Imperial Lithia Dominion, in recent years, was one of the greatest that had gone unrecognised. Apparently, the maid would occasionally attend the court behind the crown princess, encouraging her liege to speak up on social inequality, advising her plenty. And while it was often impractical to simply *fight* for the unfortunate, she and the princess had offered—on more than several occasions—surprisingly cost-effective proposals to offset the burden on the Dominion. Azure was sympathetic to those cast with misfortune, and was committed to uphold the integrity of the country.

Her contributions were far from the most significant at court, but apparently Azure had helped to shape the post-war Dominion into a government that was more compassionate and forgiving. It wasn't easy to forgive her for what had happened, or to forgive the princess, for that matter. But it was a time for reflection. She had been banished. She was never to set foot in the city or the country again after her departure. And it appeared that she would clearly be missed.

As Alpheus recalled the evening when her banishment had been announced, he remembered that more than a few of those at court had shown their concern for Azure. Alpheus didn't need any extra reason to help her, but it was comforting to know that the maid was so well-loved by her own people.

Despite the loving messages and the challenge of learning everything he could learn from Ebenezer, however, the most difficult task on Alpheus's part was to convince Azure to go on this journey. Azure didn't like the idea of lying to the Dominion, lying about leaving the country, and instead trekking southwards. And for what? To find a man whose very existence was a matter of dispute?

The wound on her shoulder was going to heal in time, but the aching pain of the alveoli would only worsen with time. She didn't know much about how she might be healed, but she seemed sure that her body was failing. The throbbing pain seemed overwhelming at certain times of the day, at which time she had probably wished she could end her life right there, rather than endure it and struggle through what might only be a losing battle. Given her usual liveliness, this miserable condition was torture. She didn't want to burden anyone, especially after she had learned that Alpheus had given up the opportunity for his name to be cleared in Zorlia.

"I'm not going anywhere," she said defiantly. "I don't need your sympathy. I don't need charity. Who do you think you are, making these decisions for me?"

Alpheus remained calm amid the shouting. He continued to smile at her affectionately.

"This is not charity," he simply said.

"You're wasting your time..., your effort, and your energy, on a *cripple*! I cannot do anything anymore! I cannot move around by myself. I cannot—" She coughed, gurgling out a mix of blood and saliva. Then she began to weep. "I cannot even breathe without constantly reminding myself that I must. I don't need this treatment. I don't deserve it."

Her temper waned as she spoke, but only because her body was failing her again. Her eyes were flooded with tears, and she breathed heavily. She clawed her fingers into her chest where her lungs were slowly clogging up. In spite of the pain, she gathered all the strength she could to swing her arm to point at the door.

"Leave!" she cried. "I don't want to see you!"

Alpheus didn't leave. Instead, he wrapped the frail young lady in his arms, who resisted at first until she succumbed to exhaustion. He gently sat her down on the bed with her legs criss-crossed. Alpheus then sat down, too, behind her. According to Ebenezer, this position was ideal for the energy transfer between people.

Alpheus thrust his palm onto the maid's back.

His sparkling light blue energy gleamed brilliantly and flowed smoothly into her body. Charged with the vibrant energy from hundreds of neurons spreading all over her body, Azure's circulatory system was effectively restored to a safe level within a short while. But despite the invigoration, she still didn't thank him. She had recovered enough strength to lash out at him, but she didn't do that, either.

"I've failed people important to me in the past," Alpheus said. "I don't want to fail you, too."

Azure's rage turned slowly into empathy as Alpheus continued. He spoke about Agnes and how she had lost her vision because of him.

"I haven't forgotten about her," Alpheus said. "I haven't given up on her. This journey to locate the physician—it's not only for you. It's for her, too."

Azure flushed, looking away. "Is she... your lover?"

Alpheus shook his head. "I see her as a sister. When we have you all well again, perhaps we can go to Zorlia to see her."

"What...?"

"You asked me to take you to Zorlia one day, didn't you? On the rooftop—we made our promise there."

Azure teared up again.

"I promised to take you there," Alpheus continued. "And I will. But first, I want you to be my guide. I want you to show me Southern Vinawell. I want to see the valley of Mt. Meridian. I want to climb all of the mountains there. Only after that, maybe, just *maybe* we'll go to Zorlia.

"Azure, believe me, we'll be together for a long time. I'm not ready to lose you."

PART IV

SIXTEEN

A new journey

Ebenezer had departed the castle earlier in the morning, and the monarch had been there to bid him farewell. Alpheus and Azure's departure didn't quite command an appearance from His Majesty, but in place of the king's absence was a much larger crowd, each one wearing ribbons of white that represented wellness. Many in the crowd were established members of the court, and all of them—in one way or another—had been on the receiving end of Azure's mischief. But they had only well wishes today, a few of them saying that their lives had been touched upon by her in ways that Azure herself hadn't realised.

One of the lords described how Azure had helped repair his relationship with his estranged daughter. Another lord, who had once been a top scholar, described Azure as *naturally wise*. Apparently, Azure had convinced him to give up being a scholar because she thought it wasn't his purpose in life. He had initially been annoyed by her persistent prying, but later on *realised* that Azure had been right from the beginning. This older lord described himself as *contented* despite no longer being recognised with the high status and merit that he had used to enjoy.

Each story varied, but the common assent was that the girl had shown them what it was to laugh. She had shown them not to take life so seriously, and not to get caught up in the perpetual flow of decisions and events that everyone was subject to. Some claimed that she had brought a dash of glee on the court, a place that had never cared for whimsy. And she had done so in the most subtle manner, never claiming any credit, or perhaps never setting out to do so.

To Alpheus, it didn't look in the slightest like Azure was being banished, and the only reminder was Gaston's warning on the day prior that no one was to lend their support to her—the convicted. And abiding by that, no one offered any parting gifts of materialistic value—that is, no one except Copper, who presented them with two black horses, his own equine companions that had been trained to endure long journeys and harsh conditions. The animals drew a draped wagon that was light in construction, a cabin the size of a compact bed. Inside was a cushioned pad that could be folded up as a seat or pulled out as a bed. The drapes were sewn to thick linen, reminiscent of sailcloth, and could be opened on all sides except for the rear. A compartment beneath the cabin was stocked with rations and warm clothing.

Alpheus watched as Azure was helped into the coach by two servants. Her visibly weak condition had some men grimacing at first, but those wry faces soon blossomed optimistic grins, for they appeared to expect nothing less for her than good fortune and a full recovery. They believed that she would live on, and that she deserved to. And that was despite their ignorance that she was heading off in search of the Passionless Surgeon, a secret kept exclusive to Alpheus and a few other people.

Azure was seated inside the cabin now with the drapes open as the people waved her goodbye. Whether it was because of the people who were there for her, their prayers for her, the strips of white ribbon dangling at their necks, or the thought that she wasn't to return, Azure was flooded with emotions. No one heard her, not even Alpheus, but she mouthed her words of gratitude more than a few times, each time with more tears flowing down her cheeks.

Copper handed a riding crop to Alpheus. "We're counting on you."

"I'm grateful," Alpheus said with a half-smile. "But... the consequences—"

"Let Azure be your only concern," Copper said, leaning in closer to whisper. "And don't worry about being chased out of the country. That won't happen. You just head down to the Harper Ranges to find that physician. I assure you that you won't be hassled by any soldiers on your way."

Alpheus nodded, recognising that Copper had undergone some trouble in order to ensure their safety. "I'll return the favour one day," he said.

"It was His Majesty's doing, actually," Copper said, still whispering. "Azure's banishment shall stand, but how strictly it is enforced is..., well, this can be adjusted. His Majesty had known this when he made the decision."

Alpheus widened his eyes for a moment, wondering if the king really had planned for this. Alpheus nodded one last time at Copper. He then leaped onto the coachman's seat, pulling on the reins. The animals neighed, and they began strolling away from the crowd.

When they reached the foot of the hill, the crowd couldn't be seen anymore. There, they happened by Zabai and her page, who were travelling in the opposite direction, apparently returning to the castle. The strongest warrior of the country seemed to be fully healed from the scramble with the Sail Band, donning her mahogany armour again. She paid Alpheus no heed, but Robinette managed a nod of acknowledgement in his direction. Alpheus reciprocated the amicability, drawing the carriage to a halt.

"Lady Zabai," Alpheus said, "would you happen to know where Marvin is?"

Zabai shrugged. "He could be anywhere."

Alpheus waited, expecting her to say more.

"The Sail Band have been convicted of multiple cases of theft in the last week," Robinette said in place of her liege. "They're most likely in hiding now."

Zabai frowned. "It may have been a coincidence," she added. "But all those reported to have been crossed were already listed as crooks by the Dominion. If you happen by Sailanson, tell him to stop undermining us. We're capable of defending our own regulations."

Zabai glanced into the coach where Azure sat, mostly hidden in the shade. She narrowed her eyes then and turned away. Alpheus watched her recede up the hill, apparently allowing Robinette the chance to stay behind a moment and say a few words.

"Go where you need to go," the young knight said gravely, "without qualms about having to avoid authority. Lady Zabai has given the order. No one is to harass you."

"Thank you," Alpheus said.

Robinette looked into the coach. "Save her," she said simply.

Azure nodded slightly to convey her appreciation. Robinette didn't return any such gesture, instead frowning slightly before trotting away. Alpheus watched her recede as well, and then glanced inside the coach, exchanging a smile with Azure.

"Off we go," he said.

* * *

They set off west toward the state of Sequiposa. According to the map, they would have to pass through several towns on their journey. They had no specific destination as of yet, and their search would only begin when they reached the mouth of the Harper Ranges at the northern end of the forest of

Central Vinawell. Most of the road along the way was conveniently paved with gravel, and that allowed them a steady pace on this first day.

By noon, they had completely left the capital city behind. Some indicators were the more sparsely lined buildings that were half the height of those in Poppaross, and the obvious decrease in the number of people walking the streets. Soldier patrols were relatively scarce, and as Copper and Robinette had foretold, no one representing the Dominion stood in the way of Alpheus's wagon. Curiously, some of the towns bordering the capital were the most affluent in the country. It was evident that the wealthy people in Vinawell preferred living at the cusp of the larger cities rather than within them, a custom that contrasted the psychology of Trubans, who saw living in Zorlia as a privilege, or at least a display of esteemed social status.

In the afternoon of the second day, they stopped at a humble stall that sold grilled fish. They had reached the border that separated the states of Astilow and Sequiposa, and it was their last chance for a nourishing meal before they would rely solely on the tasteless sustenance stored under the cabin, which consisted mainly of bread and nuts.

The modest stall was set up on the roadside with folds of old cloth sewn on wooden poles to shield the few tables from possible rain, wind, or snow. They served nothing but fish and coriander. It looked like a family-run business, an elderly couple at the grill and their adult children delivering the dishes. Alpheus had offered Azure the option of staying in the wagon, but she had insisted that she needed fresh air, which meant that Alpheus had to carry her out on his back. Though she looked better than she had the day prior, any passer-by could see that she was unwell. No one said anything about it, though. They were probably more curious about why she was in the care of a foreigner. Despite the open alliance between the two countries, Trubans were rarely seen anywhere in the country other than in Poppaross and Aragon.

Still, the people who ran the stall were more than hospitable. For the half hour during which they stayed, Alpheus was given some recommendations on the most efficient ways to get to their destination—the Harper Ranges. But with that came a warning from the elderly man that they must be wary of the bandits who frequented the road ahead.

The sun was about to set. Their journey had been without obstacles thus far, but Alpheus was conscious that these first two days would prove to be the most relaxed and carefree. Indeed, as soon as they raced through to Sequiposa, the relatively flat gravel road began winding left and right, with steep curves on the uneven hills. Adding to the challenge was the glare on the horizon cast by the setting sun that almost blinded him each time he looked ahead. Ignoring it the best that he could, Alpheus treaded forward with the next stopover firmly in mind, which was at least another hour away.

Some fifteen minutes in, however, Alpheus found himself confronted with more opposition than just the glaring sun. Behind the almost-red refraction of light before him were the silhouettes of people he couldn't identify immediately. The strangers were still a good distance away, but they were growing in size, indicating their steady approach.

Alpheus frowned, pulling the reins as the horses came to a stop. This was no time to struggle or to risk hurt. Powering their way through wasn't an option on this narrow part of the road. Fleeing with the Glider Steps was the safest option, but that would mean they would have to abandon their horses and wagon so early in the journey, which would inevitably prove disastrous.

Behind him, Azure brushed aside the drapes to see.

"Get back in," Alpheus said, a bead of sweat sliding down his right cheek.

Azure didn't listen, instead pulling herself forward with Alpheus's sleeves. She showed no fear, despite her weak condition.

"You have to relax," she said with a squint forward. "Your nerves are clouding your judgement. Look carefully."

She was completely calm, and upon seeing that, Alpheus turned to face forward again. He squinted until he finally recognised who was approaching, and he let out a sigh of relief. Before them were indeed a group of *bandits*—and they were much more potent than Alpheus feared, except they were his allies.

The Sail Band.

"How is our favourite bookworm doing?" Ash called out to Alpheus as his silhouette emerged into a discernible form.

Trailing immediately behind him were Marvin, Rover, and Tavie. They were dressed again in the way Alpheus had known them before, in modest tops woven from percale fabric and sturdy leather.

The crew offered to lead Alpheus and Azure to a place to settle in for the night, an abandoned chapel a little further down the path. Alpheus was conscious that he and Azure were pressed for time, but his companion—the one who was in fact racing against time—didn't share his urgency. Azure seemed delighted to see the thieves, especially Marvin, and encouraged the crew to hop onto the wagon.

By the time they reached the chapel, only a glimmer of daylight was still dabbing the darkened sky with colour. After lighting a few oil lamps and seating themselves on the worn-out benches, Azure finally asked about Carmen.

Marvin, who sat on his own bench at the front of the chapel, frowned. "Before we get into that, I want to get a few things straight," he said.

Azure turned her head slightly, and the bandit leader paused for a moment. "I'm sorry," Marvin finally said, his tone more solemn than Alpheus had known he was capable of.

"It wasn't your fault," Alpheus promptly inserted. "What happened that night was impossible to anticipate."

Marvin shook his head. "True. Yet, I *thought* I could anticipate it. The mission was a complete failure, and because of that, we will no longer be involved in this matter."

"But," Azure said, "what about..."

"Don't worry," Marvin assured. "With Karl and Leo in escort, the girl's in good hands. She should be in Dorellsdale by now."

"Dorellsdale...? In Trubannis?" Azure asked with a faint voice. "But... she's never been there before..."

As she trailed off, running out of breath, Alpheus began speaking for her. "I think she's saying that Carmen will have difficulty adapting to life in Trubannis. From the looks of it, the king has grown rather lenient on this matter. Carmen can probably escape prosecution if she were to return to Poppaross."

Azure nodded, but Marvin didn't seem to believe it.

"A *safe place* was all we promised," Marvin said, gesturing that he wouldn't hear anything else about it. "A deal's a deal."

Despite how simple it might be for him to grant her wishes, Marvin stood firm. He left Azure with no grounds for arguing. The maid scowled at him but Marvin showed his own displeasure with knitted eyebrows. The spark of tension between them wasn't anything new, but it was a tad surprising that Marvin was being so rigid about it.

Marvin stood up from the bench then and walked toward Azure and Alpheus. He stepped in front of them and reached into one of the pouches hanging at his belt, slipping out the glowing pearl bracelet that belonged to the princess. Under the muted ambience of the oil lamps, the bracelet illuminated magnificently, with a gloss reminiscent of a white moon. Marvin reached for Azure's wrist, taking her hand.

"There's another reason why I won't do more," Marvin said as he slipped the bracelet on her wrist. "The mission was a failure. This bracelet is a reminder of that. Let things be as they were."

Ash and Tavie leaned forward, perhaps hoping to deter their leader from gifting away their only reward for their efforts. They said nothing, though. And they soon fell back again.

Marvin crouched down next to Azure, who didn't seem to have expected a gift, either. "If you want to see your friend," Marvin said, "go to her by yourself—after you come back healthy."

Azure widened her eyes, looking a little livelier under the beautiful glow. She said nothing, however, and after a moment, Marvin retreated back to his own bench.

"I'll take the bracelet again in the future," Marvin said, dropping down heavily. "But I have something tedious to attend to, and I want you to keep it for the time being. The next time we meet is when I'll take it back. At that time, I want to see the feisty girl in you again."

"Thank you," she finally said as she brushed her fingers across the bracelet.

* * *

Alpheus found sleep elusive that night, and in his wakefulness, he noticed that Marvin and Rover had snuck out of the chapel, one after the other. He didn't think he had the capacity to worry for much more than Azure's health, but the *something tedious* that had come out from Marvin's mouth had him thinking. He sat up now and prayed that he wouldn't regret his decision that he had to find out what this was all about. Without waking the others, he quietly exited the old building.

Following Ebenezer's teachings about how to control his energy, Alpheus managed to not only sense where the thieves had headed off to, but also to compress his flow of grace to a level that no one would be able to sense his presence. He didn't think to celebrate the attainment of such a valuable skill right at this moment, though. He had pinpointed his targets' direction and distance in seconds, and was now already tracking them with guile.

Alpheus caught up to them after a few minutes, and he hid behind one of the larger trees in the area. Neither Marvin nor Rover seemed to realise that he was there. They were in mid-conversation, speaking in a grave undertone—or perhaps that was simply how any conversation with Rover went.

"You don't have to come," Marvin said, leaning against a tree. "I can bear the burden alone."

Rover snorted quietly. "Since when did you become so soft? Or did you think *I* had grown soft? The man called for the both of us. Even if I wanted nothing to do with it, he'd chase me until the end."

This was probably the most Alpheus had heard Rover speak at once, and it was the first time he had ever seen fear in him, even if subtle.

"I'll keep him busy," Marvin said. "Or... I'll die trying."

"Why do you always have to be the hero?"

Marvin shook his head. "Ro, I have a bad feeling about this. He's changed. I really don't want any more people than necessary to be involved. Besides, I need you to take care of the team."

"This is Spartamon we're talking about," Rover said with a wince. "He'll hunt all of us down if he had to."

Upon realising that the discussion surrounded the Lord Emperor, Alpheus stepped out from where he was hiding. Marvin and Rover were startled for less than a moment, their surprise likely owing to how Alpheus had managed to conceal his presence more so than that he had heard their conversation.

"What are *you* doing here?" Marvin asked.

"This is about Zorlia, isn't it?" said Alpheus. "Let me in on it."

Rover grinned. "Afraid this is beyond you."

"Perhaps," Alpheus said, feeling desolate. "Perhaps I *am* powerless. And perhaps Zorlia has given up on me." He then held a fist. "But I care. I do. I want to help, if I can."

"Get your priorities straight," Marvin said. "Azure needs you more than Zorlia."

"I know. And I'm not saying I'm going to challenge the emperor now. But to honour those important to me, I have to play a part as well."

The two men didn't seem intrigued in the least. They were about to dismiss him when Alpheus shot out a marble in surprise, trailed with the illumination of his airy blue energy. The projectile rooted into the trunk of a larch tree. And at first, nothing more happened, but soon the glow of the projectile began seeping out in all directions across the rest of the plant, almost like streams of luminous paint. The advance of the spectacular radiance didn't cease until even the tips of every leaf were joined in the same remarkable display.

"So much for trying to be obscure," Marvin said as he looked up at the spectacle.

"I wanted to make a point," Alpheus responded, as the glow gradually wore off.

"Which was what?"

"I'm a sorcerer," Alpheus said, turning solemn. "I've only recently learned to control my power, at least parts of it. I'm not bragging, but clearly sorcery cannot be belittled. And rumours say that Zorlia has become quite the popular place for sorcerers. Apparently, they're being called there by the emperor. I cannot imagine what he wants to achieve, but now that he's called for you as well… I don't know what to make of it, but I'm concerned."

The glow of the tree had completely dissipated by now.

"You said… *apparently*," Marvin said, looking thoughtful. "What do you mean?"

"The Lord Chancellor, Yeremia Schim. He has sent for Ebenezer. The two most powerful men of Zorlia—no, the whole country is at war. The ensuing clash could quite possibly reshape the land as we know it."

Both Marvin and Rover cringed slightly at the mention of the chancellor's name, but neither offered further comment.

"Just watch out for the lass," Marvin said instead, changing the subject. "You find that physician. And… if you manage that, let us meet again in Zorlia."

Alpheus forced a smile. "Yes, let us."

"Don't underestimate your task," Marvin warned. "Though I haven't personally met the Passionless Surgeon, I've heard many stories about him. Regarding this man, I'm certain of two things: he exists, and his healing ability is as incredible as the legends describe. During my tenure as a mercenary, I witnessed on multiple occasions the impossible recovery of some of my strongest enemies. After crushing or even mutilating them, some of them came back in good enough health and strength to confront me a second or even third time. *That* is the ability of the Passionless Surgeon."

Alpheus swallowed the information with mixed emotions. Marvin's description of the man had his bones tingling with both admiration and fear, and he likened the feeling to his experience of meeting the Apostle, which had itself become a distant memory. But he was thankful to hear from Marvin—a war veteran—that the physician existed. This meant that the *only* task, demanding as it might be, was to locate the man and convince him to help Azure.

"I'll find him," Alpheus said. "As for you and the crew… be careful. Zorlia might be in a more precarious situation than it was during the war."

Rover clenched his jaws tightly. "Don't underestimate us, boy. We may not have visited Zorlia for a long time, but we're not your average man."

That kind of confident assurance was what Alpheus wanted to hear. Leaving it there, he had in essence entrusted them to do his bidding—to do Reeling's bidding.

In the morning, the two groups set off in separate directions. Alpheus and Azure continued down south, while Marvin and his group departed east toward Trubannis.

* * *

Members of the Dominion had assumed that the Sail Band had left Poppaross for the petty crimes Zabai held them responsible. They didn't know that Marvin would actually enjoy a game of hide-and-seek. But with the same purpose that Ebenezer had been summoned to Zorlia by Schim, a letter penned by the emperor had been delivered to Marvin. This letter *requesting* the services of Marvin and Rover was light in tone. The emperor spoke about how deeply he cherished the camaraderie he had shared with his brothers in arms, and that he wished to rekindle those memories in the *peaceful* world of today. But Marvin had dreaded the day he would have to confront the emperor again. He expected there to be no rekindling in any form, but rather a renewal of what might be widespread warfare.

There was no escape for Marvin. Even if he ran, his band members would be chased down and taken hostage until he showed up.

The trip from the western border of the state to the eastern edge took five and a half days. Marvin finally arrived in Aragon after having to purposely detour around the city of Poppaross. During these past few days, Marvin had demonstrated a growing detachment toward the others. He struggled to act like his usual self, often quiet in the day and then isolating himself in the evening. Rover, who shared his worries, was similarly quiet, but that perhaps looked normal to the rest the team.

Marvin had noticed that Ash and Tavie had been looking forward to today, in which they would reunite with Leo and Karl, who had since returned to Vinawell. They probably expected that he would cheer up in seeing the other team members. And indeed Marvin was glad to see them, but he didn't let it show.

Aside from Tavie, everyone knew that Marvin and Rover had co-founded the crew. They knew that the two of them had once been mercenaries, and Marvin was sure that they also suspected that he was the infamous *Judge* of the *Noel Gate Incident.* Ash, Leo, and Karl had each individually worked these things out themselves, though they had never once brought it up. Marvin generally avoided any conversations about warfare, and Rover never said much about anything. It was probably surprising to the rest of them, however, that when Alpheus had spoken about the emperor of Trubannis—arguably the most influential figure of the war—Marvin had seemed uninterested when in fact he had done his best to hide some strong emotions and restrain some vivid memories, most of which were bittersweet.

The crew sat inside a seaside tavern now. The dull sky outside coupled with the heavy rain was the prelude to a solemn conversation.

"We had a good run," Marvin began. "I've enjoyed your company more than you could possibly know. But it's time to go our separate ways. Ro and I have some errands to run—matters that don't involve the rest of you. Let this be our last meal together as a team."

Silence filled the air. The bandits eyed each other, probably thinking that this was probably the worst joke ever. But Marvin's wry grin never faded, and he looked each member deep in the eyes, almost hoping to imprint them into his mind.

"All right, this isn't funny," Tavie finally said. "What's the next mission?"

Silence again. Marvin turned to Tavie, and the grateful look in his eyes said it all. He was determined to set off with Rover, and his resolve was strong. No one liked it, though, and Tavie was the first to voice her frustration.

"What's going on all of a sudden?!" she exclaimed. "How can you just decide something like this on your own? We should take a vote as a group. Ash, tell him! Leo! Karl! Say something!"

Ash frowned, and the others simply closed their eyes, realising that it was futile. They knew better than to even try convincing him given his resolute expression.

"I don't believe you can be so selfish!" Tavie yelled, rising to her feet as her hair bristled. "Go! Go wherever you want, but be sure that I'll be on your tail! I'll be in pursuit to the edge of the world!"

Marvin gazed up at her with drooping eyes that conveyed his sorrow. The next moment, he had leapt behind her, and with a light tap on her neck, he knocked her unconscious before catching her limp body before it fell to the ground.

"I'll leave her to you," Marvin said as he handed her over to Ash, who also rose to his feet.

"I don't know what this is about," Ash said with a squint. "But I want to help, and I know I can. There's no one I respect more than the two of you. But as great as the two of you are, our crew performs at its optimal level when we combine all of our talents together. I know we can help. Right? Leo? Karl?"

The big Kragan waved his large hand. "A brief disbandment won't hurt," he said with his characteristic flat tone and deep voice. "Let our leader do what he wants. Maybe an interlude would do us good."

Ash gritted his teeth, tensing up.

"Karl's right," Leo said, adding to the chorus. "This thieving business is amusing, but sometimes I think about settling down. I'd love to live in the country one day, be a shepherd maybe. It's draining to always be on the run."

Marvin smiled, glad for them. He then gestured for them to exit the tavern. The rain had stopped. Warm embraces with Karl and Leo led to straightforward goodbyes. They promised to meet again one day, and soon they treaded out from the tavern, disappearing from view.

Ash puffed out a thwarting breath. "I still want to be part of the action."

Marvin regarded him for a moment and then exchanged a look with Rover. Together, Marvin and Rover rose and turned for the door. Ash was prompt to follow, but the fact that he was still holding Tavie on his back slowed him down. As soon as they stepped out from the tavern, Marvin and Rover dashed down the pier and jumped onto the already moving ferry headed to Dorellsdale with a giant leap that simply wasn't possible for Ash, even if he was on his own and unencumbered.

Marvin turned back, eyeing Ash. "Ro and I will be at full speed. If you can keep up, we'll see you there."

Ash stood desolate at the edge of the pier, his figure diminishing in Marvin's sight as the ferry sailed away.

I appreciate you, Marvin thought. *So very much.* But what was ahead was a piece of history that really shouldn't involve Ash or the others. It was something that even Marvin himself didn't want to revisit.

SEVENTEEN

Movement in Zorlia

Julian was no longer a stranger to the court. The entitlement of working under the Lord Chancellor's direct instruction and sharing the man's perspective, including standing behind him among the court now, allowed Julian to learn what it truly meant to have power in one's grasp.

Of all the wrongs that Schim had accused the emperor of—both publicly and under more private settings—Schim seemed rather content with the fact that the emperor continued to make people wait. The emperor was still the last one to arrive to court, usually making others wait for him for nearly an hour.

Julian peered over to the empty seat across him. He swallowed as he imagined the Lord Count perched there. It had been nearly three months since the man's departure, and the order he had worked so hard to preserve was gradually falling apart. Julian had been working tirelessly with Schim to uphold the Lord Count's work, but the tension on the court had continued to intensify with every passing day. The worst part was that the discord had spilled over to the common people. The tumultuous times of the previous era suddenly didn't seem so long ago. Zorlia, in particular, was now a city clouded by fear and disarray.

Adding to the complexity of the situation was a surge in the number of magic users. What attracted them to the city was a mystery, and so far there had been no reports of murders related to sorcery. Activity had been limited to *whispers*, voices echoing deep in people's minds, torturing them with utterances they couldn't run from. These were voices of men, women, old and young—preaching for doom, warning people that they were being watched. Those who had heard the whispers—nearly half the population by now—swore that they would feel better had they seen the magic users, rather than just heard their voices.

Just as the Empire had been unable to deal with the Apostle more than half a year ago, they had no answer to this sudden rise of magic users. The

Church of the St. Bernard Order had been called to the case, and the holy faction had since responded by declaring their intention to aggressively purge sorcerers whom they labelled as atheists and heathens. Although they had yet to seize any sorcerers in the ten days since commencing the purge, there had been a significant decrease in the number of people hearing whispers. But despite their work, the holy faction had also been subject to the growing mistrust and uncertainty that plagued the city. Some had questioned the church about what they *really wanted*, while others saw the church as part of the same caste as the magic users. It didn't help matters much when one of the templars following the case was a sorcerer—none other than the glamorous Kathryn Trulips, who had been admitted by the Church since her return from Aizary.

Granted, the St. Bernard Order didn't sustain nearly as much critical scrutiny as the scholars of The Villa, who was accused of their inability to offer forward anything practical in this time of uncertainty. People were especially angered by the Grandmaster's continued inaction—the fact that the omnipotent man who had been brought up in this very city remained in seclusion, as if he wanted nothing to do with the current chaos, had citizens in a rage.

Still, the pressure on the religious body and the enlightened community didn't compare to the overwhelming load that the Empire itself had had to endure. The difference was that no one dared to condemn the Empire, in the fear that they would be silenced by violent force.

And while the haunting whispers affected not more than half the population, the threat from the south certainly had people anxious. Following the confirmed sightings of a Kragan army marching near the borders of Farella and Noel, talks of hostile encroachment—and even invasion—had intensified by the day. Allegations claimed that the Kragans had built armies and developed new weapons for an imminent attack. It might be a false alarm, but the Empire was preparing for it nonetheless. The Lord Emperor, already regarded as the greatest war strategist ever to live, had the luxury of reaching out to Vinawell and Aizary. And correspondence had been desirable, with assurance from both countries that they would side with Trubannis if Kraga was indeed to declare war.

In fact, Vinawell had already acted. A good portion of their defence had been arranged to secure the southern border, where their land met Kragan territory. This move was a serious warning to Kraga, though some commentators believed that it would instead provoke the Kragans to pounce even earlier.

Although an alliance with Vinawell and Aizary would make for a dominant trio, it was all but a front—at least for now. The Truban Empire was aware that Vinawell didn't completely trust them just yet. Aizary, on the other hand, had never engaged in warfare, and seemed reluctant to send any troops to the forefront unless conflict actually broke out. Finally, the people of Trubannis themselves were far from united.

Julian could see that the Lord Emperor's call for foreign allies illustrated how vulnerable and disunited the Empire was. It demonstrated that the proud man had no intentions to work with the Lord Chancellor, the second most powerful man in the country. And the duo of Spartamon and Schim that had defended the country eight years ago wasn't about to reconcile their differences, even against a greater common enemy. They refused to reunite and were instead looking to swiftly take out one another before the potential confrontation with the fearsome Southerners. Unfortunately, even then, the unequivocal showdown was expected to be a lengthy affair.

The Lord Emperor had seen his reputation dip once again as rumours suggested that he longed for another war, that he was ready to wage war on Kraga even if the Southerners actually meant no ill will. Commentators even went on to assert that Spartamon would conquer Vinawell and Aizary, too. The rumours played on from the folk tale from three years ago that spoke about his infinite pride, and the fact that the man now wished to propel himself to a level that equalled that of the Immortal.

Schim, however, had experienced the opposite. His popularity had soared as a result of those supporting the Lord Count turning to him as the next best alternative. Schim had won further support by accentuating the fact that the emperor had forbidden all public mourning of the Lord Count, quiet about the emperor's actual claim that it would hurt the country's morale.

The rivalry between the two men had left the court in chaos. Spartamon and Schim still attended the same court, but the rest of the court had split off into two factions: *the Advents*, who supported Spartamon, and *the Pristines*, who supported Schim. Other than a few of the more authoritative men such as Sagramore and Morlan, who carried their own weight at court, almost everyone had been forced to join one of the two sides. A war seemed likely either way—if not against foreign powers, then a civil war that would erupt in the centre of the capital.

Everyone had been entangled in the mess, and if there was any agreement among them, it was the eagerness to break the deadlock—even if it promised bloodshed.

And as the fierce struggle had been tearing through and devouring everything in its path, people had learned to adjust. A heap of people had attempted to move away from the core of the conflict, willingly taking on less significant and less powerful roles in order to avoid attention. Still others had climbed out of what was essentially sacrificial territory by increasing their own influence.

* * *

Julian shook off his daze then as the giant bell rang thunderously in his ears. The emperor was finally set for arrival, and as always, the men already in the court turned quiet and solemn, their eyes focused on the door to the right corner of the hall.

The dashing emperor swept through within moments, the air of confidence emanating from him as natural as the moons resonated with the evening sky. Lionel Lachman trailed the emperor as usual, but alongside the golden knight was a third person—a shady figure behind a stone mask.

The stranger donned heavy indigo armour with a long black cape clipped at the shoulders. His dark hair dangled down to his buttocks. He was bigger and taller than Lachman. Each step he took thudded with a force that almost shook the ground. And if that didn't win him attention, the weapon he carried certainly did—especially to Julian who immediately recognised it with a distinct fear. Dragging across the ground behind him was a dangerous metal ball—part of a sturdy flail—screeching against the stone floor, the sound drawing cringes from his audience.

Julian squinted as his heart pounded fiercely inside his chest. The eerie resemblance the stranger had to the monster of a man he had stumbled into at the prison months ago couldn't be by accident. He didn't want to believe it, but this was the man who possessed an overwhelming strength that he could only dream of.

The emperor and Lachman continued on to the raised platform, the former taking the throne and the latter standing to his left. Meanwhile, the man in the stone mask circled out to the aisle, sparing a glance at Julian—or perhaps at the chancellor, who sat in front of him. Julian couldn't tell. The newcomer then turned back toward the throne, kneeling down on one bended knee.

"If I may ask, Lord Emperor...," Morlan said carefully. "Who is this man?"

Morlan stood as an apparent neutral in the feud. He had done precious little to gain more influence, but the major move he had made was outside of the city—indeed, a fair distance away. By exercising his steady influence over Cetal, he arranged for formation of the *Cetal Legion*, the country's second largest army, to be dispersed along the Truban-Kragan border.

The emperor smiled. "The new Earl of the court," he answered. "He shall oversee the development of our soldiers. In particular, he will help Lord Breunor with the arrangement of armies."

Breunor snorted. "Help *me*? Not in a hundred years will someone like him even qualify to be my henchman!"

The masked man sniggered, without even a glance at Breunor. "Really…?" he said softly, his voice deep and coarse.

Julian jerked forward slightly. There was no mistake. That voice belonged to the warden, whose incredible strength trivialised his own meagre power.

Breunor twitched, his eyes narrowed to slits. Obviously, he hadn't expected that the man would dare to say anything back at him, let alone in a tone like that. He had been brimming with confidence in recent days.

By virtue of his efforts in making the Golden Knight Exchange a worthwhile event, as well as his deep experience in leading soldiers, Breunor had since earned himself the all-important authority to control *every* army under the Truban emblem. In theory, he was now the most powerful man in the country, but in truth—a fact of which he was all too aware—his new title as the *Final Commander* was only titular. As a veteran of war, Breunor appreciated the tough task ahead in terms of getting those armies to fight for the same cause. Each army had essentially been founded on different purposes, and their strength and culture varied drastically. It would take years, if not longer, to have them all working in harmony, especially at a time when the Empire was so clearly divided.

To tackle this difficult task, Breunor had been busying himself in classifying and sub-classifying all of the warriors affiliated with the Empire into manageable categories, including all of those he had either direct or indirect command over. He also took the trouble to identify and recruit all of those who had applied to participate at the Golden Knight Exchange. If Breunor wasn't yet able to influence the existing soldiers, then at least he could recruit new soldiers who would already be loyal to him.

It could almost be thought that Breunor could one day challenge for the throne, too.

"Identify yourself!" Breunor demanded, rising to his feet, his roaring pitch shaking the walls.

The masked man remained quietly composed, and he grasped tightly on the handle of his brutal weapon as he turned slowly to face Breunor. He dared to point the flail at him, as if proposing a personal duel. Easily provoked, Breunor swung out his bludgeon and pointed it at the man in return.

"Please," the emperor said to both men. "Is this how you treat an old comrade?"

So the warden was someone they all knew. The emperor grinned at him, nodding toward him.

And with that, the warden finally slid off the mask. Matching his shady presentation so far, a dismal countenance emerged: a frown, unfriendly eyes, the entire left side of his face disfigured from a burn. His physiognomy was far from merry, but it wasn't his unsightly appearance that had some of the people gasping in disbelief.

"You... you cannot possibly be...," Breunor said, trailing off in his astonishment.

Not everyone present knew the man, but the veterans, specifically the men involved in the war, were awestricken. Breunor wasn't the only one having a hard time believing what he clearly saw before him. Walford Bors, Breunor's most trusted soldier, grimaced as he trembled in terror. Even Schim was in shock, and so too were the Raiders, who were standing next to Julian.

"It's been a while," the man said as he turned to them. "Forgive me for my rash demeanour. It has been a long time since I appeared before such a crowd."

"It's *really* you...?!" Breunor yelped, falling back into his seat.

The emperor leaned forward with a smirk. "Some of you here may not know Pylon. Even those who have worked with him may not remember, or perhaps you are wondering if this is indeed *him*. I assure you, this *is* Pylon, the one and only *Nine Arms*, the former Right Wing of the Central Light Army."

The name reverberated across the court. Pylon had been the man's only known name until he had adopted the much more famous cognomen of Nine Arms, a name that no one at the court—not even Julian—could say they didn't know. What terrified everyone including Julian, though, were the reports that had confirmed his death—that he had been killed in the war in a frightening episode known as the *Carnage of Central Farella*, and that the man and his camp of a thousand had been stampeded and subsequently slaughtered by a Kragan army of over twenty-thousand.

Yet here he was, most certainly alive, gushing out an air of rancour that veiled the court in both confusion and disturbance.

Nine Arms was celebrated for more than just his individual strength. He was said to be incredibly efficient in leading troops on the battlefield as well. He was one of the most recognised names of the war, and also one of the emperor's most loyal soldiers. And he was already showing that now, as his narrowed eyes glared over at Schim.

"Stop that," the emperor said. "That man you once knew is no longer a mere leader of an army. He is the mighty Lord Chancellor of the Empire. At his position, he may not even remember who you are."

Schim smiled, a bead of sweat sliding down his forehead. "You really know how to joke," he said. "Pylon was one of our greatest warriors. I would forget my own contributions before I forgot his."

Nine Arms nodded, his eyes still narrowed. "I appreciate that."

"The *Muses* Cathedral," Schim continued, "just outside of Vondra Dawn, was constructed in your honour—in recognition of your contributions."

"Yes, I have visited the building. I am honoured by what it stands for."

"Your supposed death eight years ago...," Schim said, having calmed down. "It was the major sour note of our hard-fought victory. While I cannot begin to tell you how glad I am to see you alive, I cannot make sense of it. Your death was confirmed by our soldiers. How... and why? Why didn't you come back sooner?"

"Pylon came to me six years ago," Spartamon inserted. "At that time, I was as surprised as everyone is now. Since then, I have arranged a variety of tasks for him. His most recent role was a position at the prison. Indeed, he was guarding the prison on the night of Alpheus Hindlow's escape."

Julian glanced at his liege, recognising Schim's deepening grin. Schim was ready to start on his expert defamation of the emperor.

"Your mistrust is overbearing," Schim began. "To think you would mask a quality warrior like Pylon for years, to keep him from aiding the Empire, and to—"

"If I had come out of hiding six years ago," the man himself interrupted, "I doubt I would have lived till this day. As for my supposed death eight years ago... it was by no means an escapade of any proportion... I lived through hell."

Nine Arms's pupils were flaring. Turning his head and rotating slowly on the same spot, his eyes wandered round, his glare meeting almost every person present at the court. The man then dropped the giant flail to the floor, the fall resounding with a deafening thud. He crossed his right arm across his body, clawing his left shoulder. In an instant, he tore off the long cape attached behind his indigo armour to reveal that his left arm was entirely missing.

More accurately, it had been replaced by a prosthetic arm. He then went on to remove his breastplate, snapping it off aptly to reveal his torso in all its flesh. Although he was indeed magnificently well-built, the people cringed at the numerous scars and remnants of old injuries that covered his body.

"Oh, dear lord," Forredan said, turning away. "Cover yourself, please."

Nine Arms certainly didn't look like he was looking for sympathy, and he seemed to care little for anyone who had never fought on the battlefield. But his wince at Forredan now appeared more hostile than the portly statesman had perhaps expected.

Like Breunor, Forredan had actually been gaining favour. Not only had he successfully relaunched the Scorching Salamander Knights as a potent army, led by Claude Lucan and Tannon Gale, but he had also been hailed for his recent discovery of more than a dozen sites across the country that brimmed with healthy deposits of iron, ore, and other natural resources. Although cynics suspected the claim that those discoveries were recent—and that the portly statesman had already exhausted a fair amount from those sites over the years—there was little to do other than to side with the man who managed the bulk of the Empire's wealth. Even the emperor and the chancellor had grown rather genial toward him—though, clearly, Nine Arms didn't care for him.

Lucan stepped out with a hand on his hilt, ready to defend his liege with his all, though not convincingly as even he was trembling in visible fear. Julian didn't think that even Lucan would stand a chance against Nine Arms.

"Hey, hey, now!" Breunor said, leaping in between them. "We're all on the same side here."

Forredan waved Lucan back, who was likely relieved to not have to defend anyone against Nine Arms. Breunor then bent down to retrieve Nine Arms's discarded cape before gently resting it back upon the brutish warrior's shoulders.

Nine Arms eyed him. "Looks like you've puffed up," he said. "In any case, given our roles now, perhaps I should be the one serving you."

"Don't be silly. We're brothers in arms! There's no need for formalities between us."

Nine Arms grinned, showing some of his large white teeth. The notion of comrades seemed to have struck him as he looked up now to the tall ceiling.

"Comrades, eh?" he uttered softly.

Breunor shook his head, as if to share the pain. "My condolences. That battle in Farella was tragic."

Nine Arms said nothing, still visibly nostalgic.

Breunor braced himself then. "Allow me to avenge you!"

"Avenge me how?"

"We'll annihilate those Kragans!"

Again, Nine Arms said nothing, his eyes drooping down, seemingly in boredom. Julian simply couldn't read what this man might be thinking, and that frightened him greatly.

Breunor grew visibly anxious. "It had been about half a year before the war ended, right? Most of our forces at the time were focused along Southern Noel, and that was why your camp was exposed in Central Farella. We still can't see how an enemy army of more than twenty-thousand men managed to sneak their way there, and more puzzlingly, *why* they did. The major battle at the time was fought alongside the border of Noel. If they had deployed those men at Noel instead, they might have won that crucial battle. In retrospect, we could only assume that the Kragans wanted a taste of blood, a victory, because it was so rare for them. It was a shame that they selected you and your men to be the victims of their rage. Anyway, the one who led that army at the time, well, I cannot quite remember. But if we—"

"I remember that evening all too vividly," Nine Arms said, interrupting suddenly, still nostalgic. "The message had just come through to us, to stand by and prepare to move east to help out at Noel. That time, which I thought would be the most relaxed, turned out to be the end for me and my men. The Kragans ambushed my camp, slaughtering my men one by one, without mercy. Their cries of agony, their screams, the bloodshed—I remember every detail. I ripped apart my fair share of our enemies, but it was futile against an army that had completely outnumbered us."

"And how did you survive?" Schim asked.

"Well, Lord Chancellor," Nine Arms said, his focus now back on his surroundings. "I couldn't allow myself to die like that, without knowing who was behind the mission. I had to honour the lives of all those who had entrusted their lives upon my shoulders."

"Not knowing who was behind the mission...?!" Breunor said with confusion and a rising panic. "The Kragan King at the time was Bardorinoff! Who else would be behind it?"

Nine Arms snorted. "You're missing a critical point," he said. "Do you really believe the Kragans were so desperate for a meaningless victory which would cost them their defeat at Noel? They may appear rash in their actions at times, but they are a rational people."

Schim grinned. "So, you're saying…?"

"*Someone* in particular wanted me dead," Nine Arms said as he gazed across the room, making frosty eye contact once more with various men present, stopping when he met Schim's eyes. "There was no reason for the enemy to employ an army of that size to ambush my camp. It achieved nothing—well, except to remove me from this land."

"And who do you think that *someone* is—the one who wanted you dead?" Schim asked in a haunting tone to match Nine Arm's frosty gaze.

Julian swallowed as he feared for his liege, almost ready to hold him back if he said anything more. It was clearly a bad idea to provoke a man like Nine Arms given his incredible strength in addition to his quick temper.

"I have yet to confirm his identity," Nine Arms said after a moment.

"Well, when you do, be sure to tell me," Schim responded, still saying more. "I will help avenge you and your men."

Nine Arms didn't respond, though he continued to maintain his gaze on Schim. "We'll leave that for next time," he then finally said. "On my first day here, let us not talk too much about betrayal and wrongdoings. I apologise to have bored you all with my stories. Please allow me to sit back as a spectator."

"Wait!" Morlan snapped. "I want to ask about your opposite wing, Marvin Sailanson. He too disappeared after the war, and he too, I believe, is still alive."

Nine Arms frowned, growing suddenly livid. He grasped more tightly onto his weapon, suddenly trembling with rage. The emperor leaned forward, watching Nine Arms with a rare caution. Sailanson was an even more famous name than Nine Arms—notorious, in fact—and Julian jerked slightly, feeling appropriately overwhelmed by the sudden mention of the name. Was Sailanson about to make an appearance as well? He certainly hoped not.

"And what is it you wish to ask?" Nine Arms said, seemingly trying his best to calm down.

"His location," said Morlan.

Nine Arms chuckled. "I want to know, too. He has *a lot* to answer to."

"What do you mean?" Morlan asked, raising a brow.

"Sailanson… is the reason for my downfall."

That assertion was a surprise—a shock, even. The emperor was frowning in response, which could be taken as favourable for Julian and more importantly the Pristines.

"What are you saying?" Morlan asked. "That Marvin Sailanson set you up?"

"No," the bitter man answered. "But if he had come to my aid..."

"Well...," Forredan said, "there are times in war when your hands are full. You can't expect someone to save you all the time."

Nine Arms peered over at Forredan, staring down at the statesman a second time. "If I knew for certain that he wasn't coming," he said, raising his voice, "I would have arranged for a full retreat, but instead Sailanson sent me a letter, asking me to hold on until his army arrived. Needless to say, he never came."

Lachman stepped out from behind the throne, visibly agitated. "There must have been a misunderstanding! Marvin would never—"

"Then how do you explain the deaths of my men?!"

A long silence followed. Schim fell back into his seat with a smirk. Breunor, though, sighed heavily.

"Aye...!" Breunor inserted. "So, it was Marvin Sailanson's negligence, eh? What a deplorable man he is! I promise I'll kill him one day. I'll rest his head on the graves of your men."

The pledge was deplorable in itself, yet Breunor was strangely overjoyed about something. When he himself noticed that some people were regarding him with confusion, he simply claimed that he was glad to know exactly how to avenge Nine Arms.

"Lord Breunor," the emperor said. "I suppose, now, you wouldn't have any reservations about working with Pylon?"

"Ah, no. Of course not. Pylon—ah, I mean Nine Arms—possesses the qualities to... no, I mean he has much more than is needed to take on this role. As for complementing my work, he can offer his wisdom wherever he deems necessary."

"Before we dismiss the issue," Morlan said, regarding the emperor, "I'd like to know... why now? Why, Your Majesty, did you choose this particular time to reveal the presence of such a strong soldier in your ranks?"

The emperor nodded. "You are mistaken, Lord Morlan. Pylon is not my personal soldier. He works for the Empire. As for the timing, at this critical time where peace is compromised by Kraga's threat, it is important to call on any contingent talent that may strengthen our stand against our enemies."

Despite these words, Nine Arms now shared the raised platform with the emperor, standing next to the throne opposite Lachman. The man stood on the right of the throne, effectively as the Emperor's Right Wing, just as he had been during the war. Lachman, meanwhile, continued to play the Emperor's Left Wing, in place of Marvin Sailanson.

The trio's reunion would shake the rest of the Pristines as it had already shaken Schim and Julian. Nine Arms had been regarded as the second strongest man in the country after only Marvin Sailanson. Lachman was similarly once an important member of the Central Light Army. Although generally reserved, Lachman was arguably the strongest of all of the golden knights. But perhaps the thing that had Schim most concerned was the emperor's own resurgence. The man—his comrade, rival, and nemesis—appeared to have finally awakened from his slumber. The emperor, who had apparently grown jaded of his position for years, now seemed ready to defend what he believed was rightfully his. And when Spartamon set out to achieve something, Schim had once told Julian, he was almost certain of success.

There were still issues to cover, yet none compared to the re-introduction of Nine Arms and his new post as the Earl of the Empire. For the rest of the assembly, both Breunor and Schim remained quiet and carefully wary of the renewed relationship they shared with this old comrade.

* * *

Julian was among the four men accompanying Schim back to the Chancellery. The other three were the Raiders, the loyal trio who had endured the best and worst with their liege. They had been mercenaries, fighting for Schim since the war. And they were strong—possibly on par with the golden knights. Even so, they were no Lionel Lachman, and certainly no Nine Arms.

Despite their continued loyalty, Schim had shown apparent favouritism for Julian in recent times. The Raiders had realised that they might not be as important to their liege as they had previously thought. They likely found it insulting—humiliating, even, as Schim now asked them to withdraw, as he wanted a private discussion with only Julian. It would be the first time, and even Julian was surprised by the request.

The chamber here was set up not so differently to the court, only smaller. Schim sat on a grand chair on a raised platform, but a gloomy mood had cast over him. The re-emergence of Nine Arms was a shock, and Julian would attest to how much of a monster the man was. It appeared that Schim had noted his jerking reaction earlier to Nine Arms's entrance to the court.

"What do you think about all of this?" Schim asked.

Julian stiffened. "He's strong. But... he's only one man. Unless... there is more to it."

Schim nodded with a frown. "We have some history."

"I assume it's not merry?"

"Do you know how that name came about? *Nine* Arms?"

Julian shook his head.

"Besides matching the raw strength of more than nine men, he was known to be so efficient with the coordination of his arms in combat that: two became nine. It is all metaphorical, of course, but it was no embellishment. He was *that* strong."

"But he has only one arm now."

"Even with one good arm, he is a fearsome opponent, I'm sure, as you should know..."

Schim regarded Julian with a look of suspicion. Julian gulped, his eyes wandering away anxiously, careful not to reveal anything. Was it even possible that Schim had known about his involvement in Alpheus's escape? Julian was certain that he hadn't left any evidence behind that could be traced back to him.

Schim studied him for a moment longer. "Pylon was Spartamon's Right Wing," he then said, raising a hand to his chin. "And I was once Spartamon's Left Wing, which means that he was once my equal—my rival. But, of course, I became the commander of my own army afterwards. Even so, that man has the ability—the vision and skill—to lead tens of thousands."

Julian narrowed his eyes. "You seem to think very highly of him, and not only out of wariness."

"I do. And for that, I envy Spartamon."

"You... *envy* him?"

"How can I not, when he has people like Pylon and Lachman on his side?"

Julian frowned, but said nothing.

"I trust that you noticed Breunor's change of attitude just now?" Schim continued.

Julian nodded, remembering Breunor's sudden enthusiasm.

"Breunor once crossed swords with Pylon. Being the ignoramus he is, Breunor dared to challenge Spartamon for authority over the Clan of Light. No one saw the fight, though, because Spartamon arranged for it to be behind closed doors. But even without being able to see it, we are sure that Pylon completely crushed Breunor."

Schim paused there, as if to allow Julian time to swallow that information. Indeed, Julian trembled as he imagined how strong Nine Arms could be if the man gave his all in a fight.

"And Pylon wasn't the only one to serve Spartamon," Schim continued. "Lachman, too, is an invaluable asset. And then there is Sailanson, of course, the infamous *Judge*—Spartamon's Left Wing in the final two years of the war."

"The Judge...," Julian uttered softly, trying his best to hide his fear.

"I consider myself on par with Spartamon, more so since the turn of the Advent Era. My only paucity is that I've had no such luck to be surrounded by a capable support cast such as Pylon, Lachman, and Sailanson."

"What about the Raiders?" Julian asked. "Their strength rivals the golden knights."

"They are loyal to me," Schim admitted. "They are prepared to put their lives on the line. And, yes, perhaps they are as strong as the average golden knight. But they couldn't hold a candle to Lachman—also a golden knight. The difference in strength could be forgiven if they were more capable in other areas. Unfortunately, they are exclusively warriors, incapable of sharing a load of my troubles. They are unable to suggest any strategy of value. They are there to fight, and that is all."

A harsh evaluation, Julian thought, and it certainly wouldn't bode well if the Raiders had heard it. Julian had never imagined that the chancellor felt so let down, and he was surprised that Schim would share this with him, of all people.

Julian somewhat agreed with the evaluation, though. Having spent a considerable amount of time with the Raiders in the past couple of months, Julian was more than qualified to have an opinion on the matter. The trio had guided him, in rotation, and worked with him on sharpening his combat skills, which Julian was grateful for. However, out of the trio, he respected only Raphael, who he saw as prudent and cunning. Incidentally, Raphael was also the strongest of the Raiders, and highly regarded by many in the court. Schim, however, didn't appear to share the same lofty opinion for Raphael, often dismissing his strategic thinking as too conservative and safe. Still, compared to the brawny Raven and Roth, who were too impulsive, Raphael shone ever so brightly.

"You want me to be that person?" Julian asked, his pitch confident. "You want me to be your Pylon?"

Schim's eyes narrowed. "Correct. I have waited long enough. As the heir of Longinus, you must have what it takes."

"But I still cannot match any of the Raiders," Julian said, "let alone Lachman and Nine Arms."

"Combat ability is but a single measure of an individual's competence," Schim said. "Besides, that will come soon for you. I'm more interested in your ability—or, more precisely, your fearlessness toward men of power. You have managed to win the attention of Breunor and Forredan, and you dare to confront them. That alone is a rare quality, and I will need people like you... even only to dream of facing Spartamon. And if I'm to be completely honest, your sorcery intrigues me greatly."

Schim's appraisal was generous, especially when that *rare quality* he spoke of had Julian labelled by many as reckless, impulsive, and disrespectful. Julian realised he couldn't afford to be humble, however, and he accepted the praise with a simple nod.

"If you expect me to be great," Julian said, "then we have a mutual agreement."

In the back of his mind, Julian was thinking about how he had left his home on a lone journey to Zorlia. What was it that he had been searching for? Was it *this*—to soar to such heights—to be the prominent soldier serving someone who might eventually lead the country?

It wasn't, he realised. He hadn't forgotten about the massacre of Mt. Pinnacle. Julian thought not of revenge, but only that he wanted to learn exactly what had happened. He had realised he knew extraordinarily little about who he was chasing, yet he was sure that he needed power if he wanted to know more. And this—the chaos in the Empire—was exactly the place to acquire that power.

EIGHTEEN

Theatre of the Romantics

Of all the advantages that came with working for the chancellor, there was one task Julian was reluctant about—his occasional role as Lady Winter's escort. In truth, it was a task entrusted only to the most reliable, and many people would be honoured by the responsibility.

This evening, Julian was to escort Winter to the *Theatre of the Romantics* for a musical drama. The theatre itself was a magnificently revamped circular structure that seated more than five thousand spectators, on the other side of Dunn Bay across from Vondra Dawn. It was one of the few places where social hierarchy didn't matter, as the wealthiest were often seated next to the penniless. The lighting display of candles and torches on the stage was a splendid sight, but the pre-show organ music playing in the background wore thin in the midst of such a rowdy audience.

The Hourglass was the title of the drama being performed that night by a group of actors and musicians who had been touring the country, with Zorlia being their third stop after successive performances in Dorellsdale and Cetal City.

"Did you know that I am from Dorellsdale?" Winter asked Julian, who sat on her right, a pair of servants sitting on their left. Both of her servants were young girls approximately fifteen years of age.

"I have heard," Julian replied tersely.

"I wanted to see the first show there," Winter continued. "But leaving Zorlia wasn't possible."

Julian didn't respond. He didn't care for entertaining the chancellor's wife, and he didn't know how. There should be more important things to do than to sit idly for a show. Lady Winter, though, didn't seem to be offended by his attitude, as she went on to talk about her past as a regular civilian. It was widely known within the court that Winter was of Vinan heritage, and that she had been raised in Dorellsdale. She had been a nurse who assisted the Clan of Light during the war. And she had been born as Amelia Winter Neal, until she took Schim's name.

Julian knew to applaud when the musicians finally came on stage to tune their instruments, at which time Winter finally turned silent. The musicians appeared one by one behind the skene, all of them well-presented and exuding elegance in a way that contrasted with the warrior classes. Julian contemplated for a moment what it would be like to live as anything other than a warrior, and he allowed himself to relax and maybe even enjoy the show.

Barely a moment later, Julian closed his eyes and drifted toward dozing off in his seat. Just before he thought guilt might come his way, a mysterious surge of unease struck him suddenly and far more violently than any guilt could manage. His body jerked forward before it froze entirely, as if encapsulated by an overwhelming power. His surroundings disappeared into nothing—all he saw was a pitch-black emptiness. His soul had jumped out, and he was being held by an invisible hand—a power that had no physical form, a power reminiscent of the spear-wielding sorcerer, yet somehow different. Julian squirmed, and then suddenly he was returned to the theatre in the midst of the audience's applause.

Sweat rolled down from atop his head as he gazed left and right for the source of the power that had certainly been real and not simply in his imagination. Julian had hoped to run into sorcerers, but this mysterious energy he had felt just then was much more fearful than anything he had previously experienced.

The energy had come and gone without warning, yet everyone else around him were as they had been. Winter and her servants didn't seem to have even noticed that he had just now been in a trance. And no one else in the audience appeared to have experienced any strange sensations at all.

Peering back toward the stage, Julian watched as the last musician of the group appeared. She was a fiddle player in a black dress—tall, slender yet curvaceous, mature, and with long, wavy fair hair pulled up into a half-ponytail, longer locks framing either side of her face. She was beautiful, but her downturned, hollow eyes and lack of smile gave off a frosty sentiment. He watched her curiously as the show was finally about to begin.

* * *

The fiddle player was exceptional at her craft. She was the leader of the musicians, and she guided her team flawlessly. By the end of the overture, they had won the appreciation of their audience, and by the end of the first intermission, the audience had become completely captivated, Julian included. The actors were as passionate in bringing out life in their characters as the musicians were absorbed in amplifying that *life* with their melodies.

The fiddle player didn't return to the music ensemble after the third act, however. She came back instead as a character in the story—the angel that the female lead had been yearning up until then to see. In the climactic scene of the final act, in which the male lead had fallen into despair, the angel of the story descended miraculously from above the stage with large, white feathery wings attached behind her black dress and a lap harp at her chest. The cold-looking fiddle player from earlier was now a messenger of the faith.

As she plucked the gentle notes with her fingertips, she set the scene for the other musicians with yet another soothing melody. Followed by the instrumentals was the angel's serene vocals, perfectly synchronised with the melody. The name of the song was *Aria di Evaporazione Mondo*, and its lyrics spoke of a world that would soon evaporate into nothing, but would at the same time allow for the potential for a new beginning. Its purpose in the drama was to teach the male lead the reality of the harshness of the world—Julian realised—and within that, the importance of not losing faith, even in the most dire of circumstances. With every pluck of the strings, the fiddle-player-turned-angel was sending waves of optimism not only to the character of the story, but also to the audience. Her vocals echoed across the theatre, encapsulating the souls of the audience like a soft blanket and gently caressing their hearts with a tenderness Julian had never known.

The angel of the show didn't appear again until the end, when the performers entered the stage one after another to be applauded by the audience. When they were all on stage again, the performers held hands as they gave a final bow of appreciation to the audience.

Julian had never cared for music or drama, but even he couldn't deny the heart-warming, healing effect that the musical drama had had on him this evening. For more than a few moments, his troubles had been forgotten. The happy thoughts that sparked off from the music were infectious, and the peaceful atmosphere in the theatre attested to that.

People were standing up and leaving the theatre by the time Julian came back to his senses after the reverie of the performance. For a moment there, Julian had an impulse to thank Winter for introducing him to an art form that he had never previously known. But when he turned to her, her eyes were locked onto something else. At the far, top right corner of the theatre, three figures donning armour similar to Empire knights had appeared, but with a sleeker leather design of navy blue, and a long cape attached on their backs.

"They are templars—knights of the St. Bernard Order," Winter said to Julian. "And they're probably here on a witch hunt."

Julian winced as he recognised one of the three templars. He had never met her before, but the distinct silver hair and violet eyes were unmistakable. She was Kathryn Trulips—the Aizar scholar-sorcerer, now also a templar, assigned to *purge* sorcerers from Zorlia. Trulips was the first person from the Far East to join any Truban-based alliance, and it was via admittance by the most respected and powerful religious faction in the country—none other than the St. Bernard Order. In effect, she had become part of the select group made up of the most powerful holy warriors in the country.

The Order was its own independent faction. All of their members, although constitutionally recognised as affiliates of the Truban Empire, had no direct influence within the Empire. While the primary function of the St. Bernard Order was the promotion of good deeds in the name of the Immortal, the holy faction had recently dedicated their cause to the *cleansing* of the mysterious sorcerers who were thought to be responsible for the incessant whispers of doom.

As Julian watched the holy knights turn away to leave, he wondered whether the overwhelming energy he had felt earlier had come from them.

Or from someone they were hunting.

"Do you hear those whispers?" Winter asked suddenly, her gaze still on the templars who were now leaving. "Preaches of doom."

Julian turned to her. "No," he said bluntly.

"A shame," Winter said. "They say a lot about the Empire. It keeps the people informed... or *misinformed*, for that matter. And they are indeed... *terrifying*."

"I assume that Lady Winter, you are one of the unfortunate ones, then?"

Winter nodded, returning Julian's stare. "Magic users are a key factor in this war against the Advents. The faction they side with will emerge victorious."

Julian smirked. "Well, that doesn't sound very encouraging when I'm the only one on this side."

* * *

Julian headed home after escorting Winter back to Vondra Dawn. He was still living in his modest home in the outer eastern neighbourhood of Ramsgate, and the return trip took almost two hours by foot. Of course, as a prized soldier of the Lord Chancellor, he didn't have to walk. His promotion to Silver Knight had come with many benefits, including a neat dwelling in

Stapleton and his own soldiers to command. In the end, though, Julian chose only to accept the warhorse that saved him travel time. He cherished the *home* he had made with the mischievous boy Oscar, who was now like a little brother to him.

As he arrived at home, Julian was secretly pleased to see the boy hard at work practising the swordplay strokes he had taught him. Even though Oscar practised with a wooden sword, the strength and solidity of his slashes were impressive, especially for his age.

"Higher!" Julian instructed as he stepped into the humble courtyard. "*The Rise* is most efficient with a wide swing."

Doing as he had been instructed, Oscar lurched out again, noting the effect of a simple adjustment. Moving onto the next series of techniques he was learning, the boy showed Julian that he had more than just style, but substance, too.

"So, what do you think?" the boy asked proudly after he had completed a cycle of a set of strokes.

"You're doing well," Julian said encouragingly.

The boy had talent. His knack for skilled combat was unmistakeable, and his progress was proof of that. The boy could almost rival the strength of an average trained soldier.

Since Julian became a silver knight, he had also organised Oscar's enrolment into a school of the more traditional type, where he had learned to write.

"Did you help out at Dock's today?" Julian asked, after handing over to Oscar a glass of water.

"Yeah, every third day. And your old friend was there."

Julian cocked his head. "Who?"

"Sir Pole. But only for a minute."

Julian frowned as a surge of nostalgia rushed through him. It had been a while, and it was easy for Julian to say that he was preoccupied with his work for the chancellor, but in fact he had been avoiding Percival Pole. He had yet to forgive the man who had been showered with critical acclaim and unwarranted gifts from noblemen and other lords after shooting to fame in the Golden Knight Exchange. More recently, though, rumours suggested that Pole had run out of luck. A fiery argument with Sagramore over his role in the Defence Army had been the beginning of the end for him. Julian suspected that Pole had given in to his excessive vanity, choosing to indulge himself with the aristocrats in Zorlia rather than bearing the honour—but also the stress of a knight's role—in Bastion City. This open lust for social status had rebounded on Pole, as he had been instead frozen out by the Defence Army. It was thought that Pole had actively looked to submit himself to another man of power, but no one had taken the risk to recruit him since it meant that they might cross the Defence Chieftain. In fact, most noblemen—and other men of power—had issued forth in conjunction to shut out the defected warrior from any formal or social gatherings.

Pole had even been evicted from his own home in Stapleton after the Empire had revoked it on the basis that he wasn't working at all. One could assume that the drastic turn of events had turned Pole's world upside down, with his popularity sunken to abysmal levels unknown to him.

It was perhaps what he deserved. Julian only wished that after all that had happened, his old ally would finally learn his lesson. It might be too idealistic, however, to think that they could reconcile their differences.

* * *

Julian reported to the Chancellery early next morning, something that had become part of his regular routine. Schim himself wasn't there today, and yet Julian was still assigned his most prominent task to date. Raphael and Raven were there to brief him.

"You are to uproot the sorcerers responsible for the whispers of doom," Raphael said. "We have reason to believe that they work with the Advents, so you would need to be wary at every turn, especially because we won't be in support of your efforts."

Julian nodded. It was the perfect opportunity for him to solidify his position as the Lord Chancellor's *second in command*. He realised that he was perhaps only being chosen for the task because he was a sorcerer. The ability to emanate grace and, more importantly, the ability to sense it, were attributes people couldn't simply acquire with learning or with practice.

"We don't know how many there are," Raphael continued. "And we can't be sure what they're trying to achieve."

Julian frowned. "Have you been hearing the whispers, too?"

"No, but Ray has."

Raven grumbled, shaking his head. "It's so annoying," he said. "Just constant blabber about how everyone will die."

"Tell him more, Ray," Raphael said, urging him on.

The brawny man grunted this time. "Those damned magic users seem to know a lot about what's going on at the court. In between all the hokum are a lot of accusations against the Empire. No names are mentioned, but the allusions are there." Raven paused, eyeing Julian. "Even *you* are referenced… as *a friend lost to the wolves*."

Julian scoffed. "I don't like the sound of that at all."

"But they consider you a friend, it seems," Raphael said. "They might not be so hostile if you happen to run into them. And if you were to meet someone not so kind, remind yourself that you once crossed swords with Nine Arms."

"We heard about that," Raven added, with a hint of ridicule. "It's a miracle you survived a confrontation with that psychopath."

"I am fortunate to be alive," Julian admitted, realising it was futile now to deny his involvement in Alpheus's escape. "And with all the things you have taught me, I can be confident enough to accept this task. Accept my gratitude, and be proud that you had a hand in developing the strongest warrior to represent the Pristines."

Raven snorted as Julian turned to be on his way.

"Longinus," Raphael called out from behind. "Go to Arcadia. The holy men are already on the case."

Julian paused briefly, and then departed for good.

* * *

The base of the St. Bernard Order, a grand cathedral, was located in Arcadia, only four miles north-east of Vondra Dawn but separated by the Dunn River, which meant that getting there on foot took more than twice that distance.

Julian strode atop his usual warhorse, but travelling along with him today were a couple of knights, his attendants who were also his to command. Raphael had arranged for it, despite his clear dislike for Julian, insisting that Julian would need a hand. But Julian didn't thank him. Not only was he suspicious that these men had been sent to monitor him, he also thought that having other people around would just get in his way. Still, he chose not to object to it in the end. After all, silver knights were traditionally assigned attendants in a system that adhered to exemplary knighthood, with lower class knights being developed and mentored while the silver knight worked on his leadership skills.

"What are your names?" Julian asked, finally speaking, albeit without turning to face the young knights who were trotting along behind him.

"Sir!" one of them responded. "The name is Alexander Wethers."

"And me, Sir!" the other one reported. "Emery Tawzer."

Julian turned his head slightly and regarded them with suspicion, his eyes dashing naturally to the double crescent pendants hanging at their necks.

Religious fools, he thought. *That's the last thing I need.*

"Did Raphael brief you on today's task?" Julian asked, turning ahead again.

"Not in detail, Sir," Alex answered. "We never spoke with Lord Raphael, but were only given instructions in the form of a memorandum. We were to meet you outside Vondra Dawn today, and we were only told a couple of days ago by our intake leader that we were assigned to continue our training under the guidance of a silver knight."

Julian squinted. "Where were you assigned before this?"

"Sir," Emery answered. "We are both from the twenty fourth development intake of the Defence Army. Prior to today, we didn't have any direct superior."

"We are honoured to work for you, Sir," Alex added. "Our peers have admired you since the Exchange."

Julian made no response. He wasn't flattered, not even a little bit. But he was interested in the fact that Alex and Emery were from the Defence Army. After all, he knew the Defence Army quite well himself, having briefly joined as a soldier when he had first arrived in Saffron more than ten years ago. At the time, the group had been governed by the previous ruling. That was when he had first met Percival Pole, also a soldier at that time. Together, they had endured the tough and oppressive system of the Sargon Monarchy in which soldiers had been promoted through bribery rather than ability. Julian had been thirteen years of age at the time, and even then he had dared to speak up to his superiors about the unfair system, though his bravery had only led to his immediate dismissal from the faction.

All of that had changed now with the Truban Empire in power and Paltiel Sagramore as the Defence Chieftain. Going to Bastion City was the most direct and popular method of sharpening one's combat skills. It was also the most difficult for its high level of competition and rather tiresome developmental processes, which focused on solidifying every level and area of combat. Anyone with the potential to rise through the ranks likely deserved it. Like many others, Julian considered the Defence Army to be the *clean* faction of the Empire—free of the sanctimonious individuals who had entered the Empire as potential knights for reasons other than advancing their knighthood.

The intake number that Emery had mentioned indicated the time when they had first been admitted in Bastion City. With only one intake per year—and given that the *twenty seventh* development intake was announced for this current year of Advent 9—the implication was that Alex and Emery had only been members of the Empire for three years. More importantly, it meant that it had only taken them three years to become knights, which was a remarkable achievement. Compared to the Raiders, who had formerly been mercenaries, Alex and Emery appeared sensible rather than tactful, and loyal to a certain cause rather than to a certain man. Whether that quality of righteousness and sensibility was a mask they put on was anyone's guess, but no one was about to fool Julian.

* * *

It was Julian's first visit to the cathedral, and that was despite being a long-time resident of Zorlia. He had frowned at the idea of faith ever since leaving his hometown, but he couldn't help himself marvelling at the grand structure that stood before them now. The gentle flow of the ravine below and the bridge that extended over it was already a sight to behold. But the actual cathedral was still the main attraction. Supposedly more than a century old, the primarily grey, stone building erected from the riverbank with its two highest point—in the form of twin towers of black roofs—soaring to about five floors above land.

As he strode across the bridge, Julian glared in the direction of the giant double crescent sculpture that hung in between the twin towers of black roofs framing the façade, but he looked away when he noted a horse parked outside the tremendous mahogany double door. The saddle resting on the animal was imprinted with the Fenrir emblem of the Empire. Julian snorted and continued his advance, and the three men parked their horses on the opposite side of the door. Julian treaded toward the enormous double door, at least the height of five men, with Alex and Emery trailing behind him.

Upon his knock, a tiny gap opened up on the left door. Poking out was the face of a short priest. His strips of white hair indicated his old age, and the navy robe he wore—sewn with the finest of fabrics—indicated how plentiful the donations to the cathedral had been of late. The man regarded Julian for a moment, looking at him from the bottom up, finally taking note of the embossed emblem on his armour.

"Are you... Sir Longinus?" he asked, his voice a sharp squeak.

Julian nodded, hiding his surprise that the priest already knew who he was. "And how may I address you?"

"Poray is my name."

"Well, Reverend Poray, do you intend to have us stand out here all day?"

Poray scoffed to Julian's bluntness, glancing out at Alex and Emery. "Are you here because of the whispers?"

"No," Julian said, raising a brow. "But I'd like to ask some questions about that. As for why I'm here, let's just say I want to pray."

"I won't deny you entrance, but we have other guests right now. You may return in an hour."

The priest went to shut the door, but Julian slipped a hand between the gap to force it open, holding the mahogany with his palm outstretched.

"What do you think you're doing?!" the priest said, forcing the door from the other side and engaging in an almost childish tug-of-war.

"We don't have much time," Julian said.

"Sir Longinus," Emery urged. "Maybe we should come back later."

Julian ignored him and then pressed even harder, prodding the heavy door to swing open, and then knocking the priest to the ground. He trampled inside, shoving open the right side of the door as well. His attendants gawked at the sight before following him inside with quiet reluctance.

The inside of the cathedral was spectacular. Its high ceiling and spacious layout amplified any sound, and perhaps because of that, it was an ideal place for contemplation, encouraging calm and tranquillity. And when the door closed from behind, all was indeed quiet. Intersecting the two sets of neatly arranged benches was an aisle that led to a giant sculpture of the Immortal, and behind the sculpture was a sizeable mosaic window that allowed a generous amount of natural light to shine through in a design that looked like *God* was in heaven.

Seated in the front row was the other visitor, the only other person sharing the space. The stranger faced the giant sculpture, apparently praying, hands clasped together against his chin. The priest had picked himself up from the ground and though he had every right to be angry, he instead clasped his hands together, closed his eyes and whispered words of prayer, presumably to the Immortal. Julian continued along the aisle, eyeing the front row until he came to a sudden halt after recognising the stranger.

"Amen," the stranger said quietly before turning around to face Julian. "Well, if it isn't Sir Longinus."

Percival Pole.

For once, Pole didn't wear a cheery smile and his words now were spoken with an audible hint of contempt. Julian found himself standing frozen, unable to utter any kind of response. He didn't at all expect to see his old ally there.

Poray, who had finally caught up to Julian, looked back and forth between the two men, clearly sensing an air of animosity. "Don't even think about drawing your weapons in here!" he whispered in caution.

Pole narrowed his eyes, shifting his gaze to the priest. "Would you be so kind as to excuse us for a moment?" Pole asked, keeping his voice soft. "When I am done talking with Sir Longinus, I'll be leaving. I assure you that the serenity here will not be disturbed."

The priest raised a brow. "I cannot leave visitors wandering alone in here. And besides, I—"

The priest's sentence was cut short when Pole squinted and then flashed to his right at an impressive speed that immediately reminded Julian of Pole's ability. Only after a moment did Julian realise that Pole's intention was only to render Poray under the mercy and precarious position between two silver knights.

"The templars will be back soon," Poray said in submission. "I suggest you end any discussions before then." He then paced away toward the stairs on the right side of the chancel. "I ask that you remain respectful," he said after a pause. "Even in my absence, remember that the Immortal is omnipresent. He will watch over your every move. Do not invite further sins upon yourselves."

Julian snorted when the priest finally disappeared from view. "The Immortal... eh?" he said, unable to manage anything more meaningful.

Pole made no response, instead eyeing Alex and Emery. "Sir Wethers and Sir Tawzer... I see. They work for you now?" he asked Julian.

The two men nodded at Pole, but didn't address him with words.

"How have you been?" Julian finally said, his voice soft.

Pole simpered. "Your sad face tells me that you pity me."

"I heard some rumours."

"*They* know about it," Pole said, regarding Alex and Emery.

"If you turn back now, I'm sure Sir Sagramore will forgive you."

"Turn back? Why would I do that? I'm done living in his shadow."

"But you cannot go on like this," Julian said. "The court's shutting you out. All the things you've worked so hard for will go to waste."

Pole narrowed his eyes. "Those damned noblemen. They even took my home away."

"Your home is Bastion City, with the Defence Army. Go back and start again."

"Don't tell me where I should go!" Pole snapped, his eyes narrowing in fury. "Julian Longinus, I do *not* need your pity. Did you forget that it was me who brought you to where you are now? Tell me, who was it that crushed you at the Golden Knight Exchange? Who do you think you are to lecture me?"

Pole's words echoed inside the building, his wrath amplifying tenfold. He clearly hadn't accepted his drastic loss in favour. For someone who had always needed the assurance of being liked and accepted, being shut out was Pole's worst nightmare. All the pressure and spurn he must have endured had finally forced him over the edge. If there was anything to blame, it was his difficult upbringing during the times of the Sargon Monarchy. Back then, his only mode of survival had been to please those with power. And that had often included the most humiliating acts, all of which had shaped Pole into what he was today. A particular rumour, Julian remembered, involved a powerful lord by the name of Harvey, an anomalous, old man who had apparently fancied handsome boys and forced them into performing unspeakable, perverse acts.

"If there's anything I can do—"

"If you'll excuse me," Pole cut in as he shoved Julian aside, "I'll be on my way."

Pole stormed out of the building then. Julian did in fact pity him. And if there were anything Julian *could* do, it was to allow Pole to retain that small hint of self-respect.

* * *

Poray returned shortly after Pole had departed. The priest was still bitter about what had happened earlier, but he didn't seem to want to aggravate matters. He asked Julian and his attendants to sit on the front bench and follow his lead in order to communicate their prayers to the Immortal.

"I'm sorry," Julian interrupted. "But before we immerse ourselves, I'd like to ask some questions."

The priest rolled his eyes, but then nodded.

"Tell me about the Apostle," Julian said immediately, without further preamble.

The priest looked over to Alex and Emery as if to ask them if Julian was to be trusted. The knights looked away, and then Poray finally began.

"It is our right to reserve the use and distribution of the information we gather," he said. "Even if it were the Lord Emperor personally requesting information, we would not reveal anything if we deemed it inappropriate. With this so-called Apostle, however, the case is different, in that we will not claim to know any more than what the Empire issued... except for the curious fact that he was in fact once here."

This was certainly new information to Julian, and he nodded, waiting for more. If only he could somehow connect the Apostle with the whispers of doom.

"He was here once, and it was before any murders," Poray said. "He came here simply to pray. We didn't see him as a heretic. If anything, he was faithful, and was more devoted than any bishop, priest, or templar in terms of his efforts to communicate with the Immortal."

Julian frowned. "What about his death? What do you make of it?"

"His physical existence is no more. There is no doubt about that. The *spiritual aura* specific to that man evaporated at precisely the time when the Empire claimed to have eliminated him."

"Spiritual aura?"

"I won't try to convince you that there is such an energy source, as even we members of the Order are unsure of how to grasp the spiritual aura."

"What about the whispers? What do you make of them?"

"The templars are on it, but as you should know, sorcerers aren't easy to catch. We haven't yet bridged a connection between this new group of sorcerers, the Apostle, and general heresy. In the same way that it would be incorrect to classify all mortals as the same in terms of their character, actions, and purposes, it is important to note that every sorcerer is unique. For now, this is all I can offer."

Julian rubbed his chin. "This has helped plenty," he said. "Thank you."

The priest smiled, perhaps sensing some genuine gratitude in these words. But Julian didn't care about winning his favour and instead stood up abruptly from the bench then.

"Where are you going?" the priest asked in bemusement. "This is when we pray."

"Perhaps next time," Julian responded, heading for the exit. "If the Immortal was here, he would understand."

The priest shook his head in disbelief, but again opted not to pursue the matter. Alex and Emery stood, too, and dutifully bowed to the sculpture of the Immortal, then to Poray. Then they followed Julian, though clearly not content.

NINETEEN

Second in command

It had been less than ten minutes into their trip back south when Julian's party stumbled into an encounter that they would have preferred to avoid. This other group was marching up north, and among them was the much feared Nine Arms, who today was fitted with a dark mask that covered the top half of his face. With him were Lachman and a number of other knights, a total of eight men. Julian pulled his horses to a complete halt, gesturing that Alex and Emery should do the same. They all hopped off and fell to one bended knee.

Nine Arms raised a hand for his group to halt. As the new Earl of the Empire, the man had greater authority than even Lachman.

"Sir Longinus, was it?" Nine Arms asked with his customary coarse pitch.

"I am honoured that you know my name," Julian said, keeping his head bowed.

"I have heard about you. Your story fascinates me."

"I'm flattered," Julian said hesitantly.

"It appears that you just came from the cathedral," he said, gesturing north. "Might I ask what you were doing there?"

"What I did there...," Julian said, hesitating again, "was of no importance." He then glanced up at the man and the destructive flail he carried with him, immediately regretting his scanty response.

"Lord Nine," Emery said. "Sir Longinus was there to pray."

Nine Arms nodded and hopped off his stallion, treading slowly up to Julian. He leaned down and bobbed his head next to Julian's, his half-mask nearly scraping Julian's cheek. Not only was Julian suddenly frozen stiff, but the choking proximity made him unable to breathe as sweat built up rapidly at the crown of his head. Julian couldn't be sure if he was imagining it, but it seemed that an intense heat seemed to be diffusing from the man's boiling blood, hot enough to melt Julian away.

"It was you," Nine Arms whispered with a sinister undertone. "The one at the prison."

Julian jerked slightly, hiding the fact that his heart was thudding inside his chest. A surge of heat erupted in him then when Nine Arms gave him a pat on his shoulder.

"I'm sure you have guessed by now," Nine Arms said. "But let me confirm for you that I was the man you faced there."

Julian gulped as a bead of sweat slid down from the side of his face, trembling now.

"I have yet to learn who your companion was," the man went on.

My companion? Julian thought, his mind muddling in confusion. *What's he talking about?*

"But it's all part of the game," Nine Arms continued. "In fact, I find it much more exciting to hunt him down myself."

The man finally stood upright again. He stepped back toward his men, allowing Julian both physical space and breathing space.

Julian took a deep breath and then looked up. "I want to learn something for you as well," he dared to say, his face hot.

"Oh?"

"It may only be my intuition, but I suspect that there's more to the Lord Count's murder."

Nine Arms smirked. "And what do you hope to find out from me? The Count had been murdered long before I was even admitted to the Empire."

"Well, of course. But at your position, I'm sure you are close, or at least can be close to the powerful people among whom may well be the true culprit and murderer. You could even ask the emperor."

"Sir Longinus!" Lachman reprimanded. "Watch your words! This insinuation could cost you dearly."

Nine Arms raised a hand to silent the golden knight. "I guess Schim didn't rate you this high for nothing," he said to Julian. "The hearsay is that you have become his second fiddle."

Julian shook his head. "That means nothing to me. And, sadly, I am not yet acknowledged as such. But while we're on the topic, I'd like to ask: where is the *emperor's* second fiddle—Marvin Sailanson? Has he been hiding, like you?"

Nine Arms gritted his teeth fiercely in response. He latched onto his giant flail, and without any further warning, he swung it dangerously—perhaps fortuitously, but *only* onto the ground, as the immense power would have easily decimated a person. The slam instead shook the ground, sending out shockwaves similar to those of an earthquake.

Everyone froze, and Nine Arms himself held his position for a moment, the metal ball planted into the earth. Then he fixed his gaze on Julian.

"You talk big," he said simply. "But do you have the strength to match?"

Julian cringed as Nine Arms gestured for a couple of men behind him to step forward in his stead. Julian raised his arms to decline the challenge, but the two men, both silver knights, had drawn their longswords and were already leaping toward him. Julian reached for his own iron sword with a groan, glancing briefly at Lachman, who simply sat atop his horse watching with his arms folded, clearly not about to join in what would be a mere sparring contest between knights.

Julian drew his sword and started by parrying off a few initial attacks, which sparked the heavy clash of metals. His opponents then circled out to attack him from opposite sides. In response, Julian leaped away and high into the sky.

Two, Julian thought, gazing down at his opponents. *Only two.* He eyed the one on his left, a target at an ideal position for him to strike. Julian didn't think twice, deciding to thump down toward that knight. As he moved to do so, however, a longsword was thrusted at him from another angle just before he would have connected.

The other one, Julian realised with a hiss, pulling away immediately and then rolling away to relative safety. *They fooled me*. When he looked up again, Alex and Emery had joined the scuffle, fencing off the man who had almost killed him.

Julian's new attendants didn't fight for long, however, as Lachman brushed away their weapons with a simple swipe of his own longsword without even unsheathing it. When Alex and Emery picked themselves up once again, they had Lachman towering over them from atop his warhorse.

"Don't interfere," the golden knight ordered, staring them down.

Julian groaned and then returned to fighting the two silver knights. He pressured the opponent to his right, keeping him at bay with strong slashes, all the while inviting the opponent on his left to close in on him. When his foe took the bait and got within striking distance, Julian spun toward him in a surprise attack and launched a roaring inferno in his direction.

Though spectacular and dangerous, the flame itself wasn't summoned with the intention to roast his enemy. No one ended up engulfed in flames. Indeed, the inferno had missed the enemy completely. And yet its power had the knight tumbling to the ground, at which time Julian was able to swipe viciously at his feet. The other knight was quick to re-engage, however, helping his ally recover as best as he could. Just when they were growing hopeful about regaining the upper hand, Julian flashed away behind a glow of crimson red.

Everyone had become familiar with the concept of Time-Shifting, but that didn't mean anyone knew how to combat it.

Chase my shadows, Julian thought with a grin, darting away and then circling back to strike. The pair of longswords wielded by his foes suddenly seemed slow and predictable. This was the result of his training. Julian realised that he owed the Raiders a big favour, especially to Raphael who was actually patient in his guidance. Even the regular silver knight was no longer a threat to him. Julian glanced over at Nine Arms and Lachman, both of whom were expressionless, perhaps awed by his speed.

"Drop your weapons at once!" a commanding voice called out.

Julian swung his iron sword one last time, knocking his opponent's weapons off their grip, before finally coming to a pause. Behind Nine Arms and his men were a trio racing forward on white horses, now slowing to a gentle gait. They were templars. The leader of the group was a refined man who exuded an aura of vanity. Behind him were two female templars, and one of them was the beautiful Kathryn Trulips. Unlike the heavy and often full-scale armour designed for traditional knights, the templars were armoured lightly in navy blue leather. Their protective metal plates were stylishly complemented by lightly-tinted cloth. The abdominal area in particular had no metal plating at all, and was instead woven with a *blue cross* that represented the holy order, threaded into a sturdy cloth material made with the finest of natural fibres. However, it was not their dress code that distinguished them from the common knights, but the air of gallantry and holiness that seemed to stir about them.

It was a good time to end the battle. Although Julian was confident he would have won, he realised that was a meaningless fight.

"What is going on here?" questioned the other female templar.

"O' Lord Gabriel, Lady Suriel, and Lady Kyriel," Lachman said, greeting them. "We were merely exchanging our views on knighthood. Isn't that right, Sir Longinus?"

Lachman strode across to Julian, leaning down at him from his horse. "For your own good, don't go provoking Pylon again," he said softly. "And make sure never to mention Marvin again."

Julian said nothing, trying his best to maintain his composure. Lachman might have a sensible front, but the man was a mercenary just like the rest of them, and he was possibly as strong as Nine Arms. It was difficult to admit it, but Julian had always admired the golden knight. It was a great shame that Lachman represented the Advents, and was indeed the emperor's most loyal follower.

"All right, now!" Lachman said out loud. "Now *that* was a productive session!"

"You are in the vicinity of the holy order," Gabriel claimed. "I do not wish for violence or bloodshed."

"None shall be seen," Lachman assured.

Gabriel lifted his chin, watching Lachman with apparent condescension. "I warn you that indiscreet acts are unwelcome in this area, especially if you're on your way to the cathedral."

Nine Arms grunted. "Who do think you're talking to? Acting bigger than you are—how dare you speak to Lachman like that?"

Nine Arms had raised his flail-wielding arm, and the templars in turn reached for their swords. In what appeared to be the prelude to a mighty battle, Julian allowed himself a breather. The templars were on one side, and the traditional knights led by Nine Arms were on the other. Julian called neither side his allies, but in the midst of it, he realised that he despised the templars more than he had thought. Somehow, if there were a lesser of two evils, it was Nine Arms and his men, according to Julian at least.

"Everyone let go of your weapons!" Lachman demanded. "I don't even want to consider that a fight between our own knights would break out before my very eyes. The Empire and the Order belong within the same group. We are a family, and as civilised knights, I expect better from everyone."

Everyone fell quiet. And while Nine Arms seemed none too pleased, he eventually dropped his guard, slipping his dangerous weapon back behind his mantle. Only then did Gabriel wave his hand to his fellow templars that they should also ease up. To shift the focus further away, Lachman requested that the templars—who were trained in healing—to treat the wounds of the silver knights Julian had been fighting.

Gabriel regarded his fellow templars and then nodded toward Trulips, who nodded back and then hopped agilely off the horse.

Let's see what she's capable of, Julian thought, his eyes following Trulips's step.

The foreigner didn't call on sorcery, or at least didn't make it visible. The silver knights' injuries were simply a matter of dislocated joints and she effectively fixed them up with delicate twists and thrusts. After the silver knights thanked Trulips, the people dispersed. Lachman and Nine Arms continued on their path up north, together with Gabriel and Suriel. Trulips, on the other hand—after having a word with her fellow templars—travelled south alongside Julian, claiming that she had some business to take care of at the academy.

* * *

Julian and his attendants paced further south. They were fortunate to have escaped the encounter with only a few scratches, but with Trulips now in their company, Julian still had someone to be wary of.

"I've heard stories about you, Sir Longinus," Trulips said, looking over at him from her horse. "And I am glad to finally meet you."

"The pleasure is mine, ah… Lady…"

"Kyriel."

"Is that the name you prefer?"

"My templar name is most apt when I am in this armour."

Julian grinned. "In any case, your achievements supersede any name. You outranked all your peers at the academy, and you were in line to work with the Lord Count…" He paused and felt his face contort with sorrow. "Had the unfortunate incident not occurred."

Trulips closed her eyes briefly in lamentation. "Jeffery Reeling was a great man. It is a shame I never had the chance to learn from him."

"And, what do you think of his murder?" Julian asked. "Was it Alpheus Hindlow who did it?"

"No, not him," she said, firm in her response.

"You seem certain."

"I wasn't," she said, "until Lady Charlotte confirmed it."

Charlotte Hindlow was, of course, Alpheus's sister. But Julian also knew her as the greatest living scholar, second only to the Grandmaster. He had thought he would get the chance to meet her during her recent return to Zorlia. But not only had her return been brief—just a week—but she had also avoided public attention, allegedly only meeting the Lord Emperor and a few scholars. It seemed from the outside that she had chosen not to involve herself in the Lord Count's murder case at all, and in effect had done nothing to help Alpheus.

"Charlotte Hindlow confirmed it?" Julian said. "What is that supposed to mean? Am I to suppose something is true if she says so?"

Trulips looked Julian in the eyes. "Yes," she said. "Sir Longinus, it appears that you have an ill will toward Lady Charlotte, and I might suspect that it has to do with Alpheus Hindlow missing. If that's the case, worry not, for he will soon return to Zorlia."

"Did Charlotte Hindlow say that too?" Julian said with a scoff.

"Indeed."

They had arrived on the north side of Dunn Bay, where Julian halted his warhorse. The others stopped next to him.

"This is where we part ways," Julian said to Trulips. "But before you go," Julian added with hesitation, "let me ask one more question."

"And what might that be?"

"Why were you at the Theatre of the Romantics?"

Trulips appeared surprised for a moment, but then a small smile emerged. "Hunting. Hunting for heretics."

"But you're a sorcerer yourself," Julian said, raising a brow.

"And your point is?"

"A sorcerer labelling others as heretics is a first."

"So, to you, sorcerer equates to heretic?"

Julian fell silent this time. Perhaps she had a point.

"Until you see the difference," Trulips then said, "I don't see that we should share another conversation." She turned her horse, slapping the reins and trotting away. Julian watched her disappear into the crowd. He had been hoping to get a hint about the energy that had overwhelmed him that evening, but his words had failed him long before that.

Julian turned for Vondra Dawn, sharing no words with his attendants as they followed him there. When they reached the citadel, Julian realised from their astounded expressions that it was the first time that Alex and Emery had visited the imposing structure. Even the great fort of Bastion City paled in comparison to Vondra Dawn's regal and perhaps intimidating presence. Alex and Emery were looking up at the giant steeples now, which to them must have seemed to reach the skies. Actually, it felt that way for Julian, too—at least at times.

"Dismount here," Julian ordered.

His attendants parked the horses in the stable just outside the portcullis. Julian then surprised his attendants by leading them to the barracks. He had learned that Sagramore was in Zorlia, specifically to work with Breunor in order to ensure that the different armies in the Empire could co-exist. But Julian wasn't planning to see the veteran golden knight for anything to do with maintaining or pacifying soldiers. The assignment of his attendants, who had been developed in the Defence Army, was something he had to acknowledge. More importantly, a conversation with Sagramore could help him determine whether the two were trustworthy.

As they paced closer to the barracks, Sagramore's rallying calls resonated in the air, each followed by fervent war cries of several hundred soldiers. The soldiers standing guard at the gate bowed down to Julian before allowing him passage. Julian stepped in and then gestured his attendants to trail closely behind him. He scanned the open area, noting Breunor's absence. Though he no longer feared the man, he certainly wanted to avoid any direct confrontation.

Julian then eyed Sagramore, who was barking orders to the soldiers. The man was on the other side of the sandy area, and though he seemed to have noted Julian's arrival, he didn't stop what he was doing. Julian circled the wall to meet the veteran knight who barely spared him a glance even when Julian reached him. Julian said nothing, waiting with his arms crossed. His attendants stood up straight on either side of him.

It was almost half an hour after that when Sagamore finally sat back in a small shaded area. He had gotten the soldiers started on forming groups to shoot arrows, and under his guidance they were training in disciplined autonomy.

"Sir Sagramore," Julian addressed him, bowing alongside Alex and Emery.

"Sir Longinus," the golden knight replied in a forced, genial tone, his eyes turning to the two young knights. "How are the boys working out for you?"

"Good so far. Indeed, I am here to express my gratitude."

Sagramore waved a dismissive hand. "Cut the formalities, Longinus. You're no courtier. And besides, I'm not the one to thank. The Lord Chancellor requested our men—I could only pick from my best ones."

Julian fell silent for a moment, surprised and confused by the animosity on display. "Anyone hailing from the Defence Army—and I mean this sincerely—is a great man, a great warrior."

Sagramore raised a brow, perhaps surprised to hear such a compliment from Julian.

"I happened by Percival today," Julian then said softly, the name triggering visible angst upon Sagramore's face. "He didn't look so good. I think that he deserves to be given a chance. Not only is he strong—so much more than me—but he's clever, too. He would be a master tactician on the battlefield, and by that, I mean he'd be great at leading an army. So if you—"

"Say no more!" Sagramore cut in, a sudden glare flashing across his face. "I'm glad that you would value an old friend, but that boy is beyond help."

Julian opened his mouth to continue his case, but the golden knight had no intention to budge, already pointing him to the exit. When Julian failed to turn away, Sagramore himself treaded off back to the soldiers, leaving Julian alone.

It was apparent that there was something more between Pole and Sagramore than met the eye, but Julian couldn't work out what it could be. He thought to ask his attendants, but he doubted that they would know much.

"Sir Longinus," Emery said with quiet hesitance, as Julian now paced toward the Chancellery. "You were asking before about the whispers."

"And…?" Julian said without a glance back.

"I hear them, too."

Julian stopped, regarding Emery carefully. "What…?"

"I don't know if you're interested, but—"

Julian snapped his eyes wide open. "Of course I'm interested!"

Emery was visibly delighted for a moment, perhaps to have finally gotten Julian's attention. But his expression dulled soon enough as he recalled the whispers.

"They scare people, I think," he began, "because of the haunting voice and the persistent mention of doom. People associate these things with spirits and spectres, and naturally, they fear them. But being brought up as a faithful Ionian, I don't believe in any powers that claim to be greater than God's grace. And, in saying that, I've been somewhat immune to the voices that have so many people frightened. What terrifies me is something deeper. The whispers, when I listen carefully, actually speak about things in great detail. They foretell a future in which the land is ruled by sorcerers. They predict an uprising… and not only here in Zorlia. In fact, not even just Trubannis."

Julian swallowed. "Where, then?"

"Kraga… and Aizary," Emery said, his voice growing shaky. "It's all very murky… but it's those two countries that we need to worry about."

Julian grimaced as he mused about this new information. *Foreign threat?* he thought. *Kraga isn't a surprise. But Aizary? What are these whispers, really?*

TWENTY

Women with healing powers

Julian continued pacing along the grim corridors of Vondra Dawn as the thoughts of the whispers continued to badger him. He soon saw Roth in his path, who stood guard at a door of polished marble.

Lady Winter's dormitory, Julian noted. Usually, Julian wouldn't care to ask, but it was strange to send someone as powerful as Roth for such menial tasks. Julian looked the ex-mercenary in the eye, asking the question without saying a word.

Roth huffed, regarding Julian but paying no heed to his new attendants. "This should have been your job."

"It shouldn't be either of our jobs."

"The Lady is with someone from the musical drama," Roth said, making his case. "You went there with her, did you not? This is probably to mend something you did."

Julian ignored the comment and was ready to turn away when Roth added, "The peasant boy you live with is here, too."

Julian paused, turning suddenly blank.

Oscar? he thought, growing pale.

Roth blabbered on, saying something about a wooden sword too heavy for the boy's size, until Julian slammed him against the wall.

"Why is he here?!" Julian demanded, showing his teeth.

"Get your hands off me!" Roth cried, sweeping his arm out fiercely to shake Julian away. "I have nothing to do with it."

Julian expected for the worst as Roth continued barking at him. To him, there was only one reason Oscar would be here: to play the role of hostage in the case that he was ever disloyal to the Lord Chancellor. Julian stared down the door, considering smashing it down in order to see to Oscar's safety. But before having to resort to that, the door was slowly opened from the inside. A servant appeared from behind it—one of the young girls who was always with Winter.

"Lord Roth," the servant said with a frown, hushing him. "The Lady asked for silence."

"I'm sorry," Roth said, bowing slightly. "I'll keep it down."

"Jane," Julian addressed the servant whose name he actually remembered. "I want to see Lady Winter. Can you pass the word?"

"Of course, Sir Longinus," she said delightedly. "Please wait here."

She returned within a minute to welcome only Julian to proceed.

Behind the marble door was a magnificent antechamber lined with limestone pillars with freshly cut flowers stemming from each of them. Grand sculptures of mythical goddesses were positioned along polished walls of soft lavender. The overall colour converged to a light purple pigment which was less regal and more feminine.

"This way, please," Jane said, leading Julian through another doorway and into the hall.

The hall here was smaller than the one in the Chancellery. The furnishings and general decorations here were much more eye-pleasing, however, possibly because the architecture didn't have to symbolise the power and vigour of a powerful man, which would most likely restrict and constrain the imagination of the design. For one, the ground was carpeted in a warm beige unlike any other chamber in the rest of Vondra Dawn. In addition to that, upholstered lounges long enough to lie on superseded the need for any individual chairs.

At the far end of the hall sat Winter, and across from her was the fiddle player from the musical drama. They both were holding onto a musical instrument, apparently fine-tuning them. Winter held a cello, and the fiddle player was with her signature instrument. Their distinctive elegance was hauntingly similar—reserved, sensible, and polite. But their dresses didn't share the same attributes. While Winter donned a noblewoman's gown of the highest quality of woven fabric, complete with exquisite cuttings, the fiddle player sported a peasant woman's dress. And yet the fiddle player upheld that same elegance that she had as the angel in the musical drama. Indeed, Julian fell in a brief daze now as he remembered her magnificent performance that evening. The woman had played the fiddle and a lap harp with impeccable precision and skill. She had been a soothing vocalist, and perhaps most importantly, she had also played the angel of hope and despair as part of the story in the drama.

Although she was off the stage now, her dignity—or perhaps vanity—didn't subside even a little. Her long, wavy blonde hair, which she wore loose and parted down the middle, was tied from behind into a ponytail. She wore a faint smile that matched her cold, sedated eyes—hollow eyes that seemed to detach her from... everything. But despite that air of apathy, she was beautiful, with a voluptuous figure to match.

Julian blinked hard now and Oscar sprung once again to his mind. He scanned the area urgently, only to find that the boy was indeed there, sitting in a corner and looking more bored than anything else. The boy perked up, though, when he realised that Julian was there.

"Sir Longinus," Winter greeted, also noting Julian's arrival.

"My Lady," Julian addressed her, going down on one knee. "I'm here for... him," he said, nodding in Oscar's direction.

"Oh, were you looking for Oscar?" she asked innocently, waving a hand at the same time as she gestured for Julian to stand. "I apologise if we had you worried. But Oscar was with Eris, so I thought to invite him along."

"Eris?" Julian said, glancing across to the fiddle player, who returned a gentle nod.

"I don't believe you two have properly met," Winter said with a smile. "And that's in spite of your connection. She is none other than Eris Nightingale."

Julian cocked his head, unsure what the connection was.

"Oscar is my younger brother," the fiddle player said. "My deepest gratitude to you for taking care of him ever since he came to Zorlia. It is a pleasure to finally meet you."

Julian hid his surprise as best as he could. Indeed, as he thought back to the time when he had first met Oscar, the boy had spoken of a sister. He hadn't believed it at the time. And he still couldn't quite believe it even now. Julian glanced back and forth between Oscar and the fiddle player, unable to see any apparent family resemblance. The fiddle player had pale skin, whereas Oscar was relatively dark. And, of course, the fiddle player was Julian's age, much older than the boy.

"I'm sorry," Julian said finally. "What exactly happened? Why is Oscar here?"

"I was with him," the fiddle player said, turning back to her stringed instrument. "Lady Winter sought me out, and so now we are here."

That was no more information than Winter had offered only a moment earlier. Julian glanced over at Winter again, hesitating to press further. He hated to admit it, but having escorted her for the past month, Julian could find no fault with the woman. She seemed genuinely kind, and her care for the commoners was strikingly more sincere than anyone else in the court. She wasn't one to lie.

"Anyhow," the fiddle player said, eyeing Julian again, "would you kindly take Oscar back home? I will endeavour to see him again before I depart from the city."

Her words annoyed Julian, but it was unwise to show his annoyance in front of Winter. Julian glared over at Oscar as his gesture for the boy to come to him. He bowed once more to Winter and then retreated with Jane leading them back out. Oscar seemed to have noted that Julian was unhappy, and he shied away beside him.

When they stepped back into the corridor where Julian's attendants were waiting together with Roth, he shot the ex-mercenary a glare as a warning to the man not to provoke him. Roth wisely turned away, and then Julian led the others back to the main gate, where he called for their horses.

"Take him to Ramsgate," Julian said to his attendants, offering no explanation of who Oscar was.

"Julian," the boy uttered, "can I—"

"No," Julian cut in, knowing that Oscar had wanted to ask for his own horse. Emery seemed to have read the situation well enough as he offered Oscar a helping hand and pulled him up to ride with him.

"Sir," Alex said, saluting Julian. "We shall return soon."

Julian nodded, noting Oscar's pout as they rode away.

* * *

Julian had kept busy rummaging through the city for the sorcerers who were responsible for the whispers. But although he had managed to catch more than a few hints of alleged sightings, every trace of evidence had later led to dead ends. The sun was setting, and the day's work was over. Julian had relieved his attendants from duty and was now on his way to Rogers.

Oscar wasn't working at the tavern this evening. It had been three days, and although Julian had tried to avoid it, the short time each day when he had been at home with the boy, Eris Nightingale was the only topic of conversation. At times, just being with the boy was more difficult than a confrontation with some of Julian's toughest enemies. Oscar had confirmed that the musician was indeed his dear sister, and the boy had tried to explain that his sister had kept her distance because she believed that she brought misfortune to people close to her. That was a convenient excuse to explain why she hadn't come to see Oscar even once during this time.

Oscar had also confessed the *real* reason why he was in Zorlia. He had travelled from Farella with a farmer and had been arranged to live with an aunt in this city, a kind woman who had unfortunately been one of the Apostle's victims.

"I didn't tell Eris about it," Oscar had said. "If she knew, she would blame herself again. She would say our aunt died because of her."

All of it was true, at least according to his attendants' investigations. Julian had asked his attendants to take turns tracking Nightingale and inquiring about her background. Julian hadn't offered any reason to his attendants about why they had been given the task, however, but in truth, he didn't think that his investigation of the woman was independent of his hunt for sorcerers. The intense energy that had frozen him over that first time seeing the musical drama was an eerie experience that he simply couldn't forget. Whether that overwhelming energy had anything to do with Nightingale or not, he couldn't say, but Julian still wasn't ready to trust the woman.

Alex and Emery had reported that Nightingale had mostly been with her musical drama team during her entire time in the city, rehearsing by day and performing by night. Julian himself had been on the task, attending the theatre every evening. And while Julian had arrived at the theatre with suspicion each time, he had left each night in further admiration of the musician's performance.

The character Nightingale played was named *Elpis*, the angel of hope and despair, and her rendition felt closer to life each successive time that he witnessed it. Julian had come to appreciate the story more deeply, and identified not only with the male and female leads named *Hobart* and *Meredith*, but also the angel played by Nightingale, who had her own empathetic tale to tell. Julian thought that Nightingale's talent shone brighter than that of her colleagues, but off-stage she wasn't popular with the team at all. She isolated herself, altogether leaving the theatre shortly after each show. She did stay at a costly inn with her fellow cast members, though.

Julian looked up then and realised that he had finally arrived at Rogers. He pushed the door open to reveal a rather empty tavern. Dock, the tavern master standing behind the bar, noted him treading in and waved in his direction.

"Just you?" Dock asked, wearing his always jolly grin.

"Indeed," Julian said, taking a seat.

The man filled a frothy mug with beer, then slid it down the bar to Julian. "How are you getting along with the child's sister?"

Julian lifted his head. "How did you know about that?"

"I've heard a thing or two," Dock said, frowning slightly. "She's no ordinary woman. Men in town have tried to woo her—most of them brutes, of course. But somehow those men had fallen ill since... cursed, maybe."

Julian gazed down at his beer, watching as the froth bubbled over. He had learned as much in his own investigations. He had heard stories that referred to Nightingale as *the Harbinger of Misfortune*. People close to her had always been met some kind of tragedy, and most of her childhood friends had died in separate incidents. Apparently she had even brought misfortune to her parents, who had died shortly after Oscar's birth.

It was easy to believe the stories, but his attendants' prudence had brought to light another, lesser-known perspective. According to what Emery had discovered, life had never been easy for Nightingale. She had been raised in the town of Frey, in South Farella. As one of the closer towns to the frontier, the town had fallen prey to both sides of the conflict between the countries through the years. Naturally, the Kragans had been the aggressors in Frey during the war—the town had once been occupied for months. Today, Empire soldiers were stationed there, but it was said that these soldiers of Truban heritage were corrupt and potentially more detestable even than the Southerners. Part of the reason was that most of the soldiers assigned along the frontier were selected from a pool of discards that had failed to rise through the ranks. Not only did these soldiers run the town with oppression, often beating the peasants over nothing, but the word was that they also allowed *visitors* from Kraga to enter and leave the town through bribery.

Nightingale had apparently been raised in a relatively privileged home where her family had been able to afford protection from the aggressors, even during the war. Even so, on more than several occasions she had risked her life to stand up for those less fortunate than her. And in addition to freeing herself from aggression, Nightingale had also attracted a great number of suitors ever since her adolescence. She was a beautiful woman, after all, blessed with a curvaceous figure. While some of her suitors had been good men, a whole lot of them had been simply driven by pure lust. But regardless of whether those men had been hostile or not, all of those who had managed to get close to her had suffered the same ill fate—death by seemingly natural causes. Nightingale's bravery, together with the fascination for her beauty and the supposed *misfortune* that came with it, had been the very reason for the demise of the woman's loving parents. Roughly half a year after *surviving* the war, after the invaders had retreated, the Nightingale couple had then been murdered by a Kragan soldier who had been part of the army during their occupation of the town. Apparently the soldier had been wary that he would be digging his own grave if he had targeted Eris Nightingale. And in her stead, he had murdered her parents.

Nightingale had since left Frey, taking her younger brother with her. But life had never gotten easier for her and Oscar. The siblings had never settled anywhere for more than a few months. As soon as her past caught up to her—her *misfortune* having been divulged—Nightingale and her brother were driven away from each successive place as if they carried the plague. And in more recent years, the woman had finally found a place of refuge. The musical drama group was perfect for her because they were always on the move. And despite her still frosty relationship with the other musicians, Nightingale had since become a core member of the group, owing to her exceptional skill with the fiddle.

Julian sighed heavily. It seemed that this was simply another case where negative comments tended to ring louder than praise. Indeed, if what Emery had learned was true, Nightingale might just be a truly kind woman. Her fate had been seeded by one word: *misfortune*. If there were such a power in the land, Julian thought, it would be more frightening than sorcery.

And perhaps, Julian also thought, even though the possibility seemed ridiculous, *it was misfortune that had me overwhelmed that night*. He shook his head. *Idiot.*

* * *

Later that evening, Julian was at the Theatre of the Romantics once again. It was his fourth consecutive night there, and he caught only the final act of the musical drama which was incidentally the most spectacular. Upon the conclusion of the show, Julian strode to the back exit. He had waited barely ten minutes when Nightingale treaded out in a modest commoner's dress.

She gasped when she saw Julian, but calmed herself within seconds, reverting to her sedated expression. "This is not a good place to talk," she said. "Let us move to somewhere more discreet."

Julian nodded as Nightingale led the way along the bay to one of the quieter spots—a landscaped, grassy, open space. The moons were dim tonight, and the stars were hidden behind the mists. But a certain pendant shone brightly under Nightingale's dress, at her chest. Even its reflection stood out in the river.

"Are you really his sister?" Julian asked, getting straight to the point. "Oscar is a regular boy, but you are not regular in any way. Just who are you, exactly?"

"I'm his sister," Nightingale responded in her ever-bland pitch, facing the river instead of Julian.

"His *real* sister?"

She seemed to jerk forward slightly, at least it appeared that way under the cloudy evening sky. "I'm his sister," she insisted. "Just not biologically," she then added. "The Nightingales adopted me. Even he doesn't know."

"And do you see him as your brother?"

Nightingale turned to him, suddenly irate. "Of course," she snapped.

"Then why aren't you there for him right now?"

"Why...?" she said in surprise. "And I thought you would have done your research."

Julian glared harder at her.

"Did you think I came to Zorlia to see him?" she said, turning her back on Julian again. "I'm keeping my distance. I wouldn't want anything to happen to him. In two weeks' time, after the last performance, I'll be—"

Julian grabbed a sudden hold of her, wrapping his arms around her shoulders for an embrace that she was clearly not prepared for. Even Julian himself was surprised by this action.

Nightingale flung herself free, and then dealt Julian an audible slap across the face. "Are you out of your mind?!" she yelled.

Julian glanced away briefly, rubbing where it throbbed from the slap. "It itches a little," he said, "but this is hardly misfortune. Excuse my indecency, but I wanted to know what the fuss was about. Perhaps all the talk about the Harbinger of Misfortune was only a myth, after all."

Nightingale's eyes widened for a moment, but then almost immediately reverted back to her cold, sedated expression. "Don't even try," she said, and then slowing to a more chilling tone, "*you'll die.*"

Julian sighed, and then in a quick motion he drew his iron sword and slashed it across the river, causing multiple explosions above the water, sparking a spectacular display of crimson red light which reflected in both the water and the sky.

Nightingale, though, was unmoved, and said nothing, seemingly not even impressed by the power on display.

"I should have died on more than a few occasions," Julian said as he sheathed his weapon again. "If I believed in superstitious tales, then I might be the real harbinger of misfortune. If I had left things upon fate, I wouldn't be living now at all. I do not die easily. And Oscar will be all right as long as

I'm here."

Nightingale regarded him. "You have my gratitude. I wouldn't have to worry when I leave."

"No. Now that I know that he has family, I'm no longer responsible for him."

Nightingale narrowed her eyes.

"That's your role as his sister," Julian clarified.

She turned away again. "You still don't understand."

"I *do* understand. You dumped him on this aunt of yours. And what happened? Your aunt died and Oscar ended up living on the streets. *That* is misfortune, and he was subject to it even though he was sent far away from you."

She closed her eyes and said nothing.

Julian sighed again, taking a few steps closer to the water, pointing his back at Nightingale now. "Misery befalls everyone," he said. "Our lives are filled with all kinds of hardships. Poverty, desperation, war, plagues—there's too much in this land we cannot control. Misfortune is upon all of us." He paused for a moment. "The troubles met by those people close to you... They may well be happenstance—accidental."

Nightingale said nothing still. When Julian glanced back, he saw that Nightingale was simply staring into the flowing water.

"Do you really think so?" she finally said.

"I'm never really sure about anything. But Oscar... he'll be happy if you stay. I suppose I'm sure of that. So, for his sake, no more of this keeping distance nonsense. You must stay here with him."

Tears shimmered in her eyes, but she didn't let a bead drop out onto her cheeks. It was difficult for him to read her expression, but after a moment, she finally nodded.

"We'll give it a try," she said.

* * *

That evening, Nightingale followed Julian back to the home he shared with Oscar. Despite the late hour, the boy was awake. And Oscar was most glad to learn about his sister's compromise and that she'd stay in Zorlia with them, as long as she didn't sense any forthcoming tragedy. This was an ability of hers, apparently.

Julian allowed the siblings some privacy as he retired to his own room. Pausing at the door, he swept his eyes across the humble room. He saw no material possessions and not a single item of sentimental value. He had kept it this way ever since he had first come to Zorlia. He had told himself to avoid being attached to anyone or anything, and that no one could be trusted. He had valued only his own existence.

Julian then crouched down next to the bed, reaching an arm under it, and then slid out a bulky board-like item wrapped in a sturdy cloth. He swung the fabric free to reveal the extraordinary painting that had belonged to Alpheus—the one with the young boy, and the subject's view of an alternate world.

Julian leaned the canvas against his simple bed and took a step back to see it more fully. He knew nothing about art, but he found the work mystifying. He was fascinated by the young boy in the painting, the child of apparent Aizar descent as supposed by his silvery-bluish hair. With only a blanket-sized fabric covering him, the boy was next to naked—even part of his buttocks showed as his cloak was being blown in the wind.

The overall theme of the painting was bleak, and the background shades of tangerine further intensified the desolation. Still, the allure was otherworldly. It wasn't disturbing to see the horde of human silhouettes that formed the background lining up toward the figure hung on the leafless tree. They were lining up for death, and yet Julian found it refreshing. In turn, he wondered how a devout Ionian in Alpheus had managed to create such a work.

Julian had had the painting since a couple of months ago when he had snuck into the Hindlow Manor to retrieve it. Alpheus had asked for the favour in his letter of departure, which Julian had received from Agnes Gardner. And it had been a day after the Empire had issued a warrant to comb through the manor. If not for Charlotte Hindlow's esteemed status, the Empire would have torn down the entire building. Instead, the divided opinions on the court scrutinised the search to the point that it had then become a mere inspection rather than a thorough examination. Julian had heard that the people in charge had been careful not to misplace a single item of furniture. He *did* wonder, however, whether anyone had found the hidden basement where the statue of a noblewoman was kept.

Julian thought it silly now that he had actually risked going there just for a painting. Much had happened since then, and his life and freedom now were too precious to be put to such risk.

His thoughts soon flowed away from Alpheus and onto Pole. Would his once closest confidant ever return to favour again? And were they still allies? Their last meeting, of course, had suggested that they weren't.

Julian sighed and raised his arms slowly in the air, stretching toward the ceiling. He grazed the ceiling with his outstretched fingers, collecting dust, and then finally grasped thin air as he held a closed fist.

A knocking sounded at his door then.

Julian answered the door and saw Nightingale holding a serving tray and a tea set, steam billowing from the teapot—all of it likely prepared by Oscar, who had recently become a tea lover as a result of Dock not allowing him to touch liquor. Julian shifted his focus back on Nightingale, who was charming indeed. Her beauty was evident despite donning only a peasant woman's dress and having removed her cosmetics. This was also the first time he had seen her smile, which, sadly, wouldn't last.

Nightingale paled in the blink of an eye. Her eyes hollowed suddenly as she gazed at the painting leaning against the bed. The serving tray fell from her grip, crashing to the floor with a clang that made her leap with surprise. The teapot shattered and hot liquid surged out, completely soaking the floor.

Julia nudged her aside promptly and threw an old woven top on the broken teapot. "Are you all right?" he asked.

Nightingale gasped again, her eyes still on the painting. "Why... why is *she* there?"

Julian turned to the canvas. "*She*?"

"That girl."

Julian turned to the artwork with a squint. "That's a girl?"

The child in the painting looked to be around eight years of age, and with only her backside viewable, the gender of the figure was perhaps unspecified. Julian had thought it to be a boy before, on the preconception of the short hair.

"And you *know* her?" Julian asked.

Nightingale shook her head, clearly in discomfort. "I don't know what it is," she said. "This feeling... of affinity."

Julian winced, not sure what to think. "You've had a long night," he said. "Get some rest. This room is yours. I'll be in the courtyard."

Nightingale nodded at him. She seemed to have calmed down a little. Julian cleaned up the spilled tea, grabbed the painting and left, closing the door behind him.

* * *

Julian awoke to the first glimmers of the rising sun sweeping over his tiled roof. He had been sleeping on a chair in the courtyard with a light blanket wrapped around his body, and beneath that blanket he had clasped onto his iron sword with his arms crossed.

He sat up, holding the top of the throw.

Oscar? he thought, and then shook his head. *No, it must have been his sister. But... how? How did I not wake?*

Julian flapped away the blanket, rising unsteadily to his feet. He hesitated for a moment and then treaded toward his room, stepping toward the front door. He was ready to knock, but instead, he gently pushed it open. As he had suspected, Nightingale wasn't there.

She left, Julian thought as he shoved the rest of the door open, peering around for anything she might have left to indicate where she had gone. But there was nothing.

Oscar, he then thought with urgency. Julian dashed over to the next room, praying that he would find the boy there. And when he poked his head in the window, he was relieved to confirm that Oscar was dozing away.

Julian breathed a sigh of relief. He then turned away, rushing into the living area and grabbed his armour. He clinked the metal plate over his torso, clipped the cape at the shoulders, and headed outside. His warhorse was still parked where he had left him. He hopped onto the brawny equine and raced ahead toward the inn where the musical drama group was staying.

It was barely morning, and the streets were nearly empty. Julian didn't know why he bothered, but he realised that he had been in a euphoria last night when he had thought he had convinced Nightingale to stay with them.

When Julian arrived at the inn, he hurried inside, and he was about to dash through the eating house toward the boniface, but he stopped short when he recognised several faces at one of the rounded tables.

They're from the drama group, Julian realised, eyeing an attractive and slender lady and a charismatic young man who played the lead characters of the show, *Meredith and Hobart*.

Julian paced over to them. "Is Eris Nightingale with you?" he asked.

The performers winced slightly. "And you are?"

"A friend."

Hobart huffed. "I never knew her to keep friends."

"Can you just answer the question?" Julian asked, growing impatient.

"She left late last night," *Meredith* said, sharing the same annoyance as Hobart expressed.

"Even though there are four performances left," one of the other ladies added, shaking her head.

Julian thought for a moment. "Did she give any reason, or tell anyone where she was off to?"

"She's a strange one," Meredith said with a shrug. "She doesn't give reasons for anything that she does. But she *did* promise to wait for us at our next stop."

"Which is...?"

"Dawnsdale," she said, "in the state of Cellarsy."

TWENTY-ONE

Fallen warriors

Pole stepped into Vondra Dawn. No one had summoned him, but the guards at the entrance allowed his entry on the merit of his rank as a silver knight. Drunken again in broad daylight, Pole made sure to look more pathetic than ever as he shook out the last drop of liquor from the flask which had since replaced his rapier at his belt. His armour had been marred by all kinds of stains which had since discoloured it to now a dull grey. The leather underneath his armour was rumpled. Having not groomed himself for quite a while, he reeked of alcohol.

And that was all part of the act.

The guards grimaced at him as he passed by. He treaded his way toward the cookhouse only to grab a full-sized barrel of wine, which he swung atop his shoulder. The cooks gave him withering looks, but did nothing to stop him, and Pole simply sneered as he headed back out.

After shoving his way past several more guards, he arrived at the spiral stairway of the western tower. He paused there, looking up at the steeple for a moment. This was where Reeling's chambers had been, and this was where he had once shot to fame, seizing Alpheus Hindlow when even Victor Breunor had failed to do so.

But Pole wasn't there to reminisce. He was there to see someone he had managed to befriend in recent times, when everyone else had cast him out. Pole stepped into the western tower, and instead of ascending the spiral stairs, he went down toward the basement. The passageway grew darker as he descended, striding several floors down until he reached the bottom—a sizeable room stacked with nearly empty bookcases. A number of oil lamps were installed across the room, but the cobwebs and dust that filled every corner of the vault suggested that it had been abandoned for quite some time. It was an isolated nook deep within the otherwise eventful citadel.

"I brought you something!" Pole shouted, his words echoing to every recess, splitting through the eerie silence.

A dwarf of a figure stepped out from behind one of the bookcases at the far end. The small man donned a thick mantle, and when he lifted his head slightly, a grisly countenance emerged in the flickering light from the flames. The man hardly looked human, with a hooked nose, bony cheeks, pale face, a blinded right eye, and a left eye that bulged unnaturally large. And for this reason he had been assigned to patrol this vault, a place that no one ever visited.

He was Odo Rittle, the shunned sentry who had been the prime witness against Alpheus Hindlow's alleged murder.

Rittle panicked clumsily now as he rushed out to Pole. "That is too generous of you, Sir Pole!" Rittle said, gazing up at the barrel of wine.

His androgynous, brittle voice was as repulsive as his unsightly appearance. Pole giggled to himself as he unplugged the cap on the barrel of wine and tossed the cork away. He lifted the tremendous barrel up into the air with both arms, tilting it so that its contents poured down into his mouth and also down his chest.

It had been three weeks earlier when Pole had stumbled into the Soma Slums. Petty crimes such as theft and disorderly conduct were a perpetual problem in that notorious neighbourhood, but even the people there knew better than to rob a silver knight. As the man in armour lurched along the streets, the paupers scattered away like rodents. And despite his intoxication, Pole had been amused that even what he had considered the lowest of people now despised and shunned him.

There had been just one person who hadn't abandoned him, and that was Rittle. The hideous man had even welcomed Pole into his humble home more than a few times. There and then, Pole had moaned about his displeasures to Rittle, lamenting the fact that no one understood him. Pole rambled on until he lost all sense of time. And ever since that day, Rittle had become a confidant of sorts, at least as Pole continued to work in the shadows.

Pole lowered the barrel now, eyeing Rittle with his blurred vision. He stepped forward toward the sentry, but he lost his footing and crashed into him instead. The two men fell to the ground together, and Rittle's small body offered only flimsy padding. The uncapped wine barrel, meanwhile, rolled across the floor, its contents spilling out wastefully. Pole giggled, amused, and he giggled harder when Rittle rolled him away, the sentry rubbing his chest which must have been throbbing from the fall.

"I'm on patrol now," Rittle said, annoyance in his voice. "Find someone else to bother."

"No!" hollered Pole, still lying on the ground. "There's no one else! Everyone else should *just* die! They should *all* just die..."

Pole crawled to where most of the wine had been spilled, and he started licking the alcohol off the ground.

Pitiful, Pole himself realised, even as he lapped greedily at the ground. *How deep have I fallen?*

"Do you hate this world and all of its people?" Pole thought he heard then.

He looked up in his haziness, unsure whether it was Rittle who had spoken.

"Do you want to get back at them?" the voice said again. "I can tell you how."

This time, Pole shook his head and wiped his eyes as he tried to verify to the best of his ability that it *was* Rittle speaking. Pole slapped his own cheek, but failed to regain much wakefulness. Rittle repeated his offer, and still Pole groaned in discomfort as he looked around the wine barrel, then crawled in its direction after he had spotted it. But before he could reach the barrel, he found himself drenched in cold water from above.

Pole snapped his eyes wide open then, jumping to his feet. "What the hell are you doing?!" he blasted.

Rittle lowered his head. "I apologise," he said. "But believe me when I tell you this. I have a way for you to get back at those who abandoned you."

Pole winced, holding his head. "Forget it," he said. "Without power, there's nothing I can do."

"What if I lend you that power?" Rittle said with a smirk.

"You? What power do *you* have?"

"Precisely speaking," Rittle said, "it is the power of the man I work for."

"And who might that be?"

"You don't need to know who he is. All you need to know is that he can help you."

Pole snorted. "Just what are you offering?"

"I'm offering to recover everything you had. Would you like that?"

"Of course I would. But—"

Rittle turned away, pointing to the exit. "Go now. Come back again when you've sobered up."

* * *

Dig your graves now. You'll need them.

Blame no one but yourself, for you have angered the gods.

And you shall repent in the hereafter.

No one shall escape the wrath. No one...

Pole snapped his eyes open, gasping for breath. It was the same dream again—that nightmare he shared with nearly half the population.

Damn the whispers, he thought.

He looked down over the empty street, orientating himself to the height of the clock tower from which he had been sleeping. It was only early morning, the break of dawn still at least an hour away. Pole was tired, but he forced his eyes firmly open. He wasn't going to fall back into that terrible dream again, at least not until the next day was upon him.

* * *

Pole snuck back into Vondra Dawn the next evening, dodging all the guards on the way to the western tower—just as Rittle had requested. Pole had brought his weapon with him, and was now free from the influence of alcohol.

The further he went down the spiral stairs, the more sparsely placed the oil lamps mounted on the walls became, and these were the only source of light. He descended more than a thousand steps, a substantial distance that he hadn't noticed in his initial visit. The bottom of the stairway was pitch black except for the solitary candle that he held onto, which he had snatched from the wall. Though flimsy, the candle was a substantial improvement from complete darkness.

A sudden chill ran through him when he reached the door to the vault. This could be it. The grand prize that he had been working tirelessly toward for nearly three months was finally within grasp, at least he thought so. He could only pray that Rittle was more than an ignorant pawn. But the possibility that Rittle actually knew nothing made him anxious. For all that he had planned and the ostracising he had endured, he deserved some kind of reward, even if it was only a pointer.

Pole took a deep breath and pushed open the wooden door. The creaking noise reverberated eerily within the enclosed nook, and Pole shuddered at the sound. Pole didn't know whether to credit the chill to the actual temperature or to the anxiety that was threatening to devour him whole.

Every little sound he made now echoed back at him more loudly. He held the burning candle away from himself and took each step with caution, reminding himself that he had been there only the day before and that there was nothing to fear.

The man he was to meet finally revealed himself, stepping out again from behind one of the bookcases, also holding an oil lamp. Rittle was in the same mantle as the previous day, and yet seeing him when sober made Pole cringe, instinctively stepping back.

"I've waited a long time," Rittle whispered, his voice almost a hiss.

Pole calmed himself as best as he could, almost certain that the sentry didn't notice that he had cold sweat sliding from his forehead. "The offer, Rittle," Pole said. "I'm not here for small talk."

Rittle tittered, another horrible sound. "Your enthusiasm thrills me. And for that, I'll let you get back at those who have spurned you."

The sentry paced away to the other side of the vault. He was surprisingly adept at finding his way around despite the lack of light. Rittle stopped in front of a bookcase and reached his short arms into a cluster of metal bookends. A grinding sound clued Pole that the hideous man was turning some kind of mechanical knob, and the sound ended abruptly with an audible click. And suddenly a couple of the bookcases to its right creaked open, revealing a hidden passage.

"Good Lord!" Pole gasped as he walked over to the narrow passage, through which another set of stairs extended further down into the depths of the building.

"Save your excitement for later," Rittle said with a wink.

Rittle was clearly growing more excited, and at the same time more perverse. He gestured for Pole to proceed and insisted that Pole should lead the way. It was another hundred steps or so before they reached the bottom, but it felt much longer for Pole, who grew colder with every step. He still didn't know whether the chill he felt was real or not, and as they descended deeper down, the air was increasingly contaminated by a foul stench of rotten flesh and blood.

If there happens to be a monster down there..., Pole thought, a hand on his rapier. But when they finally reached the bottom, he realised that there was no such being. Instead, before him was an absolute horror, a monstrosity that was far worse than a confrontation with any monster.

Pole's stomach churned in the face of the various body parts scattered across the dreaded chamber. Mutilated corpses were chained to a collection of torture devices that had long been prohibited by civilised governments for their extreme savagery. It was an artificial hell that was no less cruel than the realms of the damned described in the holy testaments.

The frisson of horror overwhelmed Pole as he peered left and right in shock, noting that the faces and bodies were also disfigured. Eyes had been gouged out, while others had tongues stitched to the mouths. There were men, women, and even children.

Wait...! Pole thought, recognising a few faces. *Some of these men... they're soldiers.* None of them was personally acquainted with him, thankfully, but surely no one deserved this.

As Pole imagined that everything before him to be just a nightmare in his mind, Rittle began wildly whipping a metal chain at the inanimate corpses. Pole grinded his teeth in both anger and fear. He moved his hand onto the grip of his sword, but before drawing the weapon, he jerked his hand up to cover his mouth. An intense nausea rushed up to his throat, and—unable to suppress it—he vomited against the wall, his chest heaving violently.

In his agony, Pole finally turned to Rittle. "What in the hell is this place?"

Rittle calmed down a little from his hysteria, turning the question back at Pole. "Is this not what you wanted? These are the men responsible for your downfall!"

"But they..."

"They're only pawns," Rittle inserted with a smirk. "I agree that the thrill is not the same with small fries. They don't make for good specimens. They don't last. But soon, we'll catch the big ones. They last much longer!"

Pole's distress muted him, and Rittle's disgusting indulgences and unfeigned inclinations of sadism shocked him. Only when alerted by a faint cry from the crowd of victims he had thought were all dead was Pole able to grasp onto a glimmer of hope.

I could save them, he thought wishfully. The wretched wails and moans, however, sounded like they came from someone who actually wished for death more than anything.

Pole tried desperately to locate the person issuing the cry. Finally he saw that it came from a man nailed by the hands with arms spread out widely and affixed to one of the bloody walls. Hundreds of needles had been inserted into his torso, and the man was missing his lower limbs altogether. This miserable man wasn't a familiar face, and he was beyond help.

It was an unbearable sight for any sane person, but Rittle was clearly insane. Reaching into a tall cabinet which was the only piece of furniture in the room not being used as a torture device, Rittle picked out a thick needle. Faithful to the sickening demeanour he had displayed thus far, Rittle walked toward the ill-fated man and poked the needle directly into his body. The victim let out a soft wailing cry, but most likely only because he was already numb to the endless pain. Seemingly unsatisfied with his victim's passing reaction, Rittle ruthlessly ripped the needle back out, causing yet more blood to gush out from his chest. And while the bloodshed brought a wicked smirk onto Rittle's face, Pole also finally reacted with indignation, finally drawing his rapier. He leaped in the air and lashed out.

Rittle gasped, possibly fleetingly mistaking himself as the target. The strike instead prodded straight into the heart of the tortured man, killing him instantly. Pole spared Rittle no glance whatsoever, his gaze fixed upon the man whose life he had just ended.

Pole then twisted his weapon inside the dead man. "You're right," he said, staring at the lifeless eyes of his victim and secretly praying that he would be on his way toward a better afterlife. "This is a good way to correct the wrongs of society. Let him be the first of many."

Pole finally pulled out the rapier from the corpse, the swing causing blood to spray across the chamber. The atrocity around him was undoubtedly shocking, but this was a promising start. And he knew it would take much more to achieve his objective, which was to uproot the entire Empire.

He pulled out the cravat beneath his armour and used it to wipe the blood off his weapon. He finally turned to Rittle, wearing a wicked grin that had the sentry smile.

TWENTY-TWO
Valley of the Harper Ranges

It was the first day of May, or sixteen days since Azure's injury that would prove fatal without intervention. The fact that they had been warned that she would live for no more than thirty days meant that over half the journey had gone by already, and still there had been no sign of the Passionless Surgeon. Even so, their journey southwards had so far been a smooth expedition.

Alpheus and Azure had reached the northern rim of the Harper Ranges two days prior, only ten days since their departure from Poppaross. The fine horses had worked tirelessly, climbing countless hills, piercing forests, and travelling day and night for over fourteen hours per day. Luck had also played a part. They hadn't encountered any bandits or wild beasts, and even the weather had been friendly to their demanding schedule.

As her health had been holding up, Azure had managed to treat this precarious expedition as a vacation of sort. Although she was clearly weak, she had often peeked out through the drapes of the wagon to watch the serenity of nature pass her by. She was eager to educate Alpheus on the many different types of plants that surrounded them, classifying them into their specific genus, species, sub-species, and explaining some of their unique properties. Azure was familiar with both the vernacular and botanical names of the trees, shrubs, ferns, and flowers. She described the Harper Ranges as a giant garden—a *wonderland* of a twin mountain range. And her enthusiasm for the seemingly infinite nature around them only increased with each passing day. Alpheus, in turn, had queried Azure about the climatic and soil requirements of each plant in question.

The valley of the Harper Ranges was the longest known landform of its kind, which split the mountain range into eastern and western spans. The valley itself was classified by scholars as a sub-alpine region due to its high altitude where trees and other vegetation were sparse. Having referenced the map of Vinawell for study during the journey, Alpheus had drawn dotted lines over the chart to segregate the massive expanse into identifiable regions, which was necessary in order for them to avoid wandering aimlessly in a tremendous expanse that covered almost a third of the country's land.

Alpheus had circled three target areas of *high likelihood* of where they might find the physician. The first target area was at neither the eastern nor western span, but instead at a site along the northern part of the valley known as the *Terrace of Colours*. It was a beautiful, natural landform, carpeted by over a thousand species of magnificent flowers.

His second guess was the summit of Mt. Meridian, famously known as one of the Four Holy Peaks, located geographically close to the centre of the ranges and numerically being the fifth mountain on the western span. The summit of the mountain was the highest point of the ranges, and also the point from which one could oversee the entire expanse in all its glory.

His third and final guess was the flooded forest situated near the southern end of the valley, a rare ecoregion that was usually defined as a *swamp forest*. Against the limited time that Azure had left, it was a tall order to visit all of these three places, and frankly impossible to visit a fourth.

And on this afternoon of May Day, they arrived at their first stopover—the Terrace of Colours. According to the map, it was a giant meadow that stretched over an expanse equal to the size of a small town. Alpheus parked their wagon at a high vantage point that allowed them a good view of the expanse of the treaded, bowl-shaped landform. With an enormous collection of showy flowers, of which the majority were endemic, this was essentially Azure's playground within what was already her wonderland. The magnificent flower-carpeted floor of brilliant colours, together with the collective fragrance of pleasant scents lifted by the gentle winds, most likely tingled all of her senses. If Azure's health permitted, she probably would have dove into the meadow and danced upon the blooming colours. Instead, she remained sitting inside the wagon, settling for the view there.

Alpheus watched her as she marked each flower species by their vivid colours, identifying orchids, poppies, daisies, and anemones, among many others. Alpheus, though, couldn't bring himself to appreciate the stunning meadow. With not the slightest hint of human civilisation at the terrace, this stopover was clearly a failure. The Passionless Surgeon wasn't there, and probably had never even passed by. The only positive was that the meadow had brought a smile to Azure's face.

* * *

From there, Alpheus and Azure headed toward Mt. Meridian, the fifth mountain of the western span, counting from north to south. Shortly into their advance, they happened upon a series of maple trees with lush leaves standing at an average height that rivalled the great donjon of Radiance's Nest. Azure again called upon her rich knowledge of plants, asserting that the presentation of this variety of maple indicated that it was spring.

"This snakebark maple," she said, "is of genus *acer*, species *grosseri*, and variety *hersii*. The three-lobed, triangular, bright green leaves you see now turn orange in the fall. As for the hanging clusters of tiny, pale yellow flowers, and the pink-brown, winged fruits, these only appear in the flowering season."

Alpheus nodded as he regarded the trees. "How the plant presents itself in each different season incidentally describes how certain species can only thrive under certain conditions. Is that not the very law of nature?"

"Law of nature?" Azure said unapprovingly. "Can you not philosophise about everything, and instead learn to appreciate what is around you? Spring is here—the most frantic time in the garden! Every plant is trying to flower. The season is marked by rebirth, renewal, and regrowth."

Alpheus nodded and then slapped the reins for the horses to move faster.

You're the one philosophising, he thought with contented sigh, *that you can be reborn in this blooming season.* He remembered when Azure had first suffered the injury and how she had despaired. She had been disgusted at her own pitiful condition, and was afraid to be his burden. But since then, she had become a warrior who fought hard for her life every day. Since this expedition began, she hadn't complained once about her misfortune. Instead, she had taken each day as it came and had endured numerous episodes of bodily function failures, most of which were severe respiratory problems. She had remained focused on the positives like the weather, the scenery, and the excitement of the journey.

"You know what," Alpheus said, glancing back briefly to the cabin where Azure sat, his pitch cheery. "This has been a lovely journey for me. It really has. And this trek out here in the valley—it's wonderful."

Azure returned the smile. "It is," she agreed. "If I could live out here, I would."

"Now, what do you say? When we get you all healed up, how about we go see the natural wonders of Trubannis?"

"That would be… a dream, but I—"

Azure trailed off rather abruptly. For a moment, Alpheus thought she was pondering over the places they could visit. But when he turned back, he realised Azure was fighting her latest and sudden bout of extreme pain. She was clawing at her chest as her veins darkened through her skin. She was trembling, trying to cough, but instead choking dangerously, her eyes wide with fear and pain.

Alpheus pulled on the reins to stop the horses. He hopped back into the cabin, dropping down behind Azure. He thrust a palm onto her back and forced her to expel the frosty air trapped in her lungs.

The sparkling light blue energy gleamed brilliantly, flowing into Azure and soothing the blockages in her neurons. Her health had been volatile. There were times when she was that vibrant young lady again—cheeky, zealous, and enthusiastic. But at other times, and without warning, she would shut down completely. Initially, those shocks had come about once every two days, but now they came almost twice daily. Those deadly convulsions had her tensed up to the extent that her veins looked like they were about to explode. And unfortunately, every consequent episode was more severe than the preceding one.

Alpheus concentrated deeply as he became drenched in a heap of sweat. He finally released his palm, catching Azure as she fell back onto him. She had fallen unconscious, but Alpheus knew that she was better now. He laid her down and covered her with an extra cloak, and then he hopped back to the front, pulling on the horses to continue their climb.

Everything seemed so quiet all of a sudden. Without Azure's enthusiasm and sweet voice, the vibrant valley suddenly seemed dull. The *garden* around him was no longer a wonderland—it was simply uncharted territory. A foreign, unfamiliar land, in the middle of nowhere. The chances of locating the physician were slim, as they had always been.

Alpheus had become more proficient in helping Azure, but at the same time, he realised that prolonging her life by such means was harmful to her in the longer run. Despite both his own and Azure's energy were being driven primarily by the water element, his vibrant energy clashed with her dormant energy, and this regular clashing had taken a toll on her health.

The rations stocked under the seat inside the coach—although plentiful—were of the dried variety, and very lean. The basket of bread that had been neatly packed with many different shapes and sizes, were tasteless, the taste having been compromised by the additives that were necessary for the bread to be preserved for the duration of the journey. And apart from the bread, there were bags of nuts, and of a wide variety, but nothing that they couldn't find in the plentiful forests. There were also vegetables, but no meat—not even dried meat. What they had was strictly for sustenance, just enough food to sustain life and nothing more.

Alpheus had also since learned that Azure was a vegetarian, and that she never fussed about food. He refrained from his own desires for meat in order to keep Azure happy, and also to save time from having to hunt. But on this evening of the fourth of May, while Azure was asleep, Alpheus decided to go hunting. In her current condition, Azure simply needed more nutrients, which couldn't be provided by plants alone. She would have to eat some meat even if he had to force her.

* * *

Azure opened her eyes to the sight of an empty campfire. She peered up into the evening sky where thousands of stars twinkled brightly. On a clear evening, the valley offered incredible displays of celestial objects. The blue of Achelois was in a waning gibbous, but the red of Selene wasn't visible at all, hiding now as a new moon. How small she seemed under the world that revolved without end and without care for the individual inhabitants down below.

"You're awake," a voice said then.

Azure turned her head and then sat up slowly. Alpheus was walking toward her, carrying a bowl... of soup, she wondered? If she hadn't lost her sense of smell, the aroma of the soup might have had her turning to him sooner.

"I stirred together a pumpkin-based soup," Alpheus said.

Azure managed a faint smile as she received the meal, her mouth too dry at the moment to talk.

Hopefully I can at least taste some of it, she thought, taking a sip—and then biting onto something that was as tender as flesh. She spat it out immediately.

"What *is* this?!" she demanded.

"Rabbit," Alpheus said, sitting down next to her. "You need to eat it."

"No, I don't! I can't have animals dying for me. And certainly not when I was already destined for death."

Alpheus sighed softly. "As a food source," he began, "rabbit is valuable and nutritious. It is a good source of protein, niacin, iron, phosphorus, and selenium. In comparison with other meats—"

"Enough!" Azure cried, covering her ears.

Still, Alpheus regarded her with kind, tired eyes. He lifted an arm, brushing her hand softly, nudging it away from her ear. "I haven't had any meat myself," Alpheus said gently. "Think of it this way: the meat you're eating is the share that I'm not eating."

Azure regarded him for a moment. He had done a lot for her on this journey. He had planned the route, and he drove the wagon. He prepared the meals, and on top of cleansing her face and arms of daily grime, he had been a gentleman in arranging meticulous privacy and protection when she had to bathe or when she had lavatory needs. Alpheus hadn't had much sleep, either, for he had to be alert of any lurking dangers, as well as signs of the physician. And through all of this, he had shown no frustration. He had kept on a smile for her, even if it was forced.

Azure turned away then and picked up the bowl of soup again. She consumed it slowly, trying to conceal her disgust.

* * *

They continued to climb the mountain for the next four days. Around dusk each day, Alpheus went hunting. But it grew increasingly difficult. The higher they climbed, the colder it became, and there were fewer and fewer animals to hunt. In this spring equinox, the sun provided warmth for long hours, but the thick layers of winter snow still had yet to evaporate, sheets of white for as far as they could see. Even the blue sky of the day was clouded behind the mists. The freezing temperatures and the stronger winds forced them to wear warmer clothing, including woollen gloves and cloaks woven from serge.

Azure slept longer hours as her ailing condition worsened. Her face had paled, and the natural blue of her eyes paled to a soulless grey behind eyelids that seemed to grow heavier by the day. Her lips had become discoloured as well, and the cold had her numbed. And for the first time since they had begun the journey, her body reacted strangely when Alpheus worked to unblock her neurons.

Granted, she was successfully revitalised and had pulled away from death once again. But Alpheus had sat still in shock as the unconscious Azure rested against him. It was only a little, but some of the energy he had emitted during the process had spilled out. It was as if her body had rejected the foreign energy, and it was gushing out almost as soon as it flowed in.

Alpheus was no physician, but he could guess why this had happened. His research about sorcery—and, more recently, energy and the elements—had given him a good idea. The mage had once warned that Azure's condition would change, and indeed her ailment had reached its final stage in which her vital organs were slowly deactivating. It was no longer a matter of insufficient energy to drive her vital organs—it was the organs themselves that refused to be driven.

Alpheus laid Azure down in the cabin. He then quietly hopped back to the front to prod the horses on. The summit of Mt. Meridian was now very close in the distance.

Half an hour in, Alpheus slid his glasses up as he looked past the mist and over the oblique ascension of the mountain to see several shapes that resembled houses. His pulse quickened as he realised that he might have stumbled upon evidence of human habitation.

The physician, Alpheus thought hopefully as he spurred the horses to race ahead even harder. His fatigue washed away, and a hopeful grin emerged on his face. His grin broadened when he recognised the shapes as huts, albeit of humble size and build, blanketed by the thick snow. Alpheus stopped the horses and sprung off the wagon, racing to the open entrance of the first hut. When he poked his head in, however, he realised that the home had been abandoned. He scampered to the other huts, refusing to give up just yet. But each successive shelter he checked only served to further discourage him. All of them had been abandoned—empty and disfigured by the weather—seemingly for many years.

Alpheus wandered among the hovels, finally collapsing to his knees onto the soft carpet of snow under the freezing winds. He turned back and gazed toward the wagon in despondency.

It had taken five days to climb to the summit, yet today as he kneeled there, he felt nothing but disappointment. He couldn't even pretend that these poorly built huts were somehow connected to the physician.

It was already the twenty third day since Azure had suffered the injury. She only had another seven days to live, and that was with the optimistic outlook that she would even last the thirty days initially predicted.

She's going to die, Alpheus thought, contemplating the possibility for the first time. *She's really going to die.* He held his head and punched into the thick layers of snow, drawing nothing but an icy sting.

Alpheus shut his eyes, grumbling quietly until he could no longer hold in his frustration, finally screaming out across the haze. The reverberation seemed to shake the ground, but in fact, his bellowing was immediately neutralised and snared by the mists.

"Alpheus...," a weak voice said.

Azure had brushed open the drapes, eyeing him from there, clearly too weak to step out. He immediately regretted waking her, and he dashed back through the snow to the wagon.

Azure rested her hand on his. "Don't sit in the snow like that. You'll get a cold."

Alpheus was careful not to admit to his despair just then. "Just this one time," he said, inventing a reason for his outburst as he went, "I have always wanted to do that... to scream out loud. And what better place to do that than at the peak of the mountain?"

Azure regarded him for a moment, her face pale, her eyes tired. Despite her blurred senses, however, she must have noted the hovels which the mists couldn't quite hide.

"You're still a child inside, aren't you?" she then said, forcing that faint smile Alpheus had seen all too often lately. "Normally, I would let it go, but your screams will disturb the peace here. In any case, the mists are too thick. Let's get going."

Alpheus was quiet on the march down. He was ashamed to have given up, even if only for a moment, especially when Azure herself had remained so hopeful. He told himself that there was still time, and that their worst enemy in the face of adversity was self-doubt. He squinted as he looked ahead, turning his attention and hope to that final place he had circled on the map—the swamp forest that was nestled deep within the valley. It was their next—and final—destination.

TWENTY-THREE

The flooded forest

Instead of following the same route on their way toward the summit, Alpheus drove their horses to descend southwest back to the long valley that split the mountain range in two. Trekking down the mountain was naturally much easier than climbing it. They ventured back into the valley less than two days into their journey, back into the relatively warmer temperatures.

They had also reached the southern state of *Easterclem*, having trekked the entire length of Sequiposa from north to south.

And on this morning on the eleventh of May, Alpheus decided to scrap away anything that was inessential. He dumped out all of the rations stored beneath the cabin. He was confident he could continue providing nutritious meals for Azure with his improving hunting skills, which came by the way of snares. As for his own sustenance, he planned to pick fruits from the plentiful valley. He dumped out his cloak and its supplemental accessories, including an ear-covering cap and woollen gloves. One of the only spare items of clothing that he was keeping was a warm set of clothing for Azure, who donned a thick coat even now. This had become vital for Azure, because her health condition had since compromised even her thermoregulatory functions. She was unable to sufficiently produce body heat.

On the twelfth day of May, their direction toward the south brought them to the second sign of human habitation. This time, they had found a small double-storey cottage. It was half the size of the Violanola Cottage, situated in seclusion behind tall elm trees. The clue that had led Alpheus to shift his course of direction and to enter the woods was a pinch of grey smoke he had noticed wafting above the trees. As he drove the wagon in front of the cottage now, he saw smoke puffing out from a modest chimney.

Someone was inside.

Alpheus decided not to wake Azure. He took a deep breath and then hopped off the wagon, and he strode toward the wooden entrance of the cottage and knocked lightly on the door. Wishful but conservative in his hopes, he waited patiently for someone to answer the door. From what Marvin had described, the Passionless Surgeon was a man of Kragan descent, naturally dark-skinned, about forty years of age, tall and well-built. But the person who opened the door didn't match that description.

The age was about right, but it was a woman, with her amber hair worn in a ponytail with eyes of green. She donned a dark blue dress and seemed surprised to see Alpheus.

"A visitor!" she exclaimed rather enthusiastically. "It's been years!"

"Sorry for my intrusion," Alpheus said, as he glanced behind her into the house. "My name is Alpheus. May I ask if there is a physician who lives here, or nearby?"

"A physician? Are you hurt?"

"No, but my friend is."

"Then your friend is in luck!" said the woman, whose words inspired a sudden surge of hope in Alpheus. "This way."

The woman turned and then stepped away to the left of the entrance. Alpheus took a hesitant step inside and peered to the right first, into the kitchen, then to the left where the woman had gone into an anteroom. She was busy rifling through a sizeable cabinet installed on the far wall. And as Alpheus stepped closer, he realised that the furniture was stocked with many shrubs, most of which he recognised.

"My name is Hertha," the woman said, still searching. "I'm a collector of herbal plants. Whether it's a fever or even a snake bite, I have all the ingredients to brew the healing potion. Leave it to me. Your friend is in safe hands." She paused for a moment and turned slowly in Alpheus's direction. "You *do* have gold, right?"

Alpheus frowned, battling with his own impatience. "I'm sure you are very able, but I'm not looking for an herbalist. I seek the Passionless Surgeon."

Hertha brushed him off with a dismissive hand. "What? *Passionless*? What kind of ridiculous name is that?" She picked out a mucky green potion then. "I think you need something, too."

Alpheus's eyes flashed briefly but he managed to hold in his disappointment about the fact that Hertha seemed to have nothing to do with the surgeon he actually sought. Before he could bid farewell, a tapping sounded from the outside. Alpheus spun on his heels and then raced out.

Behind the horses, the drapes of the cabin were open, and Azure was lying face down, probably after having crawled her way out. Alpheus hurried toward her, held her up gently, and then sat her down against the cabin.

She's so cold, Alpheus noted with a cringe, *and her face is paler than ever.*

"What were you trying to do?" Alpheus asked ins disapproval as he held her freezing hands in his own.

"Looking for you...," Azure responded with a whisper. "I woke up... and didn't see you."

"I'm sorry. How are you feeling?"

Azure coughed. "I'd be lying if I said I was feeling well." She paused there, glancing toward the herbalist, who had followed Alpheus outside. "Who is she?"

"My name is Hertha," the woman answered, the exaggerated enthusiasm from earlier having been wiped out. "You don't look good at all, lass."

Alpheus turned at Hertha, shooting her an unfriendly gaze as a warning to her not to say anything else.

"You're right," Azure said, nodding at the herbalist. "No one likes to see a dying person."

"So, you're *really* looking for that man," Hertha said with a hand to her chin, continuing to sound solemn. "Come in. I'll tell you what I know."

* * *

A few minutes later, Alpheus found himself sitting once again in the anteroom. He hadn't noticed the fireplace earlier, but he was thankful for it now. Azure needed all the warmth she could get.

Hertha joined them again, bringing with her some herbal tea that she had brewed.

"I'm sorry," Alpheus said, "but we don't have much time. Can you please tell us what you know?"

"Calm down, child," the herbalist said, offering the tea once more. "I said I'll tell you. But first, you would have to give me an account of your story."

Alpheus glanced to Azure, who nodded at him. He sighed and then began speaking, only for Hertha to cut in, the woman insisting that he accept the tea. Alpheus huffed audibly and then finally took a sip of the hot beverage. It tasted strange, bitter initially but then with a sweet aftertaste.

It's good, Alpheus thought, looking down at the dark red drink. He took a second sip and breathed in slowly, feeling slightly refreshed.

"Now," Hertha said, smiling, "please go on. Tell me your story."

Alpheus looked up and returned the cup to its saucer. He recounted how Azure had suffered the injury, the severity of it, and their consequent search for the physician known as the Passionless Surgeon, but left out any other information irrelevant to Azure's current health condition. Hertha was nodding along as Alpheus spoke, and when he finished, the herbalist asked to examine Azure. She reached for Azure's wrist, seemingly testing her pulse. Hertha then put on a grim face as she relayed a diagnosis that took several minutes.

"It's a miracle you're still alive," she finally said.

Azure smiled, but as soon as she did, her eyelids fell and she leaned back, returning to sleep again, as if her body had requested it. Alpheus had seen this happen more times than he could count, but he still cringed, fearing as he always did that Azure might never wake up again.

"So... Hertha," Alpheus said, his words firm, "tell me, please. Tell me where to find the Passionless Surgeon."

Hertha regarded him closely. "I've lived out here for over twenty years," she said. "And I've only seen that man once—the man you seek. Four years ago. He doesn't want to be found. He might just *be* at one of those places you guessed before. The problem is he'd be hidden somewhere beneath where the naked eye cannot see. I doubt he'll be sitting in a cottage like this one."

"Are you telling me that there's no chance to find him?" Alpheus said, his voice revealing his despair.

Hertha thought for a moment. "Not unless there's a miracle," she said. "That being said, everything up until now has been a miracle. If it wasn't for the man who advised you to search for the Passionless Surgeon and train you on the delicacy of channelling your energy, you would not know how to hope. Then it was the combination of your loyalty to the girl and your knowledge as a scholar that kept her alive. And lastly, without those mighty horses, it would be impossible for anyone to get here from Poppaross—and to detour Mt. Meridian—in barely thirty days. Without those circumstances and advantages, she wouldn't have even lasted five days. And there's no reason for the miracles to stop now."

Alpheus eyed the sleeping Azure. He held a fist, feeling the double crescent pendant tied on his left wrist dangling now down to his palm.

"All I can do is pray?" he said. "Pray for a miracle?"

"You need to help create it," Hertha said. "Miracles do not befall those who do not fight for their own cause, but on those who actively seek it, through vigour and determination."

* * *

Alpheus and Azure soon set off again southwards, riding *on* one of the two horses rather than drawing the wagon with them. The swamp forest that they were heading for wasn't the type of land to allow for something as bulky as a wagon to pass through. The dense trees and the maze of freshwater swamps simply weren't suitable for carrying anything with them any further.

Hertha had joined them for a brief send off, riding the other horse. Alpheus had said that he would gift the woman the horses upon reaching the swamp forest. In exchange, Hertha had offered several potions that she claimed to provide energy equivalent to that of full meals. It was the last time the horses would work for them, and the animals continued to race tirelessly without rest. The feeling was bittersweet when they arrived at the edge of their destination. Despite having trekked toward the swamp forest in just under a day, it was time to say goodbye to their animal companions. Both Alpheus and Azure embraced the animals, patting their heads and whispering words of gratitude into their ears. And, a moment later, Alpheus finally entrusted the horses to Hertha, as he himself carried Azure on his back.

"Take good care of them for me," Alpheus said to Hertha, who nodded to him.

"And you take good care of the young lady," Hertha replied. "Now, go."

Alpheus forced a parting smile and then spun away from the herbalist, looking toward what might be the final obstacle of their journey. And indeed it all looked rather gloomy. The tall, thin trees were packed together densely, blocking out almost all of the sunlight. At this stage, anything rooted in the soil was also another obstacle, especially the Ceiba species of trees, which grew to heights that rivalled the tallest steeples of Vondra Dawn. The glut of murky swamps was already clouded with mists, despite the fact that it was still only late afternoon. Alpheus could imagine how thick the mists would become when the temperatures dropped even further in the evening.

Alpheus checked that Azure's grip on him was secure and then he dashed forward, kicking into the Glider Steps. He twisted and turned around the vegetation, his eyes wide open as he scanned for any hints of the physician. Fantastic ripples in the water trailed his soft steps as he breezed over the ponds. Swooshing by as if in a gust, it was almost like he was flying. Alpheus hoped the rapid movement made Azure feel more alive and free, even if only briefly.

It was nearly an hour later when they came to a stop under one of the larger trees with a soft patch of thick moss. Alpheus carefully laid Azure down against the trunk of the tree and he snatched one of the potions hanging at his waist, helping Azure to consume it. Alpheus then gulped down some of it before he noted that Azure had opened her mouth, perhaps trying to speak.

"What is it?" Alpheus asked gently, leaning down closer to her.

"Thank you," she whispered very faintly. "Thank you for taking me here. Thank you for giving me hope."

"We have come a long way," he said. "But it means nothing if you cannot be healed. Like Hertha said, everything up until now has been a miracle. If we continue to believe, the miracles will continue." Alpheus wrinkled his nose. "But… the smell of these swamps…"

He reached under his mantle and pulled out a tiny glass bottle the size of his index finger. It had no label, just a fancy ribbon tied under the cap. Inside was a transparent liquid, light blue in colour.

Azure blinked curiously.

"Perfume," Alpheus said. "From Aragon. The shop owner said that it's made from an extract of a flower… I think it was called the bluebell."

Azure perked up suddenly, eyes sparkling briefly.

"Now I'm not *wearing* perfume," Alpheus continued. "I'm just trying to cover the smell of the swamps."

"Bluebell," Azure muttered, her whole face now lit up. "Did you say… *bluebell*?"

Alpheus nodded, and then she asked him to run the opening of the glass bottle under her nose. She sniffed in all that she could.

"The bluebell," she said softly, closing her eyes as if to immerse herself in the fragrance. A smile emerged on her face and she opened her eyes again, which now sparkled behind tears—tears of joy. "This takes me back… back to the wet woodlands." She regarded the delicate bottle and then Alpheus. "All this time… there was this… *connection* with you."

Alpheus cocked his head, unsure about what she meant. He refrained from asking, however, conscious about not overstraining her. Nevertheless, it was pleasing to finally see a smile on her face after so much hardship.

* * *

Another two days passed by mercilessly without any sign of a miracle. It was the fifteenth of May, the thirtieth day since the injury—an injury that might well prove to be fatal. Azure was now so fragile that it seemed like she could fall asleep and never wake up again. Her neurons could hardly be driven. Indeed, her body rejected more than half of what Alpheus tried to offer.

Alpheus hadn't given up, but he was certainly growing more and more desperate. Working harder than the horses had worked, he had spent more than fifteen hours each day roaming the swamp forest in his tireless search, doing so with the weight of his dying companion on his back. He estimated that by dusk today he would have covered the entire swamp forest. He didn't let his fatigue be an excuse, though, knowing that what he endured was nothing compared to Azure's pain—or, rather, her inability to sense pain. Her body had frozen up, for the most part—she was almost completely numb. In this sense, her need for long hours of sleep was perhaps a blessing in disguise.

Running, hopping, and gliding, Alpheus proceeded in every direction where he thought they might find the physician. Exacerbating his already blurred vision was the sweat that mounted heavily from his forehead. His legs had endured hours and hours of strain, and they felt increasingly heavier. The humidity of the swamp forest combined with the heat of the warm spring day had further blighted his effort, and had indeed plagued him with a minor fever. But with all of his available will power at work, Alpheus moved along continuously, with no regards to his own health. He was numb to the soreness of his muscles, the rising temperature of his fever, and the irritatingly humid weather.

He had one thing on his mind: the Passionless Surgeon.

Alpheus was trying. He was hoping. And he was giving it everything he had. But he worried that it was still not enough as dusk fell upon them once again. With the final glimmers of sunlight fading away behind the trees, and the temperature consequently cooling down, Alpheus realised he had explored every part of the flooded forest, but with no success.

There were no signs of the physician. Not even a hint.

He slowed down now to a giant ceiba tree. He sat under it on the huge buttress roots, Azure in his arms. The mists had come again, and he could barely see the swamp before him. Even with a thick coat on, Azure's body was as cold as ice, rigid like a corpse.

So, this is it? he thought. *These are the final hours?*

The evening forest was almost silent. The dark of the night was thriving, as the moonlight could barely penetrate the dense canopy. Alpheus looked down at Azure. She was asleep, but was as good as dead. He brushed his hand softly against her hair and stroked his fingers gently over her nose, her lips, and her eyelashes, unsure why he was doing so, perhaps in the hopes of embedding her every contour into memory.

He gazed intently at the dying girl without a blink, until a droplet landed on her cheek—a droplet of a tear that was quickly followed with several other drops. Alpheus wiped his eyes to confirm that he was indeed shedding tears, numb to the feeling of them on his cheeks. He had never given up on Azure throughout this whole gruelling expedition, and hence had never even considered what or how to feel should she indeed die. As a scholar,

Alpheus had been trained to reason in terms of utility and given the duty to disregard emotions, to see things as clearly as possible. He had been raised to see everything in a logical sense, where even death was but something part of a mere cycle. But at this moment, he was unable to find any solace in logic.

Alpheus removed his spectacles, breathed in a long breath, and then began weeping openly without holding himself back. His wails resonated across the otherwise serene forest.

When he opened his eyes after a moment, he thought he saw a flicker in Azure's eyes amid the lack of light. Azure had indeed opened her eyes, albeit slightly. She was gazing up at him, lifting her hand to wipe away his tears.

"Don't cry…," she said in her most fragile voice yet.

"I couldn't do anything…," Alpheus replied in a similarly soft tone. "At the end, I couldn't do anything."

Her eyes flickered again, and Alpheus held her more tightly now. He listened intently to her faint heartbeat and breathed in synchronisation with the tiny breath she was still exhaling. He had to treasure these last moments with her.

"Look!" Azure uttered. "Look! The stars!"

Alpheus said nothing, lamenting that his dying companion was seeing illusions before death. But when a luminescence flashed across him, he realised it was no illusion. He saw it, too—hundreds, perhaps thousands, of phosphorescent tiny spectacles floating in the air around them like stars twinkling in the night sky. And yet they were within an arm's reach. The glowing spots gleamed to a wonderful green colour that illuminated the surrounding mists.

As if reacting to the shining spectacles, the pearl bracelet on Azure's thin wrist began to glow too with radiance. Alpheus sat up slowly and reached a hand out like a curious child trying to confirm whether they were fireflies, a species of flying beetles that produced light with bioluminescence.

"It's… so beautiful," Azure said.

Alpheus gently caught one of the slow-moving insects with a loose fist and then moved his hand to Azure's face. He spread his hand into a flat palm to reveal the beautiful bioluminescent glow of the insect. It illuminated her face and even briefly restored the sparkling blue of her eyes. The insect then flapped its wings before taking flight again.

The pair watched the firefly glide away to again join the thousands now swarming about. Alpheus picked up his glasses and slid them on once more. He watched on for another moment, then perked up suddenly on the realisation that the fireflies couldn't possibly survive under these temperatures, at least not naturally. This meant that someone or something had domesticated the insects.

He laid Azure lightly down from his arms and then rested her against the trunk of the tree. He then hopped several steps away, scanning to the left and right.

"We found him!" he said, his cheeks tensing up with a gratified smile. "Azure, we found him! We finally found him!" He then cupped his hands around his mouth. "O' legendary physician!" he said aloud. "The Passionless Surgeon! Please show yourself!"

Azure peered hopefully over toward the swamp. Other than the fantastic display of fireflies, there seemed to be nothing out of the ordinary.

"It has been a while," said a voice that sounded like it came from a middle-aged man with the southern accent of Kraga.

The stranger then flashed into view as a tall silhouette behind the glaring glimmers of the evening moonlight. He stepped out from behind one of the trees and into the illumination of the glowing insects as a dark-skinned man of Kragan descent, about forty years of age, tall and well-built—just as Marvin had described. His torso was covered by a criss-crossed loose fabric. From the hips down was another loose piece of leather gear, shaped like a long dress. He was equipped with steel gauntlets at both hands and attached at his waist was a thick leather belt that appeared to hold a wide range of surgical instruments. His head was an oblong shape, his protruding lips a dark grey. His narrowed upturned eyes, meanwhile, gazed forward directly at Alpheus, who was now rushing toward him.

TWENTY-FOUR

A life for a life

Alpheus hopped forward toward the man who towered over him at a height that rivalled Karl, the giant of the Sail Band. The man's dark skin tone was deeper than that of both Karl and Trajetzky. His richly developed muscles and overall broad build, which doubled Alpheus's width, suggested that the man could perhaps do more than save lives. He was probably equally adept at ending lives as well.

"My friend doesn't have much time left," Alpheus said, gesturing toward the tree where Azure was lying. "Please help her!"

"You're not a soldier," the Kragan remarked, without moving a step.

"Well… no, I'm not," Alpheus replied. "I'm a scholar, but perhaps we can talk about that later?"

The man stared at Alpheus for a moment longer. He said nothing, but then finally stepped forward behind Alpheus who dashed back toward Azure. Once he arrived at the ceiba tree, he leaned down and reached for Azure's wrist. He seemed to be testing her pulse, like Hertha had done a few days ago. The man scratched his chin with his other hand, wearing a grim expression. He then let go of her wrist after a short moment.

Alpheus expected him to say something, but instead the man grabbed Azure's shoulder and then spun her around before thrusting a forceful palm onto her back, causing Azure to spew out a spatter of blood.

Shocked and confused by this sudden action, Alpheus lunged forward, ready to protect Azure with his life, but was brushed away by the big man with a simple swipe of his arm. Alpheus picked himself up immediately and scowled at the Kragan, who simply rolled his eyes in response.

"Take a look at her," the man said.

Azure jolted, her eyes shut tightly, but her veins were almost bursting out through her skin. She tensed her hands into a claw at her mouth, retching. She battled the purge for a little while, but was unable to hold it in, and she vomited in full force… but only a breath of freezing mist emitted from her body. Her eyelids dropped immediately, and this time it appeared to Alpheus that it was really her end.

"Azure!" Alpheus cried, his eyes widened as sudden tears gushed out.

But before he shed any more tears, the big man gestured toward the coughed-up blood, which was a much darker red than normal. "She's alive," the man said with his flat voice. "After releasing rounds of poison, it is natural to fall unconscious."

"Poison....?" Alpheus said, musing. "That mist... it was the source of her failed thermoregulation?"

The man nodded.

"And that blood she just coughed up...," Alpheus continued. "Was it the part of the blood in her system that was rendered ineffective by her failing circulatory system?"

The man hardly raised a brow, seemingly taking no credit for what he had done. "Her pain is reduced," he said, "but ten hours is all she has left."

Alpheus tensed up. "Please help her! I'm sure you can heal her."

The man turned to the side. "As long as I am not presented with a corpse, I am able to heal anyone."

"I'm glad," Alpheus said.

"*Glad?*" the Kragan said, bemused. "Glad about what?"

The man's words left Alpheus briefly dazed.

You jest, he thought. *After all this, you're telling me you'll just watch her die?* He gritted his teeth. *And that must be how you earned that name: Passionless.*

"What are your conditions?" Alpheus asked instead.

The big man snorted. "And what makes you think I would deal with the likes of you?"

"You showed yourself," Alpheus replied. "There was nothing I could do, had you decided to continue hiding."

The physician lifted his head slightly. "Tell me, how did you know I was here?"

"The fireflies," Alpheus said. "When I caught one of them in my hand, I tried to inject some energy into the insect so that it would glow more brilliantly. But then I realised that it was already brimming with life. After their repeated flashing, the fireflies should have expended a fair amount of energy, but instead, they were still overflowing with energy. It was then that I was sure that they were domesticated.

"During the trek here, I've learned a fair amount about temperate seasons and their effect on flora and fauna. Fireflies are a type of insect that appear primarily in the summer season, and although it's possible for these insects to be present in spring time—especially because it's already mid-May—the swamp forest's much too cold in the evenings for them to survive naturally. And they aren't merely surviving—with thousands of them here—they're blossoming!

"If anyone were to maintain these insects, I suspected it was you, the Passionless Surgeon. I suspected that only someone like you would consciously do something like this. And more importantly, you're the only one capable of bringing *life* out of these insects in an ecosystem that is not their natural habitat."

The physician gazed at Alpheus for a long moment.

"Very well," he then finally said. "A life for a life. Give me your life, and I shall bring life back to her."

Alpheus turned blank. "What?" he managed to utter. "How is my life valuable to you?"

"It is not," the Kragan answered. "Your life is purely a balancing act. The lass was destined to die. If I heal her, the flow of life and death will be disrupted. To balance that flow, I will need to kill you."

Alpheus shook his head. "I cannot argue with your principles or philosophies, but my life is not only my own. I cannot accept these conditions, and neither would Azure."

"Suit yourself," the big man then said, indifferent. "But be warned that the lass will live for no more than ten hours. After that time, no one can help her."

Alpheus fell silent with a gape. A hundred thoughts were running through his mind, and yet he found no idea convincing enough that would have the man change his conditions.

"There must be another way!" he sputtered finally. "You're a physician! Life and death is no equation!"

The big man wasn't interested. Instead, he jumped at Alpheus suddenly, clutched his right hand into a claw for an attack. Alpheus hopped away on instinct with the footwork he had learned from Marvin, and then followed by gliding away to safety. Alpheus didn't know what this was all about until he looked up, seeing Azure held atop the broad shoulders of the man.

When…? Alpheus wondered in disbelief. *How in that short exchange did he manage that?* He frowned, peering carefully around for anything that would help him win the advantage.

"Impressive," the big man said with a squint "You remain calm, despite the uncertainty around you. Even now, you scan your surroundings for a way to get the lass back."

Alpheus said nothing, though he wondered amid his growing anxiety whether the physician was also a mind reader.

"Worry not," the Kragan said then as he turned, strolling down toward the large swamp in front of them. "I will not hasten her death, for it will come soon enough. But I *am* going beneath the surface." He paused there, turning his head back slightly. "The water here is deeper than you suspected," he then said with a smirk. "But I suppose someone with aquaphobia wouldn't believe that."

Alpheus flushed slightly. "You... *knew* that?"

"Your fear of water is the reason you failed to find me until now," the man said, continuing to submerge himself with Azure on his shoulders. "You didn't overlook anything else, from a simple tree branch to a harmless lizard slithering through the grass. Yet you never considered what was beneath the surface. You fail as a scholar."

Alpheus frowned, helpless, as he watched the man and Azure vanish from sight altogether. And he didn't realise he was trembling until he looked down at his shaking legs. The body of water before him was indeed much deeper than he had cared to guess. Was there any way he could conquer what was essentially a lake?

With a heat of unrest surging up to his forehead, Alpheus stepped to the edge of the water. He swallowed as he looked down into it, unable to see his own reflection in the murk. It had barely been a minute, but everything had seemed to fall silent after the Kragan had taken Azure away. Alpheus had known the swamp forest as a rather uneventful place, not the kind of place where life thrived. Everything appeared dull and lifeless, even dead. And now, without Azure by his side, things seemed even darker and quieter yet. The fireflies had journeyed off, taking their illumination with them. Even the glimmer of moonlight was now completely obscured by thick clouds and the even thicker canopy.

Azure really didn't have much longer to live—ten hours, apparently. And even if Alpheus would forfeit his own life for hers, the obstacle before him—the water—might prove too much for him. Not only did Alpheus have to conquer his fear of water, but he also had to learn to swim—at least well enough to navigate unknown territory, underwater, in the darkness—which was an impossible task.

He was already plagued with fever. He was fatigued. But what pained him the most was something else.

You fail as a scholar, the physician had said.

Alpheus grunted, his hand curling into a fist. He hadn't realised how much he cared about his reputation as a scholar, but those words stung him to his core. It was worse because he agreed that the words were true. He had indeed committed an almost irreversible mistake, if not having failed altogether. From the beginning, he had conveniently decided that the murky water was relatively shallow and hence deemed the swamps as nothing more than a part of the landscape. A foolish mistake, he knew.

He crouched down now. He removed his glasses again, slipping them inside his mantle. He breathed in deeply and then waved a hand in the water.

"Water need not be feared," he whispered to himself.

He reminded himself that in chemistry, water was simply a substance of molecules containing one oxygen and two hydrogen atoms. In biology, it was critical for the proliferation of life. In religion, it was a purifier, and often used to cleanse a person at a ritual. And even in philosophy, it was one of the four classical elements that reflect the simplest essential parts and principles of which anything consisted. And, finally, his own energy—it was water-based.

Alpheus shut his eyes tightly. He rolled himself forward over the edge from his crouching position, dropping himself into the water.

A plop.

Gurgling. Fierce gurgling. Coldness. Plenty of it.

Drenched completely.

His eyes snapped open then. He was submerged. It was the first time he had voluntarily elected to become so. Even if he should feel proud about it, he certainly didn't enjoy the sensation and the freezing temperature that came with it. It was only a moment, but he was already chilled to the bones. How could Azure possibly survive these temperatures in her condition? He gurgled out a second round of ferocious bubbles that surged upwards as his instincts demanded his arms to flap for the surface. The refuge of the surface seemed so far away as his legs kicked desperately for dear life. And when he finally emerged from the water, he panted and wheezed, coughing up water he had swallowed while thrashing his arms wildly.

"Dammit!" he cursed, thumping the water with a fist.

Alpheus brushed his wet hair from his face and then dipped into the water again. He repeated the same process for a second and third attempt, and each successive try saw him dive slightly deeper, but still far from what was needed to swim an unknown distance into the depths. Alpheus realised that the Glider Steps would be close to useless underwater. It might give him short bursts forward, but the energy needed to achieve such bursts would be many times greater given the water pressure. There was surely a special type of sorcery which could carve open a path, but unfortunately, Alpheus wasn't skilled at any facet of sorcery.

In the end, there was really no other option than to swim.

* * *

Azure woke in a confined, gloomy grey space. She was lying on a stone bed in an otherwise empty room. She trembled in what felt like freezing temperatures, conscious that the chill might be due to her own condition more than the location where she now found herself. She slowly sat up, and through her blurred vision under the candlelight of a solitary mounting on the wall, she saw a door at the rear end of the bed.

She wanted to reach for it, but her condition held her back. She dropped back onto the bed with a soft thud, immediately falling into slumber once again.

She didn't know how long it had been, but she woke again to the sound of the same door opening. The person who entered brought a lantern with them, barely bright enough to light up the room. While Azure wasn't sure whether to be afraid or curious, she simply lacked the energy to sit up to see who it was. The stranger came up to her on her bedside, holding the lantern in between them.

A woman.

A Kragan woman about forty years of age. Dark skin, average build, with an oval face like the physician's. She helped Azure sit up.

"I'm glad you're awake," the woman said gently.

Azure tried her hardest to keep her eyes open. "Where... am I?" she asked.

"This place doesn't have a name," the woman answered. "It was once a catacomb. And now it is master's home."

"Master?"

"Master is known by others as the Passionless Surgeon. As for me, master granted me the name Panyuk."

"Pan... yuk?"

"Here, have this," the woman said as she reached for a bowl that she had been holding with her other hand. She dug up a spoonful of what looked like soup and proceeded to feed Azure.

Azure considered the offer for a moment and then realised that no one would bother to expedite her death. She nodded at the woman in appreciation before sipping the first spoonful. The tangerine-coloured soup surged her with immediate heat, though it was not nearly enough to warm all of her body. It was more noteworthy that Azure actually thought she could taste it. On her second spoonful, she confirmed that it was indeed rich in flavour, and exactly how root vegetables should taste. When she was offered the third spoonful, she coughed up a spatter on her skirt, though was promptly attended to by the woman who used a cloth to clean the spots off of her delicate white dress.

"This dress...," Azure said, realising only now that it wasn't her own.

"Your clothes are drying," Panyuk replied.

"Drying... from what? And where is Alpheus? Where is the physician?"

As if in response, the big physician now stepped in to the room. He was holding onto a glass tube the size of his little finger, and inside the tube was a transparent liquid, blood red in colour. After passing it to Panyuk, he turned to leave the room. The man was half way out the door when Azure called out to him in a squeaky voice.

The man stopped, but didn't care enough to turn around.

"Where is Alpheus?" Azure asked.

The man turned his head back slightly this time. "I don't know. Perhaps drowned to death. Or maybe he gave up on you and left."

"*Drowned*?!" Azure yelped. "What did you make him do?"

"Rather than worry for someone else, you should worry for yourself. You are wakeful now only because the elixir has taken effect. It suppresses your pain and restores your senses, but only to a certain extent. It will not prolong your life, of which only several hours remain."

The physician walked away from the room and disappeared from view, leaving Azure dazed and confused.

"All right, drink up," said Panyuk, who passed the glass tube to Azure. "A potion."

"Wait...," Azure responded. "Please tell me what happened!"

"Swallow it first."

Again, without any fear of possible poison, Azure consumed the red potion in one gulp. It was bitter, and the aftertaste seemed to persist forever. She ignored it as best as she could, hoping to get back on topic. But as she was about to demand information from Panyuk, a wave of gentle warmth suddenly filled her body from within. The chill that had pained her for as long as she remembered was gone. Azure held out her hands to see the paleness gradually revert to the lively colour she had once known. Blood was flowing smoothly through her veins again and her heart was pumping at a comfortable rate.

"How...?!" she said.

Panyuk smiled. "Master is a genius. No one can do what he can."

Azure cocked her head slightly. Panyuk went on to explain what had happened, starting from when the physician began observing them two days previously. She claimed that she believed her master would have shown himself at the critical moment regardless of whether Alpheus had been attentive enough to note her master's presence. This ancient catacomb they were inside was estimated by her master to be at least two thousand years old. The only path to enter the building was through the underwater route that led from the only lake of the flooded forest.

Panyuk followed the facts with the consummation of the encounter between her master and Alpheus, arriving finally at the situation Alpheus was now confronted with.

"Master knows that your friend fears water," Panyuk said. "So, if your friend attempts to force his way in here, he might die."

"That's absurd!" Azure exclaimed.

"No," Panyuk said, shaking her head. "Master is purposeful in everything he does."

Without prodding of any kind, the candid woman then went on to tell Azure more about her master. His name was Olijin Pelanofzky, and according to Panyuk, the man was undoubtedly the greatest living physician and possibly the greatest in all of history. His godly ability in healing, however, predestined the path of his life to that of one he was reluctant to follow. The man was summoned since a child by the ruling Kragan government to become one of their many *tools* in their bid to dominate the land. Although he was bestowed with all the necessary wealth and resources, Panyuk suspected that her master was never fond of working for the monarch, which explained why he had opted to flee the country altogether to live as a hermit.

"Master has seen and experienced more hardship than one can imagine," Panyuk said in admiring appraisal. "I cannot comprehend his reasoning, but I trust him completely. It is not in my place to ask anything of him. Besides, even if I did, master stands only by his own principles."

Azure nodded. "Your loyalty is admirable. I understand because I, too, am a servant—a maid."

"And the scholar is your master?"

Azure flushed. "No! Of course not!" She then calmed herself, holding a hand to her chest, her expression turning despondent. "But he has been... my hero... for the last month. I wouldn't have gotten this far if it hadn't been for him."

She teared up now and sniffled quietly as she imagined the struggles Alpheus must now be facing.

"Your friend will be fine," Panyuk assured. "And need I remind you, lass, you are the one who is dying."

Azure shook her head in despondency. "He really could drown... Navigation underwater is too much to ask from someone who is subject to seasickness even atop a ferry in calm waters."

"Master told me your friend is a State Scholar," Panyuk said. "Though I am unsure what that constitutes, I believe that his commitment for your health shall see him through."

Panyuk was probably right, and Azure indeed found some comfort in her words. She was grateful for her caretaker, who only a moment ago, had been a complete stranger. Just then, an idea sprung into her mind.

"Panyuk," Azure said, grasping the woman at her sleeves. "Am I correct to assume that your master isn't as passionless as his name suggests?"

"What are you saying?"

"That there is flexibility with his conditions."

Panyuk shook her head. "No, I'm afraid not. The conditions were clear. You will only be saved in exchange for your friend's life."

Azure smiled then. "But your master never stipulated a time frame. To him, it's only a matter of principles that he must take something in exchange for his work. He isn't so rigid that he would take anyone's life, at least not right away. So even if Alpheus agreed to his conditions, he might let Alpheus live a long life."

Panyuk paused, falling quiet for a long while, until she finally nodded. "You may be right," she said. "If your friend can find his way in here, both of you can live. At least for a while."

TWENTY-FIVE

The Passionless Surgeon

It had been five hours since his encounter with the Passionless Surgeon, and during this time, Alpheus had tried everything he could to rationalise his abject fear of water. He had told himself that underwater navigation was almost natural for others. He had even tried to emulate various sea creatures by lining up his arms and legs in different ways to help him wriggle on. But rational thoughts alone had only gotten him so far.

In the end, as was the case now, Alpheus no longer thought about how he feared water or how to conquer that fear. With time pressing against him ever so critically, he dropped all his logic and reduced himself to his basic instincts. Like a beast fighting for survival, he slashed his arms wildly, focusing only on what was ahead—the path to advance.

The path to life.

Or at least he thought so.

He fought not for himself, but for Azure who might well have been murdered by the mad surgeon for all he knew.

The murkiness before him appeared endless. His thoughts were muddled, but his arms were stroking and his legs were kicking as if independent from his body. And as he was ploughing through the water, his mind gradually drifted away to past regrets, mistakes, and misfortunes—all of these thoughts urging him forward. There was so much he still had to do. Not one day had gone by without a thought about how he could avenge Reeling. He hadn't forgotten how much Agnes had sacrificed for him. He also wanted to prove to Kathryn Trulips that he was more than a dreamer. And perhaps most importantly, he hoped to lend his support to Marvin in order to prevent what might trigger another widespread war.

Alpheus looked up now, letting out a breath and gurgling out a surge of bubbles. Not too far ahead was a glimmer of light. Alpheus held his breath, almost suffocating as he pushed himself on, slashing ahead toward what he believed was some kind of sanctuary. When he whirled close enough to what looked like an opening, he kicked with the Glider Steps, emerging finally with a ferocious explosion of water that crashed about the rocky shapes cradling the water.

Alpheus collapsed to the ground immediately—on land, finally. He lied face up with his legs still hanging from the earth and dipping into the water as he gasped for breath. He didn't have the energy to open his eyes just yet, but he was ecstatic to realise that he was on land again. He brushed a hand over his chest and started unbuttoning his top which was heavy with water.

He then finally opened his eyes. He brushed his wet hair aside and then he saw a winding corridor ahead, a narrow corridor with a low ceiling where oil lamps were installed. His eyes then shifted further down, and the sight of what was ahead caused him to scramble abruptly to his feet. Alpheus grimaced as he confirmed the sight: a symmetrical line-up of old caskets were inserted into the walls.

His heart was pounding with anticipation of what he expected but still hoped not to see. But despite the eeriness, all was still and silent, save the trickling of water behind him.

Alpheus walked up carefully to one of the caskets, all of which were semi-open—most of them occupied. He reached for the glasses under his mantle, wiped them dry as best as he could, and slid them on.

The corpses had been decomposed for a long time—perhaps hundreds, or even thousands of years. It was more accurate to call them fossils. They were covered in dust and woven with cobwebs. The jewellery on them, however, had survived without tarnish. From necklaces to bracelets, all of the metal and gems looked extremely valuable. Even the caskets were constructed with a combination of valuable metals, most of which were scarce and difficult to extract, especially if they had been made thousands of years ago. The jewellery, which was prominently spherical in design, wasn't of Vinawell, at least according to what Alpheus knew. It was also common knowledge to scholars that Vinans preferred cremation over the preservation of corpses. Catacombs were unheard of in this country, as the people traditionally believed that when a person died, their soul lived on—that that was the time when life truly began. The general view was that preserving corpses prevented the dead from true liberation.

Alpheus shook his head then. It wasn't the time to think about who these people were. He looked up again, unable to see an end to the winding corridor. He prayed that there were no crossroads ahead, and he frowned deeply as he began proceeding down the corridor, taking each step carefully and softly as he decided that he had no other choice than to stay alert for any potential traps.

Alpheus eventually arrived at a sturdy steel door. It had been a direct route with no traps installed in between, or at least he had managed not to trigger anything malicious. Even so, it wasn't a journey he would want to take again with the dozens and dozens of caskets welcoming him through.

Alpheus reached for the large, ring-shaped handle of the steel door. It would be a harsh conclusion to his efforts if it were locked, and he steeled himself for the possibility. He took a deep breath and pushed. The door was indeed as heavy and sturdy as it appeared. Alpheus applied more pressure, lending all of his weight for help, when a click finally sounded. One final nudge, and the door swung open.

The narrowness of the previous corridor was no more. Alpheus found himself in an antechamber the size of his atelier. The walls and the ceiling, however, were still the dreary earth of a subterranean passage. The furnishings were minimal, and just as it had been in the casket-filled corridor, the place was lighted by oil lamps hanging off the ceiling. There were doors on either side of the walls, both closed. Alpheus's gaze finally rested on the only other person there—the big physician himself, who was dining in silence, a thick book his only companion. His meal was no feast—a humble bowl of soup.

The physician swallowed the last bit of his meal, and then finally looked up from the book. "Well done," he said, turning to regard Alpheus.

"Where is Azure?" Alpheus asked immediately.

"My offer still stands," the physician replied.

"I would give my life without a second thought," Alpheus said, narrowing his eyes. "But my life is not my own. I have much to do—not for myself, but those who are dear to me. And even if I accepted your offer, Azure wouldn't allow it. She wouldn't accept her life in exchange for mine."

"She would have no choice," the physician said. "I would heal her even if she resisted."

Alpheus fell quiet. It was absurd to him, but if it were any consolation, the physician seemed as though he would keep his word. Stranger yet was a rush of feeling that Alpheus didn't want to admit to: the way the physician spoke resembled how Reeling had spoken. Just like his conversations with Reeling, Alpheus now found himself unable to conjure up any argument. If the only way forward was to accept the man's conditions, then was this the end? But then who would avenge Reeling?

"Alpheus!" a voice called out then.

Alpheus jumped and turned to his right, from where the voice had sounded at a pleasant pitch that he hadn't heard for a such long time. It wasn't just in his head. There she was: Azure, stepping in through the door, holding a sturdy cane for support. A tall, dark woman stepped beside her, providing support to Azure. Alpheus fell almost numb as he noted that the beautiful blue of her eyes had been briefly restored in place of the grey soullessness that had been present throughout the journey. Even the paleness of her face and lips was restored to its previous innocuous hue.

Alpheus stepped toward Azure now, reaching for her hands, recognising that they were still cold, but were now much warmer than any time after she had suffered the injury. Azure was still dying, he knew, but the physician had already worked some miracle to have her *appear* healthy, even when she should have mere hours left to live.

"How...?! How did it happen?" Alpheus said in joyful disbelief.

Azure smiled in return. "And how did you manage to get here?"

Alpheus paused, suddenly very aware that he was still soaking wet. "Oh, the water. It's nothing."

Azure turned to the physician. "I'd like a private word with Alpheus."

The physician said nothing, instead simply turning back to his book again, returning to reading. The Kragan woman then led them through the door they had come through before. She still supported Azure, who was clearly still too weak to walk on her own. Alpheus followed, keeping quiet, and also keeping a suspicious eye on the tall, dark woman. After a short distance of no more than ten steps, they turned into the room where it seemed that Azure had apparently been resting in. The woman sat Azure down on the bed, which was the only piece of furniture, and then smiled at the both of them before leaving them alone, pulling the door firmly shut behind her.

Alpheus eyed the door for a moment to confirm that woman had indeed left. He then finally sighed in relief.

"Seeing you like this...," Alpheus said softly, "so much better than when you were in my care, is worth it. That man is undoubtedly the legendary physician."

Azure nodded contentedly. "I know about what he asked for—the conditions. I won't allow—"

Alpheus held out a hand. "Don't worry. With me being a criminal, my death is likely only a matter of time. At least this way, there would be some value to my life."

"You dolt!" Azure scolded with her softest yet angriest tone. "Who needs you to die for me? And if you would have listened without interrupting, you would know that no one needs to die, at least not right now."

Alpheus raised a brow, putting a loose fist to his chin.

"Listen," Azure said solemnly. "I learned a few things about him—his name is Olijin Pelanofzky. It would seem that he was *unfairly* assigned the *Passionless* name."

Alpheus couldn't agree with the assessment as he thought about his horror just now after having to plough through the murky water, almost drowning in the process. But he said nothing just yet, sure that Azure would offer more information.

"He worked for the Dynasty," Azure then said, a heavy claim given that Kraga's ruling government was seen even by their own people as brutal. "He was given everything he would ever want in his position as a great physician. But he chose to escape. He chose to hide from them. He didn't agree with their violent ways."

Bold assumption, Alpheus thought, still not offering his opinion.

"And Panyuk, the pleasant woman," Azure said. "She believes Pelanofzky would have shown himself even had you not noticed him. What I'm saying is: he's not a bad person. He won't take your life. At least not right away."

"But...," Alpheus said musingly, "can we trust her? She works for him."

Azure tensed beside him. "I trust her."

"I want to believe he is a good person, too," Alpheus said. "But the man was firm when he said he wanted to take my life in exchange for healing you. And then, he forced me to swim my way through to this place. I could have died. In fact, I'm not sure I could do it a second time. He probably expected me to die."

"He didn't wish for that... I don't think, at least," Azure said. "Intuition tells me he merely wants an advantage over you. And if it turns out that I'm wrong, that he really wanted you to die... we leave. I'll die with no regrets."

Alpheus sighed. "Either way, I shall offer my life as a start."

* * *

When they returned to the antechamber, everything was as it had been before. The Passionless Surgeon sat at the corner table, still engaged in the text before him. Panyuk, meanwhile, was busy dusting.

Alpheus walked up to the physician with Azure. "I accept," he said with quiet determination. "Allow me to give my life for Azure."

The physician inhaled deeply through his nose, and then stood up at a height that dwarfed that of Alpheus. The man narrowed his eyes and then nodded. Rather than saying anything, however, he stepped away and headed off slowly toward the door to the left, where he paused and turned back slightly.

"This way," he said.

Panyuk smiled as she scurried over to Azure. She took her by the hand.

"Master has agreed to help you," she said.

"But," Azure said, turning to Alpheus, "what about him?"

"What *about* him?" Pelanofzky asked.

Alpheus frowned. "When...," he said, glaring at the physician, "when do you plan to take my life?"

Pelanofzky grinned. "The plan was for you to die in the lake. That would have been the payment." He shrugged. "I dislike killing with my own hands. But before you rejoice, you should know I never back down on my words. I *will* kill you one day. But until that day comes, you are free to live."

* * *

Alpheus watched the second hand of his pocket watch tick. He was weary, alone in the antechamber, sitting at the small table made for one. It had been two days so far, and while Alpheus had barely gotten to know the catacomb better, he thought it was certainly a dull place, a place where day and night didn't exist. The only time reference he had was his pocket watch. Breathing itself was troublesome in an underground environment with such poor ventilation. It was beyond Alpheus to think why anyone would elect to live in such a place. It was essentially living with the dead, with all those caskets lining the corridor.

Pelanofzky was the strangest person Alpheus had ever met, and Panyuk was almost as strange, albeit without the condescending front. Panyuk had, of course, been the only person Alpheus had had any contact with. The woman had prohibited him from passing through the door to the left where the surgery was taking place, warning Alpheus that the slightest hint of encroachment could lead to Pelanofzky's immediate withdrawal from the operation. Panyuk apparently served as a nurse for Pelanofzky, too, but had been spending far more time outside of the surgery room than within it. She had seemed friendly at times, but she hadn't told him anything about how the surgery was progressing.

Other than her nursing duties, Panyuk was responsible for more than a few chores. The only chore that was slightly interesting to Alpheus, however, was her means of stocking food. She collected food directly from nature itself, usually within the swamp forest, apparently even during the time when

Alpheus had been searching for the catacomb. During these last couple days, she had invited Alpheus to join her *outside* on more than one occasion, almost as if she didn't know about Alpheus's fear of water. She prepared meals twice a day, and she had extended that benefit to Alpheus. The meals were bland and without variety, however—always roasted freshwater fish, with mushrooms on the side.

All Alpheus really cared about, however, was the result of the surgery. Although he had faith in Pelanofzky's ability as a healer, there was always the thought of *what if*. Alpheus had indeed considered swimming out of the catacomb to distract himself. But, instead, he had wandered within the catacomb itself, keeping busy by trying to estimate its age and the civilisation it had belonged to. He had sniffed around for clues, but had yet to determine much in terms of facts. The tomb was fairly empty, the only exception being the corridor of caskets and their inanimate occupants. Alpheus wondered if the place had always been empty of tools and supplies essential for the living, or if it had changed since Pelanofzky became its occupant.

Alpheus hunched forward, his chin on the table. He pulled out his pocket watch again and stared at it, watching the seconds pass him by. The second hand continued to tick away. Slow and tedious. This was perhaps the only time that he had wanted time to speed up, in a world in which he often grumbled about racing against time to accomplish everything that needed to get done. He sighed at the irony, and with a soft huff, his thoughts drifted off for a moment to Julian.

Would it be possible for Julian to speed up the surgery with sorcery? It was impossible to know, especially when Alpheus knew nothing about how Pelanofzky worked.

Alpheus was tired. His eyelids were heavy. Despite the welcome break from having to probe the Harper Rangers, sleep had been evasive, even now that he had the opportunity for rest. More precisely, Alpheus had tried to avoid sleep. He didn't know if it had anything to do with the eerie nature of the tomb itself, but every time he had managed to doze off, he had woken up terrified. Oddly, it had nothing to do with Azure—or, at least, nothing to do with anything he could pinpoint. In his hazy dream sequence, he saw the silhouette of a young girl, receding slowly into a background that was alternated between black and white. That girl would saunter away each time until reaching a certain distance where everything would suddenly explode into grainy colours that whipped about violently while thunderous claps roared through the air.

It was a nightmare. It was pandemonium. And Alpheus figured while in the dream that it *was* just a dream. But even so, he could never escape it. He had tried to force himself to wake prematurely, but to no avail. And that was only to avoid the terrifying ending, an ending that always involved the girl finally turning back—at which time the bursts of colours would splatter into blood red. Man-made structures and people—a mass of them—flashed into view. The people fought among smoke and flames, slaughtering one another. There were screams, wails, and sinister laughter. All the while, the buildings—hundreds of them—crumbled, brick by brick.

That was when Alpheus would wake up, heart pounding heavily and drenched in sweat. Perhaps when he left the catacomb, he would no longer be terrorised by this recurring nightmare.

Alpheus turned his head then to the sound of a door opening, from where the surgery was taking place. As it had been every time for the last couple days, it was Panyuk stepping out from the door. It was almost noon, and that meant that she was coming out to prepare meals for everyone. Alpheus smiled at her and was about to turn away when a glimpse of amber hair flashed into his field of vision. He perked up, peering past the dark woman to a younger lady who had stepped out behind her.

Alpheus widened his eyes, staring in wonder at the newcomer, who was almost unrecognisable to him—unrecognisable in the sense that it had been so long since he had seen her like this. She was, of course, Azure. Her hair wasn't brushed, and she wore no cosmetics, and yet she stepped out now in almost exactly the way Alpheus remembered from their first meeting in the Violanola Woodlands—that vernal quality, her unassuming demeanour, and clear sensibility. How Alpheus had missed that charming smile and those big round eyes that curbed in irises of transparent sky blue. She was truly and literally brought back to life, to the exact condition that she had enjoyed before.

Azure stepped forward to Alpheus then and wiped his tears away with her slender fingers. Her warmth had returned, too.

"Alpheus...," she said softly, meeting his eyes.

Alpheus saw his own reflection in her eyes of blue. It was no illusion. It was no dream. But he found himself unable to utter a single word.

Azure's smile widened slightly. "You look... so old," she said with a giggle. "What are those dark circles and puffiness around your eyes? And... you reek of dirt and sweat. Have you not been taking care of yourself?"

Alpheus grinned, realising that her impertinence had returned as well.

But he said nothing, instead wrapping his arms around her, holding her in a tight embrace.

"I've missed you so much," he said.

"I've missed you, too," Azure said, her pitch as genuine as Alpheus had ever heard. "Thank you for everything you've done for me, Alpheus."

A louder set of footsteps sounded then from the same doorway. Alpheus withdrew his arms and turned slowly to Pelanofzky, who wore his usual grim expression. The physician showed neither a hint of joy for his patient nor any self-satiety for achieving a feat that no one else could. He did seem weary, however. Could it be that he hadn't rested for the entire duration of the surgery?

"Do not forget the payment," Pelanofzky said, eyeing Alpheus. "Your life is now mine. One day, you will have to pay."

"Without question," Alpheus promised. "Whether or not this is only a transaction to you, I consider this a gentlemen's agreement, sealed with integrity."

Pelanofzky nodded humbly and then stepped away from the antechamber through the door to the right, perhaps repairing to his personal chamber for a much-deserved rest. Despite his own fatigue, Alpheus was ready to leave the catacomb. But in addition to wanting to postpone confronting his fear of swimming his way out, Alpheus hoped to allow Azure at least a few days to fully revitalise before heading off on another journey that promised to be just as gruelling as the one they had previously endured.

* * *

In the two days that followed, Azure spent most of her time helping out Panyuk with the daily chores. Together, they swept the tomb, caught fish, and picked edible plants from the outside. Azure had washed her own clothes, as well as Alpheus's. It turned out that she was quite the tailor, too, as she had delicately patched up every snag in Alpheus's mantle that had resulted from the gruelling expedition. Alpheus thought it ironic that, despite his painting skills, he didn't have the delicacy and patience for needlework.

Alpheus had remained reluctant to have to swim through the passage, which was the only way in and out of the catacomb. During more alone time, Alpheus was idle as he imagined what had become of Zorlia and what would become of him upon his return.

It was another two days when Alpheus and Azure were finally ready to set off. Their only regret was that Pelanofzky wasn't available to see them off. Indeed, the big man hadn't shown himself since the surgery. Even Panyuk wasn't accustomed to farewells, despite having been an affable host. She didn't seem to understand why Azure was so tearful when they waved her goodbye at the antechamber.

Azure was still sniffing as she and Alpheus paced through the winding corridor of caskets. Alpheus couldn't be sure whether to think Azure brave for seeming unbothered by the dead bodies, when Alpheus himself still shivered with almost every step of the way.

When Alpheus heard the trickling of water ahead, he sped up slightly, prodding Azure to do the same. They soon reached the endpoint where the path slanted down into the tranquil but murky water. The trickling sounded louder than last time, perhaps amplified by Alpheus's own silence as he looked down at the water with unease. He couldn't quite remember how he had managed to swim his way in, and he still wasn't sure he was able to manage it a second time.

Azure looked up at Alpheus and giggled. "Just follow my lead," she said, taking his hand and pulling him along.

"Give me a minute!" Alpheus said, pulling his arm back.

Azure cocked her head. "You'll have to conquer it sooner or later. Come on!" She reached for his arm again, but this time, Alpheus evaded altogether with a step backwards as he sensed a sudden threat more fearful than the water itself.

"Wait!" Alpheus said, frowning deeply as he stared at the water.

There's something lurking beneath.

"There's no use delaying it," Azure said, shaking her head. "Sooner or later, you—"

"No, I mean it," Alpheus cut in. "Something's down there."

He pulled Azure toward him, and together they stepped farther away from the water. Azure frowned slightly as she, too, fixed her gaze at the water along with Alpheus. As they held their breath, the water began to brew, swirling in circles. Bubbles formed. Proliferating bubbles—from exhalation. The idea of tangling with an aggressive marine creature was worse than any possible nightmare for someone who could barely swim. And yet more frightening was the thought that it could be a person erupting from the foam. Anyone who could find their way here was likely someone they wouldn't want to meet.

TWENTY-SIX

Kraga's ambitions

A ferocious whirlpool hurled out of the water as liquid splashed about, the sputter briefly blinding Alpheus and Azure. Something was enclosed within that fierce vortex.

Alpheus promptly wiped away the water from his eyes and then squinted at the still dissipating mists, where he saw a silhouette of a human figure crashed down from the explosion of water.

Alpheus tightened his grip on Azure's wrist, stepping farther away yet from the water. When the mists finally cleared, a tall man with a lean build emerged. The stranger's dark skin was a hint that he might be from Kraga. His eyes were narrowed, lips thin, chin sharp, and he had large and pointy ears. Every part of him was draped in a *houppelande* except for his head and his drenched grey hair. Unlike the noble classes, who preferred this type of cloak, his was stitched with leather rather than velvet, and in dark green rather than brighter colours like red and orange. Its hue appeared almost black under the dull ambience of the oil lamps. The scimitar attached at his waist was eerily familiar—identical to the weapon Trajetzky had wielded.

This man was older than Trajetzky, however, and unlike the narcissist, his eyes were cold and empty, lonely yet vicious, all at once exuding an air of misery. Alpheus couldn't help but shiver when those eyes peered over to him then.

"To think that the block-faced hermit actually has guests," the man said with a haunting sibilance.

Alpheus trembled, taking another step backwards, unable to mutter any words.

The man sneered, lifting his chin and taking a step forward toward them.

"Trajetzky!" Alpheus finally managed to blurt out, the name obviously surprising to the man who halted his slight advance in response. "You were sent by him," he added, venturing a guess that might win him some kind of advantage.

The man snickered and then brushed a hand over his face until he was suddenly *clawing* into his cheeks, drawing dark blue blood. The man then held out that hand and licked off the dense fluid. All the while, the marks on his face began to miraculously heal, even fade away completely, patched up on their own.

Sorcery, Alpheus thought, widening his eyes as Azure gasped the actual words.

"Trajetzky?" the man said, growing suddenly irritable. "It insults me to be associated with that milksop."

"I apologise for speaking too soon," Alpheus said as a bead of sweat fell from the side of his face, rolling down to his chin. "It was indiscreet of me." He paused, unsure about what was best to say. "Allow me to introduce myself," he then said. "I am Alpheus. How may I… address you?"

The man laughed again, this time more manically, as he held a hand over his face. "Why introduce myself to someone who will soon become a bloodless corpse?"

Alpheus swallowed as Azure trembled beside him. Intuition warned him it was time to run, and he would have had his legs not been frozen to the spot where he stood. The man had reached for his weapon, sliding it out slowly from its scabbard. As the metal glistened under the dim lighting, the man swept out the blade, slapping out a fierce gust that crashed toward Alpheus and Azure at their knees. They fell forward, and after almost stumbling to the ground, Alpheus glanced down to see that the ground had cracked open with an oblique rooting that was the full length of a man.

Alpheus felt his heart thumping as he looked up again. If the target of that slash had been a man, that man would be dead. The tip of the sword had made no contact with the ground, though, and that meant that the man had called upon a power source not unlike sorcery, an energy that formed into a sharp yet delicate wave of destructive force spurred by the swift swing of the sword. The man was no sorcerer—there was no grace flowing inside of him, Alpheus could tell. But the man was indeed drawing on powers of sorcery.

Anyone with the ability to do so is dangerous, Ebenezer had once warned.

The man's eyes had flared to a crimson red. "I shall guzzle down every drop of blood in you!" he warned with the howl of a beast, approaching slowly but surely.

Alpheus gritted his teeth, holding out a hand. "Stop! We can negotiate. Let us explain why we are here."

But the madman didn't seem to hear him, treading forward as if possessed, slurping his tongue around his upper lips. "Blood... blood...," he repeated.

Alpheus turned, prodding the terrified Azure to run with him.

"The taste of blood is best brought out...," the man said chillingly, before suddenly bolting toward them, "when boiling in extreme fear!"

The intensifying volume echoed through the corridor as the madman lunged himself forward. Alpheus kicked off to a glide in urgency, taking Azure with him as they whiffed mid-air, glancing down briefly from there to see another destructive rooting on the ground crack open. As soon as they hit ground again, Alpheus raced down the corridor back toward the antechamber. If anyone could save them now, it was Pelanofzky.

Alpheus thought he heard the man praising his speed as he was dashing away. But when he peered back slightly, he saw the man hop forward before catching onto an incredible speed of his own that brushed up a heap of dust in its wake. Within seconds, the man had drawn level with Alpheus, and after another moment, the man had flashed ahead, then stopping abruptly to block the path. When Alpheus realised what had happened, he immediately surrendered his grip of Azure, but could do nothing to save himself from the momentum that pushed him closer and closer to the madman, who had raised up an arm. Alpheus shut his eyes tightly, but that didn't save him from the inevitable collision with the madman who then sent him slamming brutally into the casket-lined walls.

"Noooo!" Alpheus heard in his stupor, both sound and vision a haze.

Azure, Alpheus thought, his back throbbing, finding himself buried into the rubble of the wall. He managed to force an eye open, peering down to his crumpled sleeves and the small patch there that had been stitched up only a day ago.

I have to protect her.

A scream sounded next. Azure's scream.

Alpheus gritted his teeth as he climbed his way out of the wall, waddling forward as fast as he could. Azure was on the ground, still unscathed but being closed in upon by the madman.

"Don't you dare lay a finger on her!" Alpheus warned, winning the madman's attention.

"Alpheus!" Azure cried, looking up at him. "Run!"

Running had never been an option. Indeed, Alpheus didn't know if he *had* any options left. His body throbbed all over, his mantle was covered in dust, blood trickled from his mouth, and he gripped tightly onto his chest where he had been struck. He gritted his teeth still at the madman who shook his head at him with derision. Barely able to stand, Alpheus finally collapsed to one knee, spurting out blood from his mouth. The madman gazed down at him, shaking his head and turning slowly toward him.

"Stop!" Azure cried out. "If you want blood, take mine!"

The man peered back at her. "A fine proposition," he said, his face contorting into a sinister grin, "for your blood must be *boiling* now!"

"No!" Alpheus cried, raising an arm that was not only just a futile gesture but was also painful enough to render him gasping in agony. "Please! No!"

The man was stepping closer to Azure. He towered over her as he slid out his sword once again.

Alpheus winced at his helplessness as he cursed quietly at himself.

Why am I so powerless?

He perked up then when something flitted in the air from behind him, bolting past him and then sparking toward the madman's sword, deflecting it from his grip, the sword then somersaulting against the wall.

The metal object that had saved Azure fell to the ground with a clang. A scalpel—a small surgical knife.

Pelanofzky, Alpheus realised. He spun and saw the wide frame of the physician emerging from the winding corridor, trampling out wearing an unforgiving grimace. It was possibly the most emotion Alpheus had seen the big physician ever exhibit.

"Do not touch my patient, Leech," Pelanofzky warned.

The madman sneered. "Your patient...? Since when did you accept patients who can give you nothing in return? Or are you telling me the lass has skills that even you, the Passionless Surgeon, would like to see passed on?"

Pelanofzky narrowed his eyes with a frown, lifting his chin. And with that, he had said more than he would with words. Obviously, the two men knew each other. But whether they were friends or foes was anyone's guess.

The madman rolled his eyes and then retrieved his weapon from the ground. "Fine," he said, studying the blade he held as he slid his fingers across the metal. "I'll let her live... but as for..." The madman paused there, peering across to Alpheus who still hadn't the strength to even lift a finger. The madman said no more as he dashed at Alpheus, dragging his sword behind him, and Alpheus could only shut his eyes and cower in response. Just as he did, however, a thunderous sound of clashing metal reverberated across the corridor.

When he opened his eyes again, Alpheus gasped at the spectacle before him: a clash between two mighty men, the powerful thrust of the madman's scimitar met by the equally impressive clutch of the physician's steel gauntlet. Even at the madman's impressive height, he was dwarfed by the enormous size of the physician, who stared him down in ire.

Angered and somewhat confused, the madman withdrew his weapon and stepped back. He gazed at Pelanofzky as if waiting for an explanation.

"You will not take the boy's life," Pelanofzky said.

"Don't tell me what I can and cannot do," the madman spat. "He's *not* your patient! You have no business here, even if I sucked out the last drop of his blood."

Pelanofzky shook his head coolly. "I cannot allow it, for his life belongs to me. His life was the payment to save the lass. No one is to take his life other than me."

The madman smirked. "And you think you can stop me?" he questioned in a chilling tone.

"You are strong, Leech," Pelanofzky said. "No one can stop you. But be sure that you will regret it if you choose to cross me."

It didn't seem the best idea to provoke the madman. But, surprisingly, he seemed hesitant about making a potential enemy out of Pelanofzky. The madman snorted and slipped his scimitar into its sheath, then turned and paced away slowly, stopping only when he reached the scalpel that had earlier saved Azure's life. He stepped onto the handle of the scalpel to flick it up into a spinning motion before snatching it with his hand.

"I have a message for you," the madman said then, pulling out a sheep-skin note from beneath his cloak with the same hand. He spun back to face Pelanofzky and tossed the sheep-skin into the air a few feet in front of him before shooting out the delicate surgical knife which was then hurled dangerously at Pelanofzky, along with the note.

Pelanofzky was quick to draw a pair of forceps from his belt, which he then used to skilfully catch his own scalpel. But despite his usual equanimity and composure, Pelanofzky trembled slightly after a glimpse of the note.

The madman grinned at the physician's uncharacteristic response. "You must have anticipated that this day would come eventually," the madman said. "I suspect that you now understand your position. Hopefully your ability hasn't declined during these years, and you can still be helpful to us."

Pelanofzky said nothing, but his frustration showed plainly on his face.

The madman had turned and seemed ready to leave. "Allow me to warn you," he said. "The King has little patience."

Pelanofzky trembled as the mention of the king had seemingly stunned him further. The madman grinned down at Azure one final time before walking past her toward the water. All eyes anxiously followed the madman's trail until he finally disappeared down the winding path. A furious splash soon sounded, confirming his departure. Alpheus finally gave in, falling face down onto the ground.

* * *

Alpheus woke to find himself exposed. He had no top on, and he was lying on his back with a bright light flashing down at him. His chest felt cool—comfortably cool. He blinked hard once more and then peered to his side. Azure was there, looking relieved to see him awake. It looked like she had been crying, though. And on the other side of him was Pelanofzky, the physician's broad physique blocking off some of the light.

Pelanofzky was wearing spectacles which he removed then before letting out a sigh. The man's forehead had built up a mass of sweat.

"Sit up," he said. "You are now fit to do so."

Alpheus groaned softly, itching from his neck to his waist, but he did as he was told. Azure helped him sit up, and when was upright, he looked down to his chest to find it completely unscathed. Alpheus brushed his hand down to his stomach and remembered how he had almost been killed by the madman.

"You are fortunate," Pelanofzky said, his tone as dull as usual. "Leech showed mercy."

Alpheus gaped for a moment. "*Mercy*?!" he then asked. "*That* was mercy?"

Pelanofzky turned to a bench lined up with a host of different surgical tools. "He used only his raw physical power," the physician said, arranging his tools. "If he had infused even a hint of grace in the attack, you would be dead."

"Grace?" Alpheus said with a frown. "How could he possibly call upon grace?"

Pelanofzky said nothing as he continued packing away his equipment. "There is still much for you to learn," he then finally said, as if that was an adequate response.

"Who is he, then?" Alpheus asked, changing the focus away from sorcery.

"The strongest warrior of Kraga," Pelanofzky said. "We call him

Leech—a reference to his consumption of human blood... and also his lust for bloodshed."

"And you?" Alpheus asked. "What is *your* post within the Kragan Dynasty?"

Pelanofzky paused there and then spun around slowly. "Let us repair to the antechamber," he said, pointing to the door.

Alpheus nodded, but as he stepped out from the bed, he suddenly became very aware that he was wearing only pants. When he looked up again, Azure presented him with his linen undergarment and mantle, folded and clean.

"All patched up," Azure said with a smile.

"Thank you," Alpheus said, slightly embarrassed, quickly fitting the clothes onto his newly healed body, and together, they stepped out into the antechamber, settling at the table in the corner.

Panyuk was nowhere to be seen, but Pelanofzky joined them after a moment, sitting across from them.

"So...," Alpheus said, "who *are* you, exactly? And what is your relationship with Leech?"

Pelanofzky returned Alpheus's gaze. "He is a Primal Soldier... and so am I." The physician paused to allow Alpheus and Azure time to appreciate the implication. "I suspect that you think all Dynasty members are just savage beasts," he then added.

"I'm not here to discriminate," Alpheus said, "but the savagery of your people has been well-documented since hundreds of years ago. More recently, during the Battle for Saffron, your people—"

"Battle *for* Saffron...?" the physician cut in with a snicker. "I didn't know you people actually call it that. Now, it is a fact that we massacred many people—more than we could count. But in our eyes, there was but one objective, and that was to seize Trubannis. Our people were the strongest. We deserved to reign."

"But...," Azure inserted hesitantly, "Kraga ended up losing the war."

Pelanofzky shrugged. "So it seems."

"What's that supposed to mean?" Alpheus challenged, growing annoyed. "Kraga lost. Despite my personal distaste for Kasimir de Spartamon, he was and still is the single greatest war commander in the land. I don't believe anyone could have gotten the better of him—not in open warfare, at least. Trubannis could never have fallen, with him as the leader, and will never fall for as long as he continues to serve as Emperor."

Pelanofzky shook his head. "You're mistaken, Alpheus Hindlow. While Spartamon is indeed a mastermind of war, even he stands no chance against our plentiful numbers. Not then, and certainly not now."

"What are you talking about?" Alpheus said with a hiss. "At the time, Trubannis had four times as many people as Kraga."

"Yes," Pelanofzky responded, "but when we consider the population trained for warfare, Trubannis was estimated at one to a hundred—meaning ninety-nine of every one hundred Trubans were powerless to defend themselves, let alone fight for their country. Kraga's ratio of trained men, meanwhile, was at one to five. Not only did we have more men, but our men were also far stronger, more patriotic—and most importantly—shared the king's vision. Every one of us believed in our right to rule. We would have crushed Spartamon and captured Zorlia as far back as nine years ago."

Alpheus grunted quietly, refusing to believe this outrageous claim.

"Then...," Azure inserted thoughtfully, "why *didn't* the Dynasty try to win the war nine years ago? Why did they surrender instead?"

Pelanofzky's grin deepened as he leered across at Azure. "The key factor was Vinawell's stance," he said. "At the time, the Imperial Lithia Dominion had withdrawn their army. But had my people advanced further into Truban territory, the foolish morals of King Steele would see him reengaged in the war—he would turn against us. While no one could have prevented our advance into Truban territory, Vinawell might have stifled us enough so that we would have been unable to achieve our *true objective* which was not only to seize Trubannis... but to dominate *the land*."

Alpheus and Azure exchanged a look of shock. While the ambition to rule the land wasn't a new concept, any talk of it hadn't ever been considered viable, or even realistic.

Not even Kasimir de Spartamon has the ambition to do such a thing, Alpheus thought. *And that is to think that he could even achieve it.*

The physician smirked. "People are like that—they have always been. There are people in both Trubannis and Vinawell who have the same aspirations, where one rules the land under a totalitarian government. The difference is that they do not have the capabilities to plan or deliver anything of that scale."

Alpheus clenched a fist. "I've seen such people in the Empire who work for their own benefit, rather than for the benefit of their people. In the face of overwhelming power, it's natural that most people would take it. As much as I want to believe otherwise, this world is full of people who would readily slaughter legions in order to reach the bloody throne." Alpheus narrowed his eyes then and turned his glare toward Pelanofzky. "I can see that your king has the vision and perhaps the power to achieve the impossible. But I remain unconvinced that the then-Kragan Dynasty could have seized Trubannis so easily. Not only did we have Spartamon, but the man had built up an incredible army. From Schim to Breunor, and from Lachman to Marvin, Jeffery and my sister—I cannot imagine this group of people losing to anyone."

Pelanofzky croaked at that, seemingly validating his point. "That group *was* a threat, but the Dynasty matched it. No, we exceeded it. Think about Leech, the man you have just met. He could better *any* of the people on your list in more ways than one. And while not everyone is Leech, the Dynasty has many warriors who are capable of what Trubans could only dream of." He paused for a moment. "And then, of course, there was no need for anyone to match the Clan of Light. A few of their most important men had long been allied with us."

Alpheus frowned, thinking these claims were growing more and more absurd.

"Your next destination is the corrupt city of Zorlia, is it not?" Pelanofzky said. "Then you shall find out soon enough."

"What's going to happen?" Azure asked with worry.

Pelanofzky glanced at her, pausing for a second. "War," he finally said. "War of the largest scale. The Truban Empire will soon wage war against the Imperial Lithia Dominion, and it will all be under the Dynasty's command and control."

Anxiousness filled Azure's face, perhaps as she imagined the terror that would follow. Alpheus swallowed with unease.

"King Wandalvic will finally be rewarded for his patience," Pelanofzky said. "The seed had taken nine years to reach fruition. Perhaps even he wouldn't have dreamed that things would fall so perfectly into place. He likely expected the Imperial Lithia Dominion to weaken, but not to the extent in which most of their most able generals are either retired or dead. The Truban Empire, meanwhile, has always been under our watchful eye. And yet, it must have been a joy to watch things unfold as the original plan."

Alpheus had fallen completely silent. He wanted to dismiss everything being said as lies but he realised there was no reason for Pelanofzky to mislead him.

Unless he's wrong, Alpheus thought wishfully. *Unless he's disillusioned.*

Or... am I the one disillusioned? Has the Empire been infiltrated since its conception? Have I been living under corruption this whole time?

"Go," Pelanofzky then said softly. "Go and learn the truth. If you search hard enough, you will find the answer. As for me, I have decided to return to Millenzburg."

"Why?" Alpheus asked, glaring at the physician. "Why are you telling us this?"

Pelanofzky shrugged. "Perhaps because you look like a lost puppy. To inject some fear into you."

Alpheus frowned. He didn't think Pelanofzky evil. Indeed, Alpheus wanted to believe that the physician had wanted nothing to do with the Dynasty. Alpheus said nothing, though, as a part of him warned that he shouldn't trust too easily.

"My life is yours," Alpheus said instead. "Let me know when you want it."

"And," Azure added, "if you are unable to take Alpheus's life for any reason, you will have my life to take back. Whatever the future holds, I shall be eternally thankful for you."

The physician offered a rare smile. "Live on well, lass. And you, Alpheus Hindlow—we shall meet again. When that time comes, be wary of me."

* * *

Alpheus leered down at the ripple that had formed after Azure's dive.

War, he had heard Pelanofzky say.

War of the largest scale. Zorlia. Corruption.

This wasn't the time to falter over something as *trivial* as his fear of water. Alpheus took a deep breath and then leaped into the water.

Gurgling again, and the familiar coldness. The feeling of being completely drenched. How Alpheus hated it. But he was determined, and he had the resolve. The question was whether or not the resolve would be enough. Perhaps it *did* help him—it *did* push him to know that Zorlia and some of those he held dear might soon be drawn into a terrible war. But what really helped Alpheus now wasn't any of those conjectures and dread, but the helping hand right before him—Azure, who had clung onto him, leading him out. For that moment, at least—despite the murk and coldness—Alpheus felt a sense of hope.

The swim seemed surprisingly shorter than the initial swim had been, and upon returning to the more hospitable landscape of the flooded forest, Alpheus and Azure dragged themselves out of the water and onto the damp soil. As they paused to catch their breath, they exchanged a smile and shared a moment of delight in noting that their trek southwards had ultimately been a success.

The joy didn't last, however. Neither of them mentioned a destination as they journeyed southeast. Alpheus couldn't break away from the agitation of Pelanofzky's words that had continued to run inside his head. The idea that the Truban Empire was infiltrated was no small matter. But he thought *not* about the wellbeing of the millions of his fellow countrymen, but about Reeling only, and how he could avenge him now that the circumstances had changed so dramatically. He hadn't posed the question to Pelanofzky, but he had since realised a duty he must perform, and that was to find—to *uproot*—that alleged emissary who had planned or carried out Reeling's murder. Alpheus had more or less chosen to believe what Pelanofzky had said, but he *did* struggle with what course of action to take.

Barely a few hours later, they arrived at a crossroads with a sign that pointed south toward the *Universal River*. It was a day's travel to reach the river, and another two days to reach the most curious frontier in the land where Trubannis, Kraga, and Vinawell met. The convergence point, however, was far less precarious than a brief geographical description would suggest. Most of the area around the boundaries was covered in dense forests with more animals and plants than people. Apparently, the mountainous forests weren't the type of land that any of the three strongest countries was keen on claiming. For decades—centuries, even—the convergence point had enjoyed relative peace, at least from warfare.

In any case, the dilemma of where to go next was growing more urgent for Alpheus. Turning back to the Vinan capital was never an option, as it was unlikely that anyone of the Dominion would listen to him. Even a trek to Millenzburg made more sense. After all, the Kragan capital might prove to be the origin of all of the chaos. But what could Alpheus possibly achieve on his own in Millenzburg which was said to be a terribly harsh place, even for its own people?

Perhaps Zorlia was the only place he could head for. It was where the storm was brewing, where magic users were gathering, and where Reeling was resting, waiting to be avenged.

Alpheus stopped then and looked up at Azure, who was walking ahead of him. He called out to her.

"I need to return to Zorlia," he said. "And that means... we might have to go our separate ways."

Azure cocked her head slightly, her expression inquisitive but also hurt. "You're going to abandon me?"

"I don't want this," Alpheus said. "But the confusion, the chaos, and the corruption in Zorlia—it's too much. I can't have you there. I can't have your safety compromised after all that has happened."

"Then what *are* you planning to do?" she demanded.

Alpheus shook his head. "I have no definite plans. But Zorlia is calling for me. I don't know exactly what to do but I think being there will help." He then lowered his eyes. "And yet, I'm still a considered to be a criminal there."

Azure regarded him for a moment. "Rest assured," she said, striding ahead again, "that I won't be relying on you to protect me anymore. But if my memory serves me right, I believe you promised to take me there one day. And whether you plan to fulfil that promise or not, I *am* going with you."

"No, Azure, you don't understand. This isn't—"

"We're going there," she said, hopping along, suddenly blissful. "But let there be a stopover. I'll take you to a happy place."

* * *

Even on foot, they managed to reach the south end of the Harper Ranges the next day. The valley had been a place where Alpheus had struggled but succeeded, and in finally leaving it, Alpheus almost regretted that he couldn't prolong his stay. In the southern state of Easterclem, there were no major cities, but plenty of smaller villages were scattered about. Azure had detoured around a couple of the villages, but had otherwise trotted almost directly south, rather than east toward Trubannis. Trekking through the tranquil plains had been rather uneventful, and although a *happy place* was the supposed destination—whatever that might mean—Alpheus simply wasn't in the mood to see anything else at a time when time itself was pressing. He actually had trouble remembering when time had *not* been pressing.

Alpheus realised that they were now climbing a hill with an oblique ascension so steep that the other side wasn't visible. It didn't seem like Azure shared any of his sense of urgency. Alpheus had tried his best to be considerate, or at least tried to act the part, forcing a smile every time that Azure had looked over to him during the journey. After all, Azure had only just been given a new lease on life. She deserved some joy. But every time that Alpheus thought he had convinced himself to allow a little more time, the physician's words rang inside him.

War, it said. *Our people will dominate the land.*

Marvin and Ebenezer were likely in Zorlia now, both of them among potentially many others drawn into what was shaping up to be a mighty struggle for power in the court. When sorcerers were added to the equation, one could imagine just how terrible the resulting damage could be. Assuming that Kraga indeed had the ambition to dominate the land and that the Truban Empire had long been infiltrated, this was surely not a matter to defer even for a second.

"Alpheus!" Azure called out to him from ahead, with an amount of joy that had Alpheus picturing her cheerful grin without even seeing it. "Hurry! We're almost there!"

Alpheus found himself smiling in response to Azure's words. He was encouraged to conclude a climb that had been more taxing than he anticipated. In turn, he wondered how Azure was striding ahead so assuredly, seemingly with ease. Barely ten minutes later, Alpheus gazed again to note that Azure had reached what looked like the peak of the hill. She had spread her arms wide open as a gentle breeze washed over her, apparently marvelling at the sight before her. When she glanced back at him with a glowing smile, Alpheus gasped, noting her beautiful sky-blue eyes gleaming with more radiance than he had ever seen.

A special plant down there? Alpheus wondered.

Alpheus dragged himself up, all the while simulating a conversation about how to convince Azure to share his urgency. Upon finally reaching her, Alpheus opened his mouth, ready to deliver his plea. But just then, a breeze of blue petals swept by softly, like waves, sprinkling out a pleasant scent that filled the air. Alpheus turned his head to follow the drift of those petals, raising an arm slightly and laying out his palm as if the petals were a springtime variant of snowflakes. The curiously familiar scent had him widening his eyes.

Alpheus then turned back toward Azure with a grin of genuine pleasure, glad that he could start a conversation that he was sure she would enjoy. But when he looked past her and the edge of the hill, he fell silent and his eyes glistened before the wonder laid out before him.

A woodland lined with fantastically tall trees and a floor carpeted by an endless sea of blue-violet flowers. Stream after stream of soft breezes brushed the vast wave of blue-violet, extending out as far as the eye could see. The lovely flowers bloomed in harmonious undulation like the gentle waves of the infinite sea. Despite himself, and amid the troubles of the world, the scenery was encapsulated in serenity.

Azure clung onto his arm then, leading Alpheus down the hill at a leisurely pace. The pleasing scent of earth and the flowering plants filled every part of the air as they traipsed along and amid the soft carpets of the wonderland. Everything that they didn't wish to be burdened with or troubled by, was somewhat being magically alleviated here.

The abundance of bell-shaped flowers embraced them in an encapsulation of optimism and hope. As they threaded and stringed their way around the fantastic woodland trees, Alpheus finally realised why Azure had brought him here. It was simply to cheer him up, to encourage him before he would have to confront what promised to be perhaps the greatest challenge in his life.

And he had thought that she wasn't aware of the gravity of the matter.

Shame, he thought. *Shame on me*.

Alpheus shook away the guilt to soak in more of the shared joy. He skipped along with Azure until fatigue got the better of them. They then crumpled down to the ground, sinking into the carpet of flowers.

As he lied on the ground, Alpheus regarded the individual flowers, which were primarily blue in colour. The violet illusion must have been caused by the density and refraction of light. The flowers were pendulous, tubular, with recurved petal tips, and borne on one side of the flowering stem. They were pleasantly scented, smelling almost identical to the perfume that Alpheus had purchased at Aragon, which he now picked out from his mantle. He held it up high behind the glare of daylight that refracted through the glass bottle, highlighting its transparent contents of light blue.

Azure, who was lying down next to him, looked over at the tiny bottle. "The perfume extracts its scent from here, the bluebell woodlands."

Alpheus sat up. "I remember," he said. "The lady at Aragon mentioned that. She sold me the perfume."

Azure smiled at him. "I'm so fond of this place," she said, sitting up as well. "But we should get going, for there is still one more stopover."

Alpheus tensed, about to remind her of the urgency of their mission.

"Don't worry," Azure assured. "It's barely a detour—east from here. But let us stay the night there. *For me*."

TWENTY-SEVEN

Azure Vera Belle

Azure was washing her face in the clear water of the stream now under the dawning horizon. She closed her eyes as a surge of melancholy rose in her. The water washed away her tears as they fell, and she was thankful that no one could see her cry.

What Pelanofzky had said mattered to Azure no less than it had to Alpheus. Azure loved her country. Her stomach churned at the allegation that Vinawell would be scrambled into an armed conflict that she was sure her country didn't want. As she imagined her people scuffled and slain, she lamented about how powerless she was. At the same time, Azure hadn't forgotten that she had been banished. She wasn't supposed to set foot in Vinawell ever again. In fact, she shouldn't be in the country even now. A return to Poppaross had somehow become a dream that might never come true. While the king and His men would possibly show her mercy if they spotted her in the country, Azure had chosen to accept her punishment. She had chosen to respect the king's decision, regardless of how reluctant she was to leave.

Perhaps the only incentive to leave Vinawell was the prospect of seeing the princess again, her closest friend and confidant. Azure had lied about not knowing where the princess had gone. It was true that she couldn't pinpoint the exact place, but the princess had said that she was headed for Aizary, far away from all the troubles of her Vinan royalty, and also away from the threat of the Kragans.

* * *

It was early morning when Alpheus and Azure arrived in Harper Springs, a small, close-knitted village with sparsely placed homes built in sheep-grazed pastures. A common animal here was the lamini, a hooved animal similar to a camel, but smaller and more nimble, wearing a thick coat of black or white with pointy ears.

Azure hadn't explained yet why they were there. She seemed to know her way around, even acknowledging a few people as they paced through the village. These people seemed to know her, too, as they reciprocated her charming smile with friendly nods. Alpheus, however, received only open glares from the same people. He found himself clinging tightly onto Azure's sleeves, as if to remind the villagers that he was with her.

"They're not fond of your kind," Azure whispered to him. "Trubans, that is."

Alpheus responded with a wry smile. "Well, I'm glad you brought me here, then."

"Had I said anything," Azure said, continuing on her business, "we wouldn't be here at all. But don't worry. No one here would ever resort to violence."

Alpheus grumbled to himself, but despite his disgruntlement, he couldn't help but be curious about the age distribution of the people in the village. The villagers were either young adults, elderly, or very young children, with no one in between. Alpheus eyed a young man, perhaps the same age as he was, supporting an elderly man who had only one leg, now walking on crutches. Alpheus grimaced slightly at the misfortune of the older man, but when that man managed to take his first step and lift his head, Alpheus was quick to turn away in order to avoid eye contact.

They soon reached what appeared the end of the village where a two-storey cottage sat. The home was well-maintained, with ornamental leafy twines running alongside its exterior—not unlike the cottage where Alpheus had first met Azure, actually. On the porch was a sizeable old sign that read: *Fragrance of the Bluebell*. Just as Alpheus was about to make a comment, Azure stepped up to the porch and pushed open the front door.

"What are you doing?" Alpheus whispered with apprehension.

Azure glanced back with a smile and then proceeded inside. "Granny!" she called.

Alpheus hurried behind her into the home. To the right was a set of stairs that led to the second floor, and to the left was a fireplace, the hearth encircled by a neat set of cosy seating, which included a couch and a pair of plush armchairs. The inviting air of freshly cut flowers, together with an air of oak, was the result of several potted plants inside an ornamental interior covered in wood, from the floor to the walls and to the ceiling. It was homely, plain, and unpretentious.

An old lady poked her head out from what Alpheus suspected was the kitchen, where a sweet aroma of rose tea diffused into the air. She stepped out to reveal her full head of grey hair, and her short form fitted into a plain dress beneath an apron. She brushed up her spectacles and squinted toward Alpheus, sending a shiver through him.

The last time he had felt such a chill was during the confrontation with Leech. And while Alpheus certainly didn't think that an old lady had the same power as that madman, this old woman seemed to breathe a sense of authority, perhaps as a domestic homemaker.

Alpheus sighed, relieved, when the old lady finally turned away from him and peered over toward Azure. "And I thought you didn't know your way back," she said, her voice hoarse yet gentle.

Azure grew teary-eyed as she beamed at the older woman, and then the two of them paced toward each other for a full embrace.

* * *

The old lady's name was Nora, and she alone had raised Azure. Despite her old age—possibly into her seventies—she seemed rather able and active. She had kept this sizeable cottage home impeccable, presumably all on her own. Not a dash of dust could be spotted, and not a single piece of furniture seemed misplaced. Her own presentation, the way she dressed, was simple yet refined—similar, in a way, to Azure.

Alpheus was invited to the couch next to the unused hearth, while Azure went into the kitchen with Nora to finish brewing the tea. The couch was comfortable, especially so when the ambiance within the cottage had him feeling a sense of *home*. Alpheus sunk deep into the seat, only to perk up again when Azure and Nora returned from the kitchen. Azure seated herself next to Alpheus on the couch, while the old lady nestled into the armchair across them. Everything had grown suddenly awkward, at least for Alpheus.

"Why so tense, boy?" Nora asked, to which Alpheus could only respond with an uneasy smile. "So, what's your relationship with my Vera?"

Alpheus cocked his head this time. "*Who...?*"

Azure giggled until Alpheus glared in her direction. "I didn't lie to you," Azure said in defence. "My full name is Azure Vera Belle."

That was certainly new information to Alpheus, who felt immediately ashamed that he had never bothered to find out what her family name was. And that was despite having been through life and death with her.

"Oh dear," Nora said, shaking her head, seemingly unsure whether to smile or to frown. "Child, you are making it difficult for me to approve of you."

Alpheus bit his lips, not sure what to say, hoping Azure would bail him out. Just then, the front door sounded with a creak. A lady with the same amber hair as Azure stepped in—someone who looked several years older than Azure, dragging along a bulky sack behind her.

"Gloria!" Azure called out to the lady.

The newcomer lifted her head, and her eyes glistened as they fell upon Azure. She then rushed over to Azure for an embrace not very different from the one Azure had shared with Nora only a few moments earlier.

"How long has it been?" the lady said, visibly excited. "When did you come back?"

Despite the tears of joy, Alpheus still didn't understand the nature of the reunion, and the scholar inside of him was frustrated about being more and more lost. He squinted now as he looked more carefully at the newcomer, thinking the face familiar. Alpheus then peered over to the open entrance where the lady had left her sack, labelled in fine writing: *Fragrances*. He then glanced out the window to the sign outside that added the words: *of the Bluebell*.

"It's you!" Alpheus said suddenly. "You're the perfume merchant in Aragon!"

The newcomer finally laid her eyes on him then. "That's no way to greet a lady," she said in reproach.

"This is Alpheus," Azure said.

The lady studied Alpheus for a moment and then nodded. "Ah, I remember," she said. "You looked so awfully pale back then that I can barely recognise you now."

Alpheus learned that Gloria was Nora's granddaughter. Their family name was Penhaligon, which differed from Azure's family name of Belle. Apparently, Azure wasn't a blood relative. And yet Harper Springs was indeed Azure's hometown, which Alpheus now learned that she had departed from over ten years ago. Although Azure hadn't returned for all these years, she had continued to write home to these two people who she considered to be her family. It was a fortunate accident that Gloria—who now called Aragon home—had returned for a visit at precisely this time.

"I'm sorry," Azure said then, turning solemn.

"What?" Gloria said, peering at her in concern. "What is it?"

"I apologise for the fact that I haven't visited for so long," Azure said, bowing her head. "And that the only reason I'm here now is because fate brought me this way."

Azure was honest with them as she detailed the accounts of her injury, their journey through the Harper Ranges, and their consequent encounter with the Passionless Surgeon. And although she was healthy again now, her audience showed a great amount of concern for her. And to Alpheus, even though he had lived through the experiences himself, he realised how perilous it sounded as he heard it reported back to him in her words.

"I owe my life to the Passionless Surgeon," Azure said. She paused there, laying her eyes on Alpheus with an expression of gratitude. "And no less to Alpheus," she continued. "He gave me reason to believe—to believe that there is value in my life."

Alpheus returned a wry smile, and then soon he realised both Nora and Gloria were regarding him anew, their eyes twinkling with that same gratitude.

"Thank you," Nora said with a nod.

"From the bottom of our hearts," Gloria added.

Alpheus flushed, not knowing what to say.

Gloria smiled for a moment longer before turning a sudden crossed face at Azure. "Come upstairs with me," she said.

Azure bit her lips, almost like a mischievous child being caught by her parents doing something impish. She then submitted to Gloria with obedience, making no protest as she followed her upstairs. Alpheus watched them disappear from view and hoped that nothing unpleasant was about to ensue.

"She needs a talk," Nora said as she sipped from her cup. "A lesson."

Alpheus turned back to the old lady now with a raised brow.

"She was lucky enough to survive this time," Nora said, "but she cannot continue to live so recklessly. Her selflessness is her best quality, but this time it almost proved fatal."

"Is Miss Penhaligon... scolding her?"

Nora shook her head. "Gloria regards Vera dearly, like a sister. She'll be reminding Vera to think for herself once in a while. And, of course, she'll also check on Vera's health, to confirm that the physician did his job."

"She's a physician, too?"

"More than half the people in our town are trained in medicine. *Impressive*—people might say."

She paused for a moment, breathing out a long sigh. She stood up with a grim face and walked over to the window.

"But it was forced upon us," she continued, looking outside. "Harper Springs is a simple town. And so is most of the state of Easterclem. We had tried our best to avoid being entangled in any conflicts, but we were naïve. In retrospect, it was fortunate that we were only drawn into the terrible war in its final years. The Kragans—our allies at the time—promised to press the Trubans from the south, and therefore help defend Easterclem if needed. For years, there was no need to defend us, but upon the emergence of the Clan of Light—the first instance of meaningful retaliation—the Kragans failed us. The Trubans charged into Southern Vinawell, slaughtering our people by the masses. Villages and towns were pillaged, looted, and destroyed. It was horrifying."

She shuddered deeply.

"Harper Springs was fortunate enough to escape the slaughter," she continued, "but the good men and women of this village were less fortunate. The Dominion impelled anyone healthy enough to fight to join the battle. In effect, all of the young people—who had the rest of their lives ahead of them—left the village and marched to the battleground. So, although the village escaped the worst, things have never been the same since then."

"And...," Alpheus said in whisper, "those people, the men and women... did they...?"

Nora turned back, eyeing him coldly. "Not a single one came back alive."

Alpheus swallowed, feeling a churn in his stomach. He had always considered the Kragans cruel, but the truth was that his fellow countrymen had slaughtered their fair share of civilians—powerless men and women who posed no threat.

And some of those victims were Azure's family, he thought in remorse. *My prosperous upbringing in Zorlia was at the cost of the many deprived children whose families were destroyed in the war.*

Alpheus had only read more into the attack of Southern Vinawell in recent years, and his readings had described it as *a minor invasion but a major conquest*. It was *the* turning point of the war, and also the beginning of the end of the war. Not only had the invasion of Easterclem slowed Vinawell's charge from the northwest, but it had also creviced Vinawell's trust in Kraga as their ally, which might have played a part in the Dominion's withdrawal from the war two years later. But despite all of that, it was difficult to fathom all of the untold heartbreaks and agonies that were the by-products of the final result.

"I am not fond of Trubans," Nora said. "I am not fond of Kragans, either. But if there is anyone I should despise utterly and completely, it is King Steele and his men. It was he who concentrated the Dominion's battalions in the north. It was he who waged war against the Trubans. And it was he who took away the children's parents.

"Don't get me wrong, young man," she continued, turning back to Alpheus now, "I didn't tell you this to get your sympathy. We understand that it was a war. It is difficult, if not impossible, to say who was right or wrong. History cannot be undone. It is more worthwhile, instead, to focus on the present and the future—and the people around us."

"And by that, you mean...?"

"Vera is fond of you. I want you to understand her more. I wish to believe that your care for her is genuine, but it aches me to see that you didn't even know her name, or anything about her hometown. Who is she to you?"

Alpheus hung his head in shame. "It's embarrassing," he agreed. "I should have known. But... it's not like that between us. We're not—"

"Is that how she feels, or how you feel?" Nora said.

Alpheus paused, hesitating.

"Either way," the old lady continued, "she has set her mind on following you. I only ask that you show some appreciation for her feelings."

Alpheus hesitated still, reluctant to agree upon anything just yet. But he managed to breathe a soft sigh of relief when footsteps from the stairs sounded. Azure and Gloria were coming back down. And as Alpheus regarded Azure more carefully then descending from the stairs, he wondered what exactly she meant to him. Why had he trekked the country from end to end for her?

I like her, he heard his own voice saying in his head. *She's beautiful in every way. Kind, good-natured, everything I could ask for.*

Is that not enough?

Alpheus turned back to Nora and nodded. That gesture was enough to prompt a contented smile onto the old lady's face, or at least to allay her worries for the moment.

* * *

As Alpheus strolled about the village with Azure, he noted that most of the people were indeed children, some just almost reaching adulthood. And all of them continued to regard Alpheus with hostile gazes. But it made sense to him now. He didn't shy away from the animosity, but he also wouldn't admit to any fault, either. He simply smiled at them as he would to any stranger. And some of them, more or less, dropped their air of ill will in response.

"So, this is your hometown," Alpheus said as they paced through stony pavements. "I always assumed you were from the capital. Well, it was only natural for me to think that when I was misled into thinking that you were the princess."

Azure stopped in her tracks. "Are you still mad about that?"

"No," Alpheus said, shaking his head. "If I were mad, I'd be mad at myself for not knowing more about you. After what we've been through."

Azure simpered. "What's with the gravity all of a sudden?"

Alpheus held her by the shoulders then, gazing into her eyes. "You have become an important person to me," he said. "And I want to get to know you better."

Azure immediately turned, perhaps to hide away from the awkward exchange. She cleared her throat and then turned back slowly with a nod. She regained her composure as she pointed toward the centre of town, where she would give her accounts as a child raised in Harper Springs. They settled at a humble courtyard, finding a seat at a modest fountain where water sprung from the feet of an angel.

"The children were spared from bloodshed," Azure began. "But it was in exchange for our parents' lives. Others honour them as heroes, but to me, they were just selfish. They died believing they had done a good thing for us. They were content even in death. But did they realise their *heroic* acts meant that we all became orphans? The thought that they *died* for us doesn't make our lives any easier now."

"But they didn't *choose* to fight," Alpheus argued. "The Dominion impelled them."

Azure shook her head. "I *know* the Dominion," she said. "I was in Poppaross for ten years. Many people, even Granny Nora, find it convenient to lay the blame on the Dominion, but that's simply not the truth. The king and his entourage would never force powerless civilians to war. Our parents volunteered to die. If we want to criticise the Dominion for anything, it should be for sending children to war."

"*What*?!"

"The orphaned children without blood relatives were taken away to the northern towns. The Dominion promised to find foster families for them, but that was a lie. Those children were instead trained to become soldiers. The Dominion saw these children as potent human weapons as they had nothing to live for and also because they were fuelled with vengeance."

"That's terrible!" Alpheus exclaimed. "And I had thought King Steele was a good man."

"It wasn't the king," Azure said with a grimace, staring into the distance. "The one responsible for that call was Ebenezer. I've never liked that man and

I'm suspicious about why he re-joined the Dominion. And I *hate* that I owe my life to him, that he was the one who guided you on how to help me."

Alpheus groaned. "Azure...," he said, hesitating, "were you... one of those children?"

Azure lightened up then. "No," she said. "It's true that I had no blood relatives after my parents died, but Granny took me in. She was my neighbour, whose son died in war. Gloria was left in her care. Although they had to cope with their own losses, they put their own sorrows behind them and encouraged me to live on. That's why I'm forever indebted to them."

"Then how did you end up working for the princess?"

Azure sighed. "Despite what Granny and Gloria had done for me, I couldn't bring myself to smile upon realising that my mother and father would never return. I wanted to show them that I was fine. But... I couldn't. I fell into a deep depression, and didn't recover until a year later, when Princess Flora came to the village. The princess, even then when she was only eight years old, toured the country to help those in need. I still remember when I first met her. Her affectionate smile brought light into my world again. She was my saviour, an angel from heaven who came to my rescue."

Alpheus nodded in agreement. "She *does* seem kind."

"Right after that smile, though," Azure continued with a giggle, "she smacked me in the face! She told me to stop acting like I was the most miserable person in the world. She reminded me that I wasn't the only one who had lost their loved ones. It was years later when I learned that she had lost both her birth mother and stepmother—the latter, of course, being the Queen."

"So, after that," Alpheus said, "you followed her back to Poppaross?"

"Yes," Azure said. "She showed me how to help others. Her altruism was infectious. She didn't treat me as a servant—rather, she cared for me and respected me as friend."

"And to return the favour, you risked everything to help her find her own happiness?"

Azure smiled, looking down and undoubtedly picturing the princess. "She helped others for her entire life. She deserves to be selfish just this one time and to live only for herself. She's a year my junior, actually, but she always felt like an elder sister to me. For once, I wanted to be the elder one."

Like a sister, Alpheus thought, as the image of his own sister streamed into his mind, followed by a vision of Agnes, who he considered more his sister than his own flesh and blood.

"While we're on the topic," he then said, "there's something I wanted to ask you about. During my first days at the castle, I happened by a strange lady who claimed to be the princess."

"*Claimed* to be?" Azure asked with a raised brow.

"You shouldn't be surprised," Alpheus said with a grin. "You did it, too."

Azure rolled her eyes. "Will you ever get over that?"

"Anyway," Alpheus said, "there was something about her. Just seeing her gave me the chills. Her eyes were hollow from the outside, yet it was as if she hid something so terrible, something beyond what anything that I could imagine. She was absolutely *enraged* when she found out that I was from Trubannis."

"That was... Princess Ingrid," Azure said reluctantly. "She is Princess Flora's elder sister, but they don't share the same birth mother. Princess Ingrid's birth mother is the Queen, who died at the hands of Truban soldiers. Princess Flora's birth mother, on the other hand, is Lady Hydrangea, who died shortly after giving birth to her."

"And what is this Princess Ingrid like?"

"I don't know," Azure said with a twitch of the brow. "I've only seen her a few times myself. Apparently, she has alienated herself since the Queen's death—which happened before I went to Poppaross."

Alpheus shook his head in pity. "A living victim of the war."

* * *

After staying the night at Harper Springs, Alpheus was ready to finally set off for Zorlia the next morning. Some of the townspeople came to Nora's cottage to see them off. They recognised Azure as their own, and in turn, they accepted Alpheus too, as a guest. Through Nora's doing, the townspeople even offered a couple of the finest laminis to them, fitted complete with saddles and reins.

"When are you going back to Aragon?" Azure asked Gloria.

"Probably in a few days," Gloria said, wrapping an arm around her shorter grandmother. "*Someone* has to be here for her."

Nora grinned, and then turned to Azure. "*Do* come back when you can," the old lady said. "This is and always will be your home."

Azure embraced her warmly. "I will. I promise."

Gloria and Nora then turned their eyes expectantly to Alpheus.

"You can entrust Azure to me," Alpheus said in assurance. "And we *will* come back. That's my promise... to Azure."

Alpheus and Azure hopped onto the laminis and slowly treaded away from the village. Azure sighed as she took one last look at her hometown. It had been only a brief visit, and Alpheus knew that she was going to miss it. He pulled his animal up next to hers, patting her on the shoulder. She smiled at him, and together they rode away into the distance.

* * *

Laminis didn't match the size and speed of horses, but they were surprisingly athletic and hardy. Their agility and nimbleness meant that they could skip through narrow spaces, natural attributes that were perfect for roaming through the dense forests ahead. The laminis were sociable and intelligent, too. Azure claimed that she had always fancied laminis over horses, and Alpheus was starting to see why as they made their way closer to the frontier.

The Truban state of Farella was only a few more days ahead, and a sure sign of their advance was on their third day away from Harper Springs, when they arrived at the end point of the Universal River. Not too far ahead was the boundary that separated Vinan territory from the Truban state of Farella.

A fair share of wild beasts and reptiles of the slithering variety ruled these forests, but few of these animals were particularly predatory toward humans. And, even so, Alpheus and Azure felt sickened now as they saw that humans had left behind a bloody trail of carcasses to rot in the wild—seemingly for sport—many of which appeared to be no more than two weeks old. Some of these victims included wild boars, but also many harmless animals.

It was always best to travel as much as possible in the day, but even with the sun at its highest point now, Alpheus suggested a brief adjournment to their journey in order to cremate all of the rotting carcasses. Azure unsurprisingly nodded her assent at the proposal, and the two of them proceeded to collect fallen tree branches in order to build a fire. It was deplorable that anyone would slaughter animals out of sadism, rather than for sustenance, and as they watched the bonfire, Alpheus realised that he had learned to appreciate animals much more than ever after meeting Azure. It hurt him to see the death of these animals, and he was angered by the thought that *people* had come to terrorise the natural order of things.

"Fancy seeing you here," a voice called out from behind some shrubs.

Alpheus turned around in annoyance, ready to accuse someone of slaughtering the animals—and to punish them for it. It was easy to point his finger in accusation, however, when he saw that it was none other than Joe Hendron poking his head out from the shrubs.

"Laminis!" Hendron exclaimed with excitement, apparently oblivious to Alpheus's ire. "I've always wanted one for myself."

"Joe...!" Alpheus greeted in a seething tone. "I assume you're doing quite well with your hunts?"

Hendron glanced down at the slaughtered animals still waiting to be cremated and then waved a finger to brush away the blame. "Hunting is an art," he said. "Slaughter is not. It *wasn't* me who did this."

"Then, do you know who it was?" Azure asked more calmly.

"Kragan soldiers," Hendron said. "Or so I would assume."

Alpheus squinted at the claim.

"I didn't see it," Hendron said. "But I *did* see a group of them here not too long ago. Apparently, they were just passing by... looking for someone named *Lord Leech*."

"Leech?!" Azure exclaimed as Alpheus trembled in silence.

Hendron peered at the both of them with suspicion. "Do you *know* him?"

Alpheus scowled. "We—"

"Actually," the hunter cut in, holding a hand out. "I don't want to know. It seems that all you attract is trouble."

Alpheus paused and then sighed, almost in agreement that that was true.

"Anyway, I assume things didn't end well for you in Poppaross?"

"You could say that," Alpheus said, not eager to explain.

Hendron shrugged. "And what brings you here?"

"We're crossing the border into Trubannis."

"But you're still a criminal there, are you not?"

"I am," Alpheus answered with another sigh.

Hendron scratched his chin. "And you're planning to go just like that? You should at least disguise yourself, like you did before."

Alpheus looked down at his clothes. He had enjoyed the liberty of roaming about freely since arriving in Vinawell, and he had been wearing platinum-framed spectacles and wearing his ponytail braided the same way he had in Zorlia. But it was indeed foolish to head back into Zorlia without at least doing something to shy away from attention. Perhaps he would have to assume the name of Albert Moon once again. As he looked up again at Hendron now, however, he remembered how he had used the hunter at the garrison near Dorellsdale. Alpheus understood that he owed Hendron, but he had no way to pay him back just yet. And yet Alpheus needed to ask for more from him. Hendron's tangible experiences in the open land would most definitely help their advance on this journey.

"Join us!" Azure suggested with enthusiasm, seemingly speaking Alpheus's mind. "I'm sure you know the best route to get to Zorlia from here, right?"

Hendron grinned proudly. "I sure do," he said. "Except the problem is that I have no interest to journey with anyone. I'm a lone wolf. Have always been. And always will be. Besides, I've had enough of Trubannis for the time being."

"Oh?" Azure said, turning suddenly cheeky. "It sounds more like you're afraid of the beasts in Zorlia."

"Afraid?" Hendron scoffed. "You should know that no beast in the land can escape me."

"I'm not convinced," Azure said.

"Hey," Alpheus whispered to her as he gripped onto her sleeve. "What are you doing here?"

Azure shook off his grip. "All right then, how about a bet, Joe?" she said. "You can take the laminis if you win. But, if you lose, you will accompany us to Zorlia. And, of course, receive nothing in compensation."

Hendron fell silent, contemplating the proposal as he eyed the animals. "A bet, eh?" he said with a smirk. "If the bet is dependent on my hunting ability, then be warned that you're destined to lose. But if it's—"

"It will certainly be dependent on your hunting ability," Azure said with a smug grin of her own, showing the impertinence that was a unique part of her. "Now," she continued, peering down at the carcasses with a hint of sorrow, "to avoid further stressing the land animals, let us base the bet on your ability to catch birds."

"Birds?" Hendron said with a squint. "They're not even worth the effort."

"Oh, is that so? Or is it because catching birds is beyond your ability?"

"Fine!" Hendron said. "But be sure not to blame me if I happen to accidentally hurt those little flying creatures. How many do you want me to catch? Fifty? A hundred? Give me some time, and I'll catch two hundred!"

Azure nodded, seemingly proud of herself. She then whistled between her fingers, a fine harmonious tune that brought about a tempest of birds that swept over the towering trees above them. The leaves rattled as the branches thrashed about. Hendron could only gape up at the skies in shock as thousands of sparrows swooped in, as if proliferating behind those trees, their accumulation almost forming a giant phoenix. One of the tiny sparrows plummeted down, landing on Azure's extended left hand. The rest of the thousands of birds hovered above, ready to pounce upon her call.

Alpheus looked up at the incredible phenomenon, too, wondering how it could be accomplished without sorcery. The incessant fluttering of wings was unbelievable. And somehow the one who had called those birds was the good-natured Azure, who didn't seem like she would ever abuse the ability. Alpheus smiled as he regarded Azure then as she tied a delicate strip of fabric onto the left talon of the sparrow resting on her hand.

"No need to catch two hundred," Azure said to Hendron, who was trying to blink away what he must have believed to be an illusion. "If you could catch only this one, you win. I'll give you an hour."

Hendron turned back to her. "An hour to catch that *one* bird? And you're *marking* the bird for me?"

Azure grinned at him. "Don't underestimate the task," she cautioned.

Azure then waved an arm to signal that the sparrows should disperse. As they all took flight, Hendron was quick to toss up a lightly tinted powder which sprinkled in the air, perhaps brushing upon some of the surging birds, their collective lift beating the leaves in a rattle as they scattered off in all directions.

"I don't know how you got those birds to come to you," Hendron said, squinting at Azure. "But I doubt you can change their behaviour. Sparrows almost always remain together in the same flock. That powder I sprinkled carries an odour. In other words, I can easily track the bird."

"Impress me," Azure challenged, gesturing for Hendron to begin.

Hendron sneered and then set off, sniffing among the trees. Azure tagged closely behind. Alpheus simply shook his head with an amused smile as he followed them through the trees.

"I've wanted to ask for long time," Alpheus said quietly to Azure. "How do you do it? How do you call... birds... and even insects?"

Azure shrugged, as if it were a common ability. "I'm just communicating with them in a way they can appreciate. It's a genuine request for help. And yes, a *request*—not a command."

"But *how*...?"

"I don't know how to explain it. There's no *procedure* involved. I suppose it's a gift the people of Southern Vinawell share—our attachment to nature and to animals. More than a few of us can communicate with them. I've been able to do this for as far back as I can remember."

Alpheus cocked his head to indicate his confusion.

"You know, Alpheus," Azure said, her smile broad. "One of these days, I'll tell you everything."

* * *

Hendron managed to do what he had promised, tracking down the marked bird sitting at the top of a very tall elm as part of the flock. Hendron grinned as he readied his equipment, swinging his knapsack forward and pulling out a long rod that shot out nets.

"I don't think you can shoot that far up," Alpheus said.

Hendron made no response. He seemed completely focused to the task at hand as he then brushed his thumb against the trunk of the tree, perhaps analysing it. He contemplated for a moment, and then he shoved his hands into a pair of sturdy gloves. He turned to Alpheus and Azure with a faint smile, as if to tell them not to blink because they might miss something spectacular.

Then, suddenly, he sprung up onto the tree and began climbing, his fluid movement resembling that of the lesser apes. He was even slick enough that he wasn't scaring off the birds. In barely moments, Hendron had climbed roughly ten stories up into the trees.

"What are you going to do now?" Alpheus asked Azure. "If he succeeds?"

Azure met his eyes and then peered up into the elm where Hendron was mostly hidden between the branches. "Well," Azure said, lifting her fingers to her mouth, "I can always do this." She didn't wait any longer, blowing another audible whistle which echoed its way up the elm.

Although they could barely see Hendron now, the leaves were rattling near the crown of the tree. It was likely Hendron jerking to the sound of the whistle, which must have sounded threatening to him. Even Alpheus had no idea what Azure had asked the birds to do this time—or perhaps it wasn't birds she called for. It could be anything at all.

Alpheus gazed up more carefully as everything grew suddenly dark. The glimmers of light shining through the tree had been blocked by an enormous amount of birds that flitted out seemingly from nowhere. The elm shook at the top, leaves rustling down to the ground, and soon it was Hendron who they saw falling through the branches, crashing down with a rod in his hand that snapped during the violent drop.

Alpheus kicked into the Glider Steps, whiffing himself up to catch Hendron from suffering the effects of a painful fall. The proud hunter had shut his eyes as tight as possible, as he might have expected death. But as

Alpheus kicked off from the trunk of the tree and breezed his way back to the ground, Hendron seemed to realise that he had been saved. The hunter snapped his eyes wide open and then stepped away from Alpheus with a grimace, perhaps unable to believe that he had lost the bet.

"Now," Azure said, leaning down to Hendron, "please lead the way to Zorlia."

PART V

TWENTY-EIGHT

Dangerous lurkers

Kraga was said to be a one-way travel destination. No one ever returned to tell stories about what they had seen there. What was brewing in Kraga was anyone's guess, and the popular supposition was that anyone from the South was evil, their land a pit nurturing unimaginable abominations. Truban conservatives had noted that there was more to it—that, indeed, they knew frighteningly little about the people who they so feared. Even Truban soldiers who had fought in the war had no better idea what Kraga was like, not when the war had been fought exclusively in Trubannis.

No one had really learned how strong the Kragan army was. At times during the war it had seemed that the Kragans had an infinite number of soldiers at their disposal. On more than a few occasions, the Kragans had managed to send out fresh armies when an already great army of theirs had fallen. It had seemed impossible to kill them off, especially as they had continued their advance toward the central state of Saffron with each passing day. This *Infinite Soldiers* phenomenon had later resulted in the ultimate defeat and demise of the Sargon Monarchy.

Kasimir de Spartamon's rise to power had only been possible due to his ability to instil in his followers the belief that they *could* win, in spite of the formidable Kragan force. Spartamon had been called *the wolf* during the war, a name that highlighted his sharp intelligence and his appetite to free others. He had reminded his men time and again that, in the midst of battle, it was suicidal to spare even a moment of thought to anything else other than the enemy soldier standing before you.

Kill your enemies, one by one, until they are all dead, had been his exact words of wisdom.

That had been the turning point in the war. In roughly four years' time,

Spartamon and his men had forced the Kragans into a full-scale retreat. The Kragans, in turn, had finally seemed to run out of soldiers. The Kragan King at the time, Tynan Bardorinoff, had then been forced to issue his declaration of surrender. And yet sceptics had continued to warn that the Kragans were plotting something, and that it was foolish to think that the Southerners had no more soldiers on hand.

In more recent years, the Truban Empire had since attempted to review the results of the war. The court, with the help of scholars, had tried to estimate the true strength of the Kragans. The problem was that they had no reliable source upon which to base those estimates. The optimists had played down the fears in the belief that, as long as the Truban Empire was united, the Kragans wouldn't dare to strike again. After all, based on raw numbers and talent alone, the current Truban Empire was stronger even than the preceding Sargon Monarchy had been in its most glorious days.

However, being united was never easy.

What had started as a spat between the emperor and the chancellor had aggravated to something far beyond what many had imagined was possible. People all across the country had started to run campaigns for unity, but their efforts had instead divided opinions even further by not maintaining a clear, unified message. Inevitably, the conflicting views had caused violent riots to erupt all over the country. In contrast, the centre and catalyst of it all—the central state of Saffron and its capital of Zorlia—had suffered the least. The court had been running as usual, at least superficially, and the emperor and the man dangerously close to usurping him had been avoiding direct conflicts with one another. And yet no one on the court was naïve enough to suspect any chance of reconciliation, knowing quite well that the only hope for the country to be unified again was if either the emperor or the chancellor fell.

All the while, in Zorlia, those chilling *whispers* of death and misery had started to spike again. The Church of the St. Bernard Order had done well since more than a month ago in terms of purging the magic users who they believed were behind the conspiracy. But they still had yet to seize even a single culprit, and the magic users had reached out even further with their messages of doom. Over three fifths of the population were now tormented by the incessant voices haunting their thoughts and dreams.

Coupled with the threat behind the whispers was an actual murder spree. In the past week, there had been over a hundred confirmed deaths cited as death by *unnatural forces*.

Dig your graves now, the whispers had said.

No one shall escape.

They will come to you from the south, others had heard—this specific remark being an allusion to Kraga. Still more whispers had referenced other details, and in the confusion and contradiction arriving with each report, people didn't know what to believe anymore.

But one thing was certain: fear was spreading.

Even with this mishap that affected both sides of the political war, the Pristines had managed to advocate to the common people that the dangerous magic users were part of the Advents. Some had gone as far as to coin the term *Advent Sorcerers.*

In any case, the court had since renewed its focus on stopping these sorcerers. They were to be purged by all means necessary.

* * *

It was the twenty eighth day of May, and an unsuspecting middle-aged man was working on shaping a blob of brown clay into shapely pottery. Though cramped inside a dim hovel, the man was humming a soft, cheery tune… at least until he heard a sudden pounding at the front door.

"Open up!" demanded a voice from outside. "By the power and authority vested in us by the Empire."

The man turned to the door, looking up in surprise at the small glazed glass on its right drawing in all the natural light he needed from outside. He frowned when he caught a glimpse of a silhouette resembling that of a knight. After nearly two years in Zorlia, they had finally come for him. The man eyed his unfinished pottery, hesitated for a moment, and then decided to escape from the back.

But he had only taken one step forward when the door swung open and another figure stepped inside, a knight whose silver armour gleamed from behind as the daylight poured in. The man shivered slightly upon the silver knight's approach and took a few steps back.

It's him, he realised—someone he had never met, but whose description was famous in his circles. There could be no mistake. Tall, athletic, and young. Dark hair in wispy bangs that covered parts of the eyes, long cape draping down from the shoulders, and that hefty iron sword clipped onto his back. This was *him*, the knight who breathed grace.

The son of Royston Longinus. The heir to Time-Shifting.

"Come, Alex!" the silver knight said.

Upon that call, the flimsy front door was then smashed in behind the man and more daylight flooded into the hovel. A knight in black treaded inside, pressing forward from the other side. The man who had been working on his pottery groaned as the encroachers inched closer. He was forced back onto the simple wooden stool next to his potter wheel, and he sat, trembling slightly.

"What is this about, Sir?" he asked weakly, eyeing the silver knight. "I may have to ask you to compensate for the damage you have done."

"Quit your act," the silver knight said. "We know who you are, *Slash*."

The man twitched a brow, but said nothing.

The silver knight then rested a hand onto the hilt of his sword. "I'm sure you know who I am. Your grace resonates with mine. We know your dealings with the Advents, with the emperor. I'm giving you a choice, Slash. I'll spare you—but only if you work with me."

"I have no idea what you're talking about," Slash replied with a bemused chuckle, no longer trembling.

The silver knight smirked. "If this is how you want to play it, then...," he said, trailing off as he clicked for a third knight who treaded in from the front door holding a boy with both hands.

"Father!" the child cried. "Help me!"

Slash immediately grew anxious but peered about carefully for options. "You wouldn't hurt a child," he said, trying to sound as unruffled as he could manage. "Not a boy of just nine years of age."

The silver knight narrowed his eyes. He then swept an arm in a zigzag motion, drawing intense heat in an instant—the steam emitting from his hands forming rapidly into a molten ball of fire. The silver knight eyed the man and then unleashed the fireball—not at Slash, but at his son.

Slash jumped to his feet immediately, waving an arm behind a blue radiance that formed a small glowing pin. He threw it into the flying molten ball, the contact igniting an explosion of intense heat that had the silver knight screaming a warning to his men, all of them turning away at once to shield themselves from the burst of fire. The loose items in the cramped hovel had no such instinct, however, crackling now as they shattered into irrecoverable pieces. Slash dashed toward his son, who he realised had fallen unconscious from the fright. He grabbed the child and then bolted out of the hovel.

Several civilians gaped at him out inside the narrow passageway, the surroundings lighted under the clear sky above. They were familiar faces, people he called neighbours who had no idea of his actual identity as a sorcerer, as an assassin. Or perhaps they *did* know a thing or two, he suspected now, which had led to this current confrontation and pursuit. He darted forward and then kicked up into mid-air, leaping onto the rooftops.

As he continued dashing ahead at that great height, Slash glanced back down to note the silver knight—or, Longinus—in pursuit emanating an aura of crimson red, sweeping his way through the unknowing civilians with a gust that left them dazed. Slash grunted and then looked at his unconscious child cradled in his arms, regret aching inside every part of him. The boy didn't deserve this. He looked up again and eyed a crowded market ahead where he imagined he would have a better chance of losing Longinus.

Slash darted in the direction of the market and jumped without hesitation as he got within reach, landing with a thump next to a stall filled with rugs for sale. The people gathered there gasped as they scattered backwards in shock. The owner of the stall—a stout woman in her middle years—didn't share the shock, however, and instead she looked furious as she marched toward Slash now, grumbling at him with violent curses.

"I don't have time, Uma," Slash said, handing over the unconscious child. "Take Peyton for me."

Uma peered about briefly. "You take care of yourself," she said, receiving the child before Slash dashed off again, shuffling through the bodies and praying that Longinus hadn't noticed where he had dropped off his son.

From the corner of his eye, Slash noted that his pursuer had stopped on the roof, apparently surveying the scene. After a brief glance back to the rugs stall, Slash was relieved to see that Uma had his son hidden away from sight and indeed had already carried on with running the stall, attracting no unwelcome attention.

Thank you, Uma, he thought as he came to a halt, having rounded to relative safety at the opposite end of the market. *I owe you one.*

Longinus jumped from the roof then, thumping down before a pottery stall, startling the patrons just as Slash had done at the rugs stall. Even behind the sea of bodies shuffling about through the hectic market, the knight-sorcerer stood out with his exorbitant height, which offered him a visual advantage even while on the ground. When Slash met his pursuer's glare, he spun and then darted off again away from the market.

Even without looking back, Slash was sure that Longinus was in pursuit. The knight's grace resonated with his own, and indeed it was pulsing stronger and stronger. His pursuer was growing ever closer.

But..., Slash thought with a squint, *you will never catch me. Not in this city. Not with all of these people around.* Slash slipped into another corner then, spinning around several mystified people who had barely realised what had come and gone. Even among his circles, Slash was one of the most nimble members. His liege—or, *The Lord Emperor*, as the others addressed the man—only handpicked men he proved worthy. And Slash was sure that his speed and inhuman ability to wedge through tight spaces were qualities that impressed Spartamon.

There, he thought, after sliding through another narrow space. *The pulsing's grown weaker. I'm losing him... for now.*

The cat and mouse game was a battle of endurance, and Longinus's tenacity was a gruelling quality that Slash wasn't going to shake off with quick turns alone. As he continued to dash away, Slash noted a street performer juggling small knives. He grinned then, turning onto a main road toward a square where dozens of entertainers gathered, a place with more bystanders than even at the market. If Slash could create enough crowd confusion, he would then be able to use his agility to slip through bodies in order to tire out his pursuer who was far less nimble than he. If he could drain out the knight's energy, there would be no fear of a potential confrontation.

Slash slowed down a little as he neared *Liberty Square*, hopping into the crowd finally when the pulsing of the knight's grace thumped harder. As he had expected, the square was bustling with a large crowd. Slash boldly dove right into one of the vast circles of bystanders surrounding an entertainer, prying through the sea of bodies while softly humming a victory tune. The curses directed at him and the scattering of bodies only served to prod him on as he flung himself into crowd after crowd. Slash could hardly repress his grin, and upon turning back, he expected his pursuer to be caught somewhere in the horde.

But what is this, he thought, as his eyes widened in surprise. The silver knight was rushing toward him, hardly slowed by the bodies in the crowd as he dangerously swept his iron sword about to clear the path, seemingly without a hint of hesitation. He had drawn no blood as yet—somehow. But his reckless abandon was enough to fill the air with screams of terror.

He's insane, Slash thought, gritting his teeth. He spun around several more bodies, leaving a gentle breeze behind him, only for Longinus to pound his way through, slamming bodies away with his other arm as if he were a mad bull. Slash groaned, realising that he had incited the wrong person to make a scene in this kind of crowd. He dashed west instead, toward the marshes.

A confrontation was inevitable, Slash acknowledged. The least he could do for the citizens of the city, who he had come to grow fond of, was to bring the battle away from them. Barely ten minutes in this next round of chasing, the silver knight had almost drawn level with him. Slash knew that his pursuer was always going to outrun him on a straight path, but at least Slash managed to reach as far as the fringe of the city when Longinus finally overtook him. With only small shrubs and no one else in the vicinity, Slash could fight without concerns about accidentally harming any bystanders.

"It's over," the silver knight said. "Work with me."

Slash smirked, relaxing his muscles slightly. "And if I said no?"

"Then I'll roast you."

"You've grown," Slash said, nodding with a squint. "Your grace burns stronger than many of our kind. Perhaps you really *can* back up your words. Tell me, Sir Julian Longinus, how did you improve so rapidly?"

Longinus grinned slightly. "Sure, I can tell you that. But first, you'll tell me why the Advents are assembling an army of sorcerers. And don't tell me that it's only to scare and intimidate people by whispering nonsense into their ears."

Slash snorted. "Nonsense into their ears? I presume you're one of those fortunate ones who don't hear the whispers, then?"

"Enough questioning from you," Longinus said curtly, pointing forward. "The one at mercy needs only to answer."

"I see," Slash said, shaking his head in annoyance. "Earlier, you said you would *spare* me if I worked with you. But let me be clear on this: I don't need any sparing from the likes of you."

Slash swirled his left arm in a circle, bringing back a fist across his chest and catching four radiating pins between his fingers in the process. He wasted no time in shooting the steaming pins out at Longinus, who rolled clumsily to the side to evade, following then with a second and third flurry that had Longinus scrambling. Upon catching a fourth set of pins, however, Slash found that the knight had propelled himself into the air behind that aura of crimson red. Slash hissed, discarding the pins and then leaping up into the air himself, kicking higher even than his youthful opponent, who looked more than briefly stunned by his doggedness. In noting that Longinus was already reaching for his sword, Slash was quick to whip out a thin green stick that he had hidden under his top, lashing it out to further stifle the other man.

The thin stick was a sugarcane branch the length of a sword, hardly a weapon—and upon revealing it, he was sure that his opponent was surprised. Slash allowed no opportunity for comments, however, whipping out multiple slashes to continue dictating the momentum, even as Longinus absorbed most of the damage with his sturdy gauntlets.

They were on their way back down then, and during what appeared to be a momentary lapse on Longinus's end, Slash stroke opportunistically, finally landing a hit at the fauld, typically the lightest part of a knight's armour. Longinus thumped down onto the ground and then kicked off with a roll. The space, however, allowed Longinus to finally draw his iron sword, and Slash only realised then that the exchange was by design. He grunted again, darting forward to resume his forceful charge. But even against the rugged iron sword, Slash reduced his opponent to merely defending—or so he thought.

It turned out that the difference in weapon size and the differences in strength between them was too large to overcome, especially as his opponent began wielding the iron sword with both hands, the additional strength allowing Longinus to thrust Slash away at a slight distance. The youthful knight took full advantage of the space he had gained, this time blasting the iron sword into a blazing weapon, the flames roaring ferociously. A little space between them was all Longinus had needed, and the knight was now also engulfed completely in that aura of crimson red, darting toward Slash with unbelievable speed.

Slash managed to block off the first and several successive swings that were powered by roaring flames of tangerine, but as its wielder himself was a blur of faint red light, Slash failed to keep up for long. He was finally crushed at his unarmoured chest with the pommel of the iron sword as he was sent skidding across the ground.

It was a single hit, but it had left Slash heavily wounded, blood spewing from his mouth as he climbed to one knee. "You really are something...," Slash said, pressing his hand up against his throbbing chest.

"So are you," Longinus said, returning his sword back behind his cape. "But the fight's over now. Talk."

Slash gritted his teeth as more blood dribbled out of his mouth. "What exactly do you want to know?"

"Everything you know... and once you tell me, I'd also like you to offer your allegiance."

Slash raised a brow, frowning deeply. "You want me to... join you? The Pristines?" Slash paused and then shook his head. "I'm flattered," he then said, "but you are naïve to think my alignment would change anything. I am but a pawn of a certain, more powerful man."

"In that case, let me ask you something else," Longinus said. "What do you know about the sorcerers marked with the endless knot?"

Slash turned silent, stunned that Longinus knew about that.

"I suppose my assumption was correct," Longinus said. "You're not of the same caste as them. They are related to the Apostle, and you are not."

"I'm impressed that you came to that conclusion," Slash said, a bead of sweat falling from his forehead. "But we know very little about them. I'm surprised, though, that you would identify them as a group. We always thought it was one person—one *being*."

"Why is that?"

"Do you remember the sorcerer who you met at the Hindlow Manor?"

"I do," Longinus said. "Don't tell me she's the being you speak of."

"No, she's one of us," Slash said. "And she had an encounter with that *thing*, after which she became dysfunctional."

"What do you mean?"

"She no longer speaks to us. She doesn't even know who she is anymore. All day and all night, she repeats these two lines: *no contest* and *they're not in the same league*."

"They?" Longinus asked. "Who are *they*?"

"The ones responsible for the whispers," Slash said.

Longinus narrowed his eyes.

"You don't have to believe me," Slash said. "But allow me to advise you *not* to dig any deeper. Worry about what's ahead of you, rather than something that's hardly even tangible. As Schim's soldier, you ought to concentrate on uprooting his enemies. I'm one of them. So go ahead and end this."

"You'd rather die than work with me? Why? Why maintain your loyalty for Spartamon even now?"

Slash shrugged, blood still trickling from his mouth. "I've lost, and whether I betray my liege or not, he will assume that I have. I will no longer be trusted or be of any use to anyone." He hesitated then. "But… I have a favour to ask of you before I die."

"What is it?"

"The boy living with me is my adopted son. He knows nothing about any of this, so I ask you to let him live."

Longinus shook his head. "No, Slash, I won't carry the burden to *let him live*. If the boy means that much to you, it is your responsibility to protect him." Longinus paused there, looking to his side. "You can go now."

Slash leaned forward. "You're letting me go?"

"I've learned enough. You confirmed to me your position as one of the stronger members of the group. Your comrade who has lost her sanity was the one I chased out of Phantom Pond. And, of course, you were the one who helped her escape that time—the mysterious man at the bottom of the cliff."

And perhaps also because you think me to be no threat to you, Slash thought, feeling both relieved and humiliated.

"So that is your understanding," Slash said instead with a nod. "You should already know that I'm not the only sorcerer on our side. And even if you are so proud to believe that you can answer to every one of us, do you think yourself also capable of holding up against *all* the traditional warriors we have?"

"*Traditional* warriors?" Longinus asked with a raised brow. "I suppose you're referring to Nine Arms and Lionel Lachman?"

Slash smirked as he shook his head. "I'm sure you were already well aware of those two. So, no, I *wasn't* referring to them."

"Then who *are* you referring to?" Longinus demanded.

Slash regarded the youthful knight carefully before rising to his feet, using the sugarcane branch as a crutch. Perhaps in a different time and place, he could have been friends with this knight-sorcerer. He had thought that if anyone were to hunt him down, it was Spartamon—not a naïve brat who didn't know his place, but at the same time had offered him the liberty to leave with his life. Slash had already planned to depart Zorlia, to turn his back to the chaos in the city. He just hadn't thought that someone who identified as a *Pristine* would allow for it. It was impossible to escape Spartamon's grasp, but even in the limited days he would have until he would inevitably be hunted down, he wanted to cherish life, if not for himself, then for his son.

Longinus had held his gaze at him, perhaps pitying him. It was ironic to Slash, though, that Longinus was the one who deserved pity, fighting alongside the rest of the *Pristines* who were destined for doom.

"Run," Slash said finally. "Run now while you still can. I can't offer you any further information. And I urge you not to pry any deeper, for I assure you that only despair awaits."

Longinus frowned but said nothing. Slash turned away then, staggering back toward the city for Peyton. They had to leave Zorlia today.

Joy, he thought as a sudden flap of warmth filled him. *It has eluded me since that day I was cursed with these powers. Grace, they call it.* He smiled, picturing his son, imagining life with the boy away from all the conspiracies that he had grown extremely tired from.

Slash paused abruptly as he heard something whistling toward him from behind, rippling toward him with a terrible speed. As he was about to turn around, he was propelled forward with a thud and a slashing sound. Slash gasped as he looked down to see an arrow rooted lethally into his chest. He grunted, turning his head back slowly with his blurring vision.

Julian Longinus?

No.

Behind Longinus was another man, another knight in silver on a black horse. The man held a bow in a gloved hand.

Slash fell.

TWENTY-NINE

Formation and formulation

Julian grunted in horror. He turned, lifting his head toward the top of the small hill where the other man's killer sat atop a mean-looking, black stallion. Hanging from both sides of the horse were sabatons, leg guards, tassets, and gauntlets—all in gleaming silver.

Orel Kite.

Despite having just murdered a man, Kite was placid as always, his crisp eyes showing no emotion as he lowered his weapon, a composite bow.

Julian clenched a fist, trying to mask his shock, at least until he was able to read more deeply into Kite's motive and the sudden turn of events. The Empire had called upon every knight to hunt down the sorcerers that they had held responsible for the recent murder spree, but the instruction was clear in that any culprits were to be taken alive for questioning. No, Julian hadn't been supposed to allow Slash to flee, but just what was Kite doing, killing Slash with no warning?

It was just a moment later when a group of knights trampled in on a team of horses, pulling their reins to a halt as they reached Kite. In a group that included silver knights Roc and Patrick as well as Golden Knight Walford Bors, there were eight in total—all of them men loyal to Victor Breunor. The bad blood between Julian and Breunor was well known among those who attended court, and had extended even to most of Breunor's men. One of those who shared the ill will toward Julian was Bors, who glanced at Julian now before turning to Kite with a look that demanded an immediate response.

Kite muttered something and nodded toward Slash's dead body. The golden knight then peered over toward the corpse and steered his stallion in its direction, passing Julian without any acknowledgement. Upon reaching Slash, Bors leaned down from his horse with a squint, and upon confirmation that the dead man was the correct person they had been hunting, he chuckled, clearly in a celebratory mood.

"You got that heretic, all right!" he said.

The other knights rode over to join Bors, many of them wearing broad grins, seemingly finding much joy in Slash's death. Julian shook his head in guilt. Slash was no friend of his, but the man was a sorcerer.

And so am I, he reminded himself, also acknowledging at the same time that Slash would have been a much tougher opponent if the older man had been wielding a real weapon rather than the sugarcane branch. Slash was undoubtedly a skilled swordsman. Not once had Julian's eventual victory been straightforward during the entire battle just now.

Incensed by the persistent laughter emitting from Bors and his men, Julian turned to the golden knight with a fierce glare. Unable to hold in his fury any longer, Julian drew his iron sword with a scream, only to sweep it out ferociously into thin air before pulling it back toward his body. He grunted and then rooted the chunk hard onto the ground which seemed to tremble, if only slightly. Finally, he fell to one knee in quiet shame. If there was anything he had learned in recent times, it was to avoid being reckless. Turning his sword at Bors now was less than wise.

Bors snorted, turning his mighty stallion toward Julian and hopping off the saddle of the beast as he got closer. He treaded forward until he stood over Julian, his wide shadow cast over him. The horn-like shapes forking out from his armour—specifically from the shoulders, elbows, and knees—might frighten a few people, but to Julian, they were nothing more than ostentatious decorations.

"You seem upset," Bors said, reaching for the grip of Julian's sword, clutching it tightly. Upon his abrupt grunt, Bors bulked up his muscles, allowing him to uproot the unwieldy iron sword with ease.

"You are a sorcerer, a *heretic*," the golden knight added, eyeing Julian with contempt. "But you are a knight first and foremost."

"How I feel is irrelevant to how I act," Julian said in response.

"In that case," Bors said, offering the sword back to Julian, "use this sword to disfigure the corpse. Show me that you can still follow orders."

Julian gawked. He rose slowly and collected his sword, peering over at Slash's dead body with a grimace. The task to disfigure a corpse was perhaps the most despicable he had ever been given.

"Go on," the golden knight spurred. "Slice that corpse into pieces until no one can recognise him."

Julian took several hesitant steps forward and then slowed to a complete halt. Finally, he turned back to Bors with a hostile grimace, raising his sword at the golden knight.

"What do you think you're doing?" Bors asked as he lifted his chin without fear. "Are you going to turn against your fellow knights for a dead man? A dead heretic?"

"I won't take orders from you," Julian replied, growing suddenly stubborn. "You lack the qualification to command me. You may be recognised as a golden knight by the Empire, but to me, you're no more than a shameless savage."

"Watch your tongue, Longinus!" Patrick inserted.

Julian glanced over to the veteran silver knight, who carried with him his signature shield and broadsword. Behind Patrick was Kite, who was wearing a smirk, seemingly amused by the exchange.

Julian returned his gaze upon Bors who was doing well in controlling his temper. "As a golden knight," Julian went on, "your task is to pass on your wisdom of chivalry and ideal knighthood to lower ranking knights. Courage, honour, courtesy, justice, and readiness to help the weak are the qualities that we should ideally represent. Unfortunately, by asking me to do something so unscrupulous as to disfigure a dead body demonstrates that you have none of those qualities. I cannot bring myself to abide by such a command, even from a golden knight."

"Say all you want," Bors replied. "At the end of the day, I'm a golden knight and you're not." He paused. "Or... are you thinking to challenge that, too?"

Julian looked past Bors onto the other knights. There were another seven of them—eight if he counted Kite. Julian sighed then, lowering his weapon.

"Why don't you just let me take Slash's dead body with me?" he said. "I'll bury him, and no one would have to know that you killed him without authority. I'm a man of my word."

"Why are you so invested in what happens to him?" Bors asked, looking suddenly leery. "Do you know something that we don't?"

"I simply don't want to do what you asked of me," Julian said, shaking his head. "Nor do I want to aggravate our already precarious alliance. And, besides, I wouldn't dream of triumphing against nine trained knights."

Bors grunted in ire, narrowing his eyes into a deep frown. And he wasn't the only one offended by the insinuation. Patrick, Roc, and Kite—who had all crossed swords with Julian in the past in fair, one-on-one battles—couldn't possibly enjoy being accused of the idea that they would try to outnumber him here. The silent glowers were a sure sign of their disgruntlement.

"And I thought you learned some manners from the chancellor," Bors said, shaking his head with a smirk. "But instead you're still out here taunting those of us who have much to teach you." Bors reached for his giant maul at his waist then. "You are an eyesore, Longinus. You need a lesson."

Julian glanced over at the other knights, none of them looking like they were about to participate in the scuffle. Kite, in particular, crossed his arms warily, seemingly growing impatient.

Great, Julian thought, regarding Bors again. *If it's just him, I might have a chance.* But as Julian prepared for a fight, he still found it difficult to fathom how he had managed to infuriate Breunor—and, now even Bors—to such a level in which every meeting between them promised some kind of violent confrontation.

Bors turned to his men. "Keep your eyes open," he said. "Watch and learn. It's rare to see—"

"We still have Marvin Sailanson to chase," Kite cut in, changing the topic. "Need I remind you, Sir Bors, to stay on task?"

Julian squinted, as the name of Sailanson had been a popular topic of late. Everyone in the city seemed to be talking about him—and his possible return. People seemed to think that the former mercenary was the missing piece to breaking the stalemate between the emperor and the chancellor.

Bors scowled. "Sailanson will be hunted down," he said. "But not before I give Longinus a lesson."

Kite hissed and then curtly turned his horse to depart. Julian glanced at the receding figure, forgetting about him as soon as he met Bors's gaze again. It was suicidal to put his mind on anything else when he was about to face off against a golden knight, the one known as the *Titan*. Julian slid his sword in front of him, eyeing Bors from the bottom up. Apparently, the man was a few years older than even Breunor, which placed him at about fifty years of age. This age discrepancy was perhaps Julian's only advantage.

They also say he's the weakest of all the golden knights, Julian thought. But despite the rumours, the man standing before him was indeed a giant, his wide build and magnificent height almost like an impenetrable tower. The giant maul he held was also every part as intimidating.

Can I really beat him? Julian thought, growing suddenly hesitant.

Julian found himself trembling in his armour when Bors rushed toward him at full strength, the golden knight's heavy stomps shaking the ground below. It was barely a moment later when Julian was forced to dash away to his side, evading the giant maul that was being slammed down toward him. Julian thought he had done well at that instance, but the maul that had missed him hammered into the ground, smashing open a crater and at the same time sending out a radial shockwave that had Julian stumbling to keep his footing. But he was then prompt in shaking away his daze, realising that this wasn't the time to be impressed or stunned—not with the giant maul batting horizontally toward him again.

Julian gritted his teeth in desperation, holding out his sword with both hands, almost hoping for the best result. While Julian managed well enough to block this next blow, he was still sent flying from the resulting force, crashing across the grass.

The difference in strength was too much for him to overcome, and as Julian got up with the support of his sword, he peered down to see that his sturdy sword had been bent out of shape and was now hopelessly crooked. His weapon was never meant to withstand that kind of force. Julian took a step back, two steps, and then another still.

How could he answer to that incredible raw strength? On his fourth step backwards, his heels nudged onto something on the ground. He glanced over his shoulder to see Slash and the sugarcane branch that the sorcerer had used. His eyes then instinctively darted back to his own sword, and specifically to the multiple dents that Slash had left on it.

I need to make him fight my way, Julian thought.

"I'll send you to join him soon enough," Bors said, still wearing the same obnoxious grin.

"You wouldn't dare kill me," Julian said with a snort. "Not when you'd be offending the Lord Chancellor."

Bors paused, raising a brow. "I *didn't* plan to do so," he said then with a grin, "until you suggested it. I certainly have no intentions to wrong Schim, at least not yet. But I suppose he wouldn't have to know that I'm your killer, when I can simply credit Slash with the honour." He paused again, shooting a glance at his men, none of them offering any clear response to the proposition—neither in acceptance nor rejection. Finally, Bors turned back to Julian.

"Lord Breunor would be glad to finally have you eliminated," he said, presumably having decided that his men, including Roc and Patrick, connived to his actions, however outrageous they might be.

Bors stomped forward, looking to pick up from where he had left off. Julian watched carefully, squinting into the distance as Bors lifted his maul into a swinging motion. At that instant, Julian flashed forward to execute his first act of retaliation—a single diagonal slice that he whipped up from his hips with supreme speed blessed by the power of Time-Shifting. The slice forced Bors to turn his swing into a desperate block, which then resulted in both of them leaping back. The exchange—as brief as it was—had apparently stunned the golden knight, whose brazen expression and demeanour had diminished.

Uncertainty, Julian thought as he himself leaped back. *I see it in his eyes. If I had been a second slower, I would have been crushed to death. To him, the exchange was incredibly rash on my part. But... he can't be sure.*

Indeed, Bors gripped onto his weapon with both hands then, more tightly than before. He did seem to be hesitating, his eyes wide in shock.

But then the golden knight grunted, erasing the doubt away from his expression, and pelting himself forward. Julian watched carefully for a second time, standing his ground and waiting for Bors to lift the giant maul once again.

I need to finish this in one go, he thought, still waiting until the giant maul would thump down at him. *Now!* he decided, bursting out his grace and an explosion of crimson red as he whipped his iron sword into a horizontal slice.

Bors didn't pull back for a block this time. Instead, the golden knight hammered his weapon down with a solid momentum, connecting at Julian's shoulder and crushing open the silver armour down on the clavicle and scapula. As Julian wailed in pain, he noted that Bors had finally allowed himself a brief grin. But that grin soon faded away into a look of shock as the golden knight glanced over to his left, where Julian's sword wielding arm was extended. Julian already knew, but Bors must have been shocked to see that he had drawn blood. And as Bors staggered back then, the golden knight peered down at the rest of his body. His golden armour was intact, but a stream of red was spilling from the fauld, at the waist.

Roc and Patrick gasped from where they were watching, as did the other knights. Bors himself was simply stunned. The wound wasn't deep, but it was burning, burning with flames that were black in colour. Julian had sliced his weapon with sorcery, and Bors could only scowl as he turned his head toward his men who gaped back at him. They didn't see how it had happened, either. And soon, the golden knight spewed out a heap of blood as he collapsed to one knee with a thud. He grunted in pain as he pressed up against the wound.

"How—when did you...?!"

Julian frowned, holding onto his broken shoulder between the shattered part of his armour, trying as best as he could to ignore the pain. Since being taken under Schim's wings, Julian had improved mightily as a warrior. The training and guidance provided to him by the Raiders had allowed Julian an astonishing surge in all aspects of his combat abilities. In particular, it was his much-improved ability to read his opponent's moves, to counter, and to take control of the battle.

"Your raw strength is fearful," Julian said, panting. "But, unfortunately for you, that's all you have. I've been taught some valuable lessons, one of which is the significance of a combatant's *reaction*—the fact that we are *animate* beings. You lack not only honour, but also the basic principle of combat, in that the techniques you learn are static, but the user of the techniques is ever-changing. Your robust style of smashing your giant weapon on others might have worked during the days of the war, but that wouldn't work against a clever opponent who would know to avoid a tug-of-war against you."

Bors grunted, more blood dribbling out from his mouth and into his beard.

"Slash didn't have your raw strength," Julian continued. "But he was still a tougher opponent than you, because he knew how to respect *me* as his opponent. He realised early on that my grace pool exceeded his, and from there, he never allowed the fight to become simply a battle of sorcery. Instead, he did everything possible to prevent me from even swinging my sword. For the most part, he shut down all of my most valuable skills."

"Nonsense!' the golden knight yelled as he struggled to his feet again. "Animate beings? Grace? Don't give me that. Strength is everything!"

Julian frowned, raising his sword again, ready to defend. But on the horizon, he noted Orel Kite racing back together with another group of knights on another team of horses. And galloping in at the centre of the group was Golden Knight Claude Lucan.

"Sir... Lucan...?!" Bors exclaimed. The shame of allowing a fellow golden knight to see him in defeat was probably more than Bors could bear.

Lucan said nothing about the fight even as he reached them, but appeared perplexed by the scene before him. Kite seemed similarly surprised by what had transpired here. It was difficult for anyone to fathom the idea that Bors would be wounded by any man around—perhaps least of all by Julian.

"I'm glad you're here, Sir Lucan," Julian said, walking toward the man and his horse. "Walford Bors and his men killed this criminal despite orders from the Empire to capture them all alive. And this very action makes me wonder just what they're trying to hide."

The bold conviction and daring implication didn't seem to faze Bors or his men. Lucan, meanwhile, finally acknowledged Julian with a nod in his direction.

"And what is it you think they're hiding?" Lucan asked.

Julian eyed Bors with a smirk. "I suspect Walford Bors is an ally of the Advent sorcerers, and so too is Victor Breunor. They're afraid that Slash—after his defection from them—would speak of their conspiracies. That is why they had to kill him."

Lucan raised a brow. "Am I hearing this correctly?" he asked. "That not only are you questioning the honour of Golden Knight Sir Bors, but even the integrity of Lord Breunor?"

"That's exactly what I'm doing," Julian said. "In fact, I dare to make the assumption that—"

"Sir Longinus!" a voice yelled from afar, interrupting Julian.

The voice belonged to Alex, who raced in on a horse of his own into the already lively scene. Alex seemed to be noting what had ensued here with his curious glances in all directions. He hopped off the horse when he made it to the thick of the action, bowing down to the golden knights first.

"Alexander Wethers," he said, introducing himself. "I'm an attendant of Sir Longinus."

"You've come at the right time, Sir Wethers," Lucan said. "Your foreman is speaking nonsense out here. Would you take him away?"

"Aye!"

"Hold on," Julian said, sweeping an arm out in frustration. "What is this about, Sir Lucan? Why are you covering for them?"

"Sir!" Alex interrupted, gazing at Julian intently with a strange desperation. "The Lord Chancellor has summoned you. Please come with me."

Alex seemed to be pleading for something, but Julian couldn't comprehend what it could be. It became a little more apparent, however, when Julian regarded Lucan again, whose face was now scrunched up in hostility.

"You have no business here, Longinus," Lucan warned. "Get out of my sight."

Julian leered back. "Didn't I just say that Bors is hiding something? He and Breunor are in line with the sorcerers!" Julian stopped suddenly, having heard himself say it out loud.

They're all in it together, he realised then, trembling with distinctive fear as Lucan's deepening grin confirmed his suspicions.

Bors and Breunor, Lucan and Forredan—all of them. They're all siding with the Advents.

I'm such a fool.

Lucan raised an arm, and his men—five of them—responded by leaping from their horses and drawing their weapons. As they pointed their weapons at him, Julian realised that there was no hope of a one-on-one battle. Lucan was a man who always chose to do things in the most efficient way possible, Julian had learned during recent months. He was meticulous, almost to a fault, and today that meant he would do everything he could to ensure that Julian wouldn't ruin his carefully laid plans.

Sure enough, Julian found himself surrounded again. The experience had grown somewhat familiar. The only surprise now was that he wasn't alone. Backing into him from behind was Alex, who had already turned his sword toward Lucan's men, prepared for a bloodbath that he didn't deserve to be a part of. It was naïve to think that Alex could help him carve out a path to escape, but it was oddly gratifying to know that there was someone in the land who would willingly fight for *his* survival.

Julian looked over his broken left shoulder. "This is my fight," he said softly, intending for only Alex to hear his voice. "When you can—run."

Before Alex could even respond, Julian darted forward, sweeping his iron sword at the three knights in front of him, one of whom was a silver knight. They vaulted backwards in evasion, only for Julian to spring himself after them, slashing out flames from the tip of his sword, burning one of them badly. He chased the other two, slashing as viciously as he could manage, all the while dragging his deadweight arm along. As he caught onto his aura of crimson red, Julian bolted off toward the silver knight—the most troublesome of the three—sweeping the metal chunk against him and knocking the man about.

Despite the outward advantage, however, Julian thought himself weak and slow as he moved around. His earlier battles with Slash and then Bors had taken their toll on him. But in the midst of battle—especially in a battle to death—it was foolish to feel sorry for one's handicap, let alone expect any handicap to be provided in return. Indeed, Julian was doing his best now to hide his fatigue and depleting reserve of grace which were a result of his previous battles. By keeping up his onslaught, Julian made sure that he appeared dangerous enough to keep his opponents guessing, with the hope that he could take some kind of advantage. The one thing that Julian couldn't hide was his broken left shoulder, but even with just one good arm, he wasn't going to lose without a scramble.

Julian slammed the other two knights away again, failing to torch them only because the silver knight had leaped in from behind. Julian grunted and then spun with dangerous speed, carrying the momentum to the swing of his iron sword. The silver knight managed to hold his own sword up to block once again, but the ferocity of Julian's strike had his hands shaking and his grip on the sword loosening.

Now! Julian decided, bursting out grace and sweeping a roaring black flame aimed at his opponent's head. Julian almost allowed himself a smile until the brutal flames splashed onto a wide metal plate, flares exploding outward from the clash.

Julian leaped back, noting that what had nullified his flames was the great shield that belonged to Patrick. The shield was likely an improvement from the one Patrick had worn during the Golden Knight Exchange, likely one that was more resistant to fire.

In any case, Patrick had joined the scramble, together with Roc. That made it five opponents in total—three of them silver knights—now stepping into a neat formation surrounding him. Julian glanced over his shoulder to where Lucan, Bors, Kite, and several others sat atop mean-looking stallions. Escape was impossible. Indeed, more foes were prepared to join the scramble, to hasten what appeared more and more like certain defeat for Julian. To their right, Alex was fighting a less eventful battle, at this moment clashing swords with two knights who had the same rank as he did. While no one expected Alex to turn the tables of the fight, Julian was impressed during his brief glance over at him. His young attendant was stronger than Julian had thought, but it was Alex's gesture to fight for him that was most admirable of all.

Julian turned back to his own fight. He raised his weapon again, the chunk of iron seeming to have grown heavier. As his opponents raised their weapons in response, Julian turned to dash away, prodding them to chase. The fastest of the foes was Roc, spurting forward with a claymore that rivalled the size of Julian's iron sword. Roc took the initiative, sweeping out that unwieldly double-edged sword to force Julian to not only turn back immediately, but also forced him into a tough clash of weapons that almost had Julian lose his footing. Julian hissed, holding a tighter grip of his weapon with the intention of returning the favour. But as he looked up again, he saw that multiple sets of blades were rippling toward him through the air. He grunted and swung his sword backwards, flashing away with urgency. His foes, however, gave him no breathing space, chasing and slashing at him relentlessly. In the heat of the battle, Julian couldn't even be sure who was who with the five men on him, but as he swept and swept for his life, he called for more grace with roaring flames splashing away upon every clash of metal.

In the blur of the action, Julian thought he spotted a shield. He circled behind the group with fantastic speed and then lent all his power to pierce his sword through the figure carrying the shield.

A growl sounded then. Julian shook off his daze and then uprooted his flame-enhanced iron sword from a chunk of flesh that only manifested to him now as Patrick's abdomen.

Julian grimaced as the veteran knight who collapsed with a thud. Remorse brewed suddenly inside of him, but he didn't have the liberty to be sorry for long as a blade seared his arm from the side, blood spurting out, the pain stinging him back into the battle. Julian hissed, dashing away again. Inside, his veins were thumping hard, almost as if they were going to explode. His one good arm had been strained to its limits.

A scream echoed in the skies then.

Patrick?

No, he's dead.

Julian slowed to a screeching stop. He peered about as he panted heavily, surprised that his foes seemed to have stopped the chase as well. The surprise soon turned into shock, however, when Julian realised the reason for the intermission. Alex—who had been fighting a fair distance away—was hollering in pain as dangerous amounts of blood gushed out from his left shoulder, the arm that had been attached now completely missing.

"No!" Julian cried, scurrying over toward him. Julian dropped down next to Alex, watching him and his trembling right hand pressing hard against the opening of his missing left arm as more blood gushed out onto the ground.

Alex turned to Julian, pale-faced and drenched with sweat. "How pitiful I am," he said.

Julian gawked in shock without a word.

"Listen to me, Sir Longinus," Alex pleaded. "The Raiders are on their way. You... *have* to... survive."

Julian hesitated. "We'll both survive," he said, narrowing his eyes. Julian raised his hand, waving it until it caught a red flame. He wasted no time in reaching his burning hand *into* his attendant's wound, immediately drawing a sharp cry from Alex that only grew louder as Julian smothered the flames deeper into the wound, not stopping until Alex finally fell unconscious, dropping into Julian's lamed arm.

Julian groaned as his own eyelids dropped. He snuffed out his flames, reducing the fire into a thin trail of billowing smoke that rose slowly up into the sky. Everything fell silent for a moment—almost peaceful, even.

But the harshness of reality soon manifested again as the ground shook, followed by a thunderous clap. Julian forced his eyes open, looking up to see Bors stomping toward him. He peered back down at Alex to be sure that he was still alive. While it might have looked like that he had killed Alex off to free him from further pain, Julian had in fact sealed off his wound to save him. But with Bors stomping toward them, Alex might not survive after all. Julian wanted to stand up, but his exhaustion had overcome any desire to flinch at the onslaught headed his way. Even his senses were slowing fading. His hazy vision was close to blurring out completely. And yet, the golden blob grew larger and larger.

To die now would mean everything was over. He would die without knowing how and why his family had been slaughtered. He would die chasing the shadow of Yesod and the other sorcerers marked with the Endless Knot.

But why?

Julian's thoughts muddled as an image of Oscar floated into his mind. And behind Oscar was a fainter image of Eris Nightingale.

Why are they all I can think about now?

Beneath the glaring sun was the blinding reflection of an enormous hammer, lifted then for one purpose only. The end was near. Death was rushing toward him. The hammer was crashing down.

Darkness. A blackout. Death.

No? Julian wondered as his blurred vision made out a glimpse of light, that flash coupled with a jangle and a tearing sound.

A set of blinding zigzag strokes followed, traced only by the sun's refraction.

Metal. A sword?

Julian didn't know when he had fallen to the ground, but crashing down in front of him was the metal head of the giant maul—detached from the haft. And following its sensational thump were pieces of the haft planted around it. Julian glanced up with the last of his energy to see a man in black standing before him, his back against Julian, a cape hanging from his shoulders flapping about violently. Beneath that strip of cloth was a familiar pair of twin rapiers.

Julian's eyes finally closed.

THIRTY

Scruples and doubts

Julian opened his eyes to see a ceiling illuminated by a flickering flame nearby. He was reclined, and his eyes darted about to survey the environment, his heart pounding when he noticed someone sitting next to him.

An ally—or, at least, that was what he had last remembered.

"You pulled through again," Raven said, his remark carrying a dab of scorn. Raven sat with crossed legs and folded arms, thoughtfully eyeing the wall on the far side of the room.

Julian confirmed to himself then that he was on a bed. He looked over to the other side to a dull, grey wall. Higher up was a window. It was dark outside, the faint glows of Achelois and Selene barely able to penetrate the thick clouds. He was in Vondra Dawn, the dreariest place in all of Zorlia—in all of the country, for that matter.

Julian squinted, knitting his brows together in shame. His left shoulder, plastered now, throbbed more painfully than it ever had before. It was then that he remembered what had happened to Alex, and also the appearance of the phantom soldier.

"Tell me what happened," Julian uttered nervously, blank gaze on the wall. "Walford Bors. Claude Lucan. Their men. What happened to them?"

"Perhaps you should fill me in first," Raven responded. "I don't know when you passed out, but when we arrived, you weren't the only one down. Bors, Lucan, Kite, Roc—all of them looked to have endured a rough fight."

It was him, Julian thought with a grimace. *The phantom soldier.*

"How badly are they hurt?" Julian asked.

"Bors doesn't look good. But the rest of them will recover in due time."

"And...," Julian said, hesitating. "What about Alex?"

"Living... minus an arm, of course."

Julian shut his eyes tightly, making a fist with his good hand.

Raven snorted. "Trash like him has only himself to blame."

Julian jerked himself up, jolting toward Raven and grabbing him by the ruffle.

"Don't you *dare* insult my men!"

"What, Longinus?" Raven asked, glaring at him. "Since when did you share camaraderie with them? Only a few days ago, you clashed with him and your other attendant."

Julian smirked. "So you *have* been watching me..."

Raven cocked his head, then swept away from Julian's weakening grasp. "The Lord Chancellor asked me to see to your recovery. I will do just that. But trust me, I wish Bors had killed you out there."

Julian hissed. "I'm not sure you should focus your hate on me. Our enemy isn't what we think they are. You wouldn't believe what the emperor has managed to accomplish."

Raven shrugged. "That Bors and Lucan are now part of the Advents? And so too are their lieges, Breunor and Forredan? This is no secret to me."

Julian frowned, trying his best to hide his stupefaction, but also his discontent about the fact that he hadn't been let in on this information.

"You didn't think you were the only one working, did you?" Raven said. "Our Lord Chancellor's sense of direction pointed us to all the right trails. When we put it into perspective, Breunor's stand is based on fear. After all, he's but a washed-up golden knight who trembles upon the mere mention of Nine Arms. On the other hand, Forredan's stand is based on greed. That fat swine only cares to go with whichever side looks more profitable for him personally. It's from the chancellor's acute perceptiveness that we discovered the collusion."

"And so what if the chancellor is perceptive?" Julian challenged, sneering at the other man. "What of it? What good is it when our enemies keep growing in numbers and power?"

Raven sighed with not exactly the blind passion Julian thought the usually fiery warrior would muster. Instead, the Raven appeared calm as he now slowly shook his head.

"If not for the chancellor, there would be no contest to speak of," he said. "Our opponent is Kasimir de Spartamon, the most powerful man of the country—of the land. He's been called *the wolf* for his sharp intelligence and fearsome ability to pounce at his enemies. He's also called *the proud conqueror* for obvious reasons. Who, other than the chancellor, could have come this far? It was never easy. But I assure you, Longinus, the chancellor gives us the best chance."

Julian held his head, silenced. Perhaps it was true. Schim had held his own against all odds for all these years.

Raven leaned in to Julian then, almost breathing into his face. "Do you regret submitting to this side?" he asked, their faces almost touching. "Are you... *afraid*?"

"Afraid...?" Julian said, and then turned away. "I *am*. How could I not be? I was almost killed. But I fear not only for my own life. I fear for the country. Everything is in turmoil. There will be war. And I'm torn—torn about the idea that the emperor is still the best person to lead the country in war, and torn that I'm here standing with the Pristines, all the while fighting a losing battle."

The only door in the room was suddenly thrust open, the metal hinges squeaking shrilly. Stepping inside was the chancellor himself. Next to him was Raphael, and behind them was a third visitor who donned a long dark robe, complete with a hood that shrouded his eyes from view. Beneath the hood was a long, puffed goatee that fell from the stranger's chin. He also held a wooden staff, and for a moment there, Julian thought he sensed a hint of grace somewhere.

"I appreciate your honesty," Schim said, regarding Julian without a mention of the stranger accompanying him. "Why is it that you follow me?"

Julian hesitated, but made no apology for what he had said. He didn't think to salute the chancellor, either, regardless of his condition, even when Raven was already on one knee.

"I never thought of myself being loyal to anyone," Julian admitted. "But between the emperor and you, I choose you, Lord Chancellor. Where the emperor would do anything to achieve his goals, you actually have a conscience. From what I've seen, you do your best to minimise casualties."

Schim nodded at what he might have seen as a fair comment.

"The odds are against us," Julian continued. "But we have yet to lose. I can't promise that I'll turn the tables, but you can count on me to grow stronger every day for as long as I survive."

Schim smiled. "I've been counting on you since the day you were admitted, Sir Longinus. I trust in your ability and potential."

"Is that so?" Julian responded with a frown. "You're keeping information from me... and you have Raven watching over me. You call that trust?"

"Longinus!" Raven berated. "Watch who you're speaking to, or else—"

"Or else what?" Julian challenged. "Let me remind you: we cannot afford to fight amongst ourselves in this little faction of ours."

"Perhaps you're right," Schim said. "I *don't* trust you, but it is simply your judgement that I cannot yet trust. You've grown strong, but we need you to be much stronger still. Indeed, I believe you have the potential to be the strongest knight in the country. I cannot lose you, and that's why Raven was arranged to *support* you. As for the collusion between Spartamon, Breunor, and Forredan," he said, pausing for a moment, "I kept it from you for *your* benefit."

"For my benefit? I almost died because of this *benefit*!"

"You almost died *not* for your ignorance—but for your softness!" Schim said with a raising voice that turned suddenly authoritative. "Did it ever occur to you to *run* from the scramble? Who could possibly have caught you?"

"And leave Alex behind?" Julian asked. "After what he came for?"

"Yes!" Schim responded emphatically. "You should have let the boy die. Let him be a sacrifice. He would be remembered for his contribution for the greater good."

Julian fell into a shocked silence.

Schim turned, flapping his maroon cape wide open and pacing toward the far wall, one hand behind his back. "We cannot afford to lose someone like you to such meaningless affairs," he said, toning down slightly. "If you had known about Breunor and Forredan, you wouldn't have been able to focus on the sorcerers. And, consequently, you would have failed to locate Slash. I accounted for that much. But I didn't account for your recklessness that almost had you killed."

Julian shook his head in defence. "This *threat* from the sorcerers doesn't even compare to the threat posed by Breunor and Forredan. What did the sorcerers ever do? Whisper into people's ears? Sure, they might have murdered a few people, but I'd think Breunor and Forredan can top that!"

Raphael stepped forward then, his cool demeanour usually a welcoming contrast to Raven and Roth, except this time when Julian had no intention to back down.

"We wish to avoid a direct confrontation," Raphael said. "The Lord Chancellor is looking to defeat the Advents *righteously*—with reason and justice. The sorcerers are critical because we plan to uncover the emperor as the mastermind behind that group—and the origin behind Reeling's murder. When we reveal the emperor's corruption, we will win the support of all neutral parties. That includes The Villa, the St. Bernard Order, and the Defence Army. At that time, Breunor and Forredan will no longer be an obstacle."

Julian clenched a fist, his lips creased harder yet. "But is it really that simple?" he asked. "How would we expose the emperor, when he's so careful not to leave any traces of his crimes? Slash worked for them, yet they didn't hesitate even for a second before killing him."

Schim scratched his chin, finally regarding the stranger standing in the back. "That's where Lord Ebenezer can give us a helping hand," Schim said.

The stranger brushed his hood behind to reveal his bald head and squinted eyes in dark circles. He stroked his puffed goatee with a slight grin.

A foreigner, Julian realised immediately, noting the blue eyes. It wasn't the first time he had seen a foreigner, but it was indeed rare to see one in Zorlia—especially in Vondra Dawn.

"Lord Ebenezer is known as the Great Mage," Schim said as Ebenezer nodded in acknowledgement. "He has studied energy flow for most of his life. His expertise has led to the ability to imitate grace."

Julian raised a brow but said nothing of his suspicions just yet.

"He can help us in our war against the Advents," Schim continued. "If Spartamon leaves no trails behind him, then let us *create* those trails for him."

"That might not be necessary," Ebenezer said. "I have reason to believe that the emperor of this country is also capable of imitating grace. Given who he is, and his feats, the man can potentially draw on more grace than even the most potent of sorcerers."

"What about the Advent sorcerers?" Raven asked. "Are they really sorcerers or did they all learn to imitate grace?"

Ebenezer glanced over at him. "It's not an easy thing to do. Those sorcerers are most likely natural."

Julian narrowed his eyes. He realised what Ebenezer was hinting at—the trick his father had taught him many years ago. At that time, grace didn't exist—or, at least, it wasn't accessible. His father had instead taught him to draw energy from moving objects—the bigger and the heavier, the better. These included flowing water and breezes of air. The concept involved drawing kinetic energy upon oneself, and then unleashing the energy into another form of power. The laws of nature dictated that every force had an opposite and equal force acting against it. Julian remembered how he had used to slow the wind by drawing upon its energy. But the very limited power he had been able to draw from the wind had made it seem as if the very act of calming the winds had actually been the magic involved.

"Grace drawn from nature is limited," Julian said, challenging the foreigner. "Sorcery is almost completely ineffective without a grace pool.

There's no way someone can draw enough power from nature to rival true sorcerers."

Ebenezer turned his gaze toward Julian. "Allow me to educate you," he said coldly, pacing to Julian and holding out a hand held in a claw. Without further warning, the foreigner thrashed his claw down at him. Julian read the intention with ease, whipping out a hand to lock onto Ebenezer's wrist mid-strike.

What is he trying to do? Julian wondered, noting that the attack carried not a hint of otherworldly powers. But as he met the foreigner's glare, he felt a sudden tingle. An itch—a jerk that was far from pleasurable on the hand holding the foreigner's wrist. A natural instinct urged Julian to pull back, except he couldn't—almost as if his hand was suctioned onto the mage.

My grace is…, Julian realised in shock, *is being drained away!*

"That's enough," Schim said.

Ebenezer snapped his claw open, the resulting force tossing Julian's grasp away. The foreigner then waved an arm in a zigzag motion that was eerily familiar, and soon enough, his hand caught onto a black flame that Julian couldn't believe wasn't his own.

"The flame was summoned with your energy," Ebenezer said, before holding out a fist to quench the fire. "Your grace pool is impressive. If you could better draw upon natural forces, you could be a real force to be reckoned with. I don't know how you practised drawing grace from nature in the past, but you're mistaken if you believe that the power there is limited. The power of nature is the power of the Immortal. If that isn't plentiful, then I don't know what is."

Julian hissed at that. "And yet what you demonstrated just now *wasn't* the power of nature," he said.

"There are consequences in drawing upon the Immortal's grace," Ebenezer said with a strange pensiveness. "I strive not to do it, unless it's absolutely necessary."

Julian said nothing to that, but maintained his glare upon Ebenezer. A long time ago, Julian's father had echoed a similar sentiment about how nature was to be respected.

Take only what you need. Take sparingly.

"Spartamon draws upon this grace from nature," Schim inserted, finally getting to his point. "I've seen him do it, long before the Awakening. It must have been the final year of the war. He called upon a source of energy that no one else could make any sense of. And only in retrospect can I see that it was grace. It was *sorcery*."

"And...," Julian uttered now, "how are we going to use it against him?"

"We will expose him before the most distinguished men of the country," Raphael said. "Lord Pierre Morlan has organised for a festive gathering on the nineteenth day of June—a day that coincides with his fiftieth birthday. The gathering is to take place within his grand manor in Phantom Pond."

Julian looked over to Schim, who nodded in confirmation.

"Morlan is no ally of Spartamon," Schim said, as if to reassure. "But he is no ally of mine, either—at least not yet. To win this war against the Advents, we need Morlan on our side. He is the final piece that we need to tip the balance in our favour."

Schim turned to Raphael again and gestured for him to elaborate.

"Lord Morlan is inviting every member of the court," Raphael said. "All other related parties—including the members of the Church and the academy—will be invited, too. The guest list should name over a hundred invitees. It appears that Morlan is hoping to create a relaxed environment, free from the fierce political war, one that could reunite the people. Wishful, but also respectable." Raphael paused, regarding Julian for a moment. "You are recognised as an important person by Morlan's retinue, and thus, you've been invited, too."

* * *

Julian's broken shoulder was still hurting and bandaged up, but he had more than half a month to recover in time for the June Nineteenth Gathering. While Julian certainly wasn't in top condition, he had felt well enough to get out of bed since the morning. And yet he had remained in his nursing room all day, for he was still reluctant to deal with the grief he had caused—to see Alex, who had lost an arm.

On the fourth day of recovery, Julian finally left Vondra Dawn, limping his way to Stapleton where he had learned that Alex was being nursed. The streets were almost empty of people, and it had been like this in the evenings for the past month, the fear of running into sorcerers daunting people and keeping them from needless wandering in the dark. Julian himself had enjoyed roaming the evening streets in order to hunt down those said sorcerers, but so far, he had only managed to find one of them—Slash, who he had found during the day.

Eris Nightingale, Julian thought, as her image flashed suddenly into his mind. Julian turned to the west, which was the direction of the theatre. Nightingale had left the city nearly a month ago, and nearly a week before the rest of the musical drama group she was a part of. She hadn't been able to let go of her past, and for that, she had chosen to run away again.

Selfish and vain, Julian had thought. *Not even a goodbye. Just dumping Oscar with gold. How insulting.* Julian cringed. *But… what is this urge to see her again?*

A sibilant whistle sounded then in the otherwise gentle wind followed by a haunting flap of fabric from behind. Julian spun to see a man dressed in full black. The only thing that wasn't black were the stripes on either side of his mask, replicating the whiskers of a beast. And yet the man's spirited presence came without a hint of grace. The man was no sorcerer, Julian was sure of that. And when the man flapped out his cape, Julian recognised the twin rapiers at the waist.

It's him, Julian thought. *The phantom. The same person from the prison four months ago, the same person who appeared again only four days ago.*

Julian held in a smile, only for the man to raise an arm pointing at him.

"You're a fool," the phantom said, his voice distorted and deepened through the stone mask he wore. "Acting like a hero to save someone else, using up all of your energy only to endanger your own life… What did you think you could achieve with that?"

"Alex isn't just anyone," Julian responded, his voice hardened. "He risked his life for me, and I had to return the favour. I suspect that I owe you the same favour if there was ever the need."

"I only happened to be passing by," the phantom claimed, waving a finger from side to side. "There won't be a third time."

The phantom reached into a pocket beneath his cape, pulling out a parchment which he then offered to Julian. And then, without any caution, the man spun around and slipped back into the darkness of the night, almost like a spectre that couldn't possibly be chased.

"Be careful out there," Julian said quietly, already sure that he would meet the man again.

Julian flipped open the parchment, which revealed itself to be a letter addressed to Breunor, penned by some Sir Russell, dated *Anaphora 2*. Julian skimmed through the words on the page, noting the mention of the notorious incident known as the Carnage of Central Farella, which was a bloody episode that had wiped out a camp of a thousand soldiers led by Nine Arms during the war. Growing curious, Julian skipped to the revelation at the end.

I hear that you are still unable to forget what happened, it read. *And I have learned that you hunted down every one of us who knows the truth. Allow me to save you the trouble of doing the same with me. The truth will forever be buried following my death. You will be the only one left to bear the mistake and the guilt.*

Julian stared at the handwritten words, musing about the validity of what was being referred to. It wasn't specifically stated, but the implication in the letter was clear. It accused Breunor of a very serious negligence which had resulted in the deaths of more than a thousand men, this same incident for which Nine Arms had apparently held Marvin Sailanson responsible. Julian folded the letter back up again, realising that if the source could be verified, he was potentially holding the key that could cause Breunor's collusion with the emperor to collapse. If Julian could manage to stir Nine Arms's vengeance, Breunor could be destroyed altogether.

Julian looked back up at the empty street in front of him, seeing nothing more than the familiar terracotta buildings and the several lanterns hanging off of them, all behind wisps of mist which swirled about the evening. The phantom had been long gone.

Just who *was* he? Why did he entrust him with such important information and even the actual item of evidence?

THIRTY-ONE

June Nineteenth Gathering

For once, Julian wasn't wearing armour. Instead, he was dressed in a noble suit with a hanging cravat and sleeves of olive velvet with gold trimmings, all beneath a draped cloth robe of a rich brown. Julian had been instructed by Schim, who he was pacing behind, not even to bring his sword. As he looked up then, Julian realised that he had rarely noticed that his liege's frame was so wide. Perhaps it was the angle from where Julian was looking, and perhaps it was because Lady Winter provided a stark contrast next to Schim.

Glancing to his left, Julian noted Ebenezer pacing in line with him. He still didn't trust the foreigner.

They had arrived in Phantom Pond, the home to some of the most affluent residents of Zorlia. Breunor and Forredan had homes here, as did Alpheus. But no one had a home quite like the former king of Cetal, whose magnificent manor sat at the end of the neatly paved road that stretched through the neighbourhood. The great Morlan Manor was just ahead, easily recognised by its unique dome-shaped half-sphere design, four or five stories high at its rounded peak. It was backdropped by the darkened sky in which the sun had all but set. The evening was upon them, one that promised to be memorable.

The dome-shaped exterior of the Morlan Manor was lighted with a collection of *twinkling stars* that formed various polygons across the spherical surface of black, as if recreating the image of a clear night sky. As they paced closer to the entrance, Julian realised that the small flames were in fact tiny oil lamps fitted into the surface of the exterior, which made for a grand lighting display. Surely it would have been a tedious task to light each one of those oil lamps, having to climb onto the external walls that curved in an extension all the way to the roof. The design was a marvel of modern architecture, but Julian found it difficult to be impressed, knowing that there had been workers spending time on grand architecture at a time when every structure in the city was at risk of crumbling down in the likely event of a civil war. Still, the building before him *was* a welcoming change from the grim steeples of Vondra Dawn.

Perhaps there was no better venue to host all of the conflicting agendas that had divided the city—and hence the country—than the home of Pierre Morlan, one of barely a handful of men who had managed to maintain neutrality in all of the disorder.

Julian's shoulder was no longer plastered, but beneath his noble garb hiding his injury from view, the joint certainly still stung, especially when he swung his arm. The truth was that he might just have to swing his arm with full force this evening. Although the evening was supposedly about Morlan's birthday, Julian wasn't about to forget that they were in the midst of a fierce political war. He expected plenty of bloodshed, and no one to offer any sympathy. The days leading up to today had been rather uneventful, and yet this nineteenth day of June had come sooner than he could prepare for. He could only hope that the Advents were less prepared than him.

A host of people were gathered outside the entrance, but all of them shuffled away as soon as they saw Schim pacing through. Among the crowd there, Julian recognised a few noblemen, but no one particularly important or high in stature. Schim most likely thought so too, for he continued treading along without pause or a comment to anyone.

The ambience was drastically different inside the Morlan Manor, especially after proceeding through the antechamber to the great hall. Other than the much brighter lighting, the air was filled with chatter and laughs, providing for a festive mood that seemed almost out of place with the guests who had been used to misery more than anything else in the recent months. The open space of the great hall was large enough to comfortably accommodate two hundred men, more than sufficient for the hundred or so guests expected this evening. Dozens of large round tables were spaced out across the floor, lighted mainly by the single grand chandelier hanging from the centre point of the enormous curved ceiling of tessellated forest glass, translucent enough for one to spot the waxing blue of Achelois and the waning red of Selene. Beneath the glass were a line of box-shaped lanterns providing further lighting. Beneath those were mural-covered walls that depicted the angels and saints. Attached to the wall on the far end were winding stairs that perhaps led to the host's private chambers.

"We're finally here," Schim said quietly.

Julian looked in the direction in which Schim was peering, first to the far right to where a group of scholars were sitting. As Schim had foretold the day prior, Yusuf Seer had come this evening, along with a few other State Scholars. It was remarkable that Morlan had managed to get members of the academy here, when they were notorious as common absentees at such events. Perhaps it had something to do with Christopher Hartland, the State Scholar who had become a regular attendee on the court and one of Morlan's closest vassals.

Julian followed Schim's gaze to the far left then.

Templars! Julian thought, noting Gabriel, Suriel, and Kathryn Trulips, who was now better known as Kyriel. At the centre of the group was the man who they called the *Holy One*—Abraham IV, the High Priest of the Church of the St. Bernard Order. It was said that the holy man shared a distaste for the Empire in the same way the State Scholars did. He had once said that he would never directly associate the holy order with any ruling government.

Schim finally peered directly ahead to the largest group present: representatives of the Defence Army from nearby Bastion City. Ever since the premature conclusion to the Golden Knight Exchange, the most powerful army in the country had been fairly quiet. Their representatives had arrived in noble garb rather than their usual chain mail. They *had* brought weapons, however, which one could see hidden beneath their mantles if one knew how to look. Their leader, Paltiel Sagramore, was the only exception, proudly donning his standard golden armour. The veteran knight made no effort to hide his long partisan, either, the fearful pole weapon springing out from the strap on his back.

Having shunned from all public events of recent months, Sagramore himself had avoided becoming entangled in the embroilment, and had in effect also pulled the Defence Army clear of the conflict. But Sagramore's inaction and his apparent indifference toward the recent troubles in the city had seen him at the receiving end of a barrage of criticism from all parties affected by the current stalemate, including the civilians. Sagramore's men, however, seemed to stand firmly behind the man, respecting and supporting his every decision.

If only Schim could manage to win Sagramore's support, Julian realised—which was exactly what his liege had been working on for years, but without success—there would be a much greater chance to dethrone Spartamon. The Defence Army was truly an enviable faction comprising some of the most able warriors in all of Trubannis. From the top to the bottom, they were—

Julian winced suddenly, remembering Percival Pole, his old friend, who was also arguably the strongest product of the Defence Army in recent years. It was a shame in every respect that Pole had fallen so deeply out of favour with Sagramore and the Defence Army. It was worse that Pole had seemingly given up on himself, which had effectively transformed him into the most scorned warrior in the country. Since his brief encounter with Pole at the cathedral, Julian had actually suggested to Schim more than once that adding Pole to their side would help them in this war against the Advents. Not only was Pole an incredibly gifted warrior—whose strength Julian knew he still couldn't match—but Pole was also possibly the most cunning—or *shrewd*—man Julian had ever known. Unfortunately, Schim wasn't intrigued in the slightest at the idea of recruiting someone who he had described as a *lamed* soldier.

While Julian never specifically looked for Pole's name on the guest list, he had learned in the days prior that Pole had indeed been listed on the invitee registry. Despite that, his old friend was nowhere to be seen.

Julian shook away his nostalgia then as Morlan treaded over with his retinue. Julian suppressed a grin, impressed that Morlan had managed to invite such distinguished guests as Yusuf Seer, Abraham IV, and Paltiel Sagramore, revered respectively for wisdom, divinity, and chivalry. All three of them had chosen not to intervene in the fierce political war. Schim had said that Morlan had been spending weeks corresponding with these men, with the purpose of having them help prevent the Truban Empire from completely falling apart.

"Good evening, Lord Chancellor!" Morlan greeted with a wide grin.

"Lord Morlan!" Schim responded with equal enthusiasm, pausing for a moment to glance back to Julian.

"Oh, right!" Julian said, having forgotten that he was holding the gift that Schim had prepared. He held the box forward and then lifted the cover to reveal the delicate horse sculpture inside. Apparently Morlan was a lover of equines, and if the man's delighted expression was anything to go by, it was true. What Julian wondered then, however, wasn't whether Morlan appreciated the gift or not, but whether any other guests had remembered to bring a birthday gift.

In any case, the pleasantries ended prematurely when a great clamouring sounded from the entrance behind them. Julian turned to note the arrival of Victor Breunor and Quinlan Forredan, arriving together in a group of nearly fifty men, probably at least half of which had received no invitation. Other than the former golden knight and the portly statesman, the group included

Lucan, Bors, Gale, and Kite—all of them in armour, as if it were a show of strength. Julian picked out Bors in particular, glaring now toward the golden knight. This was the first time he had met Bors again after crossing swords with him—indeed, the first time since Alex's arm had been severed.

When the Titan noted Julian's gaze, the man returned an inimical glare of his own. Breunor also glanced over until Morlan stepped over to them. Schim, in turn, grunted quietly from behind Julian, before steering the group away. Even as Julian followed Schim toward the men of the Defence Army, he kept an eye on Breunor and Bors.

It was upon another grunt, this time from Ebenezer, when Julian finally turned his focus back to what was before him: the conversation between Schim and Sagramore. There was clearly no collusion here. Schim seemed to be a righteous man, as did Sagramore. Superficially, Sagramore seemed to agree with Schim on more than a few things, as it was evidenced now during their conversation. Indeed, the veteran knight seemed to be enjoying his liege's company. It was a shame, however, that according to Raphael, Sagramore didn't want to be involved in the conflict between the Advents and the Pristines on any level. Julian could only imagine how well the two would complement one another if they could agree on an alliance.

It was about ten minutes later when the conversation finally ended. Schim then glanced out over toward the more reserved Yusuf Seer and then to Abraham IV, both of whom nodded back in quiet courtesy.

They hold him in esteem, Julian thought, watching the chancellor from behind. *His reputation is better than most. Really, what would Schim as emperor look like? Could he call on the academy and the holy order to support his causes?*

Could he now?

Over the past few weeks, Julian had worked tirelessly with Schim in preparation for this evening. Most of the work had only begun to fall into place about a week ago since tracking down a second Advent sorcerer. The sorcerer, code-named *Dice*, was stationed in the nearby town of Carrington. The Raiders had been tasked to capture the said sorcerer this very evening. The chancellor's plan *wasn't* to simply force the sorcerer to testify against the emperor. Rather, Schim had arranged some purposeful and crafty use of espionage to lure Nine Arms and Lionel Lachman away on this evening, which would set up the rare occasion when the emperor would be without his two most able vassals. Julian had further arranged for a group of well-trained soldiers to be on standby, to pretend to be assassins planning to attack the emperor. The objective wasn't actual assassination, but simply to force the emperor to draw on his ability to imitate sorcery.

If successful, this could well be the beginning of the end for the emperor. And that, Julian thought, would be the dawn to a better tomorrow.

* * *

It was another hour later when the charismatic emperor finally appeared. Spartamon's much-delayed arrival showed that he still fully embodied his title as the Lord Emperor. The great man had probably made sure to be the last to arrive so that he would be honoured appropriately. Indeed, most of Morlan's guests were lined up next to the antechamber now, and all of them dropped to one knee. Everything was silent, with heads inclined. Julian looked out from the far end where he was standing next to Schim, his liege likely choosing to avoid direct confrontation so early in the evening.

Julian noted the smile on Schim's face, most likely a response to the fact that the emperor had come alone—alone in the sense that Nine Arms and Lachman weren't with him. Those two were presumably in Carrington, lured away as Schim had planned. It was strange, however—even suspicious that Spartamon had come with a couple of women, perhaps his concubines. Not once had Julian seen the emperor with any women. And not once had the emperor or anyone else mentioned his concubines. Spartamon had apparently insisted since long ago, during the warring years, that women had no place at court or at any other related events. And while the great man had been at the end of some critical backlash for those remarks, the emperor had maintained more than several times that he was referring to women who couldn't fight, nurse, or scheme.

In any case, the two women Spartamon was with now seemed to match that definition of having no place at the Morlan Manor this evening. Sure, they were young and beautiful, with curves that could allure most men. But, *Spartamon isn't most men*, Raphael had said. *Spartamon's the always charismatic leader born to rule. There's an air of enchantment around him that never fails to win over his worshippers.*

The emperor strolled in with the women as his escorts. As the man reached the middle of the path that had been made for him, he slowed down and finally came to a stop.

"Rise," he said, his voice strong and commanding. "Do carry on. Let no one spoil the festivities."

The men exchanged looks, and gradually began to stand. They began to disperse and blend back into their various social circles, but not without keeping an eye on the emperor, who appeared uncharacteristically jovial, striving ahead toward Morlan and congratulating the man on his birthday. The emperor then gestured Breunor and Forredan over for a seemingly gleeful conversation that would never have taken place on the court. Something *was* different about him, and it only became more curious when Spartamon then strutted over to Seer and then to the members of the Church.

Julian stared in wonder as Spartamon managed to leave a smile on the face of every man he came into contact with.

Is this it? Julian wondered. *Is this the extraordinary diplomacy skill that attracted so many people into swearing their lives to him?*

Julian couldn't be sure. But, without a doubt, it was a striking contrast to what he had seen in his four months at the court, where the emperor had been rather indifferent in terms of tying friendly bonds with anyone. Indeed, the emperor looked blissful now and completely in his element, his eyes gleaming as he made his way around the manor to converse with even some of the lesser figures in attendance. It was as if Spartamon's words and his every stroke of movement fanned out an innate charm that drew more and more people to gather around him, literally over a dozen men by then. Julian didn't want to admit it, but compared to Schim—who many might hold in high esteem—it looked as if every man actually regarded the emperor with devoted admiration, even worship.

"Don't be drawn in," Schim muttered.

Julian's senses returned as he realised he too had been entranced by the emperor's charm. He looked up to meet Schim's eyes.

"I'm ready when you are," Julian said.

Upon Schim's call, Julian was to release a pure white dove from beneath the dangling robe he wore. On that signal, the group of nine soldiers he had trained to pretend to be assassins were to pounce on the emperor. These soldiers were lurking just outside the manor, specifically on the curved roof of the structure. They would see the white dove through the translucent glass top from the outside and would know that it was time.

Schim eyed Ebenezer, who nodded in response. Together, they walked toward the emperor, their approach prodding the neutrals to flock away. When they were only a few steps away, the only ones left were the emperor and his concubines.

"Lord Emperor," Schim said with a slight bow. "You seem to be in good spirits."

The emperor returned a smile, but barely a glance. "Why shouldn't I be? After all, this is *my* country." The emperor paused there, looking out to the guests. "And they are *my* people. There's a lot of pride in leading this lot. But I suppose you wouldn't understand what that's like."

Schim lifted his chin slightly, and then gestured toward Ebenezer. "Allow me to introduce my guest from Vinawell," he said. "Lord Ebenezer of the Imperial Lithia Dominion."

The foreigner bowed. "Lord Emperor, it is a pleasure and an honour."

"The pleasure is mine, great mage," the emperor responded. "Stories of your feats have been reaching my ears since long ago."

Ebenezer accepted the praise with a nod.

"Lord Ebenezer is here to aid us in our investigation of the Lord Count's murder," Schim said as a slight smirk emerged upon his face. "I trust that he'll help us identify the murderer."

The emperor's eyes narrowed at Ebenezer before his gaze shifted slowly back to Schim. "I'm intrigued," he said.

"So you should be," Schim responded with a deepening grin. "Ah... say, where are Pylon and Sir Lachman today?"

"Carrying out some chores," the emperor said with no change of expression. "I assume the Raiders are doing the same?"

"Yes, indeed they are. Now, if you'll excuse me."

Schim turned away, still wearing that grin, perhaps adamant that the day would soon arrive where he wouldn't have to flatter the emperor in the slightest. He eyed Julian then, flapping out his cape as the signal for the plan to go ahead.

Julian took in a deep breath and then reached beneath his robe behind his back. He ran his fingers up a pair of slender talons. A gentle touch of grace was enough to wake the bird. Julian moved his index finger up, nudging onto the bird's nape, and then pulling on a delicate string that loosened his grip of the bird. A restrained flap of wings later, the white dove emerged from his layers of fabric, surging into the air, the sudden commotion drawing immediate attention toward Julian's direction.

Julian, however, had eyes only on the bird that darted upwards into the air, breezing past the chandeliers and edging up to the glass ceiling, all while flapping its wings unsparingly. Everything suddenly seemed to turn silent at that moment. Soon, the nine soldiers he had personally trained would besiege the manor. Julian was sure that these soldiers were capable of forcing the emperor into drawing grace from nature, as Ebenezer had demonstrated, in order to defend himself.

But something doesn't seem right somehow, Julian thought, as he continued to trace the bird's upward trail along with the other guests.

It was as if time had slowed down, and the incessant flutter of the wings became almost irritable. Just as Julian grew more and more impatient, the bird too glided about searchingly, lost, struggling in its futile attempt to find open sky.

THIRTY-TWO

The return of the Judge

The white dove hovered beneath the curved-glass ceiling, swinging about the hanging column of the grand chandelier. The flapping of wings was disconcerting, both visibly and audibly. Julian looked hard for signs of the soldiers he had waiting in ambush, but there were no signs of anyone floating about outside on the roof. And then just as Julian thought he might have spotted a blurred speck through the tessellated glass, a whistle sounded from the floor. Julian glanced down, tracing the sound to a group of noblemen. Within a moment, the bird had sailed down to the nobles who then directed the bird to glide out from the great hall through to the antechamber and perhaps completely out of the building.

Morlan scurried out to the antechamber, probably to confirm that the bird had indeed left the premises. The host then paced over to the group of nobles with a smile. Few people seemed to realise that Julian had been the one releasing the bird. And, if anyone did, no one remarked on it. Soon enough, everything reverted back to how it had been. The festivities had hardly been curtailed, and there wasn't a hint of a siege.

Schim regarded Julian with a frown, as if demanding answers. Julian could only respond with a confused frown of his own amid his growing anxiety. Julian looked up again, squinting and scanning the ceiling, peering through the tessellated glass for any clues.

"Someone's there," Ebenezer whispered, nodding toward the east side of the glass ceiling.

Julian squinted upwards. Indeed, outside there was a hazy silhouette that resembled a human figure.

Why is he just standing there? Where are the rest of them?

The figure receded then, disappearing behind the blur of the glass altogether. That wasn't the end of it, however. A thunderous strike sounded on the opposite side of the room. Julian's eyes darted westward, where a figure crashed *through* the glass ceiling, shards of glass showering down on guests who were quick to scatter away in a panic. Julian recognised the full black dress that he had arranged, but the intruder certainly wasn't supposed to *ram into* the ground head first, probably snapping a few bones in the process.

Julian exchanged a look with Schim as shocked gasps filled the air. Silence followed. Men rushed toward their respective lieges, prepared to defend them with their lives. The emperor, in particular, was immediately surrounded by more than a dozen warriors, including even Breunor and Bors. The task to force him into drawing grace from nature suddenly became far more challenging, if not impossible.

Morlan sent a few men forward toward the intruder, who lay unconscious on the floor. They turned him over, only to see an ivory mask covering his face. It was shattered, but somewhat still in place.

Is he dead? Julian wondered with a squint, hardly daring to peek out from behind the crowd. *Where are the other eight?*

Another thump from above followed, with more shards raining down. Heads lifted once more as a second and a third man crashed in from different points of the destroyed glass ceiling. After a moment of pause, six more crashed through in a bunch, smashing open a destructive opening in the domed roof as more glass shards showered down onto the floor.

Nine. That was all of them.

Hurled in rather than leaping in themselves, limited to squirming and whimpering now. Julian grunted as he gazed up, certain that the one responsible for thwarting his plans was still lurking somewhere up there. Outside, however, there seemed to be nothing other than the luminance of the two moons and the stars glistening more brilliantly now through the multiple openings of the glass dome.

The festive theme of the evening had been ruined. Everyone was looking up to the broken ceiling, silent and waiting. A current of air blasted in from the top suddenly, and soon, everything dimmed—the ring of lanterns all mysteriously burned out in quick succession. Finally, the only remaining source of light—the grand chandelier—crashed down and shattered on the floor. Following a deafening clap that resonated in the great hall, heads turned forward again to see a single man lighted by the only flickering flames of the chandelier that had managed to survive the fall. The culprit had landed atop the magnificent light fixture next to the nine hobbled men, the only person now highlighted among over a hundred in the building cowering in darkness. He was a tall man in simple pants with a short shawl hanging over his otherwise unclothed upper body, and a wide headband tied at an angle. The stranger wore a wide grin that displayed his arrogance. He wasn't particularly large, but the man was blessed with a set of stalwart arms and well-defined abdominal muscles.

Julian clenched a fist but failed to call upon much strength. Although he could neither assign a name to the stranger nor determine whether he was a friend or a foe, Julian was certain that this man was immensely strong. There was no denying it when the stranger had managed to defeat the nine soldiers without even breaking a sweat.

"Sailanson...!" some muttered in awe as more gasps filled the manor.

Julian jumped slightly, his heart pounding.

That's him?! he wondered in shock. *Marvin Sailanson?*

Julian glanced to his left to see Schim's astonished expression, which was all the confirmation that he needed.

Sailanson's sensational entrance perhaps deserved a stronger reception than the astonished silence that now greeted him. But everyone in the manor, many of whom were established men themselves, were left in shock. Even Breunor, always rowdy and vain, seemed to be trembling in fear. Meanwhile, some others were reaching for their weapons, presumably to stave off Sailanson, who was an alleged monster of a man. The only man who had remained calm was the emperor, who was wearing a slight smile now, as if he had expected this. All the while, Morlan was barking out orders for men to restore the lighting in the great hall.

Sailanson spun around slowly, regarding the crowd.

"It's been a while," he said, everyone still except for the men racing around to light the lanterns. Sailanson stepped off of the broken chandelier then, all eyes following his first momentous step.

"Everything's been taken care of," Sailanson said, looking straight ahead to the emperor. "There were only nine of them."

Spartamon nodded at him. Not only was he calm, but he seemed to know exactly what was happening.

"And Watts?" Spartamon asked.

Sailanson gestured toward the wide arced entrance to the great hall. Stepping in was a middle-aged man with an eyepatch, dark wavy hair falling behind him and reaching past his shoulders over a build that was similar to Sailanson's.

"The Vulture...!" more than a few men uttered then.

Julian gritted his teeth. *Could it really be? Rover Watts?! The Lone Eye Vulture, the man who brutally tore through enemy defences in the war?*

Despite this newcomer's shaggy appearance, he actually seemed modest and sensible, at least compared to Sailanson's flamboyant entrance. And yet the fact that the newcomer seemed indifferent to the supposedly dignified men in attendance perhaps showed that he was also a man to be feared. Curiously, the man didn't directly acknowledge the emperor in any way, proceeding forward only to join Sailanson where he stood.

The emperor smirked. "It appears your skills haven't declined even in the slightest."

"Lord Emperor," Morlan said carefully. "Can I assume that you know a thing or two about what is going on here?"

The emperor smiled at the host. "A minor commotion, Lord Morlan," he said. "No one should be deterred from the festivities of the evening. The men lying on the ground are mere outlaws who I've been hunting for some time. It just so happens that they chose this day to show themselves. The damage your home has suffered is unfortunate, but the Empire will remedy any losses."

Morlan peered down at the defeated men who were finally being chained up now, and then regarded Sailanson and the man in the eyepatch.

"And dare I ask you to confirm the identity of these two men?" Morlan said.

Julian raised an eyebrow, surprised that Morlan didn't know.

"They are...," Spartamon said, pausing as he glanced over to Schim. "Well, perhaps we could ask the Lord Chancellor to introduce them."

Schim cringed slightly, and Julian cringed as well for his liege whose plans for the evening had been completely thwarted. The only positive, though, was that Julian was sure that the nine hobbled soldiers couldn't be traced back to the Pristines, regardless of whether or not they lived. Still, Schim had grown pale in the space of a few minutes. Were Sailanson and Watts really so frightening? Sure, Julian had heard the rumours that described Sailanson as a genius in combat and Watts possessing an unparalleled amount of raw strength. But surely, the rumours were exaggerated, for if it were really true, they were on a level far beyond even the golden knights.

"More than a few of us here are already well-aware of who they are," Schim began solemnly. "But I agree that they deserve a re-introduction. After all, it's been eight years." He turned to the newcomers. "Marvin Sailanson and Rover Watts," he said, "a couple of our most remarkable soldiers during the war. They belonged to the Central Light Army, but their contributions extended across the entire clan, which of course also benefitted the Secondary Light Army, which was under my command. Sailanson and Watts were consistently rated among the strongest individual combatants of all our soldiers. Always reliable in slaying the toughest of enemies, they were imperative to the country's eventual triumph. Marvin Sailanson—in particular—who served as Left Wing of the Central Light Army—was quite possibly the most able warrior within the entire army. Each time he took to the battlefield, he injected a distinct fear in enemy troops. He shook their morale, which in turn won us plenty of vigour with which to fight our battles."

Despite Schim's glowing appraisal, no one applauded. Julian didn't know whether Watts deserved any acclaim, but he knew why Sailanson wasn't receiving any plaudits. There was no way that the man assigned with the infamous cognomen as *the Judge*, thought to have slaughtered over two hundred comrades in a terrible episode later known as the Noel Gate Incident, would ever be applauded in public again.

Sailanson simpered and then slowly began to clap. "Your generous evaluation flatters me," he said, regarding Schim. "But I don't need you to aggrandise what I have done."

Schim responded with a quick grin before turning to everyone else again. "It has been eight years since the war ended, and that may seem like a long time ago. Some of us are getting far too comfortable, taking this seemingly flourishing Advent Era for granted. As for me, I can never forget the horrors witnessed on the battlefield and all of the precious lives that were lost. My deepest gratitude lies with all of those who helped make this country what it is today. It was our former Commander, the current Lord Emperor, who led us to victory. And it was fearless warriors like Sailanson, Watts, and Pylon who wielded their swords devotedly and relentlessly for their country. It was the invaluable support of the Golden Dragon Knights led by Lord Breunor, whose timely disengagement from the falling Sargon Monarchy and consequent union with the Clan of Light mightily expanded our influence. It was Sir Sagramore and his well-trained knights, who in turn supported the Golden Dragon Knights, defending our land with their lives. It was Lord Forredan, the former Minister of Whitesand, who continued to fund our armies with every last piece of gold in his possession."

"How humble of you, Lord Chancellor," Forredan inserted. "In terms of contribution, it was the Secondary Light Army under your command that fought some of the most gruesome battles."

Schim paused, glancing over toward the stout statesman. "I thank you for your kind words, Lord Forredan," he said, then turning back to the greater crowd. "But no, I do not consider myself humble. By accepting the place as the proud Chancellor of this country, I have been rightfully rewarded and honoured. And this matter of *reward and honour* is precisely what I am getting at, for I am deeply saddened that many of those people who helped build this Advent Era were *never* rightfully rewarded. Yet even more regrettable is the fact that many of those *cannot* be rewarded." He paused again, shaking his head. "They cannot be honoured, for they are dead! The least we could do is *honour* their memory, but we have not even done so."

Breunor perked up, seemingly eager about what Schim was implying. "Would you elaborate on that, Lord Chancellor?" he said. "All dead soldiers should have already been appropriately honoured. They have been cited for their valour and heroism. Their families, had they any, have been granted with more gold than they could ever use in a lifetime."

"Yes, Lord Breunor, many of our perished comrades *have* been appropriately honoured. But not *all* of them."

"And who might they be?" Breunor asked, spurring Schim on.

The chancellor turned to Sailanson. "That day haunts me still," he said. "Southern Noel. Weeks before the war ended. More than two hundred men were massacred in the space of two days. Those victims to this day have yet to be honoured."

Sailanson narrowed his eyes, and the emperor snorted. Julian realised that Schim was referring to the Noel Gate Incident, of which Sailanson was the prime suspect, alleged to have slaughtered his own comrades.

The incident had happened only days after the terrible loss that was now remembered as the Carnage of Central Farella. And while more than a thousand lives had been lost in Central Farella, the two hundred who had died at the Noel Gate were considered to be an internecine episode that was bloodier and much more sinful than anything that could be accused of opposing armies. And the accusations against Sailanson weren't without merit. More than a few people present at the manor could vouch for Sailanson's ability *and* his intent to slaughter masses of Truban soldiers.

* * *

Marvin peered about the great hall, meeting numerous sets of vengeful eyes which were locked onto him. Many of the people in attendance this evening were acquaintances from the war, or even men he had once called brothers. But his relationship with these men had clearly soured since then, these same men now looking spiteful, as if aching to release their long-suppressed wrath upon him. Some had hands on their weapons, while others moved to block his path. With so much hostility suddenly directed at him, Marvin felt a cold trickle of sweat rolling down from his forehead. It didn't look like he could escape this evening without a fight.

He squinted now, remembering how he had once been the most popular member of the clan led by Spartamon. During his time as a soldier fighting for Trubannis, his skills in combat were without rival. His courage had seen him storm fearlessly at enemy troops, and his carefree personality had allowed him to befriend all of those who fought alongside him. At the height of his popularity, Marvin had been regarded as Spartamon's equal. But his encounter and eventual romantic relationship with Theodora had later changed everything.

Kharvalenis was Theodora's family name—a Kragan name. It didn't matter to his comrades that she had a Truban mother. It didn't matter that she had never stepped foot on Kragan territory in her life. It didn't even matter that she was a skilled surgeon who never discriminated against her patients, regardless of their alliance. The discrimination against Theodora for her sensitive identity was a perpetual conundrum in the army at the time, perhaps more so for Spartamon than anyone else.

Marvin had always known that Spartamon considered him an invaluable part of his warring strategies. And for this reason alone, Spartamon always sought to defend Theodora, even when almost every soldier in the army was convinced that she was a poison to the clan. Most who knew her would agree that she was naturally benevolent, but that didn't save her from being accused of being a traitor every single time that the Kragans won even minor battles.

Indeed, Marvin had once been grateful to Spartamon who had saved Theodora on more than a few occasions from his own soldiers who were plotting to kill her as retribution for Kragan victories. He remembered the incident in which he had reluctantly slayed four fellow soldiers who had plotted to murder Theodora. After that incident, no one dared to lay a finger on Theodora again, though that was also the beginning of the irrecoverable wedge that stood between him and the other soldiers.

But his own comrades weren't the only ones who dared provoke him. In an effort to stall the relentless advance of the Central Light Army, the enemy soldiers captured Theodora alongside several prominent soldiers, including Lionel Lachman, the golden knight of today. At the time, many in the army believed that they should march on regardless of the hostages who had been taken. Obviously, Marvin didn't agree with this strategy. While the army was still finalising its decision, however, Theodora was released by the enemy unscathed, returning with a letter penned by the then Kragan King, Tynan Bardorinoff. The Kragan King requested to see Spartamon, with a professed intention to talk about the possibility of peace.

Spartamon had been wary, and so too were most of the clan members. In the end, however, Schim volunteered to attend this rendezvous in place of Spartamon, in the hope that the war could end sooner. This hope turned out to be too naïve, as Schim was instead imprisoned by the Kragans and taken as yet another hostage. Theodora was then once again accused of being a traitor, and was also blamed for the earlier capture of Lionel Lachman and the other soldiers.

Even then, Spartamon maintained his trust in Theodora. But the protest for her execution was too much even for Spartamon, who eventually resolved to give his army what they wanted. And not only did Spartamon manage to execute Theodora behind Marvin's back, but Spartamon also arranged for Marvin's capture, with the intention of minimising the internal conflict. Marvin was enraged, as everyone had expected, but his strength was far more fearful than anyone ever imagined. He managed to escape Spartamon's otherwise perfect ambush, and in turn sought to murder Spartamon in order to avenge Theodora's death.

What had happened after that was unknown to most, but Marvin found Theodora's handwritten will which stated that she was willing to die if her death meant that so many others could live. Her final words had encouraged Marvin to continue fighting—fighting for a better world. Marvin had done just that, but during the last few months of war, he barely shared a word with his fellow soldiers.

The final twist to the story came shortly before the war ended. Lachman and a few others were finally liberated, and he described his devastation upon learning about Theodora's death. He attested that the nurse was most certainly not a traitor, and indeed was the invaluable benefactor who had saved him and the other captured soldiers. Lachman revealed that Theodora was in fact the illegitimate niece of King Bardorinoff, and that she had been offered incentives to betray the Clan of Light. But Theodora hadn't given in to the temptations, not even with a sword at her neck. She instead turned the threat back at the Kragan King, warning him that if any of *her* comrades were to die, she would kill herself, which meant that he would lose a valuable hostage.

After that, a host of soldiers had wanted to offer their apologies and condolences to Marvin. More than two hundred of them gathered at the Noel Gate, waiting for days, only to ask for Marvin's forgiveness. What ensued instead was the infamous episode that everyone had heard so much about. Those two hundred men ended up slaughtered at the Gate—all of them brutally massacred. And the evidence suggested that the murderer was but a single man. Unfortunately for Marvin, he was the only one believed to be capable of such a slaughter. In truth, Marvin had been tracking down the killer as well, if not to clear his own name, then at least to find out who possessed a level of strength that rivalled or even exceeded his own. His master, who had disappeared more than ten years ago, was the only other man who could possibly overpower two hundred trained soldiers. Marvin could only wish that it wasn't him, the man he owed everything to.

Marvin blinked away the nostalgia then as he felt a cold trickle of sweat rolling down from his forehead. The hostility of the crowd was something that he had not experienced for a long time.

This isn't what I came back for, he thought as he backed into Rover, who regarded him with a look that assured him that they were in this together. Whatever might befall them this evening, they were ready to respond together, like it had always been.

"Drop your weapons!" Spartamon commanded, his demanding tone stunning everyone. "Will anyone dare to raise their swords on this festive evening? Will we be turning this jubilant celebration of Lord Morlan's birthday into a bloodbath?"

"Lord Emperor," Schim inserted. "Would you allow this murderer to leave without having to pay for his sins?"

"Lord Emperor!" Breunor added with passion. "We have to avenge our brothers. More than several of those killed at the Noel Gate were among my closest confidants!"

"He killed my father!" another voice added, before a barrage of vengeful claims shot out from all over the crowd. Vehement chants demanding for justice to be served resonated incessantly inside the vast lounge.

"Stop this madness at once!" Spartamon demanded once again, hushing the crowd to near silence. "On what basis will you apprehend Marvin? Casualties are inevitable, especially in war. As the leader of those men, I am most crestfallen for their deaths. I pity the fallen ones, but those men knew from the day they offered their services that they would live and die by the sword. I issued an explanation for Marvin's innocence nine years ago, and I will say it again now: Marvin knows *nothing* about what happened there. I personally saw him off in Farella on the same day that those men died at the Noel Gate. Tell me, how could *anyone* travel that distance from Farella to Noel in the matter of a few hours?"

Schim stepped forward. "You are the emperor of this country," he said. "And we should take your word for it. But I also know your fondness for Marvin Sailanson. If a simple lie could help him, you would say it."

Spartamon snorted. "I am fond of all of those who died that day. All of them belonged to my very own Central Light Army. They were my closest and strongest soldiers. Despite some misunderstandings, many of those had also been Marvin's closest friends as well. If anything, Marvin too is a victim of the incident, for he had to carry the burden of the most sinful of crimes, and ones that he did *not* commit."

Marvin held in a smile, wary not to be prematurely grateful for Spartamon's outwardly passionate defence of him. While Spartamon was seen by some to be a ruthless leader, Marvin was one of the few who truly feared the man for his ingenious schemes and the ruthless measures he would take in order to achieve them.

"Allow me to say a few words," Morlan said then. "I wasn't involved in the war, but because of that, I believe that my neutral perspective may be valuable."

Spartamon nodded at him.

"There seems to be many variations to the Noel Gate Incident," Morlan began. "The truth will present itself one day, and until then, I believe we should give Marvin Sailanson the benefit of the doubt. I can't say I know Sailanson well, but did he not thwart an assassination attempt just now?"

"That was clearly all staged!" Breunor inserted angrily. "To win our sympathy. Don't be fooled, Lord Morlan! And what do you mean the truth will present itself one day? It happened nine years ago! How much longer must the perished ones wait until they can rest in peace? The murderer is right here before us! I say we kill him now!"

"Kill him now!" a nobleman added. "Why did he have to hide for all these years if he didn't commit the crime?"

"Who else other than Sailanson could deal that kind of damage?" another inserted. "There's no doubt about it."

Marvin shook his head, huffing out a soft breath. The hostility meeting him now was far greater than he had expected. With Rover by his side, he didn't think he could possibly be killed this evening. But even so, it would be a mighty struggle against nearly a hundred men. If only there was a better way out.

"The evidence is inconclusive," a voice said then, deep and authoritative.

Marvin turned to his right, noting a man treading out in a set of golden armour.

Paltiel Sagramore, Marvin thought as he recognised the man. *The most revered golden knight in the land.*

Sagramore wore an unforgiving frown, despite his words. "If anyone wants Sailanson for what happened in Noel," the golden knight said, "you would have to get through me first."

The veteran's firm warning had some slightly drop their hostilities.

"You're siding with him?" Breunor accused incredulously.

"I side with what I believe," Sagramore responded before laying his eyes on Marvin again. "Don't get the wrong idea, Sailanson. I don't know if you were responsible for Noel. But I *am* certain you were responsible for what happened to my nephew. And today, you shall answer to that."

Marvin raised an eyebrow. "*Your* nephew?"

Sagramore pulled out his long partisan that was strapped onto his back, spinning it forward now. "I didn't want this," he said, pointing the pole weapon at Marvin. "I respect your ability from the bottom of my heart—as did everyone else in the country—which, of course, includes my nephew, a foolish boy who was never suited to be a soldier. He was much too kind for his own good. I still remember that it was *Anaphora 36* when I sent him to the Central Light Army, with the hope for him to grow out of his youth and naivety. But judging from the letters he wrote to me, his initial time there was miserable. I had considered withdrawing him back under my personal tutelage. But I changed my mind when one day I received a letter from him that spoke of a new recruitment in the army, a boy about his age. For once, he showed an enthusiasm to be on the battlefield, and it was all thanks to this newcomer—apparently an incredible warrior. That man was you—the great Marvin Sailanson."

Marvin frowned, having just then realised who was being referred to.

"I was glad that he befriended you," Sagramore continued. "I thought he was finally coming to grips with being a soldier. But I was wrong. That idiot boy soon found himself scrambled up in an unfortunate case of friendly fire in which two of his comrades were killed. And even though the case was apparently accepted to be an unfortunate accident, he couldn't forgive himself. His remorse led to his eventual suicide. For a long time, I believed he had only himself to blame. But in recent years, I discovered that the one at fault for the then-friendly fire incident was indeed not my nephew, but Marvin Sailanson, the commander in charge of that mission. It was *you*—the Judge! It was *you* who forced my nephew to hang himself to cover up for *your* mistakes!"

Marvin said nothing, but his visible expression of lamentation confirmed to those watching that the story being told was at least half-true.

"That's not what happened," Rover said, speaking out finally. "Marv would never do such a thing. He—"

"No," Marvin cut in softly. "The details may not be entirely accurate, but the essence remains the same. Deedee died because of me."

"You have my respect," Sagramore proclaimed with a nod. "To have the honour and integrity to confess to your crimes. Unfortunately, you are still the one who forced my nephew to his death, and that is why we stand as enemies today."

"I am sorry that this is how it stands," Marvin offered.

"What weapon do you use, Sailanson?" Sagramore demanded, swinging his partisan from right to left. "I may not be able to defeat you, but I fight only fair battles."

"Sir Sagramore!" the emperor snapped.

The golden knight glanced over to Spartamon. "This is between me and Sailanson."

"Lord Emperor," Marvin said, addressing Spartamon with this title for the first time. "I want to settle this matter, too," he said, gaze still on Sagramore. "Let us battle outside."

THIRTY-THREE

A battle of the mightiest

The crowd followed the two men out to the courtyard. No one wanted to miss the clash between the mightiest of men, least of all Julian, who anticipated an incredible battle. The emperor didn't seem to want this to happen, and despite all the haste and scramble that had led to this, seating had been arranged for the emperor, who was still accompanied by his concubines. Watts, who had come as Sailanson's ally, stood cross-armed some distance away from Spartamon. Julian afforded an inch of space next to Schim and Winter, all of them standing to watch. Everyone else, meanwhile, shuffled and scampered for the best view, all the while careful not to crowd in too close. The men who had earlier raised their weapons against Sailanson appeared content now to stand back. Sagramore was their best bet for revenge, and surely, if the golden knight ended up in defeat, they would conjure up other ideas in order to down Sailanson.

Sagramore had unbuckled his protective armour, prepared to offer a fair battle by donning only a mere leather vest. The golden knight also snatched a sabre from one of his men then and handed it to Sailanson, who accepted it without hesitation. The veteran knight was thought to be one of the greatest warriors the land had ever seen, as well as a man who held his integrity higher than his own life. In comparison, Sailanson was simply believed to be *the* greatest warrior in the land, but whose morals were questionable at best. Julian didn't think anyone expected Sailanson to cruise toward a straightforward victory, but at the same time, no one could deny that Sailanson had an obvious age advantage over the golden knight who was now in his mid-fifties.

Julian wanted to believe in Sagramore's ability to triumph. After all, the golden knight was one of the few men of power who he truly respected. He worried for the veteran knight, however, and he could only hope that Sagramore had more than just bravery and vengeance to fuel his strength against an opponent alleged to have slaughtered two hundred men in one bloody episode.

"I wield my partisan today not for the victims of the Noel Gate," Sagramore said to the crowd, "but for Disson Whitehead, my nephew. No one is to interfere. If anyone dares, I will be the first to decimate him."

"Let's begin," Sailanson said simply in response, eyeing no one else but his opponent.

As soon as Sagramore nodded at him to signal his readiness, Sailanson darted forward. With a single hop, Sailanson had sailed into the golden knight and swept out his sabre that seemed to be carried by the wind. Sagramore answered with a spin of his partisan, parrying off the sabre, the impact on contact exploding into a seething gust of air that shot out at the crowd. Sailanson swept from the right then, the golden knight responding in the same way and for the same result, with the gust blasting away to another section of the crowd. When Sailanson looked for a third swing of the sabre, Sagramore spun the partisan forward in a counter to knock Sailanson's weapon from his grip, an exchange that won immediate cheers from the crowd. But when the golden knight followed with what should have been a connecting prod, Sailanson had shaken away and darted off to a safe distance, even recovering his sabre on the way.

"So close," some commented, growing hopeful for the veteran golden knight.

"Just a little more," others said.

The battle resumed immediately, with Sagramore seemingly in control of the pace, chasing after Sailanson with a succession of purposeful prods.

Was it really that close, though? Julian wondered as he turned to study the golden knight's every deft stroke. *Incredible*, he thought. *Sir Sagramore might be the only one who could hold anything against Marvin Sailanson.* Julian squinted then as an image of his old friend floated into mind again. *Percival, you fool. If only you had been more patient.*

Julian glanced over to the emperor then, who had maintained his air of confidence and calm, as if everything was in his control—or as if he had expected all of this to happen.

Another heavy clang of metals brought Julian's thoughts back to the colossal battle before him. Julian narrowed his eyes on Sailanson, watching the legendary mercenary move—not the fastest he had seen, but perhaps the most efficient. There didn't seem to be any wasted motions at all. It pained Julian to admit it, but Sailanson was phenomenal.

Sagramore continued to wield his weapon with ferocity, speed, and precision. And despite an apparent aim to end the battle quickly, the skilful handle of his partisan didn't seem to carry the slightest hint of desperation. The golden knight's supreme offense had the spectators in awe, and it reduced the legendary mercenary to simply dodging and blocking. The golden knight was taking full advantage of the partisan's superior range, dictating Sailanson's position.

Julian held a fist, feeling the sweat in his palms, excited and honoured to witness such strength on exhibition.

After another couple of swift jabs of his pole weapon, Sagramore succeeded in forcing Sailanson against a tight corner for an opportunity to end the battle. But rather than adding to his aggression, Sagramore instead pulled back at what appeared a critical moment, grunting upon his retreat.

Sailanson seemed to have smiled in response, but Julian couldn't be sure when he saw him suddenly leap up high into the air, starting a spinning motion from the jump. As he started falling back down, the man laid the sabre across his waist with the sharp end extended from the hips, his spinning motion picking up incredible momentum. Soon, Sailanson was enveloped in a violent maelstrom that threw out blasts of air at the spectators, briefly but forcefully robbing them off their vision. Sagramore stood his ground, aiming his partisan upwards and thrusting it relentlessly forward in response. The ensuing thunderous clash of mighty metals formed yet an even stronger explosion of whirlwinds, encapsulating the two men behind a barrier of wind, which further robbed the crowd of the pleasure of watching the fight.

Sparks of light swept through the tempest followed by the cacophony of clashing metal—all of it ending abruptly upon the sound of blade meeting flesh.

Silence followed. Everyone held their breath as they wondered what had ensued behind the chaotic winds. Julian exchanged a brief look with Schim and then turned back to the calming gust.

Moments later, when things cleared to the point where the two in battle were viewable again, a few gasps sounded from different directions. Julian grimaced, sharing the same thought that everyone else must have had: Has a victor emerged?

The answer wasn't obvious. Sagramore and Sailanson remained standing, both with their weapons extended out in front of them, but both also frozen and with their backs facing one another. Curiously, Sailanson was the one wounded, with his left hand pressed up against his abdomen from where blood was spilling out. At the same time, however, Sailanson seemed rather composed, with his sabre fully extended from his right arm. Sagramore, meanwhile, held onto his partisan, which was worn out with cuts all over it. He held it with both hands, pointed diagonally to the sky.

Sagramore groaned then, spinning around slowly, along with Sailanson.

"You are truly remarkable," Sagramore said, lowering his weapon. "Your bravery eclipses that of even the greatest men I have come to know."

Sailanson sighed, discarding the sabre altogether, dropping it to the ground with a rattle. "That was dangerous," he said, glancing down at his wound, which wasn't as deep as some members of the crowd would have hoped.

Julian glanced over to the emperor, who wore a grin.

"I wouldn't want to fight you again," Sailanson said.

"You're too modest," Sagramore responded. "To possess such abilities at your age and not be vain about it. And to think you would inflict damage unto yourself in order to avoid killing me. Why, Sailanson? Don't you understand that I wanted you dead?"

Sailanson shrugged. "I promised an important person that I would never kill again."

The golden knight groaned again. "You might not want to kill, but I don't need the dishonour of having to be spared. I asked for a battle to the death. Even if you didn't take my life, I couldn't bear to live with this humiliation."

"Nonsense!" Sailanson chided, his voice and tone strong with emotion. "What you do mean you couldn't bear to live? By saying that, you're insulting all of those who fight for their lives day in and day out, including those who have since lost the struggle. There is *nothing* more important than life." Sailanson paused to calm himself. "It was Deedee who showed me—your nephew. He was far wiser than you, who cannot even appreciate the value of life."

The golden knight widened his eyes, livid once more. "You dare lecture me on what it means to live?"

Julian watched the two men in quiet confusion, wondering what this was all about. He was sure that most of the crowd were similarly baffled. How was it that Sagramore had admitted defeat, when Sailanson was the one who had been wounded?

Sailanson shook his head, still regarding the veteran golden knight. "I cannot deny that I was at fault for Deedee's death," he said. "I still remember the incident that led to it, and the two soldiers who died as a result. Although

I was deceived into the debacle, I confess that those two didn't have to die, had I been more careful. But there is nothing I regret more than not being able to save Deedee. He was too kind for his own good. Perhaps he really wasn't suited to life as a soldier. I didn't understand at the time. There's no way to undo the past, but I strive to honour him by saving those that I can."

It was perhaps more than a tad surprising to hear such words from the man tagged as *the Judge*, allegedly responsible for slaughtering legions. But as Julian and surely many others wanted to believe that those were only ornamental words, it was difficult to simply dismiss the apparent honesty and frankness accompanied by the confession.

Sagramore hesitated briefly before sighing deeply.

"Sailanson, you really are something!" the golden knight said, his lips curling up into a rare grin. "I choose to believe you. A man with such integrity wouldn't be the one responsible for what happened at the Noel Gate. I no longer have any grounds on which to avenge my nephew—not only because I cannot defeat you, but because I now understand the value of his death. I've heard a few stories about you and your thieving crew—about all the good deeds, that is. Allow me to believe that it was *him* who helped make you the legend you are today. For that, I'm sure he can rest well."

Sailanson smiled in return, though his apparent joy did not last.

"Sir Sagramore," Breunor called out, irate. "You can be best friends with Marvin Sailanson if you want. But the rest of us will not forget what happened!"

The military man then waved an arm, signalling his men to rush up from behind him. Sagramore said nothing just yet, eyeing Breunor's men as they moved to surround both him and Sailanson. Julian looked toward Schim again, but his liege simply shook his head, reluctant to be involved. The truth was that Sagramore might not need help, especially not from others when the golden knight's own men—knights of the Defence Army—had already stepped up in his defence, drawing their swords against Breunor.

"Hold it there, good men of Trubannis," a new voice said.

Heads turned toward where Forredan stepped out of the crowd. "We only want Marvin Sailanson," the stout statesman said, clicking his men forward. "If you would kindly step aside, Sir Sagramore... for we do not wish to hurt you."

"I'd like to see you try," Sagramore dared. "I want to see—"

"No, Sir Sagramore," Sailanson cut in, holding out a hand. "This is my fight. I don't need anyone to interfere. In case you're worried for me, let me assure you: they won't manage a scratch on me."

Sagramore grinned back, perhaps admitting that was probably the case. The men holding their weapons against Sailanson, however, were incensed—and rightfully so.

Fool, Julian thought. *Against almost fifty men, you'd be smothered, no matter how strong you think you are.*

And whether or not it was Sailanson who was responsible for what had happened in Noel, the man might earn himself a new crime next to his name after this evening. The supposed oath of never killing another person would surely be broken, and perhaps that was what was needed to expose Sailanson's hypocrisy, spurring everyone else on to turn against him.

A deafening clap sounded then, causing Julian and more than several others to jump in surprise. Heads turned to Spartamon this time, the emperor still seated and maintaining his calm demeanour. Next to the emperor was the other former mercenary, Rover Watts, bumping his gauntlets to emit a second thunderous clap. Watts treaded forward, shoving his way past the ring of men formed around Sailanson and Sagramore, joining the two in formation.

"Lord Breunor and Lord Forredan," the emperor said, finally standing. "Will you continue to allow lies to cloud your judgement, when even Sir Sagramore has come to see Marvin as a man of integrity? I do not wish to see dissent among my men."

Julian smirked. *Was that a confession of his collusion?*

"Forgive me, My Lord," Breunor said with a slight bow, "but I'm not convinced. The truth is that I can't think of anyone else who could have possibly slaughtered all of those men in Noel. Sailanson is the only one capable of it. We *must* avenge our fallen brothers!"

"A stubborn one, I see," Spartamon said, closing his eyes briefly. "Well, Lord Breunor, you are a knight of the highest rank. If you claim to be doing this in the name of justice, then I ask that you offer the evidence to prove that Marvin was responsible. If you insist on a duel now, then fight a fair battle. One against one. Marvin is already injured from the previous exchange. In your position, I need you to uphold the gallantry and chivalry expected of our greatest knights."

"My Lord," Forredan inserted, bowing with an uncharacteristic scowl. "This fight has nothing to do with a knight's honour. It means nothing to us that Marvin Sailanson is injured, because it is not a competition to see who is the better warrior, but a vendetta in which we want him dead! We are here to kill him to honour our dead comrades. *That* is justice!"

"A vendetta to kill me...," Sailanson said, nodding with a smirk. "Zorlia is always so welcoming."

Julian glanced over toward Schim, Winter, and Ebenezer. None of them had said anything yet, and it didn't look like they were about to. If a violent brawl was to break out now, the ultimate beneficiary was surely Schim and the Pristines.

Julian looked up again at Sailanson and Watts, and then to Breunor and Forredan. An idea came to his mind then—one that would break the current stalemate, and one that would rid the Pristines of at least one prime enemy.

The letter, Julian thought.

He slipped a hand beneath the hanging cravat, for once not reaching for a sword. At his fingertips was the suety sheepskin of the parchment.

As Julian hesitated, Sailanson and Watts suddenly darted forward, snatching Forredan by his chunky arms and leaping up high at the crowd almost like a tidal wave, but springing over the sea of men rather than crashing into them. The statesman's men turned immediately at the alert, realising that the former mercenaries were attempting escape, but the chase ended before it began as the large mass of Forredan's body was hurled back to the crowd like a giant weight crashing down. Forredan's cry of horror seemed to prod his most able vassal, Claude Lucan, into expertly sweeping open some space in which to catch the plump man. Forredan panted heavily as his men attended to him, shocked to have been handled in such a way.

Sailanson and Watts, meanwhile, had disappeared off into the dark. They had managed to leave as easily as they had come.

Julian noted that Schim was snorting softly, and he understood exactly why Schim was upset about Sailanson's escape. But as Julian looked to Breunor then, who was furious upon seeing Sailanson and Watts flee, he became convinced that the incident detailed in the letter he had in his possession was true.

We intercepted the distress call, the letter read. *We wanted glory, fame, recognition—everything that Marvin Sailanson was getting. In retrospect, he might have done it. He might have saved Nine Arms, had we not interfered. Those men, more than a thousand of them, are our responsibility, your responsibility. They asked for help, and we let them die.*

"Isn't that Sir Lachman?" someone asked.

Julian looked up. Lachman was trotting in on a mount, and so too was Nine Arms. Not too far behind them were the Raiders—Raphael, Raven, and Roth. They had managed to make it to the gathering after all.

And just at the right time, too. Nine Arms's presence was critical for what was coming next.

THIRTY-FOUR

Truce

Julian met Raphael's gaze as the veteran trotted in on a dark stallion that looked like it had been worked hard for some time. Raven and Roth's horses were similarly fatigued, as were the horses checked by Lachman and Nine Arms.

Julian wondered what they would make of the current scene in which some of the most established members of the Empire were visibly at odds and in disarray—Morlan distressed, Breunor irate, and Forredan shocked to his core. To add to that, Sagramore's partisan was riddled with cuts and dents.

Julian was sure that Raphael was already deducing something about the scene before them, but it was doubtful that the veteran would be able to guess correctly about what was happening. At the same time, Julian wondered what had happened in Carrington, and whether the Raiders had managed to at least catch a glimpse of the sorcerer known as Dice.

"We apologise for our late arrival," Lachman said as he hopped off his warhorse.

Nine Arms thumped down to the ground immediately after the golden knight, his wider frame and signature flail that swayed left and right always a daunting sight. They nodded at Morlan, the host, before trotting off toward Spartamon, bowing to him before stepping behind him. Curiously, the emperor looked as though he had not expected them there.

"My Lord," Morlan said, addressing Spartamon. "If I may, please allow me to speak for my guests when I say that I do not believe many of us enjoyed the antics you have arranged for us this evening."

The emperor glanced over his shoulder, exchanging a look with Nine Arms. "I'm not one for antics, Lord Morlan," Spartamon responded, turning back to face the host and still wearing a grin. "The only thing I arranged for was the capture of the outlaws, the nine men injured inside your manor, now guarded by your men."

"But did it have to be Marvin Sailanson?" Morlan challenged.

Nine Arms jerked forward there, saying nothing, but wearing an expression of exasperation. The emperor simply held out a hand to curb the dangerous man's impulses.

Morlan shook his head in pity. "I wish to believe that Sailanson is not as evil as some of the rumours suggest," the host then said. "But we need to settle the matter with him here—in person. If you could summon him, My Lord, I ask you to summon him to court, as soon as we are next to meet. If your intention is to vindicate him of the crimes he is accused of, then we must do this the right way. You might not have liked it, but the other lords were hostile just now for good reason. Lord Breunor is convinced that..."

Julian kept his eyes on Nine Arms, watching the man grow more and more impatient as Morlan spoke. Breunor also looked more and more timid.

It's time, I suppose, Julian decided, finally stepping forward.

"It's a shame you missed him," Julian said, regarding Nine Arms, who shot a frown over in his direction. "It's also a shame that Marvin Sailanson would miss this."

"What are you talking about?" Nine Arms asked.

Upon realising that all eyes had fallen on him, Julian actually felt a heat surging up on his back, reaching his neck and tingling him with a burning sensation. It was suddenly harder and harder to breathe. And it wasn't only the people in front of him mounting on the pressure, but also the people behind him, which included the Lord Chancellor, who was probably furious that Julian had chosen to meddle in something that even Schim himself elected to avoid.

Julian inhaled deeply in order to ensure that everyone would hear him. "I understand that Central Farella still haunts you," Julian said aloud, his gaze still firmly held on Nine Arms. "I understand that you want vengeance, and that you want Marvin Sailanson to pay."

"And...?!" Nine Arms demanded with a grunt, growing increasingly restless.

"But Marvin Sailanson isn't the one responsible," Julian said. "Yes, you heard correctly. I have learned the truth. The one to pay is someone else. And this person is—"

"Sailanson is the traitor!" Breunor inserted, showing more urgency than he ever had. "Look, Pylon," he continued, regarding Nine Arms, "I promised to hunt Sailanson down for you. He was here earlier. I'm sure he's still around. We'll just have to—"

"Have to what?" Julian cut in with a sneer. "Why are you so insistent on killing Sailanson? Is it to cover up your mistake, the one that led to the Carnage of Central Farella?!"

The accusation stunned the crowd to silence. Breunor peered about at the reaction as his face reddened intensely.

"What nonsense are you speaking about now?!" the military man roared. "You were still wetting your pants when I fought for our country's future! How dare you come out and accuse me of such indecency! There is no *truth* to what you say! It was Sailanson and his apathy for his comrades that—"

"Be silent!" Nine Arms lambasted, with a tone so stern that Breunor jumped in fright. "Let him speak. I will judge for myself whether to believe what he says." Nine Arms swung his gaze back to Julian. "Now speak!"

Julian swallowed, growing ever so tense. He knew that he was potentially holding a piece of information that would shake the foundations of what even the most important men in the country believed to be true. But as he peered about then, he truly realised the gravity of what he was about to say. The scholars, the templars, the knights, and even the Lord Chancellor and the Lord Emperor were all glaring at him, waiting, eager with the anticipation of what could be a revelation to them. Julian cleared his throat, still peering about until he picked out the giant frame of the Golden Titan from the crowd.

"Sir Bors," Julian said, calling out the golden knight. "I ask you to clarify the details when I finish."

Bors squinted as sweat amassed on his forehead. The giant warrior was Breunor's most trusted vassal, and if anyone shared Breunor's secret, it was him.

"Allow me to start with some context," Julian began, careful of every word he spoke. "At the time, Victor Breunor and the Golden Dragon Knights Army were stationed in North-western Farella, Nine Arms in Central Farella, and Marvin Sailanson in Eastern Farella. The Golden Dragon Knights were immobile, ordered to stand their ground against the Imperial Lithia Dominion, who had since surrendered. The Vinans never turned back, but as we knew, Sailanson and his army from the east were the only people Nine Arms could call upon for support. Whether Sailanson *would have* helped is debateable, but Sailanson never received the plea, because the message was *intercepted* by Victor Breunor!"

Murmurs grew then among the crowd. And while none of their words were audible, the rising sibilance riled more than a few, particularly Breunor.

"Lord Breunor never left our camp in North-western Farella," Sagramore claimed, surprisingly speaking up for his nemesis. "I was with him, and I'm sure of it. There is no way he could have intercepted a message between Central and Eastern Farella."

Julian shook his head. "Breunor didn't personally intercept the message," he said. "He simply sent someone else."

Julian reached beneath his hanging cravat for the sheepskin parchment. It was this letter—the one written by a retired knight and addressed to Breunor—that had prompted Julian to investigate the matter. The *context* he had begun with just now was what he had managed to learn in the past couple weeks.

"The evidence you want is here," Julian said as he flapped out the letter. "This is a letter penned by Sir Russell, a silver knight from the war. According to this, Breunor wasn't content with his limited role in the war. He wanted more, at a time when other armies were collecting glory on the southern front."

Breunor had held in his temper impressively well until now, and for a longer duration than Julian expected. But the military man held his rage in no more. Following a low growl, Breunor snatched a sword from one of his men and drilled the weapon forward with full steam—and his target was none other than Julian.

Julian gritted his teeth, freezing in terror. A precipitous strike from a former golden knight wasn't something he could defend at that distance. Some arms were raised among the crowd, as if they could hold off the assault, yet more out of reflex than in genuine care for the victim. Either way, it was futile to stop Breunor's deadly charge.

Can't move!

Indeed, Julian *didn't* move—at least not on his own. Shoved aside from behind, Breunor's sword seared through only his noble dress. As he was falling to the ground, Julian looked up to see a figure with a wide frame crash forward toward Breunor, pummelling the military man to the ground.

Schim.

Breunor hopped to his feet again almost immediately, but Nine Arms thumped the man from behind, clawing onto his head and forcing him down onto the stone ground.

"Lord Breunor!" Schim chided, pointing his chin down at the military man. "Your impetuous actions serve as confession to your crimes!"

Breunor didn't answer, only continuing to rage like a wild beast, howling and thumping the ground in a futile attempt to free himself. Breunor was never going to outwrestle Nine Arms, though, who then ruthlessly crushed his head into the ground, not killing him but rendering him motionless. Breunor's men, who had held themselves back until then, jumped now toward Nine Arms. And while Morlan managed to block off a number of them, including Bors and Kite, the host could do nothing when a few of them slipped past him, and raced straight to their deaths at the flail of the man they dared challenge, ending up in pieces with blood exploding out in the air in gruesome rings.

Julian gasped as a splash of blood sprayed in his direction. The crowd gawked at the grisly sight, wondering what they had been invited to—a celebration, or a slaughter. Even Sagramore was visibly shocked by Nine Arms's monstrous strength and brutal methods. Some of the scholars and the templars shrieked in response to seeing the bloodied courtyard.

Julian wiped his hand on his cheek, where a speckle of blood had landed. He glanced down to his finger and trembled at the sight of the smudged scarlet. He had thought that he was prepared for bloodshed this evening, but the carnage just now was truly horrifying.

Nine Arms had dismantled three men, all of them knights, with a simple swing of the flail. And the man had done so without even having to lift his other hand, his giant prosthetic right hand that had kept Breunor's head planted into the smashed stone floor. And, despite the brutality of the slaughter, Nine Arms was actually acting within the laws of the Empire, which granted warriors the right of retaliation—even murder—when one's life was critically endangered.

"Come at me again, if you dare," Nine Arms said, eyeing Bors, who had just escaped death.

Nine Arms then turned to Julian with a snarl that sent a chill down Julian's spine. "Continue with you story," he demanded.

Julian urged himself to abide, but could hardly catch a breath, overwhelmed by the scene before him. How could anyone remember anything after witnessing something so horrific?

"I... I... think," Julian uttered.

Breunor jerked a hand up from the ground then. Perhaps it was a miracle that he was still alive, especially as his head was still planted into the stone ground, blood slowly leaking outward from every part of his body.

Nine Arms snorted and then released his claw, allowing Breunor to pick himself back up. Bruised and bloodied, Breunor's blocky face was almost unrecognisable, if not for his mutton chops, from which a thick red was oozing down. The military man lurched about, looking here and there until finally meeting the terrified gazes of Bors and Kite, who were stained with the blood of their comrades. Breunor shook his head, perhaps in pity or perhaps to shake off his daze. He looked up again then and finally found Julian's eyes.

"Say no more," Breunor said. "I beg of you. I give up. I confess."

Nine Arms hissed, almost as if he didn't want to believe it. And perhaps Breunor *could* have denied it, especially if he could have better hid his anxiety.

"The letter is genuine," Breunor confirmed. "Only a few know. Five... six, including Walford," he said as Bors nodded reluctantly. "Tell them."

Bors shook his head and then cleared his throat. "We more or less forced the other five to retire...," he began, visibly reluctant, "but still... we hunted them down. We had them killed... one by one. Sir Russell was the only one we couldn't find. He must have suspected our intention, for he never settled in any one place. And he is indeed the author of the parchment. I don't know how Reeling got a hold of it... and why he would pass it on to Longinus."

Bors paused there, eyeing Julian with disdain. "We did all of those things to hide our mistake and to protect our honour. But instead, we've fallen deeper down into this pit where we're haunted by the souls that died there."

Julian squinted, parts of him actually sympathetic to his long-time nemeses.

"If you had intercepted that message," Sagramore put in, turning back to Breunor, "why didn't you act on it? If this is about adding victories to your list of achievements, should you not have led us south?"

Breunor spared Sagramore no glance. "That *was* the plan," he said. "I didn't allow the message to be passed onto Marvin Sailanson because I didn't want to share the triumph. I had worked out strategies with my entourage and we were ready to move the army south... but hours before that, we had learned that the enemy troops totalled over twenty thousand. If we had engaged in battle, our army would have suffered total defeat. No one in their right frame of mind would lead their troops into that kind of hell. I wanted to slay the Kragans, but it was beyond me. And by that time, it was too late to pass the message onto Sailanson, who would have been able to do nothing more than I could. No one could have saved Nine Arms and his camp. Not even if I joined forces with Sailanson."

Sagramore shook his head in pity, as did many others. Breunor might not be particularly genial, but he had been lauded as a Truban hero for a long time—and for good reason. Being the first golden knight to defect from the Sargon Monarchy, Breunor was credited as the one who had managed to convince all the other golden knights to join him in their ultimate alliance with the Clan of Light, which had proved to be a critical turn for the country.

Julian swallowed, torn in ambivalence. He could hardly believe that he almost wanted to ask the others to excuse Breunor just this time. Considering what the proud man had done for the country, perhaps this mistake of his *wasn't* the most sinful of crimes. A low growl from Nine Arms now, though, immediately devoured all of his silly sentiments. Unfortunately, the one Breunor had let down was Nine Arms—the vengeful and truculent warrior who had no mercy for anyone who crossed him. Nine Arms was a vicious man, but he was also known for holding dear the men who followed him. And in that particular incident, not a single one of his men had survived.

Many people in the crowd naturally looked toward Spartamon then. The emperor was the only one who could possibly spare Breunor. As far as Julian knew, Nine Arms still listened to the emperor's commands.

What will he do? Julian wondered, surprised that he feared for Breunor. *To lose Breunor now would hurt his chances against us. But on the flip side, Sailanson and Nine Arms, two of his strongest soldiers, would be able to solve their differences.*

Spartamon closed his eyes then, possibly whispering a prayer for Breunor. It looked like the emperor had made a decision. When he snapped his eyes open again, Nine Arms was kneeling before him, his head inclined. Nine Arms was asking for only one thing, and without speaking a word, everyone knew what it was.

Breunor and his men recognised as much. And they, too, stared hopefully at the emperor, watching for the slightest change of expression. Julian had decided barely moments earlier that Breunor's demise was the best possible outcome for Schim, but that didn't stop his conscience from questioning his own morals of being the catalyst for it. He peered over to the emperor and saw that there was no need to read deep when the clearest of signs, a frown and a nod from Spartamon, signalled the end for the military man.

"Let it be done behind closed doors," the emperor said coldly.

Spartamon stood up then, pacing toward Morlan and sharing a quiet word with the host. The emperor then treaded away with his concubines as everyone else remained still, watching on until the emperor disappeared down the paved road and into the dark of the night.

Morlan took a deep breath. "The Lord Emperor has demanded for all guests to leave immediately," he announced. "Everyone is to evacuate... except Lord Pylon, Lord Breunor, and his retinue. The court shall run as normal tomorrow morning." Morlan paused there, regarding some of the more dignified men in the crowd. His pitiful expression seemed to tell them that he had tried his best on an evening that had ended up so incredibly wrong.

"Go," he said. "Please go, everyone."

Schim was the first to nod back. The chancellor then shot a grimace toward Julian before flapping the cape behind him as he treaded off with Winter and Ebenezer. The Raiders were prompt to follow, and Julian soon caught up from behind, too, but not without a last glance at the beginning of the would-be deadly face-off between Nine Arms and Breunor.

Everyone else began moving out into the night, regardless of whether they were knights, soldiers, scholars, templars, or noblemen. No one complained. If anything, most were likely glad to leave the evening behind.

* * *

Most of the crowd from the night before were present at the court the next morning. Julian was sure that sleep had evaded most of them, and that anyone who had managed any at all had only writhed in disturbing nightmares. Members of the St. Bernard Order and The Villa, who weren't usually summoned to the court, remained uninvited. But Sagramore—usually stationed in Bastion City—conjured no excuse to escape. He was asked to stand by here in Zorlia until at least the coming week.

Breunor and his men were nowhere to be seen, and of course they were most likely dead. The court seemed quiet and still without the raucous military man around. Julian suddenly felt that he missed Breunor who had always managed to poke his head into all matters of the court, forcing his opinions on others even when no one had wanted to hear them.

Spartamon had arrived only several minutes late this morning. While his arrival was much anticipated, it was who the emperor would arrive with that had the court members anxious. But as it turned out, neither Sailanson nor Watts were with him. More importantly, Nine Arms was nowhere to be seen, either. With only Lachman by his side, Spartamon wore a reserved smile that was unreadable.

Morlan and Forredan took care of the proceedings as the court ran without any reference or even any mention of the June Nineteenth Gathering. Schim sat quietly, too, reluctant to share his opinion on the few issues raised, which were trivial compared to what had transpired on the previous night.

The affair was brief. No one dared to say much. And the result was disturbingly inconclusive for all.

* * *

Court ran again three days later, on the twenty-third day of June. The same people attended, but everyone was more or less in a clearer frame of mind. There was still no word about Breunor, but Lachman announced on the emperor's behalf that Nine Arms had returned to Vondra Dawn, and that *the matter* had been concluded. The emperor, however, had excused Nine Arms from having to attend court until further notice.

Julian looked over to the empty seat that had been vacated by Breunor.

He's dead, Julian thought, narrowing his eyes. *And it was me who sent him to his grave.* He then looked down to his breastplate, sweeping a hand across the right as he remembered how Breunor had shredded through his noble garb that night.

He had kept that torn clothing tucked under his bed, and while he hadn't seen it since, he remembered exactly where it was ripped. It was as if it were a symbol of something—a mark Breunor had left on him.

But the rest of them don't seem to care anymore, he thought as he peered across the court. No one was keen to speak about the June Nineteenth Gathering. Even as Forredan was speaking at length now, nothing he said was related to that evening. Julian eyed Schim from behind and then laid his eyes on Spartamon. They both seemed to have moved on, too, seemingly more interested in the particular matter that was being discussed.

Perhaps it was meaningless to dwell on the past. The people of the court seemed to recognise that much. Even if Breunor were still living, the man would have no influence on the fierce political battle that was brewing. What Breunor had left behind, however, was the absolute or ancillary control over every army that belonged to the Truban Empire. With him gone, that power and influence he had held—albeit something that he had never really held with a steady hand—was up for grabs to anyone prepared to scavenge for it in an open tussle. That prize pool contained a total of fifteen armies, small and large, with different purposes and visions.

The armies, too, had to choose whom to offer their loyalty: the Advents, the Pristines, or someone else altogether. It was too early to say how things would fall in place, but the only thing certain among all the uncertainty was that the struggle between the Advents and the Pristines would see a brief intermission.

This was a time to win more favour, a time to expand one's individual influence. And while the emperor was likely already in contact with Sailanson, Schim had seemed rather unenthusiastic ever since the June Nineteenth Gathering. He had refused to see Julian, which Julian believed was on the basis of his self-assertion that ended the gathering prematurely and in uncertainty. Julian would readily admit that he hadn't considered the full extent of the consequences. But, if anything, this early result was working out for the Pristines' benefit. For if there was anything the Pristines needed, it was time with which to gather more firepower.

Stranger yet was the fact that Schim had also refused to see the Raiders. The only person the chancellor had consulted was Ebenezer.

And now, as the court was dismissed, Schim was quick to disappear again. Unable to catch him, Julian instead kept his eye on the Raiders. But upon his approach, only Raphael deigned to entertain him.

"What do you want?" Raphael asked.

"Tell me," Julian said. "What is the Lord Chancellor thinking? What has happened is good, right?"

Raphael sighed deeply. "I agree that it was the best possible outcome," he said. "I can only suspect that it is Marvin Sailanson the Lord Chancellor is concerned about."

"Well, Rover Watts, too," Julian added. "But still, they're only two people. Breunor had an army—in fact, he had fifteen armies."

Raphael turned, hesitating. "Sailanson is... incredible," he finally said, trembling slightly. "He is the strongest man I have ever known... unlike anything you've seen. He really is a monster. I don't know if he killed those men at Noel Gate, but remember that there were two hundred men there—*two hundred*. It's no fable. He could have done it. He's an army of one—and one that nobody would want to be on the wrong end of."

"Even so...," Julian said in denial, unable to agree but also unable to conjure up any structured response to explain his scepticism.

"Listen, Longinus," Raphael said, shaking his head. "If both Sailanson and Watts are indeed offering their loyalty to the emperor again, the Pristines are doomed."

THIRTY-FIVE

A new direction

Julian stepped out of Vondra Dawn, dazed and disoriented. While the morning bustle of Zorlia was a familiar sight, Julian found himself in an unfamiliar situation in which there were no tasks assigned to him.

How long would this truce last? And what was he supposed to do when Schim wouldn't see him?

That phantom Julian thought, holding his head. *Just who is he?*

In retrospect, it was as if everything that had happened had been the design of that one man. If it wasn't for the parchment, things might be drastically different from how they were now. Breunor had said that he didn't know how Reeling got a hold of it. Did that mean that the phantom soldier was an ally of the Lord Count? Or was he his murderer?

Julian paused in his tracks and lifted his head to the sky, ignoring the sea of bodies streaming past him on the street. He watched the wisps of clouds float by and almost prayed for some guidance from the Immortal. Almost lost to his reverie, he then felt someone bump into him. He shook his head and looked forward, noting the rear of a figure, donning an olive-coloured robe, shuffling through the herd.

Julian sighed softly, and his instincts had him reach down to his pocket watch. He then cursed under his breath, noting that the timepiece was missing from his belt. He gawked at the shuffling civilians, struggling to digest the fact that he had been victimised by something as petty as theft.

Julian held a tight fist and treaded forward, looking for the culprit as he squirmed his way through the narrow streets. And there he was some distance away, the thief in the olive robe, still shuffling through the crowd. Julian tried to dash ahead after slipping through another group of people, only for a heavy beast to trample in his way, the mare and its driver drawing forward a sizeable wagon that carried something that smelled like barley. Julian hissed and then skimmed along the tough linen of the wagon's drapes. When he finally passed through, Julian squinted hard and noted to his relief that the thief was still in sight. Even so, it would be a challenge to get to him.

And indeed, at every chance when the path seemed to clear for Julian, someone or something emerged to get in the way. With the deluge of underpasses, overpasses, and alleyways of Zorlia at midday, Julian was unable to call on his otherwise superhuman speeds or even spurts of it, which would inevitably draw unwanted attention. The further Julian chased, the more his intuition told him that he was being lured into something treacherous. After all, not many people would choose to thieve a knight in silver armour. But just before he convinced himself to let it go, the chase was suddenly over.

Julian had been baited into a square, a perilous open area fenced in from every side by sizeable worn-down buildings, and blanketed from above with shade sails. It was a place dubbed the Felon Square—a place where crooks gathered. Naturally, there were far fewer people here than the average city street. Julian had known this shack well during his time as a patrol soldier. In fact, he had made himself a number of enemies here. Although these foes were small and humble compared to his usual enemies of late, they were still a handful upon congregation. The Raiders had once mentioned that the square was indeed regulated *by* the Empire, and more specifically that it was under the direction of the Advents.

Could Marvin Sailanson be here? Julian wondered as a bead of sweat slid down from his forehead, running over his nose.

He turned away on the thought, prepared to give up his pocket watch to the theft. It was apparent to him then that the thief had known who he was. The pocket watch was the most obvious mark of his Silver Knight rank, more so than his custom-made armour. He *had* been lured to the square just as his instincts had warned him. And as he tried to turn away then, a group of men in mantles—complete with dangling hoods—pressed into him, blocking his path and surrounding him.

"Roland," one of them addressed him with a scornful laugh, lifting his hood slightly. The face was familiar, but Julian couldn't match it to a name. "No, I should be calling you Sir Longinus."

Another man plucked a dagger from beneath his sleeves. "You're not thinking of leaving so soon, are you? After being away for so long?"

"I don't have time for this," Julian said, reaching for his sword. "Let me leave, and I'll let you live."

Julian regretted his words immediately, however, realising that he was only provoking the crooks, which was exactly what he wanted to avoid doing. He scowled, moving his hand away from the hilt of his weapon, instead lifting an arm to light a clawed hand with a red flame.

"Remarkable," said the one who had been the first to speak, flipping back his hood altogether to reveal his face—which was rather generic. "If you had held such power back then, there might not have been any rivalry between us."

Julian cocked his head slightly, thinking the face a little familiar but unable to associate it with any name. He noted from the men's expressions that they seemed more impressed than frightened. Indeed, their eyes glistened—seemingly marvelling at his powers—as they lowered their weapons.

"Just wanted to see if you still had it in you," the same man said with a grin.

Julian said nothing, maintaining his gaze on the apparent leader.

The man rolled his eyes. "You don't even remember my name, do you?" he said, shaking his head. "Times have changed, I guess. It's Buckley. Remember it."

"I'll try," Julian finally said, shaking his arm to quell the fire, dropping his guard slightly. The name actually sounded familiar now upon articulation, but Julian still had trouble remembering any kind of rivalry with the man.

"There's someone who wants to see you," Buckley said with a snort. "Come."

Julian hesitated for just a moment, but then proceeded to follow Buckley and the other men inside one of the buildings—a tavern, it turned out to be, reeking of liquor. The lodge itself was much darker than the already shaded square outside had been. It was as if the outlaws were trying to make it obvious that this was the central base of the crime syndicate.

Julian peered warily across the dimmed interior, still unable to give up his suspicion that he had been lured into a trap. The tightly packed tables were almost empty of patrons, and those few people there didn't seem to care for the group that Julian had stepped in with. Buckley gestured Julian toward the bar area at the far corner where three people sat reticently on stools, each grasping a metal mug, one of them now downing a mouthful of the beverage. They donned long, hooded robes that failed to conceal their rather petite figures. The thief in the olive-coloured robe was one of them, sitting at the left-most stool. He had broader shoulders than the other two, but was almost delicate compared to most knights that Julian knew.

But if there was anything that Julian had learned in the recent past, it was never to judge someone based on appearances alone. The mute, diminutive sorcerer was a prime example of the fact that appearances could be deceiving.

Julian stepped forward, sensing no grace in any of the men present. But he reminded himself not to make premature assumptions, remembering that Ebenezer had said that seasoned sorcerers had the ability to conceal grace. In fact, Julian was curiously hopeful that at least one of them *was* a sorcerer. The stranger on the right-most stool was holding Julian's pocket watch and fiddling with it, perhaps impressed by its craftsmanship. Then, the stranger suddenly snapped the timing device closed.

"It's been a while, Julian," he said with an eerily familiar voice. Julian gaped as he finally recognised the man before him.

"It's really you...," Julian muttered as Alpheus spun around wearing a smile that whiffed out a distinct air of grace. "You're back," Julian said, barely able to enunciate the words properly as he stepped toward the scholar.

"It's good to be back," Alpheus said, his smile growing, though still wearing his hood.

Julian reached forward and held the young scholar by the shoulders. "You look good," he said with a grin, patting him hard, and noting that Alpheus looked more mature now that he was without his spectacles. "And you've bulked up a little."

"Well, I've had a few adventures out there," he said with a wry smile.

Julian was sure that Alpheus had indeed experienced more than a few hardships during these past few months, and he felt for him despite not yet knowing what exactly those experiences might entail. More than a few questions were already forming inside his head now as joy swept over him. Amid all the drama that had happened recently, there was finally a reason for him to smile again.

Julian leaned against the bar, ready to ask his old friend all about his time away from Zorlia. But as soon as he was about to speak, the other two sitting on the stools turned to them. One of them was a young woman, Julian noted, whose blue eyes and the hint of pale hair tucked under her hood showed that she was from Vinawell. The other person, in the olive robe, was the man who had thieved him.

"Azure," Alpheus said softly in introduction, gesturing at the foreign woman. "And, Joe Hendron," he added, referring to the thief.

"He's the one you were talking about?" Azure said, regarding Julian from the bottom up. "Can he really be relied upon?"

Julian sniggered quietly. "Before we start...," he said, glancing out at the crooks spread out across the tavern. "Why here?" he then asked in a whisper, turning back to Alpheus. "You're still a convicted felon—the reward for turning you in is as handsome as it ever was."

Alpheus opened his mouth to answer, but Hendron spoke first.

"And *that*... is why we're here," Hendron said, his words carrying more than a hint of disdain. "This place is *known* to be a gathering point for outlaws. One wouldn't expect big fish like Alpheus to loiter around."

Julian winced slightly, confused by the bitterness as well as the naïve assumption.

"It's safe here," Alpheus said. "The people here used to work with the Lord Emperor. But apparently the emperor has since turned to using sorcerers for hire instead. Anyway, most of these men here are men of honour, despite their profession. My investigations tell me that they owe Jeffery—the Lord Count—some favours. Helping me now is returning that very favour."

Julian raised a cynical eyebrow.

"Trust my judgement," Alpheus insisted. "We don't have time to concern ourselves over something trivial. The troubles of the court should be our only focus. And we need to act quickly."

"And you think no one shares your urgency?" Julian said, suddenly annoyed.

Alpheus paused, downing a mouthful of his drink.

"Some do," he said. "But they have no solution to suggest, and that's the problem. I hear the whispers, too. Some of it is nonsense, designed only to spread fear. But there's also a lot in there that we can learn from."

"I don't hear anything," Julian confessed. "But... those whispers... is that where you're basing your knowledge of what has changed?"

"Some of it, yes. But we need to prioritise. Of all those messages preaching the onset of doom, there's nothing more real than the threat from the south. The march of the Kragans is sure to happen."

"Kraga is definitely a problem," Julian began. "But—"

"There is no *but*," Alpheus interrupted, his patience tested. "Kraga have had nine years to prepare. This peaceful era we're blessed with is but a gift from them." He paused for a moment. "And this gift... was part of their plan. They have bet on us to rebuild the country because it would be a greater reward for them... *when they conquer us*. And they've bet on the Empire to grow weak, they've predicted that we would fight amongst ourselves—which we have. Given what has happened here, I have good reason to believe that there is indeed a mole in the court—someone who has sworn loyalty to the

Kragan king."

He's changed, Julian thought, squinting slightly as he regarded his old friend. *He speaks as if I should just nod along.*

"Where did you learn all of this?" Julian asked, his voice sceptical.

"I have my sources," Alpheus claimed. "Without going into further details, I want you to think about it. How did the Empire arrive to this current conundrum? How did the emperor allow things to be steered to this current stalemate? Was it really only a falling out between him and the Lord Chancellor? I'd say no. It was by design... all under the direction of Syon Wandalvic, the king of Kraga."

Julian suppressed an impulse to debate those assumptions, instead remaining silent. "How much do you know about the current situation?" he asked. "About the court, I mean."

"Enough for me to act on," Alpheus said. "For one, I know about your promotion to Silver Knight."

Julian smirked. "That's it?"

"And I know that you've become the Lord Chancellor's second in command," Alpheus added. "More recently...," he continued, "a few days ago in fact... Victor Breunor fell at the hands of the man they call Nine Arms."

Julian twitched a brow, but otherwise tried his best not to demonstrate his surprise.

"I have kept up with the times," Alpheus continued, "but for *this* to work, we will need your help."

"For *what* to work?"

"We have a plan," Azure said, finally adding her voice into the mix again. "A plan to end the chaos and to set this country anew."

"Let's hear it," Julian said, opening his hands wide.

Azure shook her head. "First, you'll have to convince us that you are deserving of the information."

Julian looked to Alpheus, who simply shrugged.

"It's her plan, more so than mine," said Alpheus.

"We hold nothing against you," Hendron inserted, finally handing the pocket watch back to Julian then. "But this is a grave matter. We need to know that you're someone we can trust and rely upon completely. I mean no offence, but it was a little too easy to lure you here."

Julian puffed out a long breath, and then nodded. "That's fair," he said, receiving his pocket watch. "I've had to prove my ability many times over in the past. I never thought I would have to prove it to Alpheus, though."

"We need you to arrange for Alpheus to see Yeremia Schim," Azure said without further preamble. "We know that Ebenezer is with your chancellor. We need them to help Alpheus clear his criminal status. That is the first step of the plan, and a critical one."

Julian grimaced, putting a hand to his chin. "I could try, but don't count on it. I haven't spoken to the chancellor for some time." He paused. "Ever since my recklessness changed the complexion of things," he added.

Alpheus lifted a brow. "It certainly wasn't good to see Breunor fall," he said. "Breunor's absence only serves to protract the political war. From the chancellor's perspective, however, if he's focused on defeating the emperor, Breunor's demise can only be beneficial. It would buy him plenty of time to reassemble."

Julian made no further comment, wary not to say too much in this company. It also appeared to him that Alpheus wanted the emperor and the Advents to come through, rather than the Pristines.

Or maybe, Julian thought, *he just wants this to end so that the Empire can focus on external forces. Either way, if he cannot swear loyalty to the Pristines, I doubt the chancellor would spare any time to entertain him.*

"I'll do what I can," Julian finally said.

THIRTY-SIX

A promise to end it all

Alpheus peered out from under the hood that almost hid his eyes. No one was going to recognise him in this long, dull brown robe, the most ordinary clothing that a commoner could wear. He hadn't been wearing his glasses since crossing the border from Vinawell back into Trubannis, but he had them tucked under his sleeves in case he needed them.

It was strange to be treading on these streets again—the narrow, bustling streets of Zorlia, where one's path was never clear. And it was even stranger to be away from Azure, who would remain in Felon Square at least until his name was cleared. Alpheus hadn't forgotten his promise to show her the city. And while this certainly wasn't the time for tours—or love affairs, for that matter—Alpheus couldn't shake off the fact that the person treading alongside him now was no longer the vivacious Azure. After spending every day with the always witty lady for the past two months, experiencing with her the delights and grievances of life and death, it was naturally disorienting that she wasn't with him now. But this was part of the plan that they had conjured up together.

Hendron didn't know as much about it, though. The hunter had agreed to help, but on the condition that he wouldn't have to deal with the authorities, and that he would remain always in the shadows. Alpheus respected that wish. He believed Hendron to be a good person, but he had had to battle some inner debates before entrusting the man to ensure Azure's safety. Sometimes Alpheus wasn't even sure whether he had been a fool to have brought Azure to Zorlia in the first place, a city he himself no longer knew.

"It'll be all right," Julian said, pacing alongside him. "The chancellor is a reasonable man. If he happens to turn on you, I'll defend you with my life." Julian paused with a cough. "She asked me to promise her that."

Alpheus peered to his right, meeting Julian's eyes briefly.

"I can't say that I know too much about it," Julian continued, looking straight ahead. "But the lass is loyal to you. I can see that much. She came up to me when you were speaking with that hunter. I thought she was going to patronise me, but instead she came up to say that you are my friend—as if to remind me."

"We share a special bond," Alpheus said.

"A special bond...," Julian repeated musingly. "Did you share the same thing with Kathryn Trulips? What is with you and foreign women?"

Alpheus smiled, but said nothing. Trulips had been special to him since their first meeting. Indeed, Alpheus had updated himself with Trulips's news since returning to the country, learning that she had since become a templar known as Kyriel, aligned with the Church of which he had once been an avid follower. As Alpheus thought back, he noted that he had let Trulips down with his ideals, which she had made him realise were noble but foolish when he didn't have the means to carry them out. Alpheus had thought that his interest in her was only because she was from Aizary, when in fact he had also been captivated by her rare beauty. Despite his time away from Zorlia, and all the things that had kept him occupied, the Aizar scholar had never drifted too far from his mind.

And this was a personal conundrum indeed. Trulips had flashed into his mind on occasions when Azure was by his side. And each time that had happened, Alpheus was stung with guilt and shame. His childhood friend, Agnes Gardner, was another female companion who tended to float into mind every once in a while. More than guilt and shame, however, Alpheus was agonised every time he remembered that Agnes had lost her vision because of him. He had promised himself that one day he would take Agnes to see Pelanofzky to try for a cure.

"We're here," Julian said, stopping short.

Alpheus glanced out from under his lowered hood at the magnificent structure that was Vondra Dawn, the cluster of steeples shooting right up into the sky. His eyes naturally wandered over to the Western Tower that had formerly been occupied by Reeling, which somehow seemed taller than he remembered.

"Sir Longinus," the guards greeted with a bow.

Julian nodded at them. "This is a performer," he said, gesturing behind himself at Alpheus. "The Lord Chancellor summoned him."

The guards welcomed them inside without question, showing no suspicion of Alpheus despite him never lowering his hood. Julian led the way into the stately halls that were always dulled to a gloomy grey. Alpheus hadn't paid much heed to it in the past, but now, after his visit of Radiance's Nest, he realised how little natural light shone through into the halls of Vondra Dawn. He figured that the miserly windows were part of the reason. It was daytime now, but Alpheus could remember just how dark it had been in the evenings with such sparsely installed lanterns. It all felt rather foreign to him now.

It was minutes later before they finally arrived at a grand double door—supposedly the Lord Chancellor's chambers. The servant standing on guard recognised Julian, but appeared reluctant to welcome him through.

"Let the Lord Chancellor know I'm here," Julian said.

"Sir Longinus," the servant said with a raised brow. "This isn't a good time."

"Just pass on the message," Julian demanded.

The servant regarded him for a moment. "All right," he said, reaching for the key hanging from his belt. He spun to the door, inserted the key, and turned it with a clonking sound. He then pushed gently on the door.

"Wait here," he said.

Alpheus glanced at Julian, noting some timidity in his eyes.

So it's true that Julian's fallen out of favour, he thought, wincing then. *Can't afford wasting time*, he decided, dashing forward and twisting his way past the servant before slipping inside through the narrow opening of the double door. The servant opened his mouth in shock, but he was then shoved aside by Julian, who swung the door open wide.

Alpheus gaped at the scene before him. The chamber was an almost exact replication of the court, complete with a throne on the far end—occupied at this moment by the mighty Lord Chancellor. Standing just beneath the elevated platform exclusive to Schim was Ebenezer, who in this context looked friendlier than Alpheus remembered. Kneeling before Schim, meanwhile, were a host of men that included Golden Knight Walford Bors, together with a sizeable group of knights, totalling over thirty men.

Victor Breunor's men, Alpheus assumed.

Judging from his widened eyes, Julian was shocked, though still aware of himself enough to step in front of Alpheus. Schim had perked up, and the others spun around, snapping their eyes wide open and glaring at Julian with outright vehemence.

Julian cowered slightly, only easing up a little when Schim held up an arm.

Bors spun back angrily to Schim. "What is the meaning of this, Lord Chancellor?! I thought you said you were going to *take care* of Julian Longinus.

He might not be Lord Breunor's killer, but if it wasn't for him, none of this would have happened!"

Schim shook his head with a groan. "I didn't summon him," he said. "I haven't seen Sir Longinus since that day, and I have no plan to share this with him."

"And you expect us to just take your word for it?" Bors grumbled. "If you want us to side with you, I ask you to first kill Longinus!"

Most of the knights passionately agreed with Bors, throwing fists in the air in their strident protest. It appeared to Alpheus that Bors had replaced Breunor as the leader of these men.

Schim groaned again, regarding Julian with a scowl. When the man's eyes peered over at him, Alpheus flapped away his hood and robe in a sensational introduction that won more than a few gasps. Beneath the dull mantle was indeed a refined noble garb of the Vinan style, a dress shirt of pearl pigmentation, fluffy at the various joints of the body and with an elegant ruff at the neck. Alpheus was without his glasses, but no one failed to match his face to the criminal portraits posted ubiquitously across the country.

"Forgive my intrusion," Alpheus said, "but I have urgent matters to address."

Alpheus met Ebenezer's eyes. It was subtle, but Ebenezer's half wink suggested that it was as if the man had expected him. Schim was stunned for a moment, as were Bors and the other knights. Despite the Empire's supposed desperate hunt for Alpheus, alleged as the one to have murdered the Lord Count, Alpheus noted instead that he had become something of an afterthought to the men there.

"This is almost too good to be true," Alpheus said, regarding the men. "I thought that I'd have to convince the Lord Chancellor to seek out Lord Breunor's men, but here you all are."

Schim glanced over at Julian. "What exactly is this about?"

Alpheus held out a hand. "Allow me to answer for myself," he said with a bow. "I'm here to offer my services to you, Lord Chancellor." He paused for a moment. "I have the means to dethrone Kasimir de Spartamon."

The boastful claim was met with raised eyebrows and sneers, but Schim revealed no expression just yet.

"All I ask for in return is my freedom," Alpheus went on, noting that even Julian shot him a look of disapproval. "I demand exoneration. I ask you, Lord Chancellor—with the help of Lord Ebenezer—to clear my name. When that's done, I'll help you eradicate the Advents. It is my pledge that within fourteen days, you, Lord Chancellor, shall be the new leader of the Truban Empire."

Schim glared down at him in response and then leaned forward slowly. "Fourteen days?" he asked.

"It will likely be sooner."

"And why should I trust you? Why should I trust you have a plan that would work?"

Alpheus smiled. "Because I'm Jeffery Reeling's successor. And also because you have no one else to turn to."

Schim seemed unmoved as he sat back. "I consider the Lord Count very special," he said. "He was a unique talent. And you seem to have inherited a few things from him... not least of all his self-importance." He paused with a sudden scowl. "But my answer is *no*. You're just a dog without a bone. I don't care whether you're innocent or not. I have no time to deal with you—not four months ago, and surely not now."

The chamber fell silent. Alpheus did his best to remain calm, conscious that Julian, Bors, and the other men were all watching, perhaps thinking him naïve and callow. Rather than brood over it, however, Alpheus's grin deepened instead.

"I can see why people liken politics to a battlefield," Alpheus said. "But I *do* need your help. And, to convince you, I'll offer the people here an incentive... something that has to do with the one they call Nine Arms."

Bors perked up along with several others, but Schim raised a hand again. "Intrigue me," Schim said.

"There is no chance for Nine Arms to turn against the emperor, but there is every chance for him to compromise—or at least to delay his duties in order to settle personal matters. He didn't care for the emperor's alliance with Lord Breunor when he learned that it was Breunor who had been responsible for setting his men on course to their demise. Loyal but fiery, Nine Arms can be lured out from the emperor's range, which will then allow us to ambush him."

"You make it sound simple," Schim remarked. "I hope you have more than just a theory."

Alpheus smiled again as he regarded Breunor's men. "I do," he said. "Allow me to tell the story of my escape from prison four months ago. While I assume it has become common knowledge that Nine Arms assumed the role of a prison warden there, and that he was indeed there that evening, I'd venture a guess that you people don't know how things transpired."

Bors growled. "What does this have to do with anything?"

"Allow to me to finish," Alpheus said. "First of all, Julian was there."

Gazes darted to Julian then as he himself looked down at the ground.

"He went there to break me out," Alpheus clarified. "Julian crossed swords with Nine Arms and held on, for the most part. But it wasn't enough—*not even close.* And Julian would have been killed if not for the *phantom soldier*."

Julian tensed up, seemingly growing irritated upon the mention of the other man.

"The phantom soldier?" Schim asked with a frown.

"Yes, that's what I know him as," Alpheus said. "He dresses in black, and wields a pair of rapiers."

Alpheus smiled slightly as he noted Bors and some of his men bracing themselves. Alpheus had learned that Bors had met the phantom soldier at least once, on the day that Slash had been killed. Based on the logic that the phantom soldier had come in to shield Julian that day, it was likely that Bors had assumed the mystery man to be Julian's ally.

"I don't know who he is," Alpheus dared to confess. "And I don't know where to find him, either. *But*... the one to hunt him down is Nine Arms. I'd bet he's itching to fight the phantom again. After all, he was outdone that evening when I escaped the prison... and that alone would see Nine Arms crave for the opportunity to settle the score."

"If this phantom soldier you speak of does indeed exist," Schim questioned, "how can we know that he'll fight for us?"

Alpheus shook his head. "He *won't* be fighting for us. He won't be on our side at all. In fact...," he said, turning to Bors with a brief pause, "he's as much of an enemy as Nine Arms. That parchment Julian found was given to him from that man. *He's the one who instigated everything*. So, for our purposes, we simply watch from the flanks until they're weakened enough, at which time we'll take them both out."

"Alpheus...!" Julian interjected, holding a fist. "What are you—"

"We have a lead," Alpheus cut in, looking to Bors, who seemed to be fuelled with rage. "His name is Odo Rittle, the patrolman who accused me of murder. Since my return to the country, I've investigated these matters further, and I've found that Rittle is granted with privileges and authority that someone in his position wouldn't otherwise receive. Sources say that he commands some lesser lords, as well as a host of soldiers—giving orders as an alter ego of sorts as he remains lurking in the shadows.

"So," Alpheus continued, finally turning back to Schim, "do we have a deal?"

Schim glanced over at Bors, who nodded quietly. Alpheus had thought that Bors would have to go to Schim, and yet it was still a surprise to see the golden knight here. The two sides had probably been locked into a stalemate for days, and with Alpheus pushing them along, an alliance—precarious as it might be—looked more or less set.

"May I have a quiet word with you, Sir Bors?" Alpheus asked.

The veteran knight grunted, but then nodded and followed Alpheus to a corner while the rest of them began discussing the phantom.

"I want to help you avenge Lord Breunor," Alpheus whispered into Bors's ears, the claim causing Bors to jerk forward slightly. "But you need to do as I say. The phantom soldier is crucial to our success, and to lure the man out, you need to *work with* Julian."

Alpheus glanced over to Julian, who returned a raised eyebrow.

"When the time is right," Alpheus continued, "you can *discard* him. And by that, I mean you'd need to put Julian's life in danger. The phantom soldier is his ally. I once thought that the man wanted to break me out of prison, but every time I think back on it, I see that the phantom was there for Julian, not me. Believe me when I say that the phantom will appear if Julian is in danger. Do what you can to achieve that, but promise me—don't kill Julian. He's a friend, after all."

Alpheus looked up to the golden knight whose wrinkled eyes revealed considerable distrust.

Sorry, Julian, Alpheus thought. *I can think of no better alternative.*

Bors grumbled for a moment and then finally began to grin. "Agreed," he uttered, stepping away toward Schim. "Lord Chancellor," the golden knight said, cutting into the other conversation. "We would like to lend Julian Longinus."

Julian perked up with a grimace.

"If this is to work," Bors continued, peering over at Julian, "we would need to put our differences behind us. Consider Longinus to be the anchor of our alliance. He shall support us in tracking down the phantom soldier, and he could brief us on anything else you would like us to do. How about it?"

"Very well," Schim said. "Take Sir Longinus with you. I shall be in contact in due time."

* * *

Alpheus stepped into court behind the Lord Chancellor and his retinue, which included Bors and a host of Breunor's men. Also in the group were Ebenezer and the Raiders, only without Julian, who had been tasked with something outside of Zorlia. It appeared that Schim enjoyed the attention granted him upon treading in with a crowd of nearly thirty men.

The lords, knights, and noblemen already there held their breath upon the gaudy presentation, which showed that the Pristines were certainly a force to be reckoned with. Alpheus was quick to recognise Sagramore, the veteran cringing upon their entrance. Alpheus then glanced over to note that Forredan—the stout statesman who glowered at them now—was perhaps upset that Breunor's men had *defected* to the opposition. Alpheus also noted that he was at the end of many gawks as the other members of the court slowly recognised him in turn.

Alpheus appreciated the fact that the court had lacked more than a little lustre in the past week ever since the drama at the Morlan Manor, and that Schim was looking to build some momentum for the Pristines. Alpheus didn't trust that Schim would fight for his exoneration. Indeed, Alpheus didn't trust Schim at all. He suspected that the chancellor might instead publicise his return to Zorlia with his capture. After all, Alpheus had been confined under Schim's watchful eye for the past couple of days as Schim had worked to prepare his presentation of Alpheus to the court, and during this time, Alpheus hadn't shared a word with the proud man who perhaps rivalled the Lord Emperor in more than just authority.

In any case, it was a good time to see what had become of the Empire—or, more precisely for Alpheus, the first time he would have a real look at the country's most honoured men upon this privileged stage, a stage upon which he had been condemned for murder only four months previously.

The emperor had yet to arrive, but he wasn't late—Schim, instead, was early.

Alpheus braced himself then as Morlan and his retinue arrived. Hartland, who was quick to spot Alpheus, snapped his eyes wide open, but seemed to have done well to overcome an impulse to blurt out any words of surprise. Alpheus realised that he was certainly a surprise, but among a group that featured the Golden Titan and his cohort, he wasn't the only one calling for attention.

The ringing of the giant bell signalled the emperor's arrival. The court fell silent as all eyes turned toward the door at the far corner left of the throne. The great man stepped out in his usual regal maroon cloak that clipped at the shoulders onto the near-black set of armour, complete with gauntlets and sabatons shaped like the claws of a wild beast.

Lachman stepped out from behind the emperor, and immediately trailing Lachman was the man they called Nine Arms, whose imposing figure and deadly weapon hanging as a swivelling metal ball of death couldn't be mistaken for anyone else. His scarred face and lack of expression seemed to show that he lived for nothing but to kill. Apparently this was his first public appearance since the events at the Morlan Manor.

Bors and Kite were the first ones to tense up, but Schim raised a steady hand before them. The emperor regarded Schim and his overbearing entourage with narrowing eyes. He had noted Alpheus's presence as well, yet he had managed to maintain his calm composure.

"Why are you alongside the convicted, Lord Chancellor?" asked Lachman.

Schim grinned. "He's to be vindicated here today."

"On what claim?"

Schim turned to his left, where Ebenezer stood patiently. "If you may, Lord Ebenezer," he said.

The Vinan mage nodded and stepped forward. "Alpheus Hindlow was condemned for the Lord Count's murder for one reason: his identity as a sorcerer. But, as Zorlia has learned in recent times, there's a horde of beings that can be identified for having the same abilities." He paused for a moment, eyeing the emperor. "For instance, those referred to as the *Advent* sorcerers."

"And have you encountered one of these said sorcerers during your time here?" Lachman challenged. "If you're basing claims on hearsay alone, I'm afraid we cannot accept your case."

Ebenezer scoffed at the accusation. "If I had encountered one of them, I might not be alive to say this. In any case, I don't think that anyone can deny that there are sorcerers lurking about. Moving back to the point, if Alpheus Hindlow is a suspect, then all of those sorcerers out there deserve the same suspicion. The alleged murders of sentries Beggs and Brune and Alpheus Hindlow's escape from the prison were consequential to the cause, and hence they should be cleared altogether."

The men murmured amongst themselves. It was likely that they agreed, and indeed it was rather depressing to note that no one had really cared for Alpheus enough to point out this argument in the past four months. Perhaps the men had all assumed that Alpheus was dead.

"Not so quick," Lachman said, raising a hand. "Allow me to remind everyone here the gravity of this matter. After all, it is the murder of *the Lord Count* in discussion. Alpheus Hindlow may not be the prime suspect, but he is a suspect nonetheless. And, in my humble opinion, he remains to be the one most likely to have been the murderer. Even the slightest hint of involvement is enough for us to confine him behind bars."

Ebenezer exchanged a look with Schim, whose expression hardened.

"Sir Lachman is correct," Forredan said, raising a chunky arm. "It doesn't mean that the scholar will be executed, but a suspect is a suspect."

Some of the noblemen grumbled quietly. They had no words to argue for Alpheus, and indeed had no incentive to do so. And yet they cringed at the imperious manner in which the emperor—or the Advents—had forced the case toward their favour, just like they always did.

The emperor raised a brow at the disaccord. "Alpheus Hindlow shall be imprisoned," he declared. "I agree that the case has changed, however. And by virtue of that, he won't be subject to death—that much I can assure. The case will be investigated from the beginning, and if anyone can provide evidence to prove either his innocence or guilt, I urge you to bring it forward."

And at that, Alpheus had his wrists in shackles again. The scraping sound of the metal chains dragging along the ground was as heart-wrenching as he remembered, and the court wasted no time in having him escorted away. Everyone must have been watching him, but on his way out, Alpheus simply sighed, closing his eyes against the glares.

Despite the emperor's promise that Alpheus wasn't due for execution, he was still thrown into the same prison that housed criminals who had committed crimes that were indeed punishable by death. It wasn't something to be proud of, but upon being incarcerated for a second time in the same dungeon he had escaped from only months ago, Alpheus felt a strange sense of belonging. The experience had become a part of him, after all. The stone walls, the sturdy metal bars, the narrow corridor, and even the stench of filth that filled the air—they all had helped mould him into what he was today.

It was ironic too, that Alpheus had become somewhat of a legend here since his previous escape. Of course, all of those currently convicted weren't the same as the men who had been here four months ago—those had been executed long since. But the stories had survived, and—as it always had been—even the most ordinary stories turned into legends.

The current captives hailed Alpheus upon his arrival as though he was a king. They expected him to break out again soon, and they begged him to take them with him. The guards there had also been replaced. They no longer wore stone masks, and apparently they were far stronger than the previous soldiers.

Later that evening, when most were asleep, Alpheus sat wide awake in his cell, a lonesome figure in the dark, watching a flickering flame installed upon the corridor, waiting to see how long his stay would be this time.

THIRTY-SEVEN

Insurrection

At the court with only himself and the Lord Emperor, Lionel Lachman kept his head down, dropped down onto one knee. The sun was about to set, and his liege had been wearing a dismal expression since the morning. Lachman had said nothing to encourage Spartamon who had uttered barely a word all day. And yet Lachman believed that he knew what the emperor was thinking.

Where was Nine Arms?

Where was Marvin Sailanson?

After incarcerating Alpheus Hindlow again, a string of events had happened, none of which were favourable to the Advents. The incessant whispers that had tormented so many had finally pushed the common people past their breaking point. The whispers had always inspired a whole lot of fear, but this was about how they fed the people with more than they needed to know about the Empire—all of the conspiracy theories. While those who had been attentive to the appraisal of the court noted that not all of what was being said was true, the suspicion was that a large part of it actually was.

One of the accusations was specific to the Empire's inability to answer to the rising number of murders committed by sorcerers, which was despite Spartamon's pledge that the Empire—together with the Church—was already doing everything in their power to curb the menace. Further assertions alluded to how the court was instead occupied with the unremitting political war, and that meant that help wasn't expected any time soon. And, of course, the prophesies of foreign invasion had continued to terrify the populace.

Since the day prior, masses had rioted in front of Vondra Dawn. The people screamed about corruption and accused the court of making the same mistake as its predecessor, the Sargon Monarchy, who hadn't been united against the *real* threats endangering the country—which, in this case, were the sorcerers and the Kragans.

Already fuelled by the whispers, the people's anger stemmed further from two popular rumours that had rapidly spread across the city in recent days. The first rumour referenced the June Nineteenth Gathering and it spoke about the sensational downfall of Victor Breunor, positing that the entire sequence had been ingeniously plotted by the Lord Emperor, whose incentive for doing so was to reinstate his supreme command over the Empire's armies.

Given Spartamon's outward bellicosity and his love for war, it was easy to believe the rumour to be true. After all, Spartamon's time during the Battle for Saffron had been his most glorious and celebrated days. The armies that the great war tactician had led were merited with the title *invincible*. And it made sense that the emperor would want the power back in his hands as the country prepared for and anticipated the next war with the Kragans.

The second rumour, meanwhile, spoke about Alpheus Hindlow, and it suggested that the Lord Emperor was sure to have him dead—not for any reason other than to oppose the Lord Chancellor, who had proposed the scholar's exoneration. It had only been a few days since the emperor pledged that the scholar wasn't going to be due for execution. But to those who didn't know better, the suspicion that Spartamon had gone as far as to conspire for Breunor's end meant that any promise he made was effectively void.

In the wake of the protests, the Lord Emperor himself had come out—together with Lachman—to the front of Vondra Dawn in order to address the common people. Though Spartamon had sat astride a mighty stallion, staring down the protestors, he had indeed dropped his pride and admitted that he hadn't done enough. Spartamon had promised that he was most definitely wary of the whispers, but that he needed a *little* more time to uproot the culprits behind the whole phenomenon. The emperor had also acknowledged that their southern neighbours—the Kragans—might indeed be planning an attack, and he had vowed to crush them if they did. And yet the emperor had been reluctant to address the political war, only assuring the protestors that the troubles would all be over soon.

Unfortunately for the emperor, however, the people's mistrust was likely much worse than he had expected. It had started with only a few rash men who had dared to cry out insults before the emperor himself. They had accused the great man of answering with words only, and not actions. And soon the scuffle had taken a turn toward disaster when a few soldiers whose task was to escort the emperor had instead joined the chorus against him, crying for a revolution. Those soldiers had been contained promptly, but nothing could be done when a wooden chamber pot was hurled into the air, almost colliding into the emperor—the most dignified man of the entire country.

At the end, the protesters had been crushed, trampled on, and some of them had been killed. And while the Lord Emperor had managed to shuffle away from the scramble, he had most likely seen with his own eyes that many of the soldiers—perhaps *lesser men* from his vantage point—identified themselves as Pristines. It had been apparent that some of them had wanted nothing more than for him to die.

As if it had all been planned, the immediate aftermath of that first round of protests had been followed by a petition penned by Yusuf Seer and endorsed by the academy that *demanded* the court to bar the Lord Emperor from any further involvement in Reeling's murder case. The formal letter had argued that if Alpheus Hindlow had been held in captivity only on the basis of suspicion, then the rumours encircling the emperor equally held the great man in suspicion of potential misdeeds, sufficient to exclude him from the matter.

The insult was unforgivable. Lachman knew that the emperor must have regarded the scholars as *guileless idealists*. But the emperor had been careful not to add to his ever-dwindling reputation by making enemies with the academy. In the end, Spartamon had simply penned his own letter in response, pledging yet again that Alpheus Hindlow would be given fair treatment and adding that he also hoped that the scholar would be proven innocent.

Lachman had seen Spartamon losing favour at the court, as well. No one had dared to challenge the emperor directly, but more than a few noblemen had questioned his honour and morality with wry remarks. Away from the court, the emperor's strongest ally—Quinlan Forredan—had come to him, hinting at his inclination to withdraw from the Advents. And like the opportunist that Forredan was, his only interest had been the expansion of his own influence. In pointing out that he had the power to affect the balance of the political struggle, the stout statesman had essentially threatened the Lord Emperor into giving him what he wanted—land, gold, and power—or to risk seeing him take the Pristines' side.

It was difficult to fathom that the origin of all of the rumours and the consequent backlash was the return of Alpheus Hindlow, a mere scholar in the eyes of almost every man on the court. In truth, the emperor was hardly concerned with the scholar at all, but the emperor had been forced to ensure that nothing would happen to him—for if anything *were* to happen, the rumours would only be further fuelled. The emperor would be labelled as a dishonest leader and perhaps suffer the same fate as his predecessor—the corrupt King Robyn VI—who had been forced to vacate the throne nearly ten years prior.

It pained Lachman to see the emperor holding his head in response to the worry that was clouding his features. And yet Lachman knew that Spartamon still had the capacity to acknowledge the ingenuity of the person who had invented the rumours that had left him with no option to advance or retreat. On the one hand, Spartamon had to ensure Alpheus's wellbeing. But on the other hand, he couldn't send one of his trusted men to safeguard the prison because such an action would be viewed by others exactly as the rumours suggested.

As far as Lachman knew, Marvin Sailanson—a man he considered a friend—hadn't appeared since the June Nineteenth Gathering. Pylon, meanwhile, was conveniently away from the court for personal matters, as he had been frequently in recent times.

"The Pristines are vile," Lachman finally said, breaking the silence. "But I'm sure that if we stand the test of patience, the truth will soon speak for itself. When the people learn that they have misconstrued the whole idea, we'll have them submit to us all over again. For now, though, leave it to me to ensure that Alpheus Hindlow lives."

The emperor nodded, saying nothing, his dull expression unchanged.

"We'll win this fight," Lachman added, more encouragingly.

The emperor looked upon him. "We will," he finally responded, softly and always chillingly.

* * *

Julian threw open the door to the Lord Chancellor's chambers, furious and animated. In the chambers that hosted Bors, Ebenezer, and the Lord Chancellor himself, he had eyes only for Raphael, stomping over to the seasoned warrior and grabbing him hard by the shoulders.

"What did you do?" Julian questioned, his eyes burning.

Raphael shook him off with a heavy swipe of his arm. "What *got* to you this time?" he asked in return.

"Hundreds are dead—thousands more are injured! All because of those rumours you invented and spread."

Raphael snorted. "And what about it?"

Julian took a step back then, aware that everyone was scowling at him.

Raphael fixed up his collar with a smirk. "I spread the rumours. But the Lord Chancellor was the one who invented them."

Schim regarded Julian with a smug grin, clearly proud to have managed to defame the emperor and to have shaken the Advents' morale.

"Are you here to berate me?" Schim asked.

"But...," Julian uttered, "there must be a less damaging way to do this."

"There isn't," Schim said. "In fact, there's more to do if we are to consolidate Spartamon's fall from favour. This isn't the time to be worrying about a few civilians. Sacrifice is inevitable in this time of revolution."

Julian flinched, falling mute. He had come suspecting that his liege might be the one behind it all, and he had hoped that he was wrong—hoped that the one he followed wouldn't be so cruel as to incite those fiery civilians to protest toward their eventual demise.

How is that different from Spartamon? Julian thought. *And what was it about exonerating Alpheus?*

On the day after Alpheus had been incarcerated for the second time, Julian had asked the chancellor about the affair. Julian had offered to break Alpheus out again, only for Schim to dismiss the suggestion as foolish and even detrimental to the Pristines' cause. Apparently Alpheus had never shared any *plan* with the chancellor, either, and that was likely one of the reasons why Schim saw no incentive to help him.

"Go back to Sir Roc," Schim said, his strong tone causing Julian to tremble. "Your task is to find the phantom."

Julian frowned, but then followed with a slight bow before turning to depart. He recognised that Schim wasn't allowing him in on the plan he was sharing with Bors and Ebenezer, and he could only assume that was because it involved something unethical.

Julian could hear the violent protests as soon as he stepped outside of the citadel. Smoke billowed into the sky from the buildings closest to Vondra Dawn that had been subject to arson, apparently by the protestors themselves. Julian hopped onto his warhorse and for a moment he hesitated, but then he clenched the straps tightly and finally turned toward Soma, riding away.

Damn, he thought, scowling ahead. *What plan did you have, Alpheus? And where is that lass from Vinawell hiding? Why couldn't I find her?*

Although it was apparent that Schim had gradually been withdrawing his trust toward him, Julian still had his attendants who were loyal to him. Julian had entrusted Alex to ensure Oscar's safety despite him having lost an arm. Emery, meanwhile, had been tasked to locate the young lady from Vinawell and the hunter named Hendron. Unfortunately, Emery had lost their trails on more than a few occasions, just when he had seemed to be getting close.

Barely twenty minutes into his ride, Julian found himself in the northern neighbourhood of Soma. There were no protests here, but this place—often referred to as *the Soma slums*—was home to the poorest people in the city. The paupers were in rags. Most of those on the streets were urchins, not unlike Oscar had been when Julian had first met the boy. And these poor children shuffled away like sewage rats as Julian galloped through.

Julian soon caught up with Kite and Roc, both sitting astride their own warhorses on a narrow street, and the two acknowledged him with a glare. This lack of communication had been the way they had worked for nearly a week, and during this time, not once had Julian asked where they were headed, with Roc leading the way.

Behind the two knights who shared the same Silver rank as him, Julian surveyed a few more hovels before coming to a sudden stop. The trio had stopped in front of a scruffy building, a worn-out shack that was larger than most of the other hovels in the area.

"We're here," Roc said, dismounting with Kite. "This is his home."

"Whose home?" Julian asked as he hopped off the horse.

Roc responded with barely half a glance over toward him before he shoved open the front door, an action that seemed both tactless and indiscreet. The veteran knight stepped inside with Kite. Julian followed behind them and saw that the hovel was empty. The home was poorly lighted and reeked of stale bitterness, the smell of alcohol mingling with various food scraps. Besides a small dining table and a pair of simple stools, there was practically no furniture and no essentials to indicate that someone actually lived there. The thick layers of dust on the floor and the cobwebs occupying the corners indicated the owner was either rarely at home or that he lived filthily and with very little.

Roc and Kite then sat down on the pair of stools next to the compact table. "There's nothing here," Roc said. "That ugly dwarf must have left, knowing that we were on the hunt."

Dwarf? Julian wondered, noting a small-sized patrolman uniform lying in a corner. *Odo Rittle?*

"At least we can confirm that he's an Advent in disguise," Kite said, speaking only to Roc.

"So that's it?" Julian said. "Do we just give up now? He was our only trail to the phantom."

Roc turned a wicked grin toward Julian. "Well, Julian Longinus, we still have *you*. The scholar told us that you're the best lead we have."

Julian frowned. "What? Alpheus said that?"

Roc stood up now and took a step toward Julian. "It's ironic that you worry for him, when he surely doesn't worry for you."

Julian didn't like this hint of antagonism, but said nothing in response.

It's in everyone's best interests to maintain friendly relations, he reminded himself. *They wouldn't lay a finger on me if they...*

Julian glanced over to Kite now, who rose to his feet as well, his strong hand on the grip of his sabre. Looking back to Roc, Julian noted that even veteran knight was reaching for the hilt of his longsword.

Julian flinched and backed away a couple steps until he found himself up against the wall.

"*What*... do you *think* you're doing...?!"

"Blame the scholar," Kite said. "He suggested that we do this. The best way to get the phantom to show his face is to put you in danger."

"What are you talking about?" Julian said. "I don't even know the man."

"We beg to differ," Roc grumbled. "He saved you twice. Why not three times? Now, we know you have become quite the force to reckoned with, but against the both of us, you stand no chance."

Julian winced. "Even if the phantom *was* to appear for my sake, how would he know I'm here?" He paused then. "And, more importantly," he said, eyeing the side window, "the two of you are not enough to put me in danger."

The crimson red aura of Time-Shifting flashed for a second before Julian leaped out a window that was barely the size of the round, iron shield that Roc was armed with. Julian hopped forward, turning his head back only to see his pursuers scramble out from the door for a chase. He snorted at them, but his grin soon fell away as he turned to dash forward again.

The urchins had gathered together outside to form a human barricade. They were children—hungry and miserable children grimed with the dirt of the abandoned neighbourhood. Julian swallowed as these piteous children treaded toward him, swamping him immediately.

These children, he wondered. *Were they...?*

Julian looked up then to confirm what he feared. At a distance was Bors leading nearly thirty men striding forward toward him. The Titan had ambushed him, and he had done it well, stroking his beard behind the wicked smirk he was wearing. Roc and Kite, meanwhile, had finally caught up from behind.

* * *

Marvin had never stepped foot at court. He couldn't remember a time when he had defined winning a place in Vondra Dawn or any other citadel as glorious. But while he didn't want to be there, his host—the emperor himself—was delighted to see him. Lachman, meanwhile, was still a man with few words. Even so, Marvin noted that the honest man was as affable toward him as he had remembered.

Marvin was going to offer his services to Spartamon again after nine years had passed. He had spent the last eleven days lurking about trying to collect unmediated information on the state of affairs hurting the city and hence the country. Unlike many others, Marvin didn't believe a word of the negative rumours that the emperor couldn't seem to shake. He was certain that Spartamon would never resort to such underhanded tactics.

"You're finally back," the emperor said with a subtle smile, perched comfortably in his throne. "In the end, it is fate that links us together, Marvin. You are my most able soldier, and always will be."

Marvin frowned slightly. "You know why I came back. And, I do have one condition."

"And that is?"

"When this ends, you'll tell me the truth behind the Noel Gate Incident."

The emperor leaned back slightly. "Your eyes tell me that you suspect I was behind the case. I assume you're basing your suspicions on the promise I made nine years ago?"

Marvin winced.

"I intend to keep that promise," the emperor went on, "but I wouldn't go to such great lengths to honour that. Only after years of investigation did I learn who *he* was. I must say, it is ironic for you to be bearing the crime committed by *that man*."

"Was it really a single man who killed them all?"

"So it seems," the emperor said as he invitingly leaned forward. "I never imagined there could be someone else with such ability. I didn't want to believe it either, but he is potentially your equal. When the time comes, I will tell you his name. That time will coincide with the fulfilment of my promise from nine years ago, and I assure you that Theodora Kharvalenis will be honoured."

Marvin sneered. "I never knew what you meant, but I'd rather you not speak her name out loud."

The emperor grinned. "The next time that I do, you'll be begging me to say more." He paused then and turned to the window to the left of the throne. "Watts, why don't you come in? You're as much my soldier as Marvin is."

There was no sign of him at first, but then a head poked in behind the glass. Marvin had told Rover not to come, but he had followed him anyway, clawing onto the steeple from the outside. As Rover met the eyes of the emperor then, he slid open the window to slip inside.

"Should have known nothing could escape you," Rover said.

The emperor chortled. "Now let me summon Pylon."

Pylon arrived minutes later—the man more famously known as Nine Arms. The vengeful man never even laid his eyes on Rover or Lachman, glaring only at Marvin as he treaded in, trembling perhaps with excitement. Marvin, in turn, glared back, cautious not to be provoked. The rancour was brewing, however. Even beneath the mantle that covered Pylon almost from head to toe, Marvin sensed that the man's blood was boiling. He doubted that the brusque man gleaned any sentimental value from this reunion.

Even so, it was the first time since the war that Marvin had come together to form this group that included Spartamon, Pylon, Lachman, and Rover. Marvin was sure that they were the strongest five men anyone ever assembled, but if the past were anything to go by, the team might also be the most precarious that he had ever known, one that could implode at any time. Lachman was the pacifist of the team, but even Lachman had had a tough time trying to appease everyone.

Marvin offered his hand to Pylon then, a gesture that had the emperor grinning. Pylon, though, turned away with a grunt.

"What is it, Pylon?" the emperor asked. "Is it not clear now that Victor Breunor was the one responsible for the annihilation of your camp?"

Nine Arms hesitated, shooting another glare in Marvin's direction. "It's not only that," the vengeful man said, speaking to the emperor. "Sailanson's loyalty is contentious. I can't promise that I can work with him."

Marvin simply blinked his eyes once, with no intention to explain himself.

"I trust him," the emperor said. "Besides, there won't be any conflict of interest. Pylon, I'll have you working with Lionel. I need you to gather the sorcerers and prepare the seeds."

While the two of them simply nodded, Marvin narrowed his eyes, noting that the emperor still gave brief orders that anyone not assigned to the task wouldn't understand. Marvin looked away, realising that this was also the first time that Spartamon admitted that he had assembled sorcerers.

"Marvin, Watts," the emperor said, turning to them once again. "I want you to break Alpheus Hindlow out of prison."

Rover closed his good eye in response as his indication that he resigned to the task. Marvin then nodded his acceptance of the task as well.

"Schim shall be presented with the opportunity to deprecate me," the emperor continued. "He'll do an excellent job at it. But while he's focused on the war of words, he'll be hit with our full force. We'll crush him once and for all." Spartamon squinted. "Get moving. You shall receive further instructions later."

THIRTY-EIGHT

Troubled minds

The cramped hovel was not only suffocating, but also depressing, with no natural light shining through and barely any ventilation. The fact that it was midsummer made the temperature close to unbearable. Unable to bring a smile to his face, Marvin looked up then to the low ceiling that seemed to be pushing him down. His return to Zorlia was never supposed to be a vacation or an extension of his adventures with the Sail Band, but it irritated him a great deal to be sitting there at the small table under the faint flicker of a solitary oil lamp.

It was only their first evening beneath the prison hill. And now, as Marvin glanced over to his team, he wondered how the four of them were going to share this space for at least the next few days.

"It's not so bad," Ash said, trying to brighten up the mood. He sat across Marvin. Between them was Tavie, who had been surprisingly quiet, having made no complaints thus far. Rover, meanwhile, stood cross-armed against the wall with his eyes closed.

Marvin sighed. Although he had maintained a cold front recently, he was glad that Ash had chased him all the way to Zorlia in order to lend his support. Marvin had yet to admit it openly, but he certainly considered Ash to be a valuable ally. Indeed, Ash and his outsider's perspective on the current conflict that divided the city helped Marvin to maintain his sanity.

Tavie, however, wasn't like Ash at all. Marvin didn't know what to do with her. She seemed to have grown passionate for his causes—or, perhaps, the Sail Band's causes. But the lass was still far too naïve and unworldly to be exposed to the intrigues of the wicked men that seemed to brim more fiercely in Zorlia than in any other place in the land. In any case, Tavie had toned down from her past vibrancy. In a way, that had been a surer sign than anything else to Marvin that the Sail Band was no more.

It was at the emperor's doing that Marvin had ended up here in this crude shelter. Not only was the place sequestered—meaning that no one would think to look for Marvin there—but it was at the same time just beneath the prison hills, which made it convenient for Marvin to break Alpheus out. The only door in the cramped hovel led to a corridor filled with blocks of woven fibre. At the end of the corridor was the front of the shack that actually was a tapestry shop, one of a dozen stalls carved *into* the foot of the prison hills.

The shop itself was manned by George, an unsuspecting elderly man who was one of the emperor's long-time servants, both tactful and loyal. Marvin knew the old man from his warring years. Back then, George had been one of his many admirers. But whether or not that admiration remained, Marvin knew that if he ever showed any hints of turning against the emperor, the old man was sure to do everything in his power to have him dead.

As far as Marvin knew, no one had ever turned against the emperor. No one except Schim. Since Marvin had arrived in Zorlia, he had heard a lot of conflicting information about the rift with the Pristines. He had heard the whispers, too, and it bothered him. Marvin would admit his inexperience with political struggles, but he simply couldn't make sense of how it had come to this. The Kasimir de Spartamon he had known wasn't a man to show mercy. Spartamon had the forte and preference for swift battles, and with that, the great man should have blitzed his enemies long before they would have even assembled any kind of meaningful formation.

Unless he doesn't see Schim as an enemy, Marvin thought, staring intently at the burning flame of the oil lamp. *If this is simply about taking Schim out, wouldn't assassination be the obvious call of action? Lachman and Pylon could have done it.*

"Why are we always linked to Alpheus?" Tavie asked, breaking the silence. "Why are we always helping him?"

Marvin regarded her coolly. "Maybe one day he'll return the favour," he said.

Tavie cocked her head. "Maybe," she said. "But need I remind you what happened the last time we tried to break into prison?"

"The last time?" Marvin said musingly. "You arranged those ugly masquerades."

"I meant that it was *failure*," Tavie complained.

Marvin closed his eyes for a moment, shivering slightly. "The fight with that woman, Zabai—it still gives me chills." He turned to Rover. "Right, Ro?"

"She was strong," Rover responded with his usual frigidity. "But what's ahead of us promises to be a tougher fight."

Tavie turned sullen. Rover's words had killed the mood. The stale air and the cramped space suddenly became obtrusive once again.

"Let's get to it," Ash said then. "Our task is to break Alpheus out. I think the underground passage is the best option."

Tavie scoffed. "Since when did they have something like that, and of all places, one that leads conveniently straight to the prison?"

"Since the day we dig it out."

It sounded like an absurd idea, but both Marvin and Rover knew exactly what Ash was capable of. While Ash often reminded the others that he was a geologist, newer members of the crew never really realised what that actually meant. After all, it had been years since he had last demonstrated his extraordinary burrowing skill that had earned him the little-known cognomen of *Badger Ash*.

Marvin still remembered the astonishing lengths that Ash had gone through for the sole purpose of impressing him as his plea to join the Sail Band. It involved Ash digging out a complex network of underground tunnels, which allowed Marvin and Rover to easily infiltrate a near-unconquerable fortification held by the Kragans in southern Farella close to the frontier. In the earlier years of the crew's formation, there had been greater need for Ash's burrowing skills, but ever since adding Karl to the team—the giant who was able to draw out detailed maps of every place in the land—going underground became less and less desirable.

* * *

The group wasted no time in shovelling out the earth under their feet, following Ash's instructions and lead. Tavie had been spared from having to dig, instead tasked to man the outside in order to ensure that no one knew what they were doing. She was also to manage the dug-up soil, which she had so far dumped away into a disused church nearby.

Ash was indeed an expert in excavation, and he had been quick in identifying the best places to burrow. With his guidance, the progress was continuous, yet they were still racing against time to dig out an estimated six hundred feet of earth. The task had become more pressing after George had relayed a demand from the emperor that morning that it was critical to break Alpheus within four days' time, which coincided with an important gathering of Empire officials he was arranging.

The three of them had taken turns to rest and to revitalise. It was about midnight now, and it was Marvin's turn to rest. He had been complaining about how hot it was, and about the irony that they had been forced to work next to burning torches that lighted the way for them. Everyone wore only pants. Marvin had discarded even the headband that had become almost a part of him, and for his lofty standards, he had been rather mediocre at the task. Of course, with his strength that rivalled a hundred men, he had excavated a whole lot more than Ash, but not nearly as much as what Rover had managed to accomplish.

"Sorry," Marvin said, panting and wiping away the grime that covered his entire body. "I need a breather."

Both Rover and Ash nodded as Marvin huffed out a long breath. He then turned to leave, following the passage back toward the cramped hovel. He noted that Tavie wasn't around—perhaps she had gone out to dump more soil.

It's still so hot, Marvin thought with a groan as he wiped his face and then his body with a moist cloth. He then threw on his simple blazer before pacing into the corridor crammed with numerous bolts of cloth. Marvin didn't know the precise time, only that it was late in the evening. The near complete darkness of the corridor offered no clues, not when natural daylight or moonlight barely even poured in.

He treaded faster along the corridor then, slowing finally when a faint glimmer of light was visible ahead. He flapped open the hanging cloth that shaded the evening blue of Achelois. The moon was a waning crescent floating in a clouded night sky, its faint glow of blue touching gently upon the tapestry shop front and the open space before it.

"What are you doing out here?" George asked quietly and with a slight air of annoyance. The old man seemed to have just snapped his eyes open, perhaps from a brief doze.

Marvin glanced about and saw that the shop was closed, the strip near empty.

"Getting some fresh air," Marvin responded, puffing out a breath. "In fact," he said, "I could really do with a breeze."

"Don't go too far," George said as Marvin paced away.

We're watching you, seemed to be what he had meant.

Marvin was never one to attract unwanted attention, and he now drifted naturally away from the city centre, which he knew was still brewing with violent protestors.

I have a bad feeling about this, he thought, wandering about aimlessly. *Spartamon. He's hiding something, like always.*

The smell of terracotta wafting through the thoroughfare was one of those things that was distinctly Zorlian—and something that Marvin hated, for it accentuated the fact that he was in the Truban capital. Even the blooming wisteria vines that crept onto homes and other structures were detestable, especially as their scent mingled with the smell of terracotta, which had been baked—and, hence aggravated—by the unforgiving sun earlier in the day. Marvin had never known Zorlia all that well, and yet the current atmosphere of the city tingled deeply with his memories. Although this was supposedly a new, *better* era, everything looked nearly identical to how it had been ten years prior.

Marvin fished his pant pocket for his leather wine flask. He then looked up at the night sky to the gleaming blue of Achelois and began to drink but taking only small sips. The wine was tasteless to him. It had been that way for nearly ten years. He still couldn't forget Kharvalenis.

As he continued reminiscing the past, Marvin realised he had turned into an alleyway where a man with a wide frame stood with his back to him.

"I've finally snuffed you out," the stranger said, no longer strange as he turned to face Marvin, the blue of Achelois brushing onto his face.

Marvin raised an eyebrow, noting the tremendous composure that he expected of the man.

Schim, he noted with respect. *Is he alone?*

"What do you want?" Marvin asked, not surprised that the man had managed to track him now that he was not in hiding.

"Just a talk," Schim said with a shrug. "After all, we were comrades too, were we not?"

"Comrades?" Marvin scoffed. "My memory's not so good, but I think you wanted me dead at the Morlan Manor. I don't know about you, but that's not how I treat my comrades, Lord Chancellor."

"Let me get to the point, Sailanson. Kasimir de Spartamon is no longer the same man you think you know. He's no longer—"

Marvin raised a hand. "You've come to the wrong person," he said. "Contrary to popular belief, I don't betray the people and causes that I stand for."

"But did he not betray you?" Schim asked with a smirk. "What did he do to Theodora Kharvalenis again?"

Marvin cringed, realising with contempt that Schim knew well how to enrage him.

"Can you really forget that?" Schim continued, his voice growing shrill.

Marvin huffed out a heavy breath, and then gazed back at Schim.

"That's between me and him," he said. "If you're here to provoke me, I suggest you save the effort. I respect that you have come alone, but I have my limits."

Schim grinned. "I hear you don't kill anymore. I must admit I'm glad to know that."

Marvin clenched his fists as Schim took a small step back.

"In any case," Schim said, "you have no reason to have me dead. I've said what I needed to say, which is merely a reminder that Spartamon is not the same man we were once loyal to. While I am certain that *the wolf* moniker is still fitting in all its most powerful and positive ways, the ugly rear of this same *wolf* is manifesting stronger than ever. He no longer trusts anyone. He feels threatened by me and by you, by Pylon, and even Lachman. Do you truly believe he is the best person to lead the country?" Schim hissed at his own question. "Whatever happens after this, may there be no regrets."

The chancellor spun to leave, joining Raphael who had been lurking behind in the shadows. Marvin stood watching them until they disappeared off into the darkness.

You sly man.

But Schim had succeeded in making Marvin grow more suspicious about Spartamon. He had already thought the emperor to be a changed man. In the past, Marvin had never doubted the great man's decisions. But things were different now.

Maybe I've changed, too.

Marvin had paced back to the strip of stalls beneath the prison hill. With all of the lights out, Marvin saw only George's silhouette still sitting behind the counter.

Sleeping? he wondered.

But as Marvin paced closer, he realised that the man sitting there wasn't George at all. And behind this stranger was yet another, more slender figure.

A... lady?

The faint blue of Achelois glistened onto the striking soft amber hair of the stranger—a woman from Vinawell. She had donned a simple peasant's dress that was rather different from what Marvin remembered her wearing before. But Marvin smiled then upon recognising her, glad to see her familiar whimsical smirk.

"Finally found you, Treasure Hunter!" Azure said quietly but excitedly, beaming at Marvin.

Marvin shrugged with a return grin. "You survived," he said.

"Hold on just now!" the other man said with a glance at Marvin, and then turning back to Azure. "*Treasure* Hunter?! Didn't you say he was a bandit? And what do you suppose *treasure* constitutes? You're either a good hunter, or a bad hunter—since when are there categories for hunting?"

Azure held her head, and then turned back to Marvin. "This is Joe Hendron," she said. "He's a hunter—an old-fashioned one."

"Now what's that supposed to mean?" Hendron complained. "Is that how you introduce me? I mean, really, is that all I am?"

Azure bit her lips and widened her large round eyes. "Well, credit goes to you for finding Marvin and for luring away that merchant."

He managed to get the better of George, Marvin realised, regarding Hendron with a careful eye, and then glancing down below the shopfront to see that George was unconscious. He then returned his gaze to Azure, and a sudden frown creased his forehead.

"Why are you here, exactly?" he asked.

Azure's smile faded. "I'm sure you've heard about Alpheus," she said.

"And?"

"He needs your help."

Marvin said nothing, turning away slightly.

Azure took a step forward. "Since coming to this city, I've heard a lot about you. And—"

"Do the stories scare you?" Marvin asked, cutting her off.

Azure shook her head. "I trust you. I wouldn't be here otherwise. But I sense that you and I have different agendas. And I need you to see things from our perspective."

Hendron glanced about as if he were looking for a way out of the conversation.

Azure immediately turned to him. "Please stay, Joe," she said. "You need to listen. It's for your own good." She turned back to Marvin. "We found the Passionless Surgeon," she then said. "I owe my life to him. But this isn't about that. His name is Pelanofzky... and he's a Primal Soldier."

Marvin shivered slightly, hoping that no one noticed.

"Pelanofzky, he...," Azure continued, growing anxious as she spoke, "he claims that his people purposely lost the war, in preparation for greater things. And that is to dominate all of the land. The best place to start is to reap the benefits of the conflict in Zorlia, and Pelanofzky claims that there's a member of the court who works for them—*someone with great authority*. According to him, this entire feud was instigated by this single person. Alpheus and I are trying to find him."

Marvin squinted. "I suppose Alpheus thinks that this person is Kasimir de Spartamon?"

Azure paused, seeming to have noted Marvin's ire.

"This isn't a game!" Marvin said hotly, his pupils flaring. "Look at the city—listen to the protests—it's a total wreck! Yes, the Empire is corrupt, but what you and Alpheus have done is throw that corruption onto the civilians, who now are going out of their way to form rebellions. And of course, as human nature has it, they're fighting amongst themselves in their sad attempt to nominate some new leader. This is all wrong! No matter how ingenious your plans may seem to you, this is simply *not* how it works. I don't know what will happen to this city, this country, or even the land, but I know for certain no one needs *heroes* like you and Alpheus!"

Azure cringed for a moment, but then lashed out in return. "Do you think we enjoy this? Do you think we're doing this for ourselves? If I had a choice, I wouldn't have come to Zorlia at all. But Alpheus... he... what I'm saying is, since we learned about all these things, we have no choice *but* to help!"

"And that's exactly what I'm getting at...!" Marvin said, stopping mid-sentence. He turned away in shame, holding his head. "After your miraculous recovery, you should be treasuring your life, not risking it all over again."

Azure fell silent. Marvin looked up to the sky, his expression desolate. The clouds whiffed about slowly, shrouding away the already faint crescent. Not a speck of light shone down from above. Upon his soft sigh, however, a sparkling blue illuminated from below, a light reminiscent of the moon. Marvin looked down. The illumination had splashed over the tapestry, and the source of the light was the extraordinary bracelet wrapped around Azure's wrist. She had rolled up her sleeves to show it off, and a smile finally graced her lips once more.

Azure removed the bracelet and held it out toward Marvin. "It served as my lucky charm," she said. "Princess Flora left this for me, and I in turn exchanged it for a favour from you. It pains me to say this, but the bracelet belongs to you now. Please take it as a token of my appreciation. Do what you can for Alpheus."

Her gaze was the same as last time when she had asked him to help Carmen. Marvin regarded her for a moment longer until he nudged the bracelet back toward her.

"Keep it yourself," he said.

"But—"

"I'll do what I can," Marvin assured. "I envy the two of you. I envy what you share. If it works for you, think of it as a fool who doesn't want to see romance die."

Azure nodded gratefully, blushing a little.

Marvin smiled. "He's a good person," he said. "The land needs more people like him if it is to become a better place."

* * *

Julian was still on the run. The violent protests assembled around Vondra Dawn had made it impossible for him to circle back for the chance to run to the chancellor. But the chaos in the city also made it much easier to hide from Bors and his men, who had kept up their relentless chase for days. Julian had managed to discard his armour and disguise himself in clothes typical of lower-class commoners in a particular opportune time when he had lost Bors. The chase also had Julian venturing to the south of the city, all the way from the northern neighbourhoods where the chase had begun.

The most urgent thought in his mind was Oscar's wellbeing. Although Julian was hopeful that Oscar had been clever enough to leave their home in Ramsgate before Bors could get a hold of him, Julian couldn't allow himself to simply assume that was the case. It was early morning now, a good time to move among the day crowds of the protestors in the city. Ramsgate was just ahead. But as Julian shuffled through the thick crowd of civilians, he noted the billows of smoke ahead that looked to have originated from the neighbourhood he called home.

Someone had been there before him. Julian lowered his conical hat and continued striding along anxiously. As he got closer and closer, it seemed more and more like the smoke puffing up to the sky indeed came from the humble home he shared with the boy. The worst was all but confirmed when he finally stepped in front of his home, where dozens of people stood murmuring and pointing at the desecrated shack. The fires had been smothered—perhaps by the people living close by—but could there possibly be anything left to salvage? In the most terrible way possible, this was peculiarly similar to the Mt. Pinnacle Massacre, in which his childhood home was destroyed along with all forms of life within the home.

Please, no, he prayed. *Oscar!*

Julian clenched a fist and shoved his way past the people, dashing into the clouds of smoke and ash.

Am I too late?

He wheezed and coughed, seeing nothing but grey, until he drew his iron sword and slashed a fierce whirlwind to clear the smoke. That one swing didn't clear the fumes, but was enough for him to see the damage that had befallen his home.

The courtyard tree had turned black, and the shapes of the furniture had deformed into ghastly moulds. No walls were left standing. Almost all that was left of the ruins were the now flimsy wooden frames of the house. If there had been any personal belongings still there, they too had no chance of survival.

Oscar, Julian thought, peering around for clues as to the boy's whereabouts. He then caught a glimpse of something under the collapsed wall that resembled a hand and he dashed immediately toward it. Growing distraught, he shovelled up the wall with his sword, hurling the entire chunk to flip over in a heavy thud that blew more ashes up from the ground.

Not Oscar, Julian realised with relief as he uncovered the burned corpse of a grown man. Indeed, there were two of them, one next to the other, in disfigured metal armour that had somehow survived the flames.

Knights, he recognised. *But who? Alex…?!* He finally breathed a sigh of relief when he saw that both corpses had all their limbs intact.

"Give it up, Longinus," said a commanding tone from behind him.

Julian spun around, swatting his arm to further clear the smoke. His pursuers had caught up to him. A group led by Roc dashed in from the right, while another group led by Bors stepped in from the left, totalling close to twenty men.

Julian grunted at them, but before he could speak, Bors sneered and spat on the ground.

"Where is he?" the golden knight demanded. "Not only did he burn the house, but he killed my men as well! I'll ask you one more time: *Where—is—he?*"

Julian squinted in confusion, unsure whether the phantom had come to his aid again, apparently killing some of Bors's men.

"Julian Longinus!" Kite said, stepping forward. "There will be no more miracles this time. You're *sure* to die if you don't concede. Do you really think you managed to run all the way here? We let you go on purpose—so that you would lead us to him." Kite then drew his sabre and slashed it across the air before him in one fluid motion. "We've already wasted too much time on you. Don't make us do this."

"I don't want to do this, either!" Julian retorted. "But I *really* don't know anything about his whereabouts."

Bors growled. "We've given you too many chances already," he said, lifting his giant maul to his chest.

The golden knight swung the maul forward, which was the signal for his men to attack. Julian flashed away on instinct, darting behind one of the wooden beams of the destroyed house. Behind the still dissipating smoke, however, Julian realised that the aura of crimson red that followed him had left an evident trail. He looked up and flashed away to another beam, hoping that a second wave of translucent red would confuse his pursuers. Instead, it looked like his foes saw exactly where he was, firing several arrows that thumped into the already decayed beam he was leaning against, each thump feeling as if he was being struck.

As he peered about for an escape route, he reminded himself that he would survive like every other time when the odds had been against him. He moved his hand to the grip of his iron sword and prepared to draw.

"Stop, Sir Bors," a voice demanded then, the voice of a woman. Within a moment, the arrows that had been raining at him actually stopped.

Julian peeked out from behind the beam as everyone else turned to the surprising arrival of Lady Winter. The most esteemed woman of the country had come with a horde of soldiers that outnumbered those of even Bors and his men. Winter peered into the crowd, meeting the eyes of more than a few of the men who had been chasing Julian. Almost everyone went down to their knees.

Winter then treaded ahead and stopped at Julian, who hadn't bowed down but finally stepped out from behind the wooden beam now. Winter spun to face everyone else, lifting her chin and manifesting that powerful sense of supremacy that she must have learned from the chancellor.

"Sir Bors, the Lord Chancellor summons you," she said, her tone stronger than ever. "Take your men with you."

The golden knight didn't answer. Instead, he exchanged a look with Roc, who shook his head quickly. Kite, though, snorted.

"We have an agreement with the chancellor," Kite said. "We will work for him as long as he doesn't question our methods. You have no command over us."

Winter grimaced, her change in expression prompting the knights she had come with to suddenly surround Kite.

"You're a daring man," the proud lady said in a sour tone. "I'll be sure to let the chancellor know. But, before then, you will follow Sir Bors to Vondra

Dawn on *my* order. If you dare question me a second time, I'll make sure you regret it."

Kite seemed prepared to rebel against her, but Bors pulled him back. Apparently, the people involved in the war had a great respect for Winter, though as was evident now—Bors's expression showed fear.

"Please excuse him," Bors said with his head inclined. "We shall head for Vondra Dawn now."

When they had all left, Winter loosened up a little, relaxing her shoulders and reverting to her usual amiability. Julian finally bowed to her as he held his curiosity and worry for Oscar inside, wary of the crowd present. And as if Winter recognised his anxiety, she asked all the soldiers present to withdraw briefly, leaving only the two of them there inside the ruined home.

"I did it for Eris Nightingale," she said. "She asked me to keep an eye on her brother. That's about all I could do."

Julian raised a brow. "Where's Oscar now?" he asked.

"Your attendants have escorted him away to Bastion City."

Julian nodded and finally breathed a sigh of relief.

"It seems that the phantom soldier was here first, however," Winter said now with a squint. "And it was *he* who saved the boy before my soldiers could. But... I'm not here to tell you this." She raised her voice then. "Sir Longinus, listen well to your next assignment."

Julian tensed up upon the sudden change of tone.

"The Lord Emperor has proposed a negotiation for peace. In a couple days' time, the fifth day of July, all members of the court will be at the Luxuriant Gardens. But you will not be needed there, for you have a more important task... to get to the prison and *kill* Alpheus Hindlow. Lord Ebenezer has left the city for a return to Vinawell. No one can know for sure even if you are to use sorcery."

Julian gawked, unable to utter a word. The assignment didn't make any sense to him. Did the chancellor really believe that he would kill Alpheus? And, what was this negotiation of peace about, arranged by Spartamon? Would it be a repeat of the June Nineteenth Gathering?

"Do as you are instructed," Winter said, handing a parchment now over to Julian, "and things will be right."

Winter smiled and then left, leaving Julian with no more information other than the parchment that detailed the heavy investments that the Empire had spent in augmenting the security at the prison. This included the replacement of cell bars which were now strengthened with osmium, the introduction of specific keys for specific cells identified only by the shape of the key, and finally, more powerful guards.

Julian sneered as he burned away the parchment. Whatever might happen at the Luxuriant Gardens in two days' time would surely take the attention away from the prison. But how many other people would realise that and therefore see it as an opportunity to visit the prison to either rescue or murder his friend?

Alpheus..., Julian thought, staring hard at the blackened beams of the destroyed home. *If being the focal point was your intention, then you have done a great job.*

THIRTY-NINE

The phantom sought out by all

Julian watched the sun set as he squatted on a sizeable tree at the foot of the prison hills. He had been there almost an hour, and Julian had seen nothing suspicious over the strip of shops leading up to the ascension of the hill where the prison was located. The blue glow of Achelois was dim behind the heavy overcasts. The early evening sky, however, was free from the mists that had stifled his advance the last time he had stormed the prison.

Julian stroked a hand across his chest. The sturdy leather of the brigandine was delicate, and the light metal faulds were prosaic. The protection was lacking, but that came in the favour of added practicality and lighter weight. It was the generic uniform of the Empire soldiers, and it had been a long time since Julian had donned the garb—and the first time that it had been entirely black. The colour was crucial when his intention was to assume the form of the phantom that he had grown to admire, and also grow more and more curious about. Julian had taken the extra step to resemble the phantom by preparing the long cape which was now clipped at his shoulders. He had failed to find a mask like the original with those distinct clean stripes of white, instead having to settle for a mask of full black. Clasped at his waist was a pair of rapiers. The weapon wasn't quite a duplicate of the real pair, however, which had seemed feathery and light.

All that effort was going to waste if he wasn't able to carry out his plan this evening—his plan to *save* Alpheus—which was in direct contradiction to the instructions the chancellor had given him. It hadn't been the most straightforward decision for him to make, but in the end, it was all about his conscience, which urged him to protect and trust his friend.

It's time, Julian thought, darting out from behind the tree. He dashed ahead, flashing left and right as he climbed, leaving only a faint trail of crimson red as he did his best impersonation of the phantom, blending in and out of the darkness.

The block-shaped entrance to the prison cave grew more and more defined as he proceeded, and yet something was terribly strange.

Where were the guards?

Julian narrowed his eyes and squinted, finally spotting inanimate bodies lying by the entrance—five or six of them. It was only the early hours of the evening, but it seemed that another visitor had arrived before him and had somehow managed to advance up the hill without him even noticing.

Julian slowed his own advance, but when he decided that no one was lying in ambush, he dashed over to one of the defeated men to study the situation. There was no mistake—the chainmail shirt of interlocking loops of metal belonged to the knights that guarded the prison, and that meant that whoever had come before him had already powered down into the cave. The double door that had been swung open was yet more telling evidence that a confrontation awaited him.

Julian didn't have time to guess who it was or what they were here for. There were too many people with the abilities and motives to come there tonight. The only way to find out was to go down and see for himself.

Julian slid out one of the rapiers from the sheath at his waist, raising it slightly in front of him as if it were a cane for the blind. He stepped cautiously into the block-shaped structure lighted modestly with only a single candle mounted on the stone wall on the far end. The spare illumination of the night sky that poured in was almost vivid in comparison. He prowled toward the descending stairway, wary that there could be anything or anyone hiding in the dark. He stopped when he got within two steps of the staircase as he sensed a slight change in the air, pausing there until he spun suddenly, sweeping his weapon around with force.

The swing met a heavy chunk of metal that parried away his blow. The lump that receded back into the darkness could hardly be defined, but the brief spark from the clang seemed to have revealed a set of limbs. Julian prodded forward to chase, only to sense the sudden glimmer of a blade slicing down toward him from his left. His instincts jerked his sword-wielding arm upwards, barely blocking off a dangerous strike. He considered himself fortunate there, and yet he could do nothing to prevent the kick that followed, which sent him crashing into the wall across the entrance.

Julian picked himself up quickly, ignoring the throb of his wounded chest. The stone mask wasn't the only thing that had made it difficult to breathe. Then he noticed two figures stepping out from the shadows.

"We've been waiting for a long time," one of those in ambush said, the deep voice familiar.

Julian recognised that it was Bors swinging his giant maul from side to side, causing the candle on the wall to flicker hauntingly. The other man was Orel Kite, and they were without their respective golden and silver armour, instead equipped only with humble and dark-coloured chain mail.

Julian relaxed slightly, glad it was *only* them, and that they might have mistaken him for the phantom. Julian said nothing, instead tensing his waist and protruding his chest in the most imposing manner that he could manage. He then drew the other rapier, slashing the pair of blades destructively across the ground and tearing open a frightening fissure in the stone floor.

Bors and Kite cringed slightly, but rather than challenging Julian further, they eased up a little.

"We came not to fight," Bors said, standing his ground. "We want your help—to kill Nine Arms. We know you crossed swords with him in the past—right here at the prison. We'll need you to fight him again, but this time with our support."

Julian didn't answer, still careful not to speak and reveal his ruse.

"Nine Arms is on his way," Bors then said. "Your only option is to fight with us."

Julian flinched at the prospect. It wasn't as surprising as it was dismaying.

"He's... coming here...?" he asked, assuming a deeper voice than normal.

Bors nodded with an anxious grin. The veteran knight didn't seem to recognise Julian's voice thanks to the stone mask that distorted it, if slightly.

"You're here to ambush him?" Julian asked. "And... me? How did you know that I was coming?"

"Longinus," Kite said, and Julian thought for a moment that the other man had recognised him. "Longinus betrayed you. He left us a message that told us you were coming here."

It was certainly surprising—and ironic—to Julian that that was what Kite believed.

"And where is he now?" Julian asked instead.

Bors shrugged. "He's probably fled the city. In the end, Longinus chose to save himself."

"Did you ever think it was a trick?" Julian challenged.

"The parchment was left behind with your twin rapiers," Kite said as he gazed down to the much less impressive pair that Julian now held. "Longinus left you bare. But worry not... I've brought them for you. You'll need them."

Kite swung out the sack tied to his back to present the genuine pair of the slender swords reflecting the candlelight.

Julian froze, still wondering whether or not the phantom was assuming his name while he assumed his. "But how can you be sure Nine Arms would come?" Julian asked, receiving the weapons and discarding the pair he had brought.

Bors shrugged. "We passed by him in court, slipping out your weapon only for him to see," he said. "He recognised it in an instance. I told him to meet you here."

Julian snorted. "Clever," he said. "But as you can plan to team up with me, Nine Arms can do the same with someone else. Who's to say he'll come alone?"

"He'll come alone," Bors assured. "This has nothing to do with the Advents or Spartamon. Besides, the rest of the Advents will be occupied at the Gardens—as will the Pristines. Anyone else who might come here tonight is hardly worth a second thought."

Julian pondered this for another moment, before finally nodding in agreement. Putting aside his own history with Bors and Kite, this was indeed a rare opportunity to take out Nine Arms. With the three of them, it was possible.

The actual phantom might even come for support, Julian hoped. And he was almost certain that Bors and Kite would still focus on downing their common enemy even if they were to found out that he wasn't actually the phantom.

Julian glanced up at Bors, about to ask him how long they expected to wait. But before he could open his mouth, they all tensed up upon hearing the sudden sound of footsteps. The three of them exchanged anxious looks, and Bors demonstrated his anxiety with a cringe.

A brilliant, almost blinding golden refraction sprawled into view—the effect perhaps augmented by how dark everything had previously been. And when the newcomer stepped inside, the golden blaze indeed dulled down dramatically, yet still gleamed brighter than anything else.

The newcomer himself was a surprise visitor. He wasn't Nine Arms, but rather the person closest to him in strength, stature, and loyalty toward the emperor.

"You're really here," Lachman said as he strode forward in his gleaming armour, eyeing Bors and then the pair of swords on the ground.

Lachman hadn't dressed down like the others, and that was perhaps unwise of him considering that he would want to avoid being seen anywhere near the prison.

"The emperor has an important announcement to make at the Gardens," Lachman said, taking another step to intimidate the other men. "It is advisable that the two of you, Sir Bors and Sir Kite, attend this gathering rather than continue on whatever futile act you are planning here." Lachman then turned to Julian, who was still behind the mask. "I'll need you to leave, too."

Bors thumped his hammerhead onto his palm, wearing a grin. "You came alone now, did you?"

Lachman lifted his head slightly in affirmation, narrowing his eyes as if asking: *And…?*

"I didn't want to do this," Bors said, his grin deepening as he brought his giant maul up against his chest. "But we can't afford to have you team up with Nine Arms."

"Wait, no," Kite said, holding the Titan back. Kite then turned to Lachman. "Go, please. Pretend you didn't see anything. This has nothing to do with you."

Julian glanced over at Kite, remembering that the young knight was one of Lachman's many admirers. Indeed, Lachman was humble and had kept a low profile despite his much-celebrated standing as the strongest of all golden knights. People agreed not only to the popular consensus that Lachman was the strongest, but they also admired the man's kind nature and faithful representation of knighthood. Ever since the beginning of the Advent Era, Lachman had been visiting all parts of the country in order to promote the high standard of gallantry and chivalry expected not only of knights, but all warrior classes that belonged as part of the Empire. He was always available when help was needed, particularly known for his philanthropic work in which he often led the restoration efforts to towns or villages that had been devastated by great storms, wildfires, and other natural phenomena that affected civilians adversely.

Julian jumped slightly then as a bang sounded in the distance. Bors was on the other side of Lachman, and the Titan had closed the heavy double door that was the only exit to the prison, shutting out the shimmering moonlight that had previously shone through. Everything grew suddenly dark, and Lachman's golden armour was the one thing that was still easy to see in the flickering candlelight.

"Only you are foolish enough to be in armour," Bors said with a snicker. "Your pride is what will see you die this evening."

Julian's grip on the pair of swords had loosened. It wouldn't be easy for him to turn his weapon against Lachman, especially if this was to kill him.

But as Julian hesitated, Lachman lunged directly at him—surprisingly, he thought, since it was Bors who had just threatened his life. Julian gritted his teeth, instinctively sweeping out a blade, only for Lachman to nullify the forced initiative with a dab of his still-sheathed longsword that deflected Julian's slender weapon from his grip. The golden knight then followed by swinging an arm out that sent Julian crashing against the wall and onto the floor. Rather than maintaining that pressure, however, Lachman leaped back to where he had previously stood.

Julian promptly picked himself up, feeling little pain from the fall. But when he looked up again, he realised that he was maskless—his mask now in Lachman's hand. The chamber wasn't nearly dark enough for the others not to recognise him.

Julian glared at Lachman, angered not just at being exposed but also that the golden knight had seen through his disguise. Bors and Kite, meanwhile, were awe-struck.

"How...!" Kite uttered, refusing to believe it. "*How* is it you?!"

"I assume the real phantom must still be lurking in the darkness, then," Lachman said, glancing down at the mask in his hand and then discarding it onto the ground.

Bors growled and then hammered his giant maul onto one of only four pillars that supported the chamber. The stone pillar collapsed instantly as the walls and ceilings trembled as if in an earthquake.

"Damn Longinus...," Bors said with a long grunt. "I swear I'll kill you one day." But Bors then turned to Lachman, his gritted teeth curling up slowly into a broad smile. It wasn't the smirk that Julian was used to. Instead, that grin on the Titan's face now carried an obvious hint of unease.

"But today, we're facing a greater enemy," Bors continued. "I'll need your help. And you'll need mine. We have no choice but to fight together." He paused, glancing over at Julian once again. "If we survive this, Nine Arms is next."

Julian frowned, reluctant to agree just yet.

But Bors had turned back to Lachman already. "I'll start," he then said, darting forward to charge.

Bors thumped the giant maul down toward Lachman, connecting with nothing but the stone floor that splintered open from wall to wall, while both the walls themselves shook violently.

Bors turned his head both ways—not to where Lachman had dashed off to, but to Julian and Kite. "What are you waiting for?!" he demanded. "Fight!"

Julian exchanged a quick look with Kite and then both leaped in to join the scramble. Lachman and his golden armour were indeed easy to descry among everything else that barely reflected the candlelight. Julian simply slashed toward where the shimmer of golden twinkled, though his almost perfunctory movements gifted Lachman a handicap that he didn't need. Julian didn't want to see Lachman—who he believed to be a warrior of honour—die at the end of his blade. And as it turned out, Kite was timid too, the young knight's usual hotheadedness seemingly forgotten.

Lachman barely had to raise his longsword and was defending almost by evasion alone. Bors was the only one who respected the fight, crashing the destructive maul everywhere he could, almost as if he was looking to bury everyone with the loose stones that showered down from the ceiling.

Julian raised his arms as a shield to defend himself from the raining stones, and he noted Bors exchanging a look with Kite which seemed like a signal of sorts. The Titan then prodded forward again, hammering the maul at Lachman's feet and only missing them by inches. But as it looked like Lachman had evaded, the stone floor tore open at exactly where Lachman had jumped to, causing the man to stumble for the first time. Julian widened his eyes then as he realised that Kite had darted immediately behind Lachman, slicing his blade upwards.

They got him! Julian thought, jerking forward. But just as Kite was about to connect, Lachman spun his sword, forcing the blade to shoot out from its sheath with incredible speed—in the end, parrying away Kite who fell back with a grunt.

Bors pushed in from the other side, and Julian moved to complete the triangle surrounding Lachman.

"What was that, dammit?!" Bors cursed at Kite. "This is a battle to death!"

Kite hissed, looking down slightly. "I can't do this. Sir Lachman doesn't deserve to die."

Lachman spun slowly, pivoting on one foot as he peered at Kite and then Bors, but ignoring Julian completely. The man finally seemed wary, perhaps recognising for the first time that he had almost been killed.

"Sir Bors," Lachman said, raising his longsword and pointing it at the Titan. "Those two aren't prepared to fight me. They'll only get in the way.

And you alone cannot harm me. I'll give you one last chance to walk away. Leave now—go to the Gardens, and I'll pretend I never saw you here."

Bors snorted in offence. "Don't you *dare* pity me," he said, pointing the maul back at Lachman. "You might be strong, but I won't be humiliated." He looked over to Kite and then to Julian. "I can't understand why the young ones are so naïve, but you should know I'm not like them. I'll go all out at you. I'll fight until one of us is dead."

Lachman returned a wordless smile, bending his knees slightly as he readied for a second round. Bors huffed out a deep breath and then wound up for a full swing of his giant maul, charging forward as he did so. Julian gaped in astounded silence, realising that it was probably the first time that two golden knights had squared off.

The Titan's grit and determination was different from before, and it showed in his heightened dexterity that soon left Lachman cornered and forced into a wrestling match. Julian was sure the eventual victor would still be Lachman, despite the man's apparent struggle, both his arms shaking as he upheld the longsword horizontally against the giant maul.

Julian watched Lachman then, noting a subtle squint from the golden knight. Lachman turned his sword from the edge to the flat side and slid it down from where it connected with the Titan's giant maul, nullifying the wrestling match in exchange for the risk of the dangerous hammer crashing down upon him.

Bors stumbled forward slightly, his weapon still carrying ample downward momentum, the veteran perhaps thinking his opponent had gone mad. Julian kept his eyes on Lachman, watching the man dash inches to the right and slide the longsword up vertically to knock the maul off into the air—spinning upwards. While all other eyes must have followed that spinning motion, Julian maintained his gaze on Lachman, who then followed with another deadly slide of the sword, this time mercilessly tearing Bors at the chest, drawing a frightening amount of blood spraying out.

A terrifying scream illustrated Bors's sensational defeat. The result was then verified by a loud thud as Bors landed in shambles on the ground, drowning in a pool of his own blood.

Kite ran to his comrade with urgency and held the man in his arms. The young knight's shocked expression showed that he understood that the deep cuts on the Titan's chest would not heal. Everything was soaked in the unpleasant scarlet red.

"Sir… Bors…," Kite uttered, his eyes wide open in distress.

Bors stared only at the ceiling, perhaps heavenward. "Lord… Breunor…," the dying man said, barely making out his words. "I tried."

Julian trembled from afar as Bors's eyes closed forever. He had watched his bitter rival fight with courage this evening, and now that Bors had been laid to eternal rest, Julian felt a stinging guilt inside of him that he couldn't make sense of. Perhaps Bors deserved better than a violent death. After all, the veteran warrior was undoubtedly loyal to his comrades and the causes he stood for. But perhaps his death liberated him from his guilt of failing to protect Breunor and the burden of leading others loyal to Breunor.

Julian twitched then as he noted that Kite had let go of the perished Bors and was now on his feet. Kite raised his sabre, seemingly no longer reluctant to turn his sword against Lachman.

"No…," Julian heard himself utter.

But Kite was already lashing out at Lachman. Driven by rage, the fiery young knight sliced about viciously. And yet he didn't let his rage get the better of him, still wielding the sabre with great skill and eclipsing Bors in both speed and agility. Even so, Lachman neutralised every strike, making it look easy.

Julian groaned and then rushed to Kite's aid, certain that they would never trounce Lachman. The crimson red aura that followed Julian enlivened the dim chamber and the hacking of his twin rapiers at a speed even faster than Kite followed with red beams blazing about. Combined with Kite's already lighting quick movements, they were gradually pressing Lachman into a precarious scramble. Julian bothered the golden knight with his stronger thrusts with the intention to allow Kite to land a critical strike from any opening he might create.

Keep defending, I dare you, Julian thought, watching for any changes of expression in Lachman. *You'll soon regret underestimating us.*

As Kite intensified the pressure on their common foe, Julian pulled back briefly for a stronger swing which he swept backhanded from his left with the full force of his dominant right arm, blessed behind the breeze of crimson red.

Block this!

As if Lachman had read his intention, the golden knight countered by slamming the pommel of his sword into Julian's chest, nullifying his attack and sending Julian flying into the opposite wall. The exchange in turn delayed what would have been a purposeful strike from Kite, allowing Lachman to deal Kite the same fate as Julian, both of them crashing against the far wall.

Julian exchanged a brief look with Kite, noting the blood dribbling from the mouth of his unlikely ally. Both he and Kite looked up then at a warrior clearly far stronger than them, wondering what was going to happen next.

* * *

Lachman regarded the two young knights with caution. One of them was hailed as the strongest young knight in the country, a prodigy by any standard. The other one, meanwhile, was a sorcerer. It would be a while until either of them would pose any real threat to him, but Lachman realised that he couldn't afford to be complacent. He regretted that he had had to kill Bors. But the emperor's instructions were clear: *destroy anyone or anything that stands as an obstacle.*

"You two have potential," Lachman praised, panting slightly. "I never imagined I'd be threatened by such inexperienced knights. A lapse of concentration there would have been the end for me." He paused, swinging the longsword to his side. "One more chance. Walk out now, and pretend you were never here."

Julian picked himself up, ignoring his throbbing chest. "We don't need mercy," he said. "You said it yourself. We almost got you. A lapse of concentration, a small mistake, and you'll be a dead man!"

Lachman narrowed his eyes. The hotheaded Kite was already back on his feet and rushing at him again.

Fool, Lachman thought, shaking his head as he prepared for a second round, which he believed would be the last. *You may be fast*, Lachman thought as he counted Kite's footsteps, *but I need less than a second to draw.*

Each man had grown used to the faint lighting there, but when Lachman noted a shimmer of red behind the dashing feet of Kite, the young knight was already in his face.

That speed, Lachman recognised in awe, drawing his longsword immediately and gritting his teeth in the process. His quick draw managed to hold off the precipitous strike just in time, but even Lachman could do precious little to avoid suffering his first hit that had come by a heavy kick on his shoulder.

Landing comfortably still, Lachman turned a brisk gaze at Julian who wore a smirk. Julian had given the already agile Kite the gift of enhanced speed.

Don't take us lightly, seemed to be their message as the two of them dashed forward again now with the splashes of crimson red polluting the tightness of the chamber.

The two young knights hacked about almost recklessly as they took full advantage of their incredible speed, landing a couple of successive slashes finally that pierced Lachman's otherwise indomitable armour of gold.

There was value in your death, Walford Bors, Lachman thought as he struggled. *You managed to enrage these two not only to fight, but to raise their level.*

Lachman's lips curled up then to a grin.

It almost worked, he thought, closing his eyes and slowing down considerably, surrendering his armour to several more slashes.

As soon as he settled into his more sedate approach, however, Lachman began to fend off attacks with great efficiency. Not only did he parry off the two young knights, but he also left them stunned for seconds following each exchange, which allowed him the opportunity to counter. Lachman was doing his utmost with minimal movement, answering to multiple strikes with single waves of his arm, neutralising yet even more with casual slides of his sword. He was fighting with his senses rather than actual sensations, calling upon his vast experience to brush off attacks even before their execution.

His opponents had been tenacious, but Lachman's defence was simply impenetrable. Lachman had turned the tables completely, now dictating the tempo as he ran the offence. He was determined to batter the young knights in the same way that they had tried to batter him. The difference was that Lachman's attacks connected far more often, and at a level of strength far above what his opponents could manage.

As far as Lachman was concerned, there was never any contest from the beginning. Blow after blow, Lachman sent the young knights crashing here and there to affirm his clear dominance.

The sorcerer-knight is slowing down, Lachman noted, eyeing Julian's fading aura. *But that other one can't seem to stop*, he thought, glancing over at Kite, who was jumping at him again despite the fatigue he must be feeling. Lachman frowned, sweeping his longsword out, tearing at the thighs, drawing an eruption of blood that had Kite crashing down to the ground.

"No!" Julian cried from a distance, raising a helpless arm.

Be grateful you still have your legs, Lachman thought, staring down at Kite.

The battle was over, but Lachman didn't have the liberty to enjoy the result. He looked over at Julian whose eyes were oddly fixed on the double door that was latched closed. Lachman panted softly, maintaining an intent gaze at the only exit, which was suddenly smashed in from the outside, apparently by a gale of wind, slamming detached from hinges and directly toward him.

Forced to another quick draw, Lachman swept out his longsword to avert the danger, knocking away the metal chunk to smash against the far wall. Lachman looked up again, and in the glimmers of moonlight pouring into the chamber, he saw the man he had been looking for.

The phantom.

FORTY

Advent sorcerers

Julian found himself beaming. There was no mistake that behind that black mask with whiskers of white and draped with the long cape flapping in undulation was the phantom soldier. Julian might have replicated the stranger's outfit, but the essence of who the man was—the intrepidity and valour—wasn't something he could ever imitate.

And it looked like the phantom was armed with a new set of twin swords, the blades apparently even thinner than the original pair.

"I hate to go back on my word," the phantom said, eyeing Julian, "but it looks like you are indebted to me for a third time."

"And yet I still don't know who you are," Julian responded.

"There are more pressing matters than my name," the phantom soldier said, nodding in Lachman's direction. "You're too merciful. If you were Nine Arms, these two would be dead by now. Your gallantry has won my genuine respect."

"I appreciate the praise," Lachman answered. "But that doesn't change my impression of you. Your murder of my affiliates makes you one of my prime enemies."

"Every one of them deserved to die," the phantom said with a shrug. "But *you*—you're different, Sir Lachman. I have no desire to fight you, and I surely have no intention to kill you."

"Is that so?" Lachman asked mockingly. "I assumed that you relish the occasional fight. After all, you *did* challenge Pylon."

"He was rusty from brewing in that prison—that's why I dared. If I were to fight him again today, I would stand no chance. I'm glad he's not here."

Lachman raised a brow. "But against me, you would stand every chance?"

The phantom soldier shook his head. "I don't want a confrontation. You have shown mercy to Kite and Longinus. I ask you to extend that mercy to me."

"I can't offer you any liberty, at least not until you give me an explanation for my perished allies."

"I cannot say more than I have already said."

"Then...," Lachman said, raising his longsword, "I'll force it out of you!"

The golden knight took the initiative for once, knocking up the pair of swords from the ground and batting them at the mysterious man who easily swiped them away with his new blades. Julian gasped then as Lachman lunged toward the phantom who he thought might be blindsided from the angle. Before Lachman even got there, however, the phantom had flashed away. The golden gleam of Lachman's armour chased immediately after the shadow, and a moment later, the two men clashed blades in a thunderous clang.

Lachman wasn't fighting how he had earlier. Instead of reacting to the phantom's attacks, the golden knight had opted for an offensive tear, slashing with strong and purposeful strikes and allowing practically no space for retaliation. It was apparent to Julian then that Lachman had held back earlier. Even so, the phantom was holding his own by flashing away in sudden dashes every time it looked like he was about to be cornered.

It was too early to predict who would emerge triumphant as the phantom's deft handle of the twin rapiers answered Lachman's every strike. The phantom brushed his blades about slickly, without any fault for wasted motions—simply alluring to watch, Julian noted with admiration. The phantom's swordplay technique somehow seemed familiar to Julian, and even the phantom's relatively lean figure resembled someone he had once known very well.

Percival? Julian thought with a worried frown.

"Lionel Lachman will keep his word!" the phantom cried in between clashes with the golden knight. "But if Nine Arms arrives, we're all dead!"

Julian groaned quietly, clenching a fist. It was unlikely that Percival Pole was the phantom, and regardless of who the phantom was, Julian suddenly realised how pitiful it was to be *rescued* yet again. The thought of escaping had never crossed his mind. After all, he had come to the prison for Alpheus, to save him despite how that could adversely affect the Pristines. Although Julian was hurt and fatigued, he was sure he could still manage to get Alpheus out if he ran down to the cells. Upon that thought, Julian took a couple of hesitant steps toward the descending stairs until he was stopped and held at his ankles by Kite, who was still on the ground.

"Longinus...," Kite muttered, looking like he was about to faint. "Go... go to Vondra Dawn. Sir Roc and... and our other men are there. Bring them here... I beg you! Bring them here. We'll kill Nine Arms together!"

Although Kite was half-dead, all he knew was to avenge Breunor—and perhaps Bors. Julian glanced over to the two powerful men in battle, and then took one last glimpse toward the stairs.

Sorry, Alpheus, he thought as he threw Kite on his back and then turned to flee. Julian grunted, staggering into the open hill and out to a night sky where the heavy clouds had begun to dissipate. The glowing crescent of Achelois was beginning to emerge from the clouds.

"What are you doing, Longinus?" Kite asked. "Don't be naïve. Just let me be. Just go and—"

"Shut up!" Julian commanded.

Kite mumbled a few more words, probably of reproach, but Julian was no longer listening. In fact, he hardly knew what he was doing anymore. The damage he had endured in their battle against Lachman had left him with blood and sweat sliding and dripping from his chin, and his body was throbbing all over. Julian didn't expect Kite or anyone else to empathise with the fact that his reserve of grace was near empty, and that sorcerers too were subject to fatigue. But the truth was that he was floundering down the hill then, carrying the weight of the lamed Kite on his back, calling not on sorcery but on willpower to fight for the causes of other men.

Damned Breunor, Julian thought, huffing.

And Bors, you showed some honour in the end. I suppose—

Julian skidded to a sudden screeching stop, the weight and momentum of Kite on his back almost pushing him over the edge of the slope. Kite was still complaining, but Julian didn't listen as he looked toward the river bank ahead of them, struggling to catch his breath, refusing to believe that on the other side of the narrow stream was their most feared enemy: Pylon, more famously known as Nine Arms.

The vengeful man donned heavy indigo armour matched with a long black cape clipped at his shoulders. One hand carried the ball-and-chain flail that was as deadly as it was dread-inducing. The other hand grasped the cranium of an unconscious Roc—the very man Julian was supposed to seek to help them kill Nine Arms.

Roc's party, more than ten of them, kneeled beside them—fatigued, helpless, and defeated. Julian laid Kite off his back and onto the grass, and as Julian wracked his brain for options, Kite shouted at the madman with as much volume as he could muster.

"Mongrel!" Kite cursed from the ground. "Let go of him!"

Nine Arms grinned and then granted Kite's wish, throwing the incapacitated Roc into the stream, this action immediately reducing Kite to shocked silence. Barely a moment after Roc had sunk from view, flowing downstream, the gentle watercourse saw wisps of red. Kite clawed into the soil, still cursing, perhaps looking to crawl his way into the river. Julian hissed and then raced toward the stream, diving down into the water without a second thought. The gurgling of bubbles added to his already blurred underwater vision, but Julian stroked hard, relying on yet more willpower to get to the drowning veteran. A moment later, Julian grabbed the man's arm, wrapped it around his shoulders, and then finally thrashed up out of the water.

Julian struggled his way back to the bank, stepping on land again all drenched, dropping Roc next to the stream. He then tore off his cape and swaddled the veteran whose body was cold as ice.

Nine Arms put his hands together to mockingly applaud Julian. "But is this really the time to be worrying about others?" he asked.

Julian continued to huff, water dripping from his hair. Even he was unsure why he had bothered.

"But enough of this," Nine Arms continued. "We need to move."

Julian peered over at the vengeful man, his own body now numb from fear. "Move where?"

"We need to get Lachman, and then we'll all go to the Gardens. You'll see when we get there."

Nine Arms then swung out the destructive metal ball, hurling it out to the river, and the resulting force caused an explosion of water to erupt up into the air. The man reeled himself forward, the sensational burst of water pushing him up high and over to the other side of the bank, landing next to Julian with a heavy thump.

Julian looked up at him, the man's stalwart build always daunting. It was unthinkable to resist him, especially given Julian's current condition. Julian obediently turned back toward the prison where the fight between Lachman and the phantom was likely still going on. He took only a few steps until he glanced back slightly, down to the dreadful, prosthetic arm that came into view at every stride.

"What about them?" Julian asked, nodding at Roc, Kite, and the others.

Nine Arms paused for a second, sparing them no glance. "It doesn't concern me whether they are dead or alive," he said, pushing Julian forward. "I have no interest in people as weak as them."

Julian sighed softly and allowed himself one last glance back at Kite, who looked completely crushed—his ego utterly shattered. Kite had been lauded as the most promising young warrior of recent years, but there he was then by the river, kneeling in deflation, perhaps flooded by guilt and worthlessness.

You won't avenge Breunor today, Julian thought.

* * *

Marvin looked up with a smile, still holding the burning torch for light, proud of his team's efforts. It had taken five days to get to this point. Above them was the final barrier—a thin patch of earth that had been marked out almost like a ceiling hatch in the cramped burrow.

Marvin nodded to both Rover and Ash and then punched up into the circular patch, smashing through the soil and the apparent layer of stone. An audible gasp sounded from the top, and before anyone else above could react, Marvin threw another punch, this time smashing open the rest of the patch to force an opening that was large enough for them to emerge from. Rather than climbing out, Marvin sprung upward and landed with a thunderous thud that cracked the stone tiles. The extravagant entrance, however, came at the cost of loose soil showering down now over Rover and Ash, who were still in the burrow.

We're here, Marvin thought as he peered across the prison cave which was barely brighter than the hellish burrow he had been so desperate to escape. *But God... after all that effort, we came up into one of the cells*, he realised, hardly laying an eye on the prisoner who had retired to the far corner, shaking in fear.

Prisoners of the neighbouring cells had perked up, too, gasping and mumbling. Everyone sharing the cave—including the guards—had noted the sudden intrusion and were in the midst of deciding how to react.

Rover and Ash climbed into the cell to join Marvin. No one in the trio had bothered with masks or masquerades, for they *wanted* to be recognised. Almost all of the prisoners, with the exception of the one who shared the same cell as them, began shaking their bars like wild beasts, probably wishful for chaos to befall the prison. The guards, meanwhile—more than a dozen of them—besieged the cell from the outside.

"Who's there?!" one of the guards demanded, alert yet dumbfounded, pointing a sword in at the intruders who were indeed *locked in*, brushing off the grime they were covered in.

"He... he's... Marvin Sailanson...," a second guard said, stuttering as he stepped back, trembling.

"Sail... Sailanson...?!" a third guard said, sharing the fear of the others. "The man who killed... two hundred men?"

The guard who had been the first to speak grew suddenly pale. "That doesn't make him a man anymore, does it?" he said, shaking. "He's a... *monster*!"

Marvin frowned then, his glare meeting the eyes of the guards who were now all overcome with horror. Marvin then glanced out at the prisoners who had carried on howling like animals. He grinned and then dashed forward onto the bars, too, shaking them wildly and howling like a madman—at a volume that swept over everyone else, in turn quieting the manic prisoners.

The guards screamed, some of them in a sharper pitch than they probably knew they were capable of. They scrambled away from the cell, stumbling over each other as if they were running for their lives, though they only managed to back away as far as several feet into the opposite cells across the corridor.

Ash laughed while Rover shook his head in the back.

Marvin quieted down, glancing back slightly at his allies. "Whatever works," he said with a shrug. Marvin turned back to the guards then, making eye contact with several of them in turn. "Will you kindly unlock this cell for me, or will you see me crush it down?"

The guards exchanged looks before nodding at one another. They nominated one of the bigger men to do the exchange, prodding him forward despite his clear reluctance. The man's large fingers didn't help him pick out the right key easily, though, and the soft clanging of metal on metal only served to unnerve him more.

"Would you hurry it up?" Marvin demanded with a scowl, causing the guard to drop the keys altogether. But when he dropped down to collect the keys once more, Marvin paused.

They're terrified of me, he noted. *The overwhelming fear on their faces is no different from those helpless civilians in the war. The look of dejection, of despair. Have I really become that much of a monster?*

Marvin peered away to some of the prisoners then, noting that all of them had settled down after their initial frenzy and were now gaping out in awe.

When the lock finally clicked open, Marvin stepped out and stared down at the large guard who had *liberated* him. He snatched the chain of keys with a swipe that no one other than Rover would have seen.

"Which key to unlock Alpheus Hindlow?" Marvin asked.

"That... that one," the petrified guard said, pointing to the key with a noticeable curve on the top.

Marvin ripped the key right off and then passed the rest back to the guard. "Lock yourselves away," he said. "All of you... if you don't want to die."

The terrified guards abided immediately, proceeding to unlock the cell next to the one that had been broken into. They scrambled inside to join the prisoner already there, cramping up every inch of the modest cell.

Marvin strode along the corridor, eventually recognising Alpheus, who was the only prisoner still on his feet.

"I knew you would come," Alpheus said, looking grateful and pleased.

Marvin said nothing, only nodding in response as he turned the key with an audible click. "We have to go *now*," Marvin said, already turning for the stairs that led to the entrance chamber at the top of the hill. "Come on."

"The bookworm has survived once again," Ash said, seemingly ignorant of Marvin's displeasure with Alpheus.

"Thanks to you," Alpheus said before calling out to Marvin from behind, grabbing him by the wrist. "Can I assume that the emperor sent you?" he asked, dropping what sounded like an obvious hint of suspicion.

Marvin didn't spare Alpheus a glance and shook away the scholar's grip. "Yes," he said, irate, "but to get you out. The one you turned to, the *Lord* Chancellor, sent for assassins to have you dead."

"I figured as much," Alpheus said curtly. "After all, the emperor is working with Kraga."

Marvin held off a response this time, also holding off a grunt.

"I know you share a deep history with him," Alpheus said. "But to tolerate is to nurture the evildoer. You're no longer his Left Wing—you don't have to be loyal to him anymore."

"Shut up, Alpheus!" Rover interjected, his ferocious tone echoing through the prison. "You know nothing!"

The prisoners and the guards were still watching, all of them wide-eyed as everything fell hushed for a moment.

"I meant no disrespect," Alpheus said then to break the silence. "I assume Azure has spoken to you? I'm not sure what she told you, but allow me to iterate. I submitted myself at Vondra Dawn with the intention of expediting the political war. I want this to end. On top of that, I've wanted to identify the one connected to the Kragan Dynasty. I admit that I've suspected the emperor since the beginning, but I didn't target him. I mentioned none of this to the chancellor, either, because he was a suspect, too."

Ash coughed, likely on purpose in order to break some of the tension. "But why did you say just now that the emperor is behind it?" he asked.

"A protracted feud, the political war, benefits the Kragans," Alpheus said. "The chancellor sent people to kill me, but doing so shows that he wants to end this feud. The emperor, on the other hand, sent you to get me out. He is prolonging the feud."

Marvin squinted, holding in the impulse to argue further. He was sure that Spartamon would never ally with the Kragans, yet he was indeed torn about why the great man—the greatest conqueror in the land—had allowed the feud to exacerbate to such conditions that were so unfavourable to him.

"I'll see for myself what has become of him," Marvin finally said.

Alpheus grinned. "Let's go," he said. "I promise—"

Marvin didn't allow Alpheus to finish the sentence as he flashed behind the scholar, rendering him unconscious with a light swat at his neck. Ash raised a hand in protest, but even before he had uttered a word, Marvin slipped behind him, knocking him out in the same way.

"Ro, take them to a safe place for me," Marvin said.

Rover groaned and threw the two unconscious men atop his broad shoulders, and then strode back to the cell they had climbed into, the prisoner who occupied the cell still trembling in the corner. Rover stepped over next to the hole they had dug, turning his head back slightly when he reached it.

"Next time, allow me in on the fun," Rover said before finally slipping away from view.

Marvin nodded with a forced smile and then turned to the stairs, racing up the prison cave with a heavy heart. He had admired Spartamon and he had also feared him, but the fear had never been because of any suspicion that the man would betray the country. Marvin still didn't want to believe that Spartamon had changed for the worst. He wanted to trust Spartamon, at least still believing that the man was a good leader. In addition to all of the conspiracy theories, however, there was one more thing lingering on his mind: the question of why Spartamon had continued to tease him about his deceased lover, Kharvalenis.

Marvin soon reached the top of the prison, a small antechamber which was in rubble, most of it torn down—including one of the four wide pillars that lifted the ceiling.

What happened here? Marvin wondered, pausing briefly, as he noted the corpse of a gigantic man drowned in blood. He then stepped out to the open hill.

Fresh air, finally. But more guards lying on the ground—*are they dead?* Marvin took in a deep breath, lifting his head then and regarding the steeples of Vondra Dawn under a clearing night sky. The view seemed almost peaceful. Unfortunately, he knew too well that that was only an ornamental exterior.

Marvin sighed again and then paced onward.

* * *

Sagramore regarded the blue of Achelois under the open evening sky, the faint waning crescent slipping in and out of the swirling clouds. Barely was there a hint of Selene, the ruby red he had always been so fond of. He sighed softly, wondering how many more times he would see the moons. Life itself was so fragile. No matter the age of the land and regardless of who ruled, the moons would simply repeat the same pattern, the same phases, over and over again forever.

Sagramore stroked his puffy beard as he gazed down to where a small podium had been set, back-dropped by the gentle stream of the Dunn River and the intimidating steeples of Vondra Dawn. He was one of more than fifty men gathered now in front of it. They were at the Luxuriant Gardens, a private garden frequented by the late Lord Count. Although the place rarely saw so many visitors at once, it comfortably accommodated the guests this evening, most of who had arrived in armour and were now wearing grim faces. Schim was in attendance leading a sizeable group of men all looking eager to identify themselves as Pristines. Forredan, the wise statesman, was also present with his retinue. Morlan, the former king of Cetal, was in an entourage of seven. Completing the attendance list were some of the lesser lords who were regular members of the court.

Everyone probably had their own ideas about how the evening would turn out or how they would try to turn events in their favour. Sagramore presumed that he was perhaps the only one undecided about what he wanted to happen. He had felt helpless since the political war had first started, and coming here to the gardens this evening, he had only hoped that the beautiful landscape wouldn't end up bloodstained.

Glancing over to his immediate right and then to his immediate left, Sagramore found some comfort in knowing that he had his most trusted vassals with him, a total of seven.

Only two are missing, he thought with a slight squint as a commanding voice sounded from the podium.

"We are gathered here today," the emperor said, beginning a speech as the only person standing upon the elevated stage, "to remedy the curse that has befallen our Empire—the curse of dissension. I have only one item on the agenda today, and that is to steer us all toward unity once again."

The emperor was dressed lightly, and he carried no weapon. His charming smile as he looked down at some of the men was a genial one. Indeed, Spartamon's natural charisma seemed to have soothed some of the more impulsive men to abate their aggression. So far, the emperor had paid no heed to Schim, who had been rather quiet since his arrival. It was a curious matter, however, that the emperor had come to the gardens on his own—that is, without any of his loyal vassals, such as Lachman and Pylon.

Indeed, the entire setup was rather strange.

"This garden," the emperor said, strolling to the left of the podium, "was established during the early years of the Ode Era—well over a century ago. It still stands today, more resplendent than ever. I'm sure the king who had this built finds pride in that.

"Likewise, I am proud to have founded this Truban Empire... with you—my fellow soldiers."

The emperor frowned slightly then, turning to his right and then strolling in that direction. "There have been questions of concern about my commitment to leading this country," he continued. "But I assure you—the future of this country is what I live for. It pains me that our mighty Empire has been accused of disunity, and indeed has experienced it. I ache when I see the common people losing their trust in us. And I strive to correct this." Spartamon paused again. "Let this evening be the last of the dissension. Our goal is stability, and I assure you that when the sun rises again on my left, we shall all be family once more."

Sagramore smirked, noting many in the audience nodding along to the emperor's words. Spartamon was indeed charismatic, and his voice was powerful. He spoke confidently, and the words he spoke were what the people wanted to hear. The emperor had yet to make any proposals, but *stability* was perhaps the most important outcome for the country, regardless of where one might stand politically. Forredan, however, seemed to have his own agenda despite the rumour that he identified as Spartamon's supporter—as an Advent. And it was rather uncharacteristic of the statesman to speak so early, as he did now.

"So, Lord Emperor," Forredan said, seemingly impatient, "what are you offering?"

The emperor nodded at the stout man. "Allow me to direct your attention to the ground you stand on."

The men presently exchanged looks, but most of them then began to glance down, Forredan included. Sagramore gazed down now as well. The garden floor was carpeted not by regular grass, but by a species of bulbous plants blooming with white flowers. The floor of near-white was rather striking, and while the men had most likely noted this on their arrival, no one had remarked upon it—not in the midst of a political crisis that threatened to dissolve the city, and hence the country.

The emperor stepped down from the side of the podium, leaning toward the ground and coiling his fingers around a flower bud.

"This is a winter-flowering plant that cannot bloom in mid-summer," Spartamon said, standing upright again. "But I've made it happen. I send the best botanists here to nurture them every evening and I'm glad that they are ready for tonight."

Forredan simpered, his double chin widening. "Please, Lord Emperor, no one cares about these flowers. We care about the future."

The emperor peered over again toward the stout man, maintaining a smile. "I'm nearly there," he said. "It was about four months ago, after Jeffery Reeling passed, when I seeded this plant."

A few men raised their eyebrow, including Schim, who cringed visibly.

"It was then that I began planning for tonight. The flower is called the snowdrop, endemic to my ancestral country, Aizary. From the experience of seeding this plant, I was reminded of an important belief."

The emperor paused for a moment and then viciously tore off the flower bud he had coiled onto, swinging his arm with full force in one fluid motion. He then leaped back onto the podium and his eyes went up to the heavens.

"Come," the emperor said, as if summoning something.

A wraith-like figure flashed in toward the emperor from the right, apparently from one of the tall elm trees, its leaves ruffling. Gasps sounded as some men flinched and raised their arms. Sagramore peered about warily, raising his hand slightly as a signal for his knights to hold. No one from his group was going to act prematurely.

The newcomer was a masked man, wrapped in a long, dark navy robe—an apparent ally to the emperor, bended on one knee next to Spartamon. When the mumbles from the confused audience began to intensify, the leaves on the other trees all began to rattle together as well, the sound ringing in people's ears as if it were the incessant fluttering of a swarm of bats. The suspense made the moment feel longer than it actually was, and before long, spectres emerged from the canopies, shooting down one by one onto the podium to join the first stranger and the emperor.

Sagramore frowned as he watched the scene pan out, sure that everyone shared his curiosity—as well as his fear for the worst. What was the emperor doing, calling a dozen strangers to line up adjacent to him, six on each side? On a positive note, though, the strangers were unarmed. Beneath the long robes they wore were lean physiques that didn't match those of traditional warriors. At least two or three of them were women judging from their longer legs and convex chests. Even so, the way they had all flashed in like apparitions was haunting in that they might not even be human at all. After all, Sagramore recognised that even he couldn't manage the brief show of supreme athleticism and stealth that he had just witnessed. Adding to the animosity were the masks borne onto each one of their faces, painted with wide, sinister grins.

Beneath the podium, some men had instinctively reached for their swords. Sagramore glanced over to Forredan, and then to Schim, both of them looking ready for an unwarranted melee.

"Now, where was I?" the emperor said, narrowing his eyes. "Ah, that's right... I promised to end the dissension. So, here we are. Let the Empire be united once again..." The man paused and then snapped his eyes wide open. "Submit to me your *absolute obedience*."

The twelve strangers then shot out toward the men from the podium, sifting through the crowd like bolts of lightning, their strides trailed by a riffling luminous white that faded into the air as they passed.

Sorcery! Sagramore realised abruptly, spinning his partisan out despite the confusion. From scorching flames to prickling spears of ice, people were being attacked voraciously and indiscriminately. Destructive spells trailed by visible white energy blasted about in all directions, and even those who had identified as Advents were being shown no mercy.

Screams and cries of terror filled the air as the men fought while also wondering what force had come upon them. Sagramore grunted, barking out instructions to his loyal knights to help protect Morlan and some of the lesser lords, all the while prodding his partisan forward at one of the sorcerers—only to realise something stranger even than the ambush.

What is this sudden frailty...?! he wondered in shock, regarding his arm and then his partisan. *I can't draw on my strength at all.*

Sagramore turned urgently, watching other knights sweeping their swords in defence, their strength visibly curbed as well. Further away,

Sagramore descried fellow golden knight Claude Lucan, who was also unable to draw on his massive physical prowess and was indeed struggling in a fight against only a single sorcerer.

"What madness is this?!" Schim cried, not too far from Lucan. The chancellor was caught in a scuffle and humiliated by a series of elemental forces.

Even the Raiders, Sagramore noted, glancing over to Schim's three loyal vassals who were among the most powerful individual warriors in the country, now barely able to hold their own against the forces before them. A shriek sounded farther off to the right and Sagramore peered in that direction, watching a knight he didn't recognise pinned down face on the ground and then promptly contained with a strap tying his hands together.

Sagramore eyed one of the faceless foes tormenting a few of his own knights. He dashed toward them, spinning his polearm forward and gashing the forearm of the aggressor, successfully drawing a stream of blood.

"Sir Sagramore!" one of his knights cried, dashing toward him in support.

The idea of teaming up was correct, but Sagramore understood that they were nonetheless fighting a losing battle. None of them had ever encountered—let alone faced—sorcerers in open battle. The first challenge was to keep up with the sorcerers' peculiar movements, and the second was to respond to the elemental forces being unleashed at them. If not for their inability to draw on their full strength, Sagramore believed there was a chance that they might all be able to pull through. But as the scramble progressed, it became clearer and clearer to all of the sword-wielding men that they were on course for complete defeat and humiliation.

More than half of men in attendance—most of them knights—had already been contained, their weapons confiscated and their hands bound by a thin, but seemingly tough strap, which kept them under restraint. Sagramore, together with Lucan and a few other more established warriors, could only glare out now at the emperor who still coiled that same flower bud from earlier within his fingers.

The emperor returned their glares with a grin as the scramble went on. "This flower has been planted in Aizary since historic times to fend off predators," he said. "Its toxic scent slows the metabolism, hence the restraint on raw physical power. Grace, the power of sorcerers, is not based on metabolism. And so, one could say sorcerers are immune to the scent."

The emperor glanced away then with a smirk as Schim crashed to the ground. Sagramore noted that Forredan and almost every other nobleman had already surrendered, all restrained now by hands tied behind their backs.

"The scent of the snowdrops is detrimental to me, too," the emperor continued. "But it doesn't render me lame as it does for all of you, for I understand the basics of imitating grace."

To demonstrate exactly what he meant, the emperor jumped down from the podium a second time. He then grabbed a hold of the next knight who ran across him among the scramble, and he held the unknowing man for a moment before slapping a palm at his forehead, sending out a visible wave of luminous white through his head and out the other way, instantly killing the knight.

"Some of you would actually have to die tonight," the emperor said in a toneless voice, dropping the corpse to the ground.

FORTY-ONE

The power of grace

Perhaps there had never been any hope to begin with. Not when one was up against the Lord Emperor of the country. Yet Sagramore continued to jab at the sorcerers, holding on but rarely able to emulate his earlier gash that had actually drawn blood. His strength might be curtailed, but no one could strip away his supreme technique or his pride, which were the only things Sagramore was relying on as more and more sorcerers hemmed him in. Sagramore had no liberty to be glancing elsewhere, but with three of the twelve sorcerers tagging him and a fourth coming on soon, he recognised that most of his allies had either fallen or been contained. And yet the thrill of battle urged him to fight onward with the edge that he had rediscovered in his recent encounter with Marvin Sailanson. Sagramore knew that he might not live to see another day, and yet he had hardly ever felt more alive.

Lucan, Raphael, and Roth were among the last warriors still holding on, but a quick glance over to them made Sagramore realise that they would all soon fall. Indeed, as soon as Lucan was knocked down and then promptly restrained, Sagramore found himself confronted with both a fifth and a sixth sorcerer. His own inevitable defeat became clear then. Blasted by a roaring flame from the left and then swept by a gust from behind, Sagramore felt his hands snatched to his back and then bound tight by a tough strap. Finally, a foot forced him face-down onto the white-flowered floor.

Defeated, Sagramore grumbled as blood dribbled from his mouth. He gazed up at the podium toward their captor: Kasimir de Spartamon. The man had been called *the wolf* during the war, that name highlighting his sharp intelligence and his frightening ability to pounce at his enemies. He was, of course, also known as *the proud conqueror*. This evening, he had demonstrated that these monikers were still fitting. Perhaps it had been foolish to think any less of him. And perhaps it was his *right* to rule. It had always been.

The scuffle this evening wasn't the kind of battle upon which Spartamon's incredible and undefeated reputation was based, but even if it was, the man was on pace to maintain the record. It didn't matter how strong Sagramore and some of the others were. Spartamon had given them no chance. In the end, every one of them had been herded like sheep, their weapons expropriated—all of them forced to kneel to Spartamon's mercy, the man's condescending glare insinuating that the scene was as it should be.

"Vile beast!" Morlan lambasted the emperor, sputtering out a mixture of blood and saliva.

Some of Morlan's men heaped on the abusive criticism, but the emperor wasn't offended. Instead, the emperor closed his eyes, placing a finger over his lips to hush them. The sorcerers responded by smacking the men on their mouths to silent them instantly, which Sagramore noted was one of few actions of their aggression that didn't actually involve sorcery. Even without drawing on the powers of sorcery, however, Sagramore inferred that the sorcerers possessed a level of physical strength that matched regular knights. Add that to their supreme agility, which bettered the greatest traditional warriors he had ever known, it became clear to Sagramore that resistance had always been futile. And, finally, the sinister grins on their masks—despite being only painted on—were more disturbing and fear-inducing than they initially seemed, almost like horrifying jesters one saw in nightmares.

The emperor opened his eyes then once more. "Let the real negotiations begin," Spartamon said, his eyes darting first to Schim who flinched in response.

The challenger to the throne had indeed been humiliated this evening. Schim was bruised all over, and apart from the grime that had been kicked up at him and the other men during the scramble, Schim was also sullied by blood and sweat.

"Will you kill all of us?" Schim challenged with a scowl.

"You should know better than anyone else," Spartamon responded with a shake of the head. "I don't kill off capable men—at least not before giving them a chance." Spartamon turned to everyone else then, raising his hands invitingly. "My offer to you is the opportunity to live, *and* to reinstate yourselves as my faithful soldiers. The Kragans will come at us again, and there is no one who can lead you better than I can—your Lord Emperor. Under my guidance, we shall crush the Southerners once and for all. Anyone who desires to make history with me is welcome to..." He paused for a moment as he met Schim's eyes again. "Aye, Schim, that includes you. Your life has been mine to begin with, and it will continue to be... that is, unless you remain obstinate upon your foolish ambitions, in which case, I'll have to kill you."

Schim said nothing, not words of pleading and not words of condemnation. His intent glare, however, showed that he wasn't ready to submit.

Raven writhed forward next to his liege. "The Pristines don't fear you!" the veteran warrior said with a scoff. Sagramore saw that the brawny man looked much more injured than many others, his legs seemingly lamed.

"You employ underhanded tactics like these," Raven continued, "and you call yourself the *Emperor*? You plant flowers to curb our strength? And now you demand people to follow you?"

The emperor hardly raised an eyebrow. Spartamon instead nodded at the sorcerer standing closest to the brawny Raven—a female sorcerer, it seemed. She stepped forward and stamped her hand atop Raven's cranium, injecting that same wave of destructive luminous white into his head and killing Raven instantly.

"Nooo!" Roth cried, screaming for his comrade to wake up.

Schim and Raphael turned away, though, closing their eyes tightly. Others shivered, fearing for their own livelihoods.

"Thank you," the emperor said to Raven's dead body. "Thank you for being the first to declare your position." Spartamon turned to the others. "You have two paths before you: submit and live, or defy and die."

The captives all looked to each other for guidance. If they were to submit, they would at least survive the night. But the distraught expressions that filled the gardens showed that no one trusted the emperor anymore. Regardless of what each individual decided, it seemed close to impossible that Spartamon would be able to earn anyone's genuine loyalty.

He's been pushed to the brink, Sagramore thought, noting that Spartamon's radical actions this evening did not reflect the effortless charm that had attracted so many talented warriors to fight for his causes in the past.

The few noblemen who had been the first to surrender readily conformed to what they had recognised was a forgone conclusion.

"I submit," they had said one after another. It was a start, and it won only a slight grin from the emperor who had probably expected as much. Noblemen had always been the lesser figures in his government—in fact, they were really only on the court to promote a sense of hierarchy.

The emperor looked over to Forredan then, expecting the statesman to do the same. A nod from Forredan would prompt a large group to submit, Sagramore knew, a group that included Golden Knight Claude Lucan, among several prominent knights. Their collective submission would surely spark some momentum for Spartamon.

"Lord Emperor," Forredan said, bowing his head, one of the few men who had avoided even a scratch. "We are yours to command—we have always been, and we will always be. Let anyone who dares defy you answer to me first."

"Good," the emperor said this time, nodding at the sorcerer watching over Forredan, who promptly slashed loose the strand binding the statesman's hands with a luminous white shaped like a blade, the elemental blade fading off into thin air just moments after its purpose was fulfilled.

"Now onto a stubborn one," Spartamon said, turning then to Sagramore, who then immediately realised that he hadn't been considering what his eventual decision would mean for himself and the handful of people he actually had the capacity to worry about.

"I have been fond of you," Spartamon was saying, "ever since we first met more than fifteen years ago. Not only are you strong, but you are humble. I would be most delighted if you choose to support me. After all, it was I who bestowed upon you the title of the Defender of Trubannis."

Sagramore smirked, slightly surprised by the praise. He hesitated, not for himself, but for the Defence Army he represented and the loyal knights he had come to the gardens with.

"Sir Sagramore," one of the knights said to him then. "I know what you're thinking. Having been guided under your tutelage for all of these years, I've come to appreciate the true meaning of knighthood. I shall stand by the chivalry you have instilled in us. I choose to die in honour rather than live in humiliation."

Sagramore widened his eyes, his face glowing with pride. His vassal's words echoed his own thoughts. A few other knights agreed, shouting out their shared stance with passion. Sagramore was unable to find the words to express how proud he was.

"I don't want to die," one of them said suddenly.

The young knight who had spoken was Gareth, one of Sagramore's newest vassals—a talented warrior lacking experience on the battlefield.

"Neither do I," a second one added. He was Pelleas, also one of the younger men in the group. "The Lord Emperor has proven to be a great war general. I want to be a part of that. I want to make history with him."

The other knights frowned in response, but in the end, they said nothing, turning back to Sagramore who responded with a sigh.

"Your fate is in your own hands," Sagramore said to them. "And in your hands alone. I respect your decisions and I support them. May the heavens bless you for the path ahead."

Gareth and Pelleas gushed out a few beads of tears but said nothing more, knowing well the doom that awaited their liege and comrades.

"Lord Forredan," the emperor said, nodding to the statesman. "Show me your loyalty."

Forredan rose to his feet. The statesman groaned and then commanded a couple of his men to do his bidding. The two—knights themselves—stood from their knees, rising hesitantly. The sorcerer standing closest to them offered them their own swords that they had previously seized from them. Forredan cleared his throat, meeting Sagramore's squint, but then promptly turned away.

Better you than me, the statesman's expression seemed to say.

Forredan's men were still hesitant, but they snatched their swords finally and lurched toward Sagramore and his men who were ready to die in honour.

Spartamon ensured that there's no turning back for Forredan, Sagramore noted. He snorted quietly then. *I cannot believe I'm still here admiring his genius.* He regarded his doomed men one last time before shutting his own eyes. It would be too painful to watch them die. Sagramore didn't have children of his own. His relationships with some of the knights he had brought with him this evening were the closest he had come to fatherhood.

Even with his eyes closed, Sagramore could picture how it happened as soft grunts were followed by the sound of spraying blood. Sagramore said a quiet prayer for each one of his dear men, and he had made his peace with it when he opened his eyes again. Gareth and Pelleas, the two who had chosen to live, had stepped away, cringing just beside the podium. The other four, meanwhile, lied on a carpet of the now-bloodstained snowdrops.

No one had made a sound upon their execution. Sagramore couldn't bring himself to utter a single word, either. But he couldn't allow himself to show any signs of weakness or regret—not when his beloved disciples had died with integrity.

He trembled in anger, holding a tight fist as he looked up to meet the emperor's eyes.

"Did I change your mind, my good Sir?" the emperor asked.

Sagramore glared at the emperor for a moment longer, but then finally dropped his animosity with a long sigh.

"I respected you, Kasimir de Spartamon," he said in the calmest tone he could deliver. "You are the greatest war general I have seen. Unfortunately, you were never the ideal candidate to rule the country. You have reason to despise Schim for challenging you, but the disunity and chaos that defines the tableau you see today is something you brought upon yourself. As a war general, power is supreme—it is what respect and admiration stems from regardless of how forceful it is imposed. But as a leader of the country, kindness and compassion are more desirable attributes—of which you do *not* have. Perhaps most of us here will choose to follow you today, given the circumstances, but I am sure none of us are willing followers. You have failed as a leader."

The emperor shook his head, his brows beginning to knit together. "I'm disappointed," he said. "I really am. I was hopeful to see you spearhead an army of your own. But you have made your decision. You have chosen death, and—"

"Lord Emperor!" Morlan cried. "You can't do this! Sir Sagramore is far too important to die here. How would we defend the country if the Kragans were to attack?"

The emperor peered over to Morlan with a murderous gaze. "*Don't* interrupt me again," he warned, causing the former king of Cetal to tremble visibly.

The emperor then turned back to Sagramore. "I'll honour you myself," he said. "I'll rip out your heart with my own hands."

Sagramore lowered his head. "I'm sorry, but I won't allow that," he said. He chuckled briefly and then burst out a desperate last gasp of energy, breaking loose from the tough strap that bound his hands. He snatched his partisan back from the sorcerer watching over him and held it up high above his head. Instead of wielding it against the sorcerers, though, Sagramore prodded the pole weapon sensationally into his own chest, directly through his body.

"Come, o' sweet death," he uttered, as he dropped down with a thud, blood soaking him from the sternum.

Percival, he thought as his eyelids fluttered, the blue of Achelois still faint. *And Godric... you two are the pride of my life.*

Please don't try to avenge me.

* * *

Darkness?

No.

It was weak, but there was a flicker of light ahead. It was hard to breathe. And something was being towed.

Me? Alpheus thought, confused about whether or not his eyes were even open. *Am I the one being towed?* The ceiling was so low that he could barely sit up if he had wanted. The walls were crammed to the point that it felt like he had been sleeping in a coffin.

"You recovered quickly," a toneless voice echoed in front of him.

"Rover?" Alpheus asked, trying to shake off his slumber, his head now set to spinning as he tried to orient himself.

Alpheus peered down at his waist where a thick braided rope was tied, and at the same time realising that there was soil everywhere. His eyes followed the rope trail that disappeared off ahead, where another body was being dragged.

Ash, he realised.

Marvin!

"We've got to go back!" Alpheus cried, his words resonating in the burrow. "We've got to help Marvin!"

"You'd only get in his way," Rover said, still crawling ahead, dragging the dead weight of Alpheus and Ash along.

Alpheus opened his mouth to protest, but coughed when he inhaled some grime.

"Look, Rover," he said, struggling to get his words out. "I'm convinced of Marvin's ability to turn any situation around. And I won't pretend to know the history between him and the emperor. But need I tell you what it means to cross the emperor? Sure, no one could lay a finger on Marvin in open battle, but it only takes a backstabber and a few helpers to set even Marvin on a course for death."

Rover groaned then, and after a moment he came to a sudden stop. Alpheus poked his head up, hopeful that he had convinced the former mercenary. But as he squinted harder, he realised that it was a dead end ahead. All was silent for a moment until Rover chortled suddenly.

"Ash, the cunning brat," Rover said. "He blocked off the path behind our backs."

Alpheus cocked his head but said nothing.

"Turn back," Rover said, writhing in that cramped space, offering the torch to Alpheus. "Go. Go back and help Marv."

Alpheus nodded as he received the torch. He soon learned that he was inside the passage that the trio had dug out to infiltrate the prison cave. The idea of digging their way into the prison was ingenious and also unthinkable to him, but only because it wasn't a logically viable option. Perhaps Marvin and his crew really possessed powers beyond humans—perhaps even beyond that of sorcerers.

Alpheus crawled forward with more urgency as his headache began to soothe. Moving inside the earth like a burrowing animal certainly wasn't very accommodating, but Alpheus tried his best to ignore the unpleasant environment, reminding himself the urgency of the situation—Pelanofzky's words of premonition about the imminent Kragan attack ringing inside his head.

Minutes later, Alpheus saw light up ahead of him and also a wider part of the tunnel where he could finally stand upright. He hurried forward to confirm that the exit was at the ceiling of the burrow, an opening large enough for him to climb through. He heard the sound of prison bars being battered, possibly by the guards as they tried to settle the prisoners.

He glanced back at Rover, who nodded at him. Alpheus returned the nod and then poked his head up through the hole. He then kicked forward, springing himself up from the burrow and back into an unoccupied prison cell.

"He's back!" a guard cried, his voice carrying a hint of joy, though some of his companions began to cower in fear.

The cell had been locked shut again, but clearly the guards hadn't yet bothered to block the escape hole. Rover emerged from the cavity a moment later, the former mercenary's entrance causing the guards to flinch, most of them backing away immediately.

"Sailanson isn't with them," one of the guards said, as if to reassure his allies. "They could sit inside the cell or they could crawl back into that hole—which, if they do, we'll set it ablaze and have them burned alive!"

Rover didn't even spare the guards a glance as he stepped over to the cell door and grabbed hold of one of the metal bars. He held it for a moment before applying pressure, pulling it to his right and bending it out of shape with a long creaking noise.

Jaws dropped immediately. But, as if that wasn't enough, Rover grunted then snapped the bar right off its hinges.

Some of the guards stumbled onto the ground as Rover uprooted one bar after another, destroying the only barrier that had shielded the guards from him.

Unbelievable, Alpheus thought, stupefied, until Rover finally turned toward him.

"Go," Rover said, having created an open path. "He would appreciate your help."

"What about you?" Alpheus asked.

"Some things are not for me to meddle in."

Alpheus nodded at Rover and then caught speed with the Glider Steps, slipping through the guards and then breezing to the stairs.

* * *

Julian gaped, unable to digest the unbelievable scene that he had stumbled into. With the chancellor, the Raiders, and many members of the court held as prisoners, Julian almost forgot that he too was still being held in duress by Nine Arms. Julian met Schim's eyes, noticing the humiliation behind them.

They are..., Julian wondered with a shiver as he turned to the masked strangers watching over the defeated men, *...sorcerers?!* He peered closer to the podium then, noting Sagramore lying down, drenched in blood, with the partisan forked into his body.

No, he thought, tears filling his eyes. *Not Sir Sagramore.*

Lachman, who had made the journey across the city with them, seemed to be in shock, too, racing just then over to the fallen golden knight. During that short trip from the prison, Julian had been wondering only one thing: whether the phantom soldier had survived. Lachman had claimed that the phantom had managed to escape, despite his best efforts. But here at the gardens where Julian stood idly and in shock, he realised that all of his worries about the phantom and Alpheus would have to wait.

Lachman knelt in disbelief before Sagramore's dead body. The emperor, standing high and mighty on the podium, simply stared down at his captives.

"Why?" Lachman asked, gaping openly at his liege.

The emperor raised an eyebrow and lifted his head, pointing his chin at the golden knight. "He chose to die," the emperor simply said.

Nine Arms strode forward, forcing Julian along. "Lionel," he said. "Don't."

Lachman really didn't know about this? Julian wondered.

"Why?" Lachman asked again, this time showing his teeth. "This is slaughter. This is what the Kragans do. We are above this!"

The emperor narrowed his eyes and then stepped down from the podium, treading purposefully toward Lachman until he was towering over the golden knight.

"If you miss him that much, go join him," the emperor said quietly.

Lachman lifted his head, likely seeing only the shadow of a claw before being smashed on the chest and hurled backwards into the air. The emperor had injected a luminous white energy into Lachman in that brief exchange, now causing the golden knight to spew up a chunk of blood from his mouth.

Nine Arms fell suddenly numb, loosening his grip on Julian who was still too shocked to run. How did the emperor manage to have everyone at his mercy? And had the man gone mad, trying to kill Lachman—his longest-serving and arguably most loyal soldier?

"Why...?" Spartamon asked with a low growl as Lachman slowly fell down to the ground. "Why did you not defend yourself?"

The golden knight could hardly speak, blood and saliva gurgling out from his mouth. "My life...," he managed to make out, "has always been yours."

Lachman's eyelids fell then—the third golden knight to fall this evening. Perhaps no one should have expected any less of this evening, but Julian had already seen more than enough. He simply didn't think he was able to bear to see any more deaths, regardless of which side the victims stood.

The emperor winced at Lachman's dead body, but turned away soon enough, regarding the migrants from Cetal. Morlan was clearly shocked, but when he met the emperor's eyes, he wore a mask of disgust.

"Sir Sagramore's right," Morlan hissed. "You were never a good leader. My only regret about dying here is knowing that our fellow countrymen will have to live under your tyranny."

The emperor raised his arm, forming the same malicious claw that had taken Lachman's life. "Save your speech," Spartamon said. "You choose death."

Morlan shut his eyes, mumbling something—perhaps saying his final prayers.

"Have mercy, Commander!" a strong voice echoed from afar.

Morlan snapped open his eyes as everyone turned toward the voice.

Marvin Sailanson! Julian recognised, descrying the man who leaned forward from a branch of one of the taller trees, his loose clothing billowing gently in the wind.

More than a few men gasped as Sailanson flipped down from the tree. Somehow Sailanson's arrival had seemed to inject hope into some of the men, perhaps because he had been known as a mercurial man, who might well turn against the emperor for reasons only he would know. And yet Julian couldn't imagine the man—who was alleged to have murdered two hundred comrades—being their saviour.

* * *

Marvin peered across the landscape where so many now knelt.

How did he manage to achieve this? he wondered, noting the inanimate bodies of Sagramore and Lachman. Marvin then eyed the masked clan who watched over the captives, already suspecting that they were sorcerers. He was no expert about magic, but Marvin doubted that the power of grace alone could trump all of those knights who were now at the emperor's mercy.

"Why are you here?" the emperor demanded. "Did I not give you an assignment elsewhere?"

"It's done," Marvin said, finally looking up to Spartamon. "Just in time for me to join the party here."

Spartamon frowned. "Do I sense an urge in you to thwart my plans?"

"Depends on what your plans actually are," Marvin said, taking a step forward toward the podium.

"The snowdrops!" Morlan cried. "Stay away!"

Marvin glanced down at the budding white flowers at his feet, realising then that the flower was the reason why the knights were now kneeling in absolute defeat.

"Marvin, you're not needed here," Spartamon said, tone still calm. "Go, and await further instructions."

"I'll go," Marvin said, "but not before I appraise this empire that you have built. I need to see how much is left of what I once fought for."

The emperor snorted, but before he could speak, Pylon flung out his good arm. "Know your limits, Sailanson," the madman warned.

Marvin glared at him. "This doesn't concern you."

Pylon shoved off the young man he was holding, reached for his deadly flail beneath his cloak, and then dashed at Marvin, swinging out the deadly metal ball, which Marvin managed to evade without a flinch.

That was slow, Marvin thought. *Too slow.*

The flower.

But he sidestepped the carpeted area, Marvin noted, glancing down to Pylon's feet.

Why, then?

Pylon looked more shocked than anyone else, turning to Spartamon immediately in question.

"It is the scent, not the sensation," the emperor revealed. "And it's true that this does not concern you, Pylon."

The emperor eyed Marvin. "Our one and only duel was more than ten years ago, and while I will always be proud to know that I won that duel, I understand that a repeat is unlikely. As you should know, I never fight losing battles—so if you are set on turning against me, I will unleash *everyone* and *everything* at you." He paused, narrowing his glistening eyes at Marvin. "Do not make me do this," he said, which Marvin took to be his final warning.

Marvin inhaled gently as he took another glance at the emperor's captives. Some of those men deserved this treatment, to be sure, but this wasn't about them. It was about the emperor who had always had his way. Marvin admired Spartamon. He also feared him. But most importantly, he despised him for never trusting anyone but himself.

And he killed Dora, Marvin remembered, his eyes narrowing back at Spartamon.

"It's time to settle this," Marvin said finally, his only words of warning before he flashed into the air and then crashed down toward the emperor along with a fierce punch in his direction.

Even as the sorcerers hadn't been alert enough to immediately defend their liege, Spartamon managed to block Marvin's first strike with his forearm. The resulting impact of the clash sent out a visible wave of white energy that exploded out behind Spartamon before hurling into one of the elm trees, rattling its leaves thunderously.

Marvin threw another punch, and this time the emperor responded with a punch of his own—knuckles cracking with an explosion that burst out in all directions. The sorcerers, regardless of how powerful they might be, wouldn't be able to join the scuffle as long as Marvin remained in close distance with Spartamon whose safety the sorcerers couldn't compromise. From there, Marvin exchanged several more blows with Spartamon in a fistfight that was far from ordinary as luminous white rays splashed out from their fists, saturating the air.

I see, Marvin realised as he continued to box, feeling barely any restraint on his strength. *The Fist which draws power from nature itself is immune to the flowers that curbs only physical strength. And to think that I was the one who introduced the technique to him.*

I never imagined turning against you, Marvin thought as he watched Spartamon gritting his teeth while struggling to answer all of his punches. *And, for any neutral watching, this is an improbable clash of the greatest proportions. A clash between the central figure of the war and the most powerful mercenary who fought for him.*

But how many of them would know about the repressed gratitude and grievances I have for him. And perhaps what he has for me.

In any case, the stakes of this battle are none other than the future of the country—and the land.

I can't afford to lose.

During the warring years, even golden knights had barely been able to match Spartamon's ability as an individual combatant who was especially skilled with the sword. Spartamon was only using his bare hands now, though, as he threw out punches that sent out visible waves in the air—and with that, he had likely reminded everyone that he was so much more than a war general and emperor of the country. He was also one of the most impressive warriors the land had ever seen.

Even so, Marvin had never met anyone who he couldn't overpower. The case in point was that even Spartamon had said more than once in the past that no one could defeat Marvin on his own. Marvin was the greatest mercenary from the war, now throwing out punches that roared even more powerfully than what Spartamon could manage. Perhaps, to the onlookers who had all been tied up, Marvin really was the only man deserving of the reputation for slaughtering two hundred men.

As Marvin knocked Spartamon back with another thunderous bang, *the wolf* man finally saw the opportunity to gesture toward the sorcerers to come to his aid. Before Marvin even turned, a zephyr gently brushed Spartamon away from the dogfight.

Marvin dashed forward in chase, stopping only when a spear of ice was hurled at him from the side. Having barely evaded the dangerous spike, Marvin turned left to the source—a sorcerer who looked to be recovering from expending a heap of grace. Marvin gritted his teeth and took only a single step toward her before he sensed a scorching inferno roaring at him from above. Marvin propelled himself off from the podium which the raging ball of fire slammed down into, immediately erupting with wild, crackling flames.

Marvin escaped onto one of the elm trees as the flames danced upon the stage, lighting up the gardens with a hue of furious tangerine. The spectators, meanwhile, watched in awe, perhaps some of them marvelling at the destructive power of the fireball. Being forced to run and dodge at the same time as a dozen sorcerers threw elemental forces in his direction, Marvin believed he knew quite well now about the severe damage that sorcery could manage. Nothing had struck him just yet, though, thanks to the combination of his supreme athleticism and agility.

When Marvin allowed himself a glance back at Spartamon, he realised that the man hadn't simply crossed his arms to watch. Instead, Spartamon had naturally transitioned into doing what he did best: playing the role of general and directing the sorcerers as to how and where to attack with the greatest efficiency. As he ran, Marvin remembered one of Spartamon's famous sayings from the past.

Everyone has a weakness, and the best way to claim victory is to find and exploit that weakness.

Marvin didn't think he himself had any ostensible weaknesses, however. With his strength that matched a hundred men and the agility of a hummingbird, Marvin hardly doubted his own strength. But as he darted here and there and was forced to defend himself, Marvin realised there *was* indeed one thing that he hadn't perfected, and that was his struggles when fighting against foes attacking from a distance—enemies that threw projectiles. He didn't mind siege weapons that tossed out giant boulders, but he dreaded archers and their arrows that were shot with lethal precision, especially when there were a bunch of them.

In the past, Marvin had managed to overcome bowmen with his incredible fundamentals that had allowed him to swipe arrows away as he powered forward with reckless abandon. It was unthinkable for anyone else to do what he did, and that was one of the reasons why he was called a monster. But perhaps even a monster had no answer for these fearful sorcerers, who could be called monsters themselves. No one could make light of how deadly arrows were, but compared to elemental forces seemingly drawn from the wrath of the land itself, Marvin knew he was in trouble.

As he continued to dodge, though, Marvin recognised that the more powerful a spell, the more time it required to prepare it, and one stood vulnerable during that time. Similarly, there seemed to be a considerable cooldown time after a spell was unleashed—again, the more powerful the spell, the longer the recovery. Marvin hadn't yet been given a chance to exploit this drawback, unfortunately, as the sorcerers easily overcame it with their numerical advantage by constantly shuffling forwards and backwards as they followed the emperor's expert instructions. Indeed, the sorcerers were dictating the pace of the battle—and their success was highlighted by another roaring flame then that seared toward Marvin, scorching his shawl and parts of his chest that now billowed out black smoke from the burns.

Marvin winced, ignoring the throb of pain and skipping away again. He didn't expect anyone among the captives to realise this, but he had been moving with the intent to avoid the powerful forces from landing upon them and wounding them in the line of fire. The gardens themselves had become a wreck, certain areas whirling in flames while others frosted frozen in icy silence.

If Marvin was going to turn this around, he had to think of some other tactic. Running alone wasn't going to do it. He spun now, eyeing one of the sorcerers who was recovering from unleashing spears of ice only moments ago. If he could take down even one of them, their formation would be broken. He had to wait. He had to create an opportunity. And upon sensing another couple on his right about to unleash their next spell, Marvin cursed quietly, turning to dash away again.

As Marvin turned, however, he noted two sorcerers being blasted by what looked like bolts of lighting, sweeping their arms away and nullifying the elemental force before the power could be moulded.

Marvin spun around and saw a man. A young man. Dressed in prisoner's clothing, his hair coiled down his back in a braided ponytail.

Alpheus!

"Marvin, let me help you," Alpheus exclaimed as he breezed in with the Glider Steps, shooting out another couple of stones like drops of lightning that sparked bright the night sky for less than a second before snipping their targets with a striking static of light blue.

Alpheus isn't bothered by the flowers, Marvin recognised before glancing over to Spartamon who looked both stunned and frustrated by the new arrival. Marvin turned back to Alpheus, who was still firing at the sorcerers.

Well, of course, he's a sorcerer himself, he thought, though realising that the scholar was still unable to reliably call onto his grace—which meant that his power was close to negligible on this particular battlefield. Even so, Alpheus's presence alone had already fractured the sorcerers' purposeful formation.

"I owe you one," Marvin said with a grin, finally seeing the opportunity to dash forward at one of the sorcerers, knocking him down now with a crushing blow to the neck.

FORTY-TWO

Revolution

Some of those among the imprisoned spectators could be heard shouting cheers. It was too early for celebrations, though, for the sorcerers had regrouped once more. There were still eleven of them left.

The emperor narrowed his eyes, and the battle picked up right where it had left off. Of the eleven sorcerers, ten hemmed in on Marvin, with only one diverting off to Alpheus. Spartamon had likely realised as much, thinking that Alpheus was barely a threat to his domination.

Alpheus breezed away, trying to draw a few more sorcerers to him. He had expected the worst to happen, but he also understood that he could never have predicted that things would turn out this way. The emperor was still holding supreme power, and doing so in the boldest way imaginable. But despite the emperor's audacity, there was no way to confirm that the man was actually connected to the Kragans.

I can't die here, Alpheus thought, gliding off but still managing only to get a single sorcerer on him and seeing that Marvin was forced into a scramble against ten.

I can't let Marvin die, either.

Alpheus pulled out several more pebbles from under his sleeves and flicked them out again, only to see that he was unable to replicate the efficiency of the initial projectiles, hardly pestering the only sorcerer on him, apparently female. He hissed quietly at himself, looking up suddenly when a familiar voice called out for him to be careful. A spear of ice was hurtling toward him from up ahead.

Alpheus gritted his teeth and then spun around the whooshing spear with the hops derived from the waltz he had learned from Marvin. After his impressive evasion, Alpheus glanced over to where the word of warning had come from.

Julian, Alpheus thought, noting that his friend was handicapped and held hostage by an imposing looking man who held a dreadful ball-and-chain flail.

But this wasn't yet the time to be worrying for Julian, as another chunk of ice was crashing into him then, promising to impale him. Alpheus twisted away this time, breezing straight toward the approaching sorcerer and darting off to the right just before clashing into her. Alpheus sprung up high into the air then, his leap blessed behind a glowing white dust that trailed him. At that lofty vantage point, Alpheus peered around for Julian again. He knew that he owed Julian an apology, or at least an explanation. The best way to ensure there were no hard feelings between them was to demonstrate his loyalty.

I'll free you first, Alpheus decided, dashing down with his gaze firmly upon the fearful man standing over Julian. As he closed in on them, Alpheus wagered on the last pebble he had stocked under his sleeves, aiming at the man with the flail.

The man's huge, Alpheus thought, jerking slightly. *Those scars on his face. And that set of vindictive eyes.*

"Behind you!" Julian cried.

Alpheus turned his head slightly to see that he had finally managed to draw another sorcerer onto him—only that it was a surprise attack, the sorcerer now dashing at him from the side. Rather than hurling chunks of ice with sharp ends at him, the second sorcerer summoned a blast of wind to help send Alpheus along to where he was already headed, only much more promptly and dangerously. In fact, Alpheus was flying so fast then that he had to secrete away the pebble that he had been ready to fire, as there was no way he could aim properly, given his momentum.

Despite a strong current of air blurring his vision, Alpheus discerned a smirk emerging from the man with the flail who he was about to crash into. Unfortunately, Alpheus had no way of slowing his advance or diverting his route. Before he would clash into the man, however, Julian responded by sending a whiff of flame directly at the man holding him, which in the end, barely scratched him, but ensured that Alpheus landed safely away from harm's way.

Alpheus still ended up thumping down to the ground. But he was quick to find his footing, dashing off now past the restrained members of the court and inviting the sorcerers to chase him again. He glanced back to see that Julian had collapsed to the ground, apparently from exhaustion. Alpheus paused for barely a second, then shrieked when he found himself whirled away by another blast of wind similar to the earlier blast, but this time causing him to spin violently and seemingly without direction until the corner of his eye caught sight of the female sorcerer who now waited for him with a spear of ice at the ready.

I'm dead, Alpheus thought, swirling beyond control, shutting his eyes and praying for a miracle, which came as he felt suddenly propelled up into the air by yet another non-contacting force which replicated the same kind of energy source that had proven popular this evening. Landing clumsily at a distance away from where he had taken off, Alpheus found himself at the feet of the man who had saved him.

"Father Abraham," Alpheus uttered as he looked up with astonishment at this newcomer.

The old man spared him no glance, stepping ahead of him with his gaze fixed on the chaos of the battle. Alpheus sat up, trying to catch his breath and make sense of what had just happened, regarding the holy man who was aged but far from fragile. For a long time, the holy man had been the one person Alpheus could most confide in. And even this time, Abraham had come to his aid at the right time, which was in spite of the Church's clear distaste and reluctance to involve themselves to the troubles of the Empire. Alpheus then glanced over behind the old man where a group of templars stepped forward in a line—about ten of them.

Alpheus immediately noticed Kathryn Trulips within the group, as his cheeks tensed up into a smile. The Aizar native, with her fair skin and long silver hair, was as beautiful as he remembered. Alpheus also recognised Gabriel, the grim leader of the templars—the second most important member of the Church, after Abraham.

The holy faction's arrival completely changed the tides. The emperor seemed to agree as much, for he now commanded the sorcerers to stop, silent now as he gazed upon the holy men. The emperor's frustration must have been growing with unexpected guests showing up one after another. Some of his captives, on the other hand, were grinning as they rejoiced. The burning question for everyone, though, was how able the holy man and his disciples were going to be in terms of drawing grace, and whether they could utilise that power at the same level as the sorcerers.

"Back off, Abraham!" the man with the flail said, scowling. "This is between members of the Empire."

The old man squinted, but it was Gabriel who darted forward with wisps of cool white at his feet, reminiscent of the Glider Steps. The man with the flail whacked his weapon desperately forward at the charge, but Gabriel easily negated the strike by simply catching the otherwise lethal ball of metal with his gauntlets that protruded a visible wave of black energy.

"Pylon," Gabriel addressed the man with an arrogant grin. "Do you remember our last encounter? I've been waiting for this moment ever since."

That's him? Alpheus wondered. *The one they call Nine Arms?*

Nine Arms grunted, throwing out a punch with his other arm. This time, Gabriel drew his sword and slashed it down again with that visible black energy, tearing apart the vengeful man's limb. Nine Arms screamed in pain, and only then upon noting there was barely any blood spurting out did Alpheus remember that the man had a prosthetic arm. Still, the pain must be close to unbearable judging from how the man was pressing hard against the shoulder where the nerve endings had connected with the prosthesis. Gabriel showed little mercy, thumping him on the back with the pommel with his sword before stepping over his wounded body.

"Your time has passed," Gabriel said simply, staring down at his defeated opponent.

The captives responded with elated cheers, some of them rising to their feet but with hands still bound behind their backs. The emperor glanced over at them with disgust and then lifted his head slightly at Abraham as if to acknowledge the challenge.

The holy man regarded the emperor in return. "Let go of your lust for power," Abraham said in a benign pitch. "Confess your crimes to the Immortal, and you shall be given the opportunity for atonement."

The emperor shook his head. "Why do so many people wish for death?" he asked with a sudden sneer. The emperor then swung his arm out, sending his sorcerers out again, this time to challenge the templars. The eleven sorcerers raced toward exactly eleven opponents, as Alpheus joined the side of the ten templars.

The emperor himself dashed toward Marvin for what seemed to be a final standoff for the future of the country.

*   *   *

The sorcerers had had their way so far this evening, but they were finally being put to the test. While the templars didn't seem capable of unleashing elemental forces, their every motion seemed to carry a mystical energy that rendered them immune to the effects of the snowdrops. They were fighting the sorcerers seemingly with their full strength at their disposal, but as they were likely not sorcerers themselves, their one clear disadvantage was their inability to unleash elemental forces.

Marvin recognised that the outcome depended on him—and, of course, his opponent, the emperor himself. The proud leader of the country had been pushed to desperation, and it showed with his added viciousness, as if he were a beast fighting for survival. In between those thunderous punches were a few deadly slashes of the claw that had claimed thousands of lives in the past. There was no doubt that Spartamon was fighting with a distinctive edge, and at a level that the sorcerers and templars could only dream of.

And yet Marvin answered every attack, either by blocking or dodging altogether. It didn't matter how incredibly strong the emperor was when Marvin bettered the man in all respects. Marvin countered with unblockable pummels that sent out shockwaves that rocked the gardens. And, naturally, after sustaining a couple more heavy pounds, the emperor was knocked to the ground, falling back hard onto the podium where the flames had burned away. Jagged black marks, ash, and smoke were all that was left now. Spartamon lied defeated, his armour cracked and his long hair dangling over parts of his bloodied face.

The sorcerers immediately dashed away from their own heated battles against the templars, all of them jumping to Spartamon's defence.

"No," the emperor uttered, raising a hand which slowed the sorcerers who still stepped toward him as if following an instinct to protect him.

Marvin watched Spartamon cough out some blood as he sat up. He glanced over to the templars who had now put away their swords. The apparent leader of the Church—the old man—kept silent.

It was a comprehensive victory for Marvin, and one that perhaps merited a proud smile rather than the impassiveness his face was now showing. He had once considered Spartamon his closest confidant. Bringing the man down himself ached him in more ways than one. He stood over the defeated man then, looking down at him without any expression.

"I never dreamed this day would come," Spartamon said first.

Marvin still said nothing, contemplating on what to do next. He certainly didn't hope for Spartamon to die.

"The rules are as they were," the emperor continued, tossing out an arm and pointing at the men. "Look around you—everyone is at your mercy. You cannot escape destiny, Marvin, for you are like me—a true conqueror!"

Marvin shook his head. "I'm *not* like you. I have no ambition to rule. And I won't kill you. I'll never be able to do it."

Marvin locked eyes with Spartamon for a moment, memories rushing back to him in violent streams. It had all started in a village whose name Marvin couldn't even remember, except that it was somewhere in the state of

Cellarsy. Even in that very first meeting there had been a sparring contest, one of only three battles between them, and the only one that hadn't been about either of them intending to kill one another. Marvin had fought his most gruesome battles—as well as his most triumphant—alongside Spartamon, who had been the only man he would serve, but also the only man he considered his *brother*. They even loved the same woman, in Kharvalenis. And in regard to her, not only had Spartamon introduced her to Marvin, but the man had also selflessly elected to withdraw from the dreaded love triangle in order to avoid a stalemate.

To Marvin, Spartamon would always be someone he deeply admired, but also someone he distinctly feared and despised for all that had happened between them.

Spartamon likely shared similar sentiments even if not on the same level. In any case, the time for nostalgia was over as a group of knights galloped in on warhorses, waving flags of the Empire's Fenrir emblem. They were led by a man in golden armour and a visor shaped like the head of a serpent.

"I'll give you a helping hand!" the leading knight in gold offered boastfully, waving for his men to advance as the man himself galloped toward Schim before dismounting with an athletic leap.

The knight removed his visor, and immediately the people whispered his name—the Defender of State Farella, Sir Sebastian Dinadan. On his feet, the knight didn't look particularly tall. His build was also on the slim side, especially compared to other golden knights.

"The knights of Farella are at your command," Dinadan said, bowing to Schim and promptly unbinding the chancellor's hands.

"Sir Dinadan," Schim acknowledged, standing. "The flowers planted here are toxic. You must be wary."

"Worry not, Lord Chancellor, for I've arranged five hundred soldiers to surround the area. In the unlikely scenario that we are unable to seize control here, I assure you that no one shall leave the gardens without your sanction."

Schim chortled with pleasure, laying a hand on the knight's shoulder. "Well done, Sir Dinadan."

Schim turned his attention to the podium then, nodding at Dinadan and gesturing for the golden knight to clean up the mess.

Dinadan responded with a wicked smirk as he stepped upon the destroyed stage. "If you would step aside," Dinadan said to Marvin, drawing his heavy sword from the waist. "I'll finish what you were unable to."

Marvin watched the knight walk past him, irritated by the man's outward vanity. Spartamon was clearly no longer in the position to dictate anything to anyone, but who did this Dinadan think he was to call the tune?

Although the sorcerers were ready to and were capable of defending Spartamon, Marvin now snatched the knight's right wrist that wielded the heavy sword, forbidding the golden knight to move even an inch.

"When...?!" Dinadan uttered in astonishment and in quiet pain, swinging back. "When did you—" He stopped mid-sentence, looking Marvin in the eyes, perhaps aghast as he realised for the first time what it meant to anger him.

"Try it if you dare...!" Marvin warned, his eyes burning.

Spartamon smiled as blood dribbled slowly from his mouth. He seemed proud of Marvin, proud that he was as he had been labelled: a conqueror, a man everyone had to give heed to.

Schim grunted as he hobbled onto the podium.

"I understand, Sailanson," Schim said. "I was confronted with the same dilemma years ago. Every now and then, I think of Kasimir de Spartamon as our former Commander—the proud conqueror who led us to victory through the fiercest of battles. Unfortunately, this man before us has become a shadow of his former glory. He is *not* the Emperor we wanted."

Spartamon simpered, spurting out more blood. "And Schim, *you* are fit to lead the country?" he challenged. "You might be...," he added with sarcasm, "if for *all* these years while you were planning to usurp my throne, you have studied how to be Emperor, then you might well be!"

"I do not deny my intention to overtake you," Schim admitted. "But only for the best interests of the people. The late Sir Sagramore summed it up best. He said that you lack compassion. You might be a great general—the greatest, even. But our people don't need an emperor who rules in the same way he fights wars.

"I have, time and again, advised you to check your domineering ways—unfortunately, to no avail." Schim paused, frowning as he turned to the crowd. "I would like to take this opportunity to confess my own mistake—a costly one that resulted in the Lord Count's tragic death."

Almost everyone braced themselves. Marvin finally released Dinadan then, who was careful to check that his wrist hadn't been snapped. Marvin then peered over to Alpheus who looked mightily impatient, his blood probably boiling.

"I take the blame for the murder," Schim continued. "Because it was me...! It was me who asked the Count to do my job—to help check

Spartamon's cruel ways—and so, it was me who sent the Count to his eventual murderer…!"

The crowd exclaimed in shock at the claim, but no one responded more strongly than Alpheus, who bolted up to the podium and shoved his way past Schim and Dinadan, only for Marvin to snatch him at the wrist, albeit not with the same force he had applied to Dinadan. A few steps more and Alpheus would have been blasted by the sorcerers, all of whom were still loyal in defending Spartamon.

"Is it true?!" Alpheus demanded, raging at the emperor even as he was being held back. "Did you really murder Jeffrey?"

Spartamon ignored Alpheus and instead maintained his intent gaze on Schim in the same way that he had gazed at Marvin earlier on. But his glare wouldn't last, for he finally passed out altogether.

"Don't you dare die on me!" Alpheus demanded, still raging. "Answer me!"

Marvin sighed. "That's enough," he said with a frown. "Don't make me knock you out a second time on the same day."

Alpheus clenched a fist to suppress his fury.

"It doesn't matter!" a voice among the captives cried. "Whether or not he killed the Lord Count, Spartamon needs to die for this."

"The sorcerers too!" another voice added. "Behead them all!"

"Do it, Lord Chancellor!" a third voice urged. "Do it for Zorlia. Do it for the country!"

All the men were soon on the feet, many of them demanding for Spartamon's death. Some of them turned to Abraham and members of the Church, pleading for them to take their side. They seemed to have forgotten, however, that neither Schim nor Abraham was going to decide the emperor's fate. That decision belonged to Marvin, and Marvin knew it, as he remained in between Spartamon and everyone who wanted the man dead.

Schim winced. "Hear me out, everyone," he pleaded, raising both arms to silent the disgruntled crowd. "I share a deep history with Spartamon—twenty-six years. I know the man better than anyone. I have no intention to take back what I said earlier when I branded him a tyrant. His domineering ways resulted in many tragic sacrifices, including that of the Lord Count, Lord Breunor, and from this evening, Sir Sagramore and even Sir Lachman. Like you, I've been humiliated and forced to submit to his tyranny. But in spite of that, I'm obliged to remind you of all the good things that Spartamon has done for the country. Without him, none of us would be standing here today upon this land which otherwise would have long been conquered by foreign enemies. He instilled the belief in us that we as a country can rebound from the adversity set upon us during the bloody war. He was a genius who changed the lives of—I dare to say—every single man in the land. He saved Trubannis. He saved millions of lives. And for that, he deserves, at the very least, to live."

The speech was perhaps the fairest appraisal of Spartamon. With his words, Schim had rendered the men silent once again, appeasing them expertly.

"So what do you suggest?" Marvin asked.

Schim contemplated for a moment.

"Imprisonment... for now," he said. "I promise that no one would lay a finger on Spartamon."

Marvin squinted at Schim for a few seconds, and then glanced over at Alpheus.

Alpheus suspects that Spartamon is connected to the Kragans, he thought. *If that were true, all his achievements would be negated along with his right to live. They'd kill him without a second thought.*

Marvin then finally nodded, keeping an eye on Alpheus to make sure that he didn't speak anything of it.

"Spare Pylon, too," Marvin said, eyeing the vengeful man who was presently under the mercy of the templars.

Pylon, despite the humiliation he had suffered this evening, appeared surprised to hear Marvin's request.

"And the sorcerers," Marvin added, this time drawing a surprised flinch from the eleven who were still standing next to Spartamon. "The Empire will take none of them."

"That we cannot allow!" Dinadan bellowed, swinging an arm out in protest. "After what they—"

Marvin snorted, cutting the golden knight short with a glare. "I'm done with fighting for the day, but if anyone were to turn their swords against the sorcerers," he said, pausing for a moment as he glanced at the templars, "then let me forewarn you that I would side with the sorcerers."

Abraham and more than a few of his templars grimaced slightly at the remark, but opted to hold their position. Marvin turned to the sorcerers then, who still hid behind masks.

"Your friend, the one I knocked down, is alive," he said to them. "Take him and go."

The sorcerers exchanged looks. Sparing them was the least Marvin could do for Spartamon, who would have liked that. One of the sorcerers dashed over to an elm tree that was frozen stiff toward his unconscious ally. The sorcerers then nodded at Marvin before sprinting away into the dark of the night.

A lot of the men there growled softly as they watched the sorcerers leave. Schim didn't even look up, for Marvin was regarding him with quiet intent.

"Remember your promise," Marvin said. "If I happen to learn that anyone harms Spartamon or Pylon, I will hunt you down."

"You have my word," Schim responded with a smirk.

Marvin glanced one last time at Alpheus, finally with a friendlier expression on his face, which was an apology of sorts. Marvin then spun and walked away from the gardens. It had been a long night, and he was sure the aftermath promised to be even more exhausting.

EPILOGUE

The court of Vondra Dawn had never seen so many people. Noblemen, lords, knights, soldiers, templars, scholars, and even civilians—close to a hundred men filled the room. And yet, the most enviable seat there—the throne—remained empty.

The emperor had been accustomed to arriving late, but on this day, he wasn't expected at all. It had been four days since the revolutionary evening. Spartamon had been confined to a secret location that had been arranged by the Holy Order, and Abraham and the templars insisted that even Schim had no access to the said location. Alpheus had always had a soft spot for the members of the Holy Order, but he had since seen those same members *escorting*—basically, herding and forcing the survivors from the Gardens to the court of Vondra Dawn. It appeared even to him that the Church was looking to expand their influence at this opportune time. Abraham, known as the Holy One, had also prohibited anyone from leaving the citadel, which they claimed was to ensure that the Empire wouldn't dissolve. The court was hosting a discussion centred on the adjustments and reforms that would be necessary in order for the Empire to move forward. Until an agreement was made about what to do with the vacated throne, no one was to leave.

More people had been invited to join the discussions since the second day. Representatives of the academy were now present, including Seer and a few other State Scholars such as Willow, Black, and Reginald. Even a group of protestors who had been part of the recent riots in the city now shared the cramped space in the court.

The Church had apparently adhered to Marvin's demand of sparing Spartamon, but that hadn't stopped them from uprooting the remnants of the Advents within Vondra Dawn. The holy members dragged a group of women to the court then, a group they claimed to be the last members of the Advents—the emperor's concubines.

Alpheus gasped when Gabriel pointed a sword at one of those ladies who was fair-skinned and striking in appearance, despite the accusations against her.

"Do you submit?" Gabriel asked, tapping the blade on the lady's chin. "Or do you resist?"

The woman frowned and then turned her glare not to any of the templars, or even to Abraham, but to Schim. "I'll never betray the Lord Emperor," she said.

These were essentially the same conditions that Spartamon had offered at the Gardens: *submit and live, resist and die.* Alpheus could already see that Abraham, the man he had always considered to be the kindest man in the land, was prepared to have Gabriel push a sword through the concubine's chest if she continued to be stubborn. He would never know, however, as the woman suddenly spewed out a dangerous amount of blood tainted a thick black. The others—nearly a dozen of them—followed almost immediately, ejecting the same dark fluid.

"We won't allow you the honour," the woman said between painful coughs, turning her glare back to Gabriel.

"You poisoned yourselves?!" Gabriel exclaimed.

The woman managed a chortle as more blood dribbled from her mouth. "Zorlia is doomed," she said. "Without the Lord Emperor's guidance, you are *all* doomed!"

She choked then as several of the other ladies dropped to the ground, some of them sullying the men on the court and cursing the Empire with their final breaths.

Alpheus turned away, cringing in quiet agony. The death images of Spartamon's concubines were atrocious, but perhaps typical of the times when great leaders fell. Alpheus only allowed himself to look up again when the last of the lifeless bodies had been dragged out. He noted that many others present in the court shook their heads in shame, many of them mumbling their suspicions that Spartamon had controlled his loyal followers with sorcery—or *witchcraft*, which seemed to be an interchangeable term for them.

Forredan was the next to be escorted to court. The stout statesman had grown feeble and had aged dramatically, having spent the last few days imprisoned and without ample sustenance. It must have been beyond Forredan's worst nightmares that he would be thrown behind bars with barely enough to eat. And to be fair, the man might also have been rather unfortunate to have been considered as one of the emperor's supporters and labelled as an Advent. It was true that the hedonist had sided with the

Advents in the past, but the alliance had appeared to be for self-preservation rather than malicious intentions for indiscriminate killing. His verbal submission to the emperor at the Gardens, meanwhile, had clearly been forced upon him.

"I submit!" Forredan said then, repeating in desperation the same words he had said that evening. "I'll do anything! Just don't put me back in those cells!"

The statesman made no further claims or excuses, asking only for freedom. In the end, the court—with the mediation of the Church—decided that he deserved a second chance. But Forredan was to return to his home state of Whitesand and revert to his previous role as State Minister. The light punishment was contingent on the condition that he paid a bail to the court that was worth more than half of his wealth. Normally, it would have been impossible for him to surrender any of his possessions. But in his current hysteria, he assented to everything that the court demanded, including an agreement to part ways with Golden Knight Claude Lucan, along with his other able vassals, who were to be stationed in Zorlia or Bastion City.

After Forredan had been shown his way out, Abraham circled his way onto the elevated platform where the throne sat.

You're not taking the throne for yourself, are you... Father? Alpheus wondered, hoping that that wouldn't happen.

"Lord Chancellor," Abraham said, eyeing Schim, who sat on the right in the same chair that had always been reserved for him. "Please."

Schim smiled, rose to his feet, and then stepped onto the elevated platform to join the holy man. For that moment there, Alpheus wasn't sure what to feel, whether or not Abraham had somehow agreed on some kind of alliance with Schim. He realised, however, that while it was Abraham and the members of the Church mediating the discussions in the past few days, Schim had spoken at length on many occasions.

Alpheus peered about, noting that more than a few people had widened their eyes in delight. It looked like it was finally time for *the* announcement—the monumental moment where the country would hail a new leader. Perhaps Schim was really the only man with the merits to succeed the throne. Abraham was never going to compete for a political role, and that meant Schim's closest competitor was Pierre Morlan, the former king of Cetal who seemed to have neither the ambition nor the capacity to rule the country. Indeed, Morlan had been one of the chancellor's most vocal supporters since the discussions had started. Morlan had also stressed that he was completely behind Schim in the effort to bring a better future to the country.

The rumoured aggressive activity on the southern border also supported the opinion of Schim being the only man capable of leading the country. After the deaths of Breunor and Sagramore, Schim was by far the greatest war tactician that the Empire could call upon. The shift of power toward him was natural and no one had yet found reason to resist it.

The court fell silent then as all eyes traced Schim's hand brushing lightly upon the armrest of the throne. The man turned then to the people, grinning out at them.

"I'm flattered by your support," Schim said, his voice proud and confident. "I would be honoured to lead this country, but... I am *not* your new emperor."

Some of the audience were taken aback, though they wouldn't have to hold their breath long as Schim was quick to address his intentions.

"I won't accept the title as Emperor," Schim continued. "I don't have the credentials to be titled as such, at least not until I could settle the forthcoming conflicts with our foreign enemies. I repeat: I will not accept the credit or the title as the new leader of the country. However, I appreciate and understand the conundrum that befalls us. And I ask you to be assured that I humbly accept the responsibility to lead our soldiers in the effort to preserve peace across the land."

Schim paused, peering out at his audience who drenched him at that moment in roaring applause.

"Our first priority," he said after a moment, raising a hand to silent the audience again, "is to secure the defences along the territorial borders. We, the Truban Empire, are prepared for any waging of war. We will show the Kragans—or anyone who dares to attack us—what it means to cross the most powerful empire in the land."

Alpheus squinted into the animated crowd. The speech itself was rather customary, but he agreed that Schim had delivered it with both the confidence and authority of a great leader.

"Let there be no more Advents or Pristines," Schim then said. "There is to be no more division among the court—among the Empire. Let there be only one distinction: those who are loyal to the Empire and those who are not. And for those who are not, let them soon learn what a big mistake it is to align themselves elsewhere."

More cheers yet emerged from the boisterous audience. These were exactly the kind of words that many people had wanted to hear, especially amidst the political war that had carried on for far too long.

"On a less inviting note," Schim said with a grave expression, "I ask you to spare a moment to remember and honour all of those who have died as a result of the unfortunate feud. There have been more than a hundred casualties, and included on that list are some highly respected men. An appropriate service shall be arranged for these brave men in the coming days, but for now, allow me to read out those names, as for not one day shall I forget their contributions to the Empire."

Schim received a rolled-up parchment from a soldier, and began to read out the names of the men who had perished, followed by brief descriptions of their achievements.

The audience listened as they watched him with a hopeful expression that almost spelled out the words: *He could do it*. Even if for only this moment, the surge of optimism and togetherness was reminiscent of the time when the country had won the war nine years ago. Sure, Alpheus hadn't been old enough to fully appreciate the joy of victory at the time, but the current elation certainly matched the accounts of what he had read of people's reactions from back then. Alpheus suspected that he knew why, despite the high likelihood that the next war was just on the horizon. To the people sharing the court with him this moment, it was an incredible victory, a milestone for the country to see the internal feud finally ending. It might not have mattered to the people who even the resulting victor was to be. But at this moment, they seemed incredibly glad to know that the Lord Chancellor had effectively succeeded the throne. Spartamon was a better candidate to lead the country to war, but Schim was certainly a very skilled tactician himself. On top of that, Schim had many positive qualities the emperor lacked. Schim was modest. He appreciated what the people wanted, and he had persevered for this opportunity to serve those people who could admire him without also having to fear him. And, perhaps most importantly, it was the correct timing to take the reins during a period that had the people altogether hopeful for a brighter future.

Alpheus could only hope all of that were true. And he certainly wasn't going to wait idly to see how things turned out.

ACKNOWLEDGEMENTS

Due to life getting in the way, the release date for this book was postponed more than a few times. Writing has continued to be lonely journey for me, but also the best mode of escapism.

This second book of what I plan to be a four-book series is almost twice as long as the first book. I had so much fun writing it and hope that people would enjoy reading it. I'm trying my best not to be biased, but I really do think that this is a good read. I do love the story myself, and this is what keeps me going.

Editing was done by the meticulous Richard Larson once again. I am forever thankful for his efforts, which allowed me to write with much more clarity.

Finally, I thank my family once again for their continuing love and support.

FINAL WORD

Thank you for reading *A Revolutionary Ballad*. If you enjoyed it, I'd be grateful if you could leave a short review on Amazon or Goodreads.

I am currently writing the third book in the *Memories from Oblivion* series, entitled *Luna's Nocturne*, which is due to be released in 2020. Meanwhile, you can find out more about the series on:

www.atlas-hill.com

Thanks again for reading.

www.ingramcontent.com/pod-product-compliance
Lightning Source LLC
Chambersburg PA
CBHW022331190826
50139CB00002B/11
9780648285229